IMMIGRANTS

IMMIGRANTS

Frederick Lightfoot

For Dodo,
with as much love now as then.

Chapter One

A fiddle player who has hummed for chickens, evinces *cock a doodle doo* and a blush, two blushes. One from an acolyte, unofficial, of sorts, whose hands are mud stained from peeling turnips, patterned like two leaves, which he inspects minutely, saving him from any other attention. The other, less apprehensive, is one of resignation, predicting, though with no certainty as to what, that certain things, events, will surely follow.

Witness: 1910, a damp, grey, drizzly afternoon in winter. Through the open kitchen door the yard has a dilute yellow tinge. Dora, in the frame, out of breath, laughs then calls: "*Cock a doodle doo. The cock was crowing *cock a doodle doo* and nobody knew why. And all the time Uncle Marty was in the chicken shed again. Daddy's bringing in him. Daddy thought the old cock had flipped. I think it's dead funny. Did you hear it? The old cock, on and on, *cock a doodle doo! Cock a doodle doo!* And Uncle Marty probably singing to it." She laughed all the time she spoke, the sound coming in surges, rich yet broken.

The two in the kitchen, her mother Kate and brother Robert, immediately stopped what they were doing and blushed. Two quite dissimilar blushes. Descriptions of them whilst blushing would have to take account of the fact that Kate, clear skinned, dark eyed, and shrewd, whilst suppressing a desire to laugh at her crowing offspring, had, from first she heard the human cockerel, guessed at the discovery and dreamt of dancing: and Robert, pale skinned, delicate and reserved, possessed of the closed fantasies and fears of the undiscovered acolyte, dreamt of flying.

Kate stood up as Dora entered. "That's enough now," she said, simply but with authority. Dora shrugged and smiled at the injunction, but nevertheless fell silent. She didn't really believe in her mother's solemnity. It wasn't called for. It would be all right. It always was. Her father would pretend to be angry, but that would pass. He wasn't really an angry man, certainly never a violent man. He put on shows. He would shout maybe, but that was all right. She turned to her brother, wanting his confirmation that everything was all right, but Robert was looking down into the sink at the pieces of sliced turnip, refusing to acknowledge what was going on. Dora guessed her mother and Robert had already shared this secret. There was nothing for it but to wait for Uncle Marty to be produced.

Uncle Marty, Kate's brother, known commonly as Workhouse Marty, the street entertainer, a *talented music man*, Kate insisted on this, was duly dragged in with a paraphernalia of birds attached to his ungainly, preposterous figure. He was a lanky man with flailing limbs, a scraggy dewlap neck, and long gelatinous hair, which lay smeared like cord against the chiselled cheeks of his razor sharp face. He was covered in a filthy oversized greatcoat, that was wrapped around him in thick folds, bound together by a cord of string knotted about his waist. His chest was puffed out by a fiddle-box breastplate, just visible through the hanging collar of his greatcoat. Curlicues of chicken feathers were caught in his hair and in the filthy omentum binding his figure, lending him a wild and exotic, if bizarre, air. John Devlin, Kate's husband, held him by the scruff of the neck as if Marty were a species of cock chicken he had just strangled, whilst Marty gurgled and salivated on cue, his vocal register an intemperate cluck. John's own voice resonated in his throat before becoming remotely audible. He managed only two contracted words: "Why Kate?" An after-note of his anger hung in the air of the tiny kitchen, accentuating the taut silence. It was dispelled by the sound of spluttering water.

Robert had turned on the single tap suspended well above the large blue veined sink. As the spitting stream hit the enamel he gingerly placed his hands into the cold stream and watched the dirt wash away, the discoloured water spreading and jostling the equally stained turnip pieces. He felt cheated and disappointed, a domestic delight, that of working with his mother, had been taken from him. But he blanched at his own temerity. His father wasn't through. The sound, he was sure, would be taken for impertinence. He hadn't intended that. He hadn't intended anything. He wanted to do what was right, but had no way of knowing what that was. He dreamt he could with unclipped wings fly away.

The sound of the spluttering water released something in Kate, though, relaxed her, freed her from the burgeoning stubbornness possessing her. She approached Marty and touched him, lightly, tracing his elongated head and neck, probing the defenceless in his gestures, in the mottled skin, the blood injected eyes, the plum-purple bruise worming into the orbit. She smiled, removed a chicken feather from his hair and tickled the damaged capillaries, demonstrating them to John without anger or undue emphasis. "Sure, Marty isn't in the hen-house," she said quite calmly, almost singing the sentence, "he's in the dog-house. Isn't that right Marty? Through no fault of your own you've found yourself the whipping-boy." John finally relinquished what hold he still had, which had relaxed as Kate had examined Marty's face, though she had carefully avoided contact with his hand.

Marty held out his palm and revealed a small brown egg resting in its bowl. Dora immediately took it from him. "It's still warm!" she called out delightedly. "You know, you're just like a magician standing there, Uncle Marty, a proper magician."

Marty smiled, treating Dora's comment as praise, whether it was meant or not. He inclined towards her and whispered as if admitting her to a secret: "You know, it placed its backside right over my palm to give me that, and tried to talk to me at the same time, honest to God, clucking away as if it made complete comprehensible sense, but God knows, a chicken would leave you confused altogether. I'm sure if I'd played, if I'd been allowed to play, amuse myself with that minor pleasure, it would have laid all day long and well into the night. God knows you could do with them." He cocked his eye towards John and spoke up: "A tune for Mister John Devlin, is it? Are you ready for that? I think we've all had enough of this tom-foolery by now, wouldn't you say."

"I didn't say you could stay," John replied dully. He looked squarely at his brother-in-law then, with a sudden eruption of temper shot with uncertainty, declared: "I didn't say anything of the sort. I'm damned sure I didn't. I didn't utter a damned word."

The bruise confused him. It was new, something different, not easily associated with Marty. What had been simple, a complaint against laziness and squalor, a complaint against irresponsibility and irrationality, had become strange. Added to which, the fact he had missed it, failed to register its reality until Kate had caressed it into being, weighed on him. His anger had become chaotic and that only served to increase it. He wanted order. He needed order.

Kate read his confusion and felt for him. She recognised the look on his face, understood the dislike it revealed of things out of the ordinary. He couldn't abide uncertainties, disturbance, being put out. She wanted to assist, put it right for him, but the only way she could do it was by apology and she guessed that wouldn't be enough. She reached out and lay her hand on Marty's shoulder and quietly said: "I don't want him to go back there at the moment. He can't defend himself. I won't have him hurt. I won't have that. He doesn't deserve that."

"Feed him then!" John retorted and immediately pushed past them and made his way back out into the yard.

When he had gone Kate smiled to herself for a moment. The gesture looked tender and approving. Then she turned to the other three in turn and said: "You know, I'm pretty sure we'll dance later."

John remained absent until supper was ready to be served. Dora went for him. She had wanted to go to him earlier but Kate had refused her. She had said to give him time. He needed time. It would be all right if he just had a little time. It had turned dark when Dora went out and called to him. He didn't speak to her. He immediately threw down the cigarette he had been smoking, walked straight past her back into the house, and silently took his seat at the head of the table. Dora refused herself the opportunity to be hurt by his neglect. Her mother said that they would dance later. She had to trust to that. Besides, her father put things right. She believed that. His failure to acknowledge her, his refusal to share the meaning of his temper, would be passing. If she was patient he would explain it. That was the relationship they had. She followed him in determined to be cheerful.

Robert began the meal. He fished three pigs trotters from a pan and placed them onto a plate in front of his father. John cut into them. A stream of watery fat burst from the blubber. He scraped scraps of meat from the bones and divided it onto their plates. The pig fat shone in the firelight. Robert ladled a thin broth of onion, carrot and turnip over the meat. After that he took a small, dark loaf and broke it onto the table. His hands hesitated over the bread as if he was embarrassed by what he had done. As if by way of explanation he whispered: "It will be easier to mop like this. I thought it would be easier, that's all, easier broken up."

"Say grace, will you," John said abruptly, dismissive of Robert's timorousness. It wasn't to the purpose. It irritated him at the best of times.

Robert stood upright. He bowed his head and placed the palm of his right hand over the back of his left before his chest. He uttered a prayer in a slow, nervous, personal staccato: "For what we are about to receive may the Lord make us truly thankful. Amen."

Supper was a silent, moribund affair. The only sounds were those of the various notes of sucks and slurps it took to deal with the pigs' feet.

This was particularly the case with Marty, who kept his face so close to his bowl as he ladled the broth into his mouth he looked as if he were virtually lapping at it. By the finish his mouth and cheeks were smeared with grease.

Robert also kept his head bowed throughout, though not with any intention of eating with the enthusiasm of his Uncle Marty. Saying grace had been too much for him. It didn't sit easily with the feeling at the table. He recognised that there was always some ground between the feeling grace prompted in him and what he saw in others, but it struck him that the gap was worse during that meal than was usual. It made him nervous, ashamed even, though he couldn't account for that at all. He told himself he just had to keep his head down; keep his head down and keep such thoughts to himself.

John and Kate looked at each other from time to time, but merely eyed each other blankly, conceding nothing, neither really willing to take it on.

Dora ate as if nothing were amiss. It wasn't that she failed to comprehend the strain the others felt, but she was determined to dismiss it, eradicate it. It was absurd to her. Everything would be all right. She told herself again what she had told herself in the yard. Her mother had said that they would dance later. Her father was a dancing man. He wasn't even embarrassed when her mother told the story of how they had danced together along the quays. Her mother claimed she had seen him on the day he had arrived and knew they would dance together one day, and when they finally did it was along the very quay where she had first seen him. Uncle Marty hadn't played then, her mother said they hadn't needed any accompaniment at that time, but he had played at the wedding and they had danced to his tunes on and off ever since. Dora couldn't understand why they simply didn't admit the point and put an end to the miserable silence. They loved having Marty in the house. He got them dancing. They loved that. What could be better? They only had to say that to each other. And on top of everything, she was hungry. She enjoyed eating. She reasoned that nothing should interfere with that.

When everything had been consumed, including the blubbery casements, Kate made tea. She placed the pot between John and Marty. Marty reached for it, but before he took the handle, John placed his own hand firmly on it. "So now," he said with a slow drone of authority, "tell me exactly what happened while I pour this? And don't leave out a thing, not a detail. I want the absolute truth. I don't want any of your story-telling. Did you bring it on yourself?"

11

Marty eyed John coolly, his gaze lowering all the time he did. Eventually he uttered: "Not now, John. We won't talk about it just yet. It's hardly the right time. Let's just have ourselves a smoke. You could see your way to that I suppose."

John brought his hand down heavily onto the table top: "Tell me, damn it! I want to know why you're sitting there with a face like that. I want to know why you are in my house looking the way you do? Is that clear?"

Marty, looking up now from beneath his eyebrows, kept his attention fixed to John. He moved his tongue around his mouth, its outline visible behind his closed lips as he wiped it across his teeth one way then the other. Then he parted his lips, drew the saliva onto his palate, and slowly shook his head.

John seized his wrist and held it tightly.

Marty gave a mild tug, but John held firm. Marty looked downcast and somewhat at a loss. He said: "Your children are sitting here, John. So, well, I'd rather not, that's all. It's not the time, I reckon. I'd rather you let it go. Let's just have a smoke, John. I fancy a smoke. Come on, what do you say?"

John was incensed. That Marty should suggest to direct him was unheard of. He wasn't about to allow that. Yet, he wasn't entirely sure how to respond. His impulse was to strike out. He knew he had to resist that. He pushed his disgust to the fore. "Just what the hell are you ashamed of Marty?" he asked, goading him, wanting to throw his reluctance back in his face.

Marty didn't respond. He simply gazed passively at John. John felt some sense of satisfaction. Maybe it was Marty's fault. It invariably was when he found himself in trouble. Why should a bruise be any different? A half-smile passed his lips. He was about to speak again, repeat his insinuation, but before he could Marty suddenly called out. "Murphy!" he said, snapping the name, "Murphy! That's what! Murphy! Bloody Murphy!" He stopped as abruptly as he had begun. He looked horrified. He repeated the name quietly, as if it were an echo: "Murphy."

There was a period of silence.

John was the first to break it. As he spoke up he roughly released Marty's wrist, putting it aside as if he didn't understand why he held it. "Murphy? Murphy? Who is he? What's he got to do with anything? Do I know him?"

"No, you don't know him. Nobody knows him. He's new. He's been coming in, him and his cronies, stirring things up, causing trouble, lots of trouble."

"What trouble?"

"You know. He says things, gets them worked up, gets them so they don't know themselves. You know how it is."

"No, I don't know how it is. I've never been in the damned place. Says what? What does he say? Tell me, for Christ sake," John demanded, his impatience resurfacing.

"You know, the usual old stuff. He complains about us."

"Us? You lot? You lot in the house?"

"No, us. Us! You know. You've heard it all before, it's nothing new, but this feller gets them going, I'll tell you that. He says we're paid to come over here, paid to cut their wages, take their jobs. He tells them the only reason they're in there at all is because we're here. Tells them we've got their houses, got their jobs, that it'll be their women next. All that stuff. He gets them right worked up, though. They can't help it, I'm telling you. He's a real preacher man."

"Preacher man," John repeated, deriding the term, mocking it. If it hadn't been for Marty's bruise he might have laughed in his face. He called aloud, to his own mind objecting to Marty's condition: "It's ridiculous. No one listens to rubbish like that. For God's sake Marty. It's nonsense."

"They don't mean to, not all of them, some of them like it, mind you, but he's a tough character, and he's never on his own. He's always got his men. He scares them and gets them wound up all at the same time. He gets under their skin. I've seen it. A preacher man, I'm telling you, says God and all's with him. Crazy really. He gets to them, though, really does. I've seen it with my own eyes. He gets them right worked up. I've never seen them like it."

"So what happened?"

"Please John."

"Just tell me for Christ sake. What happened? You didn't fight him did you? Don't tell me that. Oh God, please don't tell me that. Not you Marty Boland!"

"I was unlucky, that's all, unlucky. He was in winding them up, saying this and that, and he just happened to pick me out. That was all. I was just a bit too convenient, if you like. Well, once he'd had his bit of a bash about how things are, he pulls me out and starts pushing me about, says things about my head, says it's strange, you know, the skull, a strange shape, the skull, then tries to knock it into shape. Unlucky, that's all. He was serious, though, really serious. He's a frightening man really. I won't say he isn't, won't pretend on that score. He got to me all right."

John pondered for a while, then quietly suggested: "Murphy's an Irish name."

"I think he's a Scot. His men are Scots too."

"Maybe he's an Ulster man."

"No, John, I believe he's a Scot."

"He's no Catholic, anyway," Kate cut in.

Her voice stopped John short. He turned away from Marty, but didn't turn to her. He simply gazed ahead into empty space. Her voice contoured everything Marty had said. He felt himself go cold, bitterly cold.

Marty carried on: "I feared for my life, that's the honest to God truth, but then he says I wasn't worth it, made out I was no better than some animal grubbing in its own filth. Said all sorts. But I'm not saying any of it, not repeating all his filth. He has the hell of a tongue on him when he unlashes it though, foul, really foul. The right filthy..."

"That's enough," John said quietly.

"I'm only saying. You wanted me to."

"Enough!" John repeated sharply. "I'm saying it's enough now." Marty started to speak again, but John spoke over him. "Go to bed, go on, go to bed, you can sleep in the loft. You'll be all right there. Go on. Take this with you." He took a small pouch of tobacco from his pocket and tossed it towards Marty.

Kate, Dora and Robert began to clear away, but John stopped them. "Leave it, will you! Just leave it," he said impatiently, but immediately regretted it and added, "Look, for once, the morning will do. It won't do any harm."

"We don't usually," Dora said.

"This time!" He looked around, suddenly perplexed and overcome by the situation. "Go on," he repeated, "go to bed, all of you, go on. I've already said, haven't I!"

The children stood apart but waited, unsure, disconcerted by this break with routine. They didn't know whether to approach him or not. They usually kissed him goodnight. It was a ritual, part of the day. He seemed entirely unaware of their dilemma but continued to gaze at them as if they were defying him. Kate stepped in. She commanded it. Her voice was blunt and insistent: "Go on, kiss your father goodnight, then go on!" Dora looked grateful. She went straight to John and kissed him on the cheek.

Robert, though, hung back as if shy to approach his father, uncertain of himself against the background uncertainty that the break with routine suggested. Kate was not about to allow his reluctance, though, or tolerate the expression on his face as he looked at his father, gazing at him as if he were something of a stranger. She put her hand in the centre of his back and ushered him forward, forcing him. Robert stepped up to John and with a straight back bent to him, kissing him lightly on the cheek. John nodded his acknowledgement.

The children stood for a moment longer, still waiting. Kate gestured them to go. They came to her and kissed her, hugging her as they did, then finally left, making their way from the kitchen up a narrow, steep stairway to their shared room.

Marty went straight after them, nodding to Kate as he left but saying nothing, not even looking towards John. A moment later his voice filtered into the kitchen, singing a cradle song that quickly faded to a whisper before vanishing altogether. The fire spat with pig bones.

*

Kate pressed her two hands firmly down on John's shoulders. He was solid to her touch. She moved around him letting her fingers slide across his collar bones. She pushed away the table, pulled up a stool and sat in front of him, still holding her hands against his frame. "He's probably not telling the whole truth, you know. You know Marty. He's, well, he exaggerates, makes things up, doesn't always tell things as they really are. You know that. He's always been a bit fanciful."

"I believe him."

She stroked the sharp line of his sheer jaw. He was immovable to her touch, but didn't refuse it. "At least it's finished," she said. "He's in the loft, safe enough. It's over with. No need to brood on it."

He spoke as if thinking aloud. "He could provoke a man to a great deal, I know that, I don't deny that, but not to violence. Not that. There's no cause for it. No, it's not finished."

She cupped her two palms around his jaw as if his face were a flame in their cauldron, and whispered to him: "Tell me it's finished, John Devlin. I want to hear that. I want to know I've heard the last of it. I can't tell you how I felt when I saw him. He's just a child really. You know how he is. I don't want to go through anything like that again."

"I can't say it."

"I don't want to be frightened like this, John. He looked so much like a little boy standing in the yard with his black eye. He wanted to cry. I could see that. He was just so shocked, so much more hurt than just the bruise somehow. He didn't cry but, I tell you, I did. He didn't deserve what happened to him, but it's done with, isn't it? Tell me that's the end of it. I never want to see that look again, not that child's look on a grown man's face, not that sad, hurt, wondering why look. It just wasn't fair."

He took hold of her fingers, wrapping his palms firmly around them, then answered her, his voice quiet, yet charged, excited. "Do you know what the problem is Kate? Nothing changes. Nothing ever changes. Nothing goes forward. We don't ever expect anything to change or go forward. We just take it all, day by day. Hewing and trailing, inbye and outbye. And I don't want to succumb to it. I don't want to give in to this laziness of nothing changing. I don't want to lose all the time, be a loser, never managing to do anything, just giving in, making do, thinking that's the best of everything. I'm sick of making do, sick of being the loser."

"God, you've never been anything of the sort. What the hell do you mean by that? You've never missed a shift. You're not some lousy fairground or circus man. What's made you say anything like that?"

"How long have you been here, Kate, how long have you put up with it all, Cumberland, this filthy town, this filthy backwater, put up with its view of you? Twenty years! Twenty years of nothing changing. Twenty years of getting through, surviving, taking it all day by day, and being grateful. Grateful! I'm so grateful I can hardly bear myself. I'm everything this damned country's made me and made me proud to be. A lackey, a grubber, a shoeshine boy, just a lousy bloody hagger. Christ, Whitehaven, it's never been a haven to us! They hate us here! They invite us to come here and do their filthy work and they still hate us, hate us for doing it, hate us for needing to do it!"

"Stop it!" she demanded, and at the same time pulled back against him, trying to resist his hold. He kept her hand in his, though. She stood up. The stool fell behind her. It rolled on its rounded edge, creaking against her continued appeal. "I shouldn't have let him stay. It was wrong. I know what he is. He probably got on the wrong side of someone. He can do that. You know he can. But it'll blow over. He gets picked up all wrong sometimes. It's nothing. It's just Marty. It'll be nothing."

"No, it's me. I didn't see. I missed the point."

"He'll be gone. It'll be all right. I tell you, it'll be nothing."

"He'll stay for a while. In the loft. Not with the hens. I want him to stay."

She was about to argue some more, but checked herself. She shrugged. She conceded to what he said. It was absurd not to, absurd arguing the opposite. She wanted him to stay, she wanted to know that he was safe, free from harm. She had what she wanted. It was the way it usually worked out. Marty stayed. But she couldn't be simply grateful as was usual. She wished she could. It was different though. This time it had been achieved with the reward of an even deeper uncertainty. She couldn't be grateful for that. She said: "If you say so, but you know what he's like. He'll blow with the wind. He won't be around long, and then everything will settle down as it was. You'll see. He'll be gone like always."

"Not this time, Kate. He'll stay awhile. I imagine, from what he said, that no one's going anywhere. Not without any fuss, anyways. No, no one's going anywhere." She made to speak, but John kept on. He was suddenly quite flushed with his theme. He laughed grimly. "I would, Christ, I would, Kate, I'd pack up in Kelly's coalboat and be gone, vanish away like none of this had ever happened, straight back to where I came from." He paused and smiled obliquely at her. It was a throw-away, weary gesture. "But then I'd be just as ashamed, just as angry and ashamed, as I am now, wouldn't I. I wouldn't be a hagger, but what the hell would I be? There's nothing for us here and nothing for us there. We're just lost somewhere in between, tramping from pillar to post, lackeys, a bunch of religious skivvies. We're stuck in the middle of the sea really, and we don't see it at all, don't feel the waves pulling us under. Just as well we're all strong swimmers, bred to it."

"I don't know what you mean."

He offered another brief smile. "He's a hard God, Kate, that's what I mean. A hard God, a hard task-master. And I wonder why. I really wonder why."

She smiled in turn. "Maybe I don't know because I'm not listening. Maybe I gave up when you got all knotted up and twisted." She smiled more broadly, finally pulled her hands free of him and touched his face, feeling him. She desired him and wanted him to desire her. It flushed through her. Her muscles ached. She touched him with that need. She wanted to make him dance, because, she knew, a dancer has no shame, and that made them at their best, dancing together, dancers without shame. That was how she viewed them. It was always wrapped up with that picture of their spontaneous, unrehearsed dance along the quay. It was rare that such things occurred. But they had. It had been the start of them. And then, when they had danced, held each other, moved together, they would come together again, the dance triumphant, partners again. She said: "I'm cold. I'm getting cold. I think it's time for bed. What do you say?"

Only a few coals still glowed in the grate. The air had become still and sharp. It was almost completely dark. John stood up. Their faces were close together. They could taste each other's breath. John brought her close to him. She was bursting with the desire to dance, the desire to be held by him, laid bare without shame.

"This Murphy's out to cause trouble," he whispered.

"When trouble comes stand firm," she said. He laughed. "Should we dance?" she asked. "I think I have a mind to it, after all this. We should have let Marty give us a tune. He's at his best then. Should we not dance?"

"Not tonight," he said. He immediately saw the declension of her features in the frail light and felt the weight of her against him, the weight of her disappointment. He said: "I don't think I'd be quite myself tonight. That's all right, isn't it. I'd rather be myself. You understand that." She didn't reply, but nodded, nodded then smiled, but that was barely discernible in the near dark. He led her to the stair. At the first step he laughed out loud. "You know, Kate, we should get ourselves a pig and fatten it up. That'd be something. What do you say?"

Kate made no response but walked ahead of him, up the unlit stairway, in her mind dreaming of dancing, remembering the two of them along the quays, just beginning, hearing its tune, its laughter, feeling its victory, its shameless victory.

*

Robert holds a stone aloft. It is bright in the sun. He blinks. The stone is white. He has wiped it with his fingers and against his body. It has an inscription. He recognises the language. He has seen it before. He doesn't understand it though. *Jupiter Maximus Optimus.* He reads it aloud, slowly, methodically, meditatively. *Jupiter Maximus Optimus.* He looks around at the coal banks. The collection of coal continues despite *Jupiter Maximus Optimus.* Eventually Dora stops picking. She looks at the stone held aloft. Her eyes light up. She knows immediately that Robert has discovered a treasure. She comes to him. He lowers the stone so that she can see the inscription. She touches it with her fingers and asks him what it means. He shakes his head. They both look down over the town spread across the bowl of the valley. It is white and appears polished in the brilliance of the low winter sun. Robert holds the stone aloft once more and then runs from the coal banks towards the town in order to find Father Bond.

It was that piece of stone inscribed for the God Jupiter, *best and greatest*, that brought the *foreigner*. He came in a car and when he attempted to drive up the coal banks with Father Bond beside him he had a procession behind him that trailed for hundreds of yards. They called him the *foreigner* to begin with, not simply because he was not local, only the priest had any inkling of exactly where he had come from, but because he was dark skinned and wore his hair long and carefully curled. In addition, he dressed in a style, stiff three-quarter skirt-coat with raised collar and velvet hat, that no one had seen before, and even smelled of strong perfume, which was completely unknown. He cut such a dandy figure tiptoeing across the black scree, crouching from time to time to press his fingers into the soft granular floor, that he was called Mr Fancy, and that name remained. But such was the authority of the unusually, but cleanly spoken, strangely dressed outsider, that when Mr Fancy stood on the seat of his open top car, raised his right hand as if about to offer the crowd a blessing, and announced, "We dig!" everyone applauded, politely, resolutely.

Mr Fancy was assisted by all of Whitehaven's Irish children, who lived in the terraces below the coal banks. They worked away with the small trowels that Mr Fancy provided, scraping their way through the black dust as Mr Fancy had shown them, for more of the white stone that Robert had found. In a single winter month they unearthed seventeen altars, dedicated variously to *Jupiter (Maximus Optimus), Victory, Mars, Vulcan,* or bearing no dedication at all. As the instigator of the whole affair Robert discovered that he had something of a privileged position in that he worked alongside Mr Fancy himself. He found he relished the opportunity, taking great delight in inhaling the acrid Cologne Mr Fancy wore, and in listening to his short clipped trailing syllables as he spoke. He was a representative of another world, a world which produced buried holiness, conducted itself in a manner of rarefied solemnity and seemed at ease with itself. For Robert it was all very tantalising and agreeable. It was all so far removed from his known world: it suggested unheard of borders, boundaries and newness.

Robert's fascination with Mr Fancy became acute the day they examined an altar together which bore the image of a short, squat, square figure with an enormous head, a great ball with horns. In one hand it held a spear and in the other a shield. In order to better trace the inscribed figure Mr Fancy took Robert's hand and dragged his index finger around the outline. "Belatucadros," Mr Fancy said. "The God is Belatucadros; a warrior God and also a vision of fertility." He brought Robert's fingers across the outline of the God's spear, down the elongated slender nose in the God's face, and over the God's lumpy genitals, and finally around the God's shield. He spoke quietly at Robert's ear whilst he traced the figure before him. "Belatucadros is not a Roman God at all. He was a Celtic God. He would have been the warrior and fertility God all along this stretch of coast, the whole Cumberland coast maybe. Have you ever seen such a God Robert? A round headed horned God. A frightening God, Robert." Mr Fancy released him.

Robert stepped back. Mr Fancy knelt at the altar and blew at the outline to remove the particles of black dust. Robert shook his head. No, he had never seen an ugly warrior God. He had never seen an armed God. But he was aware of an armed God. He was aware of his God, who was not a warrior God, and yet who brought a sword to sever families. In comparison to that God Belatucadros was a tiny monster.

Still kneeling Mr Fancy continued: "The Romans would worship anyone's Gods, as long as anyone worshipped theirs. Pragmatism like that was their strength. Can you understand that, Robert? That is how they conquered their known world. Belatucadros simply becomes *Jupiter Maximus Optimus.*" Mr Fancy stood up and took hold of Robert's hand once again. "Do you see that altar, Robert?" he said, leading him to a cleaned white stone. "It was erected by Marcus Maenius Agrippa of the First Cohort of Spaniards. You see, Robert, Spanish like me. My people were here before your people. Strange isn't it. A strange world, Robert, that brings a Spanish Jew and an Irish Catholic in this most unlikely of places before the altar of the *best and greatest* because the Romans had once made it their own."

"Did the Romans rule all the world, Mr Fancy?"

"No, not at all. In the time of your Christ there were many other empires: the Kushan in India; the Parthian in Persia, the Han in China. It seems the only certainty of empires is that they don't last, they die, like us all. And then people like us come along and dig them up. Does life make any sense at all, Robert? We pull out the remains of a little person, someone of no consequence at all, and we ask, what on earth has happened to you that you find yourself here? But we have no answers. All we know is the name of the Emperor, but then nothing more. So, we make a big leap of imagination and make a story. We breathe life into it as if we could make something immortal. And all the time we are trying to breathe life into ourselves because we are afraid of what we have discovered. The part is never the whole, but the whole is never entirely the part either. What are we to make of it? How do we live with such knowledge? History is a terrifying admission Robert, don't you think."

"Mr Fancy, is he not your Christ too?"

Mr Fancy laughed out loud. "No, he is not mine. And, please, call me Clemente."

That night Robert had strange dreams in which Belatucadros and Clemente became one. He was kneeling with the warrior God, spear and shield at arms, at an altar to the *best and greatest*, praying, and the *best and greatest* was not Our Lord. The warrior God, Clemente, the ugly little God, Belatucadros, denied it: *He is not mine. And, please, call me Clemente.* Robert was so disturbed by his dream that he couldn't bring himself to attend the dig the next morning. Instead he went to see Father Bond to find out why He, Our Lord, who Robert loved with an embarrassed passion, was not Mr Fancy's Christ too. Father Bond, balding and overweight, huffed and puffed his way around his study, grimaced at Robert, then finally nodded his head a couple of times, and said: "I suppose, Robert, in time we will have to forgive the Spanish gentleman and everyone like him for what they did. He is a Jew Robert and that's all there is to it."

"But wasn't He the King of the Jews, Father?"

"No, Robert, he was not."

Feeling no better informed, but already missing the scent of Mr Fancy, and the tones of his voice, Robert headed back towards the coal banks. As he approached them he felt that they were now invested with an eerie visual presence, made up of Belatucadros who had come alive in his dream. It was as if the warrior God, its shape, the hideous globe head, the snake nose, the bulbous eyes, the narrow and stern mouth, the lumpy genitalia, permeated the slag. He was not at all surprised, then, to look up at the horizon and see a figure there, arms aloft, blacked out completely by the severe sunlight, his cohorts behind him.

Robert ran to Mr Fancy who, along with the children, had stopped work and were watching the figure on the crest of the bank above them. For some time the figure simply watched them, then it began to shout down at them in an unbroken, guttural, tirade: "Come witness the bastard brats fawning around the Jew. Is it not a sickly sight? Is it not corruption? Is it not disgusting? Come witness them serving the Jew.

Come witness the popish brats and the scarlet whore drunk together on the blood of churches. Remember we have hated God's enemies with a perfect hate and we hate them now. We hate their desecration. Come witness them clawing for their heathen Gods, popery and Jew together." For a moment he stopped speaking, but before the echo of his voice had lifted from the scree he lifted his arm, pointed directly at Mr Fancy and began again: "There he is, the infidel, the heathen, the Jew, the anti-Christ, his palms still red with the blood of the sacred Lord. You can smell his corrupted body, smell his sin, smell the carnal conspiracy that festers in his body. The Jew body. It is too disgusting to contemplate what he has indulged in with these popish brats, what filthy practices have taken place, rolling together in the earth, the soiled earth. But he will be judged and so will they. We are the Israelites. The true Israelites. We must prepare the way for the coming of the Lord in glory into the cleansed body of the reformed church. I say, we are the Israelites."

During the course of this resumed speech Mr Fancy began to clamber slowly up the bank towards the intruder. He had listened dumbfounded for a while, as uncertain as the children as to what this sermon might mean, but then as the sense of the argument penetrated he had revolted at the slander and wanted it stopped. As to what he thought he would do against so many when he reached the summit he hadn't given any thought. It was a spontaneous act that had him climbing the slag, a spontaneous, courageous act. Robert viewed his progress with a mixture of fear and increased respect. Mr Fancy might be outlandish, different to any other man he had ever seen or heard, but he was heroic. He didn't understand what he was being defended against, but he recognised that it was certainly the case. Mr Fancy was climbing on his account, his and the other children. He hadn't stood still or turned tail.

All the time Mr Fancy climbed the hand of the figure on the crest remained fixed on him, frozen like a strange statuesque apparition, whilst his voice still cascaded down the bank, continuing its droning tirade. "And the brats do his work. We know what they are: a police problem, a sanitary problem, a public nuisance problem, an industrial problem. But the bosses love them, of course. Even though they live in troughs with their animals. Even though they lie down with their pigs while their parents fornicate before their very eyes. Of course they do the Jew's work." He began to laugh out loud. The sound was harsh and unreal. It seemed to roll along the banks. It was directed towards Mr Fancy who had almost reached the summit. He scrambled among the loose cinders and ashes for a hold. Eventually he was directly before the figure on the summit. As he tried to find a secure foothold to stand up the man above him pulled him to his feet, held him by the collar at arms length then screamed into his face: "Race implies difference and difference implies superiority and superiority leads to predominance. God's will be done!" He spat three times into Mr Fancy's face, slapped him three times, then hurled him back down the loose slag bank.

Mr Fancy lay amongst the cinders and ashes at the foot of the bank weeping, his exquisitely laundered clothes torn and blackened. Robert wanted to go to him, wanted to help him, except the voice above him did not cease but repeated, over and over: "God's will be done!" He found himself running with the other children towards the shelter of the terraces.

Robert didn't see Mr Fancy again. He didn't stay. There were to be no more altars unearthed. That was the last of *Jupiter Maximus Optimus*. Robert mourned its absence. He would never forget Mr Fancy. *Jupiter Maximus Optimus* had taken hold of his imagination. He pictured a dazzling world beyond the slag, a world of perfume, raiment and ideas, a world conveyed by the figure of Mr Fancy. It excited him, beguiled him, and these things made him afraid, without his having any idea as to why that should be. All he knew was that he missed Mr Fancy deeply, but considered it was better to keep that fact to himself.

*

John Devlin, his face blackened with coal-dust, gazes intently at the Irish Sea, his eyes wide open, coal-dust even lining the rims of his reddened lids. His eyes reflect the cold orange surface of the water. The sun rests just along the horizon. His gaze is severe, obsessional. The Irish Sea is not just any sea. It is dear to his heart. He is drawn to every little ship that moves upon it. And from his vantage point, Loft Pit, Whitehaven's newest and highest, perched like a fortress on the cliffs of the valley side above the town, he can see it all, the very rim of the world. He is, as if in his blackened state he were an inverse of the fast appearing moon, letting the sea influence him, dictate to him. He is recreating in his mind a journey of little ships, reading his history in it, his personality, and something of his nature. Loaded up in the stern of Kelly's coalboat, the exchange being people for coal on the Irish side, with the furniture of whole families pressed against him, he had been brought here. As Kate Boland, who was to be Kate Devlin, had been brought here before him, sometime in 1890.

She remembered vividly the sound of furniture crashing as it came around the ears of herself and another teenage exile Kate Kearney as the boat pulled from the quay and that, in the same instance, she took one last look at the only relative to see her off, her grandfather, standing alone, and saw that his face was suddenly sallow, worn and fatigued, and in that parting expression she read a message that said: *Say nothing at all. Please say nothing at all.* It was as if the crashing furniture and the silence of his expression were inexorably linked. And nothing was ever said. He died a few months later, after which Kate was joined by her elder sister Dora, two younger sisters Polly and Julia, and then, finally, by Marty, Workhouse Marty, the fiddle player, the youngest of them all.

As the thought of Marty crossed his mind John Devlin turned away from the sea and looked down over the town. A pall of thick yellow smoke and mist hung over the bone white Georgian gridiron streets. Along the valley sides the serried contours of mines, tanners and rail-yards formed vague shapes through the gloom. Below him the screes ran down to the custom built Irish houses, Ginns and Mount Pleasant. Both estates, skirting the haphazard accumulation of dock-side factories, appeared to be cut from the valley itself. Mount Pleasant was constructed like a series of rectangular caves, one on top of another, with a dwelling to either side of steps that ran from the docks to the pits above. Ginns stretched along the valley in a series of terraces, one row looking down onto the roofs of the next. Officially they were known as the New Houses, built on the cheap to house migrant workers, but were known as Ginns because of the three engines overlooking the terraces used to pump floodwater from the mines.

Below the terraces the dock basins shimmered in the sun's afterglow, the fishing smacks and barges creaking as they bobbed in the stiff evening breeze. Riding-lights ran in irregular diamonds across the black waters. Seagulls bickered around the hulls. The slender quays, *Old Tongue, Sugar Tongue, Lime Tongue, Merchants' Quay* and *Fish Quay*, stretched delicate white arms into the grey waters within the harbour walls. John Devlin took it all in with one cursory, dissatisfied look, spat at his feet, his saliva thick and black, put his boot into it and smeared it across the ground. He clasped his arms around his spare frame and began to pace along the loft.

It was not long before he heard the sound of stifled coughing coming from the steps below him. He recognised immediately from its wretched, swallowed tone that it was Bobby Kavanagh, his brother-in-law, Polly's husband. Bobby duly appeared on the top step, a large white handkerchief pressed to his lips, his torso in spasm. John waited for the crisis to subside then greeted him by simply saying his name. Bobby did likewise. They were obviously at a loss as how to say more, but appreciated the other's uncertainty. They stood together in the comparative silence of Bobby's congestive fits.

A few minutes later they were joined by two others. One of them, the elder, Gavin Duffy, Loft's union official (he also took responsibility for Fish, Canning and Lady pits) was coal blackened like John. Nevertheless, despite the industrial covering, the undeliberate disguise, the imprint of a brooding, severe face was still definable. He gazed intently at Bobby, and then, as if affronted by the show of white handkerchief, curtly demanded: "Is Kavanagh up to it? I don't want any dead-weight. Do you understand? I take this seriously. Is he game?"

"Fuck off, Duffy?" Bobby uttered from behind his cover.

John looked at Bobby. The handkerchief was still pressed to his face, but he recognised a familiar, determined look around the eyes. He was in no doubt. Besides, Bobby's retort reassured him. He turned to Duffy and quietly stated: "As much as the rest of us."

"I don't want any dead-weight. Do you understand? This is the real thing. This means something. We can't afford stiffs."

Duffy's insinuation rankled John. He felt it was an attack on him, on his judgement, made right to his face. Duffy's meaning was clear. John should have left Bobby out of it. The decision to include him was flawed. John was about to speak up, demand his case, state exactly where he could place his trust, when Duffy's partner, a young man known surprisingly for a miner as Docker, the origins of the name forgotten even to himself, began to crow the syllables of Kavanagh, the repeated taunt producing a monotonous sing-song insult: "Kavanagh, Kavanagh, Kavanagh!" (The English pronounce it with elongated syllables, the Irish with short.)

Bobby lowered his handkerchief, set his eyes sharply on Docker, then deposited a pool of discoloured sputum at his feet. It splashed like gull droppings.

Docker instinctively stiffened, but didn't step back. His expression contracted with the need to say something, but words wouldn't come. Instead he jumped at Bobby and seized him by the jacket.

Bobby held his ground and tried to shrug Docker off him. Docker maintained his hold and attempted to pull Bobby close to him, motivated by no clearer purpose than to swear into his face. Bobby's arm went back, but before he could strike at Docker John intervened. He pushed himself between them, forcing a wedge with his elbow. "That's enough!" he declared, frustrated and angered by what he considered a disastrous turn of events. His own personal dissatisfaction surfaced with his temper. This was contrary to the plan. It threw everything into doubt. That possibility disgusted him. They were wrecking his resolve. He revolted at that. He hissed aloud: "That's more than enough. I thought we had something to do? Are you afraid of it. Is that it? Is it? If you are, then clear off!"

Gavin looked on dispassionately. He had a tendency to feel superior in disputes between his own kind and rarely interfered. He told himself that he had learned to expect such things, his experience suggested little else. His class were antagonistic, instinctual and predictable. It was to their detriment, but nevertheless were qualities he could shape and direct. Characters like Docker were useful foot-soldiers (he thought of his activities as a war, a suppressed, enduring war), stupid but obedient and strong. His sort needed Gavin. He underlined their deficiencies and filled the gap. He was a leader, well aware that what he led were a rag-tag, but there were no limits to what he would claim for them, what he would claim for himself. The future could be theirs. He was suffused with belief. He was devoid of doubt. If it had been suggested that the fight had been any responsibility of his he would have denounced such an idea out of hand. He had been strict and logical, right to wonder about Kavanagh. He couldn't answer for Docker. He guessed it would amount to nothing. It rarely did. Besides he knew John would have stepped in. That was his character, his role. He wasn't entirely impressed by such a quality. It was too liable to be wayward. People like John Devlin were a problem. They had a tendency to stand alone. It was a tactic doomed to defeat. He hated the thought of defeat. It was demoralising. It poisoned everything. He had to work out how to keep John in place. Meantime he did what he did.

As Gavin looked on Docker slowly relinquished his hold. He turned to Gavin for some sign, but none was forthcoming. He released Bobby with a final shrug, but Bobby remained rooted. Docker uttered: "I'm ready!" He looked directly at Bobby as he said it, couching it as a question, challenging him.

Bobby skewed his face, half-smiled, and said: "Let's go, then."

They went from Loft by a series of meandering steps down towards the screes. It began to drizzle. The black earth became soft, sludge like. They continued down until they were amongst the dock basins, then picked their way around the stationary coal-hops, cranes, suspended jibs and chutes. Through the sketchy cloud a pale yellow moon was visible above the water. The breaking cloud fragments drifted across its surface. The waters sucked and shushed all around them. Distant voices drifted in and out of ear shot, and the further sound of the town came in and out of focus with the drizzle. They didn't speak but walked on, hunched, discrete figures, tending towards the shadows. They skirted the docks, then walked along the main rail-line which followed the coast, connecting the industrialised sea towns. Soon they left Whitehaven behind. They had shallow cliffs to their right and the sea to their left. The sea made a sound of multitudinous voices as it broke against the boulders forming the tidal break, and breezes echoed in the cliff crevices. Still the men did not speak. They smoked without sharing, without even offering. Only Docker made any sound, humming a snatch of a tune now and again, the notes flat and monotonous. After an hour's walking, sticking to the line, they came to Maryport, a town built on the mouth of a river: originally named Ellenfoot, it had been renamed after the daughter of a local landowner. As they reached the perimeter of the town Gavin stepped to the fore and took charge, pointing out the direction they had to follow.

He led them from the line through a series of banked, decrepit streets, until they came to the highest point in the town, the streets giving way to a series of well dressed squares with central gardens. From there he directed them into a closed, darkened courtyard. He stopped them, held them in the shadows and pointed to a small Presbyterian chapel. "He'll be in there," he whispered, waving his finger. "I was told. A fact. My source is good, reliable. He says he stays behind to pray. Stays alone. He's not pious though, not like that, not a holy man, not really. My source says that. Just part of the act, he says, and he doesn't like it. You see, my source prays in there as well. But he's all right. We can trust him. He's one of us."

"In a chapel?" Bobby queried, his voice thick in his throat, his chest heavy from the long walk.

"Where else would he be? Where else would he peddle his filth."

"Not in a chapel."

"Of course he's in the fucking chapel. I'm saying so. He's in there. That's what I was told. My source was very precise. We just have to walk in. He's ours."

"I don't mean that. Us. Not in a chapel. I mean..."

"Just what the hell do you mean?" Docker broke in, relishing the opportunity of having a stab at Bobby.

"Don't start again," Bobby retorted. "For God's sake, not again. I just don't think it's right, not in a chapel, that's all. That's my opinion. I should say, shouldn't I, say if I think it isn't right."

"No dead-weight, that's what I said, no fucking stiffs. I said it, made it plain at the outset. No stiffs. For Christ sake!" Gavin wailed, disgusted by Bobby's reluctance. "Are you scared, Kavanagh? Is that it? All this cheap, fucking talk because you're scared of it. Not up to it?"

Bobby shook his head quietly. He remained composed and spoke up calmly: "Sin, Gavin, I actually think it would be a sin, a sin to go into a chapel and do what we have to do. I don't see why we can't wait until he comes out, that's all. I can't see any reason why we shouldn't do that. I'm not suggesting anything else."

Gavin responded sharply: "And have the whole of Maryport watch us Kavanagh! Is that what you want? Tell the whole world what we're about? Christ! Don't be a complete fool. Not now, for God's sake. Not when we've come this far. Listen, each nation, Kavanagh, each nation has to sort out its own salvation! Do you understand? There's not a world, not half a world, not a name, nothing, not a damned thing between us. But everything between us and him. That isn't our house. It's nothing to us, nothing. Christ, we don't belong here. We don't belong here and they don't want us. Do you get it? Do you, Kavanagh, do you? We're filthy foreigners here doing just what it takes to get by. Remember, we're outside everything, absolutely everything. So you don't have to worry. You don't have to think what house it is. It's not ours. If we are going to do this then we have to go in. That's how it is. Now are you with us or are you against us?"

"Come on," John cut in before Bobby could reply. "Bobby's with us. Let's get the hell in there and get it over with. I don't like all this talk. It makes me uncomfortable, makes me itch. Come on, we all know why we are here."

It was not a place of worship they were familiar with. It contained an austerity that baffled them. The symbolism was all wrong. It made them awkward, more awkward than they had even imagined, and they had imagined all sorts. They were full of imaginings. But this was unexpected. They couldn't reason that it made their God more distant, maybe even absent from that scene. The austerity made them stop in their tracks.

They stood in a line in the body of the building. In front of them there was a stage. There was a single unoccupied cross adorning the wall above it. The stage itself was virtually bare. To one side there was a lectern, and in the centre, beneath the cross, there was a single chair. Murphy sat there. His head was bowed. He was at prayer. Or at least they assumed he was at prayer. Duffy had been told that that was what he did. He stayed behind and prayed, though it was not a holy act. They were told he was not a holy man, not pious. It was part of the act. They had caught him in the act then. He was alone.

The four approached him. He heard their footfalls. He looked up slowly. He blinked a number of times. His eyes crossed each of their faces with curiosity. There was no fear. As they came ever closer, their progress towards the stage slow and circumspect, he stood up. He continued to gaze at them steadily for a moment and then he began to lick his lips, making a large circular movement with his tongue. He began to smile. It became a wide, open mouthed grin. The pink lining of his lips showed against the black frame of beard. He looked excited, thrilled by their entrance, ready perhaps to burst out laughing.

Gavin spoke first: "We've come for you Murphy."

John spoke immediately after him: "You frightened our children, Murphy, and we can't have that, can't have that at all. We won't accept having our children frightened. Not our children. You have to deal with us now."

Murphy grinned even more widely than he had before. Then he raised his arms as he had on the summit of the slag banks and let out a single piercing howl.

As its note died away it was taken up by soft shrill laughter which answered from the body of the chapel. It came from Docker. He was excited and frightened. It made his voice shrill and tremulous. "You're a madman," he called out. "You know that, Murphy, a fucking madman. That's right, just a fucking madman!" As he spoke he took an iron drill from inside his jacket.

The grin slowly faded from Murphy's face. He continued, though, to watch their each and every movement, his eyes flickering from one to the other, his expression alert, even hungry. He suddenly howled again. The action was too much for Docker who immediately rushed at the stage and swung the iron drill at him, screaming at him to shut up, to stop his disgusting row.

Murphy watched him come and jumped back against the wall. The metal shaft came down onto the boards with a resounding thud, the hollow stage absorbing its force. Murphy stepped forward quickly, placed one boot across the bar, and landed the other in Docker's face. Docker's mouth filled with blood. He released the drill and fell back.

Bobby went to his aid, pushing his handkerchief at the blood. As he did so, trying to stem the haemorrhage, Murphy leapt from the platform and landed against the two of them, forcing them beneath him. Bobby immediately began to choke under his weight. A moment later Murphy lifted himself up and struck at them a number of quick, heavy blows, then attempted to regain his feet. He howled again as he tried to stand, striking at the two at his feet as he did, the sound now intermingled with gurgling, tidal laughter.

He was almost back on his feet and upright when John came up to him. He had been caught off guard by the speed of Murphy's assault and had not immediately reacted. But now he had regained his presence of mind. He stood face to face with Murphy and met smile with smile. He could see that Murphy was poised to strike out again. His expression was full of it. He thought he was going to triumph. He didn't fear them at all. Then, without undue force, without any demonstration, John pressed a knife into Murphy's stomach. Murphy's lips instantly parted. He breathed in sharply. His body stiffened with the sensation of pain.

John stepped back. The knife remained in place. Murphy placed his hands around the handle. He smiled again, forcing that gesture, that defiance, from himself. For a moment everything seemed caught in suspension. Nothing happened. The moment seemed prolonged and terrible.

It was Gavin who broke the mood. He wrenched at the blade and brought it out of Murphy's guts, slicing through his fingers as he did, then he immediately brought it down against Murphy's chest. Murphy breathed in with sharp gulps, but couldn't breathe out. The air sat in his body, bloating him, making him engorged. He was drowning. He spun round, suffocating, in pain, but nevertheless his eyes picked out his assailants as he spun. His expression adopted a strange relaxation, a look of satisfaction, and his breathing took on a sound like laughter.

The noise infuriated Bobby. He stood up. It wasn't easy. His ruptured breathing was still stifled in his throat. Nevertheless, he managed to get himself to his feet. He stumbled towards the stage, reached for Docker's drill, then turned with it raised in his hand, took a number of quick steps towards Murphy and brought it down crashing against Murphy's head. Murphy stood transfixed for a second, his expression one of obsolete wonder, then he fell heavily to the ground.

It took them a while to collect themselves. They stood for some time without acknowledging each other, listening to their own laboured breaths. Even Docker forced himself to his feet. He kept one hand pressed hard against his mouth. His chest rose and fell rapidly. And then, as if it were at some predestined signal they gathered around the body. They remained hesitant, scared to touch it, scared to kneel and verify to each other that he was dead. Any doubt was somehow welcome. They knew that he was, though. They knew the truth of their silence. There was no escaping it. They had killed him. They had done what they had intended, though they had never openly admitted to each other that that was their ultimate purpose. All the same, they knew that was what they had agreed to. A pool of blood had leaked from his stomach and chest and a purple clot was apparent on his smashed head.

Again it was Gavin who broke the solemnity. He threw down a sixpenny piece and said: "That's for the statute of Kilkenny which fined an Englishman sixpennies for killing an Irishman." He withdrew the knife. There was a gasp of air. It was a lifeless gasp. It escaped from the hole in the chest. Gavin held the knife in his hand for a moment or two, then knelt down and wiped it with Murphy's jacket, taking pains to ensure the blade was clean. When he was quite satisfied that the weapon was free of Murphy's blood he stood up and held it out to John, handle forward. John gazed at it for a moment, unable to meet the steady intensity of Gavin's expression, which was vividly apparent behind the now thin veil of coal-dust. He reached out took hold of the handle firmly and held it perfectly still, allowing Gavin to remove his hand. He then thrust it quickly back inside his jacket. Straight after Gavin told them to get the hell out of it.

They went back along the line the same way they had come, their pace quick but not rushed. The further they came, the further they left Maryport behind them, the more certain they became that they were in the clear. It could be days before Murphy was discovered. There was nothing to connect them with the scene. They had not been seen. They had acted. They had taken something on themselves and they had succeeded. It was something they had done for themselves and for each other. They became quietly, personally exhilarated.

When Whitehaven came into view John stopped. The others went on and then also stopped, waiting for him. He took the knife from his pocket. He had bought it himself. It had no history as far as he knew. He had acquired it because he always had a mind to keep a pig and thought it would be good for butchery. He smiled grimly at the thought. He turned and looked towards the sea. The others walked on a little further. He knew they were leaving him alone to decide about the knife.

31

They had nothing to say about it. They could live with it or without it, but they conceded the decision was his.

A slim disk of moon was visible above the sea. It swam through the waves. John threw the knife into the water. He failed to hear it as it went beneath the surface. He listened as the waves broke against the boulders, a speech of unintelligible syllables from a sea dear to his heart. He smiled at the sound, smiled at what they'd done, smiled because he was going home to dance with Kate. It was, after all, March 17th, 1910, Saint Patrick's day.

Chapter Two

1912, two years on from any accusation or reprisal regarding Murphy, and John Devlin stepped rather gingerly into the kitchen of his own house clutching a shabby sack to his belly. He stopped short at the sight of Julia, Kate's sister, enormously pregnant, sunk in a chair by the fireside.

She was the youngest and most attractive of the Boland sisters, and also the most troublesome. Headstrong and witty, and in her own words, *the least prone to backwardness,* she had married Jones, an Englishman and a Protestant, which had demanded that she had had to fight her sisters, and when the time was propitious forgive them, which she had managed, and in so doing had won them to her.

Jones, an attractive blond haired miner, prone to sarcasm and violence, led her a dog's life, shaped by episodes of binge drinking and beatings, followed by the emotional excesses of his penance. All of which might have been guessed by the sisters but was never verified as Julia refused absolutely to discuss her marriage with any of them. She was particularly adamant over the point regarding children which, as the years passed, seemed would never happen, so that now, in her thirties, they worried that she was too old to be starting. And as it happened the pregnancy had been long and difficult, marked by fatigue and sickness. She was now weeks overdue.

It seemed to John she sat in great discomfort, constantly stroking her vastly swollen, awkward belly. It made him shy and tetchy. It was a trouble he was powerless to influence, one he was therefore afraid of. It was with a certain embarrassment that he watched both Kate and Marty, Kate seated opposite Julia and Marty behind her, also stroke and attend to her body. He could scarcely look. Julia, however, immediately fixed him with a mawkish grin and said: "And how's Mr Devlin doing, I ask myself, if he's not going to speak?"

Robert, who had been sitting at the table, quietly reading the same passage over and over, from a book he had borrowed from Father Bond, *With our tongue we will prevail, our lips are our own; who is Lord over us?* started at the sound of Julia's voice, and with a look of some apprehension suddenly turned to his father. Dora, beside him, placed her hand over his as it lay on the page. He immediately looked down and stared at the back of his sister's hand. She smiled indulgently towards her father.

John was taken aback. Robert's timidity towards him confused and irritated him. He quickly took in the faces around the room. There was a mournfulness he couldn't quite penetrate. He presumed it was to do with the baby, but was at a loss as to know how to pursue the issue. He felt certain he was being deliberately debarred. He looked at Julia. She was still grinning at him, her expression coquettish and expectant. "Will you never give word to a body," she demanded crisply.

He shrugged. "I'm doing fine Julia but, more to the point, what about yourself?"

"Well, Mr Devlin, I'm in the same state I've been in for a while and I'm afraid I'm getting sick of it."

"Will it be much longer?"

"Well, who knows Mr Devlin? These things work their own way out."

"I wouldn't know."

"Of course not," she laughed.

"It won't be long now," Kate cut in authoritatively.

"So there you are," Julia said. "Now we know."

"Of course, Kate will know, Kate will do best," Marty eagerly joined in. He turned to John, smiled feebly and added: "Kate knows."

John eyed Marty impatiently. Marty's preening of Julia made him uncomfortable. It was unusual for a man, inappropriate somehow, being so obviously tender, in front of anyone. Marty got away with things. He used his eccentricity. It rankled John. "Are you in the loft?" he demanded, insinuating that it might be better if he took himself there now.

"No, John, I think I should help Julia along. It's a terrible load she has on her, you know. A terrible load. A helping hand, John, a helping hand."

"All right, all right!"

Julia, with the combined assistance of Kate and Marty, struggled to her feet, and then with both hands supporting her back walked up to John, stood swaying in front of him and grinned again: "It seems I'm not the only one carrying something of a burden. What are you hiding, man? You're more than cagey about it, acting like a common thief!"

For a moment John looked dismayed and somewhat bashful, unclear about what he should say, but then meeting Julia's quizzing look straight on, something relaxed in his demeanour and he smiled. In fact, within seconds a general excitement possessed him. He didn't say anything but knelt down and emptied his sack onto the kitchen floor. A small stunted pig rolled out onto the slabs. "I've got myself given a little runt," he announced triumphantly. "It would have just gone to waste. There was no sense in that, no sense at all." He looked up, keen to discover the impression his acquisition had made. He found Dora already beside him, bent over, eager to view it at close quarters. He seized on her interest. "Do you know what a runt is, Dora?" he asked, taking hold of her hand and drawing her to her knees beside the animal. "A runt is too small to cope with the rest of the litter, so we'll have to feed it. We'll have to rear it as if it were just like a baby. Can you and Robert manage that?"

Dora simply grinned.

Julia burst out laughing and made for the door, calling out: "Your man has his pig at last, God help you! God help you! You'd better get on with it Kate, or he'll be hell to live with." She let herself and Marty out, still laughing as she went.

As soon as the door closed behind her John looked up at Kate and demanded: "Is there something wrong with that baby?"

Kate picked up the runt in the palm of one hand and studied it. "Of course not. It's late, that's all."

"She's too old."

"Maybe."

"She doesn't look well."

"It's been a long pregnancy!"

"It was a long time coming."

"It's here now."

"But there's nothing wrong?"

"Oh, feed your animal, for God's sake, and leave the babies to those that know!" she snapped, laying the runt back on the kitchen floor.

"You and Dora feed it," he ordered, and immediately got to his feet. "I have a box to make. Robert come with me."

Robert was reluctant. As soon as his father had suggested that he and Dora would have to look after the runt he had set to work. He had immediately poured a little milk into a jug, and had already started to spoon the liquid into the piglet's mouth, holding its jaw in order to do so. The pink muzzle was wet with it. He looked up from the animal, obviously disappointed, his expression suggesting that he was already doing his bit, doing something he could manage. It was with a certain sensitivity that Kate took the spoon from him and gently ushered him to the door. John hadn't waited for him, but was already outside. He had no inkling of Robert's hesitation.

The small yard, between hen-hut and toilet, was a litter of junk. John collected anything he could lay his hands on, working on the premise that it might be useful one day. He sifted his way through various pieces of wood, picking out those that might fit together. As he did he spoke to Robert, his tone casual, undemanding. "What did your mother and Aunty Julia talk about?"

"I don't know."

"Were you not there?"

"I didn't listen."

John stopped and turned to him, his speech quickening. "You didn't listen?"

Robert lowered his eyes, quailing before the directness of his father's attention. In his mind he expected to be struck, and had already accepted the sting. The thought was strange, but not unusual. Robert often felt that he was about to be beaten, though he invariably never was. It was a habit of thought, a habit of imagination. He had no idea where it came from. His father wasn't violent with him. Unlike the majority of boys of his age Robert had never been leathered with either belt or strap. The reality of that fact didn't lessen either his apprehension or his sense of guilt. Those were imaginative customs. "No, I didn't," he answered gently, though with discernible force.

"What did you do?"

"I read?"

"You read? What? What did you read? Tell me."

"*With our tongue we will prevail, our lips are our own; who is Lord over us?*"

John didn't respond and remained silent for a while. He just gazed at Robert, his eyes crossing Robert's pale face, the apprehensive, thoughtful expression, the awkward, exposed pose, trying to work out what had happened to him to make him like that. That a son of his should be so obviously downright holy. It didn't make sense. How did he have such a son? After all, he had personally killed a man, stuck a knife into his belly, and felt no shame. Certainly he had dreamed of the killing, and wouldn't deny that the dreams were often bad, so much so that when he awoke he regularly had great difficulty shaking the dream off and separating it from reality, but despite that he wouldn't have changed for one second what he had done, what he had needed to do. And yet, Robert wasn't just holy. It wasn't holiness that made him stand there like that, refusing to admit what had been said. He was tough and truculent. He could see that. There was that tendency in his voice. Tough, truculent and moody. He liked that. He smiled at Robert and quietly said: "I'm really proud of you, you know. You know that, don't you? Really proud of you."

Robert lowered his face and blushed.

John made no further attempts to quiz him.

A couple of days later Aunty Dora arrived on the scene. She was the eldest of the Boland sisters, and was generally taken to be the most formidable, though that opinion of her was largely as a result of the matter of her appearance. Gazing out from beneath her white starched bonnet, rimmed with great clips, which kept her grey rope of lifeless hair in a perpetual bun, she appeared a brooding, ponderous, woman, possessed of a spirit of apparent solemnity. Yet, beneath the craggy, implacable, rather masculine integument, lurked a sharp, tender, woman, that only the tiniest amount of gin released. Her home-comings inevitably inaugurated a family party. When she had worked in hotels, wintering at the end of the season with each sister in turn, these parties were a weekly occurrence. Aunty Dora would sit cradling a gin bottle, one of the many she provided, quietly contemplating the proceedings with her adamantine features, until suddenly she tore off her coat and she was up to Marty's fiddle, going to it until the party concluded in the early hours. Now that she worked in houses her visits were more sporadic, yet still instigated a series of family celebrations, each sister taking it in turn to be host. What was unusual, unheard of, in fact, was for Aunty Dora to turn up unannounced, as she had done now.

Kate let her in and left her in the kitchen. They hadn't spoken on the doorstep. She didn't remove her coat, but went and sat by the fire and gazed into its flames. She made no acknowledgement of John or the children, neither looking at them nor speaking to them, despite their obvious surprise. Even by her standards such reserve was unusual. Dora began to smile, refusing to be discountenanced by such unusual behaviour. After a few moments she actually moved to be closer to her aunty, and sat scrutinising her, her frowning expression quizzical and interested.

37

Robert took up his book and moved off into a corner and began to read. His eyes fell on the text: *With our tongue we will prevail, our lips are our own; who is Lord over us?* He read it over and over. Eventually it had no meaning. It was simply a pattern and a texture, a piece of music. He let his imagination drift with the words. It removed him from the kitchen, removed him from having to know anything. The text was his flight. He wished he never had to return it.

John had been washing. He was stripped to the waist. He looked at Aunty Dora for a minute or so, trying to make sense of her presence and her strange behaviour, but couldn't work out either. Eventually he spoke up, expressing his surprise at seeing her, his surprise and, he supposed, his pleasure. He made a point of the supposition. He didn't know. He didn't generally take to surprises.

"I'm not stopping," she responded abruptly, as if telling him he need have no fears on that account. Then, before he could defend himself, she repeated it, speaking gently, almost warily, correcting herself. "No, I'm not stopping, you can rest assured on that score. Not long, anyway."

"That's a shame. A few days, at least. Wet our lips."

"I've come to see Julia. She's pregnant, you know, heavily pregnant I'm told. I should have seen her before now. I've been lapse."

"It's taking a long time."

"Yes, it's taking a long time. It's taking a very long time. I need to see her."

"What will you do?"

Aunty Dora turned from the fire in order to look at him, in order to face him down and let him know that she wasn't there to answer his questions. She was there in order to see Julia. To her surprise she met Dora's attention and obviously hadn't expected that. Her attention was evidently so wrapped up in something that she hadn't even seen her from the corner of her eye move into place. Still, she returned her attention steadily and the two of them contemplated each other for a while, each one as quizzical as the other.

Aunty Dora spoke first. Her tone was quiet and relaxed, yet had an unfamiliar quality, an edge of something, disappointment, disbelief, Dora wasn't at all sure just what, but she sensed it. "My little Dora, not so little anymore, a woman, God help us. A little woman. How did you get so old? How did that happen? Just about a woman. Well, do you intend to go though all this rigmarole and have children?"

Dora smiled broadly, not so much amused by the question, as wanting to mitigate the strange note she heard in her aunty's question.

She replied simply, but with frank enthusiasm: "Yes. I do. Lots! Yes, lots and lots, I reckon!"

Aunty Dora continued to gaze at her for a moment, and then something relaxed in her deliberately taut expression and she burst out laughing and at the same time shook her head. "God help you!" she pronounced. "Dear me, God help you! And God help your mother and father."

As far as anyone knew Aunty Dora had never had a man. She certainly had never admitted to any relationships with men, and really no one believed it possible. She was too solid, thickset and set in her ways to be imagined with anyone else. She had always been a spinster. She was made for it, born for it. She appeared a large, fleshy, overseeing virgin. She told stories of what went on in the kitchens of hotels and below stairs in the houses, the travelling salesman and delivery men and all their crack, but it was if she wasn't really there, not as a player, just a watcher, a welcome, likeable watcher, but just that. It didn't make her bitter or angry, rather patient and reflective. Her sisters loved her, loved her for her virginity. It marked her out, made her special in a defined way. There was something so obviously reliable in it, something predictable. She wasn't at the whim of what other people might do. She wasn't prone to crisis and emergencies. It was something they could trust in. She was always the same. It made her a virgin sentinel.

It was this break in predictability that John found so difficult. He couldn't work out what it meant and that irked him. It was obviously to do with Julia, but as to what he realised he wasn't going to be told. He was debarred. He couldn't stomach that. An image of Marty preening her weight crossed his mind. He snapped out, speaking over her continuing laugher: "What will you do?"

Her laughter stuttered to a halt and she fell silent. The silence made the small kitchen seem suddenly sombre. She turned to him and gazed steadily at him, her features set against him, hardening all the time she looked at him. She pressed her lips together, breathed out gently and then very quietly stated: "Whatever, John Devlin, whatever. I'll do whatever."

John was about to protest. It was outrageous. He insisted to himself that he had every right to know what brought her so far. He had to understand. He couldn't accept his exclusion. He was about to rebuke her for that refusal and demand that she talk sense to him when Kate came in, dressed for going out. She nodded at her sister, confirming that she was ready and then in a very matter of fact tone said: "We shouldn't be too long. We're going to see Julia."

"I know, she's pregnant," John responded tartly.

Kate turned to him with some surprise. "That's right," she said firmly, "she's pregnant, and we should see her. We are her sisters, after all."

John made no response. Kate and Aunty Dora stood for a moment, seemed to simultaneously but independently decide that there was nothing more to say and left without another word. As the door closed behind them John hurled his bar of carbolic into the sink. The water splashed up the window, the wall and across the kitchen floor, drips running down his torso to his waist. "Damn it!" he shouted. "Damn! Damn! Damn!"

The two didn't knock at Julia's but let themselves in. Jones rose quickly as they stepped into the kitchen. "Oh, it's only you," he said with some annoyance, grimacing as he sat back down. "What do you lot want?"

"Go to the bedroom, Julia," Kate said, quietly but firmly.

Julia began to protest.

"Go to the bedroom as Kate says," Aunty Dora cut in.

Julia didn't move, but sat upright, looking nervously between her two sisters. Aunty Dora repeated her injunction, but with an added note of obvious impatience. At that show of temper something in Julia snapped, and she felt her resistance drain away. She was too tired, too heavy, too not herself to want to interfere with what Kate and Dora had planned. She didn't have the fire left to wonder. Besides, there was something wonderful in conceding to them. She wanted to be cared for, wanted them to take charge. She felt as if years of senseless dispute fell away with that act of acquiescence. In an instance she became a little sister, a baby sister. Any lingering segregation, consequent to her marriage to Jones, a separation they all would have denied vehemently, was finished.

Without a further word she started to struggle to her feet. Kate and Aunty Dora came to each side of her to assist. Jones simply looked on, amused. "Have you come to pull it out?" he said. "Some old Irish trick for getting the damned thing over with."

Kate and Aunty Dora ignored him. They kept their attention on Julia, watching her all the while she made her cumbersome way from the room. She hesitated in the open door, and turned back. She was seized by a sudden sensation of panic. She struggled with it. She wanted to come back. Her thoughts were chaotic. She looked at Kate, her expression imploring readmission, but Kate pressed her, encouraging her. "Go on, go on, everything will be all right. Promise. You'll see. Go on, and close the door behind you." Eventually she lowered her eyes, and pulled the door slowly to behind her.

"What does she have to do?" Jones spoke up. "You haven't told her what to do."

Aunty Dora turned from the closed door towards Jones and gazed at him steadily for a moment, as if trying to come to some judgement about him. He repeated that they hadn't told her what to do. How the hell was she supposed to know? Aunty Dora replied quietly: "You've told her that, though, haven't you, told her what to do, time and time again, I believe." He shrugged, set his face against her, then scowled, shook his head and turned away, dismissing her. She stepped up to him slowly. She stood over him and waited. Eventually he turned his head towards her. He was going to let her know just how irritated and impatient he was becoming with this intrusion. He'd had enough. He wasn't about to play stupid games in his own kitchen.

However, as soon as he turned his face towards hers, she struck it, first one way and then the other, with a short iron bar she had secreted up her sleeve. In an instance she succeeded in transfiguring his beautiful face, making a sop of it, leaving two raw wounds. Jones leapt up with the second blow. With one hand he clutched at his face, his fingers spread claw like, clutching at the parted flesh: with the other he hit out blindly. He caught Aunty Dora in the eye socket. She tottered back. As she did Jones wiped his hand across his face, trying to clear the blood from his own eyes, readying himself for what might follow. However, before he could fully focus Kate, also armed, was on him.

She struck him across his raised hands, across his face and across his head. She struck him with a resentment she couldn't contain. She was wild with it. Her pent up distaste at Jones' concealed cruelties overwhelmed her. She wanted retribution.

Jones fell to the floor beneath the weight of her blows and crawled for the cover of the table.

Kate screamed at him as he sought his refuge. "You're a lucky man, Jones," she said, banging the table top above him. "A very lucky man, because up till now John Devlin and Bobby Kavanagh and Peter Kavanagh do not know the truth of what goes on here but, God help me, if there's a next time they will. Do you hear me? If anything should happen to that girl or baby from what you did to her you will answer

41

for it. First to us and then to God. Do you understand?" She repeated herself, screeching her words: "Do you understand?" Jones groaned.

At that moment she heard Julia on the stair. She immediately composed herself, rushed from the table and met her before Julia had chance to descend more than half-way. She reassured her that everything was all right, but then went on and forbade her leaving her bedroom until the following day, unless it was because the baby was on its way. In response to Julia's obvious dismay she demanded that Julia trust her. For a second time, sensing the sheer determination of her sister, Julia obeyed. She had already made the decision. She would do as her sisters told her. She had no resistance left. She was too worn out. She was grateful to be able to obey. She turned and made her way back to her room.

As Julia made her way up the stair Kate rushed back to the kitchen and set to work to wash both Aunty Dora and Jones.

Aunty Dora's eye wept profusely. When Jones hit out he had struck her tear duct. The damage he inflicted with that blow proved to be permanent. The duct never functioned properly again. A steady stream of unemotional tears was destined to wash Aunty Dora's face for the rest of her life.

When Kate had finished washing Jones she put towels beneath his head and left him in his semi-conscious state under the table. She then took a plate of bread and cheese and a cup of milk to Julia and told her she would be back soon enough and stay with her, and in the meantime to stay put. She added that she would empty the chamberpot herself when she returned. Julia didn't bother to argue.

Aunty Dora didn't return home with Kate, but immediately left for Saint Anne's arriving back that same day. They didn't mention what they had done on parting. Kate touched her cheek though and wiped away the gathering tears. Aunty Dora shrugged. The fact of tears was meaningless to her. She could work just the same.

Kate went home to make supper. It was obvious that John would have liked some answers but he made no demands. There was something about her demeanour and her busying herself, a sense of something that seemed like satisfaction but wasn't, though as to what it was he couldn't say (he also thought she seemed dissatisfied), that told him not to try.

She said absolutely nothing about what had occurred.

*

David Jones had watched Julia's swelling belly with dread, as if it were a disease. The more she grew the more she was drawn into it, absorbed by it, and became separated from him. The liveliness, laughter and forgiveness which typified her evaporated and left a quiet, but agitated, self contemplation. She was enthralled, absorbed and moved by her pregnancy. It seemed as if she had entered a dream world from which he was debarred. He watched her personal excitements, hesitations and whims with incomprehension: a spy in his own house. And each day it seemed she conceded more and more of herself to this mysterious thing, this thing which, for him, had no real life, no reality. He could not perceive it as child, something newly alive within her, something of him, but simply her exclusion from him. He began to retaliate.

He drank every night, came home drunk and insulted her. At first it was a mere calling of names, infantile insults of her altered body, pathetic name calling, not yet brutal. She cradled herself, made herself immune, ever more distinct from him, defying him with the serenity of her pregnancy. And then he struck her. After that he needed to be more drunk so as not to have to face the consequence of the previous night, by turns everything becoming previous, until nothing made any sense, except the gulf between them, the two worlds they occupied, the spiral of abuse they were living. A spiral which went so far that in the end he kicked her in the belly twice. It was then that Julia went to Kate and Kate sent a telegram for Aunty Dora. After that there was only silence in the house.

Nevertheless, it was Kate he sent for when the time came, sending a neighbour with the blunt message: Tell her she'd better get here. She dropped everything and rushed off around Ginns cobbled streets, leaving a quickly scribbled note for John. Within minutes she stood breathless in the small drab kitchen, bent over her labouring baby sister. There was no sunlight in the houses of Ginns as one house shadowed another. Julia got to her feet and clung to Kate, pressing her face against Kate's neck, letting her tears run across Kate's breasts. "I'm scared, Kate," she whispered, and kept repeating. "I'm scared, Kate. I'm scared." With each spasm they gulped together, held each other fast as the wave passed, then shuffled forward, trying to step away from the pain. As they shuffled together Kate caught glimpses of Jones over Julia's shoulder.

He gave no sign that he thought or felt anything. He simply stared from his still pulpy face, continuous, sullen. Perhaps this image of them embracing, attempting to share the load, was the ultimate demonstration of his exclusion, an exclusion he had so woefully failed to resist. He felt as if he had almost no place in his own kitchen. He told himself it all might have been different but for the fact that she was a foreigner. That was his mistake. To think that such things didn't matter. Of course they did. She brought her sisters beneath his roof. They were a bunch of drabs. Their talking got on his nerves. As long as Julia had fought them it had been all right. It made sure that she wasn't one of them. But she had returned and turned her back on him. This damned change in her body had driven her back to them. It suddenly struck him that her turning back to them underlined something that had been staring him in the face all along. She wanted the baby to be hers, hers and theirs. She wanted it to be one of them. An Irish Catholic, foreign baby. That was why she was so hung up on it. It wasn't surprising that he felt so little for it. That was how they wanted it. They had cut him out. They wanted him out of the frame altogether. It sickened him, sickened him to see the confidence with which the sister carried herself in his kitchen. It was all so different, so far removed from the early days when they had kissed in secret, secretly making love, as if they were residents in a different world altogether. The baby in her ruined all that, wiped it out. Now she acted as if she didn't remember, maybe worse, regretted all they had done. Nevertheless he couldn't take his eyes off her as she was helped across the dark room towards the fire, Julia whispering all the time, whispering at her sister's ear. Jones could see her speaking, but all he heard was the sound of wood snapping and somewhere far off a dog howling. He had no notion that she was saying, over and over, that she was scared, so scared.

"It's all right," Kate assured her, massaging Julia's body folded against her, "you've started, that's all. It's good. It won't be long now."

"But I haven't. I just want to go to the toilet, but I can't. I don't know how many times I've been out in the yard."

"Come with me. We'll see."

They made their way from the kitchen and went to the bedroom, leaving Jones alone without a word. He followed them with his eyes until the door closed, then simply stared into space. His thoughts ran to nothing. His isolation was complete. He had nothing left to think about. The closing door sealed their separation. Julia was gone. The baby went with her. She had kept it to herself. He felt nothing. There was only a nagging sense of despondency, a recollection of his battered features. He mourned his damaged looks. It wasn't a tangible thought, though, just a state of mind.

Once in the bedroom, Kate lit the small gas-mantle above the bed, then helped Julia to lay down. As she helped her onto the mattress she pulled her loose fitting smock away from her and exposed her large rounded belly. It was bitterly cold in the room and the air was musty damp so she wrapped coats around Julia's shoulders. Julia continued to complain that she was scared and that she didn't want to dirty herself. Kate laughed aloud and said: "You're well on, little sister, that's all, really well on, doing fine."

"I want the toilet, Kate," Julia protested weakly, no longer feeling she had the strength to manage it. She let herself become heavy against the mattress, not relaxed, but not so resistant.

Kate stroked Julia's face with one hand, and her now exposed belly with the other. "I'll send him for the nurse. She'll give you something, something to let you go to the toilet. It'll be all right. You'll see. Stop fretting for goodness sake. It's going to be all right." She laughed again, gave Julia's face one more rough massage, then left her in order to go down to Jones in order to tell him to fetch the midwife.

In Kate's brief absence Julia pressed her hands into the mattress, lifting her weight off it, and screamed out loud, not moved by pain so much as the fear of being alone. The room seemed to be closing in on her. She could feel her heart beating like a drum beneath her breast. When Kate returned she clung to her arm and refused to relinquish her hold. Kate stroked her. "Don't let me dirty the bed, Kate," Julia gasped. "Please God, don't let me dirty the bed. Take me to the toilet, please."

"You're all right," Kate insisted, "doing all right. It won't be long." She held Julia's face tightly between her cupped palms, smiled at her and declared: "You're doing really well, little sister, believe me. Trust me."

It wasn't long before Jones returned. He stood in the door frame for a while unable to speak, once again simply staring at the embracing sisters, but no longer making anything of it, no longer comprehending that he had an opinion of them. He was an obstinate, obsolete witness.

"Well?" Kate demanded sharply.

"It's cold in this room."

"It will have to do," Kate snapped. "We don't really have any choice, do we. Well, did you see the nurse?"

"She said she'll be along soon."

"No, David, go back and tell her I need her now." Jones didn't move. She shouted at him: "Go on! I want her now!" For a moment the look on Jones' face became fierce, but at that same moment Julia screamed out loud. He took another step into the room, but then stopped dead. He stared at Julia's tensile figure, and for a moment a likeness of her expression of pain appeared in his features. He was enlivened by it. He remained until her panic subsided and she again breathed normally, then, as the note vanished, its urgency paled, and she once again nestled against Kate, he became himself once again. He shrugged, gave a mild, meaningless grimace and left.

When he was gone Julia looked up tearfully at Kate. "I've wet the bed," she said hopelessly. "I can feel it! It's wet! After all that, I've wet the bed."

"It's nothing," Kate insisted. "It's a feeling, just a feeling. I'm telling you. Trust me. You're all right."

Julia sighed deeply and lay back heavily across the bed, repeatedly admonishing herself for wetting the bed.

Kate watched dismayed as the purple circle she knew was the reluctant baby appeared. At first it was small and appeared briefly, only to vanish and then reappear. But each time it appeared it grew larger, until it finally ceased disappearing altogether. Very rapidly it became a visible head. Kate placed her hand over it. She wasn't sure why. She had no sure knowledge of what she should be doing. She just felt compelled by a need to cradle this first revelation of child. She felt the soft bone of the skull, and blood and mucus trickling between her fingers. Julia seemed unaware of what was happening. Her arms were raised, pulling against the bed head, her screams coming now in quick succession.

Soon an entire crimson head, a misshapen squeezed ball stained with blood, became visible. Kate held it firmly. She fought her own repugnance. She could not abide this sight of the head strangled at the womb. It seemed to suggest that birth was terrible, altogether too hard. As she held the head she wished that Julia would stop screaming. It was too much. She couldn't help her. She was crying herself, and she knew it, but she was powerless to stop. She had to fix her attention on the baby. Everything else would have to wait. She slowly rotated the head as the baby continued to come and so brought its shoulder, arm and hand into sight. Eventually she felt the baby pushed hard against her hand and in one swift motion it lay complete between Julia's legs, sticky, soaked, crimson and very still. It seemed scarcely alive, suspended there helplessly between two worlds. Julia too seemed to sink away.

For a moment Kate felt incredibly alone. Neither Julia nor the baby were with her. She was terrified, unclear about what she should do next. She found herself simply watching the baby, which as far as she could tell wasn't breathing. Then, suddenly, with a remote but ferocious cry it began. Within seconds the outburst ceased, but then began again more strongly, and this time continued without cessation. Kate went to a drawer and brought a pair of dress making scissors. She knew they were there. Julia was a seamstress. Kate knew where she kept her things. She brought them back to the baby. She lay them down beside it, then tore at the sheet with her bare hands, tearing two ragged strips. She tied two ligatures on the cord an inch apart, then picked up the scissors and brought it to the leathery tissue. She hesitated for a moment and then pressed hard. The cord was stiff and firm between her fingers. It resisted as she cut. She bore down harder. The scissors sliced through. Blood splashed against the sheet. The ligatures remained firm. She picked up the separated baby and placed it amongst the coats over Julia's chest. Julia squeezed the child to her then pressed its head against her nipple. When the mouth was attached she lay back and closed her eyes. As the baby suckled she sank away ever more deeply before Kate's eyes.

The blood came before the placenta. It came quickly and persistently, blood and liquor staining the entire visible sheet. Black clots ran into the liquid. Blood dripped onto the floorboards. They sounded out against the hissing gas, large leaden drops. Kate felt a wave of panic pulse through her. She knew it was bad, the worst thing. She screamed aloud, screamed at the blood to stop, screamed for help which wasn't there, screamed at her fear. But for all she screamed she knew what she had to do, knew what was possible. She leaned over Julia and massaged the womb, running her hand gently and thoroughly over the belly, feeling her fingers press into the pliant flesh. Then she pulled at the cord hoping to bring the placenta. Still the blood came. Again she massaged the belly in order to make the womb close, but still the blood came.

She stopped. She listened to the rhythmic drips still landing onto the boards. She lifted Julia up. She was heavy and reluctant. It was difficult holding her. Her face was clammy, shimmering, tainted grey. She saw a sudden frank paleness break through the initial grey mask. She was shockingly beautiful. Kate let her back down onto the mattress. She took the baby from her and walked from the room. Jones was standing at the bottom of the stair. He was still alone. It crossed her mind that he had never left. She went down to him and said: "Tell her she was too late." He didn't respond, but she knew he had understood. He was no longer separate. For all he stood completely still, seemingly impassive, she recognised the total and terrible loneliness that seized him. She had to look away from him. She walked towards the door, hesitating only long enough to say: "I'm taking the child, David. I don't think you'll stop me. And we'll take care of the bidding. Do you understand? We'll see to it. We'll do all the funeral bidding." He made no answer. Indeed, he made no discernible response. He simply looked at the stair, rooted to the spot, as if he were a corpse himself. She let herself out.

*

The moon glowed behind scattered cloud, a fragment, its sheen filtering through the vaporous sky. She clutched the baby to her, nestling her face into its face as if it were a cloth on which she could wipe her grief. She inhaled baby smell. It was simple, sweet and clean. She inhaled time after time, taking in the glorious aroma of new born skin, then suddenly threw back her head and roared with a terrible moan of pain. Her sister was dead. It was too much. She held her sister's baby in her arms. It didn't make sense. The baby meant something else. She looked at it bundled up in its cloth. It was a wrinkled, bruised old man. It needed loving. It needed its mother's memories. It had to take from her thoughts all the colours, scenes and misgivings that she had. But it could only have one. The grey luminosity of dying. She groaned again, but the noise was less. She was too empty to howl aloud. Besides, it didn't feel right again. She was too confused to make any sense, or any decision, even that of complaining, of resorting to the most basic protest of all: shouting, screaming, denying. It was over, for the time being. She touched the baby's face again with her own, her wet cheek making the barest of contacts. She closed her eyes. The touch ran through her, thrilling her, yet at the same time wounding her.

She remembered Julia's touch, a baby, her little mechanical hand pawing at the still, empty air, clutching at the strange fearful world, yet gurgling, surprised by everything. And Kate knelt there, beside her box, looking up at the unboarded corner of a shuttered window, listening, catching glimpses of moonlight, the moon itself, hazy blue, its outline sharp against the frost charged dark. And later thinking the moonlight was scary, a secret thing, not a nice thing at all. Never that. Moonlight was only spoken about in whispers and never in front of them, the children. But they knew the songs and the chants and the right things to think. The gombeen men were bad men, bogey men. Everyone hated the gombeen men, so the children made wild tales. What the gombeen men would do to you if they caught you, the monsters, the gombeen men.

The gombeen tune went through Kate's head. It was always there. She smiled at the easy recollection, then despaired at the same thought. She was always filling in, learning the past from the present and the future. Her future and now Julia's baby's future. The gombeen men were only small-time traders, money-lenders and shopkeepers, who had saved enough to buy up tenancies when the old landowners went bankrupt after the great famine. They were the worse kind of landlords, certain of how far they could rack rents, certain of their right to do it.

Julia was born in the year of the worst harvest since the famine, the great famine. They were evicted the same year. Kate remembered her father as a damned man. She had heard the phrase at some stage in that year, 1878, a four year old, hearing things, overhearing, guessing at everything. If he was damned it wasn't his doing. He might have been a different man. Who's to say what man he might have been. But he was a landless man. Kate ran through the idea. What would John be if he were a landless man? Well, of course, he was, but he had his house. That was the difference. Naturally he didn't own it, but it was his. He wasn't barricading the door.

And Julia, standing behind the door, not laughing, not crying, but both, making something new, something quite wonderful. But that was later. In the other cottage. Who owned that? Not her father. Her mother's father. He managed to do all sorts. He had strips of vegetables, his own pigs, even produced his own liquor. He was quite the man really. But they weren't always there, and never together. Kate was usually there with Polly. It was Marty who was always with Julia. How would she ever tell Marty? He was too simple. He wouldn't understand a baby, what a baby could do. He wouldn't make sense of it. He would pine, lie down like a sickened dog and waste. Because that was how he loved her, really, like a dependent dog. Even when she was raging with them all over Jones it never included Marty. That was the stupidity of it all. Their old trusts and alliances were never in doubt. They would never have disposed of all the things they held in common. The four year old panting behind the door, not laughing, not crying, but both, her expression turbulent, apprehensive but uncowed. Like her face for Jones. Kate remembered that clearly, her for Jones face, her feisty, yet hurt, declamatory expression. It was at once an outcry, a criticism, a plea for sanity. And yet, she didn't remember what she had done that day thirty years previous. She didn't remember the story, just the face, that beautiful face, and the odour of hay and root vegetables. The odours, just that, smells to draw a face.

Thirty years, behind the door, truculent and vulnerable. The same face running along the river bank. Chasing or running? Always that conundrum. Julia, wild and wilful, yet scared and easily hurt. And Jones kicked her. She was like a flower. She was a flower. A flower that grew out of nothing. They weren't beautiful people. Dora was like a man. Polly was heavy and quaint. Marty had a certain look about him, but not handsome, not a flower. He was like a snake at times, maybe a lizard in the early sun, his lean, slippery face, peering about with that simple, surprised expression he had. And for herself she couldn't answer, or certainly wouldn't, though she would never have hidden from a reflection. But Julia was a flower, fresh and light coloured, a yellow flower, a yellow bog flower, a rock rose. Why was she running by the river? She was always up to something, yet never really bad. She was always alive, that was for sure.

She pressed the baby close to her chest, held high, just below the chin, wanting to keep it close, near to her face, her mouth, her breathing.

She was all the difference with their father, the damned man. Who said that? Was it a complaint or a piece of flattery? She had always taken it as flattery, well, a flattery of sorts, something to explain a man driven by obsession, a man driven to terrible things. There were suggestions that someone had been killed, a landlord's agent, beaten up and left for dead. It went along with the other things that went on in the moonlight. The maiming of cows. It was cows that took the land. Cows were better off than they were. At least they were wanted. So the cows got it. Strange to think that. Such pathetic creatures, with big sad eyes, like people really, being maimed, hurt. Terrible what ordinary men can do? What was John capable of? She refused to think any further. John was more singular than her father. Her father didn't think. She never remembered him like that. He didn't speak. He grimaced the day out. He was simply driven, possessed by disappointment, but John was more than that. He wouldn't let disappointment better him. That was more dangerous overall. But as long as he was never tested she need never worry about the cows.

But Julia could shake the disappointment, make it go away, albeit briefly. It was just something between them. Maybe it wasn't as vague as all that, nothing particularly strange between father and daughter, other than a willingness to insist on it. But when Julia tugged at his arms, put her arms out to be carried, insisted on piggy-back rides and games of hide-and-seek, would he not have shrugged the others off, and in the shrugging symbolised something about not being equal to hide-and-seek under someone else's roof. She managed it though. But then, she was a rock rose.

Kate didn't know how true it was about the landlord's agent. She had never thought it through, what her father, her landless father, was capable of. It struck her now as entirely feasible. She had come too far to think anything else. She had been the first to give it up and emigrate. That made her complicit in something. She wished she could return to that shadowy world of not knowing, of not conceiving that it could possibly be the case. He was never formerly accused of anything, certainly never stood trial or went to prison, but it was there, lurking in everyone's memory, until he died, worn out, unfit to keep on, no longer sure of himself, living from small job to small job, hand to mouth, no longer the father he had set out to be.

She threw her head back with a sudden sensation of anger. How could it be that anyone should have to live like that, so out of touch with themselves? He must have grown up with bog sounds, curlew, snipe, turf spades, the crackle of small fires, and learnt to hate them, or worse, considered them never worth loving in the first place.

Julia had stood behind the door crying. Again, behind the door, sunlight breaking through the window, the sound of crows among the trees just a short walk away from the cottage. The same figure, the same expression, a rock rose, weeping, behind the door, as if she could bar the thought, the occurrence, the truth. She was always so plainly alive, so possessed of rich and varied thought. Weeping, behind the door, the evicted baby, as if she knew, the door was everything, the passage between one life and another, the emigrants' route.

And the door led to Jones. Kate always knew it was irrational, but she blamed herself for Julia and Jones, blamed herself for the fact that her sister, her evicted baby sister, had to put her faith on the line for the sake of a man. If she had never made the decision to emigrate then she was sure Julia never would have, nor would any of the others. Somehow she had become the driving force of the family. She wasn't sure what that meant. She rejected completely the idea that she was the mother. She was nothing like her mother. She had been a quiet, reflective woman, easily misconstrued as being simple, but that wasn't the case at all. She wasn't Marty. He was a one off. Where he sprang from was impossible to say. Kate remembered her mother as a secretive, whispering woman. If she spoke at all to her neighbours she conducted her conversations as if in perpetual fear of being overheard, and given that she would characteristically wear her shawl over her head and hold it pinched at her chin, afraid of being recognised. God knows what she could have known that she should have been so nervous of it.

Maybe Kate was like her father. Maybe the forces that drove him to become possibly suspect of killing a landlord's agent, a landless man, moonlighting, fighting for the rights of land he had never had, was the same instinct that drove Kate. It had been a valiant and a frightening decision to go to England, to head off in Kelly's coalboat, a teenage girl. But what choice had there been? Her grandfather couldn't keep them all, and he was the only one left. It was ridiculous the amount of dying. It didn't make life precious, not then, but rather absurd. Why give yourself to anything when the norm was to have it snatched away? What was the point of dignity when there was no reward? What was the point of heroism? But then there was John Devlin. John Devlin gave her the fight, the reason, the fear. And Jones must have given the same to Julia. And he kicked her. What was that kick about? What had dragged him so low? Was it perhaps them? He had only ever been tolerated, never accepted, never made to feel at home. And home was important. Julia had stood behind so many doors, not laughing, not crying, but both, making that simple statement that home meant something. Time, place and person had to stand for something.

Now, when she thought about it, Jones and Julia, it didn't make any sense. Once again grief had wiped away a story worth telling, had dismissed it as all so much cant. But she defied grief. Julia's story was a great story. She had stood up against the bullying might of her bigoted sisters and won her case. She was as loved as ever, the yellow rock rose, with her rash temperament, her desire for living, life.

Life, life, life! Christ it was all so little to ask for. A desire to be herself. A desire not to let the unbending world grind her down.

She was a player. She was skittish. She was cheeky. She was annoying. She was wilful. She was lovely. She was... She was Kate's dead sister.

So many faces flashed through her mind; behind the door, beside the river, looking at Jones, the funny pride, the telling smile, the satisfaction. Oh Julia! (Why on earth had she been hiding behind the door, and why had she run along the river bank? How were such things lost?) She howled again, but it was all inward, tearing her insides as if she were a sounding chamber, her body a space for her mind. It erupted in her and threatened to choke her. Julia's name, just her name, ran over and over in her mind. It was a demand that death return its victim, an

52

acknowledgement that that could never be, and a prayer for her soul all at once.

The baby began to cry. Kate held it away from her in order to look at it better. Already it was demanding something. She shook her head. She couldn't satisfy it. It was learning a very stark message within an hour of being alive. It didn't make sense. Maybe nothing would make sense ever again. Maybe that was the whole point. Nothing could ever make any sense. That was the delusion they all lived under. Only a home made any sense, and that was something none of them had ever really had. When all was said and done they had only ever been kicked out of pathetic little hovels.

Unless Julia had managed it? Unless by marrying Jones she had belonged in a way that the rest of them could not even envisage, let alone achieve? She had been so satisfied to have Jones. After all, he was something of a beauty, and in all honesty something of a charmer. It couldn't last, of course. Once he started drinking his good looks became a little puffy, his skin injected, the supple flesh flabby. But the figure of the man was still to be gleaned, a recollection just beneath the surface. It appeared in the turn of the head, occasionally. The reason for so much upset and complaint. Jones, the beautiful Protestant miner. And he was Julia's. She had made him hers. And, perhaps, if the child had come earlier, if it had sealed that hard won marriage, maybe it would have been different. Maybe that was the way life had to be conducted, seizing any possibility as it arose, before it could be snatched away, before a bunch of misguided sisters could ruin it. Poor Jones.

It was to her credit, then, that she had Jones. There were plenty who would have liked to have had him. He was the symbol of how far Julia, the baby evicted in the year of her birth, had come. She was his equal, his better, his prize.

Kate smiled grimly to herself, the sound of the raging baby grating on her ears. The strange incomprehensible realisation dawned on her that she didn't hate Jones at all; in fact, quite the contrary. She saw him through Julia's desire for him. Her desire for the arrogant, beautiful, limited creature that he was. There were very few like him; blond, perfectly featured, self-assured men. And Julia had had him. He was hers. He was Kate's little sister's man. She couldn't hate him. He was too much an ornament of a man; too much an ornament that suited the grasping hand of a baby put out at arrival. No, she didn't hate Jones at all. In fact, she would be delighted to acknowledge that she was bringing up his child.

She didn't know how she arrived home. She couldn't recollect her journey through the streets at all. The only thing that crossed her mind were the lingering pictures of Julia, but she knew she couldn't afford to go over them again. She was brutally matter of fact as she spoke. For her own sanity she had to be. She told John that Julia had died, died in childbirth, but that it had all been very quick and easy. She added that there was nothing for it but to bring the child home. Before John could speak she busied herself accommodating the baby.

"He is called Patrick," she said to John as she emptied a bottom drawer to serve as a cot.

"You can't take another man's child," John remonstrated.

"I know it's the name Julia would have wanted. It was my father's name. You know that. She was always close to my father. I'm sure I've told you all about that. She used to recite the gombeen chants for him. You would have liked my father. He was a man of principle. You know that though."

"But Kate..."

"Jones cannot look after a child," she snapped, then immediately looked at John tenderly and quietly whispered: "He is all the children we lost, John, believe me."

John knelt down at the drawer beside Robert and Dora and gazed at the baby. He thought of Julia, heavy, flippant, so comfortable by his own fireside. He closed his eyes. He let out a howl of pain, a single grotesque syllable dying in the silence. When it passed he said: "We should go to Jones." His voice trembled.

Kate rested her two hands onto John's shoulders and said: "No, leave him be, it's better like that. He doesn't need reminding. God knows how I'll tell Marty?" She closed her eyes, bit her lips and whispered to the inviolate air: "Our son is crying."

John answered: "They both are."

*

It was to be months later before Kate saw David Jones again; apart, of course, from the day of Julia's funeral. That had been a day of gifts.

Dora accepted the first of them from a lean, wizened, barrow-trader, called John Darcy, who spent the winter with his mother in Ginns, a grim, reclusive woman reputed to be a witch. He stood on the doorstep, proffered a broad rectangular smile, exposing a line of yellow stalked teeth, gave a floppy ostentatious bow, then handed Dora bootblack and sill from his small four wheeled trolley of broken china, spoons and battered pans. His message, delivered in a florid cadence: "In lieu of obsequies from the Darcys." Before his trolley trundled on Dora brought the baby for him to hold, which he handled with solemn satisfaction.

The coffin had a small wreath of entwined rowan and holly, the rowan berries already orange, which Robert had plaited and Dora had tied with a red sash. It remained on the lid as the coffin was lowered into the ground. Kate watched as the dark green leaves and spent berries vanished under a mound of soil which was iced and granular like crystal ginger. It fell heavy and crisp. She looked away. The vision of Julia, her expression keen, secretive, beguiling, standing behind a not fully closed door, flashed across her mind. She wanted to scream aloud, give voice to her frustration, her inability to make sense of hurt; but somehow, without having any obvious rule to pick on, she knew such outbursts were forbidden. It was tantamount to religious fury, religious revolt, and that was certainly unacceptable.

She scanned her surroundings. Everywhere, the marsh surrounding the graveyard, the disordered bowls of fields pockmarked by iron-ore workings which sank away beyond the rim of marshland, was white with frost. It was all singularly beautiful. The broken landscape was complete in its winter element. She recoiled from the thought. It was all misplaced. Its beauty was unnecessary. It concealed a more vulgar reality. It was a painful beauty. She groaned deeply. Was she going mad? Would she ever feel right again?

She forced herself to look back towards the open grave. She realised that Jones had gone. He had been standing close to the edge, peering in, gazing emptily in front of him. It was the same way she remembered him looking up the stair towards the room where Julia had died, a man aware of his loneliness but devoid of understanding. He hadn't spoken to anyone throughout the whole ceremony, though he and Kate had acknowledged each other. But that had been a simple meeting of eyes: a meeting of eyes that agreed on the terrible nature of things and admitted that they personally couldn't say more. Nevertheless, though she would never have denied him his right to be there, indeed, to herself she remained very true to her thinking that she didn't at all hate him, his presence troubled her. She was scared of his awareness of Patrick. What if he discovered his feelings for him? She didn't doubt he was capable of it. But it couldn't be. The absence of hate she felt was conditional on his acceptance of giving up Patrick. She hadn't yet given a single thought to the future, whether she would ever want him to see Patrick or not, whether indeed she would want him acknowledged as the father. She couldn't think so far ahead, not yet. She chose not to remember the fact that she had thought she would be proud to bring Patrick up as Jones' child. Things had moved on since the night Julia died.

So, now she looked for him urgently, angry at herself for being caught inattentive. She just caught sight of his figure as he passed through the gates. She saw that he marched out alone. He never gave a backward glance. She eyed the gates for some time to satisfy herself that he had really gone.

She was brought back to the grave by the sound of a small wooden cross being hammered into place, a gift from Peter Kavanagh, Polly's son, which bore the inscription, *In God's loveing care,* (accurate spelling not being one of Peter's gifts).

Later, when they had all returned to the house on Ginns, Father Bond brought gifts: a miniature of the *Holy Family* which he unsuccessfully tried to get Patrick to hold, and a small, white backed, *Book of Psalms* inscribed with the words, *With the love of our Lord Jesus Christ, Maximus Optimus,* which he gave to Robert. Robert accepted it with a look of shy, restive pleasure, and quickly scuttled off to a corner to view his prize in shameless secrecy.

The final gift of that day came once again from John Darcy who brought his trolley onto the terrace of Ginns after dark bearing a small home-made Christmas crib lit from behind by numerous candles. "In lieu of angelus, Mrs Devlin," he called up the steps ceremonially. With the baby in her arms Kate said to Robert beside her: "Say, thank you, Father. Thank you, Uncle John Darcy." He balked at the tone of command, the apparent disappointment at his gratitude, in her voice. However, before he could speak, before he could make amends in her eyes, Marty started to sing down the steps: "Ding, ding, ding." The angelus, however, remained unsaid. The crib was taken indoors and set up for the baby to gaze at.

No one mentioned David Jones, either to criticise or understand him. He had simply, to all intents and purposes, ceased to exist for them. His desertion of Julia by the graveside merely served to confirm that. But for Kate, his leaving had been the ultimate gift of the day. In all probability, if anyone had criticised David Jones she would have insisted that she loved him as Julia would have wanted.

Some five months later, on a particularly warm day in May, Kate found herself on the cinder plateau at the base of Lady Pit waiting for him. At precisely 2.45 p.m. that day an explosion had occurred in the main shaft of the mine precipitating fires along the galleries. This was the presage to the worst disaster in the town's history. It struck the fledgling Catholic community of Ginns and Mount Pleasant, a small community almost exclusively employed in the mines, to its core. Scarcely a family was immune to the event. The scale of the tragedy was so immense it became the reality through which they thought. This was particularly the case for Robert.

He had been walking along the coast at the time pondering his own ambiguous future, in his hands the book of *Maximus Optimus*. He had spent the last hour coaxing Patrick with spoons of milky slop. In the intervening months from Julia's burial Patrick had progressed from being a sickly baby, prone to colds, diarrhoea and vomiting, to an irritable baby with an intermittent brassy cough and shrill cry. Robert had had to escape, particularly when the milky slop was all brought back, to the personal, yet chaotic peace of his psalms and the sea.

He stopped by the dockside and read the anticipated words: *The words of the Lord are pure words; as silver tried in a furnace of earth, purified seven times.* He was, as always, enthralled; the words belonged to him, spoke of him, were his. He was surrounded by silver: its threads dappled the water, merged, elided and divided again, shone from the blistering skin of a row boat stranded like a great shining turtle between the slips of two quays, and from the painted hulls of the fishing smacks sitting heavily and calmly in the waters.

A loco went by shunting chaldron wagons towards the plateau of Lady Pit. It shone like silver, its grating sound was silver. Robert immediately followed its laborious noisy movement, leaping from sleeper to sleeper, between two perplexingly ever merging silver threads, easily transmuted in his florid mind into a wonderful, if ineffable, destiny.

And as he leaped his belief in God had never been so vivid as it was at that moment. It was a product of his own developing spirituality, his transactions with the natural and mechanical world, and his sense of bewildering and exhilarating creativity. He was in love with life as only a romantic could be: a sad, wistful lover who sought the transport of prayer. God in all words: God in all movement: God in all shade: God in everything. He could feel it, see it, reach out to it. Distance had ceased to occur. God had put everything in touch.

He let the coal-hops move away and walked down to the water's edge. He put down *Maximus Optimus* and put his hands into the water. It was also God, flesh of God. He scooped it into the air. It fell in silver drops. He dreamed of the water rising, rising over the town, rinsing it of debris, like a baptism, conferring the freedom of God. The image was wild and beautiful. He was enthused by it. He seized up his book and held it against his chest as if it too were flesh. He began to praise God, extolling earth, sea and sky, extolling life emergent. And as he sat there praising God, praising God in his own laconic, nervous yet restive fashion, he heard the strange wailing angelus, the clang, clang, clang, from Lady Pit. He stood up immediately, without thinking, and started to run towards the sound.

There was already something of a crowd gathered by the time he reached the cinder plateau, yet still they came, streaming from the screen-sheds, grub-houses and along the road from the town; every one of them bewildered, uncomprehending, and already terrified. Robert pushed through the disorganised mass searching for someone he knew. He found his aunty Polly, slumped heavily on the ground, still black from working on the screens, staring mutely at the pit-head gear. Robert knelt down beside her. He knew that Peter Kavanagh was below ground. He made no attempt to speak to her. He knew it was useless to try. He was relieved that was the case.

The siren ceased. The vigil began.

He gazed at his aunty Polly for some time, studying the rapt contours of her face. She was too absorbed to be aware of his interest. Indeed, she made no acknowledgement of his presence at all. He tried to gain some inkling of the thought taking place behind the expression, but could make no sense of it. She was too inert, her being too far away. Eventually, her continued lack of acknowledgement made him awkward, and he increasingly felt self-conscious and out of sorts.

An image of himself staring at her suddenly struck him, and he guiltily turned away from her as if he had been found out. He immediately looked everywhere, all at once, wanting to rid his mind of that picture of himself. He took it all in quickly. He saw flurries of incomprehensible action in all directions. His attention darted from one group on the plateau to another. He was drawn to each centre of movement and murmur, drawn to try and decipher and make sense of what was said and done. And as his eyes roved around the terrible scene the realisation quickly dawned on him that it all excited him. Each tiny staged drama produced its own distinctive thrill. He balked at the possibility. It horrified him. It was inexplicable. It was, though, undeniable. His thoughts were running wild. And as his wonder increased so he suffered it.

He felt it particularly as the volunteers lined up in order to make a descent down the shaft. There was no shortage of them. Gavin Duffy, the Loft Pit union official organised them. For the first team he drew on the Loft, Fish and Canning men, which included his father and Bobby Kavanagh. He knew his father was on night-shift. He never slept well during the day, so he was almost certainly awake, but he didn't have to be there. He had come of his own accord. He must have. He could have waited to be called. As Robert looked on he instinctively knew that there was no way he could go and speak to them, no way he could wish them luck, indeed, no way he could even wish for their safety, and yet as he realised this he also felt completely at a loss to understand why. All he knew was that it had something to do with the blankness of their expressions. It seemed that the whole group of them had decided to brazen it out.

This was particularly notable when they were ushered together for photographs and were forced to wait for the camera to work. He could sense their awkwardness and impatience, their desire to have the thing over with, but they gave no vent to it. They simply held the same adamant stare, the front row all posed alike, one knee to the floor, an elbow resting on the other, the back row standing upright, arms to the side, each taking his cue from the other. He knew as he looked at them gazing squarely at the camera that they resented its intrusion. They were going down the shaft and that was it. It wasn't really a decision. It was something they had to do. They hadn't bargained for the camera. It made them self-conscious about themselves and they didn't want that. He recognised their relief when the agony of the portrait was over.

His attention rested on his father. He looked clumsy and apprehensive posing for the camera, certainly not at his best, yet he was probably the most forthright amongst them, his arm hanging casually over his bare raised knee. (He had on a pair of short flannel breeches knotted just above the knee.) But he knew the apprehension was at the camera, not at what was to follow. He knew his father would not admit to being afraid. He was too strong to consider that. And then for the first time in his life he questioned that thought. What did it mean? Did he admire that in his father, his frank refusal of fear, or did he at heart resent it, mistrust it, disbelieve it, or maybe just wonder at it? To refuse fear meant that he would have to refuse doubt. Surely that was unwise. Wasn't a sense of doubt necessary in order to understand anything. Did his father understand things? His thoughts ran up against a blank wall. He struggled with it. Surely this wasn't the time or the place to consider such questions. He quickly came up with an answer. His father certainly understood things, but his understanding was very personal, very much his own. He felt cowed by the thought. His father seemed like a giant, a man alone. He gazed at him with renewed admiration, fearful, reserved admiration.

He saw the clumsiness fade as the photograph was finished. His father stood up, breathed deeply and seemed to flex all the muscles in his body. His shirt sleeves were rolled up above the elbows and the muscles of his forearm stood out, as did this muscles exposed between breeches and shins. He was obviously preparing for his descent. Robert recognised a quickening and relaxation in his father's expression as he accepted the *Mecco* breathing apparatus he was offered. He immediately put the silver helmet over his head. It seemed as if the anonymity of the glass face, the external metal lungs and bronchus made him altogether more sure of himself. Along with the other volunteers he even agreed to pose again for the cameras. His stance was entirely changed. He gazed towards the lens, his hands at his hips, balancing his weight jauntily on one leg. He appeared quite carefree standing there, peering through the bowl of his mask, before stepping away with the others in order to move towards the shaft.

As Robert watched them march off in the direction of the brick buildings housing the shaft, the still images of the photographs remained in his mind. They were embedded, two fixed, ornamental pictures. They provoked a feeling of intense, uncomfortable sadness in him. It seemed to him that what they caught of his father, his father and the other volunteers, was already past. They could never be those men again. It was too late for them. They had struck their pose and moved on. And the pose had been consigned, given to that moment, that plateau, that eerie silence, that seeming nothingness. And it could never be reclaimed. The past didn't allow for it. The past could not be reclaimed. It took your opportunities, your passions, your endurance, and swiped them away. Only the camera challenged it. But it only left pitiful remembrances: awful little, strange, brown tinted, mechanical figures. And each figure seemed to ask the same terrible question. What happened to your hope? He hated them. Robert knew that he could never look at the cinder plateau, the haphazard buildings, without sensing that an outline of his father died there. He wanted to go to him, but to what purpose he couldn't really have said. He wanted to stem something. But it was impossible. The moment passed. The men went on. His father kept on marching. There was a shadow with him. It was impressed on Robert's mind. In witnessing the taking of those two photographs he had learnt a lesson of personal, tragic fatalism. From that time he would weave it into his equally personal love of Christ, the crucified, suffering Christ. Christ was the symbol of it all. His church was full of such frozen, expiatory figures, pale Madonnas, shadowed Christs, the host of saints. His Christ, the Christ he loved above all others, was the one that suffered earthly agony. His Christ was the Christ of the five sorrowful mysteries.

As the volunteers stepped out of sight Robert placed his hand on his aunty Polly's shoulder. His need to do something had become too great to ignore. She turned to him mechanically, nodded once, though with no sense of recognition, then returned to her self-absorbed contemplation. Robert relinquished his touch. Almost as soon as he had reached out to her he was embarrassed by it. It was unlike him. It was a gesture he would never have felt himself capable of making. He certainly had no means of knowing whether it had been accepted or rejected. Had he overstepped the mark, or was he old enough to have offered her that touch? He didn't know. He was suddenly filled with a strong desire to escape it, rush away from it. And not only from Aunty Polly but from the whole plateau, from this previously inconceivable world. He remained exactly where he was though. Escape was not an option. It was his part to share this burden, whether he felt able or not. That was the sudden burden of his growing up.

As the afternoon wore on he waited with an ever growing sense of discomfort, a sense of being personally preposterous. His discomfort wasn't relieved by the appearance of his mother and sister. He hadn't seen their approach. His first awareness of his mother was the feel of her hand across his face, her fingers probing the lines of his cheek and jaw. She stroked Polly at the same time with her other hand in the same urgent, troubled manner. When Polly looked up at her Kate immediately sank down beside her and embraced her, dragging her fingers from Robert's jaw. He watched them slowly rock together, a low monotonous wail issuing from Polly, a counterpoint of solacing hush from Kate. Not a word was said to him. He was at a loss. He turned away from them.

The shadow of his sister fell across the small group. She had remained standing, watching the embrace between her mother and aunty. Robert looked up at her. He blinked in the sun. He wanted a sign of what he should do. She could see the need in his expression. It was the wrong time for him to feel that need. She had nothing to give. She ignored him and concentrated her attention on the two women, and at the same time quietly rocked Patrick in her arms. The baby was sleeping. Robert maintained his appeal, urging her to take notice of him. Eventually she conceded and turned to him, and for a brief moment her expression became enlivened. She obviously wanted to give him the solace he required, but it was too difficult. As soon as she acknowledged him, agreed with his discomfort, her own panic burst to the surface. She suddenly turned away and rushed off with the baby without saying a parting word to anyone. Robert badly wanted to follow her but was unable to move. A sudden presentiment of fear, triggered by Dora's hasty departure, swept over him. At first he began to shiver uncontrollably and then he hunched over himself, stared hard at the plateau floor and began to cry.

As the tears dripped across his eye sockets, then fell to the waste ground, he felt a hand press hard into his shoulder. He looked up. The priest, Father Bond, gripped him. He seemed infuriated. "Are you praying?" he demanded, his voice coming in a low croaking whisper. "Are you praying?" Robert shook his head. "Then pray," he said in the same demanding tone, then with a sigh of fatigue and with sudden gentleness repeated: "Then pray, Robert, pray!" Nothing more was said. He blessed Kate and Polly and moved on to the next family. As he stepped away Robert put his hand against his heart and held the solid spine of *Maximus Optimus*. It was as much as he could do. Prayer was out of the question in such an alien world.

He recognised that it was certainly an alien world. He had never given much thought to the idea of his father being underground, working underground. It took the accident for that to become an element in his thinking. It was as if suddenly the fact that his father returned home covered in a film of black dust assumed a meaning. His father spent the greater bulk of his life buried. He was underground, beneath the earth, like corpses were beneath the earth. But what did that mean in reality? He didn't know. His first thoughts were primitive. A man and a pick in a glittering cavern hewing without undue force at the rock. It was an absurd idea. All he had to do was look around to give the lie to that notion. The mine workings were great warehouses full of pistons, compressors and gigantic wheels. There was obviously thought, intelligence and ambition incorporated into the pit. There was something frightening in that realisation. It reduced the men. The pit was bigger. It robbed his father of his fearsome aspects. He was even pitiful. His figure, moving towards the shaft, now struck Robert as a dazed, limited figure. He fought against such a disgusting thought. It was wrong. He told himself that his father, and the other volunteers, were heroic, powerful men. They had to be. They were down there, wherever that was, doing whatever it was they did. He longed to pull back the cinder plateau and reveal the hidden guts of the workings, the hidden guts of them all. It drove him silently crazy that he simply did not know what went on underground, it struck him as a terrible omission.

It was late afternoon when the first men came up, casualties and corpses blackened alike. Peter Kavanagh was with them. Despite the confusion at the pit-head Polly had not missed him. He was alive. He had helped carry someone to the surface. Robert watched her as she pushed through the chaos of bodies, virtually falling forward the whole time, to claim him. He saw their meeting.

Peter, who was larger by far than anyone else in the family, stood like a great blackened statue before her, reluctant to be embraced. He was trying to say something about the man he had carried. Polly dispelled it all. She took hold of him with two hands and pulled him to her. He raised his arms, which had obviously been burnt, above her head, allowing himself to be embraced, perhaps tolerating it. The gesture, however, was hurried, troubled and severe. No sooner had they touched than she released him and tried to lead him away. Once again Peter resisted her entreaties, but Polly was not to be gainsaid and began shouting at him. It didn't take much. A few seconds after her outburst Peter followed her. They walked silently together, without any further show of emotion, without any acknowledgement of anyone else, across the cinder plain, away from Lady.

Robert watched them disappear towards the vague silver tracery of the white-washed town. As he watched their progress, two clumsy silhouettes, he was sure he understood his aunty Polly's need to escape, understood her involuntariness. It seemed to him that sometimes it was very difficult to be alive, that it was almost a matter of shame. One's own life was always balanced against that of another. He pulled himself across the cinders and knelt beside his mother. She turned to him and smiled incompletely, her expression hollow yet terrified. He pulled her face to his shoulder. She sank into him gratefully. Neither spoke. They remained together, scarcely moving, maintaining their silence throughout the long afternoon whilst bodies continued to be brought to the surface.

At first the recovery rate was rapid and the deputies were at a loss as to how to cope with so many corpses. The best they could think of doing was to place them uncovered in the coal sheds. But then, as the afternoon wore on, the recovery rate declined and they transferred them to the Methodist church for collection.

It was almost sunset before John Devlin, Bobby Kavanagh and the rest of the initial volunteers emerged from the shaft. Robert was the first to see his father. He got to his feet immediately. Kate, however, remained where she was, seated on the cinder floor. Robert was at a loss. He couldn't understand what she was suggesting. He needed her with him. He couldn't go on his own. He felt that he was unequal to it. He had experienced too much disgust, disgust at being one of those waiting, to feel equal to it.

The feeling had grown in him throughout the long weary vigil. It had begun with the reunion of Aunty Polly and Peter Kavanagh, and from then steadily took possession of him so that by the time the sun had sunk to the surface of the water, bathing it in the deepest blood-red wash, his sense of disgust was absolute. It pervaded and tainted everything. On any number of occasions he had thought to pull out his copy of *Maximus Optimus*, read once again the twelfth psalm in which the word was purified seven times only to touch it and thrust it back into his pocket with distaste. Nothing made sense. The world that had been his when he sat by the water praising God had been taken away. In its place was a mysterious, savage, remote, inexplicable nether-world. There was a world that went on underground that he knew nothing of. His not knowing was unforgivable.

He took hold of his mother's hand. "He's there," he whispered. "He's come up."

She looked up at him. "Then go to him, Robert," she said, her voice extremely tender, calm yet authoritative. "Go to him."

"I can't."

"Go to him, Robert. Go to him now. I have to stay here."

They gazed at each other for a few tense moments. Robert couldn't understand. Surely, for them, the vigil was over. Why did she refuse to even stand up? The waiting for them was complete. Surely she didn't have to sit on like this with the other women. They wouldn't expect that, nor would they want it. But as he looked at her he sensed that she was quite possessed of a determination to stay put. It showed in her face. There was clear lucid resolve. Then as he continued to gaze at her he recognised a tremendous sympathy governing her expression, a sympathy for him. She was urging him on, urging him against his self-disgust. She seemed to be saying that she understood his reluctance, but it was unwarranted. He smiled at her gratefully. Whatever she was thinking obviously had purpose. She was surprising like that. He couldn't resist her, no matter the difficulty it caused him. He nodded towards her, shrugging his compliance to her wishes, and went off to meet his father.

John was standing with Bobby Kavanagh at the pit-head. They seemed confused, unable to move, uncertain as to what they should do next. And as Robert went up to them he knew, he could see it in his father's expression, that his presence merely added to that general sense of bewilderment. He immediately convinced himself that what he saw in that distracted look of his father was the same sense of distaste that he had felt himself. His father too was disgusted at him. It was inescapable. It brought Robert up short. He stood and gazed at his father for a moment. He bit his lip. He tasted his own blood. They would see. He was always making himself look foolish. He told himself he had to say something. If he didn't the disgust might well overwhelm him. There was nothing for it. He simply could not fly away. He stepped forward and spoke up as strongly as he was able. In fact, he only managed to speak quickly. "Aunty Polly has taken Peter home. He's safe. He was one of the first to come up. Mother is still sitting, waiting. Thank God you're safe. Thank God."

At first Bobby Kavanagh said nothing. He pursed his lips as he thought through what Robert had told him, then without warning he gave up a brief, intense, flow of tears. "I'll have to go," he said, speaking through his sobs, edging away from them as if he were backing away from emotions he knew he needed to quell, deeply embarrassed by his display. John simply nodded. He understood. It was all right. Bobby was an emotional man. That was understood. He didn't need to say anything. But Bobby had no need of John's understanding. He was already on his way. He walked briskly, then broke into a run, following the same line as Polly and Peter earlier.

Robert waited. It was just as he had done all the long afternoon. Eventually John looked down at him. At first he seemed scarcely able to take in the reality of his being there at all, then he took a few weary steps towards him, placed his blackened palm firmly against Robert's face and held it. He gazed at him intently, looking straight into his eyes, his own filled with wonder, doubt and concern. He tried to speak but failed.

At that moment they were joined by Gavin Duffy, who carried a board which read: *All's well in this airway*. Gavin grinned at John. His expression seemed at the same time to be both delighted and malicious. It made a grimace of his tawny features. He declared fiercely: "We'll have something for this, by God, we'll have something for this." He flung the board across the cinders and marched away, showing no fatigue despite the labours of the long afternoon. He made his way to the coal sheds to assess the disposal of the bodies.

John ushered Robert away and said: "Let's get out of here. I've had enough." Robert led him to Kate. John spoke immediately, repeating similar words to Kate as he had to Robert. He'd had enough. He needed to get away. His tone was weary but triumphant.

"I can't, John," Kate responded calmly. "Jones is still down there. He didn't come up. I'm sure of that. He's still down there. Someone will have to claim him."

John's face fell. Robert wanted to reach for him and somehow halt that declension, but it was too late. The rupture was instantaneous. "Come home, damn it!" John insisted through clenched teeth. "Don't make me have to tell you to come home."

"I can't, I have to claim him, I just have to," she said firmly, eyeing him directly, imploring him to try and understand her, understand the relief she felt at his being there, her relief at being allowed to wait for Jones. She spoke gently. "Go home and sleep. I'll be along shortly. I just have to claim him. I owe it. I owe it to Julia. I owe it to Jones."

John flustered to discover a reply. Numerous things came to mind, but nothing was right. He gave them all up with a frustrated shrug. He stomped off across the cinders.

Kate smiled at Robert and with obvious satisfaction declared: "He'll be in our house by morning, Robert. He'll be in our house. It'll all be over by the morning. Now, go with your father. He needs you." Robert recognised that it would be unwise to cross her. He set off as she had commanded and went after his father. He didn't walk with him, though, but rather someway behind.

By the next morning Kate had her wish. Jones was brought to the surface in the early hours. She had his body taken directly to the house, where she herself washed him, laid him out and commenced the wake. She undertook the funeral bidding herself, going from door to door in Ginns requesting attendance at Jones' burial. She planned a funeral tea of ham sandwiches, funeral bread and Madeira cake. These were the usual local things. It was only fair to Jones. Nevertheless, she insisted that he was to have all necessary exequies, a proper Catholic burial in all respects, and as he had no family to speak of the matter was closed.

*

They kept his body for a week during which time all the members of the family, including Aunty Dora, came to pay their respects.

Father Bond came and said prayers over him. He asked Robert to accompany him. Robert watched, strangely bemused, yet enthralled, as the crammed figure of the priest hunched over the dead man. Their faces came close together, priest and corpse, lit by the same failing candles, suspended in the same sepulchral gloom. They looked the same. They were possessed of the same fleshy, waxen density, the same taciturn gravity. Robert wanted to laugh, laugh at the strange reflective quality of the two men, and yet the very thought of laughter filled him with dread. It was completely new to him. He had always felt something akin to rapture in Father Bond's presence. He corrected himself. He insisted in his own mind that it was that familiar sense of rapture he craved now in this rarefied situation. He forced himself to attend to the priest.

He concentrated his mind and closely studied each hushed invocation, each movement of body and mouth of the priest, in order to regain his own bewilderment and wonder at such power. However, as Robert's gaze flickered with the candles between the two faces, and the priest's lips and hands, the priest unexpectedly hesitated. He looked right across the face of Jones toward Robert. His expression was probing, carefully taking Robert in and weighing him up. He smiled and began to speak, his voice quiet, even and precise. "Faith is very serious for you, Robert, isn't it." Robert quailed under the priest's attention and couldn't answer. The priest stood up from the corpse of Jones. He gave his attention fully to Robert. He repeated his statement in the same quietly formal voice: "I said, faith is very serious for you, Robert, isn't it."

"It has to be, Father," Robert stammered.

"Of course, it has to be, but then, it isn't like that for everyone, not even many priests, I might say. It doesn't make them any the less priests, not bad priests, certainly not, don't get me wrong, not at all, but not everyone has the same seriousness that I detect in you."

"Am I in the wrong then, Father? I feel that I am really."

"Dear God, no. No, no, not at all. Isn't that what I'm saying. The church has need of young men whose sense of faith is serious."

"But that isn't possible, Father."

The priest flared: "What do you mean? You are not equipped to talk about what is possible and what isn't."

"The likes of me though, Father? In the church, I mean."

"Anything is possible, Robert. Faith can move mountains. Have you never thought where it could move you? Do you have that kind of faith, Robert? Could you take it the whole way? Could you move a mountain, Robert? Of course not. But how far? Tell me, Robert?"

67

"I don't know," Robert stammered shyly.

"You don't know. Then, Robert, think about it. Find out."

"How?"

"Ask yourself, of course," the priest snapped. "Ask yourself, then come and tell me. Remember, confession and delight! Faith is confession and delight! Come here, Robert, read to me."

Robert approached the priest gingerly. He was made to stand over Jones, brought closer than ever before to the tallow features. They looked so smooth, so exact, Jones' face spared, if little else. Father Bond stepped behind him, penning him against the coffin, then passed him a small bible and instructed him to read.

Robert began in a slow, faltering, whisper. Then as he read on his speech rose to a shrill gasp, eventually becoming regular and strong, until finally the words passed his lips with ease: *"Know ye not, that so many of us as were baptised into Jesus Christ were baptised into his death? Therefore we are buried with him by baptism into death: that like as Christ was raised up from the dead by the glory of the Father, even so we also should walk in newness of life. For if we have been planted together in the likeness of his death, we shall also in the likeness of his resurrection: knowing this, that our old man is crucified with him, that the body of sin may be destroyed, that henceforth we should not serve sin. For he that is dead is freed from sin. Now if we be dead with Christ, we believe that we shall also live with him: knowing that Christ being raised from the dead dieth no more; death hath no more dominion over him. For in that he died, he died unto sin once: but in that he liveth, he liveth unto God. Likewise reckon ye also yourselves to be dead unto sin but alive unto God through Jesus Christ our Lord."* He paused, then with renewed embarrassment uttered: *"Amen."*

"Amen," Father Bond repeated with satisfaction. He went on warmly: "You did very well, Robert, very well indeed. I am pleased with you. Remember it."

As the priest praised him Robert looked over the shapely, lustreless features of Jones in the failing light, inquiring of him, wondering if he would witness evidence of his prayer in the dead man's face. He could see no recognition of his words. He closed the book and passed it to the priest. He thanked him. He inched his way from the coffin. As he did he said: "I will remember, Father. Thank you."

"Come to me."

"Of course, Father, I will."

"Remember, confession and delight! Confession and delight!"

Robert stepped into the kitchen and looked around at the gathered mourners. They seemed content and relaxed. He was certain that what they were doing, their respecting Jones, was correct and enviable. The light of Jones' face faded in his mind's eye. He smiled. He went to his father and said: "Don't forget, I'll be down the mine this summer. I'll be a miner." John made no response. He merely looked at Robert for a brief moment. He felt quite bereft of any reasonable response. The announcement seemed of such intent to Robert. He didn't understand that. He could make nothing of the timing of Robert's statement, nor give to it any particular importance. Of course Robert would be down the mine in the summer. It didn't need to be said. It certainly didn't need to be said with Jones still lying in the adjoining room. He nodded his acknowledgement, then quietly moved away. Within five minutes he was laughing with Aunty Dora.

After a week in the house Jones was buried alongside Julia. Kate had insisted. It was a hot day. They could hear frogs in the rush at the graveyard limits, their infernal belches conjoining Father Bond's obsequies, rising like waves of heat to the noise of skylarks. As Kate took in the calm beauty of all that lay around her she was entirely satisfied. On the same day a stopping was erected in the return airway. A stopping had already been built blocking the mother gate, the main route to the face, in order to starve the fire that still raged of oxygen. Sealing the return airway closed the mine forever. As a result of this six hundred miners lost their jobs. As the return airway was sealed the last remaining woman on the cinder plain, who had been brought food and drink each day, once by Robert, only to have it removed the next, at last gave up the vigil. Final figures recorded that one hundred and thirty six miners, men and boys, died as a result of the explosion. The majority remained entombed in Lady.

Six months later there was a public funeral for all the men and boys who had died together. The procession was led by a line of caged canaries held aloft like lanterns. They were followed by the banners of the Union of Mine Workers, and the Salvation Army playing the death march as soldiers and mounted police in dress uniform led in a ceremonial coffin. The coffin was placed on a wagon platform decked with a black cloth and sprinkled with dried white flowers as aimlessly as confetti. Behind the coffin came the mayor accompanied by the mine share holders. In his pocket he carried a letter and a hundred pounds from the Queen Mother. At the steps of Mount Pleasant the procession turned along the

Strand and passed by the harbour towards the Protestant church of Saint John's. The houses on Mount Pleasant had closed curtains.

*

A grey mist hung over the valley in broken rolls. The mists were streaked pink. Over the roofs of Ginns the mist spread into one thin covering. All colour ran out of it. It hung between the terraces. Robert looked back, tracing the route he had taken. There was a steady line of others climbing the bank towards the sheds of Loft. They seemed identical as they tramped uphill, dressed in the same flannel shirts and shorts. The only sound was the slow, haphazard fall of their clogs on the cobbles and then the cinders a little further on. Robert looked away and took in the whole town. Between the rolls of long trailing mist its contours were clearly visible, but still soft and fused under the early morning light. It was as yet only five fifteen. The light was only beginning to spread across the valley. The previous day had been hot and airless. It seemed as if today would be the same. The sea beyond was a still, flat plain of lead. He had seen it the previous evening shine like silver. He had felt his habitual joy confronted by the scale of God's creation. As he gazed at the sea and remembered it glimmering in the sunlight a line of a Psalm, one of the many he had memorised from his book of Maximus Optimus, began to go through his head. *O God, thou art my God; early will I seek thee: my soul thirsteth for thee, my flesh longeth for thee in a dry and thirsty land, where no water is...* He progressed so far when he heard his name called and abruptly stopped. He turned immediately. His father had also stopped and was calling down to him. He said that if he expected to be underground by five thirty then he had better get a move on. He didn't sound particularly irritated. Robert gave up his psalm and plodded on after his father who had already turned and was marching on to the pit-head. It was Robert's first day at work.

A few minutes later he was standing in the cage beside his father. John handed him a palm full of chewing tobacco. Robert looked at in his hand for a while. He didn't know what he was supposed to do with it. He didn't use it. He didn't even smoke. He thought he should perhaps try. It made him strange. He was always making himself strange. He thanked his father. John looked down at him and told him to put the bacca in his waistcoat pocket. It was for later. It would help collect the coal-dust. He would have to chew and spit out. It was the only way. He fingered the bacca into his pocket and as he did the cage began to wind down.

Loft was a recent mine. Its first shaft had only been sunk four years previously. It stood high on the cliffs overlooking the town and the sea. Each shift he worked allowed John a view of the sea dear to his heart. Sometimes he looked at it, but mostly he didn't bother. The shaft went down for upwards to a thousand feet. Its workings stretched out three miles beneath the sea bed. Its workings extended into those of Fish and Canning, effectively making it one great mine underground, with numerous galleries and tunnels. The mines were owned by the same family. The miners regularly transferred from one pit to another depending on the owner's need.

Robert felt his heart-beat race as the cage descended. He was already terrified of making a fool of himself. The other miners knew what they were doing. He automatically assumed that they had always known what they were doing. By the same token he assumed that he would never know what he was doing. There was a great deal at stake. He was to work with his father. His father was a hagger, cleared the coal at the face. His previous apprentice had been moved on. Apprentices moved up through a hierarchy of jobs as new ones started. His father was in charge of a small team of four, two qualified miners and two apprentices. On Thursday his father would get the pay-chit recording the weight of coal they had shifted, the number of props they had put in and the number of yards the face had moved forward, and then divide the money between them as he saw fit. His father had been all through it with him. Robert was certain the chit would be for less than it had been and it would all be his fault. He was convinced he was going to fail. He couldn't begin to imagine how his father would react. He wished he didn't have to work with his own father. It would have been easier with someone else. He didn't want to let him down. He didn't think it was avoidable.

He was surprised to find that the temperature was the same at the bottom of the shaft as it was at the top. He didn't know whether he expected it to be hotter or colder, just different somehow, the difference underlining the fact that he had entered the other world of the mine. His father instructed him to go with the other apprentice and collect the horses. As soon as he had given his orders he left him and headed off inbye towards the face some three miles away.

Robert stood still for a while. There were men heading off along the main road. There was a darkness waiting for them. He was reluctant to leave the shaft bottom. The distance covered preyed on his mind. He had come so far down. He had never dreamt it possible. He was buried deeper than his imagination had been able to take him. A cold damp sweat broke out all over his body. His throat ran dry. He felt tears welling up in his eyes. He could hear his own voice screaming inside his head. He was frightened and out of sorts. He couldn't believe what he had done. He had committed himself to this. He would have to do this every day for the rest of his life. He felt tears trickle across his cheeks. He would have given anything to be back in school, to be sketching pictures of the Holy Family, scrawling out stories of Israel in Egypt, telling tales in his awkward spidery handwriting. He was sure he had made the greatest mistake of his life. But what choice did he really have? He would have been lying to himself to imagine that there had been another option. For a moment he thought he heard Mr Fancy's strange, yet exquisite voice. He turned quickly. There was just the grey emptiness of the pit floor. The other apprentice urged him to get a move on. He didn't understand. He couldn't have mistaken the voice of the apprentice for that of Mr Fancy. The other apprentice stepped away. There was nothing for it but to follow.

Robert knew the other boy. They had been to school together. He was called James Minnigan, Jim. He was a year older. He was long and lean, a slow, ponderous boy. He had started as a trapper, minding the ventilation doors, opening and closing them as men, horses and wagons made their way through. The trappers just sat in the near-dark listening for the sounds of traffic coming inbye or outbye, to the face or from it. John had said Robert could do better than that. He didn't have to start off doing such tedious work. He had Robert apprenticed to him. As Robert trailed Jim Minnigan he wondered what he thought about it. Perhaps there was some rule that everybody started as a trapper and he had broken the rule. He hated the idea of being out of line. It was all strange enough without the burden of privilege.

The horses were looked after by Jimmy Dent. He went down the mine every morning at three to see to them. He was a quick, impatient, precise man who showed no particular affection towards the animals. He gave a short speech of initiation.

A horse was an animal over 14.2 hands in height. Anything less than that and it was a pony. In Loft they used both horses and ponies. The horses were Clydesdales and the ponies Galloways. They had four stables with room for forty odd animals. It was important not to spook the animals. If they cut loose underground someone was likely to be killed. It happened from time to time. It was important to keep the animals in check and under control at all times. You had to show it who was boss. It was important to remember that the horses couldn't see, so you had to keep the noise familiar. At the end of the shift the horses had to be washed down. Finally, it was up to Jimmy Dent which horse you took. He was in charge. He ended by saying that they would probably remove the horses from all Whitehaven pits in the near future and that was no bad thing. They were brutes and stupid animals.

Robert wondered how he was supposed to see if the horses couldn't. He asked Jim Minnigan. The other apprentice burst out laughing. The horses were blind. They were always in the dark. They only went above ground during the summer holiday or during a strike and when they went above ground they couldn't see. The sunlight blinded them.

Robert looked over the large creatures with a sense of deep, unnerving wonder. It was atrocious that they should be blind. He approached them gingerly. He wanted to see their eyes. He didn't know what to expect. Blind sockets, probably. He came close to one creature. It turned its head and peered at him. Its eyes were normal. Jim Minnigan burst out laughing behind him. He had obviously worked out what Robert was looking at. He turned to Jim questioningly. He explained that they weren't literally blind. They still had their eyes, at any rate. But they couldn't see. They certainly couldn't see when they went into the sunlight. He wasn't sure about below. They maybe saw something through the gloom. What was there to see though? It was only tunnels and more tunnels. The horses might as well be blind.

When he had finished explaining about the blindness he said he would have to show him how to prepare a horse. He added that if they didn't get a move on the horse keeper would give them both a leathering. Robert was about to say that he wouldn't dare, after all his father was below ground with him, but Jim seemed to be too much in earnest to argue with. It was obvious he had suffered his share of beatings. Robert wondered whether his father would be in a position to defend him. What were the rules? It was something of a shock to him to be even considering such a question. Did it mean that his father's authority might be limited? It wasn't a good thought. A cold shiver passed over him. The underground world terrified him. It unnerved him that he should wonder about being defended. What would his father make of that? He would feel let down. He was always letting his father down. He didn't mean to. He knew it to be the case though. He felt the tears well up in his eyes again. He hated it. He hated being underground, hated the feeling of being so out of sorts and lonely. He rubbed at his eyes. They began to burn. Already they were being impregnated with dust. He thought of the tobacco in his pocket. Should he be chewing? God, he didn't know. He didn't know anything. He was buried without a clue.

He was roused from his forlorn reverie by Jim who punched him on the shoulder. Robert turned to him. Jim signed him towards some gear hanging from the stable walls. Jim told him that he would show him how to dress a horse. He instructed him to watch closely as he wasn't going to go through it again and again. He had one chance so he better make the most of it. They had to get down to the coal-face. If they missed getting some weight out they would get a hammering. They didn't have time to mess about. Jim collected his equipment and gestured Robert to do the same. He approached two horses standing side by side. They had obviously been selected. Robert wasn't sure how that had happened. He hadn't heard Jimmy Dent say anything. He had obviously gone off somewhere. It unnerved Robert all over again. He was convinced he would never get used to all this.

Jim proceeded to explain the process of preparing a horse. Firstly the braffin, a collar with reins attached, was placed over the horse's head. Then limmers, leather straps, were tied under and over the horses body to keep the braffin in place. The limmers were shaped like a wish-bone with the horse positioned in the middle. The end of the limmers were attached to the coal-tubs by means of an iron-peg. Their first job was to take empty tubs inbye.

When both horses were dressed Jim Minnigan led his away. Robert simply waited. He listened to the slow heavy footfalls of Jim's horse as it made its way along the main road. A moment later Jim shouted back to him to get going. The horse reared back slightly against his restraining hand. Robert turned apprehensively towards it. He looked into the horse's face. Its large doleful eyes were fixed on him even as it reared back its head. Robert whispered to it. It was all right. He told it he was nervous too. He asked it to come on. He pulled slightly on the reins. To his amazement the horse began to step forward. It responded to his hold. It was amazing. He followed Jim and together they collected their empty tubs and then began their slow progress inbye along the mother gate. Robert marvelled at the enormous strength of the animal as the weight of the tubs was taken.

As they progressed inbye the darkness intensified and the temperature began to rise rapidly. The heat seemed to be coming from the very rock walls. Robert began to sweat. He wanted to strip off his waistcoat and shirt, but didn't know whether that was allowed. Pretty soon the flannel was saturated and stuck to his skin. His mouth was full of dust. He couldn't really see where he was going. He let the horse lead the way. He put his trust in the animal. He was sure Jimmy Dent was wrong. The horse seemed quiet and intelligent. He didn't mind thinking Jimmy Dent was wrong. He was a bully. It clouded his thinking. It always did with characters like that. So many men on Ginns were the same. They shouted their mouths off, but they never stopped to think. They weren't like Mr Fancy. Their words didn't seem connected to a particular idea or point of view the way Mr Fancy's were. He conjured up whole worlds when he spoke. Suddenly the sheer banality of much of what went on around Ginns struck him. At the same moment he determined in his own mind that he would take up Father Bond's offer. He would go to him and maybe learn something of the incomprehensible music of Latin. Maybe he might even learn Spanish. He had never heard Mr Fancy speak Spanish. He wondered now how he had missed that. He had failed to seize the possibility. Now he could only wonder. It would be good to learn. He longed to be in Father Bond's parlour now listening to the priest recite, even if it meant that he would be asked to recite himself. He wouldn't refuse. He would start with the first words of *Maximus Optimus. Blessed is the man that walketh not in the counsel of the ungodly, nor standeth in the way of sinners, nor sitteth in the seat of the scornful.* Better still, he dreamed he was kneeling in the body of the church. There was the smell of beeswax, incense and tallow. The light was a kaleidoscope of colour, rich reds and blues, as the sunlight broke through the stained glass windows. The images of the saints, Our Lady and Christ himself gazed down, but indirectly, intimating their grace, modelling it, the knowledge of a peace that passeth understanding. It was shadowy in the church, its corners were hidden and mysterious, its images flickered, but it was perfect, a haven, an escape, asylum. *In the Lord put I my trust; how say ye to my soul, Flee as a bird to your mountain?* In comparison to that lofty heaven Robert was convinced he was now in narrow hell.

They passed through numerous doors. They opened mysteriously as the horses approached and closed behind them the same. Robert could scarcely see the trappers sitting in the dark controlling them. It crossed his mind that it might be preferable to be able to sit there all day, keeping to the shadows, hidden away. His father said they wouldn't be using trappers much longer. The new seams would be approached by a longwall face and not board and pillar. They wouldn't need trappers for that. Maybe that was why the horses would be going. Probably that's what Jimmy Dent meant. Robert wasn't sure. Anyway, his father hadn't wanted him to start off as a trapper. Robert hoped the horses would be there a while longer. He had taken to this animal. He called ahead to Jim Minnigan wanting to know if the animals had names. Jim shouted back that of course they did. He was leading Sammy, whilst Robert was leading Little King. Robert stood more upright and led the animal with a greater sense of pride. He was leading a horse called Little King. There was only one true king. The horse must have been named in his honour. Even here the Lord was revered.

It was stiflingly hot at the face. The face workers, his father included, were clearing coal that had already been cut. The actual cutting was done on the cutting shift, usually the night-shift. John had tried to explain it to Robert before, but Robert had not really visualised it. It struck him now as very strange that any distinction could be made between night and day when the reality of such was so far removed. He stood there and mourned the light and the space, and at the same time the seclusion of the main road. Despite everything, as he had travelled inbye a sense of calmness had gradually affected him. He had been able to daydream. His mind had run with his favourite words. The darkness had become peaceful and containing. But now he was back amongst a crowd he began to panic again. He would be expected to perform and he was sure he would not be up to it. He would let his father down. He was convinced of that. He would be made to feel ashamed. He always was made to feel ashamed. It weighed on him.

The seam was about three feet in height and about eighty yards long. Small teams of men worked at their allocated section. It was his job to take the empty tubs for filling then move them to a siding to form a rolley, a carriage used to take the tubs outbye. Robert stood and watched the hewers clearing the coal. They were stripped to the waist. The dust and sweat formed a lining of black grease. Despite that, when the stark light caught them at a certain angle, their bodies glowed. They spoke in snatches. They shouted and swore. There was a pattern and rhythm to it. He couldn't work out what controlled it, but he sensed it was there. They all understood it. He could only watch. He could only stand back and fear exposure, fear being called on to do something he wasn't fit to do, or even worse be something he couldn't be. More than the physical labour he dreaded the jokes and the banter that went on. He couldn't shout. He didn't joke. Unintentionally he made himself different. He let everyone down. A phrase from Maximus Optimus went through his head: *Preserve me, O God: for in thee do I put my trust.*

76

When they stopped for bait his father approached him. Robert had no sense of time. It seemed to him he had been underground for endless hours. If it was only bait time then there was still a long time to serve. He thought ahead. If every day felt the same, then he would certainly go mad underground. The time was unendurable. He couldn't stand it. He was sure it must show in his face. He knew he must look tiny and insignificant, a frightened little school-boy. He tried to put a brave face on it. He even tried to smile. His father gazed at him for some time. It was obvious he wanted to say something, but was really at a loss as to what would suffice. Father and son were awkward with each other. Eventually John spoke up. His voice was quiet and not without sympathy. He told him to remember to chew his tobacco and to drink plenty. He said it would help. He placed an undeniable emphasis on the word help. Robert felt himself surge at the word. His father knew how he laboured. He felt tears come to his eyes yet again. He didn't know whether his father would be able to see that in the dim light. John added words to the effect that it was always hard, at first, hard for everyone, but eventually you got used to it, people got used to all sorts. He had no sooner finished talking than he turned away abruptly and went off shouting towards a group of men. His voice came to Robert in loud surges, roaring louder than most others.

Still, Robert didn't feel at all rebuked. He had expected that, but it hadn't happened. He had been forgiven. It was unmistakable. His father had forgiven him. He felt light and exhilarated. His father was surprising. He never gave him any credit for that, but it was true. He was an unpredictable and surprising man. He told himself he had to remember that.

As the shift wore on they came into more contact. Together they tied up the tubs to be hauled to the rolley track. Robert was sure he was being helped out. He hadn't expected it. It struck him that it was a strange, novel world being underground. There was no doubt that had he been able he would have gladly exchanged it for some other, yet he had discovered something about his father and already he was thinking that he would not have wanted to miss that. It was a feeling rather than an idea, not something that could easily be put into words. It was a feeling that got him through. For once, at least, he didn't feel at all ashamed.

Towards the end of the shift he had to lead the horse back outbye. It had to pull the rolley of tubs. It was a slow plod back to the shaft. Nevertheless the horse was faster than the returning miners. They stepped sideways into manholes as the horses and tubs passed. Robert hadn't really noticed the manholes before. They were gaps in the side of the roadway. He looked back along the mother gate. There was a long stretch of impenetrable darkness, and then, unexpectedly, one by one, like so many stars flicking into place in the night sky, lights appeared as miners stepped out from the manholes. After that he kept looking back. He felt he was at the head of a candle-lit procession. They were all following Little King, a horse named for the Lord.

When the tubs had been deposited at the shaft bottom he took the horse back to the stable. Jim reminded him that he had to wash it down. There was a gutter of water diverted to the stable, pumped out from the inbye for the job. After he had washed and dried Little King Jimmy Dent took charge. Robert wanted to say something. He wasn't sure what, but something favourable about Little King. He had been frightened of the horse at first, but there had been no need. Little King was a splendid animal, intelligent and gentle. He caught sight of Jimmy Dent's sneering countenance and knew it was pointless. In fact, it was with some reluctance that he handed the horse back.

He returned once again to the shaft bottom, went up in the cage, then ran all the way home. Once he was home he went to his room and lay on a prodded mat, one of the rag mats his mother was always making, and fell asleep. He didn't know how long he slept for. His mother woke him. She spoke firmly, but smiled all the time. He had to get himself washed and then come for his meal which was ready and waiting. When he had finished eating he went straight to bed. He cried himself to sleep.

The second day was better. Time went more quickly. He no longer had the sense of not knowing what was happening or what was to happen next. He took empty tubs to the mother lode and brought full ones back. His only regret was that Jimmy Dent allocated him a different horse, a plodding characterless animal called General. He missed Little King. Little King was the Lord's horse.

*

Marty played on the opposite side of the Market Square to McClean's. McClean's: barber, tobacconist, authorised emigration agent. It was a large white building painted over with the flags of the Cunard Lines, Toncastle Steamers, Union Coast Lines and Mays Shipping: and in bold blue letters: *McClean Shipping Agent, To all parts of the world by any line of steamers: South Africa, United States, New Zealand, Australia, and Canada.* It was the scene, on the last Friday of every month, of the emigrants' party, held before the midnight sailing, destination, eventually, the South African mines. McClean himself, a pyknic shaped ex-sailor with untrimmed beard, who wore a billycock hat and polished clogs, who was usually to be found frequenting capstans where he leaned, smoked long stemmed pipes and chatted to the hobblers, fishermen and coalmen, or otherwise pulled toy boats on lengths of string at the shoreline, provided trestles, braziers and sold under the counter rum and poteen. The emigrants and their families, mainly iron-ore miners, provided food. Marty, regaled in a billycock hat for the occasion, kept beneath McClean's counter, was the emigrants' violinist. Bobby's *emigration,* on the last Friday in October 1913, consequent of the Irish *big strike* which closed the Irish ports and thereby closed most of the market for Whitehaven coal, was also the occasion for the announcement of Peter Kavanagh's engagement to Anne.

Bobby's decision had been sudden and rash. It was Gavin Duffy who, in a state of euphoria, had predicted the upheavals the Dublin strike would create. It had been on the day of the great funeral. As the cortege made its way from Mount Pleasant Gavin Duffy, John Devlin and Bobby Kavanagh slipped away and made their way to the shoreline. John Darcy was already there collecting seaweed which he said he boiled and ate with fried eggs; and McClean was also there pulling one of his home-made boats, a large clipper ship with white sails.

Duffy's emotional volatility at the time was pronounced. He stood close to the water line and shouted out in temper towards the waves as if there were someone out there to hear, denouncing the funeral as a charade and an insult. His language was foul. After he had shouted for a few minutes, visibly working himself up, he suddenly burst out in a round of raw, forced, self-abusive laughter. Then, as the laughter stuttered to a close, he declared through clenched teeth, still to the oncoming waters: "Well, to hell with them all, fuck them! The time has come. Connolly and Larkin have the transport and docks organised. One big union for the whole of Ireland. They'll paralyse these pits. And then there'll be one big union here too. Do you hear me? One big union, for the whole lot of us. Larkin and Connolly are due to draft an appeal to the British workers calling for an all out strike in support of the Irish workers. We'll all be one. There'll be an alliance of socialists, nationalists, trades unionists and suffragettes. Those bastards won't ever beat Larkin and Connolly and they won't beat us, not when we're all together, not this time. They can't beat one big union. We're too organised to be beaten this time. I'm telling you, this is the start. Everywhere is going to erupt. And the explosion is going to grind this country to it's knees. It'll be the end of empire, the end of the owners, the end of everything!"

John's response had been to ignore Duffy, as it usually was when Duffy was in those moods, and think quietly to himself the Fenian maxim *ourselves alone*. Bobby, on the other hand, had been thoroughly shaken by Duffy's pronouncement. He hadn't heard of the *big strike*, or its leaders. He went up to Duffy, manhandled him to get his attention, and demanded to know more. Duffy was scathing over his ignorance and sneered at what he called Bobby's *cooly mentality*. "I only worry about Polly," Bobby claimed in his own defence. Duffy berated him with a sneering parrot call of *Pretty Polly, Pretty Polly* to which, much to Duffy's further chagrin, Bobby refused to rise. "You don't know a damned thing, Kavanagh, except your parrot cooly mentality!" Duffy went on mercilessly, goading Bobby to respond. Bobby was inflexible, repeating over: "I only worry about Polly." "Christ man!" Duffy exploded. "There's going to be a war in your country, a fucking war! Do you not hear what's going on? They say 500,000 unionists have signed the Ulster covenant against Home Rule and they have the best of England with them. So Ulster will fight. They'll have Bonar Law's Tories and the British army with them, and all you can say is you're worried about Pretty Polly. The police are clubbing down workers in O'Connell street. Christ, Connolly was in prison on hunger strike just last month fighting for the Dublin workers. Do you hear me? Hunger strike! The ultimate sacrifice. And he won. He's in Scotland now canvassing for those same workers. Things are happening everywhere and all you can say is what about Polly. Fucking hell, Kavanagh!" Bobby stuck to his theme. "But if these pits close what about Polly? I worry about what happens here." With that Duffy spat at Bobby's feet and marched away, pausing only briefly to purchase a fox-pelt from John Darcy, which he had seen on his trolley and for some reason had taken a fancy to.

Bobby turned to John for support. "What do you say Devlin?" he demanded. John shook his head. His imagination was alive with what Duffy had said. He was trying to picture home, trying to cast his mind across the same sea Duffy had berated. What would it mean? What would he have to do? What would he be called to do? He couldn't work it out. He had to know what he personally should do. It was the way he dealt with things. If there was a war, which seemed very likely, how would he be called on to fight? "I don't say anything," John replied. "I don't say anything at all. Not yet. I don't know what any of it means at the moment. Not yet, anyway."

Before Bobby could say anymore, he lowered his head and he too began to make his way from the shore, leaving John Darcy to collect his supper, McClean to play with his boat, and Bobby to ponder his future. The very next day, without confiding in Polly, Bobby booked his passage to South Africa to work in the gold mines. Three days later he was attending his own emigration party.

That night he was unusually calm. Even the simple act of breathing was less laboured than was normal with him. To begin with he stood apart, leaning beneath a street lamp, simply inhaling the various acrid smells, a combination of horse droppings, tannin and smoke, that always characterised these parties. He was content. He was going. It was done. For one night he expected to be pampered. He waited until the trestles had been set and watched as Polly and Kate laid out brawn, brazier baked potatoes, and stewed crab-apples, and John stirred up cinnamon spiced rum that he had bought from McClean's shop. Only when these preliminaries were complete did he go to them.

Without speaking he took his place by Polly. He reached out and grasped her hand. Polly's hand squeezed around his. They thrilled to each other's touch, but then immediately felt embarrassed by this obvious show of affection. It was too raw, too naked, too obvious. Nevertheless, neither of them withdrew from it. There was too much feeling between them for that. For one night they would put their own need first. So they stood, hand in hand, despite feeling awkward and uncertain about it. And even as their children began to join them, coming from the dancing square, they didn't relinquish the other's touch, though it obviously gave them some discomfort to be seen.

There were seven Kavanagh children, Bobby's guilt, wonder and satisfaction, ranging in age from the eighteen year old Peter to the ten year old Stanley. Between those two came Cath, June, Tom, Alice, Breda and Stanley. On this night Peter was the last to show. He held Anne's hand with the same inexpert attention as his father held his mother's hand. The whole gathering collected around the mock opulence of the trestle and waited. No one was sure what to do. There were all the trappings of a party, but no one was quite clear that they were allowed to enjoy it. No one quite knew who should take the lead. In the end it was Bobby who broke the silence. He smiled and simply said: "I'm not going to say anything. You do realise that? Not a word."

They all thought about that sentiment for a moment, wondering whether there was an expectation to respond, or even whether it was right and proper to respond. Finally John Devlin took it on. "Well, in that case, Bobby Kavanagh, slink and reprobate," he said, handing Bobby the jug of cinnamon rum, "I'll insist on you drinking my good health." Bobby took the jug in one hand and drank deeply. He finished to applause. He passed it back to John and John in turn swallowed hard. He then passed it on to Peter.

Peter relinquished his hold of Anne and took the jug in both hands, cupping them around it. He held it for a while without drinking. Eventually he looked bashfully at his father and quietly said: "I have something to say."

"Good lad!" John Devlin declared.

"No, I didn't mean that," Peter said, turning quickly to John, quite flustered by his enthusiasm. Then he turned straight back to Bobby and said: "Of course, good luck, God speed! Of course that." He immediately put the jug to his lips and drank quickly, gulping at the rum.

Bobby watched and waited, but Polly was not so patient. It was obvious that Peter had more to say. She needed to know just what that was. This night was hard enough without the added burden of mysteries. She spoke up, demanding that he explain himself: "What else, Peter? There was obviously more." Peter took the bottle from his lips. He held it for a moment longer, then suddenly thrust it forward and offered it to her. Her expression alone told him how she scorned his offer, indeed, took it as something of an insult. She was not to be deflected, though, and stuck to her theme. "I asked you what else?" she repeated.

Peter shrugged. He had meant the offer to be teasing, nothing else. "Well," he began, stretching out the word to its limit, "it's just that I wanted you to know, well, we wanted you to know, no, no, me, that as of tonight Anne has agreed to our engagement. Me and Anne." His announcement was greeted with complete silence. He couldn't understand it. He had expected an instant response, and a warm response. He looked from one parent to the other. He stared hard at them, willing them to respond. Eventually he demanded it. "Well, what do you say? We're engaged! I want your response."

His plea went unanswered for a moment. Eventually Bobby spoke up, his voice hushed and distant: "Tonight is my going away."

"I know that," Peter insisted, "I know you're going away. What difference does it make?"

"It could have waited," Polly cut in.

"No it couldn't. He's going away. When could I consult him?"

"You haven't." Bobby said. "You haven't consulted me, you've told me. I'm going away and you tell me what you're doing. You've taken it all on yourself without speaking to anyone. If that's how it is before I'm even gone how will it be after?"

A sudden thrill of temper shot through Bobby. Everyone was aware of it.

Peter was at a loss. Being challenged was not something he was used to. It went against the grain. He had always been indulged. He was used to that. Everything he wanted usually came easily to him. He was a striking boy, a big, strong, attractive boy, and everyone admired him, everyone was happy to please him. In many ways he was Bobby and Polly's boast. A great strapping boy, despite Bobby's physical failings. He had never really encountered this from his parents before. He struggled with it. He wasn't about to accept it. He prepared to shout them down. He didn't have any other response. He braced himself for the encounter.

However, before he had begun, Anne spoke up. She seemed to physically separate herself from everyone else there and gave all her attention to Bobby. She spoke quietly and evenly. "We're asking you now, because you're going away. It has to be now. That's why. Tonight, I mean. We're sorry it was like this. I'm sorry." She peered at him after she had finished, her expression contrite and rather wistful. It added to her. Even without it she was already lovely.

As she gazed at him Bobby held up his hands. He couldn't help but surrender to her. Her apology was too much to resist. She whispered, as if she just wanted to speak to Bobby, though everyone could hear: "It's the accident that did it. It makes you realise that, well, you have to seize what's best and good. We are good together Mr Kavanagh. I'll be best and good for him, I promise you. That's the only good that could have come of it."

Bobby tried to smile, but it remained only half-formed on his lips. She had shaken him. Recollection of Peter down the shaft, still along the galleries, had hit him. He felt suddenly aimless and confused, certainly breached.

"Your blessing?" Peter pressed him, still agitated by his parents' response.

Bobby nodded, conceding to it all. He felt embarrassed that he had felt otherwise, embarrassed to be so revealed.

Polly said: "I didn't want to be happy tonight, it's not easy. But I am, happy for us. That's it."

"I'm sorry," Anne said, "we got it wrong."

Polly shook her head. She turned away and looked across the dancing square. Its lights dotted across her face, but she couldn't focus on anything. Her mind was half-deranged with the ambiguities of life. That she should be so happy and so sad at one and the same time was beyond understanding. But so much was beyond understanding. It wasn't usually something she would even try to work out. It would be an unaired thought. But tonight she knew it. She was filled with the utter strangeness of her life. She continued to shake her head. It wasn't aimed at Anne anymore.

Perhaps Kate didn't understand that because she took Anne's hand firmly in her own and pressed it hard. She was approving her and wanted to let her know that was how she felt.

Eventually Polly turned her attention back to Anne. She saw Kate and her hand in hand. She asked: "And what of your own family? Will they have an opinion?" The question sounded more brusque than she had intended.

"I live with two aunties, Mrs Kavanagh. It was good of them to take me in. My mother died just after the New Year. She hadn't been well for some time. She thought the world of Peter Kavanagh though. I'm just so pleased they met before she passed away."

Polly didn't respond. She knew Anne was indulging her. She wasn't disappointed in that. It showed Anne in a good light. She was disappointed in not knowing, though. She objected to being told that Anne's mother approved of her son and she didn't even know they had ever met. It wasn't right that her son conducted himself in such secrecy. It showed him in a bad light. It meant that they had made mistakes. They had been too free with him. How much more did she not know? Did all of her children hold secrets? It was a difficult thought. It implied that the day would come when they would not be hers anymore. Indeed, it had already occurred. Peter had felt fit to withhold Anne from her, withhold the approval of Anne's dead mother. She couldn't accept that. She knew it was irrational, but she objected to Anne's mother's approval. She turned to Peter and looked him over steadily. How was it that she felt such contradictory things at the same time? She was angry with him and pleased with him. She welcomed Anne and resented her. She was glad and she was unhappy. It didn't make sense.

Peter shrugged at her interest. He was sure everything was normal again. He was sure he was her big boy again. He skewed his face at her playfully. She continued to gaze at him steadily. He dismissed it again with another shrug and turned away from her. He held up the jug of cinnamon rum to his father. Bobby took it, sniffed it, and as he put it to his lips uttered: "Good luck, God speed." He took a single deep drink then passed it on to Robert.

Robert took the jug gingerly. He was surprised to have been included. He hadn't expected nor really wanted it. Up until that point all of his attention had been taken by Anne. To his devotional, pious mind her contrition appeared heroic, and in some way troublesomely angelic. He couldn't rid that idea from his thoughts. Her slender, pliant figure, right down to the pared tip of her nose, which moved as she laughed, suggested the fanciful idea to him of an angel from a miniature of the holy family. And as he watched her, particularly now that she was laughing, serving the Kavanagh children brawn and potato, he felt a deep, real embarrassment growing inside him.

He couldn't understand it. Why was he embarrassed? It disconcerted him. It somehow undermined what had been simple and rather wonderful. It crossed his mind that he should perhaps express something of this to Father Bond during the next of their weekly lessons. They had begun just after Robert had started to work. They were quite the highlight of his week. The priest had regularly suggested that he might attempt to express something of his religious thoughts. Robert wasn't exactly clear about what the priest had in mind. Maybe the way he thought about Anne was a clue. Maybe that was a religious thought. No sooner had he considered it than he dismissed it. The idea was absurd. Father Bond didn't want to know such things. There was no way he could find the words to express what he meant. He wasn't sure that he really knew himself. It was far easier sticking to Father Bond's game of guessing at the meaning of the Latin texts he was made to read aloud. He was never really close but it all amounted to a repetition of *Hallelujah* and that satisfied them both.

The jug abruptly arrested his thinking. In fact, it filled him with dread. The problem was that it was inescapable. It had been offered, therefore it had to be drunk. He put it to his lips and sipped. The cinnamon was pleasant, but the rum abrasive. He immediately began to hack. Anne turned to him and laughed out loud. He told himself it was not meant unkindly. As he coughed John took the bottle from him. Robert was perplexed. He felt exposed and shied away from looking at his father. He would never know the look of sympathy and pleasure that passed across John's face. He would only ever recollect that the bottle was taken from him.

John immediately passed the bottle back to Bobby. As he did he commented on the fact that it was virtually empty and said that he was going for more. He left them saying: "I'll even get some for that itinerant who said to McClean: Lend me a tanner and I'll buy you a drink."

"And so he should for all the work Marty does!" Kate called after him.

"Work?" John scoffed, shouting over his shoulder without turning back.

"Yes, work!"

As she called out Gavin Duffy stumbled towards them. He had been drinking hard. His manner was mulish and ponderous. He echoed her word, making it into something of a query. As he did the greater part of his attention was directed at Bobby. His expression was greedy, his eyes taurine, his mouth agape. Eventually he laughed out loud and jeered. "Work is it? Oh yes, work! Off to work for pretty Polly."

Kate checked him. Though, in general, she had a great deal of time for Duffy, she found his moods, his personal piety, distasteful. "So you've come to see him off, Gavin," she said, coaxing him, trying to smooth the waters between them.

"I've come to see him go all right!"

"And wish him well?"

"To call him a coward, a traitor and a blackleg!" He burst out laughing. It sounded bluff and abusive.

Peter spoke up over it. "Clear off, Duffy, this is family."

"No, no, I've got more to say, a lot more."

"You've said enough, now clear off."

"What do you say, Bobby? Clear off? Do you want me to clear off? Do you?" Bobby didn't answer. He had made his decision. It had relieved him. He didn't need to explain. He had had no other choice. He was surrounded by that lack of choice. They were feeding off a very staple diet. Duffy could goad him all he liked. He had nothing to say. He waited.

Peter stepped forward, but Polly checked him. She lay her hand on his shoulder and shook her head wearily. She said: "Mr Duffy will leave us alone now. He's said what he had to say, but he's finished now. He knows how it is. He knows it's bad enough."

Gavin laughed out loud again, the sound pitiless and brutal. He said: "Don't take on son, listen to your mother, really, let it go, you'd only regret it." Peter made another move, but this time Anne stayed him. She took his hand in hers and gripped it tightly. Gavin went on. He couldn't help himself. He was too wound up to control himself. Besides which, he was drunk. There was no reasoning with him. "Actually, I tell you what son, you ask him why he's clearing out. Go on, ask him. Ask him if he'll tell you what's happening back home?"

"I know what's happening at home Duffy," Peter responded.

"Do you, do you really? You know the British army is about to take charge, do you? You know they'll probably shoot Asquith and Redmond, and then they'll clamp down everywhere they have a fancy. You know all that do you? Well that's good. I'm pleased, really pleased, because we have to be ready, we have to organise and we have to stand firm. That's what this is about." He turned his attention away from Peter to Bobby. "You see, it's not the time to be running away. Do you get it? There's war in your own country, man. War! Don't you understand? Don't you care? Don't you feel any damn thing? Are you not ashamed? Have you no conscience? Christ, Bobby, what about it?" He couldn't go on. His voice stopped, suspended at this point.

Bobby remained implacable. He had no doubts. He had no choice. He didn't have Gavin's privileges, but he wasn't about to explain that. He knew that Peter was looking at him and was questioning him, but Peter didn't understand either. How could he? He was too young. He was untested. But he would know soon enough and would come down on the side of reason, the side that made sense of a second emigration. He smiled at the thought of it, the thought of being correct. Peter caught it and frowned at it. Bobby didn't care. He had nothing to explain. He wanted to damn them all. He had made his pact with necessity and the rest of it could go to hell. He would do what was right by Polly and the children. It simplified life. He would ensure their survival. That was it. Nothing to answer.

John Devlin returned with another bottle. In the meantime he had had a couple of swift drinks with McClean and was in high spirits. Indeed, like Duffy, he was really quite drunk. On seeing Gavin he called out to him: "Are you after drink you unstable troublemaker and hell raiser!"

Gavin looked around vaguely. His mood had swung from excitement to despondency. He felt suddenly wounded by everything, and unequal to any more. He had spent himself. His enthusiasm and obsession had become flat. He assumed it was because he had drunk so much. It was always the same. He invariably ended up feeling depressed. He shook himself, trying to pull himself together and think straight. As John came up to him a light of recognition lit up his face briefly, then instantly dimmed. He said: "Oh, to hell with it, Devlin. These parochial bastards will give up the ghost. Why should I care? I can still think, even in this smutty world, I can still think. I have that regularity, Devlin, that stamina. Isn't that right Devlin? Isn't that damn well right? Stamina."

"I dare say so, Gavin, if you say so. But I'll just nod my head for now."

"You do that," Gavin responded wearily. He was smarting deep down inside himself. He turned to go, but then hesitated, looked back and said: "Good luck, Mrs Kavanagh. Good luck." He immediately turned away and staggered across the square with short, heavy steps.

Only John Devlin felt inclined to laugh. He wasn't about to let Gavin's maudlin exit spoil his humour. He challenged the mood that he recognised had descended on the rest of them. He turned on Bobby: "Come and have a drink with me for Christ sake, before you go and leave me to the likes of that." He strutted towards the square where the iron-ore miners were dancing beneath the electric street lights. He turned and called back: "Come on, and bring the boys." Bobby shrugged. They couldn't refuse. They went to drink another jug of cinnamon rum.

Polly was left with Kate and Anne. Anne began to tidy up the trestle top.

As Polly watched Bobby stroll towards the square she whispered: "He was very loving."

Kate smiled. "Of course he was."

Polly shook her head. "No, I mean, he was very loving." She appealed to Kate for understanding. A sense of timidity and shame was mobile in her solid figure. Kate laughed at her. "Is it right, Kate?"

"By God yes," Kate declared, feeling the weight of her own desire spurt into existence.

"Why does it take going away, though, our Kate? I don't follow that." Kate shook her head. "You know why he's going, don't you." Kate chose to say nothing. She thought Bobby Kavanagh's decision rash and untimely. She had no opinion on what Gavin had said, but she was certain that Bobby was wrong. Nothing had yet occurred to make her think otherwise. The mines still worked. Life went on. She felt nothing in the wind, no more than was usual. And besides, it troubled her that if one went, one of her own, then others might be inclined to follow. She was sure she would go mad if John left her, and that she might never forgive Bobby Kavanagh if he did. She shook her head at Polly, refusing to be drawn. Polly said: "He's going because he's got such a lousy chest." She smiled grimly. "His lousy bloody chest."

"I don't understand."

"He just needs to keep going."

"So far?"

"He's scared. He's always scared. He dwells on things. He doesn't forget that our mammy had to give children away."

"To family."

Polly didn't hear but carried on her eulogy: "I try to calm him, but it's just him. Always nervy, always on edge, always scared."

"It makes him loving."

"Yes, it makes him himself, God help him." Polly looked for him across the square. He was standing with John. He still had his composure. "I think I'd better go and dance with him. What do you think? Should I or will I make it worse for him?"

"I think you would know best," Kate replied. Polly said no more. She set off and walked towards Bobby. Kate turned to Anne. "Are you going to dance with your man?"

"Do you think I should?"

"Why not?"

"It's their dance, isn't it."

"It's free."

"If you say it's all right?"

"Oh, for God's sake."

Anne shrugged her compliance. Kate wasn't there to take any notice. She had already set off towards the square determined to dance with John. Anne came a few steps behind her.

Bobby and John were both quite drunk, consequently they were scarcely at their best, stumbling more than dancing, but still they managed a few rounds before the party broke up for the midnight sailing. Gradually everyone on the square began to disperse. The slow clop clop clop of the hired carts echoed around the square as the iron-ore miners headed toward the harbour. Bobby took Polly's hand and said: "I still have nothing to say. I hope you won't begrudge me that." He began to follow the carts. He had a single bag. John Devlin carried it. He collected it from McClean's. McClean was asleep beneath his own counter. He was talking in his sleep. Kate took the Kavanagh children home. Robert went home to Dora who had remained there with Patrick. He was keen to tell her about Anne, yet at the same time was timid of how whatever he might say would sound. He rehearsed his words all the way home.

That night, as Bobby boarded his boat, taking leave of Polly as if they were acquaintances, Peter made love to Anne for the first time. They lay together amongst the lobster-pots in a shed off the *Sugar Tongue*. Anne sobbed in a suppressed ecstasy of pleasure and pain as the empty peaceful night gathered around her. They slept until dawn and the voice of the dock workers roused them. As they stepped onto the harbour they were almost surprised to find Bobby's boat gone. They each went home gingerly. Little did they know that it would be less than a year later when Peter would be sailing himself.

Chapter Three

John stared at his face in a cracked mirror above the square sink. Flies crawled along the window sash and crane-flies beat the glass. The room was airless. The late summer heat had dragged on without diminishing well into September. As if drained by the heat he stared at his own reflection for a long time. He was preparing to shave but as always recently the cracked mirror brought to his mind the face of Tumelty. Tumelty known as Docker. Tumelty's face in two distinct portions of his broken mirror. He rubbed the heavy dark growth around his cheeks. Unusually for a miner he shaved every day. He claimed to be uncomfortable otherwise. In truth he was a fastidious man who lay great store by appearance and would have felt he was letting himself down by not shaving every day. Consequently, he had to come to his mirror each day and encounter Tumelty.

Eventually, he sopped his face with soap and moved close to the cracked pane. As he did so he caught sight of Robert standing in the doorway behind him watching him. He proceeded to shave. They neither spoke as John scraped away the thick black stubble. When he was finished he threw cold water over his face, shook off the drops and let the rest remain to drip over his torso. He turned to the window and pushed the upper sash behind the lower. The air remained heavy and warm. He shook his face again and breathed at the open window. Outside the kitchen window everything was bathed in crystal light, the sky all blue.

He turned back to the sink and began to fill it with cold water. As it poured he splashed it over his shoulders, chest and arms, sprinkling water all around him. The floor was patterned with a series of drops. He rubbed a block of soap against himself until it formed a thick layer of cream, his skin smacking, moving like elastic beneath his palms.

Sensing that he was never going to be acknowledged Robert decided to speak. It wasn't easy for him. He half-guessed the picture in his father's mind. After all, it was also in his own. He couldn't remember a time in his life when he had approached his father in this way. He had agonised over the temerity of it. But finally he had been unable to contain himself. His passionate mind was filled with a new wonder.

He spoke very quietly. "Peter is talking about joining up, boasts about it, really. He says he's going to marry Anne then go into the army." John carried on washing, giving no indication whether he had heard Robert or not. Robert continued. "Did you hear? He's going to marry Anne, then leave her. Do you think he should?"

John turned on Robert and stared at him for some time. His expression was stern, fixed and immovable, yet at the same time fragile. In his mind he was willing Robert to say more, urging him to flesh out that stark statement. He just didn't know what he was being presented with. The note of interest in Robert's voice both infuriated and scared him. But Robert was too unnerved by his father's attention to be able to carry on. It had been difficult enough just broaching the topic. So, realising that Robert wasn't about to say anymore John spoke up. "You tell me Robert. You have lessons. You give me a reason for it. You explain it to me. Maybe that would be better."

Robert wanted to give it up. His stomach was turning. He expected that if he said more then his voice would fail. He would be humiliated. He was always humiliated. It was almost natural with him. And yet, somehow he knew he had come too far to back down. This time he would have to answer. He couldn't fly away. Not this time. "Peter Kavanagh says it's only right to help out poor Belgium," he faltered, speaking in low tones of sulky, nervous defiance. "They haven't done anything to anyone."

John continued to stare fixedly at him. He responded with a slow determined voice that rose gradually in volubility until it was an excited rush. "You understand more than that Robert. You're almost educated. You have all those lessons. They must stand for something. Tumelty is dead. He's not going to be brought back. They did that. Do you understand! They did whatever they damn well wanted. They did it! Cut us up! Made meat of us! No arrests. Nothing! Belgium! Christ! Belgium. Don't do this to me! Bloody hell, are we supposed to forget that? Are we? Forget Tumelty, forget poor Tumelty? Well?"

Robert gazed hopelessly at his father. He knew what Tumelty's name meant. He didn't need to be reminded of it. Not like that. He understood. But there was also Peter. He had to stand up for Peter. His defence of Belgium had been so passionate. Poor defenceless Belgium, he had said. Belgium like Ireland. He had said that. Surely his father would appreciate that. Belgium like Ireland! Peter Kavanagh knew what he was talking about. He said that Mr Lloyd George had said it was a crusade on behalf of the little five-foot-five nations. A crusade! And he would know. He was a Welshman, after all. Wales like Ireland. Belgium like Ireland. A crusade! Everybody thought so. Peter Kavanagh said everybody was for the war. All the Christian churches, the unions, everyone. Surely his father would listen to someone like Peter Kavanagh. He had certainly won Robert over.

Not that Robert had needed a great deal of winning over. Certainly not by Peter Kavanagh anyway. He had learnt to hero worship Peter Kavanagh in his own particular and passionate way. And in return hed earned approval, indeed affection from Peter. In fact, they had formed a somewhat unlikely yet evident friendship. It started immediately following Peter's engagement and developed as the year progressed. By the time the event with Tumelty occurred their closeness was such that they had held hands without embarrassment in the face of the enemy.

Mention of Tumelty, though, stalled Robert. In some ways it intimidated him. He knew that Tumelty obsessed his father's thinking, but he wasn't convinced by the nature of that obsession. He was certain it was more personal than his father would ever have owned. Tumelty had certainly provoked a rupture between them, father and son. They were still living it.

In the period following Bobby's leaving Gavin's predictions seemed to be proving true. Reports suggested that Ireland was on the brink of chaos. Even Kate had to accept that she had wind of things, events that made her feel uncomfortable and deeply fearful of the future. Bobby's decision now seemed somewhat more sensible and less rash than it might. That understanding only heightened her sense of dread. She just couldn't countenance emigration for John. The fact that local problems could be caused by events back home was just too difficult to comprehend. There was no doubt about it. The Irish strike was hitting the Whitehaven mines hard. Each one was working to reduced hours. It was impossible to see how the situation would end. Events moved with such rapidity.

An unlooked for consequence of the strike and the deteriorating situation in Ireland was the effect it had on militant Protestantism in Whitehaven. There had always been Orange Lodges around the area, their numbers made up of Northern immigrants who entered the established church and Presbyterians predominantly from across the Scottish border,

Murphy being a product of its Calvinist fundamentalism, but they had scarcely troubled themselves with *the Irish streets,* the Catholic streets, Ginns and Mount Pleasant. However, as the Dublin strike developed and the shipment of coal increasingly declined this changed.

Throughout the spring and summer of 1914 *the Irish streets* became the target of various attacks. At first these were mere propaganda incidents, the daubing of slogans, Carson's words appearing on walls and doorways. *Ulster will fight and Ulster will be right.* There were minor acts of vandalism in the night; fences knocked over, vegetable gardens kicked over, animals let loose. However, following General Gough's mutiny in the Curragh barracks Dublin, March 1914, where he announced his refusal to move against the armed camp of Ulster, things took a turn for the worse. Certain shops became closed to the women of *the Irish streets.* Children found themselves running the gauntlet when they strayed from home. Incidents of beatings began to increase. Matters came to a head when an Orange Lodge chose to march through Ginns. Orange marches were not uncommon but never before had they opted to march anywhere near *the Irish streets.* Carson's slogan *It must be war with honour* was obviously to be put to the test. In Ginns the barricades went up.

Robert remembered the preparations keenly, remembered them with an unsure mix of pride and shame. Sandbags and rocks were piled in doorways, whilst a mountain of furniture was stacked across the street. The expressions on the faces of those involved in the work were grim and resigned. Except for Uncle Marty's, of course. He remembered Uncle Marty clearly. He was grateful for him, grateful for the fact that he made no pretence of being brave. In fact, he mooched around the preparations in a state of near panic, unashamedly frightened. His skinny frame had never seemed so crimped and fowl-like. His angular, auk features were sealed tight and the wet disks of his eyes were more pronounced than ever. Dora comforted him. Indeed, she scarcely left off touching him, wrapping her arms around him and hugging him tightly like a mother with a child. Finally John ordered him home to the loft. There was no judgement in the command. Robert respected that. There was only affection, albeit a formal, circumspect affection, but affection nevertheless. John even refused Gavin any opinion on the subject. He simply but categorically made the point that Marty was his responsibility and no one else's. Gavin didn't argue the case one way or the other. There was too much else to do.

Shortly after Marty had been ordered home to the loft the sound of drum and pipe could be heard coming towards them, though still some distance away. As the music drifted up the Strand Robert remembered it as pleasant. It was a brisk, variously patterned hum, and the repetition of its rhythm was strangely compelling, given the uncertainty it provoked. But, as it progressed, as it grew in volume and intensity, it became ridiculous, grotesque even, its insistence increasingly perverse and barbarous. Then, as the first lines of marchers appeared along the fringes of Ginns streets, led by suited staid looking men with bowlers and rolled umbrellas, he made out the words they were singing. He immediately reached for Peter's hand, and felt it taken, unresisted. He would always be grateful for that acceptance.

Poor Croppies ye know your sentence was come
When you heard the dread sound of the Protestant drum
In memory of William we hoisted the flag
And soon the bright Orange put down the Green rag.

He didn't know who gave the order to start stoning the marchers, but they all began at once. He remembered the relief of it, though, the exhilaration of it. They even started to laugh as the missiles continued to hit their targets. He could still bring Peter's laughter to mind, its notes strong, sharp and bitter. He echoed it as best he could. The very real pleasure he felt at that moment was bewildering to him. It was an instance of the gross variances within himself. He had to admit to himself that he found the violence both compulsive and repugnant. It had compelled his thinking ever since.

From that day on he had experienced recurring dreams, dreams in which he was the tormentor, the inquisitor, doling out justice to a fiery mob, a rabble. He was vengeance, he was discord, he was anger. In some dreams he was sure he was rank with sin, and in others he was equally sure he was expiated of all sin through the very self same acts. It was an imaginative limbo, a purgatory he couldn't dictate, and one he was convinced he couldn't truly comprehend.

There had certainly been no hesitation to be involved in the stoning. He roared and hooted as the Orangemen scattered. He cheered as Docker, Tumelty, dragged the isolated Lambeg drummer to the ground and beat him with a fragment of stone. No one expected or could have anticipated what was to happen next. No one would have believed it possible that the marchers would draw their ceremonial swords and run at their opponents. They slashed and wounded at will. They were greedy for it, bent on some ceremonial revenge. In the ensuing chaos there were over a hundred casualties, many of them serious.

For the first time in his life Robert had actually felt hatred for other human beings. It was overwhelming. He hated the grotesque creatures in their formal garb, hated them completely. His sense of morality was virtually shattered. It was to be many weeks before he returned to his lessons.

The carnage came to an end when a number of shots rang out and both sides were forced to run for cover. No one knew where the shots came from but following them Docker was dead. His body lay in a heap beside the tasselled podium of the fallen drum, his face a gash. Moments later John Devlin went out into the street to carry him away. He took him into the first house he came to. Robert followed him in. If there had been anyone else in the house then they were hiding because no one came to them. Robert remembered the disturbed ramblings of his father, the way he continuously muttered, repeating over and over again: "Tumelty, his name you see, must tell Mrs Tumelty, Tumelty, see, Tumelty? He was never christened in the name of water Docker. Tumelty. Christ, Tumelty."

It was obvious that in death the correct name was important to John. Such a detail was an element of his correctness. It was both a way of thinking and a way of life. It was the same correctness which made him attend mass, union meetings and shave everyday; the same correctness that made him demand of Robert that he say a prayer over Tumelty's body. He had been more than insistent in his request. There was an element of desperation in it that Robert had found bewildering. Robert's refusal that day was a source of a continued unspoken rupture between them.

So, remembering Tumelty, remembering the terrible forces that were unleashed that dreadful day, it was with great difficulty that Robert continued to challenge his father. He knew there were good reasons to pass. The moment might be more propitious some other time, some time when he had not just looked in his cracked mirror, some moment when he hadn't been brought face to face with the recollection of Tumelty's parted crown. And yet the recollection of Peter's hand holding his, his large palm wrapped around his own smaller palm, outweighed every other consideration. He had to be true to Peter. He owed him that. He had allowed him to put his faith in a single difficult gesture. His gratitude was such that he would even challenge his father: challenge the severed head of Tumelty.

He tried to speak kindly, nevertheless. He wanted his father to appreciate the gravity of Peter's decision. Surely his father would see things as Peter did. They were natural allies. But even as he thought these things, he knew that his father would see Peter's volunteering as treachery. Nevertheless, having come so far he determined to see it through. He finally responded to his father's demand. He said: "Peter says it would be unforgivable to leave a poor little country like Belgium on its own. The papers are full of what the Germans are doing there, really horrible things, terrible things, cutting off the hands of babies and women, raping and killing nuns. Father Bond says it's because they're Lutherans. I don't know if he meant it though, I couldn't tell."

Despite himself, John found he couldn't help but respond. "He probably meant it all right, but he's wrong. It's not because they're Lutherans. That's a stupid notion. It's in their blood. They're a military people. Junkers, Prussians, brought up to it. Always have been. It's nothing to do with religion. Besides, the stories are probably exaggerated. Christ, they're probably just a pack of lies, a pack of lies concocted to make people like Peter Kavanagh rush off to fight the British empire's battles for it. I thought more of Peter Kavanagh. I did really."

"That isn't fair. Peter knows what he's doing. He says only cowards would abandon a country like Belgium. It's only a little country. It needs help. I've already said, he's very clear that Belgium is a country like Ireland. He seems to understand that. He makes that point all the time. He's right isn't he. Right about Belgium and Ireland. Little countries. He has a case, doesn't he? Lloyd George said just the same. Come on, you know Peter Kavanagh."

John's hands moved slowly across his body pulling at the muscles that patterned his sinuous frame. The word fair was burning in his mind. He wanted to scream aloud his objections, beat them all away, take control and make his case, win it for himself, and yet he could do nothing. The world was proving too big for him. He couldn't take hold of it, stop it, stem it, or open it up. It was beating him. So he just stood, his mind aching, devoid of speech, gazing at Robert.

The soap cream ran in blackened drops across him. He was contemplating Robert from that point of rupture between them. Robert knew it. He knew just what picture flashed across his father's mind as he looked at him. He knew he saw his refusal to say a prayer. He had never asked why. That question seemed too difficult to broach. Once again John avoided the question of prayer over Tumelty's body and instead eventually asked: "What do you think, Robert? You keep telling me about Peter Kavanagh. Peter Kavanagh is his own man. What about you? I want to know what you think, not what Peter Kavanagh thinks."

"I don't know," Robert responded. He had intended humility. He didn't really know. He was working something out. He was flattered to be asked. It said something of his difficult decision to speak to his father at all. And having been asked he wanted to express, in as honest a way as he could, something of what for him were the consequences of Tumelty's death. It was something that tormented him and stopped him being himself. He said: "I have always thought it a sin to take a life. *Thou shalt not kill* never seemed difficult before Tumelty. I don't know now. I don't know what I'm free to think, anymore. I really don't know. It shakes me right through."

"They killed him."

"I don't know who killed him," Robert replied quickly, and then added with a quiet wail, "We don't know."

"Don't be stupid!"

"Well, it wasn't the Belgians," he snapped, and as he did something snapped with the sentence and his resolve failed him completely, evaporating away as if it had never been. He felt a release of tears in his eyes. He couldn't hold them back. He spoke through them: "The Belgians haven't hurt anyone. Peter Kavanagh said they haven't done anything..." His voice trailed away to nothing.

"Peter Kavanagh," John echoed bitterly. "To hell with Peter Kavanagh!" He became silent. He looked at Robert for some time, just staring at him, taking in every changing nuance in his expression, though without comment or interpretation. Then, as if he had arrived at some decision, he stepped up to Robert and put his arms around him, despite the fact his torso was still smeared with a lining of soap and water. "It doesn't matter, Robert. It really doesn't matter. Duffy tells me that the Volunteers are signing up in their thousands. The unions are more patriotic than the bosses. It's all over. Why do anything? Why ever do anything? Tumelty died for nothing. His face like that for nothing. Everything we do we do for nothing." He laughed bitterly. "Duffy can't believe it. All of his talk of revolution, the strikes, the civil war, the suffragettes, all in one big union, his blessed *one big union*, has come to nothing. Oh well, to hell with it! You're always better on your own. At least you can only let yourself down. So, to hell with it!" He gently pushed Robert away, repeating his last phrase beneath his breath as he did so.

He went back to the sink, looked into the mirror, ran his palm across his cheeks and in a clear voice said: "Of my country I am ashamed." He turned to Robert, his expression once again inflexible, and spoke to him formally: "Anyone who fights for the British Empire is a mercenary, a traitor and a fool."

"And your son?" Robert replied quickly, though his voice was fearful and tentative.

John picked up his towel and walked out without saying another word. Robert went to the sink and released the water.

*

Anne placed the seasons final bedraggled daisies and buttercups in a vase in the window. Sh'd picked them long and thick with leaf so they clustered together. The sun in the window was bright. The small yellow and white flowers shone like a mantle over the dull tangled stems and the grey pot vase. Robert watched her arrange them. She smiled, pushed her hands through her thick curling hair and turned to him for approval. He applauded silently. She looked back at the vase and screwed up her nose sceptically. Robert was thrilled. He loved the nipped tip of her nose.

Ever since the day of Peter's departure Robert had become Anne's regular visitor, coming to her each day, dividing his free time between the church and Anne. Anne's married life had lasted no more than two days, but she was at least mistress of her own house. At first it had been decided that she would move in with Polly but Anne had wanted Peter to come back to their own home. Peter had managed to rent a house on Ginns. It was furnished spartanly but Anne set it as her task to make a home of it in time for his living there. She was building for him. She became a regular visitor to the town's numerous junkshops and pawnshops. She proved particularly adept at fashioning furnishings and decorations from the most unpromising materials. She brought flowers into the house. When he returned the walls would have the aroma of spring and summer. The papers had stopped saying it would be over by Christmas and that it was more likely to be a long war. Two days sustained her. Two days, if necessary, would serve as the memory of two years, twenty years, longer, if need be, as long as she could believe it.

She put the final touches to the flowers with her fingertips, then turned to Robert and in a matter of fact, impersonal voice declared: "I have no right to be angry. I know that. It has to be right. It was what he wanted."

Whether he believed her or not he wasn't so sure. She said it rather too often to be entirely convincing. It was a common theme with her. Still, she never openly displayed any anger. Indeed, her manner always seemed calm and sincere. But he doubted her. Whenever she had said it before he had turned his face away from her. In his mind he was turning the other cheek, turning the other cheek to her. But as to what stung him, her denial of anger or its reality, he wouldn't have been able to say. The truth was that the smart he felt was because he invariably imagined that her anger or her denial of anger was for him. It was about his decisions, his frame of mind, his ideas. He found his musing painful, yet at the same time perversely satisfying.

To his somewhat florid way of thinking the idea he conjured, that he was turning the other cheek to her, was symbolic of the many contradictions which tormented him. The idea of what turning the other cheek, giving oneself to the punishment, actually meant, preyed on him, nagged at him and gave him no rest at all. Was it not also tantamount to simply turning away, refusing to see, to hear, to feel? Of course, turning away was the path of devotion, he knew that, the saints achieving seclusion, separation, but wasn't that also turning away from life itself? The path to life, though, was not so clear cut. He couldn't fathom it. His thoughts ran wildly with vague notions of suffering and grace. Were they coexistent? He wanted to be in a state of grace. He was absolute on that point. But did one have to suffer to achieve it? And if it was right to suffer then did it have to be embraced with open arms?

In his mind the confusion had one picture. He lived with it constantly. It was never far from his thoughts. He returned to it time and again. He knelt before it. It was the image of Christ crowned. A king bearing a diadem of thorns, arms spread wide, his face averted, his eyes resting on no one, expressing suffering, servility and forgiveness. He knew it was the most beautiful thing in the world. It was perfection. The God, the man, his agony, his passion, his suffering, pinned to the cross. It had no equal. An alternative to forgiveness was intolerable, barbaric, unendurable, animal. He had to believe in the regularity, the moral certainty, of his faith, and yet, despite all of his reasoning, he was afraid of what it might make him. He no longer knew himself. And somehow Anne embodied all of his misgivings and confusion. When he was with her he suffered, yet was certain he was in a state of grace. It didn't make any sense. In reality he knew she had no inkling of punishing him, indeed had no opinion about what he thought about Peter's decision to fight one way or the other, but still he dreamed it, lived it, endured it.

He turned back to her. She was smiling, her expression easy and complacent, as if she had spoken without thought, and it was now over.

Robert spoke out severely: "Of course you have the right to be angry. Everyone has the right to be angry. Why not? If anyone feels they've been wronged, then they have the right to be angry. If they didn't we would never be rid of wrong."

Anne turned her face away and looked along the sun drenched blackened terraces of Ginns. Her expression gave no indication of her thinking, but Robert was sure he had wounded her. His eyes filled with tears. He had broken faith with himself and broken faith with Peter. Peter had come to him personally and specifically asked him to look after Anne. He had been placed in a situation of trust.

He put the palms of his hands together and spoke to her gently, endeavouring to somehow retrieve the situation and restore the trust he had been given. "Don't be angry," he said. "Don't ever be angry. It's not how you are."

She looked at him and again smiled, smiled as she had smiled at the buttercups and daisies.

*

By the beginning of October the long summer had ended. The days were shortening quickly and the long spell of dry weather was replaced by squally showers and winds which cast a dismal greyness over the valley. The atmosphere over Ginns was thick again with grease and soot, the rain mixing with the smoke constantly issuing from chimneys around the docks. On a dull Thursday evening in the middle of the month Peter's elder sisters, Catherine, just turned seventeen, and June, sixteen, came to visit Anne in the house on Ginns when they had finished work. They were both employed in a workshop producing gloves, painters' aprons and men's shirts. Anne assumed they had brought her some goods to finish. Catherine had for a long time brought homework for Anne.

It was through Catherine that Anne had first met Peter. Anne had always been a homeworker, finishing off after the basic sewing had been done in the workshop, felling, lining and folding gloves, finishing collars and cuffs. She hired her own Singer machine at 1s.6d a week. (Peter had promised to buy it for her as soon as he was able.) Most of the homeworkers went to the factory to pick up their work, but as Anne's mother had been more or less house bound for a number of years before her final illness killed her in January 1913 (she had suffered from a chronic congestive lung condition as far back as Anne could remember), Anne had been reluctant to leave her on her own for too long, so Catherine had got into the habit of taking it to her, or more likely, whenever he was free, Peter would take it across town. It was a combination of the facts of the mine explosion and Anne being forced to move into the loft in the house of two maiden aunts, retired seamstresses, that accelerated Peter and Anne into announcing their engagement. The war had speeded that into marriage.

Anne was delighted to see them. Though she would never have said it, life for her in Ginns was lonely. Her days were usually only broken by the habitual visits Robert paid her after his shifts. She was grateful that he came, but also fatigued by him. He was such a serious, self-absorbed young man. She hated thinking it, because he was also motivated by a great deal of affection for her, affection she returned, but he was so tortured by his own reflections he was profoundly wearing. She had never really known anyone like him. He took nothing at face value but had to try to work it out, take it apart, see the inner workings and mechanics.

Of course, there were elements of that about herself. She knew that. Indeed, she was convinced that it was that aspect of her personality that drew Robert to her. She had been on her own too often for it to be otherwise. The small world of caring for an invalid mother was an insular, closed, reflective world. She had had time to work out how she would deal with any potential life that was offered her. Her conclusion was that she would treat it well. Life being so precious it had to be treated well. The war was therefore an anathema to everything she believed. She had watched her mother struggle with her small reserves of energy for years, watched her struggle to meet the ambitions she set for herself each day, and she clearly remembered the look of defeat which was invariably imprinted on her mother's face. But there was never any hint of self-pity, only ever disappointment. Her mother was a woman certain she had so much to give, but who simply couldn't manage it. She had imparted this energy to Anne. Anne would succeed where she was handicapped. Anne was her mother's true self. Anne was also her own self. She was both the product of her frustrated mother and her frustrated upbringing. And the war had given her the opportunity to do life well and then snatched it right away. It had taken Peter.

She put her energies into preparing for his return. It was a means of being true to herself. She was driven by a desire to make the house something for him. After all, he had taken her from the loft. He had saved her from the tedium and constraint of her aunts' house. They were both elderly, much older in fact than her mother, and had lived together for years. Indeed, they seemed quite eccentric, living each day with strict, formal routines, everything having a set time and order, breakfast through to dinner. The house had an order and solemnity to it that was quite life denying. The old women, surprisingly given the time spent with only each other's company, spoke very little, and then only to pass laconic comments. They had been quite indignant that Peter should be bringing Anne work, being both quite convinced that there was something improper about the fact. Besides, he was a miner, albeit a Catholic one. They could never approve. He was a different sort of Catholic. He was Irish, foreign. The likes of him had changed the town. It had never been the same since the immigrants. When Anne did eventually tell them that she had every intention of marrying him she had expected some kind of a scene, but she was wrong. They shrugged at the information as if it confirmed some secret prediction between them. All in all, it simply meant that Anne had been a minor hiatus in their lives, a nuisance, but a temporary one. Anne went into marriage with just herself.

She got on very well with Catherine and June, but couldn't escape the feeling of being far older than them, far older than she really was. She was only a matter of eighteen months Catherine's elder, but it felt like so much more. She found them playful, a bit brazen and childish, and not a little jealous of the fact that she had her own home. Catherine and June were close and gave each other confidence, indeed, egged each other on. They were sometimes very direct in the way they asked questions about *our Peter*. How did our Peter start going out with you? When did our Peter first kiss you? Is he a good kisser, our Peter? And what about the rest? Is he all right in that direction, our Peter? The *our* rankled Anne at first, but she quickly stopped caring. He was her Peter. Only she could answer their questions. He was hers. They teased her for being married so young, and were man mad, but it was all good natured. They all loved Peter, our Peter. He was everybody's hero. Anne was uncomfortably satisfied at that, proud and bitter all at once.

It turned out that they hadn't brought her any work, but acted as if it were simply a social call. Anne was surprised. They hadn't made any social calls before this. There had always been some pretext, a batch of gloves, some shirts or aprons, usually something, even if it was only as an excuse, but there wasn't even the pretence of an excuse. (Anne was sure Polly made them bring the smallest amounts of work just to keep an eye on her. Polly had not given up her insistence that Anne go and live with her lightly.)

They didn't sit down. Catherine stood by the window and June leaned against the grate. They passed a few brief comments about how nice she had the house, how nice and her only doing finishing work (the piece rate for home-working not working out nearly as favourably as that for the workshop). Anne repeated her often delivered maxim that she would have the house right for his homecoming.

Catherine picked up her words and, as if it were only a casual question, asked: "Have you heard from our Peter much, since he went off soldiering?"

Anne had received a number of letters since he had gone, at least two a week. She thought shyly of them as Catherine asked. She read them constantly. She could see them in her mind's eye inside a biscuit-tin in a bedside drawer. She took them out every night, said a prayer and then read them over, before settling down to sleep. She imagined that Catherine could read her mind and was laughing at her. The one thing she was certain about was that she had no intention of sharing them. She wasn't easy with that thought. She knew that they needed something of him as well, but that wasn't going to be her letters. Reluctantly she replied that she had heard from him a number of times.

"And what does he talk about?" June asked.

"Nothing special, you know... Nothing, really."

"Does he not talk about the war? Doesn't he tell you all you need to know?"

"No, not really. Not the war as such. Well, he hasn't really seen much of it, not really. Not so far as I can tell."

"He's a proper soldier, though, our Peter. He'll end up in the thick of it soon enough."

Anne shuddered at the thought. She didn't know what it meant for him, but she knew it couldn't be good. None of it could be good. The war couldn't be good, no matter what anyone might say. Life was too precious. She refused to answer. Catherine and June were irritating her. They seemed slightly more juvenile than usual. She realised that whether she liked it or not, marriage separated her. It made her a woman. It gave her knowledge. It gave her rights.

Catherine spoke up again. "Of course, he's gone for a proper soldier and he's a hero like any of the others. Well, I bet he's a better hero. Do you hear me? I bet he's a better hero."

"What are you talking about?" Anne said, turning from one to the other. June looked towards Catherine. Anne followed her attention and also looked at Catherine. "Well?"

"You know the Whitehaven News want letters from anyone who has relatives at the front?"

Anne didn't reply. She just gazed in the direction of Catherine. She couldn't make sense of it. How could anyone want her precious letters? How could anyone see them? It was impossible. There was too much of him in them. They were his flesh, his lovely words. The thing was a joke.

June spoke up, obviously reading. As she did Anne turned to her. *"We invite those of our readers who have friends and relatives serving as soldiers with the British Expeditionary Force to send to the Whitehaven News any letters they may receive from the front. The letters, which will afterwards be returned, should be accompanied by the envelope in which they were received, together with the name, rank and regiment of the writer, and the name and address in full of the person to whom they have been written. No reference to the regiment or their position in the field will, of course, be published."*

Anne remained confused. She didn't know what to say. She wasn't really sure what Catherine and June were getting at. Eventually she uttered: "Why, why do they want them? I don't understand. Why?"

"Because they're local heroes, of course," Catherine replied. "A lot of lads went off together and the news men want to follow their story. Everybody wants to know. They're our soldiers, fighting a terrible foe."

"Uncle John says it's the only way anyone can get any news. He says the big papers aren't allowed. I don't know. He's a bit sour though, isn't he. You couldn't take what he says."

"Mr Devlin's a clever man."

"I'm sure he is, Anne, but it doesn't mean he's not a miserable bugger."

"But why are you telling me?"

"Our Peter's a hero," June insisted. "He deserves it just as much as all the other lot."

Anne gazed at her but made no reply. There was a long silence. June looked beyond Anne towards Catherine. Eventually Catherine very quietly suggested: "I'm sure it would make the family very proud, especially Mam. It would help her, I know that. She misses him something terrible. And it would help. Help her."

Anne turned to her. Catherine's figure was just a silhouette against the window frame, her features indecipherable.

Later that same night, after she had said her prayer Anne took her letters from their box. She had made no promises to Catherine and June other than that she would think about it. She opened one of them. The page was covered with awkward, poorly formed, poorly spelled words. They were scarcely literate. But they were hers. His each and every word was for her. How could anyone else know the meaning of such ineloquent but perfect phrasing? As far as she was concerned he was a poet. She knew that was fanciful, but she also knew what she meant. His letters had secret depths, hidden depths, intimate depths. How would anyone else see that? Why should they? The idea was monstrous. She began to cry as she read.

Dear Anne, We're living in tents and running up and down fields with bits of sticks. If this is what it's all about I don't know why there was so much fuss. I wish there hadn't been. I don't get all that stuff. It was like the night Dad went. They didn't have to be all stuffy and shirty like that. I couldn't work that out. I still think about that. But what a night, eh lass. The best night of my life, you know. We weren't awkward or out, were we. Not us. I miss you, lass. I miss the feel of you beside me. It was only a couple of days, I know that, but it's like you're imprinted on me. Christ, listen to me. Can you imagine the lads knowing what's going on inside my head, eh. Funny that. I wonder what's going on over there in theirs? I never had time to think like this, did I. I don't know that I should. I just keep saying your name. I want you to know that. Does that make sense? Oh well. They're a good bunch of lads here. A real bunch of heroes, eh pet, all at the foe with their bits of sticks. Quite a squabble. The Boche won't stand a chance when we get at them, will they. No, they're good comrades really. The officers are sticklers mind. Really old, all of them. Only the old fellers do the training and a few Regimental Sergeant Majors. Easy to get on the wrong side of them. Easiest thing in the world. I wish I'd seen me dad, like. I'm not chuffed about that. I've done the right thing though. I have, haven't I lass. It'll be better when we pack in all this running round with sticks. They say it'll be the real thing soon enough. The real thing, eh. That's a thought and a half, I think. Oh Anne. Christ, I'm off again. You got a lovely name though. Bloody good name. It tastes great lass. Anne. Lovely. I know it maybes didn't feel like a proper wedding. I know there was no fuss or out like that and I wish me dad had been there. He would have been as proud as out. But I'm pleased we did it. I think I'd be going out of me mind now if it wasn't for that. You know that don't you. I'll make up for it. When all this is done with, and me dad's home, we'll have ourselves a right good do, the best the families ever had. We'll have us a time that nobody will ever forget. Everyone says this business isn't going to take very long and then we'll have all the time in the world to make it up to everyone. Shame about me dad. Look after me mam. God bless. Make sure our Robert looks after you. He's a good lad, you know. Tell him I'll whip his backside if he doesn't keep an eye out. I'll write soon. Love Peter.

She folded it carefully, lay it in her lap then took another from the box and began to read.

My dearest Anne, The train down to Folkstone was a funny old business. It felt like a day out at times and then, well, totally different. I think it was worse for them that had people seeing them off. The station was mad. I've never seen out like it. I was pleased you weren't in all that pushing and shouting. London's not for the likes of us. But at least I've seen it. I've seen all sorts I never thought I would. I've been on a train five times. Five times. I've never been anywhere till now. I can't believe it. When I get back I'll make sure we have a few trips. You had a few trips with your mother in her brighter days didn't you. But then you're from the posh end of town. I'm only teasing you. No, we'll have some grand trips when I'm through here, I promise you. Maybes we'll get all the way to Blackpool. You've been to Blackpool, haven't you. We never got anywhere. Never had the money really. All this lot are making plans for when we're finished here. Get the job done and then get back to real things. So, a promise, first thing we do is go for a trip. Some of the fellers had never seen the sea before. Can you believe that? Never clapped eyes on it. I really can't imagine that. It was like being at home. Well, home with soldiers and all the rest of it. You wouldn't believe what they pack into those boats. It's a wonder they float at all. Some of the lads spent best part of the crossing hanging over the side. I wasn't too clever myself. It's a bit different being on it than under it. I'm a miner not a fisherman, that's for sure. God lass, but I miss you. I can't believe how sentimental a lad I am. You wouldn't credit it would you. I's not daft though. You have to keep your wits about you with this lot. It's all rules and regulations in the army line. A lot of it's bloody stupid, but you have to watch yourself. I suppose there's a reason for everything. They know best, eh. They bound to really. Seen it all. I've seen nowt. Not really. Seen a bit more now, but nowt really. The London lads I've met are all right. Full of it like. Our train was all northerners though. From all over the shop. God knows where really. You stick to your own section really.

They're right good lads. There's a lot of lads from home. Not lads that I knew mind. Not a one, but they know what you're talking about. Christ who ever heard of Cleator Moor? Who'd want to? We have a laugh about it. There's some jokers here, I'll tell you that. Jokers, whingers, old fannies, the lot. What a cargo, eh lass. But I think we'll be all right. They're good lads. Is our Robert doing his job? I can't see him among this lot. I don't mean out by that. He did all right with that Orange mob. Christ that seems an age ago. Mind you, there's some right holy lads here. One feller, John, dead devout, Proddie like, got nick-named John the Baptist, just Baptist now, and doesn't mind a bit. Lots of the lads got themselves nick-names. I'm just Peter though. Suits me. I don't want any of that funny stuff. I'm Peter and you're Anne and they go together like. Peter and Anne. I'm off again, you know. I love your name, like. Can't stop saying it. Oh, look after yourself lass. Keep smiling eh. Keep it up. Love Peter.

She folded it carefully and lay it on top of the other already in her lap, then took out a third. She held it for a while, before opening it. She breathed deeply as if inhaling the aroma of the paper, indeed, as if the paper contained some scent of him. A vague outline of him was imprinted on her mind. She couldn't understand why his image wasn't more vivid, but consoled herself with the thought that the mind just wasn't like that. It didn't contain vivid pictures. If it did it might reduce the need and the desire for the real thing. And that just wasn't the case. She longed for him. She wanted his physical presence. Certainly she felt embarrassed by her desire, but she wasn't going to lie to herself. She was hungry, desperate and aching. She throbbed with desire. Christ, they had only been married two days. Why shouldn't she be angry. But not at him. He wasn't to blame. She began to cry. They were bitter, angry tears. He wasn't there and she could only form a vague impression of him in her mind. It was an unreal outline of him writing, struggling to spell words, struggling to make her image in his mind. They were far away from each other now.

She opened the third letter and began to read.

It's a long road leading to the front line. I don't know if we looked smart or just downright stupid all neatly turned out, all spick and span, polished buttons and the lot. God, they're sticklers for all that stuff. Shave every day or else. One lad lined up on Pay Parade with a bit of stubble and had to do Field Punishment Number Two, running round in full pack with his rifle over his head till he was only fit to drop. No need for that. He needed his pay to get some blades. I don't like all that stuff.

Still, I mind myself. Some lads said you had to be careful on the road because the Germans shell it from time to time. No good telling us. We weren't in charge. Nowt we could do about it. A shell went off right in the middle of the line. What a carry on. Men rushing all over the shop, lads shouting all sorts. Just a mess really. There was this poor horse just kept stumbling about. It wouldn't go down. In the end one of the officers shot it in the head. It went down like a stone. I'll never forget that poor hoss. The rest just had to be pushed to the side of the road. Then we...

She stopped reading. She folded the letter, placed it on top of the others, then put them back into her biscuit-tin, wiping her face on her apron as she did so. She put the tin back into her bedside drawer underneath a pile of linen. She lay down in bed and fell asleep trying to create a fully formed image of him in her mind.

She dreamed of horses.

Two days later she was approached directly by a journalist from the Whitehaven News, Mr Clough, who told her that he had been generously informed that Anne's husband was currently serving at the front. She thought his choice of words strange, to say the least. She queried why he said generously.

He gave a speech: "I say generously, Mrs Kavanagh, because I fully understand the nature of a loved one's communication. It is necessarily something intimate, something special between two people. But they are also our boys. They've gone out from this town to do battle with a terrible foe for reasons of justice and liberty. Poor Belgium. Oh yes, poor Belgium. And I think you would agree that we are entitled to know just what is happening across in France and Belgium. I'm sure you see the justice of that as well. Mrs Kavanagh, there are no reporters at the front. The powers that be are attempting to keep our lads from us, and the small papers are not going to stand idly by and let that happen. I have connections with many people who work on local newspapers and we are all determined to stand by our boys and hear their stories. I know for a fact that the *Formby Times*, the *Southport Visitor*, the *Crosby Herald*, the *Daily Post and Mercury* and the *Liverpool Evening Express* - I have close ties to the Mersey area Mrs Kavanagh - have already published numerous missives from the front, celebrating the contribution of their heroes, and it is the same in all areas across the country. We at the Whitehaven News feel it is our bounden duty to match that, Mrs Kavanagh. And we also want to be fair, Mrs Kavanagh, fair and decent. I would never want it said that we failed to flag up the contribution of a brave Catholic lad. Oh God, no, I wouldn't be happy at all if your husband should in any way be overlooked. You'd never get that from us. What do you say, Mrs Kavanagh?"

She didn't really know what to say. She was rather bemused to be called Mrs Kavanagh quite so much. To her mind that was really reserved for Polly. Polly was Mrs Kavanagh. She was Anne. He called her Anne over and over. Mrs Kavanagh was someone else. Thinking of Polly brought to mind that Catherine and June had said she would be pleased, proud even, to have his letters in the paper. Could she really ignore that? She couldn't escape the fact that maybe she was being selfish in keeping them to herself. Catherine and June certainly thought so. This Mr Clough would think so to. The weight of opinion seemed to be against her. Nevertheless, she wasn't ready to give them up. She just couldn't do that. In the end she said: "I will have to ask him, Mr Clough. I can't just give you his letters. Not without asking. It has to be his decision."

Mr Clough raised his hat and left.

She wrote to Peter and told him of the journalist's request. She was careful not to mention Catherine and June's opinion that it would help his mother. She told him only the barest outline of the request. The Whitehaven News would like to print his letters, what did he think? Much to her surprise and disappointment he wrote back saying he had no real objections. She was dumbfounded. He said it would be good to talk about the other lads. He listed a few names. She was appalled. They were invading her privacy, the privacy she had won with him despite everything. It spelled the end of their secret marriage. She cried for days after. The thought of what he had agreed to kept striking at her, suddenly clouding over her thoughts, the way the death of her mother had clouded over her thoughts. She wondered whether it would carry on the same, striking at her long after the event. But there was nothing for it but to reconcile herself to his decision. His letters would be given to the newspaper. Not the old ones, just the new. She put it down to his naiveté. She knew he was naive. That was a part of who he was. Peter Kavanagh, big, soft, naive, trusting Peter Kavanagh.

Two weeks later she saw his first letter in print. She bought the paper and took it round to Polly. As Polly couldn't read Anne read it out to her. Polly looked at the print as she read, a look of amazement and respect on her face. That her son should be in print, his words there for all to see, was more than she could have dreamed possible. She found it bewildering and wonderful.

He described how he went down through the communication trench at night with his platoon to relieve another platoon in the front. He went on to describe how he went out with a small party to repair the wire. He spoke about men Anne had never heard of before, Tate, Ackroyd, Baxter, Gadd, Wilson. He said he was thinking about her all the time he was out there, fumbling in the dark between the two rows of opposing armies. He didn't say Anne, though. He didn't describe how he repeated her name over and over. As far as she was concerned it might have been written by anyone. She didn't recognise it as her Peter anymore. They had even corrected his spelling. She wailed at the fact that they had corrected his spelling. As she did Polly put her arm around her and tried to console her, telling her he would be all right, he was made of strong stuff.

Anne quietened herself, nodded at Polly, folded up the paper and gave it to her. Polly told her that she should keep it, but Anne was insistent. "It's yours," she said. "Really, it's all yours. He would want you to have it. I'm sure of that."

Polly took it gratefully, but was unable to speak.

The newspaper returned all of Anne's letters as they said they would and she continued to store them in her biscuit-tin, but she rarely took them out to read. They were too painful.

*

During the early weeks and months of Peter's absence Robert's greatest pleasure was in spending time in the church with Anne. They went together two, sometimes three, times a week and always on Sunday. After Sunday mass they went to eat with either Polly or Kate. He felt decidedly proud, unashamedly so, standing alongside her in the congregation. It was one of the few emotions of self-satisfaction that did not fill him with shame. He considered that they were sanctified, elevated as a family through the sacrifice of one of its members, Peter, to the wider family of the church. His going to war symbolised to Robert's mind the unique union of suffering and grace. It made them all one. Everything moved towards oneness. Everything strove to be combined. He was most particularly satisfied when Anne found a reading or a hymn particularly pleasing. Then he understood the process all the more, the process of binding together.

The joy he felt in their shared experience was never greater than when All Saints and All Souls came round and they decorated the altar

111

together. They collected acorns, willow, holly and mountain ash. Anne prepared the furnishing. Robert watched her as she knelt before the altar and, with the same simplicity with which she decorated the house in Ginns, placed sheaves of willow around its base, binding the ash stalks with her fingers. When she was complete she stood up and raised her arms for his approval, looking all the world like a supplicant. Her shawl fell from her shoulders. Her breasts swelled beneath her blouse. Robert was enthralled and mystified. The altar had never appeared so beautiful. She had never appeared so beautiful. They were joined. Anne was the altar's flesh, its humanity. Yes, he thought, faith was human, she was breathing its clear fresh air, it rose in her breast. He imagined her taking from its feast of bread and wine. It made sense. One had to turn to life. He applauded her. She smiled gingerly and pulled the shawl back over her shoulders.

It was shortly after All Souls that Anne announced that she was pregnant. Her breasts had indeed become fuller. Robert became an ever more frequent visitor. In the absence of the father, together with his memory of her image before the altar, her pregnancy struck his religious imagination as somehow miraculous. His love of God and love of Anne had finally become incontrovertibly one. His love of the unborn baby was something akin to his love of Christ himself.

Only weeks after Peter had left for France Bobby had come home, returning late one night, without warning, having come overland from Liverpool by train. He lay down in bed beside Polly without a word. It was the night of his leaving all over again. As far as Polly was concerned if it was not Bobby beside her then it was his ghost or at least a dream of him. And the morning was to prove the extent of the dream when she discovered the pillow and sheets blood stained from Bobby's coughing. It was evident that he was not likely to get out of that bed again. Polly went to work on the screens, telling no one of his return, having scarcely come to realise it herself. However, it was fortuitous that she did not keep her ghost like husband a secret for long because it was soon apparent that she too was pregnant. Mother and daughter-in-law would share their confinement. The Devlins watched over them.

Kate fussed around Polly. She made her avoid full moons, dogs, or any other omen she believed could strike into the womb and she watched for her cravings, noting them, wanting to fathom the desires sparking inside her. The unborn child, she admitted, was never out of her mind. Polly was unperturbed. She stroked Kate's hair as Kate fussed over her, whilst whispering consoling words, constantly attempting to reassure her. She knew full well that it was Julia who was never far from Kate's mind. She refused to admit, though, that Julia was never far from her own thoughts. Kate never brought Patrick to the Kavanaghs and Polly, though she would never have expressed it, was glad.

While Kate fussed and pampered Polly John sat with Bobby. He rinsed the towels Bobby used for catching the phlegm he constantly spat out using a bowl left in the room for the purpose, until the water became too discoloured and clotted to manage, then he took it outside, emptied it in the ash-pit and refilled it with clear water. Bobby had deteriorated so rapidly since coming home the miracle was that he was there at all, let alone that he was due to be a father again. Both his lungs and heart were finished, his body completely water-logged, even his scrotum had split. A doctor came and punctured his legs with metal tubes to drain away the fluid, but the process was painful and the respite brief. He didn't speak much, the effort being too great, therefore only occasionally complained, usually repeating the same broken phrase: "Gold is a terrible thing to get onto your chest." At those times John held him by the shoulders, helping him void the blood from his throat that came with speech. Sometimes Bobby simply lay back across his pillows and moaned. At those times John moved to the window and watched the smoke rise over Ginns from the rooftops below and remained there until the only sound he could hear was the return of stridor. Only then did he feel able to go back and sit again by the bedside. He wanted to ask Bobby about the mines and the black miners, but Bobby was never up to questioning. No one openly admitted that Bobby was dying, but John knew he would never find out about the gold mines. No one admitted that Bobby knew.

Robert kept an ever vigilant eye over Anne, noting the observable changes in her body. Her breasts expanded, filling her blouse. Her belly became neatly rounded, the weight low and forward, so Kate said it was certainly a boy. He tried to serve her whenever she would allow it. For instance, if her ankles swelled he lifted them onto a stool, if she was tired he cooked, or saw to any other domestic chores she let him do. But this was rare. More usually she was energetic, more often than not engaged in some project she had set herself around the house, decorating, arranging and rearranging the furniture, cleaning, polishing; making shawls and baby clothes from old sheets, embroidering bibs and caps. She always looked to Robert for approval, which was always given, though he was nervous and shy about doing so.

She assumed he found pregnancy a serious, perhaps even a solemn event, but the truth of his awkwardness was her. He loved her. He loved

113

her with the full force of his fanatic imagination, as both a woman, an evident sexual woman, the constant flux of her changing body emphasising that, and angel, an angel beyond reach. His feelings caused him real suffering. He fought with them, but never won.

The worst moments were when she received letters from Peter. On the whole Peter was rarely mentioned. For Anne to talk of him was to admit that he was not there: for Robert it was to admit that he was. She wrote regularly, sending him little keepsakes of home and small parcels of food. When she received his letters she was secretive and read them in private, before handing them over to the newspaper, which she did in the most cold, formal manner imaginable. Robert dreaded these letters, every new delivery confirming the fact that he was jealous of Peter. With the arrival of each one he would go and sit in the church and attempt to rid his mind of the picture he had of Anne and replace it with the image of the tormented Christ. He always ended by praying for the safety of Peter Kavanagh, though when he left it was with an angel in his thoughts. Like Anne he told himself that he wasn't going to read Peter's letters, but like her he always did.

*

Dear Anne, I got your jam all right. All in one piece it was. The postboys are amazing really. We get all our parcels. We get all the papers. They're only a day late. Can you imagine that. All the way here and you get the papers a day late. It's better for the London and Kent boys. They don't feel so far away from home at all. I tell you they're bad to understand half the time, especially when they've had a few drinks and start cracking away. Same for all of them I suppose. You can feel a bit left out. It's all right when you stick with your own section. Well, you're all the same aren't you. It means something that. It's like you've grown up together. There's some lads here become the best mate's I've ever known. They stick up for each other. I like that. You just wouldn't believe it. I don't know what would happen if it wasn't like that. I really don't. It seems the only thing that keeps it all from going mad. There's some queer things happen. I don't mean things totally out of the blue, but just things you weren't ready for. We've just had a to do with a lad called Wilson, first name Wilfred, terrific bloke, helps me all the time, a happy go lucky sort of bloke. A well-built lad, worked in quarries before all this. God send really. Great with a shovel and a pick. Just what you need in all this. We'd been taken out of the front line just before light. Five days of it. Five days of wettings and filthy food. A few spuds and cabbage. And that's the best of it. It's no picnic. Christ, no. But we stick at it. Anyway this poor lad Wilson couldn't stop puking when we got back here. First of all he went grey, really grey, like a ghost, and sweaty all over. You could see it like beads all over him. I thought he was dying. Honest to God. Poor bugger. And then he starts vomiting. Christ it was awful. He just couldn't stop. Well, there was me, Walter Ackroyd, a calm clever bloke, worked in a pay-office, and John Tate, a good lad, the religious lad, quiet, but not offish or out, helped him get his kit off and tried to get a bit of water down his neck. Poor Tate got vomit all over his arms. I was nearly sick myself. He really couldn't stand. He was out on his feet really. A big lad like that. The last you'd expect. Mind you, like Walter said, he'd been on latrine duty all morning. God, what a job. There's just buckets down there. The stink is unbelievable. I think you get used to it. There's not a lot of choice. You can smell the trench a long time before you get to it. Poor Wilson must have had his fill anyway. We were trying to get him to sit down when the Sergeant orders us to back off. A man called Close. Not a big feller, Close, a very neat, quiet sort of a bloke, but a real stickler. They're not all like him, but a lot are. I suppose they have to be, keep the likes of all us lot in line. Close seems to enjoy it though. He stood in front of Wilson asking him what was wrong, not barking at him, but keeping on and on. Wilson couldn't speak. In the end he just collapsed. The three of us picked him up and lay him comfortable. Close didn't say much more, just ordered us to sort him out. Well, he's had a good dollop of your jam, and he's had a damned good slice of Tate's cake (Tate's mother, what a bake) and he's had Walter's chocolate, so I reckon he was having us all on. Laughing his head off about it now, chocolate and God knows what else, all over his chops. I really thought he was going to die. Can you imagine being killed by latrine duty. Dear me. We're having curry now. All the boys love curry. I didn't know what the hell it was, but it's the best you get here. It's a change from bully beef or Maconochie. The German's love our bully you know. Whenever they raid our lines they always go back with as much as they can carry. Can you imagine that? I'm sick of the sight of it and Jerry can't get enough of it. Still, at least they feed us eh. No complaints on that score. Christ, the food's the best of the lot. I love grub up. I really do. You'll have to do curry lass, it's all right. Then again. Take care. Peter.

Dear Anne, Honest to God you'd think this war was all about holes and ditches. I'm always in one or the other, crawling about. It's crazy really. I try to think about being a miner. You know what I mean. I'm a man who made his living underground and that wasn't safe, and it was dark, and it was hard. But the trick doesn't work. I'm crawling about on the top, mud up half the time, wet through, half-frozen, and somebody's trying to shoot me. Except it's all dark and I can't tell what's going on, so it seems like a dream. When I sit back here and close my eyes, I can remember it all, but it's all so mad, flares going off, whizz-bangs and Jack Johnson's going off. We do everything at night, you see, so it's like it's not happening. And you're so tired it's, well, it's like dreaming. A nightmare more like, I suppose. We came down the support trench just after dark. We were detailed to repair the fences. It was a hell of a night. There's a real medley of sound you know, all the different sounds you get in a barrage. You can work each one out. And the grounds flying up all round you. So you see the fences in flashes. And with every flash you're looking for the enemy. Christ, what if he should appear, standing in the flash. I'd have to shoot him down before he shot me down. It gets harder to keep that simplest fact alive. I'm here to do a job. The goal of this strife is to vanquish the foe and therefore conquer. Some of the officers try to keep the message fresh. They tell us we must be ardent and show valour and be manly. Well, we're all that. Damn sure we are. I suppose all the other stuff. I don't know. Don't know what they're talking about half the time. They're all right really. Mainly posh kids. Kids though. They're either ancient, and look it, or are a bunch of posh kids. I quite like the kids. They do their best. They really do. Most of them are there with us. You know, you see them, and they know what it's like. It's not easy saying what it's like, because it doesn't make any sense. I can't feel what it's like and I'm here. But when it's dark, and there's all the noise, and people shouting, screaming sometimes, and things are happening so fast you can't hold on to anything, then I feel really strange, like I'm not really here. Well, no, I'm here, but not here. Oh God, I don't know. Tate always says a prayer, right out loud. A lot of the lads snigger, but deep down you know they're all listening and are really happy to listen. Dear God, he says, I'm going into great danger, please guard me and make me act like a man and bring me back safe. And after that he looks as smug as out. He really believes in it. And maybe he's right. Christ, I don't know. I know I should pray. I know you'd all want me to, but I don't find it easy. Not like Tate, anyway. I bet our Robert would say a prayer like that, right out loud, for everyone like. He's a good lad. Walter reminds me of our Robert. Walter's a thoughtful lad, bright and on the ball. Is Robert doing his duty? I hope so. God I do. We lost a lad called Robinson last night. Bit of a podgy lad really, big round, freckly face. Sort of lad you nod at and say hello. White, white, podgy skin. God knows how on this grub. Nice sort of lad really, harmless, bit shy probably, inclined to overdo it sometimes to get in with someone. Always a bit too keen to get in your good books really. And we lost him. Big, soft doughy lad like that, left out in the holes and ditches. Close sent me and Wilf, you know, Wilson, back out to look for him. I couldn't believe it. We'd been crawling around for half the bleeding night repairing the fences and then he tells us to get back out and find Robinson. It's not the done thing. Christ, he could have been anywhere. Close thinks everybody's a malingerer. He does. He reckons we'd all do out we could to get off with things. Well, maybe we would, but we do our bit. By rights he should be one of the battle police who patrol whenever there's a set to. He'd love that, making sure no one had second thoughts. Can't understand what gets him going really. We're on the same side, for God's sake. Anyone would think that we didn't want to get the job done. He must have a pretty poor opinion of us. He wasn't getting at me mind. I know that. He's always been a bit funny with Wilf. I don't mean since that day he vomited all over Tate. Christ, Tate forgive him. Tate would forgive the Kaiser. Well, maybe not. No, before that. I just don't think he likes jokers and he is a joker, Wilson. He's a good lad. I don't know what the Sergeant's problem is. I know he doesn't laugh himself, but that shouldn't mean you don't let the rest. Tate says that Close is a religious man. I really can't see that. He says he's a Catholic, straight up. He's nowt like our Robert. He's mean. It's the only word I can think of. Really mean, mean with himself. We didn't find Robinson. Of course we didn't. Poor Wilf crawled through a ditch of bodies. He said his arm went up to the elbow in guts. He wasn't joking. In fact, he hasn't joked much since. He was a bit shaky about it all. Close ordered him to pull himself together. I suppose he has to. Close, I mean. Maybe it's not easy. Well, it can't can it, giving orders. Not orders like that. Poor Robinson. We always have a look in the morning, but it's just to see what the other lot have been up to, see if the lie of the land has changed at all. No chance of seeing Robinson. He'll have to stay there until we push forward across the graveyard that keeps us apart. I don't know when that'll be. They're always talking about the great push. I can't see it. No, it's all about holes and ditches and sticking it out. It'll be a case of who goes barmy first. Well, I feel quite sane in daylight. I just wish I could get a better kip. There really isn't anywhere in the front trench. It's just about midday so I'm going to get my head down. It's pouring down at the moment, but

I've got my groundsheet so I'll manage something. To be honest I could kip on a greasy pole. Goodnight, Peter.

Dear Anne, Just had morning stand-to. Just got my morning tea. I'm set up, aren't I. Funny old business. All we ever really see is sunrise and sunset. Lovely one this morning. A lovely pink morning. Can you believe it, but I actually felt good. What on earth goes on inside a body's head. Lovely sunrise over Picardy and here I am chipper. What on earth is that about? It's dry I suppose. Maybe it's just that. A lovely fine dry day. Just the day, well, we all know that. But it didn't happen. Not this morning. But if they'd decided to come this morning we'd have been ready for them. We're ready every morning. Every morning and every evening we're ready for them. Why they won't come for breakfast or tea I don't know. But someone must know. Someone must know just about everything. I don't know who, but someone. There's too much goes on for no one to know. There's soldiers moving in and out all the time. Some are chosen to be in reserve, others for this and that. That can't all happen on it's own. So there must be some sense behind it all. I don't suppose I'll ever meet him, the one that knows what's happening. I wonder what he has in store for me next. I nice long kip back at Amiens I hope. It's very solemn at stand-to. Normally you wouldn't say a word. It's like being at church. You know, up, down, let us pray. Lord have mercy, Christ have mercy, Lord have mercy and all that. Let's pray to God there isn't a field-grey line on the horizon getting thicker and thicker through the mist and half-light. We all imagine it. And if it was us. Gloria. We believe in one God. Christ, am I getting holy. I don't think so. It cuts both ways. Sometimes you think like this, then other times your faith is in a very different idea altogether. Bang, bang, bang. It was a bit different this morning. Not weird, but just something. A lad called Gadd, Harry Gadd, (have I mentioned him before?), stood on the parapet and went really mad. I'm sure he thought he was in a pub asking someone outside. Come on, you bastards, he shouted, I want to sort this out. On and on he went screaming his head off. Funny thing is he's the biggest whinger in the platoon. Honest to God. Famous for it, in every section. Young officer, Mills, said he'd send him home if he could. It's not funny. Gets you down really. Absolutely everything. Mills said he lets himself down, lets his comrades down and lets his country down. He just whinges about that. Should be a laugh really, but it isn't. And there he is, a one man army, wanting to take on the whole host single-handed. Walter pulled him down. Lovely man that. Reminds me so much of our Robert. Not that he

118

shows any tendency to holiness. Not at all. He's just quiet and thoughtful.
Well, usually. He has his moments like the rest of us. Shouldn't be here
by rights. Wants nowt fighting in a war like this. Too decent altogether. I
think it must be hard if you're a thoughtful sort of bloke like Walter. He
never complains mind. He kind of sorts lots of things out. Keeps things
straight like. Keeps us out of trouble at times. Anyway Walter pulled him
down and tried to quiet him down a bit. They both got Field Punishment
Number 2 for that. Christ, can you believe it. Walter was only trying to
help the lad through a sticky patch. Funniest thing of all is that Harry
didn't seem to mind at all. Never said a word. We've never known the
likes. Gadd not to complain. What's all that about? You know, we just go
from meal to meal here and little things happen in between. Gadd and
Walter are clearing the latrines right now. That's not the punishment.
Well not all of it. Not by half. I should offer to help. To hell with it. The
dawn doesn't feel as good as it did. I'm really up and down. Up and
down. Gloria. Love Peter.

Dear Anne, Fantastic new bloke here. Local. Family out Frizington and
Cleator Moor way. He's a real striking lad. I'm sure the Whitehaven
News will be interested in this. All your readers. I thought he was a bit
stuffy at first. And he wouldn't mind my saying it. That sort of bloke.
Spick and span when he came in. They all take a bit of a ribbing, new
recruits. Bound to. Well, they're like outsiders for a while. It doesn't last
long, though. Well, in steps Hugh, Hugh Glyn, a miner. A miner. Knows
what it's like to be underground, knows the route inbye, outbye, digging
the mother lode. The trenches aren't going to be a surprise to him, are
they? The others wouldn't get that. So they all starts in on him. You
know, nice this, that and the other. Hugh Glyn says, I'm sure it'll take
no time at all until I'm just as disgusting and uncouth as the rest of yous
and maybe a bit worse. True to his word. Works hard. Doesn't shirk a
damned thing and yet isn't a skivvy. It's been great meeting up with him.
The other lads are really grand, but to know your own streets and the
same characters. He's a bit of home, isn't he. I told him about getting his
letters printed in the press, but he didn't really answer properly, just said
we'd have to wait, that maybe he'd have nothing to say. I put him right
on that score. There's plenty to say. You probably don't understand the
half of it, how could you, but it doesn't mean it can't be said. We're doing
a job here, maybe a good one, maybe it could be better, I can't say on
that score, but you should know about it. These lads all deserve a medal
if you ask me. Even moany old Gadd and that's saying something. To be

honest he's never been as bad since that day on the parapet. Walter says he's crossed the Rubicon. I was buggered if I knew what he meant but Hugh did. I have to hand it to him. He's bright as a button for a miner. He's funny really because he's almost military. The way he stands and stuff. Almost formal, like, and very neat and when he talks it's a bit like an officer. I don't mean the accent, that's home, but the way it sounds as if it's for everyone to hear, like he's earning a bit of respect. Something like that anyway. Caesar, he says, Caesar leading his army against his own kind. I hadn't even heard of Caesar. Well, that's not exactly true. One of the bosses at the pit had a mastiff he called Caesar. Never did know why until Hugh Glyn told me the story. He seems to know all sorts. God knows why a miner should know all this stuff. He just says his dad was a bit of a stickler for books. Books and birds. Keeps finches apparently. Gold finch, green finch, chaffinch. God you should hear Hugh Glyn do his bird calls. It's a bit strange, I'd have to say that, the sound of a man singing like a chaffinch in the middle of this lot, but what a sound. It's all so daft you end up feeling all right. He tried to teach me. God almighty. What a laugh. I haven't laughed so much for a long time. He had the whole lot of us singing like a flock. A charm of finches he called us. A charm. What a man. Let's hope it's a lucky charm, eh lass. I think it might be. He got us all some bacon for breakfast this morning. Now, how on earth, I asks him? Diplomacy, says he, diplomacy. He's a gem in this man's army. I'll keep the readers informed. See you lass. Love Peter.

Dear Anne, We've been involved in all sorts recently. God it's been a time and a half. I've been stuck in a ditch the best part of two days. We couldn't move. I don't know whose bright idea it was, but we've been out each night in hunting parties. Bring back some Boche they said. Christ. We were right in the firing line. Once we were out of the saps they just tore into us. We were simply cut up. I don't know how anyone escaped. I saw poor old Gadd go down. It was terrible really. I know he moaned all the time, but that made him someone. I felt sick right through. Bullets and shells were coming down on us so we couldn't move. The idea of making an impression on their lines was ridiculous. They don't seem to plan these things right. They can't do. God knows how many have been killed and for what? I can't work it out. A lad called Baxter, a big lad, done a bit of fairground fighting, was in the hole with me, him and Hugh. I don't know what we'd have done without Hugh. Baxter had been shot all down the side. He was moaning all the time. Terrible, pitiful moans. And from such a big lad. Honest to God, a great big, hulk of a fellow, whining like a baby. I maybe shouldn't say this but I heard him call for his mother. It must have been in his sleep like. Poor bugger. And Hugh looked after him all the time, talking to him, whispering about this and that, trying to wipe his wounds. Not that he had anything to wipe them with. A few filthy cloths cut from God knows. But he didn't give up on him. By God he didn't. Come on lad, keep your mind on the job. Hold on there and we'll get you back. I swear I couldn't have done it. I was too tired for all that. You know, when you get pinned down like that your mind does strange things. Sometimes I thought I was back in Indian country. You won't know Indian country. It was the Wild West when I was a kid. Fantastic place. We used to fight there with bows and arrows and bits of wood. A young lad called O'Flynn nearly lost his eye one summer. We used to steal turnip and cabbage from the fields and stay in Indian Country all day long. It was like a cave in the ground. I reckon it must have been an old disused mine. Never thought about it much at the time. I thought about it all the time in that ditch, listening to Hugh keeping that lad Baxter going. He didn't make it in the end. He was crying like a baby at the last. That was a bad show. Poor bugger. A great big prize-fighter crying like a baby. Lots of them here would have had a go at him for that. You have to do the manly thing, whatever that is. Hugh told him to cry. Go on, son, he said, you cry your heart out if it'll make you feel any better. I said to Hugh it was good what he did, saying all those things, not making him feel bad crying like that. He kind of smiled at me, which was a bit strange, and said there's nowt wrong with crying, not when crying's the right thing. The right thing? I don't know. Close was raging when we got back. He said we were a shambles. We hadn't managed to get one German. I don't think he can talk to us like that anymore. Not after what we've been through. I was raging. I was ready to hit him, but Hugh held me back. Saved my life, I suppose. I was ready to kill Close. I don't think I've turned into a whinger, but he can't say things like that. Not now. Poor Baxter was crying like a baby. Real little squeals and moans. I couldn't stand it. We're living in hell. I'm in hell now. And he speaks like that. Well, I'd better finish at that. I'll probably get into trouble because they read our letters anyway. I don't care. Walter says they don't read them all, just a selection, just to check. He reckons they won't bother mine too much. Too many errors to bother with. I'm not sure what he means. Why do I understand so little? What the hell is that about? Hugh is for ever putting his arm around me, or patting my back like I need looking after or something. Why? I don't follow. Poor Gadd and Baxter. They're still out there. Maybe they'll be out there forever. Love Peter.

Dear Anne, Sorry I haven't written earlier but I got myself into a small spot of bother. Don't worry about it. It's all over now. It was my own fault. I shouldn't have said anything. It's not my place to say anything. I'm a soldier now. A few nights ago the enemy launched a series of heavy raids on our lines. I was down a sap with Wilfred and Walter. We tried to stay our ground, but they just kept coming. It's hard to describe them really. They're just over there like grey wolves, a pack of grey wolves, shadowy and strange. It's terrible when they come at you. It doesn't make sense, because they're from over there, from the other side of the wire, from their side. They should just keep that correct. What the hell do they want charging over here? They should keep to their own. We'll just wait it all out. Oh God, I know that's stupid. I'm just not thinking straight. It's just that it's us and them, and they shouldn't really come together, but they do. The whole point is that we do, and yet we don't. They're not visible like that. And then surprisingly there they are. At times you're so close it's unavoidable seeing a face, a proper face, with eyes and a mouth and everything. And even then it still isn't quite real. I don't know what it would take to make this real. Maybe it can't become real, so it'll just go on and on. Anyway it was obvious we couldn't stay put for much longer so Walter says we should fall back. Wilfred was down there with the Lewis Gun. Extra four Francs a week for lugging that thing around. He volunteered for it. Well, it needs someone big to manage it. He loved it like, in charge of the new gun. Dead proud he was. Secret weapon and all that. So when Walter says we should fall back Wilf's all for it really, so as he doesn't lose his gun. Course, Close went mad when we got back in the main trench. He ordered Wilf straight back. Wilf didn't really hesitate. But I wasn't having that. I pulled him back and told Close it was too much. There was no way Wilf could get back along that sap at the time. We'd have to win it back with a main effort. Close lost his head. He doesn't normally go wild. I told you, he's quiet and creepy. But not this time. He accused me of refusing an order. I wasn't doing anything of the sort. We rowed for ages. Well, it felt like ages. Meanwhile Wilf went back up the sap. I should have been with him really. I was too busy rowing with Close. Later I was put on Field Punishment Number One. I don't suppose the readers want to hear this, but I don't care. I was crucified on a wheel and fed nothing but bread and water. Well, it should have only been bread and water but Hugh gave me whisky and beef. I don't care though. I don't care at all. This isn't a proper war. It's just for them. They've changed this war. This isn't how it started. I don't know what the hell all this is about now. Christ why should I care? Wilf died that night and I was too busy rowing to do anything about it. What the hell was going on that he was sent back down that sap and why did he go? Just to get me off a court-martial? There wasn't any evidence that I'd refused an order. Wilf died. Wilf died. What kind of war is it? Christ what can you say to that? I miss you so much. So much love, Peter.

*

Kate's worst fears over Polly were fulfilled. Just days before term the baby's heartbeat could not be heard. Despite the fact that Polly had half expected it, so many people had been afraid of it, she was greatly effected by its loss. When Kate came to her she found that Polly could scarcely open her mouth without crying. "I didn't even get to touch it, Kate," she moaned and wept, and continuously ran her hands across her face and into her hair. "Not even to touch it. I didn't touch it." On the other hand, Bobby, lying on his sick-bed, was relieved. He had suffered terrible guilt that his dying legacy was yet another mouth to feed. No one quite knew what the child dead in the womb might mean. The doctor said it would probably come away in clots. They waited for it to come but it never did. From the moment the fever began it was only days before she was dead. Bobby outlived her by two more days. In dying he was inconsolable. During the periods when he was lucid he sobbed and moaned, blaming himself over and over for the baby and for killing Polly. Then, as he drifted into periods of semi-consciousness, he was agitated and restless, crawling around the bed and on occasions tried to climb the wall. He remained distressed to the very end, struggling even against his terminal breaths.

As Bobby endured the final moments of his hard dying Anne's baby was born. John, who was with Bobby to the very end and Kate, who was with Anne through what proved to be a long arduous birth, claimed that the two events must have been simultaneous. Anne's baby boy took its first breath as Bobby heaved his last. Kate insisted that the soul of Bobby was with the child. Whether they really believed it or not, the magical possibility was something of a solace to the Kavanaghs and the story stuck. For Robert, who remained Anne's constant attendant, the idea of the birthing breath and the dying breath being coexistent was a mystical, thrilling notion. It was as if the promise of the resurrection

123

had been acted out and revealed in the child. He looked on the child as nothing short of a miracle.

The baby was a fit, heavy, demanding boy. It cried constantly to be fed which very soon Anne did openly in front of Robert. So often did the baby require feeding he otherwise would have spent his visits leaving the room. Those acts of feeding, the swollen smooth breast obscured by the temporarily silent respiring baby, were precious visions to him and affected the way he thought. From that time on he began to pray to the Madonna as much as to Christ. He felt certain, despite the war, that the purpose of life was not death but birth. Was the life of Christ not the story of the revelation of birth. The birth of the mortal in the stable, the birth of divinity in the eyes of the Kings, the birth of mission in the temple, the birth out of sin on the cross, the birth into immortality with the resurrection. The resurrection was birth. It existed for him. The baby was the central core of his devotional frame of mind. The baby was God's gift, God's love, God's mystery.

The birth and the deaths made it imperative that an urgent letter be written to Peter. Anne had wanted to write as soon as Polly had died, but both Kate and John had advised against it, suggesting that she may as well delay as it would probably only be hours before Bobby joined her. She thought they were wrong, but allowed herself to be guided by them. As Bobby's dying went on she became absolutely convinced that they were wrong and that Peter should have been given the chance to be there with him. To herself she accused John Devlin of a perverse jealousy in wanting to keep Bobby's dying to himself. However, any notion that she might go against their advice was ruled out by her labour. When it was over, and Bobby was dead, she was absolutely certain she had made a drastic error. He might have been there for the birth as well as the death. He had been excluded from what was rightfully his. She didn't know how she could make amends. She set to writing within hours of the baby's birth, but found she couldn't manage it. The words just wouldn't come. She simply could not state side by side that Peter had become a father and an orphan. In the end she gave it up and asked Robert to write in her name.

She gave him an idea of what she wanted to say then sat in the window and cradled the baby. There was a vase of rhododendrons by her hip. The room was heavy with its perfume. She couldn't look at Robert as he wrote the letter, but simply nodded in profile as he composed its contents aloud. Her eyes strayed along the rooftops and along the streets. Cats lay stretched on the hot slates and dogs lay on the cobbles beneath the shade of walls, whilst the street itself was full of children. The sound of their shouting filtered into the small room. It made her want to cry. She rocked the baby and turned more fully into the window, attempting to shut out everything but Robert's voice.

"Dear Peter," he began.

She corrected him: "My darling Peter."

"My darling Peter," he repeated, pausing for a second or two for any further response. She said nothing. He continued slowly. "I think we are blessed this early summer. It's obvious to me now that you knew it was a boy I was carrying. He is called William as you desired."

Robert looked up at Anne in the window. He couldn't see her face clearly. The sunlight was profiling her. She sat completely still. On the first day she had known she was pregnant she wrote to Peter asking him to name the child. After weeks of waiting his answer had been a single name, a boy's name. *Despite the Kaiser we'll call him Bill. William.* From then on Anne had no doubts that the baby, as Kate confirmed, would be a boy.

Robert shook his head and continued. "He's a fine, strapping, lively, beautiful boy, the talk of Ginns. You can be very proud of your son as he will be of you Peter..."

"My darling Peter..."

"My darling Peter... I have begun this letter many times and just as many times abandoned it..."

"Say that you have helped me."

"What?"

"Say it. Say that I asked you to help."

"Why?"

"Because I will never deceive him over anything, not again. I think he's been deceived enough. I'm not going to deceive him over this."

Robert again eyed her dark figure in the window before continuing. Deception was so strong a word. It alarmed him. She alarmed him, saying what she just had. Did she recognise it in him, in the way he looked at her. He wanted to see her expression, but her face was turned away. There was nothing for it but get on with his task. His voice was rather more diffident as he spoke aloud. "It is so difficult to write what I must write and I'm afraid you must read... my darling Peter, that I've asked Robert to help..."

"He supports me in this."

Robert was aware that her face had turned towards him once again, but still he could not discern her features. "He supports me in this," he repeated. Again she averted her face. "Despite all of your wonderful letters, which everyone appreciates, it's impossible for us to realise what it must be like for you there surrounded by death..."

"Don't say that," Anne said quietly, without turning to him. "Leave that out."

"I'm sorry, I didn't, well..." Robert began, embarrassed by her instruction, thinking she meant his allusion to death.

She seemed to recognise the cause of the discomfort in his voice and said: "Don't mention his letters, the fact that everyone reads them. Don't say that. Start after that."

Robert hesitated before once again starting. A thin film of sweat had formed around his torso and his mouth was dry. He couldn't understand why he had become so nervous. He took a couple of deep breaths to compose himself and began again slowly. "It's impossible for us to realise what it must be like for you there surrounded by death, and I hope you never despise us for our lack of understanding. We try as best we can, but I'm afraid we'll never truly appreciate what it is to suffer."

Anne's eyes turned to Robert and stayed on him. He met her gaze briefly, but was embarrassed by her attention, and quickly lowered his eyes. They both recognised that he was speaking for himself. She let it go. She didn't mind. It was their letter, one she hadn't managed herself. "Go on," she prompted. "It's good. It says just what I want."

He went on as instructed. "Knowing this, it is with the greatest reluctance and difficulty that I must add two more deaths to a world too involved with death. Two deaths that I'm afraid, my darling Peter, may be worse than any you've experienced. Your dear mother died with child. Her blood was poisoned and the fever was too much for her to fight. Mercifully your father was released from his terrible illness. They are still together Peter and I am certain watching over you at this very minute. Both your aunty Kate and I wanted the family to come to us but Catherine and June are insistent that they won't be broken up. Alice has been in the factory with them since Easter and young Tom is finding plenty to do along the dockside. There's no shortage of boats to load or unload at the moment or ships needing coaling. I don't know if it's what he wants for the future, but he's doing all right for now. So they should manage fine. Catherine and June are really grown-up now. Well, they won't have it any other way. They'll look after each other, I'm sure. I know your aunty Kate never lets a day go by but that she's there." Robert paused. He looked towards Anne. She made no response. He considered for a few moments then continued. "I can't say anything else without crying. Think only of the day that you'll be home for good and can watch Bill grow up into a man as fine as his father. Et cetera."

"Thank you, Robert. I will copy that as it stands."

"You can change what you like."

"There's no need. I told you, it says just what I want."

"It's a strange letter to send to the front."

"You think he really is surrounded by death?" she asked, her voice quiet yet strong and defiant.

"I do. He says so in his letters."

She stood up and calmly left the room. Robert heard Bill cry and knew he was being changed.

*

Peter was given ten days leave. On a hot mid-afternoon in July he stepped into his house on Ginns. Anne and he just looked at each other for a moment and then smiled. They stepped up to each other and still without speaking began to undress each other. He kissed her and stroked her, hungry to make up for their curtailed honeymoon. But then, when she was not quite entirely naked Bill began to cry. They both stopped and listened for a moment, then Anne began to smile. Peter made a move to kiss her again, but she whispered that she would have to see to the baby, adding that it wouldn't take long. Peter was quietly furious. From that point on he grew increasingly irritable and impatient with Bill's constant need for attention. On the second day he commanded Anne to leave him be and let him cry, but Anne wouldn't hear of it. Peter slammed out of the house in temper. When he returned an hour later Anne laughed and told him that it struck her that son and father were very similar. She began to make it up to him, but he shunned her. She simply smiled and told him it wouldn't always be the way it was. He looked at her as if she had said something truly terrible.

With everyone else he was taciturn and remote. Catherine and June had come round as soon as they heard he was home, and as soon as they were let in began cheering and shouting as if hailing a returned hero. He was after all a soldier from the war, a soldier who wrote for the papers. He told them to shut up on the instant. When they tried to coax him to be a bit more reasonable he lost his temper and ordered them out. As they were leaving he told them he just wanted to be left alone, and instructed them not to call again uninvited. When they were gone Anne smiled at him and suggested they were simply proud of him, and that perhaps he should indulge them. He didn't respond.

Unsurprisingly he was the centre of attention at Bobby and Polly's burial. They had all read his letters. Now he was there in the flesh. They could see how the war had really treated him. The war made him into a figure of curiosity. Only John Devlin refused to admit that he was interested in Peter Kavanagh. In private he told Kate that he wished he had never been given leave for the funeral. He made the vaguely comic remark that he had already spoiled Bobby's sending off once before. Kate told him to stop being so ridiculous. She then gave him a short lecture on the need to separate family and politics. He shook his head. He made a short speech back. He could never condone anyone fighting for the British Empire. He told her it was a war of aggression and conquest, not defence or liberation. She scoffed at him and said it didn't matter to her whatever he said because she knew that he read Peter's letters just the same as they all did. He made no reply.

Bobby and Polly were buried together at the same time. The miners' union provided the bearers. Gavin Duffy organised it. He tried to say something to Peter by the graveside, but Peter didn't respond. Gavin left it. Peter was the same with everyone who spoke to him. He made no response, but simply continued to stare into the hole where the two coffins lay one on top of the other, Polly below, Bobby above. Eventually he was left alone. Even Anne thought it better to move aside and give him some time alone. Besides, Bill was crying again and she sensed a quickening in Peter's expression as he began. She took herself to the side of the graveyard and began to feed him.

As she sat beneath the hedgerow at the field's edge Catherine joined her. She didn't sit but remained standing, gazing towards Peter. She didn't speak for a while and Anne thought it better not to prompt her. Experience had taught her that it was sometimes better to say nothing where death was concerned. Eventually Catherine said: "He's changed isn't he. Our Peter, I mean. He's not the same at all."

Anne lifted her head from the suckling baby and looked across the field towards Peter. He remained in the same fixed position, an informal guard, gazing into the hole. She smiled and shook her head. "He's sunburnt if that's what you mean. He's got a lot more colour. He's not underground all the time anymore. He's out in the daylight."

"I don't mean that. You know I don't. He's hard and, well, I don't know, just hard."

Anne gave a small laugh and again shook her head. "No, he hasn't changed a bit. Not from where I'm sitting. I don't deny he's seen a thing or two, things that a man wouldn't normally see in the ordinary way of things, but he'll sort that out. He's just Peter."

"Well, I hardly recognise him as the brother I knew."

"I told you, he's sunburnt, of course you don't recognise him." Catherine was about to say something else, but Anne spoke again before she was able. "What do you think he's looking at?"

"Mam and Dad, I suppose."

Anne stood up so that she was beside Catherine. They both gazed at Peter for a while longer, then Anne shook her head. "I think he's looking at something he's seen, and he can't really tell us. There's more underground than your mam and dad for him. That's why he's staring like that. Holes and ditches he said."

Catherine shrugged. "He sends his letters. He says there what goes on."

Anne frowned and shook her head. "He doesn't tell us anything, not anymore."

It was at this point in the conversation that Mr Clough and a photographer from the Whitehaven News appeared. They saw the two of them rush across the field towards Peter, still standing by the open grave. They could guess from the reporter's gesticulations that he wanted a photograph of Peter standing over the grave. He was evidently suggesting the pose he wanted Peter to adopt. It was then that Peter began saying something to the reporter. They couldn't hear what he said, but he was obviously annoyed. They could see him pointing and threatening. The next moment a brief altercation ensued. It didn't last long. During it Peter snatched the camera away from the photographer and threw it away across the lines of headstones. It ended with him knocking Mr Clough into the open grave, and the photographer running away, pausing only long enough to retrieve his camera. Peter stood poised over the grave for a moment as if he intended pursuing Mr Clough into it, but then he turned and fled from the scene. Anne went running after him. The bearers from the miners' union helped Mr Clough from the grave, Gavin Duffy taking the lead.

Anne called to him as she chased him, but he kept on. Eventually she caught up with him at the gates. She lay her hand on his shoulder in an attempt to halt him. He turned round fiercely. His face was a grimace of agony. She cried out his name in sympathy. It seemed as if she were calling to him at the edge of a precipice. He simply gazed at her with the

129

same contorted face, unable to relinquish it. Eventually he shouted out: "I'm not a fucking hero. I can't stand all that stuff. I hate them. What the hell do they know?".

"Of course they don't know. None of us know. But we all care."

"Well I don't want your care. What the hell do women know about it?"

"We know what the waiting's like. We know all about that."

He closed his eyes and threw back his head. "Jesus Christ! Jesus Christ! You cannot conceive what I've seen."

"And I don't want to Peter Kavanagh. I just want you home, safe, everything normal again." He opened his eyes and glared at her, glared as if what she was saying was inexcusable. She refused to be gainsaid. "Yes, normal. Do you understand? Normal! And I'll fight for that."

He was about to say something more but Bill began to cry. He threw up his hands in frustration and went on. She trailed him for a while, but Bill's screams grew in volubility, so eventually she sat down on the roadside and tried to comfort him, refusing on this occasion to give him the breast again.

A matter of days after Peter had returned to his platoon Anne received a letter from him.

My darling Anne, Even now I can still feel the shape of your body. I wake up from these half-hearted kips and I can feel you. God, but we had a grand time of it. I never knew out could be like that. Honest to God, it's like you're still with me. Even with all the chit-chat and row and stink you get here I've still got you against me. Oh Christ Anne, Anne. And this is just for us. I don't want any of that lot getting their hands on us anymore. I'm sorry Anne, but I don't want you to let those bastards have my letters anymore. I hate them. Listen, sorry. I've started again, all right. I'm not going to tear it up, because I can't afford to waste the paper. You can't afford to waste anything here. Most of the lads use their letters for toilet paper. You see them sitting there reading it over for one last time and then down it goes. You maybe didn't realise that we see things like that. There's no secrets here really. Except the feel of you like a bloody miracle still on my fingertips. I don't know how you've done that lass. Oh but Christ it's keeping me going. I'm sorry about all that business. I let everybody down, didn't I. I let you down, let myself down, but most of all I suppose I let me mam and dad down. I wasn't really thinking of them much. I just couldn't stand that damned weasely reporter feller. I couldn't bear him. I hate them all, you know. They got in the way. I didn't get to talk to you. Not proper like I wanted. I was going to tell you about a lad called Baxter. Did I tell you about him? See, I can't remember. I don't know what I wrote about half the time. Don't know what I've said and haven't said really. Well, everything just goes round and round. One day it's one and then another. I should never have let them get my letters though. What was I thinking of? From now on, it's just us. I'm sorry if you're disappointed, but that's how I want it. Well, anyways. Baxter died, died before my leave. The stupid thing was I think I expected to see him still here when I got back. Came as a shock for some reason. Great big fine lad he was, done a bit of prize-fighting, and such a laugh. Daft really. I hadn't really forgotten. Well, how could I? Hugh and me were with him. All that coaxing and keeping him going, all for nowt. Walter took it pretty bad. He's a thoughtful feller at the best of times. I didn't reckon they were such big pals, but I suppose they might. Most lads tend to pal up with someone. A bit stupid really. We just try to survive from disgusting meal to disgusting meal. We want nowt making pals, but we do. I don't know where I'd be without Hugh Glyn. God he's a level-headed young lad. He told me Walter got himself really down for a few days there, while I was away like. Apparently Walter said it was already too late for the likes of us. He'd get himself into hot water for defeatist chat like that. It's not too late. It can't be can it, but I'm right scared that's it's going to go on and on. We're 800 thousand men here you know. Well so Walter reckons. I hate that. It makes me like nowt. Absolutely nowt. Just another regular feller that should be back home with his missus. I didn't mean to act like I did. It wasn't just that bloody reporter. It was everyone really. Except you. And the wee feller, of course. I've got nowt against the wee feller. He's a bit of a crier like. But he'll soon grow out of all that. He's going to be a big lad isn't he. Poor little blighter really. I don't think our Cath's going to speak to me ever again. Well, to hell with her! What the hell does she know! All those bloody people smiling away and those stupid old fellers. What the hell do they know? If the Prussians sent a few Zeppelins over the water with a bit of gas they'd all change their bloody tune wouldn't they. It's like a bloody cork-screw down your throat. It burns your eyes out and burns your innards. You drown with your throat all clogged up. They wouldn't like that, would they! I'm sure as hell they wouldn't. The flash bastards. Wanting to take my picture! The local hero page. Well, I'm sorry if it puts you out lass, but as I say I'm finished with that business. I don't want them having any bit of me. Not a bit. I don't know how I'll ever make it up to my mam and dad. I've never seen my dad since he went away. There's all sorts of things I want to ask him really. Trouble is I can't

131

even get a clear picture of him in my head. Honest to God I can't. What the hell is that about? He was such a lovely feller really. He wasn't the strongest, but he had such a heart. Mad about his family. I should have said all that to him. Our Cath and June are a bit forward with themselves I noticed. Well, Aunty Kate will keep an eye on everything. Is Robert still doing his bit? I didn't take much notice of him really. Funny, but we were kind of friends for a wee while. But, well, he seemed more serious than ever. I couldn't stand that either. There's no pleasing me is there lass. It felt a bit odd coming back here. It was like coming home, seeing all the lads, catching up like. And they all wanted to know everything. They're a good bunch, they really are. You'd like Hugh. What a feller. He borrowed three blankets the other night. No blankets in the front trench. They're scared we'll get so cosy we'll miss the other lot coming our way. I can just imagine being cosy here. You never heard the amount of daftness you get here. It's just one thing after another. It might have been all over if we'd been in charge but it's left to a few soppy posh kids and old horse men. The kids mean well, I suppose, but what do they know about out. It's all so bloody stupid. Well, if they read this one you'll most likely not get it. To hell with them though. I'll say what I want to my wife. You're the best of me Anne, and I let you down lass. I let you down badly. And I wouldn't have done that for all the world. Christ I love you. You're a smasher, you know. I'm sorry I acted like I did. I really am. But I'm not sorry I nailed that reporter. I can't abide the likes of him. And that Duffy's just as bad. Well, I'll let that go. Dad would have liked the miners seeing them off like that. Jesus, you know, I can't get my head round it at all. They didn't harm anyone. Christ almighty. Why both of them Anne? It doesn't make any sense at all. They were decent all their life. I can't make head nor tail of it. They're dead and Baxter and Wilson and Gadd are dead, and maybe all the rest of us. Oh Jesus, Jesus, Jesus, Anne, what on earth am I going to do? You're still with me lass. Oh Anne. Your husband Peter.

She carefully folded the pages in neat equal sections then pressed it against her breast, smiling, smiling long and hard.

*

During the hot summer days following Peter's departure Robert would bring Patrick and together with Anne and Bill they would walk along the cliffs further than the lighthouse so that the town was out of sight. Here the cliffs were sheer sandstone stacks, topped by gentle grassy banks. The sound of feeding gulls barracked the cliffs. Robert liked the constant hostile throb of the jabbering birds. It was a background against which he could talk, a background against which he could say things about the war which were occupying his mind. He would put Patrick on the grass, stand, survey the birds and wait for his cue to speak. Patrick, who was now three, and speaking only a little, remained a sickly infant, given to chills, coughs and vomiting. He was more or less content to sit on the grassy banks without moving. Occasionally he would cry for no apparent reason, then Robert would cradle him. When Patrick cried Bill cried. On one occasion Robert picked up the sobbing Patrick, burst out laughing and said: "The cliff of the crying babies."

"You make it sound terrible," Anne said.

"It is terrible. Listen to the ferocity of those birds. They make a sound like babies, call out like babies, and all the time they're watching each other, bickering, fighting, stealing, killing. It's a war of sorts, a war of survival, with no commandments at all."

Anne was not amused. "Is that from one of your lessons, Robert?"

Robert was unrepentant, and responded with sincerity. "No, that isn't something I've read, something I've seen. I've watched these birds and I've seen the hunger in their eyes and seen it was terrible. I used to think that if something was terrible then God would stop it, but God can't stop it, He can't stop anything. He's left all that to us. That's the wonderful mystery, Anne. He can't stop the war. He didn't make the world like that. He put good and evil into the world and sometimes they're almost the same thing. It's up to us to decide. We have to find the path of good and hope we're right. If we are it'll lead us to Him. But it's not clear cut. It leads us into dark as well as light. It takes us to war as well as peace."

"Be quiet, Robert," she said firmly, though without any real anger. She found his words vulgar and certainly misplaced, but recognised an ache in them, a childish, ill conceived ache. He was a soft frightened boy trying to understand himself. She took his hand and stroked it. He blushed deeply. "I don't like you speaking like this," she said. He was about to protest, but she spoke over him. "We both just hope and pray that it will soon be over. That's the main thing, that it's over and life can be normal again. That's all we want. The day when Peter, and all the other lads, can all come home and be where they should be, not in some God forsaken other place. That's what you hope for as well Robert. I know that. I can see it in your face." Robert made no response.

133

This conviction that war was not intrinsically bad but part of God's design grew in him. War was Nature. It existed within human beings the way good existed within evil and vice versa, the way suffering and grace existed one within the other. It was a compatibility, a unity, that one had to strive for. To fight for something intrinsically right would expurgate the soul. He knew that the following year would see him able to fight. He was almost afraid that it would end before he had witnessed it.

He spoke to Father Bond about his beliefs. He still kept up his studies with him, which in the main consisted of sitting in the priest's study reading aloud to him. Usually the priest closed his eyes and rested to one side, looking for all the world as if he were sleeping, a pose that he would regularly maintain long after Robert had concluded. Sometimes, though, he kept his eyes on Robert throughout the whole reading. Robert found his attention unnerving. He could never interpret what Father Bond's misty, grey eyes were registering. Their gaze seemed altogether too inward to take account of Robert, swimming freely in the wet bath of their orbits. Even when the readings were concluded he would offer only the briefest of commentaries. Robert fluctuated between believing the man to be either profoundly devout or simply ignorant.

On this particular day the priest chose to have his eyes closed. Robert read the opening of the Gospel of Saint John. Robert had a personal liking for the Old Testament, but the priest seemed almost indifferent to most things other than the Gospels. Usually when Robert concluded he kept his attention essentially on the book in front of him and patiently waited for the priest to rouse himself from his holy reverie, but on this occasion he turned to him and quietly asked: "Father, is this a good war or a bad war?"

Father Bond opened his eyes instantly and flashed a sharp, inquisitive look across Robert's face. Robert was somewhat taken aback by the vividness of the priest's attention. He turned back to the Gospel as if the question had not arisen.

A moment later Father Bond said: "So, you are thinking about this calamity which has struck us, are you Robert?"

Robert didn't reply. He felt embarrassed under the priest's scrutiny. He shrugged slightly.

"Tut, tut," Father Bond continued, "that will not do, son. I give the question back to you. Do you think this thing which is happening in France and Belgium is a good thing or a bad thing?"

"I don't know."

A quick smile passed the priest's lips, then instantly vanished. "It is a bad thing. But maybe that was unfair of me. You wondered whether it was a good or a bad war, which is maybe a different question. I have only answered that it is a bad thing which is happening. But that maybe isn't what you are asking me. So, what are you really asking Robert? Is it a just war? Is it a glorious war? Is it a correct war?"

"Yes, I suppose I'm asking that?"

"What, all of those questions, or just one?"

"I don't know."

A another smile flashed across the priest's face, only to vanish as quickly as the former. "What sort of war?" he mused, and as he did he eyed Robert closely all of the time. He seemed possessed of a quick, sharp intelligence of which Robert had hitherto been unaware. Robert felt caught out, presumptive and arrogant. "A glorious, just, correct war? For whom? That is the question, I suppose. That is the struggle for your father isn't it. He doesn't comprehend the words. It's like a foreign language to him. And that's awful, awful for him, awful for anyone. He is bedevilled by terrible ironies, the worst of which is that just by living, by managing to get by, this place becomes home. That is a terrible, brutal prospect for a man with his genius for understatement. Does that beg any questions of you Robert?"

"I'm sorry, I really don't know what you mean Father. What has my father got to do with it? He won't even talk about it."

"Does that not strike you as significant, Robert? Does silence not cry out to you to be acknowledged? Have you not learnt to hold communion with silence? *In the beginning was the Word, and the Word was with God, and the Word was God.*"

"I'm sorry Father."

"You're sorry? Sorry for what, Robert? Sorry that you have failed the silence? Do you know what you achieve when you read Robert? Do you know the authority by which you reach into the darkness? You have a gift for it, and yet you are unaware of it, a gift for dealing with silence. Oh Robert, my son."

"I'm sorry that I've let you down, but I don't really know..."

"It's all right Robert, don't upset yourself. You're not the only one who can't work things out. Faith, Robert, faith."

"Yes, Father," Robert assented with some difficulty, struggling against the need to either fly away or cry.

Father Bond looked at him with some sympathy. "I am being hard Robert. Faith tells me to be true to the customs of beauty and justice, which is the basis of all of our Christian progress. But faith also tells me that an angel fell, and the fall from grace produced a hard, bitter, brutal shock. Grace and disgrace contend in the same flesh. We all bear the germ of moral cancer. The darkness and the light both beckon, one attempting to obliterate the other, yet the one is always predicted by the other. We are sorely tested Robert. Only Christ could succeed, that is why we place our trust, our reliance, our weakness in him. Pray, Robert, pray."

"I sometimes pray that it won't end before I've had my chance. Is that wicked Father? Is that truly bad?"

"Of course, son, you are on the path towards blasphemy," the priest replied wearily, and as he did closed his eyes and again tilted his head to one side.

Robert waited for a moment, unsure of what he should say or do. He opted to simply gaze at the face of the priest. Was his expression content or complacent? Robert couldn't say. Eventually Robert turned back to the Gospel and continued his reading from the point at which he had left off. Father Bond smiled quietly, revelling in his most favoured words, revelling in the voice that spoke them.

Robert never mentioned the war to him again.

*

On an unusually fine, sunny day towards the end of September Robert called on Anne with the intention of inviting her to walk with him along the cliff tops. As Patrick was too chesty at the time to chance taking out Robert was free of him. He was in exultant mood. He had worked a first shift so it was dark when he went underground. The daylight that met him when he had finished had been unexpectant. He had stood on the promontory for some time simply looking over the town. It was peaceful and compact. Its parts fitted together. There was a lazy sheen to everything. It sang of God. He felt like a bird. He closed his eyes and dreamt he was flying. He imagined himself climbing higher and higher, leaving the town far below, growing ever more distant. He heard a distant chorus calling to him. He opened his eyes. The light rushed in. He ran home to wash, before going to Anne. He wanted to share this glorious day with her.

When he arrived at the house on Ginns he was still in ecstatic mood. He was delighted that his mother had advised him not to bring Patrick. His constant crying would have been at variance to the day, to the way he was feeling. He felt larger than was usual with him. He had stature. He was sure he had grown. He was certainly too wrapped up in himself to recognise that Anne was uncharacteristically preoccupied.

He spoke to her about the sunshine, the pattern of light along the surface of the dock basins, the feeling as he came to the surface and felt the warmth and tone of the day. She scarcely responded. He went on and was rather more daring than he would have believed possible for himself. He told her his first thought was to be with her, to go with her onto the cliff-tops, to the top of the world he called it, to share it with her. He added that they should take a break from the war.

At first she carried on in the same preoccupied dreamy fashion as she had when he first came in, but then she suddenly concentrated on him. She stared at him hard for a while and then demanded: "What do you mean Robert? What are you saying to me?"

He felt instantly deflated. He was aware of himself shrinking in size, dwindling before the criticism of her attention. He mumbled: "I just thought it was a lovely day." Her expression became even more hardened. He felt compelled to try to retain something for himself. "I got carried away." He smiled weakly. "I thought I could hear angels singing."

"You and your bloody God, Robert. I don't know that I can stomach either today."

Robert smarted at her comment. He was sure he was about to cry. His eyes burnt with the expectation. He couldn't speak. He desperately wanted to run out, but his body had become a lead weight. He suffered his own continued presence. She recognised his discomfort, but for once she couldn't help his misplaced infatuation. In fact, she felt motivated to hurt him more. She wanted to ridicule his facile admiration, his holy tendency, his childlike enthusiasm, but in the end she was simply too weary to be bothered.

"I think you'd better go Robert, don't you. I don't know that Peter would be happy you coming over here quite so much as you do."

"Do you not want me to come back?"

She glared at him fiercely. She wanted to shout at him, berate him for his solemnity, his God, himself. She was too tired for him. He demanded sympathy and understanding and she didn't have that energy. She was determined not to indulge him. Still, he just stood, awkward and nervous like a scolded schoolboy. "Go on, Robert, you can leave me alone. I don't want you today."

He was about to say something. His face was flushed red, hot with the possibility of what it might be, but then he suddenly turned tail and fled. He ran from Anne and Peter's house, leaving the front door swinging behind him. She called after him that she was sorry, but he didn't hear. He was far along the road by the time she had stirred herself, before she considered what she had done.

Having no clear notion of where he was headed he simply ran for some time, but then after a while the effort to keep on became too great to continue. He ground to a halt. The light had turned mildly grey, the sun having fallen steeply in the sky. There was a slight tinge of cold in the air. He panted and breathed deeply. He couldn't understand his hurt, nor why it had been inflicted. He felt foolish and childish. She had ridiculed everything he had ever felt. He stumbled on in a haze of tears and embarrassment.

Without planning it he found himself at the porch of Saint Joseph's. He stood there for some time refusing to enter. He swore under his breath, berating himself for his belief, for being who he was. He couldn't stand it. But then the violence of his temper suddenly subsided and was replaced by a vague yearning space. It was as if he were suddenly filled by a terrible emptiness. He couldn't bear it. He went in. He needed the familiarity of his church.

He walked down the central aisle and stood before the altar and the tabernacle for some time. He was at a loss. The things he loved seemed willing to forget him. He told himself he was crying out to the Lord, but it was Anne's words that replied.

He turned himself and faced a statue of our Lord, pinned to the cross, pinned to the ignobility of crucifixion. The face was beautiful. Its eyes searched a gloom Robert could not even envisage. The suffering went deeper than anything he had ever perceived. He began to cry all over again. His pain was awful. Again he felt like flying away. What was he doing standing so brazenly before the tabernacle? He went down on one knee, genuflecting to that immense power, then he went into a pew and kneeled down. He rested his head into his palms and groaned aloud. He vowed before God never to speak to anyone again about good and evil, right and wrong. He was to be mute on all such matters. He determined never again to feel enthusiasm. From that time on he would be reserved in all matters. The alternative was too painful.

He sat on until the body of the church was almost virtually dark, but couldn't bring himself to leave. In the early evening Father Bond came in and lit candles around the altar. As he turned to return to the vestry he saw Robert. He looked at him for a moment, then continued on his way without saying a word. Robert immediately stood up and departed.

He walked back up to the exit to the mine workings and looked over the town. It was fundamentally silent. Only an occasional voice drifted towards him. He had never felt so lonely. He closed his eyes. Of course, it was impossible to fly. Earth dragged you down. There was no escaping its pull. He stayed there sometime more, then made his way home telling Kate he would go straight to bed as he had endured a hard day. She left him alone.

When Robert rushed away from Anne she stood still for a while, rooted to the spot, determined not to respond to him. It was only as the silence of the room intensified around her did she follow him to the door and call out her apologies. She didn't call very loud. The business was too embarrassing. She went back in, locking the door behind her. She didn't want any further disturbance. She went to her bedroom, took out her biscuit-tin and picked out Peter's latest correspondence. She lay back and simply held them clasped between both hands, pressed below her breasts.

As she lay there terrible images came to mind. It didn't matter whether her eyes were open or closed, the same drastic picture goaded her. It was horrible. A distorted, mangled face, its jaw bone revealed, the bundles of muscle gaping: its eyes staring and sad, so deeply sad, so deeply lonely. And the trouble was it was true. She had seen it. She had seen it and stared at it, as so many others had done. She had stared and tried to be sympathetic, tried to say something to those beseeching eyes, but she was horrified. She was like everyone else, terrified and revolted. She hated herself for that, and tried to excuse herself. It had been so unexpected. She hadn't had any time to think it through. But it was no good. She couldn't extract the pity from herself that that face was due. She let herself and it down.

It! She couldn't even think of it in broader terms. It was disgusting. Except, it had the most timid, tortured eyes. She found herself pleading with the image that pressed itself into her thinking. Why were you there? Why did you wander around that market-place, exposing yourself to such wonder and revulsion? How could any human being suffer so much? And if it were Peter, her Peter, her big, bold, beautiful Peter? Beautiful?

How long would that survive? Perhaps he was already mutilated, his bones and muscles open to the world's criticism. She virtually screamed aloud at the thought of that wound coming towards her, approaching her with desire, with a need to touch her, kiss her. No, no, no, she repeated to herself. And at the same time, as she challenged that vision from coming close to her, so too she turned it on herself.

She was the one being disgusting, the one disregarding common human tenderness. She had made vows. She was charged to love him through all circumstance. Their union was absolute. They were no longer separate beings. She owed him her body if he sought it. What did all her hoping mean, otherwise? What did all her house building mean, otherwise? It couldn't all be simply facile.

And yet, still the thought horrified her. Her whole body heaved with the affront of it. Her skin was covered with a film of cold, drenching sweat. Her heartbeats thumped at her chest. She stood up and paced aimlessly around the room, carelessly touching objects and surfaces as if she could discover some release from the torment of her thoughts. And then, finding no release, she screamed aloud, a shrill terrified outpouring. It lasted a matter of seconds, then she was silent. Following that outburst she found that her heart was quieter and that she was in some control of herself.

She went to the window, opened it and breathed at the air that flowed in. It was cold and sharp over her damp body, but refreshing. She inhaled and exhaled deeply for some time. When she felt entirely calm she stripped off her clothes and wiped down her skin with a towel.

She returned to her bed and slipped under her sheet naked. She was no longer assailed by the picture of the wounded soldier who had wandered round the market. The terror had gone, though she was aware that there was a seed still remaining, a seed that could erupt at any moment. After all, the soldier she had seen wasn't the first. They were not uncommon at all. She wasn't even convinced that he was the worst. Certainly his wounds, his terrible disfigurement had been pitiful, but the real pity was in his eyes. He was so punished by onlookers. And she had been one. She felt deeply ashamed. She had so much betrayed his need. How could she have been so callous? She told herself that she would never again react with anything less than tenderness. That thought brought her back to Peter. She struggled to control her resurgent panic. She pleaded. Please, not him. It wasn't a prayer, just a bland hope.

She opened one of the letters that she still grasped in her hands. She hadn't even relinquished them to undress. From the moment she began to read she felt something of the reassurance his presence brought. She always heard his voice as she read. It was as if he were there speaking to her, that they could never really be so far apart.

Darling Anne, As soon as I put your name down, I'm off. I think all this malarkey has made me a bit soppy, lass. You'll soon sort all that out, I reckon. The days are long here. There's all sorts of rumours flying round. I can't go into all that. Well, to be honest, I don't know nowt. You get the feeling that something's in the off, but Christ knows what. Lots of the lads say it's too late in the year to bother with out now. I can't get my head round another winter here lass. Bloody hell, eh! Still, we'll do what we have to, same as always. I know what Walter meant now. I got it all wrong at first like. When he said it was already too late for us. I thought he was being defeatist like. And to be honest, you don't get any of that sort of chat. Lads get fed up, but they all reckon there's a job to do like. Nobody puts up a fight about that. There's still a pack of them heroes here, like. Most of us have lost all that rubbish. We're workers, that's all, digging away to the end. He just meant that in a few years it'll all be forgotten. Well, it will, won't it. I don't suppose Wilf's folks'll forget, not properly like, but even they won't keep on forever. Well, you can't, can you. We all know that. Nobody'll give tuppence for what all this carry on meant. It won't exist. And all these lads dead. I don't know how many. I don't suppose anybody'll really know how many. They just go out, like, at night and you never see them again. You get it in your head that there's a magic place out there where all the missing lads go. Kids fairy tale sort of thing. Daft the things you get in your head, really. Poor old Wilf. That bastard Close. Lots of the fellers think Close's all right, you know. They trust him to do the job. You know what I mean, they want to press on and get the job sorted. I think he's just a bastard. I hope he reads this one. He can do what the hell he likes to me. I'm through with being bothered by the likes of Close. No one talks bad to me over petty things, not now. Not after poor Wilf. Christ, pet, can you even begin to imagine the sort of place these lads would have made if they'd all come home together. What a thought, eh. Bloody hell, but we would have put a bomb under the whole damned lot of them, wouldn't we. Christ knows what a palace we would have set up. A palace for you, and for my mam, if she'd a lived to see it. But we're not all going to come back together are we. We're going to come back in dribs and drabs, an arm missing here, a leg missing there, an eye over there, well you know. And we're going to be told where to go and what to do. See, that's what Walter means. It's too late for us now. We're kind of old and grey and faded. We'll stumble about and hide in corners, too afraid to come out, an embarrassment, something to be shoved out of the way. And we'll just take it all. I'm sure we will. Hiding in the shadows. We just don't have any scrap left. We're all fed up, I reckon, with trying to work it all out, trying to make sense of it like. Well, sick of any crack about making plans. What the hell could we plan? That's a joke isn't it. What a bloody joke, though. Well, we've all written our wills in the back of our pay-books. Fat lot of thinking had to go into that. I've got nowt, but I want the best lass in't whole world to have it. I've been a smasher, haven't I. I push a reporter feller into my own mam and dad's grave, make a bloody fool of myself, and haven't got bugger all for nowt. Bloody hell, bloody hell! Christ lass, I'd tear all this up, but I can't really afford the paper. Bear with us, eh. Bloody stupid, writing wills. They're all out of date by the time your ink's dried. All the lads want to give their mates something. Nowt much. A keepsake. But your mate's dead. He hasn't got any use for the stupid bits of rubbish you might want to give him. What a caper. No use at all. What the hell could we give anyone anyway? All we've got is crap. We've got nowt, nowt at all. To be honest, we're just a pile of shit to be shot up. Just because your mates die doesn't mean out happens. It doesn't, does it. Poor old Wilf dies and nowt happens. There's no medals like, just for getting yourself killed. That's just stupid like. It's not regulation getting yourself cut up. If ever I needed to be told I was nowt, well I've learnt it here, right enough. I know it now. I'm nowt. And I'm not going to change nowt. But, Christ if we'd all come home a whiles back. Well, I've already said that. No, I reckon you just have to enjoy yourself. I remember a while back I was out between the lines and this German came charging towards us. Big, grey feller. I shot him just at the top of the leg, but he kept coming. God knows what he was going to do. Kick us to bits by the look of him. I reckon I had a few seconds to sort out what to do about him. Well, I gave him his life. I shot him in the leg just above the ankle and brought him down. If he came at me now I'd shoot him between the eyes without thinking twice. That's how it is here, and that's how we'll get through. I don't know how long they've got planned to keep us here, but we'll do the job, you just see. Oh Christ Anne. I don't know that I'm the same lad. Bear with us eh. Cut us a bit of rope, like. God but I miss you. Your loving husband, Peter.

His last correspondence was a Field Service Postcard, Form A.2042. On it there were a few printed phrases. *I am quite well. I have been admitted into hospital... sick / wounded... and am going on well / and hope to be discharged soon. I am being sent down to base. I have received your letter / telegram / parcel. Letter follows at first opportunity. I have received no letter from you... lately / for a long time.* Peter had crossed out everything except, *I am quite well.* He had signed it *Peter Kavanagh* and nothing else.

Anne sank down onto the mattress, pulled the sheet right over her, curled into a ball, still with Peter's letter and postcard pressed against her, and began to sob, great heaving sobs.

*

In October Anne received another Field Service Postcard. This time he had crossed everything out except: *I am quite well. I have been admitted into hospital... wounded... and am going on well / and hope to be discharged soon.* Again it was signed simply *Peter Kavanagh.* She studied his signature for some time trying to decipher the extent of his injury from its rounded, messy lines. As far as she could tell it was the same. He was always a poor writer. In fact, he wrote with the hand of a much older person, the ink lines wavering and uncertain, the tilt marked but uneven. It gave no inkling of its sender.

She had thought about this happening, but had always done her best to dismiss it from her thoughts. What she had never expected was the numbness she felt. Whenever she had allowed herself to rehearse this most dreadful of moments, she always imagined herself engulfed by howls of fear, protest and pain. But they wouldn't materialise. She was suddenly bereft of all thought and feeling. She couldn't understand it all.

She looked towards Robert and held out the card for him to take. He was no longer the constant companion that he had been, but they had made a satisfactory peace. It had been down to Anne to go to him and apologise and try as best she could to explain the anxieties that had led to her outburst. She had accurately predicted to herself that if she appealed to Robert's ability to forgive then she would win him over. In reality, it didn't take much. He suffered their brief estrangement terribly. For the duration he felt totally adrift from known landmarks. He loved Anne deeply, more deeply than he could ever openly admit, even to himself. Whether he believed in her contrition or not was immaterial. He was too grateful to care. He needed her good will.

Since the day of their rupture Robert had ceased altogether to mention the war. Indeed, he scarcely mentioned the war to anyone anymore. The question of justice, of good and evil, had left him. They were now part of his imaginative world, his world of faith. He had answered all of his own questions. Grace was suffering, suffering was grace: evil was good, good was evil. His faith was more abstract than ever. He lived with an inner framework of moral codes and connections, held together by a vague reality which was beyond his known experience. For him God had always had that quality: now God was present in the war, His mystery, His scale, His commandments, His test. Robert lived with the hidden conviction that the day was coming when he would be intimate with the trial God had set for him and so many others.

He was something at a loss as to know how to respond to the postcard that Anne handed him. He read it over and over, delaying the moment when he would have to respond. Eventually he lowered the card in his hand and looked towards her. She appeared remarkably calm. He couldn't work out what that meant. Was she so shocked she was no longer thinking? Or was she being strong? He didn't know. It was outside of his understanding. He knew he had to say something though. She had readmitted him to her most personal experiences. He had to be worthy.

"He says he's all right," he said in a quietly encouraging voice. Only the slightest movement of Anne's facial muscles suggested she had heard him at all. He went on: "He says he's hoping to be discharged soon. It must be all right if he puts that. He wouldn't say it, would he."

"He doesn't say it," she replied hastily, "That public thing says it. What else could he put? What if he's mutilated Robert? What if he's disfigured? What then? How will he cope with that?"

"There's no reason to think it. He doesn't say. He would say. He's bound to."

"He should never have gone," she snapped, her voice accelerating as a tide of emotion began to rise in her. "What the hell is he doing there fighting other people's fights for them. He should be here. This is where he should be doing his fighting. It isn't fair. It just isn't fair. Two days, two lousy days. What's that, for God's sake!"

"He thought it all through. He's very brave, our Peter. Really brave. He'll be all right."

"Brave," she snapped, deriding the word.

"You think he's brave don't you Anne?"

"Am I allowed to think anything else Robert?"

Robert nodded his comprehension of what he assumed she meant. In fact, he took it at face value. Of course it was brave. It was the height of bravery. He handed her back her postcard as if it were a testament to that fact. She quietly raged at him, but made nothing of it. Robert needed her sympathy, not her scorn.

She took the card and told him she would have to go to the Kavanaghs. He offered to go with her, but she wouldn't hear of it. She needed him to mind Bill. She said it as if it were important that Bill was not with her, as if he needed to be protected from such news. He accepted anything she suggested, pleased to be her servant. He stayed with Bill and she went alone.

She found the Kavanaghs in lively mood. Breda and Stanley were describing how they had seen some prisoners of war. Catherine hadn't believed it at first, but Tom told her there was a transit camp a bit out of town where he had heard prisoners were kept before being taken on to Scotland. He knew for a fact that they were shipped in after dark, through the harbour. He didn't say whether he had been involved himself in bringing them ashore, but he was very certain about his information. He said that if you lay awake you could see them being led through the town in the early hours. Catherine made a fuss about it, describing such goings on as disgusting, making out that they were all at risk. What if they escaped? Tom dismissed her fuss as nonsense.

Anne didn't like breaking their friendly family row, but what could she do? She decided to hand the card to Tom. He took it and read over it. He looked at Anne and nodded as much to say he knew how to handle it. In fact, he made a short speech in which he stated that Peter was obviously all right, but had evidently received a minor wound. He insisted that they had no need to worry. It was more than obvious that he was all right, he had written the card himself. Whoever heard of soldiers sending postcards themselves unless they were all right.

Catherine made another fuss over the news. She wailed and moaned aloud. She embraced June and made a few dramatic statements to the effect that they needed to find out more, much more. Anne felt distanced from it all. She took the card from Tom and made to leave. She only barely reached the door when Tom stopped her. He whispered that he had meant what he had said, and that he believed he would be all right. He said that he felt it in his bones. He grinned as he said it, adding the meaningless phrase: you know our Peter. Anne wasn't so sure, but she was grateful that he had said it. She smiled in return and again made to leave.

Once again she was stopped This time it was Catherine who detained her. She called across to her. She informed Anne that she and June were going to Gretna to work. Apparently there was a large armaments factory there and they needed women to keep up production. She said it was great money. Anne merely smiled, but didn't feel able to offer any other response. Catherine wasn't through though. She said she was only telling her in case she wanted to come. Didn't she want to work in an armaments factory, earn good money and help the war effort? Anne didn't know what to say. She had never thought of anything like it. She shook her head and edged her way through the door. Catherine's voice trailed her, telling her that Peter would be pleased she was making bombs and ammunition and that she should think about it. She hurried out.

Having escaped the Kavanaghs she didn't know what to do. She couldn't face going back to the house and sitting with Robert. She told herself that the day was altogether too dreary. It was grey and damp, though not particularly wet. Everything had the bleak air of mid-autumn. The trees were just about bare and life had ceased. She couldn't seal herself away, and she couldn't settle herself down to do any sewing. She was too agitated for that. Instead, she decided to go and look at the prisoners. She knew where Breda and Stanley had meant and set off immediately she thought of it.

It took her little over twenty minutes to reach the camp. It was housed on a piece of scrub beside some disused mine sheds. They were obviously sleeping the prisoners in the sheds when required. The holding area wasn't large. At most it would hold a few dozen prisoners. She didn't count them, but she reckoned that there were probably twenty that she could see.

They stood close to the chicken-wire, simply looking out. Their expressions were drawn. They seemed weary and uncertain, though not particularly scared. They just didn't know what might happen, so they looked out. The majority had close fitting woollen caps, but some had bare heads. Their hair was cropped close to the skull. It gave them a gaunt, rather fearful look. Many of them still wore dirty bandages to various parts of their bodies, arms, legs, or across their faces.

Anne inched closer. They seemed framed, standing there behind the wire, motionless, so still. In fact, as she drew closer she saw that they were in a cage within a cage. There was a small chicken-wire frame erected within the larger compound, and all the prisoners were inside the small cage. There was something very strange to Anne in that, in the fact that they were inside a cage within a cage. It was off centre, as if they were somehow suspended in the core of all these intersecting wires. And they just stood at its edge, looking out, saying nothing, doing nothing, just looking. She went right up to the outer wire and put her hands up as if she were about to lay them against the fence, though she never actually touched it, just implied the gesture. She began to whisper. Are you all right? Are you all right? There was no response. They seemed caught, the prisoners and her, in a strange dreamlike proximity. They brought her close to Peter, and yet they were removed from her. They were the enemy, and yet they looked pitiful and worn. Indeed, they were perversely lovely, beneath their filthy grey top-coats, their woollen hats, within their pared expressions. They smelled strongly male. She stood there for some time, her hands raised, poised to touch the wire, though never committing that indiscretion, until a soldier came from the sheds and shouted at her, demanding to know what she was doing. She immediately turned and fled, terrified as she ran away of being shot in the back.

She never told anyone of her encounter with the enemy. She wouldn't have known how to word it. They seemed quite saintly to her, standing patiently below the grey skies, behind the chicken-wire. How could she have explained that to anyone? Not even Robert could have comprehended that.

*

Throughout the winter and into the following spring the war became ever more distant and remote for Anne. She never received proper letters from Peter anymore, only postcards which obliquely suggested that he was all right, but gave no information as to where he was or what he was doing. She knew he had had spells of leave, but had not chosen to come home. He had stayed in France on one occasion and gone to London on another. On one postcard he had mentioned being in hospital in London for a brief spell but nothing else. She found it a terrible burden. There was no one to confide in anymore. Catherine and June had gone to Gretna. They wrote that they were having a good time and earning really well. They had to admit that their skin had turned a nice yellow colour, right down their legs and even onto their toenails, but it didn't look too bad, and their hair had become a golden colour. It wasn't stopping them having a laugh. In fact, it was all right for them. Those that started with grey hair ended up with it turning green. Gold was quite acceptable. They sent photographs to prove that they didn't look too bad, but as the surface of the photograph was a rust coloured brown anyway it was impossible to tell what colour their skins or hair were. Again they invited her to join them. Of course, it was impossible with Bill. They probably knew that well enough. It was easy to invite her knowing she never would come. Even Robert was lost to her. Certainly, he still visited her regularly. He remained true to his promise to Peter and true to his devotion, but he made no attempt to know her thinking. He was entirely preoccupied by his own destiny. She found herself more and more in Kate's company. Kate was obviously interested to hear about Peter, but her real concern was Robert. She had an inkling of his thinking. She knew it would create a rift with John. Anne and Kate gave each other what strength they could.

Ever since the day of Anne and Robert's rupture the war had become a silence within him, a living silence. He only awaited the day when he could go. He would prove to her, to Anne, how much of a man he was. He would show everyone. And the nearer the possibility came, so too did his conviction. When he prayed that Easter it was as if he had discovered once again the utmost beauty in Christ. Each station of the cross felt like a renewal to him, a birth into a new humility. He felt strong again. He felt as he had that day he had looked over the town and imagined he could fly. As always, faith had renewed him, made him strong again. Beneath the fourth station it crossed his mind he should tell Anne he loved her, but he quickly dismissed such thinking and, without even looking at her, quickly passed on to Simon taking the cross.

When news of the Irish rebellion became known Robert could not even look at his father. They no longer spoke. When Clarke, MacDiarmada, Connolly, Pearce, MacDonagh, Ceannt and Plunkett were executed it was already too late to say anything at all. By the start of the autumn Robert had gone. They had not exchanged a word. The absurdity of their prolonged silence was underlined by the fact that by the time Robert was eligible to go he was conscripted. Kate apportioned no blame. She understood that as inevitably as father and son were put apart so ultimately would they seek reconciliation. The women held the centre.

*

Epiphany. We came here under the cover of dark. Everything here takes place in the dark. I don't know why. Don't know why it all takes place in the dark or why I'm here. Why am I here in this place, in this cold, in the dark? It's very solemn all this moving about in the dark. We could hear the sea long before we could see it, the usual sound, battering, soothing. As a kid I dreamed of letting it loose, a child's badness, before I learnt goodness, and here it can be done. The Belgians opened the Nieuport sluices and checked the Germans along the Yser. Apparently, the Yser is a stones throw away, but I don't know. I can't see it. I can't see anything really. Still, a Belgian infantryman pointed out the prospect stretching from Nieuport along the coast to Oostend and inland to Bruges. He told us that once the whole area had been inundated to stop the advance of the Duke of Marlborough. I didn't understand a word, but one of the men in the section is a teacher and speaks French. I don't understand why a teacher who speaks French is also a soldier, but he is. French is like Latin, like music, I think. It sounds lovely to me. I wish I could speak such languages. I wonder if Spanish is the same. I never heard Mr Fancy speak his language. He had a lovely voice, a beautiful voice. I should have asked him to speak to me. I should have asked Father Bond to teach me Latin. I don't know why I never got round to asking him. I always meant to. Maybe I'm just lazy. I've asked Shaw to teach me French. He says we might manage an introduction. He must believe me very stupid but I'll prove him wrong. Shaw proved the Belgian wrong. He told him that it was Marshall Vendome, a Frenchman, who flooded the plateau. The Belgian shrugged and then laughed out loud. To be honest he didn't seem bothered. He just carried on in the same easy going way, pointing to places we couldn't see, nattering away to Shaw. I asked Shaw what on earth he was on about. Shaw was a bit offhand. He snapped at me. He loves his country, he said. And that was it. That was all the explanation he would give. It's not like Shaw. Shaw has a wonderful way of speaking usually, really lovely at times, says bits of poetry, and all sorts, just as he fancies. He says he's really fond of somebody called Shelley. I don't really follow the bits he says, but it sounds wonderful. I wish I understood. It's like listening to Father Bond read the gospel. He's not a bit like Mr Fancy though. He's not fancy at all. He's plain and pleasant. He's such a calm, peaceful man. I'm pleased he's here. We're bedded down in sand-dunes, waiting for daylight; then, I don't know what. It's so cold, too cold to write. I can't believe how cold it is. My body feels numb. It's unbelievable the cold. It makes your muscles ache right inside. There's no end to it. I can't feel my fingers. I'll never be warm again. I'll never feel right again.

Pop. The dawn was misty, grey and pink, everywhere flat, a spoil-bank, a causeway or embankment a feature. Along the Yser I could see the vague outline of Nieuport, whether in one piece or not, I couldn't tell, ours though, the right side of the river. The tide was going out and the sand froze behind it. It was so cold. I've never been so cold. Shaw began to smoke. He could hardly hold the cigarette between his fingers they trembled so much. Shaw's ash landed in the lap of his coat. Older soldiers don't seem concerned by what lands on them. They simply strip every morning and wash it away. They frighten me. They've killed another man face to face. They must have. They don't brag about it, but they're not bothered either. Nothing bothers them. They laugh, but they're not really amused or happy. It's too difficult to understand really. I try to do as they do. I don't think I really pass muster. It began to snow. It collected on the ice. At first it was just a few flakes, like ash on our coats, then a great swirl. It was so cold. I didn't think I'd be able to move. Then one of the Belgian soldiers came through the storm to our group. He just nodded to the C.O., then went off again. He didn't wait or anything. We were fell in and brought to the bank of the Yser mouth. We couldn't see further than the other bank. It was just like night again. Everything here takes place at night. I'm still a miner really, doing things in the dark, traipsing inbye then outbye, without really working out why. I'm never in the light. What have I done that I'm always in the dark? We hadn't been waiting long when a small skiff came through the storm. As it came closer we could see two men in it. It ran right up onto the shore. We helped the Belgians pull it in. When we'd brought it up onto the bank we were ordered to escort the two to Poperinge. We all smiled. *Pop* is at least five miles behind Ypres. We knew the food would be all right. We didn't expect to stay though. It was a long old trek getting here, twenty miles or so, and the two wanted to hurry. It wasn't possible, not in the snow, we could only be slow. Maybe that was the explanation, maybe because we lost the track along the dykes we were following. I don't know. Anyway, as we trudged along I asked the sergeant who the men were. He got really angry and even clipped me across the ear. It made my eyes smart. I couldn't help crying. I was just so cold. I think I'm a bit weak really, maybe a bit cowardly. I'm terribly afraid of my cowardice. Shaw put his arm around me. He was smiling all the time. He made light of the whole thing. He said nice things to me. I don't know what I'd do if Shaw wasn't here. We had beef and good tea when we got here. Proper tea is a real treat. There are so many people here. I didn't realise. I haven't seen this side of things. I think it's better to think there's nothing like this, nothing behind the front lines. War should be thoughtless, I think. I keep having to remind myself that today is Epiphany. It's so easy to lose track of time. I wonder if the weather was like this when the Wise Men discovered Our Lord? Across to Ypres it's dark, nothing in the sky, no stars, thank God. Tomorrow we return to our platoon. *Arise, shine*

150

out, Jerusalem, for your light has come, the glory of the Lord is rising on you, though night still covers the earth and darkness the peoples.

January 31st. Three inches of snow today. It is so cold. I've never known anything like it. Perhaps I've never really known what winter is. I must be very soft. I mustn't complain. Everything is holy. Septuagesima is three Sundays from Lent. Then I will fast. The duck-boards overflow with water, then freeze. Shaw tells me not to moan, at least we have the duck-boards, otherwise we would never have our feet out of water, and apparently they haven't always been here. I said I was a miner and used to being up to my waist in water. I shouldn't have said that. I don't know why I did. It's not true. Inundation happens, but it's never happened to me. It was always the dry heat with us. We were scared of fire, not water. I just didn't want him to think bad of me. They're so hard the older soldiers. They frighten me. I hate being frightened. I can't help it. I don't want to make a fool of myself. But Shaw is all right. He's been here a long time but is still nice. He looks after me really. He stopped me taking my boots off yesterday. I'm so stupid really. I've been told umpteen times that my feet would swell and I'd never get them back on. The others laughed. Shaw was nice. I don't know what I'd do without Shaw. Lots of men have frostbite. I don't really know what it is. I know the toes go black and fall off. I should ask Shaw but it just seems so stupid. When they go home I wonder if they say they were shot? I bet they do. It's supposed to be a war. I wonder which church Shaw used to go to? I don't really know anything about him. I'm too frightened to ask. I don't talk much to anyone. It doesn't matter. Nobody talks really. They never talk when it's snowing. They don't talk they just make jokes. Endless jokes. Sometimes they're funny, but they're not always funny. Sometimes they're a bit cruel really. They all do it though. Make jokes. It wears me out. I can't make jokes. If I try I make a real fool of myself. It was the same down the mine. I could never make a joke. The jokes down the mine were the worst thing. I wish I could fit in a bit better. Why can't I make a joke?

Sexagesima. Lots of men began diaries. New Year started it. Most of them have stopped already. Is it vain to keep a diary? I just thought I should. It's a chore really. It's easier to do nothing. But I shouldn't do nothing. It's a sin to do nothing. I should write home. I used to. When I was first here I wrote all the time. But what can I say to them? I can't tell them about the war, it's not really allowed. I ended up telling them about the weather. I don't want to tell them that. At least I don't have to tell Daddy there are so many Irish here. Apparently the army has adopted the Red Hand of Ulster but not the Harp. I suppose he'll get to know all about that, but I'm not going to be the one to tell him. I've done enough already. I hope he doesn't feel bad about not saying good-bye. It wasn't his fault. I'm sure he loves me. I don't think anything else. I'll never forget that first day down the mine. He was so surprising. I think about that often really. It helps a bit now, really, somehow. I'd like to write to Anne. She loves getting Peter's letters. I don't think she really liked it when they were in the papers. I could say things to Anne. I don't know what really. Just things. Maybe it is vain to keep a diary. I don't suppose I'll keep it. I'll throw it away when it's finished. I probably won't keep it up, anyway, not there in the trenches. It's easy now we're in reserve. I wonder if Anne would like to read my diary. I like to think of her reading it. When I write I imagine her voice reading it aloud. That would be nice. I'll write as much as I can for Anne. She'll know then, what it's like here, what it's like for me. I'll try and make her proud, proud of me. That would be something.

People are different in reserve. They talk a lot more. It must be the food and tea. We have to listen to Reid all the time, but no one seems to mind. Reid tells all sorts of stories. He's been here the longest. I don't know if they're true or not. He's been to Paris and all over. He said the French army turned up in taxis in the beginning. I can't believe that. Just another of his tales. He said all the French soldiers had to be collected from brothels. I didn't know what a brothel was. I made a fool of myself. I'm sure I did. He's always talking about women like that. Nobody minds. Reid says he's going to show me the interesting quarters of Paris on our next leave. He winked as he said it. Does that mean he's joking or not? It would be nice to see Paris, maybe once. McAllister and Davies both say they are going to Paris. Geddes says he's been. Nobody believes Geddes. They pulled his pants down to embarrass him. Geddes is twitchy at the best of times. He has a skinny face and his eyes and nose twitch constantly. I don't know why everybody gets annoyed at Geddes, but they do. Reid organises card games. We play for cigarettes usually, and sometimes for one of his Paris postcards. You get to keep it for one night. He says they're about seventeen years old. I won once. The picture was brown. A young girl stood at a large mirror. The mirror was enormous, fixed in a wooden frame, arched at the top, with four great carved legs on small wheels. She was holding each side of the glass along the arched top. There was a hanging basket full of flowers above her to the right. Beside her there was a small round table with slender legs and on top of the table there was a little vase with three roses. There was the leg of a chair with a striped seat just in the corner beside the little table. The girl's hair was in a bun with slides holding it in place. Her arm covered one eye of her reflection and her fringe came low over the other. Her nose and mouth were sweet. She was naked in the mirror, one breast sideways and one forwards, with a little triangle of hair just visible. Reid asked me if I wanted a name. I said I didn't. I don't know what he was laughing at. I didn't want to look but I did, I didn't mean... *Forgive me, Father, for I have sinned...*

February 13th. They drill us in the snow. We know how to be drilled. Drilling is all right because we're in reserve. The rest of the time we fill sand bags. So many sand-bags, mountains of sand-bags. We know what it means. We watch for premature spring. We are all fed up and yet glad of winter. No one wants a premature spring. Perhaps next year. Perhaps the year after. Something happened while we were sand-bagging. A man called Moore, a bit of rough character from our platoon, always swearing and carrying on, tells stories and jokes all the time, started bullying me. I don't know why. I hadn't done or said anything, not that I know of. I don't get up people's backs, I don't think. I don't mess about or anything, don't bother anyone with anything. He's never had a go at me before. I don't know what got into him really. He knocked me round a bit, swore at me and said I was a little cheat, a red-neck bastard, but that you'd never know from my accent. He said his brother-in-law had been in Dublin, and didn't come back, so he knew all about it, knew all about me. He just kept on and on, swearing and prodding and pushing me. God knows what it was all about. I didn't know what to do. He was too big for me. I couldn't have done anything about it even if I'd tried. Right in the middle of it Sergeant Brough came along. He saw what was happening straight away, but he looked away and started to whistle *It's a long way to Tipperary*. I thought there was no hope for me. I couldn't believe it really. Sergeant Brough is all right most of the time. He's a bit hard but then he has to be. I couldn't believe it when he turned away. I thought he was maybe scared of Moore. I felt really sick and, I have to be honest, I started to cry. I was wrong about Sergeant Brough though, thank God. As soon as he turned away Davies and McAllister came behind Moore and grabbed him around the throat. Moore struggled but Shaw and even Geddes joined in. Davies went a bit crazy actually. He was punching and using his elbow in Moore's face.

Davies and McAllister pulled his legs apart and told me to kick him. I couldn't. I couldn't do that. Davies did though. Moore screamed really loud. Brough was still whistling but then he turned to Moore and said: *Did you fall over soldier?* Moore could scarcely talk but managed to nod his head and squeeze out a *Yes, sir.* Soon as he heard that Brough went straight off. Davies and McAllister pulled Moore to his feet and let him go. Later Moore gave me a bar of chocolate. He said he didn't realise. He tried to talk to me for a while, but I didn't know what on earth he was going on about. He went on at me about my next leave. He seemed to be saying that he thought I'd be killed if I went home. Asked me if I knew that there was a place in London for the likes of me. The likes of me? I didn't know what to say. He gave me a pat on the shoulder when he left. Maybe he's a bit war crazy. It was good to have the chocolate though. Davies and McAllister are finishing it now. I don't know what got in to Moore. He was friendly enough afterwards. What makes men act the way they do? What didn't Moore realise? Maybe it's something they've seen. Maybe I'll know soon enough. The likes of me? I don't really know what most of them are getting at half the time. I feel like a little boy really. They make me feel like that. It's like I'm no good at things really. Well, the things they're good at. It's like down the pit. They all know what they're doing. They just get on with it. They're so strong. I could hardly lift the sand-bag. It frightens me really. What if I let them down, let them down badly, what then? Is that what he meant? The likes of me? It's terrible here really. I miss sitting in Father Bond's study, reading, listening to the birds outside his window. He always wanted me to read Saint John. He never tired of it. He's right, though, it's so lovely. *In the beginning was the Word, and the Word was with God, and the Word was God. The same was in the beginning with God. All things were made by him; and without him was not any thing made that was made. In him was life; and the life was the light of men. And the light shineth in darkness; and the darkness comprehended it not.* I wish I could say to him how lovely that is. I don't think I realised. It would be nice to read that to Anne. I hope she's all right. Poor Anne.

February 14th. In reserve but ordered to the salient at night. The G.S. wagons drove us from camp into Ypres. The road is cobbled, the trees bare. We passed the shattered walls of an asylum. It's all in bits. Everything is in bits. Bits of wheels, bits of walls, bits of trees. The snow covers a lot of it, but then it falls between all the cracks and crannies and leaves a strange disordered pattern. It's very odd. It doesn't make sense.

Everything is holy. I have to get on. We assembled in Ypres main square. It was pretty dark. There were just the lights from the cellars. They made the snow blue. Lights went up and down along the ridges of the enemy lines. Every few minutes another light went up. It's spectacular really. You'd never say that though. Even the sound of them bursting across the sky is lovely. I suppose in the day they can see everything that goes on in this city. God knows what there is to see though? It's such a funny place. It has no people, no real people. They've all gone. Now it's just the army. It's different outside the city. The farmers went, but they've come back. They'll be in the fields in spring. It's a funny war. We left the city on foot and marched right into swamp. It wasn't easy finding the duck-boards in the dark because the snow was level with the tops. We kept falling over. Still we kept running, though as always we stopped every now and again for no reason at all. We went towards the left sector. The canal which skirts Ypres and passes between the asylum and the town ran to the left of us. We had a funny job really, not supplying ammunition to the front, or anything like that, but reporting on the trees. We were told to make our way behind the reserve trenches towards Pilckem Ridge and beyond, as far as the Yser. We had to recross the canal which went behind enemy lines at Pilckem. We were to count, describe, and in the dawn, photograph trees. I suppose we've been asked to do stranger things. Something for the spring. Shaw said a platoon always gets a photograph of the line in front weeks before an attack, so you know which corner to run at. I don't want to think about it. I'm such a coward really. I rely on my book of Maximus Optimus. I read it constantly. I should thank Father Bond properly. I never did really. I copy bits so as to remember them better. It's easier than thinking of something to write sometimes. *I looked on my right hand, and beheld, but there was no man that would know me: refuge failed me; no man cared for my soul. I cried unto thee O lord: I said Thou art my refuge, and my portion in the land of the living.* It all went wrong though. We'd been running for a while and come to one of those funny stops. Everybody was listening, everybody quiet, just waiting, but then somebody lit a match. I saw the flame in somebody's cupped hands down the line. Everyone howled. The match was extinguished. We began to run. I could hear the duck-board crack, then the snap of machine-gun fire across our track. We scattered, diving this way and that. I jumped into a ditch. McAllister was beside me, pressed against me. In the pauses in the firing I could hear men still running across the snow. Then the firing stopped. It only went on for a minute or so. It's winter. What's the point. I stayed in the ditch though, still as I could. I could have slept and probably would have if McAllister hadn't been there. Perhaps he was thinking the same. We would never know. I pushed my fingers through the snow until I felt ice. We would have been lying in water. Someone was dead. I heard the scream during the firing and then the moaning and then it was quiet. It might be days before we know who. We were in the ditch quite a while, hours maybe. Maybe we did fall asleep, I don't know. Anyway, the light seemed different when I eventually saw somebody skulking along the duck-boards. I pulled myself up. It wasn't easy. I was frozen stiff and could hardly move. McAllister did the same. It was the sergeant who'd led the party. He came right by us. He didn't notice us at first though, just walked straight by. He was obviously looking for something. He looked so wrapped up we thought he'd cracked up a bit and kept quiet. A minute or so later he came back down the track. He caught sight of us that time. He was raging. He gave us a hell of an ear full. I assumed he'd been searching for the dead man, but I should have known better. He'd lost the camera. He was crazy about that. I thought we'd go back. After all, most of the party was missing and the camera gone. But he was having none of it. We had to look at the trees. What do they want us to say? What can we say? The trees are pitiful. The forest gives no shelter. There is no shelter. Our Lord was nailed to a tree like this. In fact, there are few trees along the sector. Perhaps there were. There is spoil. The land is too wet. Only poplars knit the horizon. As the first colouring of indigo sky lit around us we could see the serried rows of poplars along the plains. As the light increased we could see beyond the canal and beyond the Steenbeek river into the flood plain. Perhaps three miles away was the Houthulst Forest. We ignored it. Our report: *As with previous reports of the area east of Ypres around Hooge to Becelaere, so here too, area shows a great diminution of trees.*

At the Yser we cut back inland. The dawn lit up the snow fields around us. Morning mists hung over a succession of pale grey ponds. As we passed them we found that they were all frozen. Around the edges the ice was brittle and white and in the deeper water there were large clear sheets. The water is winning the battle. Soon it will all be water. It's coming. The appalling thing is I felt suddenly happy here. I couldn't help it. The crystal ponds were so beautiful in the early dawn. I imagined so much, felt so much. It was stupid. Lord, give me that courage though. *Yea, happy is that people, whose God is the Lord.* For a short while I was all right. I wasn't afraid of letting anyone down. I even thought Anne might be just a bit proud of me. It didn't last though. I'm not worthy. I get so scared. Later, when I lay sleeping in the barn a sergeant came and screamed at me to get my arse moving or face a Field Punishment. It was a pleasure to swear and turn over and sleep deeply. I will be with a working party again tonight.

Quadragesima. Then the devil taketh him up into the holy city and setteth him on a pinnacle of the temple, And saith unto him, If thou be the Son of God, cast thyself down: for it is written, He shall give his angels charge concerning thee: and in their hands they shall bear they up, lest at any time thou dash thy foot against a stone.
All this ice and snow, but no water to drink. In the forward trenches we rely on supplies. They don't bring enough. We have more whisky and rum than water. We chip bits of ice and suck it. My teeth sting when I suck it, but it's better than melting it. It's better not to know what's in the ice. Shaw told me that the ice has bodies frozen in it and that blood has run into it, but it doesn't stop him. Can I call this a fast? I don't know. Ash Wednesday came and went. No change. Today is the first Sunday of Lent. I am shy to think of the Lord in the wilderness. I don't want to be vain. I don't want to be proud. It isn't easy. God forgive me. *The tempter came to him and said: If thou be the Son of God, command that these stones be made bread.* I am too proud. Father Kellet came along the trench. There are lots of priests at the front. There aren't nearly as many Protestant ministers. I don't know why that is. He offered me communion. I turned away from him. I felt very ashamed. He's a good man. I quickly knelt at his feet in the mud. He's a beautiful looking man, a young man, with blond hair and an athletic figure. He's always very calm. I get angry at that, I don't know why. I asked him about the ice. He told me that if I am thirsty then I should drink. I wanted to know whether he would use the water. I'm so vain these days. What is happening to me. I must remember. *Thou shalt not tempt the Lord thy God.* I must fast. Our Lord fasted in the wilderness. I mustn't forget my obligations. *Blessed be the Lord my strength, which teacheth my hands to war, and my fingers to fight.*

*

Dora said grace: "Make us grateful for this meal which we hardly deserve but for your kindness Lord. Amen." When she had concluded she looked at her fist of hands. The fingers were white and the knuckles crimson. She waited. Eventually she heard her mother echo her amen.

She turned towards her. Her mother occupied herself in the task of pouring melted butter into a well of dry mash potato. Beside the potato were two unfilleted mackerel. Their eyes were creamy grey and popped at the sockets. The poached flesh was amber beneath the bruised skin. It was her father's job to share them out; but even when the well was full the fish remained untouched. She turned to him and found him looking patiently at her, waiting for her attention. "We don't usually bother these days," he said.

Smoke bellowed from the chimney. The air was tinged with it and dried their throats. Dora coughed and hid her face. She was determined not to display the apprehension she felt. "I just thought we might, tonight," she said softly, letting her tongue run along her sticky palate. "It's right, isn't it."

"If you want to pray then pray. If you want me to say amen I will. You understand that."

"I don't want you to do anything," she replied, wanting to sound far more bold than she felt. "I just don't want to act as if Robert is dead."

"He isn't dead."

"Then why are we afraid to pray?"

"I said, if you want to pray, then we will pray."

"That's not what you mean," Dora declared, openly despairing at the thought of Robert, her checked emotions flooding into her voice. "You mean you don't care. What if he does die? What then?"

John eyed her steadily. He was hurt by her accusation, but could think of no other way of dealing with that hurt than by staring it out. She recognised the hurt she had given him and broke under his gaze. She took her eyes from his. There was a short period of silence, then he uttered: "Pray for me." His voice was hoarse, little more than a retarded whisper. "Yes, pray for me," he repeated a few seconds later, though this time with more strength. Then he pushed back his chair, stood up and quit the table. He went to the fire, spat into the coals, then went out into the yard. The mackerel remained untouched.

It was raining hard. It bounced off the yard floor. Very quickly his jacket was heavy with it. He reached for his cigarettes tucked away in an inside pocket, but then realised the absurdity of it in that rain and begrudgingly gave it up. He cradled himself and looked into the falling sheet. As he gazed through the deluge he saw what looked like a figure on the wall. It was completely covered by a grey pall. It made no movement, but sat immobile. It looked like a peering ghoul. John picked up a piece of wood and went towards it.

As he came near the figure spoke to him. The voice was familiar and melodious. "A flood night for certain, Mr Devlin." John recognised Marty's voice and immediately burst out laughing, amused as much by his own caution as by Marty's ridiculous appearance. He nodded and agreed wholeheartedly that it was a flood night. Marty went on: "You're a man in a good humour, though, I can see that."

"No."

"A man to build something, though. A shelter, an ark, a trench, perhaps."

"I was coming to block you."

"Well, I hope you've changed your mind, on that score. Jesus, I wouldn't be a party to that at all."

"I suppose I might have changed my mind," John replied brusquely, then realising he still held his weapon threw it down. "Anyway, what the hell are you doing perched there spying on me?"

"I wouldn't have been spying on you at all if you hadn't come into the yard there. You got yourself spied on and no mistaking that."

"Did you not have a mind to come in?"

"No, to be honest, I did not."

"Why not?"

"Well I knew I could, like, if you know what I mean, and decided against it. To be honest with you, I wanted to feel a bit of rain."

"Christ, you'll have felt that plenty of times, Marty Boland. You should be expert enough by now."

"But never sitting quite so still like."

"You're a mad dog, you know that, mad altogether. God knows where your head came from, at all."

"And what would you be going saying a thing like that for?"

"I'd be saying it because of this thing draped across my wall."

"Ach, it's only an old sheet I'm wrapped in," Marty replied dismissively, then began pulling at the trail of material hanging across the wall. Two black orbits marked where his eyes peeped beneath the cover. "The priests would call it a bandage. I'll tell you the truth though, it's hopeless against the old water, I'll give you that, right enough."

"Come in, for God's sake, and have a bit of mackerel and champ, will you."

"No, John, I'd rather not."

"Ah, to hell with it!" John snapped, and without any more debate pulled at the sheet where he believed Marty's ear to be, and dragged him from the wall, across the yard and into the kitchen.

159

"What in the name of God is it," Kate screamed, backing away from the sodden, grey sheeted figure standing dripping in the centre of the kitchen.

Dora remained seated, still affected by her effort to talk about Robert.

"Only this half-wit," John replied, pulling the covering from Marty. Once exposed, Marty looked a forlorn beaten figure. He was limp with cold. His face was scrubbed red by rain, its indentations raw, and his hair was fast against his cheek bones. John ushered him to the table and pushed him down onto a seat. As he did he looked over the untouched meal. "I think we should eat," he said, an element of contrition colouring his voice. He looked at Kate and Dora in turn and appealed: "I think we should all sit down together and eat. What do you say? Will this champ warm? It will, won't it?"

Kate didn't reply but immediately picked up the pot and lay it close to the fire, then waited for the pool of solid butter to once again melt.

Marty sang softly, under his breath:

"There was an old woman who lived in a lamp
She had no room to beetle her champ
She's up with her beetle and broke the lamp
And then she had room to beetle her champ."

As he sang Dora stood up and went to take his fiddle case from him, which he held pressed against his chest. She was deeply relieved that the crisis seemed to be over for her father, and wanted to show that, as far as she was concerned, it was over for her too. Much to her surprise he was quite reluctant to yield the case and clung on to it. "Oh, come on, Uncle Marty," she pressed, trying to prise the thing from him, "it's time to eat. Let me have the case."

He held on tightly to it, then when she finally relinquished her grasp, he threw his hands into the air in a theatrical gesture and with his face fixed, uttered: "I don't feel worthy. I'm not worthy. No, I'm not worthy at all. Can you not tell, for God's sake? Not worthy at all." His voice trailed away to an undertone, and was taken up by the display of a soundless sob.

Dora pulled up her chair and quietly sat down beside him. She stroked his raw, gaunt features and tried to console him, though she couldn't comprehend this unusual outburst. "Look, we'll all be eating together. I don't know what you mean, but it'll be all right, you see. It'll be fine."

160

As she continued to stroke his cheek she looked up at her father, hoping to glean some meaning for Marty's utterance. John merely shrugged. He set to dividing the cold mackerel and sharing it out. When all the fish had been divided onto the plates Marty looked up at him and with a childlike, timorous expression, meekly asked: "Can I eat?"

"It's only a smattering of fish, for Christ sake!" John snapped, uncomfortable with Marty's strange behaviour. He was sure it was a symptom of real madness. He always suspected Marty of being half-mad, and supposed it was something that was likely to get worse over time. He was deeply uncomfortable with it. It was something that was beyond his control. He hated anything beyond his control. His instinct was to banish it. But how did you banish madness? The only possibility was to have Marty locked up. That was out of the question. Kate would never hear of such a thing.

Kate took the lead now. She simply suspected Marty of playing the fool and she wanted none of it. She roughly placed the bowl of warmed champ back on the table and as she did demanded: "Would there be any sense at all in asking just what on earth you were about, Marty Boland, and don't feed me any of your old fairy-tales?"

Marty had already already begun eating the fish. He had been using his fingers. He laid his hands down and let them rest directly on the mackerel flesh so that his palms were covering it. He very quietly said: "I was thinking about Robert. I was thinking that it was his birthday and all. That's the sum of it. I was thinking about Robert. I wished I could wish him a happy birthday, that's all."

There was a brief silence. It was Kate who broke it. She retorted: "Thinking about Robert is no reason to act like a damned fool, no reason at all."

"I was just wondering, Kate, that's all..."

"Shut up!" she snapped indignantly, and at the same time banged her hand down onto the surface of the table. "We don't know. He doesn't say. He doesn't manage to write anymore. That's all. But he's alive. We would know if it wasn't the case. We write to him. So that's all. No more. I don't want to hear anymore." She stopped speaking and stood very still. She knew her outburst was about to overwhelm her. She fought against it. Hadn't she just said that she didn't want to hear anymore. Robert would have his own, peculiar reasons, reasonable only to himself, for not writing. And as they would make sense to him they would have to accept that. Yet still the tears came. "To hell with it," she muttered, leaning on the table for support. "To hell with it all. What

161

damned right have they to take my boy? He's no soldier, for God's sake. Robert would never make a soldier."

John stood up and put his arm around her and held her below the armpit, supporting her. He spoke up strongly, his voice reverberating around the small kitchen. He knew he was speaking to himself as much as to them: "He is alive. And he'll be back. And when he's back everything will be as it was. And we'll celebrate then. Do you hear? That'll be the time to celebrate, when he's with us."

Kate turned to him. Her face was puffed and blotchy. "Why doesn't he write, tell me, why doesn't he? I don't understand that."

John couldn't answer. Dora recognised that he couldn't and spoke for him. "So as not to worry us, of course. Why do you think? Besides, he'll be busy. You know Robert, always on with something. He won't realise that we might appreciate a letter. You know Robert. He's a bit thoughtless at times, that's all."

John looked down towards Dora as she spoke and smiled. When she was through she smiled back. They knew that their antagonism had vanished, and that their compact had been renewed through Kate. He reached down and took Dora's hand. Kate noted it. She sighed deeply and then laughed. The sound was stubborn and it was weary, but it wasn't niggard. She said: "Robert will have his head in a book, I suppose. Of course he will. That's what he's like."

"Where else," Dora agreed.

"It's one of the things we love about him. And I'm not heating this again, so will we all sit ourselves down and eat."

John said: "You can say grace again Dora, if you like."

Dora recited quickly, without ceremony: "For what we are about to receive may the Lord make us truly thankful."

"Thank you," John said. A few seconds later he quietly added: "Robert will do well enough as a soldier, you'll see."

They ate in silence. Before the meal was complete Patrick started to shout from the front-room where he slept. Kate shuffled off to answer him taking some mackerel with her, saying that maybe he was a little hungry. John lay his fork beside his plate, and watched her as she went off to answer his summons. His features folded into a fixed grimace. A moment later he became aware of Dora gazing at him. He picked up his fork and resumed eating without saying anything.

*

162

March 15th. We are weary of snow. Day after day it falls. Premature spring is a joke. The world is an empty bowl of snow. It's entirely quiet. Nothing seems alive. Everything has submitted to the snow. I'm so cold. So cold. Nothing new. I'm too cold and stiff to move. I just want to stay still. It's too terrible this cold. It never ends. I'm sick of myself. I feel tearful lots of the time. I wish I didn't. I want to say to someone that I'm cold, but not these. What's the point? They know. They're cold. We're all cold. We don't talk. We have no need to talk. We know that we're cold. Do they know I'm afraid? I'm sure they do. I'll try to be worthy. I'll try. Maybe they're afraid too. Who knows? Maybe that's why they're so sarky and bad tempered. We don't talk. That's how it is. Dear Lord, help me not to let Shaw down. Make him proud of me. Help make me act like a man. I'm on a high bridge and can only go forward and I'm afraid, so afraid. *My heart is smitten, and withered like grass; so I forget to eat my bread.* Make me not afraid. I'm so cold. Oh God, I'm so very, very cold. *My bones cleave to my skin...*

Palm Sunday. On this day Christ rode in triumph from the Mount of Olives into the city of Jerusalem. The multitude lay their cloaks across the ground before Him so that He could ride over them and they cut palms and lay those across His path too, but that wasn't His triumph. No, it wasn't the fact that He was worshipped that was His triumph. The triumph was that He kept his bargain, kept faith with the prophets and with God and with all who came after. He entered the city as it had been written. *Fear not, daughter of Zion: behold the king cometh, sitting on an ass's colt.* And already He knew He was to die. He can never have doubted it. He had no choice but to ride into the city, knowing only too well that crucifixion awaited Him. And John said that Lazarus was with Him and the priests wanted to put Lazarus to death. But how can you kill a man who has been raised from the dead? How can you kill those promised eternal life? *O Lord, do not leave me alone, my strength, make haste to help me!*

I think Shaw saw me cry. I had to walk off. I tried to see Father Kellet, but was told he was in the front trenches. He's always in the front trenches. He never seems afraid. I must learn that. It's right that I should learn from him. He is my priest. I should look up to him. Why don't I always look up to him? He's obviously better than me. How else would he be a priest? I don't know what gets into me at times. I walked away from the camp into the open country. There was a very heavy fall of snow. It swirled all around me. I couldn't see. The winter is endless.

When it let up I was surrounded by fresh white fall. It had no marks or prints. Mountains of blue-grey cloud hung across the skies and down to earth at each horizon. I felt concealed within snow and cloud. I felt hidden and secret. It was lovely. I had no need to say I was afraid, no need to speak at all. I was away from it all, safe. I suppose it was stupid standing in the snow feeling like that, but I couldn't help it. I just felt for a time that the war wasn't the most important thing. It was so lovely making fresh footmarks, disturbing the gently rested snow. It was just lovely finding myself so alone. Thank God I hadn't been in a forward position. I knew they would have missed me at camp, but Shaw had seen me cry and would have seen me all right. If I'd been at the front they would have shot me. But not here. Shaw would have said something. I imagined I was entering the city of Jerusalem mounted on an ass, and had no doubts but had kept faith, without vexation. I looked across all the skies. I'd never seen cloud so beautiful, skies so wide. I fell into the snow. I could hear the blood pulse behind my ear. The clouds spun overhead. I swept the snow with my forearms. It was soft. I lay still. What would Anne have thought seeing me lying there with a war going on near-by? I watched the cloud drift across the sky. I prayed, I prayed with so much love. I love you, Jesus, I love you... *O my Father, if this cup may not pass away from me, except I drink it, thy will be done.*

When I got back to camp Davies asked me where I'd been. I told him that I'd been to mass. He seemed embarrassed. He pointed out that I was soaked. I laughed and reminded him it was snowing. It's started again.

Easter Day. Pearly spring. Not a cloud in the sky. The frost has hardened the mud. Christ is resurrected. *We did eat and drink with him after he rose from the dead.*

April 16th. We have been fumigated, fed and got drunk on cheap red wine. We can hardly believe our luck, being so far from the front, billeted in a farm in a small village near St Omer and ordered to rest. We are lying in straw in a cow-shed finishing off the wine, eating chocolate and smoking. It's still raining. It's rained for days. We listen to the insistent rattle on the cow-shed roof. The air inside is heavy and warm with the airless odour of animals. We all wish it would stop raining. If it stopped raining we would explore the village some more. The rain makes me think of the front. I try not. Perhaps spring will never reach the trenches. I remember the Senegalese soldiers crouching in the trenches, the rain soaking their blue coats. They were completely numb with cold, their faces dark, lean and so very sad. They get treated very badly. I can't understand why they are here. I would send them home. I must ask Shaw where Senegal is. Do they believe in God? Shaw explains many things. He told us this morning that he heard they're shooting foxes in England. He heard the Captain complaining about it. I didn't know what he was talking about. It had something to do with losing the sea, getting supplies through. He explained that food shortages must be serious if they're shooting foxes. He said that was why we went to the coast at the start of the year. He reckons they'll be planning to win the Belgian ports and the U-boat bases this summer. I don't understand. I didn't say anything. I wonder what they're doing at home. I must write. I hope Anne is all right. I was supposed to look after her for Peter. I think of Anne often. I can see her settling the thick curls of her dark hair in the sea breeze. I keep my faith. I will write to Anne. I will write to my mother. But what will I say? I pray to God they're not hungry at home. It's so confusing. Surely they can't be hungry at home too. The war is here, not there. They want nothing being hungry. I must write. But how can I write? I've nothing to say.

April 18th. Sunshine. Everybody in a good mood, Reid telling jokes. He says very rude things. He asked me if I had a girl back home. I told him that there was plenty of time for that, I was in no rush. He got angry at me. I don't understand. I don't have to be like him.

Pentecost. Three words of French, *bonjour, au revoir, merci,* such strange words. I haven't done very well. Shaw has given up on me. I'm so lazy. I can't bring myself to do anything. I'm lapse in so many ways. I don't write home. I scarcely write in my diary. I have nothing to say. I can imagine Father Bond shouting at me, saying confession and delight, remember, confession and delight. I want to be good. I want to do what's right. It isn't easy. I don't know. I'm frightened. I'm too frightened to pray. We're near Hill 60 and there's so much noise. Shaw reckons I should point out that I'm a miner and get into Hill 60. He can't understand how I wasn't put with the engineers. But I can't stand it. There's shouting all the time, men swearing, screaming bad words, screaming over the parapet from the entrance saps. I want to cover my ears but I don't want to be a fool. I can't stand all the shouting. I can't stand all the machines. The sound never stops. Engines, pumps, the earth grinding, shaking with the motors, drilling somewhere, but where? I'm a

165

miner, but where? It thumps all of the time. I never experienced a mine like this. The earth throbs with the workings. What's happening? And then the shells. All of the time. It never stops. My cot shakes. I hang in it. I'm frightened of falling, frightened to move. What shall I say? I want to write to Anne. I miss her. I miss my mother. I want to say... I want to cry. The noise doesn't stop. I mustn't be lapse. I must ask Shaw, but later. I'm tired now. I need to sleep. I need to pray. Everything is holy. *The Spirit of the Lord fills the whole world. It holds all things together and knows every word spoken by man, alleluia.* Confession and delight.

Trinity. Lying in my cot, alive with lice. Dry dust falls between the timbers. Foul smelling water gushes underneath. Everyone shits and pisses in it. The cots are wire-meshes strung to the walls of the saps leading into Hill 60. We've been delivering ammonal. The place stinks with it. Foul water, excrement and ammonal. We've been ordered to get some kip before we're moved back out. Sleep is impossible here. There's too much noise. There are too many voices along the galleries. We listen to each other's voices. Someone says the fields are full of buttercups. Someone else says that the French are mutinying. Lots of us have heard the same. It's all rumour, of course. Word has come up the line that the red flag flies over the French camp at *Chemin de Dames.* We don't know what it all means. There's a lot of excitement, and everybody is afraid. Are we going to be alone? We're afraid of being alone. We feel it lying in our cots. There's a phrase passing around the galleries: *Replace me; I'm tired...* Despite the noise and the stink I don't want to leave here. I don't want to leave this bunk. The stink is all right. Why not? There's stink wherever they send you. Shaw's right. I'm a miner. It's safe underground. I should say. I can't leave Shaw though. I have to be with Shaw. I'd go mad without Shaw. Maybe we'll stay here awhile. Who knows? To hell with the noise. I don't care if I don't sleep. I just want to stay underground. I could dream that I was leading Little King inbye. He was such a quiet and intelligent animal. I loved Little King. He was the Lord's horse. He didn't seem blind underground, making his way along the main road. I never thought I'd miss Loft, but I do. I miss it so much. There's no use crying, is there. Who would hear me among this lot? *You are blest who gaze into the depths. You are blest in the firmament of heaven.*

June 17th. I've been in battle. I expected to say more. Somehow it was all familiar. I'm vain, puffed up with it. I'm become untouchable. I wish

I felt differently. We were prepared on the night of the sixteenth. Past midnight the artillery pumped across the sky. It continued relentlessly. I crouched in a tent in the rear. For a few minutes Shaw held my hand. Shaw is a brave man. It was like being with Peter waiting for the Orangemen. I remember that was so good. Peter taking my hand, Shaw taking my hand. They are so good. They are real mean, I suppose. But I've been in battle. I'm real. Shortly before three in the morning the shelling abruptly stopped. There was a rosy glow as weak streaks of dawn seeped into the sky. Clusters of flares went up from the German trenches. Stillness everywhere. And then the earth began to rock as if the sea had finally burst across Flanders. Had I dreamed of letting it loose? But I've dispensed with childlike badness. Before us a large black mass rose into the air suspended by scarlet flame. It remained for seconds. Flame lit the whole countryside. No sound. Before me men rose out of the ground advancing towards the eruption. The barrage commenced. Shells began tearing at our trench. We crouched low. We wanted to be deeper underground. We wanted back into the earth.

We didn't move forward until late afternoon. In battle the earth moves. It's the movement you fight against. Fountains of soil spout across the field. We advanced through this fire into the woods around the rail-line. We were already further than the German support trenches. Rifle fire sounded through the distorted trees until dusk. There were endless screams for stretcher bearers. We found ditches among the trees and lay down. The noise faded. All the time we waited for the counter attack. I prayed in the ditch for it to be over. *He shall cover thee with his feathers, and under his wings shalt thou trust: his truth shall be thy shield and buckler. Thou shalt not be afraid for the terror by night; nor for the arrow that flieth by day.* I wanted to sleep. We were ordered to dig in before dawn. We worked beneath the spidery shadows of the trees, deepening and widening the trench. When dawn broke the wood was shelled again. We crouched in the trench unable to move. We had no way of knowing what was happening. The shelling didn't stop. We remained dug in. We stayed there for three days unable to move. The trench floor ran with piss and shit. We were numb from the damp. We hated each other. We were relieved on the third night. Battle is a case of enduring filth. *A thousand shall fall at thy side, and ten thousand at thy right hand; but it shall not come nigh with thee.*

*

167

Pansies, marigolds, primroses, irises and stock. The flower harvesters moved through the cord stems filling their baskets, Anne and Kate together, maintaining a slow constant progress along the cliff plateau. Even at the moment of coming to the cliff edge they had not thought of the nature of the naming of clustered petals. There were no *Virgin Mary* or *Rainbow Goddess*. There were only flower-heads of yellow, blue and white. Anne threw flowers down the walls of sandstone simply to see them fly, to see them descend towards the vast boulders at the cliff base, not as any gesture towards sea or sky. Sea and sky were one, pale blue and lined with trails of white, like an elaborate writing. The flower-heads spun to a level where nothing was read or desired to be read. The sea breeze flung the small stems and blew their skirts against them. Seagulls circled and rose on currents of warm air, moaned and cried against the great bellies of rock where guillemots were deserting the ledges for the open sea. Their black and white droppings daubed the crevasse fractured cliffs.

"Pansy, marigold, primrose, iris, stock," Anne murmured, carelessly tossing the flowers beyond the edge. Kate watched as the falling flowers progressed, catching on ledges or gorse, or were blown back towards the banks from where they had been picked. And some occasionally fell beyond view. The waste appalled her, but she couldn't bring herself to challenge Anne. No longer picking herself, she walked away keeping close to the edge. Anne continued. Kate remained aware of the dull monotony of her voice. It disturbed her. She called against the sound of the cliffs: "Don't bother naming them, Anne. That doesn't matter."

Anne turned to her and said: "Robert called this the cliff of the crying babies." Kate listened but made no response. "I told him that he made it sound terrible. He said it was. He said it was a war of sorts." She paused. She instantly regretted what she had just said. She had been angry at him for saying it. She shouldn't have shared it with Kate. "He just meant the birds, of course," she continued, by way of a corrective. "Just the birds. I see the guillemots are leaving. I wonder how they sleep out at sea?"

Kate stopped walking and looked down at the ledges where the guillemots had bred. So, Robert had an opinion about this. He had spoken about it. He had called it a war. It was something she didn't know, a thought of his she had never shared. It was difficult to discover aspects of him, words and deeds, of which she didn't know. She had a strong desire not to be ignorant of him in anyway. She felt mildly jealous of Anne. She told herself that it was ridiculous, but there was no getting away from it.

She watched the birds fly low over the light coloured sea, off into the distance. There were boats along the horizon almost too small to see. She looked back at Anne. She was waving at the little ships. She was laughing to herself as she did. She became aware of Kate's attention. "Do you think they can see me from out there?" she laughed. "How do I look? Like a soldier's wife?" Her hair blew across her face.

"No, not at all," Kate responded ruthlessly.

Anne pushed the bunches of hair from her face. "No?" she asked, smarting from the answer.

"Peter isn't a soldier. He's just fighting in a war."

"Is there a difference then?" Anne demanded, retaliating against her rebuke. Kate didn't answer.

They both stood and looked out to sea. They felt the swell of air as it rushed through the globe of the cliff. Below them gulls flew in and out of interconnecting lines, creating imaginary shapes in the air. Shapes they created and then let fall to the gentle but explosive foam below. And they both thought the same thing without sharing it with the other. The gulls did cry like babies. It was a sound they were both familiar with. And Robert had named it for them. He had perhaps stood where Kate was standing now and had named it. She took a handful of marigolds from her basket and cast them down the cliff, imitating Anne as if she now understood her. The flowers were a gift, an act of devotion, because he had been there, because he had named it. She watched the flowers scatter on the breeze and fall. The sea gaped. The little ships had sunk from view.

Anne spoke to her. Her voice was pensive. "Do you worry much, Aunty Kate, that they'll not come back?"

Kate continued to watch where the marigolds landed for some time before answering, the florets moving like fingers through the gorse spines. Eventually she said: "I worry that they'll come back and not realise they are."

"You mean crazy?"

"No, tainted."

"Not Peter and Robert, though, surely."

Kate shrugged. "We don't know, do we. We don't know anything about it." The gulls cried. She clapped her hands at them, irritated by their relentless demands, but they merely circled on and on.

169

"I despise not being able to say that it's wrong," Anne said sharply. "I resent that."

"Why not say it?"

"Who would hear me? You, the birds?" Anne turned back seaward and stared into the depth. "I'm the one who'll go crazy. I don't know what's real at all, Aunty Kate. I don't know where it all ends, and nor do you. We know nothing. Nothing at all. It's not fair." Kate came to her. She was disturbed by the recklessness of Anne's emotions. She took her arm. Anne stared in her face. The crisis was not complete. "The sun's shining for God's sake! Look at it. Where is it? Where is the war? I don't even know where the countries are. I don't know anything. All I get are his blasted Field Service Postcards. Apparently he's been in London. He's been injured. He's been... Oh, what do I know what or where he's been? What do I matter that I should know? Who the hell am I?" She broke down and hunched into Kate. As she did she continued staring at the distant horizon, as if appealing wordlessly to it for a clue. There were no little ships, only a bar of the softest light. "All I know is," she said, catching her breath, "that he's in the world somewhere and the world is horrible. Horrible! It's all a world of lies! Just lies! He's in the world but what the hell is the world in?" She turned her fury to the seabirds and began screaming at them, repeatedly calling to them: "Shut up! Shut up!"

"Shush," Kate said, and at the same time as she tried to soothe her she led her away from the cliff edge. She told her to lay her basket down and sit on the grass. The grass was leathery and springy. The sea breeze dropped and with it the gull sound sank, muted beyond the crown of cliff. Only occasional solitary birds glided up, peered over the rim of grass, and cried at the spreading earth. The sea consisted of the horizon. It was as quiet as the sky. The sky was still, without drift or drag. Skylark song was everywhere. The two women didn't speak. They composed themselves by looking at sea and sky. Little ships returned to the horizon. They gave up the desire to piece land with land. It was too much. Eventually they lay back on the grass. They didn't sleep, but simply lay together.

Shortly after they had lain down Dora came. She knew where they had gone and had come looking for them. She carried Bill in her arms and Patrick held her skirt. She squinted down at the two and said: "Lord Singer's circus is coming into town. I thought you might want to see." Kate sat up immediately and skewed her face at Dora as if she disputed the news. Dora insisted: "I saw the cages myself coming along the Strand, but no animals."

Kate stood up and looked towards the town. Beyond the workings of Loft pit she could see a tracery of its grand houses and dingy streets. She turned to Dora. "Why?" she asked, her tone startled, incredulous.

Dora laughed. "Why not?"

"They want nothing here at this time," Kate said adamantly.

"Perhaps it's just what everybody needs," Anne suggested.

"I don't want anyone to go," Kate said decisively. "Not this time. Maybe next time." She paused, eyed Anne and Dora in turn, then smiled as if to say she had not gone crazy, it was just that it struck her as somewhat improper. They would not have contradicted her. "Come on," she said, "we were picking flowers when we weren't wasting them."

She looked at the boats dragging through the slow silver waters of the horizon as if she half suspected an ark of bringing strange beasts to their shore. She walked away and began stooping at the stems of wild flowers. She avoided looking into the valley. She resumed her picking as if it were a way of not seeing a circus animal. The world was simply no place for the fabulous or magical. She wanted everything to remain as it was, so that when Robert returned the cliff of the crying babies would remain simply a name for mothering sea birds, not a place where an ark came to ground. She continued to pluck the flowers with a restrained fury. Dora and Anne followed her, and the quiet harvest of flowers, without symbols or names, was sustained. Patrick ran across a plain of daisies kicking and screaming. Bill began to cry. Anne took him from Dora. Kate looked back. The sea had disappeared below the edge of the cliffs. The space between sky and earth was endless. Dora knit a chain of marigolds and placed it around Bill's neck.

*

July 25th. Thunderstorms. I don't think our artillery has stopped since the 15th. Can it really have gone on for ten days? Maybe I'm mistaken and it just seems so long. It's not so easy keeping track of the days. We've come under constant air attack. There's been much destruction. Trenches and entanglements have been destroyed, dugouts smashed. One of our forward telephone dugouts was wrecked. We saw the earth explode. Sergeant Brough asked someone to help bring in the wounded. No one moved at first, but then Shaw went. I followed. I have to be with Shaw. I feel so out of place without Shaw. All we found were legs, three pairs of legs severed at the waist. I think for a time we must have all three gone mad because the sergeant let me go into the dressing station for a doctor. He screamed insults at us and ordered us to bury the damned things. The dressing station smelled. The aroma was incredibly sweet.

August 2nd. An ammunition wagon had only been there for a few seconds when a shell killed the horse underneath the driver. We all stood there for a few minutes just looking at the bulk of the animal lying heavy in the wet, sludgy ground. Then I went up and tried to unharness it and cut the traces away. There was no point. It didn't help. It had a dead face. Its eyes were open and blind. There was no light there at all. I just stared at those big eyes looking dully back at me. Horses are better off down the pit than they are here. They have such a terrible time of it. There are so many dead horses and dead mules. The place stinks with dead animals. Sergeant Brough said: Never mind, sonny. Why the hell did he call me sonny? I realised I was on my knees. I don't know why, but it felt embarrassing. I couldn't move, though. I was crying and I couldn't move. Damn it! I couldn't move and I couldn't get Little King out of my mind. I thought it was Little King on the ground in front of me. That's all I could think, that it was Little King in the mud. Little King the Lord's horse. It was all too terrible. I cried and cried. Why did he call me sonny? I miss Little King. Shaw helped me up. I can't say anymore.

August 10th. Over the top. There were men lying in the mud. They were all wounded. Their faces just looked up as we ran past. There were Germans as well. We just pressed on. We were told to move. We were spread out in open formation a few yards apart. There was firing all of the time, but it seemed someway off. There were men falling either side of me. I didn't understand. I couldn't work out where the firing was coming from. Someone came up on the right of me. As I turned to see who it was he went down. I didn't see his face. I didn't stop. I traipsed on for a while longer but then I couldn't go on any further and I fell into a ditch. I found myself squirming in thick yellow mud. It stunk of gas. Still, I put my face down into it. The noise didn't stop though. It was both close and far. At times remote and then all around me. It was strange, drifting in and out of earshot like that. At times I didn't know which way I was really facing. I don't know how long I'd lain there when I felt something drop down beside me. It must have hit me on the side. I didn't really feel it, but it must have done. It can't have been the sound of something falling in the mud. The mud swallows everything. The mud even swallows shells. They make a strange muffled uproar when they blow. I lifted my face out of the quagmire and looked around. My heart missed a few beats. I thought it most likely to be an unexploded shell. There was a tin of Woodbines beside me. Someone was standing over me. I looked up. It was Father Kellet. He just stood there, looking down at me. His expression wasn't severe, but it wasn't sympathetic either. He simply gazed at me. It wasn't as if he seemed desperately interested, or bored for that matter. He was simply there and he'd thrown a tin of Woodbines beside me. I lifted myself up so that I was on all fours. As I did, I expected him to smile. I don't know why. I don't even know what I thought the smile would mean, but I know I waited for it. It didn't happen though. Nothing did. He just continued looking down. I suddenly thought I should have said something. I was sure I was failing in some response. But that was crazy. I was in the middle of battle. I was crawling through mud. Surely there's no response. I couldn't have got that wrong. I got to my feet but remained bent over. The machine-gun fire was coming thicker than ever. I still couldn't work out exactly where it came from. Father Kellet began to walk forward. He took slow steps. He didn't seem at all concerned for his own safety. I quickly snatched up the tin of Woodbines. I called to him. He turned. I tossed him back the tin. He caught it in both hands, shrugged then immediately turned away and continued forward. Within seconds I'd lost him amongst the mud, wire and smoke. I couldn't move. In that instance I hated him. How dare he walk on in that shameful manner as if it was nothing. It wasn't fair. Personally I wanted to run back. I couldn't face any more mud and bullets, the slops of men's guts trailed in the quagmire. It was too much to ask. And yet the priest had wandered on. I shouted out loud, objecting to it, but then found myself charging forward again. I couldn't go back, not when he had gone on. I screamed as I ran. Without knowing how, I got myself back with my own platoon. When I caught up with them they were making for a pillbox some hundred yards or so ahead. We went about fifty yards and were told to get down. A moment later we were told to get up again and take it. As we got up we came under heavy machine-gun fire. There were men falling to both right and left. We kept on. We came right up to the parapet. I saw Geddes jump in. A second later I saw him impaled on a bayonet. It came right through his chest and stuck out of his back. I saw the look on his face. He was surprised, that was all, ridiculously surprised. He wasn't whinging at all. He was just too surprised for that. The German fired. I lifted my rifle and aimed at the German. Before I could fire he went down. There

173

was firing from everywhere. All the Germans were shot down. Geddes lay on top of the German who had bayoneted him. I saw someone lift him off. His chest was wide open. His lungs were hanging loose. He was dropped back onto the German. The pillbox had a heap of dead bodies in its centre all laying together, one across another, arms and legs intertwined, wrapped around each other, strangely still and peaceful. As I continued to look a shell went off a few yards from the pillbox. A shower of mud splattered across it. Someone screamed at us to move forward. I hesitated. I didn't want to leave Geddes. He was always so edgy and twitchy. The scream went up again. I started running. The field kept erupting in showers of mud. I was sure everything was going to sink into it, slowly vanish beneath its filthy, stinking tide. Geddes would be buried with the Germans. They would have the same filthy grave. Then the shelling became so heavy we had to take cover. I ended up here in this stinking pillbox with nine others. We're from the same platoon but I don't know them that well at all. We've been stuck here for hours. It's almost dark. We'll spend the night here now, I presume. We'll be safe enough. The walls are incredibly thick. It's German, of course, so it's well made. The entrance faces the German lines, but that doesn't matter. It's far from comfortable, though. It's only about five feet high and the bottom two feet are flooded. The water is rancid, full of old tins and shit. Luckily there's a sort of concrete shelf just below ground level. We're all huddled on the shelf, four officers and six men. There isn't room to lie down or even sit properly. We're just crouching, watching the night sky fill in over the battlefield. Outside the pillbox there's an enormous shell-hole full of water. There's a dead German in that. I think he must have been there for some time. His body is bloated, his skin ruptured, coloured creamy yellow like beef fat. At times he floats and then he sinks, only to appear again a few hours later. I can't work out why that should be. He's there and then he isn't. A bit like Father Kellet. I have the distinct impression that I won't see Father Kellet again. I'm certain he's dead. I don't know why. Just a feeling. He really was such a beautiful man, not at all as I would imagine a priest. I wish he'd heard my confession. I really want that now. I want his forgiveness. I know I'll never have it though. Strange what you just know in battle. I pray that I'll find Shaw in the morning. I know Shaw is still alive. As much as I know Father Kellet is dead I know Shaw is alive. I'm so sad when I'm not with Shaw. Somewhere out there he'll be sheltering in some water-logged hole. Or maybe some of them fell back to safer lines. I must find him. I'll go mad without Shaw. There's a partially formed moon overhead. It's

174

visible in the brief breaks in the cloud. It seems to have been overcast for weeks. The drizzle never stops. It's light, but drenching. I can feel it now, soaking through me. It hasn't become completely dark. It's never completely dark at this time of year. It's simply grey and blurred. Flares go up continually. There's no darkness, no silence, no rest. I don't know how I'm going to stay here like this all night. My body feels broken already. I must stick it out. Tomorrow I'll find Shaw. I must keep faith. This is the trial God set for me. *Thou hast caused men to ride over our heads; we went through fire and through water: but thou broughtest us out into a wealthy place.* I should pray for Father Kellet. He was such a beautiful, athletic man. Forgive me Father. I cannot pray here. My back is broken and I can no longer feel. Tomorrow I will pray. Tomorrow I will find Shaw. Tomorrow I will go on.

August 12th. It's rained for days. Thunderclouds rolled across the sky, the plateau always dark, any time of day. We had to run across the plateau. That's all we've been doing. Running, running, running. Our coats were water-logged and incredibly heavy. It made me hot and feel sick. I was grateful to drop into a trench. I just lay there. A window of sky opened up and became increasingly blue. I lay in the mud. I felt cool and then I felt cold, so very cold. I wanted to be sick, and then I wanted to sleep. I jump from need to need. It's crazy. I feel I'm going to shit myself, but I never do. In fact, I'm bound up most of the time. I don't know what I'm feeling. I realise that when I'm running all I think about is going to earth. I tell myself it isn't fear, but what is it? In the end I was sick. I had to lie with the smell. *In my distress I called upon the Lord, and cried unto my God: he heard my voice out of his temple, and my cry came before him, even unto his ears. Then the earth shook and trembled; the foundations also of the hills moved and were shaken, because he was wroth. There went up smoke out of his nostrils, and fire out of his mouth devoured: coals were kindled by it. He bowed the heavens also, and came down: and darkness was under his feet.*

August 13th. Wire holds men up long after they are too heavy to stir. They moan out loud but are not real. They have strange clumsy postures. We scream back at them. We are pitiless. Of course, many are German. *He shall go to the generation of his fathers; they shall never see light. Man that is in honour, and understandeth not, is like the beasts that perish.*

175

August 14th. Yesterday I used the word *honour*. God forgive me.

August 17th. We ran from shell-hole to shell-hole. The holes are full of water. It stinks. Just putting one foot in front of the other is hell. It sinks into mud. My whole body is covered. I'm covered from head to toe in filth. I can't feel myself anymore. As I lay in the hole I heard the rattle of a harness in the distance. There was an ammunition wagon coming up behind me. It was unmistakable. It was like a sign. I know it was wrong. But I'm so tired. I can't keep pulling my legs through the mud. I've no energy left. I'm exhausted. I just can't move. I knew I was close to the roadway. It would be so easy. If I just put my leg out the wagon would go over it. I could plead it was an accident. The sound of the harness grew closer and closer. Eventually, as I looked back, I saw the heads of the leading horses. I began to ease out of the hole. I slithered along the mud floor. And then I stopped. I pressed myself into the filthy floor. The ammunition wagon went clattering by. I didn't have the guts to do it. I just lay there shaking. I'm such a coward. How will I ever be able to look at Shaw again? I cried with my face in the mud. I stood up and trudged on. There was shelling all around me. I walked on and on, pulling my feet out of the quagmire, slow step by slow step, going nowhere.

August 20th. We've fought against mud for three days. It's endless. This whole land is under water. We've scarcely moved at all. That's hard to accept. After so much effort to have moved nowhere is inconceivable. We can no longer rise. We lie in the mud. We watch the walls trickle towards us. It mixes with our shit. Shaw is leaning against me. Showers of mud slop over us from the deluge of shells. I press my book *Maximus Optimus* against me. I'm still alive. How is that? I'm with Shaw. I have to be with Shaw. I'm afraid. I'm so afraid. How am I still alive? *Lord bring me up again from the depths of the earth.*

August 21st. McAllister came walking towards me from the mud and smoke. I shouted at him as he passed. I wanted to know where he thought he was going? I didn't really expect him to hear me through all the noise but somehow he did. He answered me. I heard him. I clearly heard him say Paris. He said he was going to Paris. Paris! I saw him fall. He was hit in the back. I hope they don't find his body. *O Lord. What profit is there in my blood, when I go down into the pit? Shall the dust praise thee? Shall it declare thy truth? Hear, O Lord, and have mercy upon me:*

176

Lord be thou my helper. Lord thou hast turned for me my mourning into dancing.

August 24th. Relieved. I don't understand.

September 14th. We're in reserve. We don't talk much. We don't have much to say, besides we're scared about falling out. We want to do as we like. There are no masters here. Except Shaw. A school-master. I asked him things about himself. I was surprised he answered. I'm not sure what that means. Shaw is married. His wife's name is Alice. He has a daughter. She is also called Alice. Shaw's name is Walter. I am Robert. He doesn't have a usual church at home. He doesn't believe in God. I wish he'd told me nothing. I wish I'd never asked. I want him to be proud of me. How can that be? I'm so afraid. I'm afraid of Shaw. Nothing makes sense. I'm still alive. I wanted to tell him about Anne, but I didn't. I didn't really have anything to say. *O God, Remember thy congregation which thou hast purchased of old; the rod of thine inheritance, which thou hast redeemed; this mount Zion, where in thou hast dwelt. Lift up thy feet unto the perpetual desolations; even all that the enemy hath done wickedly in the sanctuary. Thine enemies roar in the midst of thy congregations. They have cast fire into thy sanctuary, they have defiled by casting down the dwelling place of thy name to the ground.*

October 6th. We were brought back to the Salient at night. The traffic to and through Ypres is endless. The wagons shunt forward beneath skies coloured bright with Very lights. We can hear planes above us. We don't want to be shot from the air. It's possible. There are more and more air attacks. We're silent so as not to be heard. It's better like that. It's always too soon to be sent back to the front.

October 7th. We left Ypres on the Menin Road in the early morning. It was still dark. Artillery batteries lit up the sky and revealed the extent of the bog all around us. We could see abandoned machinery sunk into it. The roadside was littered, though everything was pushed to one side to allow passage. Men and machinery moved down the line. Not far from the town we passed the decomposing bodies of dead mules. They too had been thrust to one side. They were swollen with gas. The stench was terrible. There were other bodies too. The rains began. Very quickly they became torrential. The bog rippled under the downpour.

We were assigned to a dressing-station positioned beneath the ridge where the village of Hooge had been. The village isn't there any more. There were more than a hundred of us and we waited for stretchers. We were detailed to collect the wounded, but there weren't enough stretchers to go around. We had to wait for the wounded already in the station to be looked at before we could start.

We went as far as the wooded area beneath the Passchendaele ridge south of Poelcappelle. Mud everywhere. Wounded everywhere. *Consider and hear me, O Lord my God: lighten my eyes, lest I sleep the sleep of death.* The mud was red. We kept falling into it. Eight men had to carry one stretcher. We kept dropping our man into the mud. The shelling began again. We were showered in mud. We couldn't see. We dropped the stretcher and began to run. An officer screamed at us to go back. He held his revolver at us. We had no choice. We went back and picked up our man. When we reached the wooden road it was easier. We took it in turns of four at a time so that we didn't become exhausted. We reached Hooge quickly. He was dead. *I am poured out like water, and all my bones are out of joint: my heart is like wax; it is melted in the midst of my bowels. My strength is dried up like a potsherd; and my tongue cleaveth to my jaws; and thou hast brought me into the dust of death. For dogs have compassed me: the assembly of the wicked have inclosed me: they pierced my hands and my feet. I may tell all my bones: they look and stare upon me. They part my garments among them, and cast lots upon my vesture. But be not far from me, O Lord: O my strength, haste thee to help me. Deliver my soul from the sword: my darling from the power of the dog.*

October 8th. Lying in mud. I'm sinking into it. My legs are buried. I crawl up the crater bank, but just slide back into it. I've given up. I'm just going to lie here and write my note. The shell-hole is filthy. If I was on my own I'd certainly drown in it. I've just seen two kids drown. It's incredible, terrible, I don't know what. Even to me they looked like kids. I must look the same. We are all each other. Of course, we're all covered in mud, so we all look the same, all are the same. Like us they were in a sea of mud. Their arms were stretched out like pilgrims at the feet of Our Lord. We couldn't reach them. We were supposed to be collecting the wounded. That's why we're here. We were sent to collect the wounded. It was impossible though. Shaw was screaming. He wanted them to hold on. But hold on to what? There was one small sapling, that's all. How does one small sapling survive in all this mess and destruction? It was pointless trying to bend it over. It was too far from them. They'd dug their rifles into the mud and wrapped their arms through the sling, but it didn't hold them. They kept sliding in. We needed ropes. But we came under heavy fire. We had to take cover ourselves. By then only their faces and hands were showing. We had to dive into a pit as well, dive into this stinking hole. As the shells hit the mud it stirred up sickly sweet smells. The air was full of it. The first smell was the sweetness of rotting mules. Not sweet. But not filthy. Too far gone to be filthy. Nearly sweet. Then there was the smell of chlorine. It's like peardrops. For a moment I was in a sweetshop. It's always there in the mud, waiting to be stirred up by the shells, the smell of peardrops and dead flesh. It's inevitable. There's always gas and there are always dead animals. The animals get blown to bits on the roadways. They have a terrible time. They're such an easy target. I've seen shell after shell explode in the middle of the mule teams, six mules getting it at the same time, their dismembered bits flying in all directions. It's terrible. I often imagine how it would be if Little King were here. A blind horse ploughing into the mud. I suppose he would just keep on and on. He was such a loyal, lovely creature. That's the trouble though. He would just keep on and on. Maybe the mules would be better off if they were blind. They shouldn't have to see what they see. Of course, we'll probably all be blind by the time we're through. The mules are horse and ass. Our Lord rode in triumph on an ass. And now the shell pits beside the makeshift roadways are full of their decaying bodies. They are in a pit. I am in a pit. Shaw is in a pit. We are all in a pit. What on earth are we doing here? I am a miner, Shaw is a teacher and we are both in a pit, and we have just seen two kids drown in a pit. What is happening? He isn't talking to me. I guess he's thinking about the kids sinking in the mud. He'll be blaming himself. He won't be fair on himself at all. I can see it in his eyes. He's seeing me through, though. I know that. He directs me. We have the stretchers to hold on to. It makes no sense. The ridiculous thing was that in all this mess we stumbled into Reid. It was just before we came across the two kids. There we were, our section, supposedly evacuating the wounded and we came across one of our own. He was ripped from the shoulder to the waist with shrapnel, his stomach on the ground beside him in a pool of blood. He begged Shaw to shoot him. Shaw would have shot him, as well. I know he would. I could see it in his face. It was the same look he has now. But Reid was dead before he could have drawn his revolver. There was a long, quiet wail. I'm sure he said mother, holy mother. I'm sure. There was so much noise though. Reid shouldn't have been shot

179

up like that. He was with us. He was collecting the wounded. Reid was all right. He'd been here from the very start. He probably had his cards in his pocket. Where will they send those? To his mother? What will she make of them? There are two planes overhead fighting it out. They're stuttering and awkward. On the other side of the pit someone has started to sing. *O for the wings, for the wings of a dove, far far away would I rove.* His voice is low and lovely. It shakes Shaw up. He looks confused, as if he can't work out what the other's doing there. Apparently Shaw knows him well. He tells me that he sang in a church choir before the war. But how does Shaw know that? Shaw doesn't believe in God. I can't understand. What does Shaw believe in? Why is he in the pit? The singing is lovely. It keeps fading though. The singer is wounded. Should we not take the stretcher to him? What are we doing? We are sliding in mud. It smells of peardrops. It smells of dead mules. Those poor kids must have choked on it. Kids like me. How is it, drowning in mud? I try not to think of it, but I can't help myself. I imagine it covering my face. It's horrible, disgusting, the smell, the touch, the suffocation. I can't stand thinking it, but I can't stop. I can't stop seeing it coming at me, covering my face, me, all of me. Oh, if only I was underground leading Little King inbye. I would stay there forever. I would never come up again. I should never have come up at all. *I am counted with them that go down into the pit: I am as a man that hath no strength: Free among the dead, like the slain that lie in the grave, whom thou rememberest no more: and they are cut off from thy hand. Thou has laid me in the lowest pit, in darkness, in the deeps.* The singing has stopped. One of the planes is spiralling to earth. I watch its downward flight until it disappears from view. As it falls, for some reason, I have the strangest but clearest impression that I'm not going to die. It's not a voice or anything like that, just a feeling. I know it though. I'm not going to die. I'm not going to be killed. I should be rejoicing. But Alleluia won't sound. The earth stinks in my nostrils. I slide down the bank again. Shaw holds me. He has no expression. He stares into space. He must be seeing mud covering his eyes too. Oh Anne, I don't understand why I'm writing all this to you. I'm sorry. This wasn't my promise, this wasn't my promise at all. Forgive me. I am making a mess of everything.

October 9th. The front. The trench walls are collapsing. Behind me a man is shitting in an empty bully beef tin. I can smell him. I don't know how many times he's had to shit now. I think it's the tea. They bring it up in two gallon petrol tins. It always tastes of petrol. Then you shit for hours. They've started to bring lime with them. They spread it on the back of the posts so that they're not crawling in our shit. It's not our fault. What else can we do but chuck it over the edge. Sergeant Brough is with us. He kept his eye on me for a while then pulled a face at me. He looked quite curt really. I thought I must have done something wrong. But then his face changed and I thought he wanted to be kind to me, but didn't find it easy. He certainly wanted to say something. I suppose he doesn't have much time to reckon what we're all thinking about. I don't envy him really. He's got to get the job done. It can't be easy. In the end he told me that he thought I had learnt to be a man, matured quickly. I guess he won't call me sonny again. His voice faltered. He's not as severe as he'd like to make out. I don't believe it, though. I believe the opposite. I said nothing back, though. He gives the orders. *And I said, O that I had wings like a dove for then would I fly away and be at rest. Lo, then would I fly away and be at rest.*

October 10th. I'm so lapse in my devotion.

October 11th. The mud absorbs the shells as if they're duds. That makes us all slightly braver. Shrapnel and gas are not so repelled. If their shells are lost in the mud so too must ours. This will go on forever. The war will go on forever. I'm still here. I don't understand. What does God have in mind? He is a jealous God. Lord, if I have sinned... *The sacrifices of God are a broken spirit.*

October 12th. Today we drove forward. All day we battled through the mud. The dead lay on the dead. The wounded lifted their rifles in the mud to show where they were lying. A forest of rifles appeared in the swamp. A new forest in place of the old one. I sank up to my waist in the mud. It was impossible to dig in. Why do I walk through the valley of the shadow of death untouched. I'm going mad. I can't stand much more. O Lord. *All they that be fat upon earth shall eat and worship: all they that go down to the dust shall bow before him: and none can keep alive his own soul.*

At the end of the day we were no further than the morning. I'm lying in mud. I can hear moans around me. The shelling will never stop. Shaw came looking for me. *Why do you seek the living among the dead?* I said. I believe I've embarrassed him. He's concerned. He cares. I reached out for him across the mud. We are too numb to feel.

October 13th. Of my country I am ashamed.

October 14th. Shaw died today. Nothing to say. Amen, perhaps.

October 15th. Why do you seek the living among the dead? I have an answer for Shaw. Because the living and the dead will be together at the end of eternity. Tomorrow I will be with you in paradise. Confession and delight!

October 16th. I can go no further. Oh Anne, I wish I'd told you how much I love you. Forgive me. I have sinned grievously. I wanted to be so brave for you, I really did. I think I wrote all this for you really, but thank God you'll never get to read it. That would be too much. I don't want you to know the worst. I've let everyone down so badly. I've proved worthy of nothing. Father, forgive me. *Let the enemy persecute my soul, and take it; yea, let him tread down my life upon the earth, and lay mine honour in the dust.*

Chapter Four

John waited for Peter to speak. Peter appeared lazy and retarded. He slouched uncommunicatively in his seat. They were in the bar of a public house together with Hugh Glyn, the local man Peter had come across for the first time in France. They had spent much of their war together and had been demobbed at the same time, spring 1919. Hugh was an avid man, with dark, regular, features, who carried himself with a spare military style. He took a packet of cigarettes from his pocket, took one himself and threw the rest onto the centre of the table. "Just the job, Mr Devlin, if you have a mind," he suggested, smiling mutely. Peter Kavanagh snatched it up. He hung a cigarette loosely from his lips, then tossed it back down. John was appalled, but felt unable to respond. He no longer knew what to expect as characteristic. He could only wait. He took a cigarette himself, slowly and deliberately. It was something of a respite to do so. Hugh lit them and then he sat back, inhaled deeply then sighed aloud: "The pleasure is immense, Mr Devlin, immense. I cannot say."

John swallowed. His throat was raw and the taste sour. Without looking directly at either Peter or Hugh he began to speak. "I was against it," he said, his tone deferential, yet not undefiant. Hugh Glyn shrugged and drew again on his cigarette. John pressed on: "You know, England's trouble, Ireland's opportunity. That's what we always said. We believed it back then, really. Well, still, well, you know..."

Hugh looked weary. He spoke with awkward compassion. "My father's Irish too, Mr Devlin, so I know something of what it was like. Only something, mind you. I wouldn't presume, you see. We just have to fight the war set out for us. It stands to reason, I suppose. I won't say too much about mine, I don't think I can. I don't suppose that makes any sense at all, but, well, there it is."

"I lost my son," John said abstractly. He was uncertain how to pursue it. He felt debarred from claiming anything through it.

"I know," Hugh said with obvious sympathy.

Peter spoke up, his tone derisory and challenging. He said: "Robert was a bit of a priest."

Hugh eyed John steadily and said: "Brave men fight wars, Mr Devlin, no other type. They might be mad men or idiots, but brave, all the same. I met all sorts, some who'd had enough, some who'd had too much, some who couldn't get enough, but I reckon they were all pretty brave."

"He was a dreamy boy," John said. "A bit serious, I suppose, but very principled. He loved his church, but what's wrong with that? It meant a great deal to him." He voice faded. He struggled with it. For the first time he was confronted not so much by what he had lost, but by what he had had. Images of Robert flooded into his head. Suddenly it was as if he saw him at all ages at once. And he saw himself with him. The trouble was, he didn't come out of the memory very well. He recognised himself as impatient and dissatisfied. It was all so unfair, so wrong. He had failed to see what Robert was. Why had he been so blind? He moaned aloud, unable to check himself: "He was a good boy. He was such a good boy."

"He should never have left Anne," Peter snapped, dismissively and somewhat mercilessly. He had no intention of offering his uncle platitudes. He was incapable. No one deserved such facile sympathy, such easy forgiveness.

Hugh dismissed Peter by quietly insisting: "Be proud, Mr Devlin. Be proud."

Peter was not through though. He sat forward and eyed John with a taunting, jeering expression and demanded: "I wonder what frame of mind a priest would bring home? Do you reckon it would be all light and halleluiah? Glory be and Our Father."

"He isn't coming home Peter," John replied.

"But if he had?" Peter insisted, with a sudden snap of temper.

"He wasn't a priest, he just liked his church."

"Oh, fuck the war!" Peter said, instantly weary of his own malice. He slumped back in his seat. He was played out and dejected. He uttered under his breath: "Fuck the fucking war."

Hugh smiled at John and said: "Naturally."

Peter continued mumbling. "I just wanted to know, that's all. I didn't mean anything by it, for Christ's sake. He might have said something to her, prayed with her, something like that. I'm damned sure I won't."

"Has she asked you?"

Peter looked up sharply. He seemed startled that John had questioned him. He spoke with a sense of incredulity. "I can't step into the church, can't get across the threshold, it gets right up my nostrils." Suddenly he grinned. The gesture seemed reflex, beyond his control, as much a result of embarrassment as malice. Still, John thought it looked ugly. Once again his tone became taunting. He looked squarely at John and, still grinning, said: "My nostrils are full of the farts of dead mules. Can you imagine dead farts? The foulest fart imaginable."

John returned his gaze calmly. He said: "Father might surprise you."

Peter skewed his face, but didn't respond. John felt his cause hopeless. He was sickened by the listlessness he felt. He couldn't understand it. He was devoid of the motivation to stand up to Peter. He just didn't have the will to resist either his cynicism or his insults. He tried to tell himself that he was simply being patient, patient with someone who had probably been through hellish things beyond his comprehension. But he wasn't convinced by himself. Peter depressed him. The more he was in Peter's company so the greater became his sense of inertia. He found it irresistible. Peter brought him down to the depths. And in the depths there was no order or sense. He tried to visualise Robert, to put some truth and reality into this gloom, but it didn't really work. He simply groaned inwardly and grieved in a stark, lazy fashion. He didn't want to mourn in that way. He wanted to claim something for Robert. In his heart he condemned Peter Kavanagh, but he would never have said so. He warned himself to be patient and tolerant. He smiled. It was a weak, forlorn gesture.

Hugh caught sight of John's hopeless smile. He recognised how much he was struggling, and how much worse Peter was making it. He thought it was crazy. They were both struggling. They should face that together, not apart. He thought they might benefit from some time together. Maybe he was in the way. He stood up and put his palm around John's glass and suggested another drink. The force of the gesture was such that it was as if he had figuratively put his arm around John himself. John nodded. Peter simply swallowed his remaining beer and put his glass down. Hugh smiled and excused himself.

John and Peter sat without speaking. Without a glass to pick up they were more awkward than ever. They were at a loss as to how to broach the silence. They avoided looking at each other, but fidgeted uneasily and looked around the room instead, their eyes catching each other only in passing. It was Peter who finally broke the dead-lock. He spoke up,

185

his voice hushed and halting, as if he had no idea where his words were taking him. "I don't enjoy anything, you know. Really, nothing. I can't bring my mind to anything. It's... well... Christ. Anne's welcome home. Well. Welcome. I can't stand it really..."

His voice faded away. He looked down. He ran his hands restively along his thighs, across his face, then down his torso. He tried to speak again but gave it up before a word had passed his lips.

John responded quietly, his eyes now focused on Peter: "Give it time. She's done it all for you. Give it time."

Peter threw back his head hurriedly. He laughed mercilessly. "I miss it, you know, I actually miss it. Can you believe that? I fucking miss it."

"Why not?"

"I'm no fucking priest. I don't feel the urge to pray."

"I suppose not."

Peter couldn't say anymore. His expression was just a gape. What more could he say? His admission was too awful. As he gazed at John, staring into the heart of that confession, into the heart of its implications, Hugh returned. Peter immediately slumped back, again lapsing into his state of aggressive, restive awkwardness.

John eyed that act of petulance with curiosity. It disgusted him. He felt suddenly sour, more estranged from Peter than ever. "She lives for you," he uttered quietly.

"What the hell do any of these women know? What the hell does anybody know?" Peter responded tartly.

Hugh looked over the two of them as he placed the glasses of beer on the table-top. It was more than evident that John and Peter had not managed to reach any compact. He felt for both of them.

"A hard job, not knowing," he suggested, as he sat back down, without looking at either of them.

John couldn't comment. Peter's weariness and contempt was ultimately too much for him. It went against the grain. He wanted to shake him into some semblance of the man he remembered him to be, but the very fact that it was something remembered meant he was unable. He couldn't possibly know what had brought Peter here. So, as much as he couldn't condone it, at the same time he couldn't challenge it. He would just have to mind his tongue and try to work it out.

Hugh pitied their struggle. He couldn't quite work it out. He felt himself torn by contradictory loyalties: one to a near past, the dreadful years he had endured with Peter, and one to a more remote past, a domestic world that demanded their return. He knew that somewhere between those versions of his life story lay his future. He attempted a reconciliation. He spoke to Peter, but it was for John as well. "You're not being fair, Peter Kavanagh. You're not being fair at all. You're not being fair to damn good people. Christ, man, you're not being fair to yourself. You need to get your head round that. Not knowing isn't a crime, it's a burden, a bloody hard burden. I wouldn't like it. You wouldn't like it. Mr Devlin doesn't like it. You can't have it everyway, can you? So, they don't know, but they care. You can't have a go at them for caring. Tell them, if they don't know, or shut up. But give them a break. You're acting like a fucking fool, excuse me Mr Devlin, and you're no such thing. Christ, no such thing at all."

"Am I not?" Peter said, a derisory smile quickly crossing his expression.

Hugh turned to John and simply nodded. In its brevity and precision it was almost a military gesture. There remained a military quality, an alert, formality, to all Hugh's movements and gestures. John was pleased, relieved to receive that sign of alliance. He took it as that. He also read it as a signal not to disturb himself too much. Hugh would see that Peter was all right. It was a token of promise. John responded with a brief smile.

It was during this quiet exchange that Gavin Duffy approached. He immediately offered his hand to Peter. Peter simply gazed at the outstretched palm, his expression bewildered and disgusted. Gavin let it remain for a moment longer, then shrugged and put it in his pocket. As he did he spoke up: "I just wanted to say that I was sorry. Some sad things happened while you were away. I haven't had chance before to say my piece. Well, it wasn't really possible, not with you and the reporter feller, well you know what I mean. I'm speaking for myself mind." He extended his attention to Hugh as well as Peter. "I speak for the miners in lots of things, you see, but I'm speaking for me now. Well, I wanted to say I was sorry, that's about it."

Peter looked up at Duffy. His expression remained quite unchanged. He couldn't immediately speak but eventually forced out the statement: "You hounded him, Duffy, hounded him!"

Gavin immediately sat down beside John and leaned right up towards Peter and said: "I did nothing wrong."

"You hounded him."

"No, I never did. I never lied. I just said what was happening. Bobby understood. It was never personal. Bobby understood that. Nothing personal. We were never like that. There could never be anything personal between us."

The colour suddenly drained from Peter's face. He gazed at Gavin steadily for a moment. When he spoke again his voice was subdued but forceful. "I believe you helped kill him. You're guilty of that. I find that personal. I find that very personal."

"That's nonsense, Peter, and you know it is. That's really wild talk, and doesn't do anyone any good. Bobby understood, Bobby always understood, politics was the issue, politics was the only issue and it still is the only issue and it always will be the only issue. Don't look backwards, lad. There's nothing to be gained from that. Now we have to work on what's the best plan for getting you lads back to work."

Peter continued to gaze relentlessly at Gavin, the colour still absent from his face. Hugh intervened. He didn't understand the enmity Peter obviously felt for Gavin. He had never before heard anything disturbing about the death of Peter's father. He knew it had happened, but had always believed it to have been an ordinary natural death. He wasn't unconvinced that this was yet another example of Peter's unsettled behaviour, so he was sure he shouldn't jump to any conclusions. Gavin seemed all right to him. Nothing out of the ordinary. Besides Gavin was talking about getting back to work. Hugh was certain that represented the normality they all needed. He knew he needed to be back working himself. He said: "We've got our free insurance policies to see us through for now. Then, as soon as it can all be sorted out, well, we were led to believe that our old jobs would be there waiting for us, that the National Union and National Federation are there with the set job of resettling service men."

"Where were you?" Gavin asked.

"Whinn Hill iron-ore mine."

Gavin seized on what Hugh said with enthusiasm. "God, man, you have the best union in the whole of Britain. Since 1914 they've negotiated three hundred per cent wage increases, and they burnt out a lot of scab labour in the process, I'll tell you. The iron-ore boys always got what they wanted in the end, made the Ministry of Munitions pay for what they wanted. Well, they didn't have much choice, did they?"

"Bastard!" Peter uttered.

"Three hundred per cent!"

Hugh spoke across them. There was an idea he needed to air, to test out. He said: "I didn't think to mine again. There'll be new opportunities coming up, won't there? I thought I'd look for something in electronics.

That's where the future lies. There's something new coming along that's going to be really big. Radios. They'll all have radios soon in the south. I'd like to make a radio. I'm telling you, every house in this country. Well that's what they say. I read it. Lot's of lads I knew want to get into electronics."

"Three hundred per cent!" Gavin repeated triumphantly. "Remember, the Triple Alliance had planned the most thorough, class based strike for the autumn of 1914. Don't lose sight of that, lads. The war just postponed it, that's all. It didn't make it go away. Not one bit of it. I reckon the war was a damned good side-show that's made us even stronger than we were then. We'll really get something out of all this, I'm telling you."

Peter stood up. He had no real purpose. He was confused and tearful. He didn't look at Gavin, rather he just looked down, ashamed of his emotions. He said: "Side-show? A fucking side-show? Christ! Fucking hell! Well, I'm pleased, Duffy, pleased you made them pay, so fucking pleased for you and the likes of you."

"Sit down, Kavanagh, it's all right," Gavin said, not without sympathy. "We know you've been through a great deal. I'm only saying. You have to make it count for something. Of course, make the bastards pay. By Christ, make them pay. Why not. You've done all the work. You deserve it."

Without warning Peter turned over the table and immediately made for Gavin. He shouted out: "Fuck what you're saying, Duffy. I don't want to hear it. I don't want to hear anything from you anymore."

Gavin jumped back, tearing himself from Peter's grasp. Quickly and reflexly he struck Peter two sharp blows to the face. Peter's nose burst. Peter wiped his hand across his face with a slow disdainful movement. He smeared the blood across the lower part of his face as he did, then flicked his palm away. Gavin waited. Hugh stood up and with surprising ease pushed Peter back down into his seat. He turned to Gavin. Gavin held up his hands in a conciliatory gesture. He was claiming innocence. He hadn't started anything. He hadn't wanted any of it to happen. Hugh struck him in the face. A line of blood appeared in the corner of Gavin's mouth. He immediately smiled, spat out, then quickly lunged at Hugh. Hugh struck him a number of swift blows to his body and head and brought him swiftly to his knees. Then, with Duffy crouched before him, he stopped and turned to John. He looked suddenly lost and frightened.

John had stepped back. He had felt entirely powerless to intervene, and was shocked by his inability. He couldn't ever remember having only been a bystander in a dispute like this. He had been totally powerless to stop the violence. He had failed to protect a member of his own family. He had stood aside whilst his own kind had slugged it out. He was appalled by himself. It was a new and disagreeable experience. But now Hugh was reinstating him. He was saying that he needed his help. Hugh was appalled by the position he found himself in and needed some means of escape.

John acted quickly. He was deeply relieved to be able to do so. He pulled Hugh and Peter away and ushered them to the door. Before leaving he looked back. Gavin had picked himself up and was sitting down where Peter had been. He gave an indiscriminate wave. John merely nodded. He went out. He took them home.

Anne was with Bill at Kate's. John had not considered that. Their meeting was awkward and not without incident. As soon as Anne caught sight of Peter's face as he stepped into the small kitchen where everyone was gathered she let out a pained moan and went to him. She tried to comfort him and touch his wound. How could he have let anything happen to his lovely face? He had managed to see through an entire war without damaging it. All her old nightmares flooded in. She felt a wave of shame as she recalled them. She had to soothe him, soothe him in order to rid her mind of her former fears. But he would have nothing of that. He shrugged her away, snapping that it was nothing and that he had seen worse, much worse. It was the exclusivity of that remark that echoed around the room. He wouldn't let up. At every opportunity he punished them with the war, punished them with their not knowing. She stepped back from him. There was an awkward silence for a moment. Peter knew he was responsible. He had an urge to turn his back on them all and simply walk out, but instead he tried to smooth it all away by lifting Bill up in his arms. Bill immediately began howling and kicking. Anne quickly snatched Bill away from Peter. "Why would he not," she declared, comforting the child, "confronted with a face like that? Why wouldn't any of us confronted with a face like that?" She took Bill's hand and sat with him apart.

Dora immediately offered to bathe Peter's face. He was about to argue the need, but Hugh spoke up and said that it would be just the job. He looked directly at Peter and repeated himself. It would be just the job. It was his phrase. He smiled and nodded at Dora to do as she had suggested. Peter reluctantly acquiesced.

Peter's truculence with Anne concerned John. It suggested that Peter's mood was more than passing. It wasn't reserved for the pub

190

and men like him who had never been to France. It was more general than that. For Anne to have reacted the way she had meant that she had already experienced too much due to Peter's mood. It didn't bode well.

The only relief to the gloom he felt came from the presence of Hugh. He busied himself by bringing in some water for Dora, and changed it whenever she suggested it was needed. As he went back and forth to the sink he made sure he caught Bill's eye and whistled bird tunes in his direction, singing for his benefit.

Kate insisted that everyone stay for dinner. Peter was reluctant and made numerous excuses, but Hugh over-ruled him and declared that it would be a marvellous idea, just the job.

Peter and Anne did not exchange a word throughout the duration of the meal. Hugh took it on himself to maintain the conversation. He chose to entertain them. He directed himself mainly towards Kate. He told her about his father, a man, he said, who was in love with birds. It was a love that knew no limits. He went into great descriptions of the characteristics of the caged song finches his father kept. He passed his days grooming them, pampering them, listening to their song and imitating their song. He suggested they were well called a charm of finches. He also suggested that, from his own point of view, the song the birds sang sounded sweet and dreadful. Sweet and dreadful! Having described his father's passion for birds he put on a rather grave face and went on to say that for all of his father's talent with birds he was decidedly incapable of caring for his own feet. He then went on to describe a list of ailments to which is father was prone, each one of them related to feet. Kate dismissed the whole list as the commonplace failings of a widower and said she could well imagine.

After dinner Hugh went into the yard to smoke. Dora joined him. For a while he scanned the mauve, cloud scattered sky, inhaling deeply, as if unaware of her presence, but then without formality he began to speak to her. His voice was even and measured, yet tinged with mockery. "We have to keep on hoping and praying, Miss Devlin, hoping and praying. What do you say?"

"I'm sure we do," Dora responded lightly. "But would that be for anything in particular, on your behalf?"

"That everything will fall out more or less as we left it, not entirely, but more or less. Hoping and praying." He threw down his cigarette, then turned to her and laughed quietly. "You're quite the healer of wounds, you know. That was a most impressive display, and I've seen a fair amount of wound care, what with the bandages around the birdman's feet, before you go and ask. I'd be a dab hand at it myself if I gave it a go."

"You're having me on, having a bit of a laugh, I'd say."

"No, I'm serious. I'm a deadly serious man."

"No, you're not, but never mind."

He held up his hands, surrendering, then laughed out loud. His entire expression was mobile and frank. He spoke to her confidentially: "Peter was brave and fierce, you know. Today, I mean. I don't know the gist of it, but he struck me as brave and fierce. We shouldn't be too high and mighty with him."

"Did it do any good?"

At that moment Marty climbed the back wall. As soon as he saw them standing there he bowed in their direction, the gesture deliberately slow and ceremonious. He then took himself into the chicken-shed. A pig squealed, made disgruntled noises for a while and then there was silence.

"It's only Uncle Marty," Dora said in a entirely matter of fact tone. "He likes sleeping in the chicken shed."

"Oh Jesus, thank God for finches and fowl, and all the beasts of the field," Hugh suggested.

Dora agreed.

*

Hugh's courtship of Dora was quick and serious, so much so that within four months they had set a wedding date. It was to be in six months time, by which time Hugh calculated he would have managed to save enough money to be able to put down a rent deposit and buy a few pieces of furniture. He had taken a job alongside Peter down Fish Pit. John Devlin secured their posts. He had transferred to Fish from Loft shortly after they had received word about Robert. There was no further mention of electronics, or building a radio.

Both John and Kate approved. They approved of the match, they approved of the haste and they approved of Hugh. They welcomed him into their house everyday. In fact, they came to rely on it, to rely on him, his nature, his spare, yet frank optimism. They could never have said so, yet his appearance, coming out of the war, helped in some symbolic fashion to allay the loss of Robert.

On the other hand, it was with increasing concern that they watched Peter and Anne. Although Peter was working, his inability to adapt back to normal civilian life became more apparent with each passing day. He was moody and cynical with everyone, but with Anne he was quite relentless. It was as if the more she tried to reach him, the further away he had to go. He couldn't stand her sympathy, her patience, her desire to soothe him. At times he would almost rave, his voice hushed but possessed, levelling the most ridiculous accusations against her. He claimed she was sick of him; she kept herself apart; she had been seeing someone else while he was away. At first she tried to defend herself, but that only sent him into brief but intense rages. She gave up. At other times he would withdraw into himself and not speak at all, but simply stare into space. These periods of distraction could last for days. She hated his silence more than his noise. For everyone else they were periods of respite. At least they didn't have to witness him criticising her. At no time did he show much interest in Bill, except sometimes to shout at him. Bill soon learnt to avoid him as best he could. Anne struggled with his moods and was obviously worn out by him, yet would hear no criticism of him. She repeatedly told Kate that all he needed was time, and offered the reassurance that he never lay a finger on her. She believed he just had to get it all out of his system and then everything would be all right.

He had only been home a couple of months when she announced that she was pregnant again. She was delighted. Everyone shared her optimism. The pregnancy suggested that the situation should improve. But nothing did change. If anything, things were slightly worse. He became self-righteous and accused her of being selfish and reckless. She had no right to be pregnant. The world was not a fit place to have a child. She had not thought what it would mean to him. He was openly indiscreet in blaming her sexual frustration for the pregnancy. Interrupted intercourse wasn't good enough for her, as it was for most women. She winced at his accusation, but didn't defend herself.

On the whole John and Kate, remembering what he had been and who he was, pitied him, but often they despised him. Whenever they personally witnessed his treatment of Anne or Bill they hated him. But they found it impossible to talk to him. He was too truculent to approach. Hugh would have confronted him on any number of occasions, but Anne had asked him to say nothing. During the first days of their demobilisation she had spoken to him in the Devlin's house. She had suggested that he must understand more than anyone what Peter was going through, and put her case that she was sure all he needed was time. He agreed with her, but as the situation developed he found it increasingly difficult to stand aside. The better he knew Anne, the more difficult it became. He had to keep reminding himself that she was right, after all she was his wife, she would know, that all Peter needed was time. He remembered what he had been in France and grieved for him. In general they prayed and hoped for restoration, and in the main even managed to love him for himself.

As the pregnancy progressed Anne became ever more tired. She was often tearful, and sometimes scarcely able to move herself. It appeared a particularly troublesome pregnancy. No one could really decide whether that would have been the case anyway, or whether it was Peter who caused the problems. Anne would not hear a word against him. She told herself that he would be himself again. She was certain the baby would do it. She told Kate on numerous occasions that really he was just his old self. She said you could see it in his face and deep in his eyes. It was there when he turned his face, like another visible face altogether. He was the same frank, energetic boy that had announced their engagement on the night Bobby had gone away.

On one occasion she was very tearful and told Kate that his face was as lovely as ever and then, as she cried, accused herself of being a shallow, undeserving person. Kate consoled her without having any idea what she meant. She couldn't even begin to guess at the accusations Anne was levelling against herself. Anne had gradually learnt to blame herself for Peter's behaviour. She had so much wanted him to come back physically whole that she convinced herself that she deserved his mental struggle. She had to prove herself worthy.

Kate was sceptical but wished it was true. She tried to see the old Peter in him, see what Anne insisted was there, but it eluded her. She only saw his temper and his impatience and she didn't understand. He didn't deserve Anne. He didn't deserve the fact that she never criticised him or gave up on him. She asked Father Bond to speak to him. He said he would pray for him. She understood.

The baby was due shortly after Hugh and Dora's wedding, but came a month before. Anne went into labour in the evening. Kate went to her. She brought a midwife with her. She had learned to dread birth. As Anne was examined she stood by the window and looked out through the slightly drawn curtain. There was a large yellow moon. It seemed to fill the sky. Kate closed her eyes and prayed. After she had made the sign of the cross she went to Anne. She knelt beside the bed and rested her hand, then her ear on Anne's belly, letting her face press against Anne's skin. Within seconds she burst out laughing and said: "I can hear the baby cry, I can hear it cry in the womb, and you know what that means, it's a sign of greatness." She immediately stood up and made to leave. She was inspired to tell Peter what she had heard, certain it would do him good. She paused at the door, laughed out loud again and said to the midwife: "Babies are reluctant in this family, so keep a good watch on it. This one is crying in the womb, so mind it." She made the sign of the crucifix once again, then went to tell Peter that she had heard the baby cry in the womb and that it was a sign of greatness.

She found Peter quivering against a wall. At every sound from Anne he flinched and felt for the solidity behind him. Kate went to him. She took hold of both of his hands, brought her face directly in front of his, smiled at him and said: "It's all right, I heard it cry in the womb. Do you hear me? I heard it. You know what that means?" Peter just stared at her. Her words were incomprehensible to him. She tried again, but she had no sooner begun when Anne screamed out again. Bill began to cry. Kate had not been aware of him. She turned towards him and saw him crouched in a corner. She made to go to him but Peter held on to her, Bill's crying having roused him from his terrors. He smiled at her. The gesture struck her as in some way pitiless and filled with rage. He turned to Bill and shouted at him furiously, instructing him to be quiet and get himself to bed.

"I'll take care of him," Kate said softly. "He'll be no bother."

"And I told him to go to bed. Now, get to bed, like I say!"

"He's scared, Peter. He doesn't understand."

Peter pushed Kate aside. "I don't want him here. He shouldn't listen to this. It isn't right. He wants nothing being here. What the hell is he still doing here?"

"I'll take care of him," Kate repeated, her whole body heaving with the weight of emotion the frightened child invoked in her. She was tremulous and enraged. She moved toward Bill as she spoke and immediately embraced him, holding him fast against her. Once she had claimed the child she turned on Peter, her disapproval of him finally triumphant, and bitterly declared: "You are a monster, Peter Kavanagh, a monster. I never thought I'd see this day. You don't deserve happiness." He made no response. He was again subject to Anne's birth pains. Seeing that he was so preoccupied, Kate ushered Bill from the room. As she left, Peter repeated his injunction that Bill get to bed, his words though were scarcely audible. When the door closed he began to cry.

At the same time as both Peter and Anne cried Dora also cried. She made love with Hugh for the first time. They had walked along the harbour, past the coaling stations where the sluices dropped through the harbour walls, past the tramps asleep amongst the lobster pots, out onto the promontory towards the lighthouse. The moon was enormous above them. It was repeated on the surface of the water. They stopped every twenty yards or so in order to kiss. They were eager yet nervous, tormented by their own tenderness. Indeed, they were fearful of the feeling they had for each other, fearful without knowing why. They touched compulsively and hastily, with tenderness and sadness, both of them blissfully unaware that what they were expressing was a fear of losing the other. Their love had brought them to the brink of marriage, the brink of each other, and now they were scared they might not make it.

"It isn't enough, is it," Dora whispered, her breath crystal in the cold.

Hugh shook his head. He lay his cheek against hers and said: "Someone said it would take us a hundred and seventy years to reach the Rhine, a hundred and seventy years, Dora. But I'm here now, and I can't quite believe it. Yes, I want more, but I can't ask. I won't. You know I won't. Christ, I've never felt anything like this. It goes right through me."

"You make me shake, Hugh Glyn, every inch of me," she said, encouraging and coaxing him. "I like that. I like it so much. There can't be anything wrong in liking it, can there? There can't be anything wrong at all. I don't mind about the consequences. It's all right. It really is." She stepped back from him, without relinquishing her hold on his fingers. She drew them up into the air so that they were both at arms length from their point of contact. She smiled, then gently drew him towards her. She led him to one of the numerous sheds along the promontory.

She found making love with him more painful than she could ever have imagined. She had never experienced such a commingling of hurt and pleasure. Later, as they lay together, listening to each other's breathing, a harmonious counterpoint to the surf, she knew that her pleasure of him would always be marked by hurt and pleasure. Her joy would be tempered by the fear of losing him. The loss of Robert made that certain. Nothing was reliable. There were no certainties. Even the strongest looking edifice was fragile. Everything could be sundered. By the same token, she knew that to give herself to him was no sin. They owed each other as much of themselves as they could give. They made love again without pain.

As Hugh and Dora made love Anne's baby was still-born. When Kate and Peter went into her she was rocking it in her arms. Kate was frightened. She motioned to take the baby, but Anne smiled and said: "Don't worry, I understand, but he deserved something all the same. Look, he's a little boy, a beautiful little boy. He would have made a fine brother for Bill, wouldn't he, poor little mite. Honestly, don't worry. I just want to let him know we love him, that's all." Kate smiled, relieved that Anne was so lucid, so completely herself. She agreed. Peter knelt by the bed, lay his head on Anne's lap and began to cry. Anne stroked him with the same motion as she rocked the baby.

Later that night Peter took the baby from Anne and wrapped it in a blanket for burial. As he stood with it in his arms Bill came to the door. Peter immediately shouted at him to go back to bed, but Anne held out her arms for him and beckoned him to come to her. She said: "He'll stay with me Peter. I need someone. Don't send him away. Not now."

Peter left the bedroom without another word. He took the baby to the graveyard and buried it on top of his father and mother's grave. He stood there for some time staring at the newly mined earth, the moonlight silver on the loam. There were dead flowers in a plain pot vase. They hung over the rim, the dead heads touching the soil. The water in the vase was rancid. He picked them up and threw them aside, angry at himself for allowing them to be still there. He knew it was because he had visited the grave so infrequently. He let Anne do that for him, but she had been too tired of late. He knelt down and touched the soil. His fingers ran along it in urgent inquiry. He was aware that he felt no grief. How could that be? He squeezed some soil in his palm and gripped it tightly. Had he lost so much? Had so much been taken from him? It was too much? How could anyone lose so much? Suddenly he found himself crying, crying against the great absence he felt within himself. He fell flat against the ground and began beating his fists against the loose soil covering the grave. When the frustration and rage burnt themselves out he continued to lie there, immobile, prostrate, for some time, feeling the soil against him, disabled by it, unable to relinquish it.

When he returned to Anne she was still awake. Bill was curled beside her. He took off his earth stained clothes and lay down with her with Bill between them. He reached out and stroked her. He spoke to her quietly and tentatively. He asked her if she loved him.

"Yes, I love you," she replied. "I love you more than ever."

"I love you more than all the madness."

"I know you love me."

"Are you happy?"
"Yes, I'm happy."
"Even tonight?"
"Especially tonight. Tonight of all nights."
"I'm scared."
"I know."

He nestled against her in order to sleep, and she held him, securing him. They slept together, all three, long after the dull heavy dawn had filled the room with weak grey light. Ten days later Anne died of an embolus.

*

Hugh and Dora wanted to cancel their wedding when Anne died, but Peter persuaded them not to. He came to them immediately after her funeral. When he spoke he was cold and precise, but not without passion. He insisted that a wedding would do everyone good, that it was just what they needed. He was adamant that Anne would not have wanted anything else. As he spoke they remembered him as he had been a couple of hours earlier, standing over Anne's open grave, his figure very still, without any outward show of emotion, Bill clinging to his arm and Peter allowing it. His expression was steely still, suggesting resignation, yet at the same time profound aggression. Dora had found the display quite terrifying. She asked Hugh whether that was how a soldier was tutored to show his grief. Hugh didn't think so, but didn't disagree. He merely shrugged. Peter's grief frightened him too.

Hugh knew that he should go and see Peter and talk it through. The promise he had extracted from them, that they would go ahead with the wedding, was premature. Anne had only just been buried. Peter wasn't thinking straight. What would everyone think? They couldn't start their marriage under a cloud of disapproval. They were both troubled by the sense that it just wasn't right. But, at the same time, they were desperate for it to be right. They wanted nothing more than to be married. Any idea of delay struck them as ill omened and devastating, personally devastating. They hoped beyond hope that Peter's forcible insistence that they proceed was the permission that everyone might agree to. In their hearts they doubted it. It was plain that Hugh would have to talk again with Peter. The days passed, though. For some reason he kept putting it off. He told Dora that Peter needed time alone, that it was too soon to start bothering him with their burdens. To his own mind, though, he couldn't work out whether his reluctance was due to the fact that he simply couldn't face Peter's grief, or the worry that Peter just might have changed his mind. He knew it was unwise and maybe cowardly, but for a while he did nothing. He just waited. Eventually Dora pointed out that if he left it for too long they would have to cancel whatever. Hugh finally braced himself and went to Peter.

It was a cold, bright winter morning when Hugh went to Peter's house on Ginns. The light was crystal bright, and the still air fresh. It solidified and outlined everything. Long shadows crossed the street, the low sun only lighting strips of the upstairs and roofs of the terraced and banked houses. In the shadow it was bitterly cold. Children ran up and down the street. They were playing at soldiers, or cowboys and Indians. He wasn't sure which. The shouts and halloos of their imagined charges and retreats filled the street. A number of dogs ran with the children. Their barking was excited and shrill. Each noise sounded brittle in the icy air, liable to fracture, remote yet overwhelming and piercing. He stood at the front door for some time, listening to the street games, to the chaos of sound.

He was in shadow. The difference in temperature between the sun and the shade was incredible. He felt his body heat retreat inwards. But still he waited. He groaned aloud at his hesitation. It showed him up in a bad light. He had deserted a comrade, a friend. He had committed an unforgivable crime. But why was it? Why was Peter's loss so unapproachable? It didn't make sense. He was a soldier of the Western Front. He had seen death till he was dull and docile at the sight.

In his mind's eye he could see a narrow trench, only wide enough for one man to walk along, two to stand and wait. It went straight up to shoulder height, and then angled away to either side, higher than head height. He could see a line of men, each of their faces vividly real for him, just waiting, staring without speech at the dirt before their eyes. It was as if he could float along the trench and see each of them, recognising them as he went. Their faces. So much seem wrapped up in their faces. Ponderous, hardened, weathered, sincere, uncertain, beautiful faces. And each one was dead. It was a trench of ghosts and he was their medium, bringing them to life, permitting them to come back, to share another moment in the cold of a brilliant winter's day. He didn't call to them, though. He wasn't summonsing them. They were just there, wherever that was. And they would be there forever. They would wait in that slit trench until the end of time, staring, wondering, conceiving the inconceivable future.

It was all too pat to say that the trenches they dug were their own graves. It was all too obvious. And besides they took a more comic line than that. No one ever stated the obvious, only the offbeat and the wild. They made lurid and wild jokes. They laughed at grotesque and ugly things. They laughed at being afraid. What else was there to do? A confession is forever. A joke quickly passes. Life is fragile. Death is meaningless. The one should not interfere with the other. He grieved inwardly for those faces haunting him, haunting him with their gentle good looks, their civil manners, their trusting affection, their eager charms. They were a terrible responsibility to carry around, but he wouldn't desert them. They deserved that. They were his amateur army of ordinary special men. Their secrets were safe with him. He would speak no evil, hear no evil. He had to signal his intent. He had to go into Peter's two up, two down house and share his grief over his beautiful wife. She had died in a different world. They were free at last, free to break down and cry, free to break down and say it didn't make sense and that it hurt and was dreadful and appalling and ruthless and...

And still he hesitated. He was aware that he was beginning to attract attention. Women reddening their steps or polishing their windows were eyeing him strangely. Why was he waiting at the widower's door? What more was likely to happen? They were imagining stories about him. Surely such a long wait must have some significance. It couldn't simply be the cowardice of a friend's hopelessly inadequate sympathy. It couldn't simply be that this man on the door-step was so frightened of the future, because of his friend's mourning, that he was almost paralysed by it. How on earth could Anne die? They hadn't come through a war for that! It was too dreadful to contemplate. He considered shouting to the women, calling on them to say whether they could make any sense of anything. The cry came into his mind. He was on the verge of speaking out. But he stopped himself. He wasn't like that. His sanity was intact. He was grateful for everything. He was a lucky man. He couldn't give way to stupid whims like that. It wasn't fair on anyone. He looked up and down the street, smiled and nodded, generally acknowledging anyone who cared to notice it, then dusted himself down and made his way into Peter's house. He didn't knock. There was no need. He was a friend. He would be expected.

He went past the front-room straight into the back-room. It was even more shaded than usual. It scarcely managed any sunshine at the best of times, positioned as it was under the shadow of the higher terraces, but Peter also had the curtains drawn to so, despite the fact that they weren't heavy curtains, only pale flecks of grey light penetrated the gloom. The room was also bitterly cold. There was no fire burning. Nevertheless, Peter sat in a chair gazing down at the empty grate as if he were looking into a heart of flames. There was an ashtray rested on one of the arms of the chair which had overflowed so that ash and stumps had fallen onto Peter to one side and onto the floor the other. Bill sat on the floor under the window-frame. He was making something out of pieces of sticks and a sheet of canvas. Hugh assumed it was a kite. He looked up from his work when Hugh came in, but then straight away turned back to the task in hand before Hugh had a chance to acknowledge him. Peter didn't stir.

Hugh simply stood and waited for a moment. He looked around the room. Even in the limited light he could see that it was dirty and untidy. There were used cups and plates left about, already effected by mould. The grate was full of cinders and ash. Bill looked like a street urchin. Peter was dishevelled and grimy. He took another cigarette and lit it. He threw the disused match at the grate. As he smoked he made no attempt to reach for the ash tray, but let the ash drop on himself. Hugh continued to watch for a moment longer, then he picked up the ashtray, tipped its contents amongst the cinders and ash and placed it in Peter's lap. Peter looked down at the empty bowl, then up at Hugh. He made no show of recognition. He drew deeply on his cigarette. More ash fell down his front.

Hugh wanted to say something, to speak out against the squalor that Peter was creating, but he couldn't. He just couldn't find the words to begin. As he stood there, looking down at Peter Bill came and stood beside Peter's chair. In the grey light he looked sallow and worn. Hugh thought he was becoming one of the dirty, surly, abandoned kids of the very poor. He revolted at the image of the child. He was so patient in his neglect, so patient of his boredom and so patient with the fact of being bullied. Hugh asked him if he had eaten. Bill looked at his father, seeking permission to answer. Peter carried on smoking. Hugh asked again, his tone pressing and obviously angered. Bill shook his head once. He immediately looked again at his father. Hugh marched into the kitchen and began to search for something to feed the boy. He couldn't find anything. He pulled at cupboards and drawers, but there was nothing other than an occasional patch of mould that had maybe been a piece of cheese or a piece of bread. Finally he gave it up.

He marched from the kitchen, through the back-room and straight out into the street. Even in the shadow of the street he had to blink after the gloom of the interior. He looked up and down. He went up to the first woman who caught his eye and asked for something to eat. The woman looked horrified, and was about to give him a piece of her mind, but he spoke over her, his tone severe, bitter and saddened, condemning her and everyone else in the street. He said that there was a little boy starving and they were guilty of letting it happen. He also said that he was guilty. They were all at fault. They all shared the same awful shame.

She gave up any attempt to respond and went indoors. She closed the door behind her. He waited and when she didn't immediately return he thought about approaching the next woman he could see. However, just as he was about to give it up, she emerged once again and gave him a plate with a piece of cooked bacon, black-pudding, cheese and bread and a small jug of milk. He took the offering with a sense of both gratitude and embarrassment. He began to explain and excuse his presumption, wanting to say something about his failings and Peter's family's failings and about his haste, but she shook her head and simply stated that everyone understood that Peter Kavanagh was having a hard time. She concluded by saying that she was sorry. He simply nodded his appreciation of what she had said and done, then made his way back into Peter's.

He found Bill still standing to the side of Peter's chair. He immediately held out the plate for him. Bill wouldn't take it, though. He gazed at his father, clearly frightened that he might do the wrong thing. Eventually Hugh shouted at him to take the food and eat it. Bill turned to him quickly, terrified of Hugh's raised voice. Hugh repeated his injunction more quietly, speaking through clenched teeth, insisting that he take it and eat. Bill seized the plate and dived down, back beneath the window-frame. He began to eat, not at all like a wild animal as Hugh had expected, but slowly and daintily as if he wasn't too fussed to eat at all.

Hugh watched him for a moment, then smiled at him. Bill returned the smile, albeit briefly and circumspectly, but nevertheless it was apparent. He struck Hugh as a lovely child, a real combination of his mother and father, Anne's generous nature and airy good looks, and Peter's solid masculine good looks. It was unacceptable that his true nature should be subject to such abuse. He had heard that his first breath had been Peter's father's last. Surely that meant something to Peter?

Hugh turned to Peter. He wanted to say something on Bill's behalf. However, before he fully realised what he was doing, he had seized Peter by the collar and was glaring in his face. But no sooner had he done it than he remembered Bill, squat on the floor below the window. He turned to him. The boy was staring at him, shuddering with fear. Hugh immediately released Peter and stood up, then backed away. He whispered towards Bill that it was all right, nothing was going to happen and he should keep on with his food. Bill continued to gaze for a moment, then resumed his slow careful eating.

Hugh turned back to Peter. Peter was looking straight at him. Hugh thought he was trying to smile, but the gesture would simply not materialise.

"You have to snap out of this, Kavanagh," Hugh uttered. "You can't treat the boy like this." Peter raised his eyebrows and again Hugh thought he detected the glimmerings of a smile. He went on. "Anne would never forgive you, you know. You know that."

"She said she'd never been happier," Peter said, though his voice was so mute it seemed he was simply speaking his own thoughts aloud, rather than speaking to Hugh. He screwed up his face at the thought.

"Anne was a happy person. She was full of spirit," Hugh suggested, wanting to affirm what Peter was saying, but no sooner had he said it than he thought how much her loss meant. He quietly said: "Your loss is terrible. I shouldn't, well..." He couldn't go on.

Peter eyed him carefully. He smiled outright. "You always want to make everything all right, don't you Hugh lad. Always the fixer and patcher."

"I don't know about that."

"Oh, I do. I'm telling you. Always wanting everything to be okay for everyone else. Does everyone else matter so much to you Hugh lad?"

"There's nothing wrong in that."

"No, not at all. Nothing wrong. But does it really matter? What's it all for at the end of the day, huh. Nothing at all. Absolutely bugger all. We're all still dying, Hughie lad. If they're not dying of the pox, they're topping themselves. Corkindale hung himself last week. A woman screamed at him in the street. Who wouldn't eh? He's got no fucking nose and half a jaw missing. Not surprising is it that she screamed and that he strung himself up. I've lost count of the number that have gone from pox. Before long we'll all be gone. So, all your efforts are for nothing, Hugh lad. There'll be no one to thank you at the end of the day. So why bother? First of all you lock yourself away, let the disease eat through you, whichever one you've got, then when you've had enough..." He stopped speaking but placed an imaginary pistol at his temple and squeezed an imaginary trigger.

"Anne won't thank you for neglecting yourself like this."

"Anne isn't here, Hugh lad. Had you failed to notice? She's gone, cleared off and left us. Didn't you work that one out when you marched in?"

"She hasn't cleared off at all. She'll be watching you, watching you every minute and second, and she won't be too proud. She'll be disappointed in you Peter, disappointed the way you're going on with your own lad. I don't think she'll understand that. I don't think any of us could understand that."

Peter groaned aloud and sank back in his chair. "Christ, they always want something, Hugh lad. They're never satisfied. Always something. Anne was always running round after him."

"He's half-starved Peter."

"So what?" Peter suddenly snapped. "So what? What life has he got to look forward to, eh Hugh lad? Is it so bloody rosy? What the hell difference would it make if all the filthy rabble didn't make it? There's nothing for them, so why pretend? He's cried and cried, badgered his mother, interfered and got in the way for nothing, because there is nothing, nothing at all, and that's if he's lucky. He might just have what we had. Oh, Christ. Go to hell with it."

Hugh didn't speak for some time. His attention kept passing to Bill. He could obviously hear all that was said, but continued to gaze ahead as if it were not about him. He had learnt to disassociate himself from Peter's rage. It was dreadful to see the compliance that appeared like trust apparent in Bill's expression. It wasn't fair. Maybe Peter was right and he did want to make everything all right for everyone, but what was wrong with that? Maybe he would never be truly content until everyone was, but he didn't see that as in any way a bad thing. To hell with Peter Kavanagh! And yet, he wanted it to be all right for Peter Kavanagh as well. He had an image of him that would endure through all alteration and damage. The image of a well-meaning, optimistic, singularly happy young man. He had been robbed. Hugh wanted to give it all back. He quietly said: "You've been through a lot Peter. I can't pass any judgement on you. You'll always be my comrade, my friend, the best friend a man could have. We all miss Anne, so God knows what you're feeling. I'm sorry. I wish I could take a bit of it, but I can't. So I don't know what to do. I want to help, though. I want you to let me help."

"We can never work out surviving can we. I've tried to do it, but I can't make head nor tail of it. Why have I come through it? What the hell was the use of getting through? I'll never get to the bottom of that."

"No, you're right. I can't work it out. And I ask myself the question all the time. But maybe it's not for working out. Maybe we have to pay for it."

"Wrong word, Hugh lad, wrong word."

"Is it? Is it?" Hugh asked with a sudden show of noticeable passion. Peter simply shrugged. He didn't feel able to insist on anything. Hugh went on in the same quietly inflamed manner. "I've got to do things right, Peter. Do you understand? I've got to get it right. I've got to do things well."

"You'll do that right enough, Hugh lad," Peter suggested with more than a hint of sarcasm.

"Well, first things first, and that's why I'm here really, I've thought it through and I'm convinced we'll have to postpone the wedding."

"No!" Peter replied flatly.

"It's not right Peter. Everyone loved Anne. What are they going to think? I don't want that hanging over my wedding."

"It doesn't matter what other people think. What the hell do they know about anything?"

"But it does matter. Don't you see? You can't just rubbish what people are thinking. People make it good or bad for you. People make the world you live in. Don't you see. They give you your permission and they take it away. That's what the problem was for Corkindale. It's not right, but it's how it is. They make you or break you."

Peter hung his head. He gave a low, forced laugh. "She said she was happy. Happy!" He looked up at Hugh. His expression was horrified. "I didn't make her happy, did I? I was hopeless. I can't believe I was so hopeless. You should have seen her the night my dad went away. Oh God, Hugh. You should have seen me. I just want to go back to that for a minute, just to tell her, to say to her, to say I'm sorry. Christ I'm so sorry. I am sorry Hugh. I'm so sorry and so ashamed and I can't get back and I can't get to her and... Christ Hugh. I'm burning up, here, burning, all my insides. And I just... Oh Christ, Hugh!" He moaned aloud, gripping frantically at his chest, as he let out his searing hopeless plea and then he began to cry. The tears filled his eyes and stayed there for a moment, then despite himself began to race along his cheeks. He swiped at them as they fell as if they were appalling.

As he cried Bill moved cautiously from below the window-ledge and came and stood by his chair. Peter turned to him. As Peter's eyes fell on him Bill looked terrified, but he had obviously chosen to refuse himself the option of running away.

Peter pulled Bill to him awkwardly. He looked up at Hugh and pleaded: "Please, Hugh, for Anne's sake, don't change your plan. There's no time, no time to waste. You know that. She would want it more than anything. I don't care about the rest of them, but I want what Anne would want. For Christ sake don't cross Anne. Please don't cross Anne."

Hugh thought for a moment, then quietly conceded: "I'd do it for Anne." Peter smiled gratefully. "Mind you, I think Kate will take a bit of persuading, and John too, for that matter."

Peter flared with anger. "Well don't let her, for Christ sake. It's not her choice, is it. It's Anne's decision. Christ." He stopped speaking. He suddenly gave a terrible smile, his face agape: "I'm guilty for ever Hugh lad, guilty as sin."

"We can all be forgiven Peter, but maybe it takes time."

"I never want to be forgiven though. I killed the best thing, the most wonderful thing I ever had. I killed it dead. I don't want to get off with that. Never." As he said this he held Bill away from him at arms length. For a few moments Bill still leaned against Peter's outstretched arms, but then he gave it up and went back to his construction on the floor under the window. Peter smiled grimly. "I don't want forgiveness in this life, or any that's to come. I don't ever want forgiveness. Do you understand? I'm through with things like that. I killed her. I killed her dead. And I thought the dead didn't have any hold over me anymore, but I was wrong, very wrong. And now it's too late. I'll never get to say any of what I should have said. But that's all right. That's my punishment. It should be more. It should be a lot more. You get it right, Hugh lad. Well, try anyway. Let's be honest, you haven't got a hope. Who's to say you haven't got a dose, Hugh lad, or were you so good in France?"

Hugh shook his head a number of times, then quietly stated: "There's always hope Peter, it's a state of mind."

"Get married for Anne's sake. Tell me you'll do it for her."

Hugh nodded his agreement. He waited a moment longer, but finding he had nothing more to say excused himself. Before leaving he went over to the window. He asked Peter if he could open the curtains so that Bill might have some light in which to work. Peter didn't answer. He was again staring at the empty grate. Hugh took that as an agreement.

As he drew aside the curtains a pale pearly light gradually filtered into the room. He looked down at Bill's work. He hadn't made a kite but a funny canvas doll with stick arms and legs, and a flat round face with poorly drawn circles for eyes and mouth but no nose. Hugh smiled at the creation. Bill picked it up and nursed it like a baby. Hugh left them each to their consolation.

Back in the street he was approached by the woman from whom he had asked for food. She had obviously been waiting for him. She said: "I never realised. No one realised. The lad's had a rough time."

Hugh nodded his agreement. He didn't know whether she meant Peter or Bill. He smiled in gratitude. "Keep an eye that he's fed, and let me know."

She smiled and placed her index finger to the side of her nose.

When Hugh left Ginns the street was in total shadow.

He was right about Kate. No amount of his suggesting it would convince her that the wedding should go ahead. She thought it quite out of the question. After Anne's death she was certain they were cursed. She had prayed, but it had not proven enough. In the week leading up to the funeral she lay in bed unable to sleep. She found herself whispering to Robert, asking for absolution for them all, though she could not articulate their sins. John was aware of her insomnia and, having heard her prayers, knew her thinking, but he said nothing. In the back of his mind there was always the unconfessed killing of Murphy. In the immediate aftermath of the killing he had often had bad dreams, dreams in which he was always on the precipice of exposure. He dreamed that he had covered his tracks well, and was sure he was about to be released from the possibility of discovery, when, usually for the smallest of errors, it was all about to go wrong. His crime was to be revealed. He was never actually accused in his dreams, but the moment of revelation seemed to go on and on interminably, and that moment of anticipation was the nightmare. When he awoke from these dreams he invariably found them difficult to shake off. For days he would find it difficult to separate dream from reality. However, once the outcry and interest died down he was relieved to find that he was less haunted by dreams, though he was never entirely rid of them. Following Robert's death they had returned with a vengeance. They were even more difficult than ever to shake off. His dreams were now more vivid than he could have believed possible.

Such was Kate's objections, tacitly supported by John, that Hugh considered that only Peter himself could hope to achieve any change of heart in her thinking. He duly went back to Ginns. He was somewhat relieved to find that the curtains were open and there was some semblance of order in the house. Peter told him that some women along the way came in and helped straighten things out for him. Hugh was quite moved by the information. It confirmed something in his thinking about doing things well. He thought the women really quite wonderful. When Hugh told Peter that Kate was quite inflexible over the subject of the wedding Peter assumed it was that news that had made Hugh so emotional. Hugh instantly recognised that Peter was angry over the matter and suggested that he was not at all surprised by Kate's attitude and that maybe Peter should think it through one more time. However, he quickly realised that Peter was as adamant as Kate and didn't press the point. Peter declared that he would go to Kate directly.

When Peter went into Kate he refused to listen to her concerns and flatly refused her dissension. He pointed out, in no uncertain terms, that the decision was his and his alone. Anne was his wife. She was his loss. He didn't really see why he had to share that loss so completely with others, to the point where someone would feel it right to cancel their marriage. Kate didn't approve of his tone or his words, they weren't just *someone*, and they didn't assume a *right*, but she didn't argue. He was altogether too volatile to argue with. She didn't want to even consider the ramifications of refusing him. Reluctantly, then, she agreed that if that was what he wanted, then the wedding should go ahead. He insisted it was not what he wanted, but what Anne wanted. With rather more grace she gave her assent on that point.

As it turned out the wedding was a great success. John Darcy began it. He turned up on Kate's doorstep a week before the event with a roll of cream coloured material, a square of embroidered lace, and a tin of ivory buttons on his trolley. His response to Kate's suggestion that the items must be stolen was a dismal display of grief. Seeing his response Kate was then profuse with apology. He eyed her starkly and somewhat defiantly, an attitude quite uncharacteristic of him, then puffed out his chest, and declared: "Your job, Mrs Devlin, is to make the dress. My job is done. I don't think you understand that Mrs Darcy and myself love that girl. No you obviously do not." He turned to leave, but Kate stayed him. She was solemn and contrite in her gratitude, and humbly told him she would never forget his gesture. The truth was he had awakened in her a sense of the seriousness of the impending wedding. He had made it real for her. Up until then, to the point where she held the material in her hands, it hadn't really existed. It had been a factor in Anne's death, not something in its own right, something precious in her own life. The lace and ivory changed that. She immediately took herself to the Kavanaghs' house to seek help.

Catherine had come back home, having spent over two years working in Gretna in the munitions factory, and was now back in the clothes factory. June hadn't come with her. She had apparently gone to Glasgow in the first place, in the company of another girl from the Gretna works who had promised her that she would be able to secure her a position in the Singer factory, having herself worked there before shifting to Gretna. But apparently that hadn't worked out, and June had somehow found herself in Manchester. She had started there by working in service in the house of a local politician, but was now working in a large store. She detailed all these events in letters which she sent sporadically, addressing them on all occasions to Tom, presumably as he was now considered the head of the household. She enclosed two photographs, one of her holding a feather duster, and the other holding a jar of sweets. In both she gazed impatiently, yet mischievously at the camera, as if she were only just managing to stop herself from laughing. She didn't ask to be reminded to Catherine in her letters. Catherine never verified or contradicted what June wrote. Her only comment was to say that it was just like June to send photographs of herself, she always was a bit vain like that. It struck everyone that Catherine and June must have had a falling out, but when it had first been hinted to Catherine on her return she had insisted that that was not the case at all. However, she never spoke much at all of what they had done with themselves in Gretna. In fact, she was altogether a quieter, more sedate, young woman than she had been. She had soon settled back into her old routines. The only change in her daily pattern was that she now went to the factory with Alice, and no longer needed to bring homework for Anne.

With the help of Catherine and Alice, both experienced seamstresses, Kate was sure she could surprise Dora. She explained her intention to Catherine and they set to work immediately. They worked throughout the week in total secrecy. When the job was complete Kate was overjoyed with their achievement. The dress had a neat shaped bodice, patterned with the ivory buttons, interlaced with ribbons of lace, and from the waist down it was an extravagance of material. They had fashioned the remaining lace into a mantilla large enough to drape down to Dora's waist. When Kate and Catherine presented it to Dora she immediately broke down. When she learnt where the material originated from she promised to kiss John Darcy and his mother, despite the fact the old woman had never lost her reputation for necromancy with the passing years.

And it was the dress, more particularly the mantilla, and her hair braided with bluebells, symbolising constancy, which were noted as Dora approached the altar. She felt the strength of the attention on her and revered it and revelled in it. For Hugh, her progress to the altar, her slow, sure steps, coming inexorably to him discontinued, once and for all, the unfinished war. They laughed as they greeted each other. They felt free and at ease. The past was put aside and was replaced by the future, and they didn't feel any guilt at doing it. They just felt an incredible liberty in their coming together.

John Devlin felt embarrassed. He recognised their intimacy, and through it remembered the desire that had brought him to Kate. He felt exposed thinking about it, standing there at the altar, in full view of the congregation. He was relieved when he was able to shuffle back to his pew and bow his head in respect. Shortly after, as he listened to the readings – they had chosen the *Song of Songs* - he felt moved by desire and piety. He was filled with joy and sadness to equal measure. He could scarcely comprehend it. He knew as he listened to the words that a part of him was complete. The very sensuality of the passage underlined the fact. A large part of his job was finished. His children were gone. One was dead and one was going to another man. He was through. It made him feel old and yet satisfied. At the same time, he was being brought back to Kate. The *Song of Songs* was their song as well. It was enthralling. He was through with so much and yet the future remained unpredictable, not negligible. The future remained his. He would have to steer his guilty heart through it. The story never ground down to nothing. As the reading progressed, he never felt stronger.

> *O that thou wert as my brother, that sucked the breasts of my mother! When I should find thee without, I would kiss thee; yea, I should not be despised. I would lead thee, and bring thee into my mother's house, who would instruct me: I would cause thee to drink of spiced wine of the juice of my pomegranate. His left hand should be under my head, and his right hand should embrace me.*

When the service was complete Father Bond accompanied the couple to the porch. He embraced them at the door, then opened it for them and told them that they were now on their own. His remark disquieted them. They looked out warily, hesitant to cross the threshold. It wasn't yet spring, and the chill of winter remained. Dry leaves blew around the crucifix in the courtyard and the pale porcelain figure of Christ looked frozen. In the end Father Bond burst out laughing and told them to get out, he needed to change. However, by the time the wedding party had made its way up the valley side to Ginns he had managed to rejoin them. Before they went into the Devlin's house he made John read. John felt awkward and his voice faltered, but he got through somehow without failing:

Set me as a seal upon thine heart, as a seal upon thine arm: for love is strong as death; jealousy is cruel as the grave: coals thereof are coals of fire, which hath a most vehement flame. Many waters cannot quench love, neither can the floods drown it: if a man would give all the substance of his house for love, it would utterly be contemned.

When he was through there was a moment's silence, and then a stuttered ripple of uncertain applause broke out. The noise was quickly stifled by the priest who immediately raised his hands to quell it, obviously disapproving of such a show. He told them he would say a blessing. They felt embarrassed and interpreted it as something of a rebuke. "Dear Lord, Bless this couple and help them discover your truth, through the sacrament of marriage and bring them ever closer to your love. Bless the table at which we are about to eat, and the food that you have provided. Thank you Lord. Amen." They were relieved to be dismissed by the amen, and were grateful to enter the house.

Kate and Dora had prepared the meal themselves, which consisted of baked kidneys, spiced herring, bread and teabrack, and for Hugh, John and Peter, the speech makers, rabbit pie. Marty took on the role of unofficial Master of Ceremonies. He was decked out in a beret and top coat, acquired especially for the occasion from a Dutch sailor for the price of half a bottle of poteen. By the end of the day he had offered to sell both on separate occasions to McClean and later Gavin Duffy. Gavin was there as a particular invited guest of Hugh's. Before the meal was complete Marty called on John to start.

John felt awkward and nervous as he looked around at the familiar faces. He knew it made no sense. They were friends. He was in his own house. Eventually, he laughed at his own hesitancy and raised his hand as if to quiet them so that he could start, though they were already silent.

He immediately laughed again at that. Gavin egged him on from the back of the room. John burst out laughing and invited Gavin to take his place. Gavin raised his hand in acquiescence. It was just the spur John needed. "No," he said, beginning in earnest, though his voice trembled, "I don't want anyone else to stand here. As terrible as it is to have to get up here and face the lot of yous. Well, I think a man worries about his daughter." He stopped abruptly. He looked about the room, though he didn't register any faces. He needed time to compose himself. He quietly berated himself for being so foolish, then continued with noticeably greater authority. "I know that a man who is anything of a man worries about his daughter. Of course he does. It's only natural. You just want to protect them, make sure everything's all right. You know, good. Of course, you always think that someday she'll get married. You have to think about it. It's only natural. You have to think that someday she'll bring a young man home. And it's not a nice thought. Well, it isn't, is it. A daughter is precious, and you get scared, really scared. You get to wondering just what sort of man he might be. Who will you have to welcome into your house? It isn't easy not being able to choose for her. I know you can't. That's what I mean. It's a headache. And it's not easy when you're in a different country. I don't need to explain that. You know what I mean. There's a lot of things different, and you're not quite yourself in some way. Well, that's by the by. Still, I'll be honest with yous, I never thought I'd be standing here speaking of a soldier, ex, British. And I'll also be honest with yous and say I'm not disappointed. Perhaps we're lucky to have a soldier, ex, British, at all. Maybe we're damned lucky. We'll have you Hugh and welcome. I like you son. I'd like to drink to you." He raised his glass and toasted: "The bridegroom!"

Hugh didn't wait for Marty to call on him but stood up immediately. Even as the toast was still being repeated around the room he began speaking. He addressed himself entirely to John, his tone confidential, apologetic even, but pressing: "I hope to live up to some of that, Mr Devlin, I promise I do. Listen, I tell you this, I was at work yesterday and some of the lads there were kidding me on about today and all and, well, eventually they got round to asking me whether I'd be in uniform or not. Well, on the whole they're a great bunch of lads so all I said was, no, no I wouldn't be in uniform. I think they were a bit surprised really. I reckon they must have seen this suit before. Anyway, what I didn't tell them, but what I'll tell you, Mr Devlin, in confidence like, is that any uniform I ever had was wrapped up with stones a year ago and dumped at the bottom of the dock when the ship we called *the big ship* pulled in and I was demobbed. It's not that I'm ashamed of what we did, but I'm not proud either. I don't know the rights and wrongs of it, how could I, and I don't care to work it out now. All I know is it's finished. A new start, then. There are people who think marriage is the end of something, well, I don't think so. Marriage is not a destination, it's a journey, and I tell you, Mr Devlin, I'm a happy man starting that journey with your daughter, particularly with your good wishes. I won't ever let her down, Mr Devlin. You're all just the job, just the job." He hesitated and for the first time acknowledged the others crammed into the small room, as if he had only just registered that they were listening too. He laughed out loud, embarrassed and surprised by himself. "Crikey, listen to me. Look, I'd just like to say thank you to everybody here for... well, coming to see us off. That's it. It'll do. It's just the job I reckon." He sat down quickly and bowed his head, unable to face applause, yet relieved and pleased that it was so forthcoming. Despite his lowered head he felt entirely content.

Marty fiddled *Love is pleasing,* and nodded towards Peter, inviting him to say something as best man. Peter was reluctant to accept and remained where he was, apart from Hugh, Dora and the rest, amongst the crowd of guests, his back to the wall. They made room for him. He looked around timidly, as he realised he had been exposed. A momentary flash of anger spread across his face as if he felt he had been betrayed. Still, he knew it was inescapable. He had to say something. It was the done thing. It didn't matter what he thought, he had to do it. He had to do it for Hugh, for the man who had sustained him, seen him through in order that he could be here. He quailed inside. Standing in that crowded, dull kitchen it didn't seem worth it. It was a terrible admission. He fought against his own repugnance. He made abortive attempts to speak, but failed each time. But then with a sudden burst of energy he spoke up quickly and abruptly, a few sharp, broken phrases: "No salutes Hugh. That's behind us. An order, though, a civvie order, mind, the only orders for you now. Be happy. All right. That's all. That's all there is to say. Be happy, happy for the whole lot of us. Good lad." He fell silent, inhaled deeply and drank without toasting, avoiding the attention of those around him. As he drank a burst of applause broke out, at first uncertain, but once begun it quickly assumed a momentum, until it finally became rapturous.

When the applause died away and the guests got back to eating and drinking Hugh went to Peter. He took his hand and embraced him. John watched their embrace grimly. There was so much meaning in it, so much that spoke of their shared experience, their separation together from the others in that room. His thoughts turned to Robert. He felt his composure begin to crack. It was all he could do to master himself and not start to weep. Robert, his quietly sensitive, thoughtful son was absent. He had never heard a speech over his parting. He had not even received a farewell. How on earth had he let that happen? What demon had possessed him to put anything before the life of his son? That was why he had bad dreams. It was nothing to do with Murphy. He had killed Murphy to protect his son and then he had casually thrown him to his fate, acted as if he had disowned him. But it wasn't so. He had never disowned him. He tried to tell himself that, but it was difficult to make a convincing case. He wasn't even sure that he had ever owned him, had ever tried to understand what went on inside his head. What wonderful thoughts he might have heard had he only had the mind to listen. Of one thing he was certain, he had never stopped loving him. He had been inadequate in showing it, but it didn't mean it wasn't the case. Surely Robert would have known that. Surely he would have known that he was loved. But it was too late to know for certain. Now he could never know, never be told. Robert by rights should be in paradise. It was a place he would never know. He had given up his God and failed to make that sacrifice count. He felt tears on his cheeks. He had to get out. He didn't want to be drawn to speak of Robert to anyone. He felt he had said enough for one day. He went out to the yard ostensibly to smoke, in essence to hide.

Hugh and Dora planned to leave after the first dance, their first together, but stayed longer and danced some more. After the first few tunes, which they danced together to everyone's satisfaction, Hugh danced with Kate and Dora danced with her namesake.

Aunty Dora, smelling of gin and weeping crocodile tears, still had her bonnet on but had stripped off her coat, which meant that now she had started she would be up until the music came to an end. Dora wanted to know how long she planned to stay and was surprised to learn that she intended to be gone by the morning. She rather grandly announced that she was needed. Dora asked her to come and live with her.

Aunty Dora laughed out loud: "And I thought you were going to have a whole load of children. Or have you given up on that mad idea you had as a girl?"

"There'll be room."

Aunty Dora shook her head and laughed out loud again. Yet, something in Dora's expression told her that she was serious. She gazed at her with deep affection, and rather wistfully said: "No, I'll be back in the house tomorrow. That's where I belong, for the time being. I couldn't see myself anywhere else for a while. I tried to leave once, got myself a job in a factory, but, when it came to it, I couldn't do it. I'm a big woman. I need a house, even if it isn't mine. I wasn't born to be the woman of my own house. We none of us were really. I'll be back there, in my place, thank you, all the same. It means a lot to me mind, that you'll be in your own place, no gombeen men knocking at your door. That's all the world to me. It'll be all the world to your mother. We've come a long way."

Dora ran her fingers across her aunty's cheek and wiped away the trickle of tears from her cock eye. "There'll always be a home if you want one."

"I know," Aunty Dora said, and tried to laugh but failed. She was content and she didn't want to query it. She had learnt to be content, to be what nature had made her, a weeping, homeless virgin. She spoke for the sake of saying something. "It's a warning, you know, this old crooked eye of mine."

"About what?"

"Christ, I don't know, but they're tears aren't they, so they must mean something. Tears always mean something. Just take care of each other, that's all."

"We'll do all right."

"John and Kate will like grandchildren. They'll do everybody good. I find everybody a bit flat at the moment. Your children will laugh at my cock eye, and make up stories about where it came from, and that'll be great, I tell you. That'll give me a bit of a kick. It'll make me a bit of an old oddity, but what the hell. I suppose I will be." The dance came to an end, but they remained together. "You have your great bunch of kids. I think it's altogether mad, mind you, but John and Kate will love it."

Dora nodded. Aunty Dora was right, she was sure. They would love it. Nothing could be the same again, not without Robert, but they none of them were through. They were all just a bit more mature. She gazed around the room wanting to take a look at Kate and John. She missed her father for the first time. It perplexed her. She turned back to Aunty Dora. "We'll be going soon, get on our way," she said. "Remember, there'll always be room."

Aunty Dora didn't answer, but simply kissed her on the forehead and broke free. She went to Marty, and immediately started clapping to the resumed tune. She didn't look back. She wasn't able.

Dora searched for her father and eventually found him still in the yard, smoking, staring up at the sky.

"You're missing your daughter's wedding party," she said.

"I can hear it through the door. Have I been missed?"

"I missed you."

"You shouldn't miss your father on your wedding day."

"You've given up on me already?"

"You can always come back."

"I will. All the time."

"But not to stay."

"No, not to stay."

"The house will be empty without you. There'll be nobody now. Well, except Patrick." John paused, then turned to her. "I never spoke to Robert, you know. I think that's unforgivable. How could I not have spoken to him? I wanted him to be like Peter, you know. When they were growing up, I mean, and when they were young fellers. And look at Peter now. Why didn't I know he was special, Dora? Why wasn't I told?" He paused and shook his head quietly, without any force. "What am I saying, Dora?" He grimaced, looked up again and laughed. The sound was harsh, mocking and self-abusive. He went on: "Do you think he's up there, Dora? Do you think he's anywhere? The sky is a great big place to hide someone. I can't really believe they've hidden a whole heaven up there, somehow. But he believed it, didn't he. At least, I think he believed it. I don't know for sure. I don't think I believe it. Do you believe it? Maybe I shouldn't ask. Maybe I don't want any answers. I never listened before."

"Come on," she said, cutting him short, "I'm going now. You have to kiss me and wish me God speed."

They kissed. They said no more. They had nothing to say. They were content with each other. John stayed in the yard. Dora went to find Hugh. She walked back into a heated row between Peter and Tom.

Marty continued to try and fiddle, but the sound of their raised voices, particularly that of Tom, made it impossible. The music came to a stuttered, elastic, somewhat comic halt.

Tom had obviously been drinking quite heavily. His voice was slurred and his gait unsure. Dora had no idea what had started the fuss, but she recognised the substance of Tom's tirade against his elder brother. The sense of what he was saying was disconnected and jumbled as new thoughts came into his head, but it was obvious he had a great deal to get off his chest.

He accused Peter of being wrapped up in himself, of arrogance and selfishness. He threw up his hands and asked about June. Why did Peter never think to ask about June? Did he not care? Did he not care about anything other than Peter Kavanagh? Of course, no one had seen or done anything, except Peter Kavanagh. Wasn't that the point? No one was worthy of Peter Kavanagh any more. The big brother was so full of himself he didn't have time for anyone else. Well, it wasn't Tom's fault he hadn't been to war. It wasn't his fault he had managed to stay on the dockside whilst the great hero was fighting in the great war. Well, if it was all so awful, why wasn't he glad for all those who had missed it? Why did he have to keep ramming it down their throats as if they had committed some crime, some sin against Peter Kavanagh? Why had he hounded Anne with it all? Did he not realise how she had missed him, pined for him, loved him?. Even when he turned out to be the arrogant fool he was, she had still loved him. God only knew why? Well, he could stop it. Stop lording it over everyone. Stop inflicting his self-pity and his self-righteousness over all of them. He had had enough. He had kept the house together, kept the Kavanaghs as a family together, and he didn't take to Peter strolling in as if he were the rightful head of everything. Time had moved on. Did he realise? Did he realise anything any more? Well, did he?

The tirade drew to a climax of shrill, repeated questioning, the same demand being made over and over. Did Peter Kavanagh realise anything anymore? The remarkable thing was that throughout Tom's entire outburst Peter had only raised his voice to instruct Tom to be quiet. Of course, whenever he had, it only served to work Tom up to ever greater volubility. He made no attempt to argue back or defend himself. And, what was perhaps most surprising to most of those who listened as Tom went on, Peter did not hit out. He was now marked as a potentially violent man, but he made no show of it.

In fact, it was only when Aunty Dora went to Tom to try and coax him to be quiet, and Tom thrust her away, that Peter made any move towards his brother at all. However, it was Hugh who intervened first. He had allowed Tom his say. He wasn't sure he would have known how to stop it. But as soon as Tom pushed Aunty Dora, and he recognised that Peter was about to respond, he stepped in. The last thing he wanted was a wholesale fight at his wedding feast.

He wrapped his arms around Tom, pressing Tom's arms to his side, and side-stepped him away from Peter, whispering at his ear all of the time, telling him that it was all right and that it was all over. Within

217

seconds Tom was weeping uncontrollably. He moaned that he was always disregarded. Everyone went on and on about Peter Kavanagh. But what about Tom Kavanagh? He had done his best. He didn't know what had happened about June, but he had done his best. He was worried about June. For a moment he bleated her name. At that point Aunty Dora stepped in again. She took over Hugh's hold on Tom and began to dance with him. Marty picked up her cue and began to fiddle. After that, it was all over. Tom went through the steps of a stupefied dance and shortly after Alice took charge of him and led him home, hugging him tightly all the way, where he immediately slumped in a chair and promptly fell asleep.

As Tom danced with Aunty Dora Dora went to Hugh. She smiled at him, full of pride and curiosity. She suggested he was quite the man for sorting out everyone's problems. He shrugged. He looked across at Peter. He was drinking on his own. Hugh turned back to Dora and shook his head, then laughed. This is just the job he said, just the job. They left without any further fuss. They merely went to Kate in order to say their farewells, but they were dismissed by her before they could speak. After that they let themselves out.

The wind along the street remained strong. Low fragmented cloud blew across the sky. Dora pulled her dress up into her arms and began to run towards home which was rented on the slope of Mount Pleasant. Hugh came right behind her. Before the year was out their first child was born and as it was almost Christmas they called her Mary.

*

Mary, born 1920, before the year was out. Her birth marked the end of the post-war industrial boom. At the same moment she was born industry collapsed. Within three months unemployment doubled. By June 1921 it stood at two million. It marked the end of optimism. It also marked the end of power. In the summer of 1920 a threatened general strike had forced the government to withdraw planned support for Poland against the Soviet Union. The dockers refused to load the boats. The labour movement had stood firm. Councils of Action had been set up across the country demanding that Britain would not go to war against the Worker State. The government acquiesced.

The economic downturn changed all that. In response to continued agitation from the miners throughout the winter and on into the spring the government returned the mines to private ownership. The owners

218

immediately cut the wages and returned to the old system of district rates. In April, after the miners demand for equalised rates had been rejected, there was a lockout. The triple alliance was called upon. However, when the owners offered a standstill on current wages and further negotiation over a national pool for future wages, the railway and transport workers called off their strike. It was Friday, the fifteenth of April, Black Friday, a date of shame for the labour movement. The miners were on their own.

It was also the day that Peter Kavanagh searched through Alice's bedroom to see if he could find any clue as to who might have made her pregnant. Since her admission a few days previously that she was pregnant (she insisted that she didn't know how far on she was, which only made matters worse in most people's eyes) she had steadfastly refused to name the father. Peter had only learnt about the pregnancy that morning. Catherine came to him and said she needed to speak. He had had little inclination to listen. He was too involved in the lockout. He had found a role for himself, encouraging the men to follow the union line. He had no illusions about the fact that he basically bullied them. In fact, the truth was he enjoyed it. He enjoyed the possibility of retaliation. It allowed him to vent an incredible retribution. It made him dangerous. He didn't have limits. He didn't suffer anyone to give him limits. He was driven by a disregard for all and everything.

Strangely enough, it had been Gavin Duffy who had managed to get him involved. Inevitably they came into regular contact. They worked in the same place and frequented the same pubs. Duffy was always conciliatory. Peter did his best to ignore him. It was the situation in Ireland, the war of independence against Britain, into which Ireland had gradually slipped since January 1919 when Sinn Fein members had refused their seats at Westminster and instead set up a Parliament in Dublin, that had altered things and put their relationship on a different footing. Michael Collins led the Irish Republican Army in a increasingly successful guerilla war against troops and police. Just after Hugh and Dora's wedding the English government reinforced the Irish Constabulary with ex-soldiers. Stories soon circulated throughout the Catholic community of the atrocities they committed. There were terrible incidents of burning, torture and killings. Most of the families in the Irish streets still had some family in Ireland. The community was incensed. It was difficult for people like Peter and Hugh. They were torn between contradictory loyalties. They tended to say nothing. In public at least.

Dora would always remember the terrible night Hugh smashed up the cellar, leaving a debris of broken glass and shattered wood, where boxes and barrels had been reduced to shards. When the storm subsided he lay on his knees and shivered without restraint. The outburst terrified her and yet impressed her. His very lack of restraint was so passionate she couldn't help but wonder at the depth of him and appreciate it. If anything, she was rather jealous of it. It was an aspect of him that she had to take on trust and share as he decided. She had always surmised that there was a dangerous, unruly side to him that his usual manner belied, he was too passionate for it to be otherwise. She held the vision of it dearly.

Matters came to a head for Peter in the shape of Duffy. They were in the same pub. Duffy had drunk quite a bit. He regularly drank to excess, as did most of the miners. Peter was not surprised when Gavin approached him. He usually did. Peter didn't really know what the approaches were about. He assumed it was Duffy's way of making amends. Not that he ever apologised for anything. Far from it, in fact. He certainly didn't shrink from talking about Bobby, but would invoke his memory as justification for all manner of his activities. Over the months he portrayed a picture of Bobby as a committed, passionate man, a man who took his responsibilities to heart. Peter tolerated Duffy's overtures. He didn't really pay them much heed.

He was surprised, however, to be approached by an uncharacteristically contrite, almost tearful Duffy. He simply came up to his table, nodded at him and then stood and gazed at him. After a moment or two he casually commented on the fact that Peter was sitting alone. Peter shrugged. Gavin suggested that it was good to sit alone and keep to your own company. It was the best thing altogether. Peter merely responded that he hadn't really thought about it. He didn't have an opinion either way. He thought about it at that moment though, in the few seconds before Gavin spoke again he thought about it. Was he alone out of choice or because others chose to avoid him? He didn't know. He told himself that he didn't care. He repeated it. He didn't care. He was sure it smacked of the truth. As if he knew exactly what Peter was thinking Gavin repeated that it was the best thing to keep your own company. He qualified it by saying that it saved a person from chronic disappointment.

Gavin then made a short impassioned speech about what was happening in his country. As far as he was concerned it was being raped and brutalised. It was being bled at every turn. He tossed his head

220

roughly from side to side and threw out questions, one after the other. Maybe it wasn't the right struggle? Who knew? Maybe you had to fight the struggle given to you, not the one you wanted? Maybe everything would always be a compromise? Maybe the main prize would always be out of reach? One thing was certain though, he hated and detested the ex-soldiers who were tearing his country to pieces. Peter didn't respond. He felt too sympathetic to Gavin's mood to challenge him. He was obviously suffering. It was a side to Gavin he wasn't familiar with. Gavin came up close to him. He whispered forcefully. The worst thing of all was that there were soldiers from their very own town, no, no, worse, from their very own streets who were opting to volunteer. For the sake of a few shillings they were willing to shit on all of them. He came right up to Peter's ear and spoke sharply and bitterly. Bobby Kavanagh would never have stood back and allowed that to happen, he uttered.

Peter pulled back his stool and brushed past Gavin and went straight out. Gavin went back to the bar to get another drink. By the morning three ex-serviceman had been badly beaten, each one left unconscious. Gavin never openly asked Peter about it, but there was a tacit understanding between them. Gavin continued to be polite. Peter was more indifferent than hostile. Gavin had increasingly approached Peter to assist in union matters. Peter obliged. He was always quite dispassionate. Gavin said he liked that. Peter didn't care what Gavin liked. He didn't care what anyone liked.

His mind, then, was on the measures Gavin had prescribed for him to resist the lockout when Catherine informed him about Alice. She took some time to get to the point. She hummed and hawed for a while, uttering words to the effect that she wasn't sure about what she was doing, implying that she had counselled against it, against involving him at all, but had finally come to accept that it was the right thing. Still, she didn't want him going off like a madman. He shrugged his indifference to whatever it was she had to say, but she knew he was desperate to know, and knew she had made it so. She even pointed it out. She told him flatly that she recognised the lie of his coolness. She knew what he was like. A hot head, a bully and an idiot. He didn't defend himself, but simply pouted his mouth as if he had a foul taste on his lips. It was then that she sprang the news about Alice. It was almost as if she were deliberately working him up. He refused to play her game. He shrugged and said nothing, gesticulating that it was of no concern to him. After that she informed him that she was refusing to say who the father was. Again he made no direct response. She became suddenly exasperated.

Who was going to pay for the upkeep of a child? She couldn't afford it. She was only just clinging on to her position by the skin of her teeth and a bit of guile. Tom had little enough to occupy him on the dock. So, would Peter take it on? She jeered as she asked him that, shook her head and suggested that she thought not. Peter's laconic response was to say that she should give her a slap. She put her face squarely in front of his, and coldly told him to give her a slap, if he wasn't too busy to care. He jumped to his feet and ordered her to follow him.

Catherine had no idea what he intended. The closer they came to home the more concerned she became. She had been incensed that Alice refused to name the father. That's all she wanted. She couldn't understand why Alice would refuse to confide at least in her. She was the elder sister. It was sheer frustration, and a hint of anger, that had persuaded her to go to Peter. She regretted it bitterly. There was no telling what he might do. She even told herself that she feared for Alice's life. She tried to calm him down as they marched along but he blanked her out.

In the event he more or less ignored Alice, the only real acknowledgement he made being to call her a whore once, but nothing more. There was certainly no physical contact. He instructed her that she stay put and not move a muscle. He proceeded to the bedrooms and began to pull out drawers, tipping their contents onto the floor, and stripping cupboards of all their contents. It was Catherine who complained at that, pointing out with some indignation that many of the things he was so carelessly scattering were either hers or Breda's. He carried on regardless. She insisted he cease immediately. He gave her a withering, hostile glare and demanded she shut up. From his original indifference he seemed to have worked himself up into something close to fury.

Along the bottom of the bed there was a large bedding-box. He lifted the lid and tossed its contents over his shoulder. After a moment or two he stopped and slowly got to his feet. He had unearthed a few scraps of paper that looked as if they might be letters. They weren't folded together or tied up, nor were they particularly hidden, other than for the fact that the bedding-box was rarely used. He opened them out and read each one. They were directions of places to meet, just notes with one or two instructions. There were only three. None of the three were addressed directly to Alice, and two had no signature, but the third was signed. Peter couldn't make out the name. He pushed it towards Catherine. She looked over the little note. It was an instruction to come to the delivery door of the factory at seven. It was signed by Mr Henderson. He was the manager of the sweat shop where Alice and Catherine worked. He was married. Catherine held her hands at her mouth as she gazed at the note. She looked at Peter fearfully, then begged him not to do anything hasty. He lifted his hand to strike her out of the way, but stayed himself and merely pushed past her.

He leapt down the stairs and banged into the kitchen where he had instructed Alice to wait for him. She looked up tearfully as the door swung open and he stood in the frame. He held the note out towards her. She looked at it apprehensively, then shrugged her incomprehension. He went closer to her, still with the note extended before him. Still she eyed him with the same naive apprehension. Finally he stood over her. He quietly demanded the truth. Very calmly he explained to her that if she didn't tell him the truth he would give her a very serious beating. She shook her head. He lifted his hand.

Before he struck her, however, Tom rushed in. He had been hanging about the dock, hawking for any available work. Breda, who had been indoors when Peter came, had gone straight to him, not knowing anything else she could have done. He shouted at Peter to stop. Peter swung round viciously and glared at Tom for interfering. Tom stood his ground though.

"Is this what you're reduced to Peter, smacking women, your own sister, who you should be looking after?"

"Who you should have been looking after," Peter retorted. "She's under your roof."

"And I will."

"It's a bit late for that, isn't it, Tom."

"Not for me, it isn't. She'll be all right. I've already told her."

"Are you so flush, down on the water front, Tom, that you can afford another man's bastard?"

"No, we're not flush at all, but I've given my word. Now, I think you'd better go. I don't want words like that under this roof."

Peter flared up in response to the summons. "Don't push me Tom. I won't stand for that."

"I wasn't pushing you. Stay then, if you want, I don't care, just calm down. We'll sort it all out. We're a family, aren't we?"

Peter shook his head. "No, I can't stay. I've got someone to see." He screwed up the note in his hand and let it drop to the kitchen floor. He marched forward and deliberately pushed past Tom. Tom sighed deeply as he went, slamming the door behind him, then smiled at Alice. She gave a weak smile in response. Catherine picked up the notes and threw them in the grate, saying that everything would be all right. Tom didn't ask how Peter had found out. He guessed it was Catherine's doing. He didn't know why she had told him, but it didn't really matter, he knew that Peter would have had to find out sooner or later. His knowing made no difference. He was master of that house.

Peter went straight to the sweat shop and waited for Henderson. He knew him by name but not by sight. He assumed it would be easy to work out who Henderson was, though. There were very few men worked in the rag trade. In the early evening the women began to leave, not altogether but in dribs and drabs. Eventually, at seven o'clock a man let himself out through the door at the back where deliveries were made. He was a tall, lean man, relatively well dressed, his clothes certainly clean. He had a pinched, sallow face with a slightly comic, morose look. Peter bounded straight over to him. He had every intention of questioning him, but when faced with Henderson's droopy expression it seemed somehow pointless. Henderson was obviously a married man. His demeanour said as much. Or so Peter told himself. Speaking to him was therefore futile. He even thought of simply walking away. Henderson obviously had no idea why he was being accosted. He was almost snivelling with fear, despite the indignation he was attempting to weave into his voice. So Peter took a step away, but suddenly his whole being erupted in loathing at this man, at his clothes, his position, his marriage, in fact, everything about him, and he swung back suddenly and struck Henderson in the face. He heard the crack as the jaw gave way under the blow. Henderson fell to the ground screaming in agony. Peter ran.

Much to his surprise Peter didn't live easily with the assault. He awoke each night following, having dreamed that the police were banging at the door. He lay awake, listening to the silence, certain that at any minute the calm would be broken by the imagined sound. In the ensuing days he even concocted plans to go to the sweat shop and make enquiries about Henderson, saying he was just an interested party. He dismissed each scheme he considered as absurd. The one thing he never countenanced was going to Catherine or Alice and asking them if they had any news. In fact, he even began to suspect them of being in league with Henderson. He kept asking himself why it was that they weren't in the factory at the time? How had they managed to have free time? It didn't add up, unless they had in some way set him up. It even crossed his mind that Alice wasn't pregnant at all, but with that thought came the realisation that he was losing his mind. He tried to take a grip of himself. He knew how important that was. He reminded himself that his comrades, the men he fought alongside, were still dying, only now they were killing themselves. They had fought for people who didn't want to admit who they were, didn't want to concede any responsibility or debt. They wanted them all to kill themselves. Well, he wasn't going to oblige. He might be on his own, but he would survive. He would keep his sanity.

On the third day following the assault Catherine called on him. He couldn't really work out her mood. Was she angry, upset, disappointed or what? He couldn't tell. He had expected her to fly off the handle with him, and condemn him for his rash, violent outburst, but she didn't. She was calm, but forceful. She told him that she knew it was him, knew that he had broken the jaw of the manager, Mr Henderson. She said that it was a mistake, a big mistake, but that it didn't matter. As far as she could tell only she, Alice and Tom knew the truth of the situation, and they would say nothing, but they wanted Peter to keep out of things. He caused too many problems. He jumped to assumptions. He was too quick to act. He didn't think. He let himself down. Then she modified what she had said and told him that it was she herself who wanted him to keep out of it. It was her decision. She had an idea or two of her own. She did finish by threatening him though. If he interfered further, then she would certainly admit to someone, she only said someone, what she knew about Mr Henderson. He felt a wave of temper flash through him, but he resisted it. For once he controlled himself. As she left she shook her head at him and told him to pull himself together and grow up. As the door closed behind her he was sure he had never felt more childish and he was determined never to feel that way again. For the next few weeks he never went near the house that had been his parents. He busied himself with the lockout. Gavin kept him busy.

While Peter was busy persuading men to resist any call to return to work June came home. She arrived late in the evening. It had been a clear, fresh day in late May. Despite the fact that it was late the light was only just fading. There were mists rising from the docks that were slowly settling over Mount Pleasant and Ginns. A greyness shot with pink coloured the streets. There were still kids playing around doorsteps and groups of men on each street corner, but everyone was hushed, as if speaking in whispers. Only an occasional shout broke the still atmosphere, but they seemed to come from some distance. She didn't try the door to see if it was open but knocked. She had a small, battered hold-all. Catherine answered her knock. It was the first time they had seen each other since leaving Gretna.

The two women just looked at each other for some time. It didn't seem in any way a battle of wits as both were completely devoid of expression. If anything, they seemed to be willing to try and out do each other with patience. In the end it was June who spoke first. She was quiet and fatigued in the way she spoke, disappointed.

"Am I not welcome then, after all, Catherine?"

"No, you're not welcome, not by me, anyway."

June pursed her lips, gave a brief, blank smile and shrugged. "When it comes to it I don't know what to say. I've gone through it as well, God knows how many times."

"You could start with sorry."

"Kick off with a lie. Start as I mean to go on. Carry on the way I have. Kid everybody. Make out that it was all a ball. In that case I'm... No, not this time, Catherine. I'm damned if I do and I'm damned if I don't, so I'll have the damning I choose. No can do."

"As wrapped up in yourself as ever. No idea what it might be like for someone else, for me, for instance."

June shook her head mournfully. "Who the hell do you think this is, standing on your doorstep? You don't know me. I bet you scarcely recognise me? I'm a stranger. I could be anyone to you. You think you might vaguely know me, remember me from somewhere, but you don't really know. Your memory's shot to hell."

"I remember absolutely everything. I remember vivid details. Everything is impressed on my mind. And you certainly are fixed in my memory. You're right, though, you don't look the same. You look a bit frayed around the edges, a bit dog-eared, I'm pleased to say, but apart from that it's the same miserable bitch I carry round inside here."

June smiled. "You still like me, don't you?"

Catherine shook her head very slowly.

"Oh I think you do, Catherine. And you still hanker for things, don't you. You can't quite get it out of your head that you've missed out. Well, you have sweetheart, missed out on everything. Just look at you."

"I look myself right in the eye when I look in the mirror, do you?"

"I look at myself all over, every inch, and I grin from here well, to there... " She laughed as she pointed firstly to her ear and then vaguely to some distant geographic idea. Then she brought her hand to her mouth, pressed two fingers gently against her lips, as if she had accidentally committed an indiscretion and said: "I bet you've never stripped to the skin in front of a mirror in your life. I bet you've never seen yourself taken in a mirror, and seen the smile of satisfaction on your own face as you were."

"You're disgusting."

"Am I? And what do you base that on, I wonder? Is it the lovely flush and flare for life I see around me? This really is the luxurious life isn't it."

"And you've had better, I suppose."

"Sometimes, and I've had worse. I've had much worse. Does that make you feel better?"

"It doesn't upset me."

"No, I'm damned sure it doesn't. That's honest of you anyway. I'll tell you something, though, I wouldn't give up my worst for your best."

"Whore!"

June suddenly flared in response: "Never! You can't accuse..."

Catherine spoke over her: "Thief! Liar! Cheat!"

June turned away, and glared fiercely towards the quickly darkening sky.

Catherine crossed the threshold and came up close to her so that she spoke right into her ear, speaking in a low but sustained, furious whisper. "I got all the blame for the money, while you did a bolt and scarpered off with one of your soldier friends."

"How the hell did I know they would look through your things?"

"We were sisters, for God's sake, sharing the same room. Of course they looked through my stuff. I was lucky just to lose my job and not end up in prison. I still don't know how I got away with it."

"Bad for morale, unpatriotic."

"What?"

"Filching from the offices of a munitions factory. Not the done thing sweetheart, not in time of war. Wouldn't want that on the front cover. Might signal the fact that someone realised there was nothing in it for them. No, they would always have hushed it up. That was the beauty of it."

"We were doing all right."

"Skivvies."

"The money was good."

"The trouble with you is you've got no dreams. I did you a favour. You always wanted to come back to this. I opened the door for you."

"I didn't come straight back. I couldn't."

June eyed Catherine with curiosity. This was a part of the story she really wasn't aware of. She smiled broadly, delighted by the possibility.

"I'm here now though, and yes I'm content with it, if that's what you mean."

June screwed up her face in disappointment. "Why don't you tell the truth. The only reason you're still mad at me is that it wasn't one of my soldier friends I scarpered off with, it was your soldier friend."

Catherine glared in defiance. She heaved with anger. She almost certainly would have slapped June had Tom not come to the door at that moment and called out June's name in astonishment.

"What the hell are you doing, nattering all night out here? Come in, for God's sake. You're letting all the cold air in."

As Tom stepped back, holding the door wide for them, June turned to Catherine. She looked at her for a moment and then smiled with what seemed an expression of genuine warmth and sympathy. She whispered: "He was no good. He dumped me in Glasgow. He wouldn't have made you happy."

"You have no idea what would have made me happy."

June shrugged and smiled again: "Oh I don't know, maybe I do." She looked up at Tom and called out briskly that she was coming. She went indoors without looking again at Catherine. Catherine waited outside in the street for some time, peering through the thickening mist. She couldn't make out the identity of things: figures were indistinguishable and so were known landmarks. After a while she began to smile. She threw her head back and looked above the narrow channel of the street into the night sky. The mist brought it down to earth. She reached out as if she could touch it. She grasped at nothing. She looked into her empty palm. She didn't stop smiling. She clenched her hands and opened them quickly as if discarding something, then went indoors closing the door firmly to behind her.

Christine and June remained aloof with each other for the next few days. If they were in a room together they scarcely spoke beyond what was necessary. What neither admitted was that Catherine had written to June and requested that she come home. She had some notion that June would know what to do about Alice's pregnancy. Although she never openly admitted it to herself, she had some vague idea about an abortion. She thought that if anyone would know about how to go about it then it would be June. She knew for a fact that June herself had gone through an abortion in Gretna. They had been friends then, as well as sisters. She had gone with her and knocked at the back-door of some

228

half-drunk ex-midwife. Everything had gone to plan. It had been a secret that bound them together, bound them to their liberated life. The bond had not survived much longer. She had had to fish out June's old letters, which Tom kept in an old tin under his bed, in order to find her address. In the event her letter was forwarded three times before June received it. The miracle was that she received it at all.

June hadn't been altogether certain whether to respond or not. The problem, as Catherine described it, of Alice being pregnant was meaningless to her. Young women were always getting themselves pregnant. Sometimes they married, sometimes they didn't. Usually parents took on their children's children and brought mother and child up as brother and sister, or sister and sister. Of course Alice couldn't do that. Sometimes the priest could be relied on to spirit the child away, as if working some great moral miracle, and no one was ever the wiser. And sometimes the offending mother might find herself in an asylum for mental defectives. It was the way things were. But as the days went on, the fact that it was Alice who was pregnant began to hit home. Who would stop the priest interfering, or save her from the mental hospital? There was no mother and father. If it was left to Peter to sort out what might he do? He always saw things in black and white, as far as she recalled. The war might have changed that, but she couldn't bank on it. Catherine was obviously concerned or else she wouldn't have written. She began to think of it as something of a mission to go and see her little pregnant sister. Of course it was over six years since she had seen her. She wasn't a little sister, fourteen years old, anymore. She was a woman of twenty.

In reality she wasn't leaving much behind. She had been asked to leave service for unacceptable indiscretions, and had been living hand to mouth for a while. Despite her protestation to Catherine to the opposite she had recently succumbed to the necessity of prostitution. Catherine's letter came like a sign. It offered the possibility of return. She hadn't thought of it. She had told herself all such paths were closed. She took one more client and bought a rail ticket from Manchester to Whitehaven.

She told Catherine that she had no intention of staying, yet nevertheless went to the old factory and inquired about work. She was seen by Mr Henderson's deputy, a dry, middle-aged spinster who informed her that she was looking to lay people off, not take any on. She went on to deliver a short lecture. She had to understand that she could not take herself off, then return as the whim took her and expect to pick up where she had left off. The great industries, the industries that had made Britain great, were no longer what they were. The Indians made their own shirts, and they made them far more cheaply than any home market could. The world was changing as they spoke. She was dismissed with a flourish of the arm.

Throughout this time June never spoke to Alice about the pregnancy. She acted with complete indifference to it. In reality she bided her time. Eventually during the late afternoon of a day in the beginning of June she found herself alone in the house with Alice. She took her opportunity.

The weather had been hot for a number of days and had turned humid and stormy. There had been a sequence of torrential showers throughout the day. Alice was sitting in the kitchen. The door was open into the yard. She was watching the rain slant across the frame. It was so heavy it was like a curtain. It was too hot to close the door, despite the fact that rain water bounced onto the kitchen floor. June stood by the window with her back to it and looked at Alice. Her features were blacked out against the light of the window. The sound of the downpour hitting the yard accompanied her speech.

"Tom'll be soaked down on the dock. He wants nothing soliciting for work in this weather."

Alice turned her attention away from the door and the rainfall and looked towards June. She looked as if she had been roused from a dream. "He has to do what he can. He can't afford to wait for a nice day."

"No, I suppose not. Still, it's a pity to get soaked."

"Where's our Catherine? I thought she might be back from work by now. Things have been a bit slack lately."

"I don't really know. She must be gone somewhere with Breda. The pictures maybe. And I guess Stan's with Tom."

"Most likely. They don't often go to the pictures, but it's been known. I suppose you're right. They wouldn't want to take me."

"I don't see why not."

"I've become the black sheep."

"Become?"

"Well, you know... "

"Oh it's all right. I know who was. It doesn't take much, does it?"

"Well, I don't know if it's not much or not. Maybe it is. Catherine seems to think it's a lot. Kate Devlin thinks I'm a disgrace."

"Did she say that?"

"No, but I can see it in the way she looks at me. I know what she's thinking. What a wicked, terrible girl. What a sinner."

230

"I don't suppose she is really."

"Maybe I'm wrong. I don't hold it against her. She's been very good to us, acted the mother without interfering. She's been good like that. Never took over, but never left us alone."

"Would it bother you, being considered a sinner, I mean?"

Alice smiled. The smile was commensurate to her speech, both had a strangely serene, dreamlike quality, as if she felt removed from things. "Would it bother you?"

"You mean, does it bother me?" June corrected her. Alice shrugged. "Well, whatever," June suggested. "No, it doesn't bother me. God and all that's fine when you're a kid, but when you get older other things matter. I wouldn't give up what I've done for a second."

"If you could go back would you still leave?"

"Sooner."

"Why?"

"There's a lot to do. I should have given myself a head start. I'm like an old woman already. Catherine says I look a bit dog-eared. I dare say she's right."

Alice laughed gently. "You're only just twenty-three, June, whatever are you talking about?"

"Is that all? I thought it was a lot more. I was sure it was a lot more. I feel like an old woman sometimes."

"You look great, the best of the lot of us. You'll get a proper man whenever you want. Catherine reckons you're too flighty. I reckon you're just enjoying yourself for a while, and then you'll settle down properly."

"Settle down! Fat lot of good that would do me. Settle down for what? Just to set my sights on being used two or three times a week for a couple of years, if I'm lucky, till he drinks himself into not bothering anymore, then what, sit and wait for the angels to come and redeem me. No thank you."

"You're not serious."

"About what?"

"Well, I don't like to say really. Men using their wives, in marriage like."

"Of course I mean it. What else do they do, but whip it out before you've even got started. There's no pleasure in that. I knew a girl in Manchester went off with another. She told me it was the best thing she ever did. The first time she'd ever been properly satisfied. She offered to show me how they did it, but, well, I just couldn't. I was tempted mind.

231

In fact, if I ever see her again, I might just take her up. What do you think of that Alice?"

"You're awful, our June," Alice laughed, "really awful."

"No, not at all, you just don't know do you, I mean till you've tried something. I don't mind trying anything once. A lass and a lass, fancy that. It might be quite something."

"I don't think I should be listening to this."

"It's all right. You're not a kid sister anymore."

"Well, you wouldn't catch me doing any lass and lass stuff."

"Have you never thought about it?"

"Course not."

"Well, I have. I've thought about it a fair bit since that lass told me. I'd never thought of it before, mind you. I'm sick of being used in the same old way, though."

"You shouldn't say these things, June. A man and a wife, it's different. I don't believe what you say. They don't all use their wives."

"Mind you, it's a damn sight better they whip it out than leave you with a kid you never asked for. Oh I'm sorry, Alice, that was a bit thoughtless of me. I didn't mean that. I shouldn't have said anything. I'm really sorry."

Alice didn't reply immediately. She looked back through the open door. The rain had eased to just a few heavy drops. The yard steamed. The atmosphere was still heavy. The sudden hush was intense. "I don't care what you say. I don't care about any of it anymore. Why should I? I know it's wrong. I know that. I've made my peace with that. I know what it means and I'm prepared. So, I'll never see God, but I won't be the first, and I don't suppose I'll be the last. I'm not proud but, well, I don't think I'm ashamed either." Her voice trailed away. She looked, to June, as if she were suddenly lost and lonely.

"It's not that bad," she said, cajoling her. "Let's be honest, it's quite the norm."

"Oh no, June, it is that bad."

"Look, I'm telling you, it isn't that bad. Don't let them get to you and make you think bad things about yourself. You were unlucky that's all. You got caught out. You'll be a bit sharper next time."

"You don't understand."

"Of course I understand," June said impatiently, bored by Alice's naive protestations. "I've been there all right. I'd have been in the same boat, except in my case I did something about it. And it was all right. Apart from some burning up here for a few days it was all right. And I

232

haven't been caught out ever since. So, stop telling me how awful it is. You're not the only one. No need for all this mystery and suspense. It makes a fool of you really."

"It's not the same."

"For God's sake, Alice, it really isn't anything."

"Tom's the father."

There was instant silence. June gazed at Alice blankly. She didn't know what to say. Alice stared at the open door. She had desperately wanted to say what she had just said, but had told herself it was impossible. What she had said was the unsayable. She both regretted saying it, and at the same time felt relieved. She was delivered of it. Satisfaction quickly replaced any other feeling.

Eventually June spoke up: "Tell me you're joking," she uttered, and then instantly repeated it with far more force, and then yet again with real violence.

Alice gazed ahead. The rain had started again. At first it was slow, but then very quickly became another torrent. She turned calmly to June. "Why should I grow up into some pathetic old spinster? Why?"

"What on earth do you mean? Why should you?"

"Because I don't know anyone. There isn't anyone. There's no men around here, not free like. They're all dead, aren't they. I don't know any men at all. Not one I would look at. I don't see why I shouldn't have what you've had. You were proud enough of it a minute or so ago."

"Jesus Christ Almighty!"

"No, leave all that out of it," Alice declared, her voice shot with emotion. "I don't want to hear all that from you or anyone."

"Our Tom!"

"He was lovely," Alice said with an agonised wail. "Absolutely lovely."

"Shut up! Just shut up!" June shouted at her, her mind in total confusion.

Alice leant towards her. She was either determined to defend herself, or motivated to taunt June. "He never used me, do you understand. He never once used me."

June glared down at Alice who was straining towards her, proud of her crime, relishing it. She attempted to speak but had nothing to say. Without thinking about it she slapped Alice across the face. Alice wiped her face where the palm had struck her, looked up at June and laughed. June slapped her again. The laughter immediately ceased. June struck her again. Suddenly she found herself repeatedly striking her. She could hear herself telling Alice to shut up. What she didn't really understand was what it was she didn't want to hear.

Alice fell away from her and sprawled across the floor. June took a step to keep striking her where she lay, but stopped herself. Alice recoiled from her. Suddenly Alice swore at her, calling her a bitch over and over. June made another move to silence her. Alice quickly pulled herself across the floor towards the open door, jumped to her feet and ran out into the rain. June stood perfectly still. The sound of the rain filled the small kitchen.

June stood alone in the small kitchen for some time. Still the rain drummed against the yard floor. She was at a loss as to what she should do. She had never expected in her wildest imaginings to have heard what she just had. What was she supposed to do with such knowledge? She was crucially aware that she had won the admission from Alice by disclosure, by painting herself in a certain light, a light that questioned the rules and standards. How was she to be true to herself? What would that mean? Suddenly it struck her that she didn't know herself at all. She hadn't chosen the steps laid out before her, she had stumbled along like a blind person groping in their own darkness. She didn't know what she thought about herself. Opinion had been shaken out of her by circumstance. Alice was at once more naive and more deliberate. In her quiet, yearning fashion she had chosen to abandon everything, to live without God. It was all so much more reckless and shameless. She was suddenly filled with a terrible regret that she had hit her. Who was she to do such a thing? She was hardly a saint. She had to go after her, but where would she have gone. She could only imagine that she would go to the dock in order to warn Tom that she had let slip their terrible secret. She told herself that she had forgiven Alice completely, but as for Tom, that couldn't be the case.

She ran down to the dockside. The rain kept coming. It bounced off the quays. The ground steamed with the heat. There were large pools and slicks along the dock walls. The water ran black with coal-dust. The atmosphere was rank with foul smells, fish gut and mineral. The air vibrated to the sound of the deluge on the water in the dock basins. Her clothes adhered to her body, making a second clammy, uncomfortable skin.

She ran along the Strand, running between the rail tracks, around coal wagons, ducking beneath the frames of the coal loading bridges and the coaling sluices, past the sheds and carts, searching every figure and face as she went. She raced along the quays where fishing smacks were being unloaded, despite the persistent rain. She pulled at the dockers, insisting on seeing their faces, to check whether she had come across Tom. On any number of occasion surprised dockers raised their hand to her and chased her off. The rain blinded her. Her hair was plastered against her head. She had it in mind that she should find Alice before Alice managed to speak to Tom. He shouldn't discover that their secret was out.

She ran back and forth along the quays and around the basins, but couldn't find either Alice or Tom. Eventually she stopped running. Her mind kept going. Perhaps Alice had already seen Tom and they had decided to hide away somewhere together. But if that was the case what were they hiding from? Her? Had she somehow become the foe?

Now that she had stopped running, she stumbled about aimlessly. On numerous occasions she ran into someone working on the quay edge. She was shouted at and pushed, but she didn't care. Something altogether larger and more incomprehensible was happening to her. She felt she had played a certain part and missed the truth of a blatant reality that was staring her in the face. Everyone was capable of recklessness, everyone was capable of going beyond return, even Alice, even here, among the tedium of ordinary lives. Ordinary lives! There was no such thing. There was luck, mishap and disgrace. One had no control over any of it.

She had wandered for some time when, purely by chance, she saw Alice. To her own mind she had stopped looking. She didn't really know what she was doing. She was simply wandering, letting her thoughts drift as she drifted. And out of the blue there she was, huddled on the patent slip, situated on the east Strand. She was hunched into herself, with her shawl draped over her. She looked like a beggar. June went to her. There were nets laid out across the slip waiting for repair. The seamen had obviously given in to the rain and abandoned repairs for the time being. There was only Alice on the whole slip.

June stood over her for a while without speaking. She knew that Alice was aware of her. She had stirred as her figure crossed her area of vision. She didn't acknowledge her though. She remained shrunken beneath her heap of wet clothes. They remained together, without speaking, as still as each other for a long time, the rain washing over them. Everything served to make them numb: the event they contended with, the weather and the scenery. It all ran to silence with them.

June struggled to hit on a sequence of words that might make some sense, but none would reveal themselves. In the end she asked: "Have you told him then, that I know?"

Alice didn't immediately answer, but she stirred, moving her heavy figure slightly. Eventually she nodded and whispered: "He knows."

"So, where is he?"

Alice looked up and glared fiercely at June. Her voice was suddenly raging. "He's gone! He's cleared off, of course! Are you pleased? Is that what you wanted? To get him out of the way?"

"No, that isn't what I wanted. I don't know what I wanted."

"Well, why did you interfere?" Alice wailed. "Why did you make me betray him, betray me? We didn't hurt anyone. We didn't do any harm. We love each other."

June revolted at the word love. It was too much. It was too perverse. She had discovered her limit. This was beyond sanction.

"Of course you love him, he's your brother. That's proper love. The other is filthy. I can't condone the other. Don't ask that of me, for God's sake."

Alice called out powerfully and painfully. "We love each other. It's clean and it's real."

"No!" June screamed.

"Yes!" Alice countered, even more forcefully.

"It's perverse and ugly and filthy! What about the baby? It'll be a monster! Do you not understand? An absolute monster! A freak and a monster!"

In one quick, smooth movement Alice rose to her feet and attacked June. She clawed at her throat, all the while screaming her opposition to what June had insinuated. They pulled and tore at each other, both channelling all of their pent up frustration into the physical release of violence. After pulling and tugging at each other for a while, they began to wrestle, both trying to squeeze the life out of the other. June felt all the air rush from her lungs and struggled to take a breath. She was drowning in Alice's grip. With a growing sense of panic and urgency, she put all of her energy into an almighty shrug. They both lost their footing and fell to the ground of the slip. Both still kept their hold. They wrestled on the floor, gradually rolling down the slope. Eventually they rolled, still enclosed together, into the harbour waters. They continued to struggle, despite the waters breaking and reforming around them. Both of their heads went under. They came up sputtering and struggling. Again they went under, dragged down by the weight of each other's continued assault.

They remained under for some time before again surfacing with a great roar of relief. This time they parted. They had no energy left to fight. All the air had left their bodies. They breathed quickly and deeply, desperate to replenish the life in them that was so dangerously expelled. They crawled from the water on all fours, separated by a matter of feet. Once free of the water they came to a halt, still on all fours, breathing with their heads bowed like animals inhaling the aromas of the near ground.

Eventually, having filled their lungs and felt their heart rate reduce, they lifted their heads. They moved in unison, recovery and repair occurring almost simultaneously. They looked at each other and without thinking fell into each other's arms and burst into loud, complaining tears. They embraced for some time, as if scared to release the hold of the other.

June got to her feet first and helped Alice to hers. As she did she began to speak, wanting to apologise, make amends for the terrible situation they found themselves in, but Alice, with a deal of nervous fumbling, put her fingers across June's lips and stopped her. They made their way heavily, dripping and frozen, back to Ginns.

They never relinquished the hold one had on the other as they climbed from the docks. They continued to breath deeply, luxuriating in fresh air. The rain had ceased as they embraced on the slip. The air was filled with tangy aromas.

The kitchen door was still open just as they had left it. Obviously no one had returned. June stripped off Alice's wet clothes until she was completely naked. There was the rudimentary shape of a forming bump on her belly. Her nipples were dark and protruding. June took a towel and began to wipe down Alice's body, very gently and with great tenderness. She was particularly careful around the protuberant belly.

As June wiped her dry Alice began to undo June's clothes. Again June attempted to speak, but Alice stopped her with the same movement of her fingers to her lips. Soon June was completely naked too. They stood and looked at each other for a minute, then Alice lowered her head and softly kissed both of June's nipples. The nipples swelled against her lips. She smiled.

She stepped away from June and collected all of their clothes from the floor and hung them over a clothes-horse. She brought a paraffin heater from the corner of the kitchen, which had been buried under sheets and towels, and dragged it roughly towards the centre of the kitchen. The paraffin sloshed about as she pulled. June just watched, still enjoying the moment of her nipples being caressed by Alice's lips. Alice lit the heater then placed the wet clothes close to it. Within seconds steam began to rise from the saturated garments. Alice then went to the pantry and returned with a bottle of gin. They very quickly drank two large glassfuls. She left the bottle on the table, then reached out and took June's hand and led her from the kitchen. She directed her upstairs, and together they lay down in bed, alongside each other. They lay simply embracing, nothing more, and within a short while fell asleep, exhausted by fighting, thinking, desiring and gin.

When June woke up the room was filled with a thin haze of smoke. She was confused. Everything was so strange. All the events of the last few hours ran through her mind in a matter of seconds. She looked down at Alice. She was asleep, stretched out, one leg under the sheet, the rest of her exposed. And then there was the smoke. Suddenly, the reality of the grey haze began to register. She jumped from the bed and rushed to the door. As soon as she opened it there was a great onrush of flames. They ran up the walls and wrapped around the banister. She felt immediately the intensity of the heat. She slammed the door to and rushed to the bed and shook Alice.

Alice woke with difficulty. June tried to pull her from the bed. Alice assumed that for some reason this was a resumed assault from June and pulled the sheet around her as if that might afford her some protection. June became frantic. She shook and pulled at Alice, wailing all the time that the house was on fire. When the realisation of the situation finally dawned on her Alice rushed to the door and would have opened it but for the fact that June leapt beside her and placed her back firmly against it. Dumbfounded Alice gazed meekly at the door-handle. She looked cowed and passive, like a child who had just been scolded. She really didn't understand June keeping her there. It very rapidly crossed her mind that this was her punishment, something that June had decided on.

As she was thinking it through, June grabbed her by the shoulders and gripped her tightly. She explained in a slow, commanding voice that they would have to jump from the window. There was no way out through the house, the downstairs was already engulfed. The door would hold the fire for a little while, but not long. They had to be decisive and brave. June wasn't sure that Alice was even listening. There was no light of comprehension in her face. She took her arm and led her to the window. She could see that there was already a crowd gathered in the street below. As soon as they were seen the crowd began to call to them. She flung open the window. A host of voices all shouted at once for them to jump.

June turned to Alice. Alice smiled. All panic seemed to have left her. She was composed and calm. June felt a surge of incredible, uncomplicated love for her. She moved to kiss her, but as she did the door gave out a loud, piercing crack. They both turned. It still held, but was framed by a rim of intense brightness, its shape slowly dissolving into flame.

It was now Alice who urged June. She pushed her gently closer to the window and commanded her to jump. June hesitated. The door cracked again. Alice now shouted at June to jump. Spurred on by Alice's urgency June quickly put her legs over the window-ledge, sat for just a moment and then launched herself towards the crowd. She was received by numerous male arms which, knitted together in order to make a fleshy net, managed to cushion her fall, though not entirely prevent it. She was cradled and rushed to earth in one quick movement, then left flat on her back. She immediately lifted herself up in order to watch Alice make her escape, but much to her confusion Alice wasn't there. Her figure wasn't in the window frame.

She got to her feet, still staring at the frame. Then she looked all around, her eyes flicking between the window-frame and the crowd. Alice certainly hadn't already jumped. She would have been there with her. They would have been side by side, arm in arm. They would have been defiant. They would have been strong. They would have outfaced the disaster. She didn't understand. What was going on? What had they done to Alice?

She walked forward towards the house. The crowd parted for her. Some people continued to look up at the window, and a couple kept on calling to Alice, but the great majority looked at her. Of course, she thought, she was naked, so they were bound to stare. They would seize that uncommon, freakish moment and steal it for themselves. Already she would be the stuff of their smutty imaginings. The stories would be doing the rounds as she stood there. Well, she didn't care. It was known. She had experienced it in dreams a thousand times, experienced the grossness of being unclothed amongst a crowd, naked without really knowing why. It was just like this. People looking, some pretending it wasn't happening, some lowering their attention when she looked back, others brazenly staring her out. Well, let them look. She didn't care about being naked, she didn't care about them, not anymore. They were only jealous. All she cared about was Alice. Alice had to be protected, made safe. It would all make sense with Alice.

As the name came into her head she screamed it aloud, screamed it with all her might. But there was no answering appearance. She fixed her attention firmly on the window, willing Alice to appear, mumbling under her breath short expletive demands that Alice get herself to the frame. She tried to scream again but couldn't. Her voice choked in her throat. At the same moment as her voice failed, she heard a scream from the open window. It wasn't her name though. Alice wasn't answering. It was a scream of pain. And with that scream Alice finally appeared at the frame, but just for a second, her naked outline turning in flames, and just as suddenly as she had appeared she was gone again.

As Alice vanished from sight June dashed towards the burning house. She was determined to break through the fire and reach Alice. She had to attempt it. She couldn't let this happen. She could never live with this. There had to be an opportunity, though the moment might be brief. She never crossed the threshold, though. She was held back by a line of the crowd. She kicked and struggled, but couldn't break through. Eventually she was forcibly dragged away, screaming Alice's name, two men holding her arms and two holding her legs.

She was dropped in the middle of the street. She crawled onto her side and looked up at the window. It was covered with flames. She slowly got to her feet. She continued to gaze at the house. The flames broke out over the roof. It was at this moment that the fire-brigade arrived. As the crowd stepped back to allow them access, a blanket was draped from behind around her shoulders. She took hold of its edges and pulled it tightly across her. She turned to see who had covered her. It was John Devlin. He put his arms around her and held her in a fast embrace. She tried to cry but couldn't. She rested her head against his chest. She closed her eyes. She tried to visualise Alice naked beside her, her figure almost completely exposed, but not quite, her skin pale, tender and soft, but all she saw was a body ignited like a torch.

The house was completely gutted. Two bodies were eventually removed. Stanley had not been with Tom. He had managed to secure a morning shift in an earthenware pottery factory that needed casual labourers. He had intended the money as a surprise. When he had finished there he had spent a couple of hours in the pub, and then gone home to sleep it off. June had no idea that he was asleep in the room next to theirs when she trailed Alice up to bed.

After the funeral of their two charred bodies both Catherine and June went away. Neither said where they were going. They hadn't exchanged a word to each other. No one had any idea where Tom was. It was over a year before he got in touch. He wrote to the burnt-out house. He addressed his letter to the Kavanagh Family. Breda took charge of it. She was living with the Devlins. He was in Ireland, living in Dublin. He was working on the docks. He said he was doing all right. He made no particular mention of Alice. He didn't specifically ask about her or enquire about the baby. He added a footnote for John Devlin. *Tell Mr Devlin there's a great deal a docker can turn a blind-eye to here. They reckon the whole of Europe is just awash with explosives. There'll be a hell of a fire over here soon. God knows how it'll be when it all blows. I never came across so many disgruntled people. I feel as if I know my mam and dad so much better. I'm pleased I found myself here. I might just make a name for myself, in a quiet sort of way like. Tell him that. And tell him I'll back the right side. He needn't have any worries on that score. I'll do the right thing.* He didn't include a return address. Breda kept the letter for a week and then burnt it. She wept as the paper caught and then rapidly went up in flames.

*

Tom's letter arrived at the same time as Free State troops opened fire on the Four Courts in Dublin where dissident Republicans, the *Irregulars*, had set up an armed camp. It had been tolerated for two months but when a party from the Four Courts kidnapped a pro-treaty general, Collins, the *big fellow*, legend of the war of independence, ordered the attack. The Irish Civil War, between *Irregulars*, still loyal to the 1916 Republic, and *Staters*, those in favour of the Anglo-Irish Treaty giving the Free State dominion status under the British Crown which had brought the war of independence to a close, had begun. The immigrant Irish in Whitehaven were caught in a state of shock. Over the ensuing weeks occasional scuffles broke out amongst the miners, but nothing serious. On the whole the majority felt it was prudent to keep their opinions to themselves. The Irish community was a small one. The civil war threatened to tear it to shreds.

On an evening in late September Kate went looking for John. He had come home, washed, eaten his meal in complete silence, then gone out again. He didn't say where he was going, only that he needed to go for a walk. She waited for over an hour and then went after him. At first she had told herself that he had simply taken himself for a drink, but she knew that was unlikely. It was the day before pay-day. He had no money. She worried that he was getting himself mixed up in something. Tensions were mounting throughout the Irish streets. At some point something was likely to happen. She didn't want John to be right in the thick of it, though she wasn't sure how she could avoid that. Still, she checked all the pubs around Ginns, just in case. As she expected he hadn't been seen.

She went down into the town and wandered around the docks. There was a large steamer, the *Cornwallis*, docked for coaling. There was a great deal of activity around the quays because of it. It was a military ship. There were soldiers strolling along the dock walls, dressed in full uniform. She had never seen so many soldiers around the quays before. It was quite an event. There was a photographer taking pictures for the local papers. There was a great crowd of kids gathered around, watching the coal fall through the sluices into the ship's hold. She pushed through the crowd, trying to catch a glimpse of John. As far as she could tell he wasn't there. After half an hour she gave it up.

She abandoned the docks, passed the tannery and climbed up the steps of Mount Pleasant, and beyond to where the cinder plateaux of Fish, dead Lady and, highest of all, Loft surmounted the whole of that valley side. She wandered round the pit-heads, past Fish, then Lady, then finally on up to Loft. She saw a lone figure standing on the promontory, looking out to sea. She chastised herself for being a fool. Where else would he be, but looking across that sea?

She approached him. She could hear her own footfalls clearly on the cinders. He didn't stir. She knew he must have heard her. She went and stood beside him. Still he didn't move or even acknowledge her. Eventually she said: "There's quite a commotion down on the docks, a ship coaling, full of soldiers. They look quite smart parading themselves all around the quays. Full of themselves, of course, but, well, they're only kids, really."

"Peter Kavanagh caught me at the end of the shift. He was wondering about the war." He didn't continue. Kate refused to be drawn. They waited for a while. Eventually, realising that Kate was refusing to ask questions, he went on. "He was wondering why we were all still here. He says he doesn't understand that, at all. There's war in your own country, man. War, he says, don't you care?" He gave a sour grimace. "Don't I care?"

Kate smiled. "That's what Gavin said to Bobby the night he sailed. The exact same words."

John turned to her. "I don't remember that."

"You were probably too drunk, Mr John Devlin, too far gone, drinking the health of the unhealthy man."

"Ah, God, poor Bobby. What would he make of all this?"

"He would be too busy grieving those poor children."

"I think that's what I meant."

"I'm sorry. I thought, well, there's no need to say, well..."

"Have you ever seen a more beautiful sea?"

"I've never seen any other sea, at all, and unless you've been deceiving me nor have you."

"I mean tonight, tonight with the last light and everything. Look at it, the colour of green, like metal, but flecked all over with those bits of lights. To think that's there all day, the whole great mass and weight of it, and me underneath it, worrying away like a dog in a hole. What on earth's going on over there, Kate? We didn't come so far away just to stand here and not know what the hell is going on. Can you believe they're killing each other, actually shooting each other down? It took a lot of lives to get this far. They should have remembered what they died for. You can't sign them all away like they didn't matter."

"Father Bond says all we can do is pray."

"Well, Peter Kavanagh reckons we should be doing more, a whole lot more."

"What, just what does Peter Kavanagh reckon?"

"Making a stand, taking sides, being there."

"And what the hell does Peter Kavanagh know?" Kate retorted. "He wasn't born there. He's from here. This is where he belongs. He fought in the British army, for God's sake. Remember that. He was one of the first to go."

"So did Robert."

"Well..."

"Isn't that the problem?"

"Robert just did what he thought was right."

"Us, I mean us. We don't really belong anywhere. I couldn't go back there now. What would I do? Would I even have the right to fight? I don't know. I don't know that I would anymore. You know, I thought Collins was the man, and now that he's dead I don't care. That can't be right though, can it? That can't be fair. But what the hell is fair? I don't know. Am I the man that came here, Kate? I don't know any more.

243

Maybe I lost a bit of me, out there somewhere, in the water, a whole chunk of me sunk, never to be seen again."

"Oh Jesus, John Devlin. You're the man that danced with me, over there, along that quay where those soldier lads are swanking a bit now. That's what I know. I don't seem to recall there ever was a bit of you missing, not an important bit, any roads."

John smiled: "I've never known Duffy so quiet. I think he's in a bit of a trance half the time. He does well, really. He says our fight is here for the union, with the bosses and owners. He does well to say that, really. I thought he might say a whole lot more, but he's just as lost for something to say as the rest of them."

"It won't go on. It won't last."

"And then what?"

"We'll pretend it never happened." John laughed briefly. Kate went on, speaking over him: "Of course we'll pretend it never happened because it didn't, not for us, and when they come to their senses, which they surely will, they'll realise it didn't happen for them either. They got carried away with something they never should have. Well, we haven't got carried away because there's too much else to get through. I'm still mourning those kids too. All of them. You mark my words, it'll come all right."

"I don't think anything will ever be the same again."

"No," she said, "nothing is ever the same again, of course not, nothing, you're a bit older and I'm a bit older and a lot has happened, things we can't get back, things we can't change, but that doesn't mean stop, or start, or anything else. It just means that. Nothing is ever the same. I wouldn't be working days in the cloth factory because my children don't need me anymore if everything was the same. I wouldn't be anything, for God's sake. That's all."

John reached out and took hold of her hand. They stood in silence, side by side, looking over the sea, watching the sun sink into it, a large, orange, molten ball, veins shifting through its intensity. Kate was resolved in her own mind that she intended to speak to Peter Kavanagh and remind him that what he was saying was devoid of originality, and that he should keep other people's thoughts to himself. The only ideas worth having were your own ideas. Other people's ideas led to trouble. She would tell him that.

As she stood on the promontory Peter Kavanagh was slapping Catherine Kavanagh around the head, and putting her out into the street. She had returned to Ginns in the late afternoon and had wandered around the streets, passing the old, burnt-out house numerous times as she did. Eventually Breda had appeared, making her way to the Devlins' from the Guinea Warehouse where she had been working since the early morning. She stepped in behind Breda and took her by the arm. Breda let out a scream of surprise as she turned to see who had waylaid her. Catherine put her hand across her mouth and told her to be quiet. Breda was full of questions, though. As soon as Catherine lowered her palm she began. Where had Catherine been? Why hadn't she been in touch? What about June? She was just about to say about the letter they had received from Tom when Catherine very firmly told her to shut up. She wanted Breda to do something for her. Breda fell quiet, and pulled herself free of Catherine's hold. Catherine's tone had rankled her. How dare she appear out of the blue like that and speak in that manner. Didn't she realise the torment Breda had been going through?

Catherine recognised the anger in Breda's movements and tried to console her. She was sorry, but she didn't want to talk to anyone, not yet anyway. Again Breda had numerous questions but Catherine simply put her finger to her lips and refused any explanations. She said she wanted Breda to see Mr Henderson for her. She had something, a letter, she wanted him to have. A note of urgency entered Catherine's voice. Breda asked whether Catherine was in trouble. Catherine shook her head simply, and merely suggested that it wasn't trouble as Breda understood it. In the end Catherine persuaded Breda to go to the sweat shop where Catherine and Alice had once both worked together.

They stood outside for some time. Women were coming out in dribs and drabs, two or three at a time. It was the usual thing. The women left as they finished their work for the day. Eventually Catherine recognised Mr Henderson's deputy leaving. She ushered Breda forward. Breda hesitated. She wanted to know why Catherine couldn't go herself. Catherine shook her head and simply said she knew what she was doing.

Breda reluctantly went into the sweat shop. The machines were idle. A few people were still packing things away. She asked for Mr Henderson. Someone sniggered and pointed to an office at the rear of the shop-floor. She knocked. A man's voice told her to come in. She pushed open the door and stood in the frame. Mr Henderson turned to her and slowly looked her over. He quietly stated that the factory was closed. Whatever her business was it would have to wait until the morning. He didn't have any time. If she was looking for a position she needn't bother there were no vacancies, times were very hard. Breda just stood and gazed at him. He was a tall, slender man, with a lean, suspicious face. He eyed her coldly, his eyes narrowing. He waved his hand to dismiss her. She noticed his jaw line was somewhat lopsided, giving him a twisted, curious look. She said she had a letter for him. He didn't reply but gazed steadily at Breda, looking her over more closely. Then he stepped up towards her and stood over her. She didn't look into his face. She handed him Catherine's sealed envelope.

He looked it over for a moment then tore it open. He read it over once then screwed it up in his hand and shoved it into his pocket. He suddenly reached out and roughly caressed Breda's chin, his thumb and fingers pressing into her jaw bone. Breda tried to shake her head but he still held her firmly.

He started to speak. His voice was cold and drawling, but wary and nervous. As he did he grabbed his hand away from her. "I suppose you're another one of them. I was sorry about your sister. She was a good worker. She wasn't bad at all. Tell Catherine Kavanagh to go to hell. I won't be blackmailed like this. Tell her she can say what she likes. I don't care. She can't touch me. I'll tell my wife she's mad, mad because of what happened. But I won't be threatened. Now, get out. She has no business here."

Breda took a few steps back. She looked directly at him. She saw his pinched cheeks becoming more hollow as she looked. He was sweating. He was obviously frightened. She smiled and said that she would tell her. She turned and made her way from the office. He called after her. His voice was thin and shrill. "Good. You tell her. I don't owe her anything. If you're looking for something for yourself then that might be different, but I can't promise anything, do you understand..."

Breda didn't look back. His voice trailed her as she made her way from the factory.

Catherine hadn't moved. Breda went up to her and said: "He's sacred, a nervous man."

"What do you mean, scared?" Catherine demanded.

"I don't know, do I? He just seems a funny, frightened man, that's all. I don't know why. I don't know anything about him, do I? You haven't said. I know you're trying to get something out of him."

"What did he say?"

"No, he says no. He doesn't care what you do. You've got no business here. Is this to do with Alice?"

Catherine didn't answer. She groaned in frustration and set her face in a show of obvious temper. She marched off. Breda followed. Catherine led them straight back to Ginns. She went to Peter Kavanagh's and burst in without knocking. He was alone, sitting in the kitchen. Catherine flew at him and started beating her fists around his head. She accused him of interfering in things he didn't understand, accused him of being a bully and fool. She howled that Henderson didn't want to know anymore because of him. He caused such pointless trouble.

She wasn't remotely through with her assault and accusations before Peter rose to his feet and slapped her around the head. He pushed her back out of the kitchen, slapping her all of the time. Breda started to cry out and also backed away ahead of Catherine so that she was back outside first. Peter didn't utter a word until he had ushered Catherine back to the front door at which point he took hold of her arm flung her into the street and told her to get out and never come back.

Catherine lay in the road sobbing. A few people stood and watched. Breda knelt down and tried to soothe her, but Catherine swung out her hand to keep her away. After that Breda maintained her distance. Catherine continued to sob. Breda called out that she didn't understand. What was going on?

Catherine looked up at her. Her face was dishevelled, blotched by tears, her skin puffy and pink. "I didn't mean to threaten him. I only wanted him back. But he never answered any of my letters. I thought everything would have settled down. I just wanted it to be like it was. I made a mistake, that's all. I should never have gone and I should never have come back. He said he loved me, you know. Don't think I was his trollop. It was never like that. He said he loved me, but Peter broke his jaw. Peter thought... Oh it doesn't matter what Peter thought. Peter doesn't think. Peter never thinks. We're all bad, I know that, but Peter's the worst. Do you understand? We're all hopeless but Peter's the worst of the lot."

Catherine got to her feet unsteadily. Breda went to help her but Catherine shrugged her away. She flared up in temper and demanded that Breda leave her alone. She wanted everyone to leave her alone. She was through with everything. She started to stumble along the street. Breda called after her, but didn't follow. She didn't want to be pushed aside again. She watched Catherine pass out of view.

When Catherine was gone Breda knocked on Peter's door, but she didn't wait for an answer. Straight away she made her own way along the street where Catherine had gone. She didn't know whether Peter answered or not. She returned to the Devlins. They were both out. Patrick was indoors. He looked at her sheepishly as she went in. He always had a puzzled, frightened look about him. For a brief moment she thought he looked just as Mr Henderson had looked and wondered what that frightened, perplexed look was all about. She gazed at him steadily for a moment or two trying to work it out. As she did the look of anxiety on his face worsened. Finally she smiled. She asked him why people were always fighting with each other? It didn't make any sense. He looked horrified.

Breda never mentioned to anyone that Catherine had been home, and as far as she could work out Peter never alluded to it either. It was as if they had tacitly decided to pretend it had never happened.

Chapter Five

The birth of Mary was followed by Hugh, Martin, Julie, Jane, Catherine, Annie, Robert, John, Patrick, born before each year was out. A decade of children, a decade of bringing children to John and Kate as if they were bringing new offerings to the altar. A succession of births which prompted Kate, on being presented with the quietly respiring Annie, the seventh Glyn child, in the summer of 1926, in a mood of exhilaration, wonder and fear, to declare: "And what do you expect to bring them up on? Miracles!" Her declamation was made in consequence to the culmination of one of the worst periods in mining history. Under her breath she added the fearful supplication: "Clay to God, how will yous ever survive?"

Since the mines had returned to private ownership, March 31st 1921, there had existed a state of permanent conflict between the miners and the mine owners. The conflict was always a topsy-turvy affair depending on the perceived fears of the government of the day. Following the *Black Friday* humiliation of 1921, when they had been abandoned by their *triple alliance* allies the transport and railway workers, miners had eventually been forced to accept wage cuts and longer hours, despite holding out alone for a seventeen week strike. The 1921 lockout ended on worse terms than the miners could have secured by negotiating in the beginning. They lived with a permanent sense of defeat and outrage, and struggled in grinding poverty.

Three years later, May 1924, due largely to the prompting of Labour's first short-lived administration, installed in January of that year, saw a better deal for the miners. However, it was a deal that the owners sought to reverse only a year later. On June 30th they gave a month's notice to end the existing agreement. The new offer involved sharply reduced wages. The miners refused. The owners threatened a lockout planned for July 31st. Twenty-six hours before the lockout was to begin the new Tory regime capitulated and in a state of panic circumvented the lockout with the promise of a nine month subsidy in order to maintain existing wage rates and the setting up of a royal commission to investigate the entire industry, giving the miners the victory of *Red Friday*.

However, the government had merely been buying time. While the commission spent the winter preparing its 300 page report the regime, fully believing that the unions were inspired by Communists, obsessionally egged on by such anti-Communist evangelists as the home secretary, Joynson-Hicks, *Jix*, and chancellor of the exchequer, Churchill, who denounced the working class as *the enemy* and when the time came demanded their *unconditional surrender,* made contingency plans for the coming year. The country was to be divided into ten areas, each with a civil commissioner who could exercise complete executive powers, with an emergency transport system in place to ensure food supplies. When the commission reported in March 1926, recommending an immediate reduction in wages, which was supplemented by the owners demand for longer hours, conflict was inevitable. The miner's secretary, A. J. Cook, answered: *Not a penny off the pay, not a minute on the day.* On May 1st miners were locked out. On May 2nd the government pulled out of negotiations with the union general council. On May 3rd a general strike was called. The general strike lasted nine days. The miners stuck out alone for another eight months.

"We'll survive," Dora smiled, offering the still sleeping baby to Kate. Kate eyed her sceptically, admiration, fear and even resentment stirring within her. It was obvious that Dora thrived on pregnancy, and she was glorious in success. Kate, however, suffered her daughter's pregnancies, each one weighing heavily on her. To give birth in the midst of such a crisis was more than she could take and made her discomfited and morose. "Oh take her, for God's sake, will you," Dora rebuked her.

Kate took the baby and nestled her fingers through its covering layers to reveal its face. "Jesus," she said, delighted, "it's smiling in my arms."

"Wind, Mrs Devlin," Hugh teased, handing Catherine to Dora, though he kept Jane in his own arms.

"Would you remember that you are a man and not considered expert on these matters, Mr Hugh Glyn," Kate retorted.

"Would you ever let me forget it!"

"Perhaps if you did forget it from time to time, you wouldn't have quite so many mouths to feed."

"Mrs Devlin, my children are the roots of me," Hugh replied with formality, as he placed Jane on the flagged floor.

Kate was abashed. She looked down at the small, flabby, features of Annie, her mouth and eyes puckered, and accepted it probably was wind. She snapped: "I know that."

At that moment Mary and Julie began to fight. From the moment Kate had taken the baby they had hung to her skirt, wanting a glimpse of their sister, each attempting to oust the other. Finally, they had come to blows. Both turned to Dora, sobbing, claiming their own right. Kate exploded: "Clay to God, will you never give your mother any peace." Both children screamed with increased vigour.

Hugh sought to alleviate the situation by offering to take the children to see the pig. John picked up his hint and quickly suggested that they feed it. Dora laughed out loud, evincing reproving looks from both Kate and Hugh to which she responded with even more helpless laughter.

John, Hugh and the children went out into the yard. Patrick was already there, gazing into the makeshift sty at the mooching pig. He cast two furtive, baleful eyes across the intruders, then moved aside. He was a wiry, pallid boy who scarcely spoke unless forced, and then in pained, bashful, niggard phrases.

John whispered to Hugh in a rather disgruntled, dismayed manner: "You wouldn't believe the beauty his father was."

"Does he know?" Hugh asked.

John shrugged and frowned indecisively, yet sternly. "He knows, he must know. Why the hell else would he act like he does? But no, he hasn't been told, not right out. Kate wouldn't have that, would never agree to it at all, wouldn't even consider it, but he knows."

"You would?"

"He'll have to know sooner or later. He can't keep pondering us like this forever. He's not one of us, and he knows it. Sometimes I think he hates us. And after all we've done for him."

Hugh felt discomposed, but couldn't articulate it. He looked over the dilute, recalcitrant figure of Patrick and felt sympathy for him. His own son, Hugh, his eldest and named after him, had gone to stand with him. He was half Patrick's age but was already quite tall against him. He was nervous and uncertain, and kept turning to his father for encouragement. He was always the same. With his neat, fine features, solid build, his hesitant, well-mannered bearing, he made an impression, but that inevitably made him uncomfortable and self-conscious. He seemed to Hugh vulnerable and in need, somehow quite fragile. Hugh felt a fierce, terrible love for him, that in turn made him feel weak and rather helpless.

He approached the two and, half crouching, put his arms around them, pulling them to him, Hugh falling willingly against him, Patrick resisting. Hugh would not be gainsaid, though, and drew Patrick in. Patrick eyed him distrustfully, unable to believe in the embrace. Such was the look on the boy's face that Hugh felt an urgent need to make him believe in it. He couldn't make sense of his remoteness. It frightened him. It was an affront to his view of things. Children should not be disappointed or feel blame. There was time for all that. If the war had taught him anything it was that there was time for all that. It didn't have to come from your own making. He wanted to make it right for Patrick. Somehow, if he couldn't do that, it might bring into question his ability to do it for Hugh. He had to get through to Patrick. The problem was he really didn't know how. He didn't know what to say. He decided to use the animal in front of him. He said: "Your pig's doing grand."

"It's not mine," Patrick replied abruptly, obviously confused by and uncertain of Hugh's interest.

"But you help out, you do plenty of chores, so in my eyes, and your father's, it's yours as well."

Patrick shook his head. "It's not mine," he repeated. "I like pigs, though. I'd like to look after it. I'd look after it if I was let."

Hugh let out a small grunt of disappointment, but quickly qualified it by saying: "You're doing grand."

John joined them. He patted young Hugh on the head and asked: "Would you like to feed it? Not that there's much to give it, just a few potato and turnip peelings, but it'll have to make do."

Hugh stood up, his hands still resting on the boys' shoulders, and looked steadily at John. He was attempting to work through in his own mind what the relationship between John and Patrick amounted to. He believed John Devlin to be a profoundly decent man, and yet he seemed to have a blind-spot over his adopted son. He couldn't work it out. It suggested a dark, troubling dimension to his father-in-law. Even if there was something that rankled John, surely it was consigned to a now remote past. Patrick was not to blame. The phrase came to his lips, Patrick is not to blame, but he couldn't say it. If John was aware of anything unusual in Hugh's scrutiny he gave no acknowledgement of it. In the end Hugh had to change tack. He was working himself up into a state of emotional crisis, a crisis compounded of sympathy for Patrick and concern for his own son. He had to let it go. It wasn't the time or the place. He said: "I'm sure we could collect a bit of swill if we tried."

John frowned. "If you brought any swill here I'd probably eat it myself." He burst out laughing. "If you get your hands on any swill, Hugh lad, you take my advice and give it to your own, they'll be the ones needing it."

"We'll manage."

"Will you?" John scoffed, as he brought a small bag of peelings to be fed to the pig. "I hope you're right."

With the appearance of the pig feed bag Mary, Martin and Julie came to the sty. John let them each take a handful of peelings. Hugh leaned over and dropped his into the animal's trough. Mary and Julie threw theirs straight at the pig. Martin launched his in the air one by one as if the bits of peel were numerous missiles. Hugh tapped him on the ear, but Martin continued regardless. Patrick declined to be involved. When they had each taken a second handful John stepped back and left them to it. They immediately began to bicker over the bag. The sound of the grunting pig, nosing for the scraps, interspersed with their quarrelling.

John rolled himself a wafer thin cigarette then busied himself, rearranging some of the junk in the corner of his yard, the festooned pile his pride and joy. From it he had already manufactured a small chicken run and the sty, as well as boxes and cupboards around the house. He spoke as he rummaged, between draws of his roll-up. "They're good kids, Hugh."

"They'll do."

"They'll do all right. She's got a point, though. It's a lot of mouths to feed."

"We'll get by," Hugh said easily, his eyes fixed on them all the while. An after note of his emotional concern remained with him. It girdled him, wrapping him to them, indivisibly, annulling any vestige of a previous life, subsuming it to them, his desire summonsed in them. He called to John, repeating: "Of course, we'll get by."

John stopped what he was doing and turned to him. "We're on our own, you know, as always. There's cheap coal coming in from Poland and Germany. They don't need us. They've made damned sure they don't need us. Maybe we should have accepted the deal."

"Don't let Duffy hear your defeatist talk, he'd never let you forget it."

"What will he say when we all starve?"

"He'll blame the others for not being solid."

"They were with us though."

"Not for long."

253

"We had a promise of a Wages Board."

"No we didn't."

John smiled: "No, we didn't."

"Were you testing me out?"

John shook his head. He drew on the remains of his slim cigarette, until there was too little to hold in his fingers then crumpled what remained and let it drift away. He stared ahead. He was pensive and fearful. He looked over his rubbish but didn't touch it. He said: "We have a hard God, Hugh, a bloody hard God. I don't know what we did to deserve it, but it's the case all right."

"Jesus, don't drag God into it, keep it between them and us, it's enough."

"They'll always win, you know that."

Hugh shrugged. "You don't believe that?" he said, questioning rather than stating, not used to defeatism, or even compromise, from John.

John gave a forced smile. "Maybe we're better off on our own. I like to be able to handle things myself, in my own way, even if it gets me into trouble. I don't like having to rely on others. You know where you are when you can handle something by yourself."

"Some things are too big to do on your own."

"When trouble comes, stand firm."

"Well..."

John couldn't answer. His thoughts had drifted off, back to Murphy. He had been able to respond then. He had seen the problem and taken matters into his own hands. But what had that amounted to? He had accepted damnation for the sake of a dead son. He had stood up for a country that had ripped itself apart with civil war. He had endured sell outs, compromises, back peddling and defeat. He had achieved nothing. He was still charged by the same fear, the same urge, the same lunatic desire for a freedom that remained immaterial and illusory. It sickened him. He kicked out at the wood-pile and snapped a board. The sound jolted him. It brought him back and made him aware of Hugh watching him. The other's expression was unsure and troubled. "Don't worry," John said, "I'd do it all again." He raised his head to the rooftops, his fists at his stomach and called out: "Do you hear? I'd do it all again! To hell with the cost! I'd stand up for my children whatever. Do you hear?"

The children turned to face him, but Hugh signed to them to concentrate on the pig. Despite his father's injunction still young Hugh

254

stole occasional glances at his grandfather, and Patrick openly studied him. Hugh looked on. He was concerned, non-plussed, uncomprehending, but he couldn't intervene. He didn't know how. He didn't know a fraction of what went into that outburst, but he wanted to. He needed to. He quietly asked: "How can I help?"

John lowered his face slowly, and with obvious deliberation allowed his fists to open. He was downcast, beaten by his own outburst. "It's all right. I'm fine. I'm just worried, worried about all of us. I don't like relying on others, you can't trust to it. They'll sell us out, Hugh. Other people let you down."

"Not this time."

"Before the war Peter's dad went to South Africa."

"I know."

"He couldn't take not knowing. He didn't really feel free to do anything else. That's an awful burden. He had a big family too."

"Are you saying I should go to South Africa?"

"No, God no, no. Jesus, I thought it was wrong for him. It killed him. He came back dusted and never managed to get out of his bed. They killed him."

"He was never well from what I've heard."

"He was a good man. I loved Bobby Kavanagh. He would have done it all again. Christ, I'm telling you..." His voice faded away. He was close to tears. He squeezed his fists at the base of his stomach again. "They're trying to kill us all."

Hugh spoke up. He tried to be calm. He wanted to reach the elder man but didn't know how. "We won't let them."

"Won't we, though."

"No, damn it," Hugh declared, with sudden volubility, "we won't."

John merely nodded. He tried to smile, but that proved futile. He turned towards the children and watched them. Except for Hugh and Patrick they were absorbed by the pig. Hugh quickly turned away under John's steady attention, and concentrated his attention firmly on the animal. Patrick, however, met John's gaze head on and engaged with it. It became a trial of strength. Hugh was aware of it. He recognised the absence of contact between father and adopted son, but felt powerless to intervene. He couldn't guess what had brought them to this pitch. He could see they were disowning each other, but couldn't comprehend it. He hated having to witness it. As a means of bringing the confrontation to an end he said they had to be getting on. It was like breaking a spell.

255

John turned to him, his face flushed, his tone mocking. "What's the rush, Hugh lad, you have all the time in the world."

Hugh refused the challenge. "I keep busy. They keep me busy."

John raised his hands immediately, surrendering, surrendering his mood, conceding. He had gone too far. He hadn't been fair. "You did well to listen to all my rigmarole," he said.

"No harm in listening."

"Do you think I should ship off to South Africa?"

"I'd tie you up first."

John smiled.

As the Glyns made their way back to Mount Pleasant Hugh took his father's hand and asked: "Why did my grandfather hold his stomach like that?"

"Grown man's trouble," Hugh replied. "You'll understand better when you get older."

Late that night the Glyn children began to hold their own stomachs. Mary complained first and Hugh sat with her. She had an urgent desire to defecate but when she tried the attempt proved painful and ineffectual. She strained over the pot for half an hour, but only managed to produce foul smelling water. She sobbed, both with pain and in embarrassment. Eventually the three other elder children woke up. They shared the same room and bed, the girls one end, the boys the other. Martin woke next. He produced the same watery waste. When Hugh and Julie woke with the same urgency to empty their bowels there was a panic to possess the pot. Hugh brought the one from his own bedroom so that Mary and Julie had one each. Hugh and Martin went outside. Jane, Catherine and Annie slept on undisturbed in his own room. He told Dora that it was nothing and she should stay asleep. The children's condition, though, did not improve. Hugh, Martin and Julie developed mild fevers, Mary's raged. Her stomach cramps became unbearable. In the morning Hugh sent for the doctor and the priest.

Father Bond appeared first. He gave each one a blessing. The children stayed in bed, Mary's condition remaining noticeably worse than the others. When the doctor finally came he diagnosed dysentery and gave instructions that the children be kept in their own room away from the others and given only water. He was sure that they would all be up and about soon. Only Mary gave any cause for concern. She had no colour, called out in pain, and muttered incoherently. As the others improved she remained the same. Towards the end of the first day she had a convulsion. Hugh tried to embrace her, her hot, clammy body

256

stiffening and relaxing in his arms. He spoke to her and tried to soothe her. He moaned helplessly as he held her. He stayed by her bedside. He fell asleep kneeling beside her.

Hugh, Martin and Julie improved quickly and were up and about by the second day. They slept in the kitchen whilst Mary was ill. She remained the same for four days. Hugh stayed with her the whole time, watching over her, only sleeping fitfully. He told Dora to keep herself and the babies away. Father Bond came each day, the only visitor other than the doctor Hugh allowed. She had three fits in all during that illness and was to have occasional fits until she was thirteen years old and began to menstruate.

In the semi-light Mary's colour looked ghastly, grey, pallid and moist. She lost weight quickly. Her neat figure was emaciated. She was lost in the bed, despite turning and moaning and kicking her way about it throughout the night. Hugh wiped her with warm cloths. He stroked her face and whispered to her. All the time he wanted to take it on himself. He had never felt such tender, raging love. He now understood something of what John had said. He wanted to be able to resolve this himself. He feared and resented having to rely on others. He would never forget the agony of hope, the fury of prayer.

On the fifth day her fever subsided and she improved rapidly. By the end of the day she managed to leave her bed. Father Bond came that night. Hugh spoke to him in the dark outside her bedroom door. "The miracle works, Father. I must tell Kate." Hugh slipped into the bedroom. Father Bond made the sign of the cross. Hugh did not see. He simply heard the priest's heavy, laboured breaths through the half open door, and willingly praised his God.

*

Once the *polite class war* of the national strike was over the miners, who had been left to themselves, were brought to the point of starvation. After a long battle of resistance they were forced back to work under conditions worse than those offered in May. They had to accept longer hours, lower wages and district deals. In the Whitehaven mines the deals were particularly severe. By the summer of 1927 miners were still struggling to pay off their debts. It was the year Mary was to make her first holy communion. There was no money to buy her a dress. Father Bond insisted that it was *corpus Christi, the Eucharist*, which mattered, not adornments, aware that few families could afford such luxuries, yet it remained a cause of embarrassment for those involved. After much soul-searching Dora took her wedding-dress, stored as if it had been a holy relic, and cut it into pieces, fashioning it into four meagre communion dresses, one for Mary and three to be distributed. Hugh, despite his insistence that she wait, approved.

The advent of *corpus Christi* brought Father Bond to Peter Kavanagh's. Bill was now twelve years old but Peter had never allowed him to make his first communion. He never articulated his opposition, indeed, never forbade Bill from attending mass, which he did with Kate and Dora, though Peter rarely attended himself, he simply said there was no need. Kate and Dora implored him, and even Hugh approached him, but he remained deaf to all entreaties. Nevertheless, despite his fervent opposition Father Bond turned up at his house every year to solicit a change of heart.

It was a fine, clear, warm evening when Father Bond knocked at the door on Ginns. "I was wondering when you would turn up," Peter greeted him offhandedly. He immediately stepped back inside, leaving the priest on the doorstep, though he didn't close the door to him.

"I'll come as long as it takes, Peter," Father Bond said, following Peter into the kitchen. It was dull and cool, the evening light failing, the room itself meticulously clean and tidy. Bill saw to that. Already he had taken on the tasks of cooking and attending to the housework. Peter scoffed at his domesticity. To the priest's surprise he encountered Gavin Duffy already comfortable in the small room. "Well, well, Gavin," the priest uttered, discomfited by Gavin's presence. He was acquainted with the historic enmity between the two men. "I can't pretend I'm not surprised to find you here."

"I could say the same to you, Father."

Peter interceded. "Is it Bill you've come to see? I'll give him a shout. He's around somewhere."

Father Bond turned fiercely on Peter, determined not to be trifled with: "You know perfectly well that I have not come to see Bill but have come to see about Bill."

"Go on then, you might as well get on with it."

"Don't adopt that tone of voice with me," the priest retorted. "You carry a grave weight of responsibility on your back. It is as much your salvation I am concerned with as Bill's."

"Well, I'd rather you didn't concern yourself with mine," Peter replied, as he slumped down heavily at the table. He hunched over himself, took a pack of cigarettes from his pocket, took one, then threw the packet to Gavin.

Gavin took one, lit it, inhaled deeply, then reached across and lit Peter's. He threw the dead match into the perfectly raked grate, then as if as an afterthought turned to the old priest and asked: "I'm sorry Father, were you wanting one yourself?"

The priest shook his head, aware of the hostility, the offensiveness of the offer. He eyed the two men pointedly, then spoke in a low, but strong and clear voice. "I'm wondering to myself why two of my congregation, two strapping fellows like yourselves, two grown-up men, should be acting like sniggering school children."

Gavin's demeanour fell, the priest's comment arresting his thinking. His expression looked contrite. The priest smiled. He felt triumphant and awaited an apology. Gavin met him face on. He spoke firmly, but without undue excitement. "Perhaps, Father, because you are not wanted here, but we don't have the sense to kick you out."

"We, is it?" the priest queried, casting his attention at once to both of them, challenging them.

Peter took him up. "It can hardly have failed to have met your attention, but I've not invited you to sit down."

"No, it has not failed to reach my attention. I was, of course, wondering why?"

Peter met the priest's attention for a moment or two, then wearily broke the contest. "I can't be listening to you at the moment, Father, that's all."

The priest seized on Peter's wavering. "You can't go on denying Bill the beauty of the communion, Peter. You are not that man. I know that." He eyed Peter keenly. He felt he was standing between Gavin and him, though what compact he was blocking he couldn't guess. He just had an insight that he had interrupted some alliance. He went on, soliciting Peter: "You haven't given up on the holy catholic and apostolic Church, Peter. You believe and accept the Credo. You haven't given up on the mass, I know that, I've seen you."

Peter looked up at him. He was at once angered and pained by Father Bond's comments, yet he was unable to speak. He couldn't deny his periodic submission to the mass, but equally he couldn't explain the need that drove him there. He couldn't openly declare his desire to reach Anne, her face, her body, her voice, her touch. It wasn't the done thing to make such a confession. Nevertheless, it was the reality of his worship. It was the promise of her presence he stole to, nervously, even begrudgingly, but ultimately absolutely, his eyes scanning the altar, the statues, the candle flames, for a hint of her, the woman he knew once dressed the church. But it invariably proved an empty promise and left him more lost, bereft, and tormented than before. Surely the priest knew that. Surely he recognised the desperation that drove him to the aisle. He didn't need to say it. He didn't want to say it. He shook his head.

"For God's sake, Peter," Father Bond went on, sensing the anguish, "let the lad come to the Lord's supper."

"All right, all right!" Peter called out, unable to contain himself, or to his mind, save himself. "Let him do whatever he damn well wants. I don't care. Let him decide. It's his life. What is it to me? See him. All right. See him!"

The priest raised his hand as if conferring a benediction, though in reality he merely wanted to stem the emotional tirade.

Peter fell silent, but eyed the priest furiously, resenting what had been so easily drawn from him, and added, under his breath, but violently: "See him! Let him do what the hell he likes! What do I care!"

Father Bond turned away, intending to go and find Bill and deliver the good news, but before he had taken a step Gavin spoke up. He was solemn and reasonable, yet greedy. "You haven't got us at our best, Father. It's been a hard fight and we're all tired. We've been brought close to defeat, and right now we're concerned by what's next. But we're working things out, working things out in our own way. So, you see, we're not quite ourselves."

"I know you've had a rough struggle, Gavin. I understand that."

"Well, I'm not so sure you ever can, Father, but I don't care about that anymore. Things have moved on. You'll see, Father. Things never looked better."

"Don't lose yourself, Gavin. You're a good man."

Gavin smiled, despite himself. He refused to respond, though. Father Bond waited just a moment further, then excused himself and went in search of Bill. He found him instantly, beating a retreat from the other side of the kitchen door. He called to him to come back and told him that he was to make his first communion. Bill was too nervous to reply. Father Bond demanded his answer. Bill nodded in agreement. The old priest was satisfied. He said no more, but let himself out. Bill went immediately to Kate to tell her the news. She recited *Hail, holy Queen, mother of mercy* in gratitude.

When the priest left the house on Ginns Peter and Gavin remained silent for a short while. Peter spoke first. He was self-berating and disconsolate. "I wouldn't make much of a cadre would I? I let the old man walk all over me."

"Not at all," Gavin responded warmly. "You said you didn't care."

"I don't."

"Well, then, it isn't worth making a stand over it."

"I didn't think it was enough."

"Don't expect too much from yourself immediately. You will be taught the disciplines of thought and argument in good time." Peter looked doubtful. Gavin laughed. "You've come a long way, Peter Kavanagh. Your part in the recent conflict was invaluable. The men from Fish would never have been solid without you. You have a way with you, Peter. A good way."

"I bully them, Gavin."

"Not a bit of it. They trust you. You have a way with you. They look up to you."

Peter took another cigarette from his pocket, and lit it. He opted not to offer Gavin one. He took a number of deep draws on his cigarette, then said: "I can't believe I'm talking to you like this Duffy. I don't know why I'm getting into this at all."

Gavin eyed Peter steadily: "Because you know that this is the door to the future. This is a party of a new type, Peter. It's disciplined, organised, uncompromising, ruthless. And we have to adopt those principles to support it, to ensure its ultimate victory. And it will be victorious Peter. Of that there is no doubt. The price of defeat is too great, Peter."

"Do you envisage anything else but defeat, Duffy?"

"I don't envisage defeat at all, Peter. We live in the antechamber of ultimate victory. Marxism guarantees the scientific and historic inevitability of success. October offers the proof of it. The worker state is a reality Peter, not a theory, a living, functioning actuality. And they are in terror of it, absolute terror."

"I'll be honest, Gavin, I get confused by what you say. I can't always get my head round it. It's all so precise and definite. I tell you, I feel uncomfortable, Gavin."

"Of course you do. It wouldn't be any good not to. There are things that you have to work out, disciplines that you have to adhere to. You'll have to take orders, accept others' decisions, sink your differences to overcome, have the courage to act, know what is expected of you by history and economics, give up yourself for the good of the whole, learn the skill to organise, and also have the courage to fail and to pay for failure."

"I don't know," Peter complained, still smarting from Father Bond's exposure. "I don't know that I have the personality for it."

"Give up your personality, Peter Kavanagh. Give up your own petty gripes, give up your own petty wishes, give up yourself. Give yourself to something far greater, Peter. Give yourself to the Party. You could never be wrong with the Party, Peter. The Party is bigger than any of us. It's a home Peter. A home in which to think every thought you ever needed. Learn to concede to it, and you will discover a freedom greater than you ever imagined. You couldn't regret it, Peter. I promise you. It's the dawn of a new age, Peter. October has started it. It can't be stopped. Not now. The machinery of history is turning. It's your destiny Peter. I can see it in your eyes. You can see it in your mind. You don't want to concede it. It will be our greatness, Peter. What do you say? Are you ready to submit? Are you ready to meet the challenge? You won't feel defeat again. You know that. What do you say?"

Peter looked at Gavin with wonder. He could hardly believe he had let the man into his house, and yet that past had all burnt away and nothing of it remained. The Peter Kavanagh who had been present when his father chose to go to South Africa no longer existed. His marriage, his son, the war, Fish pit, had each taken something of him. There was very little left. He had no personality to contend with. The war had blasted his very shadow from the dirt. He needed consolation, and here of all people, Gavin Duffy offered it to him. Not only to join the rank and file of the Communist Party, to be simply a paid-up member, but to be one of its cadres, an active worker carrying out its orders. His organisation of the Fish men had brought him the opportunity. He smiled grimly at Gavin, though he didn't feel like smiling. In fact, he felt chilled. He didn't know himself anymore. He had lost contact so long ago. He remembered lying on his mother and father's grave desiring some resolution for his empty soul. It had never appeared. He nodded his head. His voice came, low and firm. "I'm ready, Duffy. Ready for anything. I'd like to kill the bastards that sent me to war."

Gavin offered a calm, unenthusiastic smile. "No need to say that, Peter. No need to say anything anymore that you're not told. That's the wonder of it, Peter."

Peter nodded. "I accept that."

Gavin stood to leave. The evening had deepened as they had spoken and the kitchen was now quite dark. "I'll be in touch," Gavin said. Peter looked up at him. Gavin's expression was brooding and intense, yet satisfied. Peter made no response. Gavin left. Peter sat in the ever deepening gloom for some time. The air became chilled, the atmosphere dense. He wanted to cry, but knew he couldn't. Anne was so far from him. Why had she gone so far away? She was the only thing that made sense of anything? He still remembered her on the night his father left. He could still see the impression of her face. It wasn't absolutely clear. But it was her. A face and a style, a look and an attitude. Christ, she was so beautiful and lively, so frankly in love. What had happened to that? Why did the world intrude? Why did it take away and give so little?

He closed his eyes and screwed up his face. He couldn't stand his loneliness. He thought of crashing his fist onto the table, but at the point of raising his arm he stopped himself and held himself in check. Such gestures were meaningless. He knew that. He knew that all of his gestures were meaningless. He had lost all meaning. Well, in the future he wouldn't need any stupid gestures to see him through. He was one of the Party now. What the hell did it matter! They could do what they liked with him. He didn't mind. He knew that they were fundamentally right. He had no differences with Gavin anymore. Gavin had been right all along.

He sat in the chair, in the dark, for the rest of the night, sleeping for short lengths of time, dreaming of inconsequential things.

Gavin made his way back to his single room cellar dwelling on Mount Pleasant satisfied with his night's recruitment. Despite the enmity he knew Peter Kavanagh felt towards him he actually liked Peter. He found a dismal intensity to him that appealed. He wasn't sure whether it was real or apparent, but was willing to find out. He knew that Peter was no great intellect, but believed he was capable of conviction and devotion. Besides, he needed a comrade. He was too much on his own. He didn't mind the challenges, but he recognised that it weakened his position. With someone like Peter on his side he knew he would be able to talk to the men with greater ease. He felt that things were falling into place. The glaring injustice of the mining deals could only serve to politicise his reluctant class. The future beckoned. It had a shape and a pattern. He was filled with certainty.

The Communist Party was the perfect vehicle for his pessimistic desires. He envisioned a future of pious justice and equality, a future devoid of gimmickry, of personal ambition, of individual desire, one where free thought and action were willingly proffered to the realisation of the socialist state. The serious man, one of many, of the whole, would come into being. Life would be ordered, rational, composed, complete and regular. His soul thirsted for it. If necessary he would coerce his class to adopt perfection.

When he reached his cellar he lit a candle and took up where he had left off in reading Lenin's *The Agrarian Programme of Social-Democracy in the First Russian Revolution, 1905-1907.*

By the time corpus Christi came around Peter had not uttered another word to Bill about the matter. Needless to say, Peter did not attend the mass but went to work as if it were any other Thursday. Bill went alone. He stood outside the porch, and waited. He felt self-conscious and absurd. He was dressed in Hugh's suit, which had only been amateurishly altered. Kate Devlin had done her best, but Hugh couldn't afford to let her cut it, so all she had been able to do was tuck away the excess material as best she could. Besides, she wasn't a skilled seamstress, she just minded a machine. Bill's discomfort was made all the greater with the appearance of Mary's class. They were all so much younger than he was. They marched towards him from the adjoining school, keeping in a formation of strict pairs, each one dressed in makeshift shabby garments. He stepped back, below the porcelain Christ, and desperately tried to smooth the material of Hugh's suit where it was pinned at the wrist, but all to no avail. It remained lumpy and obviously folded. As the children came closer to him he considered walking away from the whole affair, and regretted ever having agreed to it in the first place. But before he could execute any escape Mary approached him. She was on her own. She explained that she had refused a partner and that it had been allowed. She reached out her hand and took hold of his. She smiled and drew him away from the shadow of the porcelain Christ, then led him towards the porch.

As they stood for the entrance Antiphon Bill said: "You look lovely."

Mary laughed and replied: "You are almost a man, stood there like that, Bill Kavanagh."

"Clay to God," Kate snapped from the pew behind, "be silent!"

Mary raised her head, not at all discountenanced by her grandmother's rebuke. She was right, one had to be silent. She smiled. She had never felt so lovely, nor so old. After all, she was wearing her mother's wedding-dress. She felt that all eyes were on her. She was about to be called to take the body of Christ. Her small chest heaved in anticipation. She slipped her hand into Bill's. She found his palm warm and moist, and assumed he must be scared. She looked at him. He was rapt and eager. She squeezed his palm.

The Lord fed his people with the finest wheat and honey; their hunger was satisfied.

"Amen," Mary said loudly.
"Shush, child," Kate snapped.
Mary smiled to herself. Was she still a child? A child to be seen, but not heard. She didn't think so. She held her head aloft to pray.

Lord Jesus Christ, we worship you living among us in the sacrament of your body and blood...

*

In the spring of 1928 McClean acquired a motorbus, a 1920 charabanc, 40 h.p. with torpedo-de-luxe body and solid tyres, named Lady Grace. Despite being in his sixties he was still open to a new departure. Times were good for McClean. Emigration kept up at a steady pace. He still sold tickets to all corners of the globe. Mine workers were his mainstay. Since the strike of 1926 there was a constant pool of unemployed miners. This gave the owners the whip-hand. They hired and fired as contracts dictated. Men like Peter Kavanagh and Gavin Duffy, men who had gained a reputation as troublemakers, found themselves constantly in and out of work. Others just waited for their own turn. No one doubted it would come sooner or later. People knew there was money to be made in the newer industries. The *Daily Herald* told them how well workers were doing in the motor industry (a million privately registered cars were on the roads) and electronics (as Hugh predicted everyone had a wireless), but that was somewhere else. Emigration to McClean's far-flung corners of the world was a more realistic proposition. 1928 was a good year.

The motorbus was a local marvel. Opinion regarding McClean was modified. He was a man of means. The motorbus was a substantial piece of equipment. McClean altered what had come to be regarded as the habits of a lifetime. He no longer took his customary post on the quay, nor did he frequent the shoreline with his toy boats. Overnight the motorbus made him a modern man. He conducted tours around the impressive machine. He told everyone who came to admire it, *It's not brand-new, but it's almost brand-new.* He had picked it up from a Carlisle omnibus company who had invested in even newer machines. He impressed everyone with his new found expertise. During his tours he would go into detail about the various design points of his acquisition. He stated how design had become standardised to a two axle system, the rear axle for driving and breaking, the front one for steering. He spoke knowledgeably about the need for a low centre of gravity in order to reduce the possibility of tipping. He had people on their hands and knees measuring the space between the base of the vehicle and the ground, whilst he stood proudly back waiting for their calculations. The only noticeable survival of the old McClean during these tours of inspection was his tendency to call the bus a vessel.

However, from May until June the vehicle sat outside McClean's shop in the Market Square and didn't move anywhere. It was inspected everyday, McClean wiping his palm here and there, removing any specks of dirt or water splashes, then every few days he would polish it thoroughly, but it never moved. Stories began to circulate that McClean had been cheated and the machine didn't work and it was only pride that stopped McClean from admitting as much. McClean's motorbus became more notorious with each passing day. There was even a joke and a children's song that did the rounds, the gist of both being that you'd never get to heaven on Billy McClean's bus. Marty prospered by the machine. The Square was noticeably busier than it had been for some time. He changed his busking position to McClean's side. Out of courtesy to McClean, the founder of the good times, he never played the children's song.

Only Kate refused to take a proper look at the machine. She had no grudge against McClean personally, but she viewed his shop with a feeling close to repugnance. She never forgot the fact that it was from McClean's shop that Bobby bought the ticket which, to her mind, killed him and in turn killed Polly. She was sure that had they lived the Kavanaghs would not be the broken tragic family they were. She lived with constant trepidation of more emigration. It was always in the back of her mind that John might not think himself too old to consider such a step. He couldn't bear himself when he wasn't working. And it would have been no surprise to her to learn that Hugh had bought his ticket. He was clearly devoted to his family and wouldn't leave them lightly. But what wouldn't he consider if he could no longer provide for them? Unemployment might yet force him to desperate measures. Kate didn't exactly boycott McClean's shop, she just didn't go herself. If she needed cigarettes, gas-mantles or fire-lighters she got one of Dora's children to go for her, usually with the unusual instruction that they didn't stand and talk. It became part of their routine to go to Kate and ask whether she had any *messages*.

Then, in the beginning of June, the Square resounded to a new and unusual sound. The motorbus had been started up. The simple truth was that McClean lacked a driver. He had never driven a motor vehicle himself, and certainly had no intention of starting now. It wasn't at all the sort of vessel he felt equipped to move from one point of anchor to another. Eventually he struck a deal with Harry Jacques, one of the very few mechanics in the town, that he would maintain the vehicle and drive it on week-end excursions. Consequently a new sign was painted outside McCleans: *Week-end Mystery Tours*.

As far as McClean was concerned the Mystery Tours were a great success. His customers came from the better quarters of the town. Even the mother of the owner of Fish, Canning, Loft and half a dozen other mines, a grand old matriarch in her eighties, condescended to take a trip in McClean's bus. The tours took in the traditional tourist haunts of the better off; places like Keswick, Silloth and Grasmere. On one trip Jacques ventured as far as Bowness-on-Windermere but the trip took all day. There were complaints that it was dark when the passengers were returned to the Market Square, and the bus overheated on two occasions. On the second occasion Jacques had to walk with his empty can until he found an obliging farmer.

It was Marty who suggested, albeit in passing, that McClean was forgetting who his friends were, and that he might like to put a watch on his precious profit making omnibus, just in case. McClean dismissed Marty's hints outright. Of course people had a tendency to be vindictive about success, it was a part of human nature, McClean understood that, he was a successful business man, but to take reprisals over it was absurd. Marty simply smiled knowingly, cocked McClean a wink and went back to playing. McClean scowled and marched off. Nevertheless, he woke throughout that and subsequent nights and rushed to the window to peruse his valuable purchase. Consequently, in pursuit of a sound night's sleep, a new sign went up outside McClean's during the summer holidays, Cheap Week-day Excursions. The word cheap was underlined. For McClean it was a masterstroke. It gave him income at a time when the bus would be otherwise idle, and at a time when Jacque's was free to drive. It got the grumblers off his back, whoever they might be, and even went so far as to make him look like a philanthropist. It also saved him the fuss of approaching Father Bond about the church's opinion regarding pleasure trips on a Sunday. He hadn't bothered about his regular Sunday mystery tours. Those customers were all Protestants. They could sort out their own salvation. The proof of the success of his move came when Marty whispered, *Good man*, to him as soon as saw the sign. McClean was delighted with himself.

So, on a day at the beginning of August the Glyns, Peter, Bill and Breda Kavanagh, John and Patrick Devlin and Marty Boland climbed aboard McClean's fabulous bus, along with other miner's families. McClean had designated it miners' day and charged a special fare. He was enjoying the role of friend to the community. Marty went along as an unpaying guest. Their destination was just a matter of a few miles down the coast, the wide sands of St Bees. They were all used to walking there. Throughout the summer scores of people would walk along the summit traversing the miles of sheer sandstone cliffs which separated St Bees and Whitehaven, the cliffs Robert had called the cliffs of the crying babies. From St Bees onwards the coast flattened into a vast coastal plain, with wide sandy shores all the way to Lancashire. From Whitehaven northwards the coast was rocky and devoid of any true beaches. St Bees was a different world. To go there in McClean's bus rather than walk was an unheard of pleasure. Even Peter Kavanagh had dispensed with his usual moroseness and needed very little persuasion from Hugh to come along. Only Kate refused to travel by motorbus, though she still made the journey, on this occasion preferring to travel by train. It was more expensive than McClean's bus, but such was her protests that in the end John agreed to meet her there. She claimed she simply could not trust McClean's contraption. In reality it was simply another manifestation of her protest against McClean's continued business. Any trip courtesy of McClean was one too many.

They set off early in the morning. It was already hot. It had never really cooled through the night. There was no movement in the air. Everyone knew it was going to be another scorching day. Still, as the bus motored along a draft of cool fresh air rushed through the interior. The sound of the air, plus the sound of the engines, and the noise of the wheels on the road and through the body work, meant that everyone had to shout to be heard, but that only heightened the excitement of the trip. The children, in particular Mary and Martin, were shouting with the thrill of it all.

The Lady Grace had an aisle by the kerbside window with a platform up to rows of bench seats. John found himself squeezed against a window with all the younger Glyn children fidgeting and fighting beside him, each having their moment of climbing against him to look out at the passing countryside. Dora had placed Robert on his lap. He knew it was deliberate. He had never really accepted that she had called one of her children Robert. Of course, it was the most natural thing in the world. Names passed through generations. That was the nature of naming. The same characters popped up years apart. One was an echo of the other. The baby she had in her own lap, born in the February, was named for him. He was the John of the future. He would carry on his grandfather's name. It would be a blessing and a burden. Names always were. She was already pregnant again. He might look around the motorbus and predict the names she might choose. Who was left? Marty, Peter, Breda? But Robert wasn't right. Maybe that was too much of a burden. It was too much to expect to carry the weight of a dead man, a man who had acquired mystery and suspense around his name.

He knew no other way of describing it. His memories of Robert remained raw. It didn't matter that over a decade had passed since his death. He was still learning about his son. The son he never said goodbye to. The son whose dreams he had never considered. The son whose visions he had never asked to see. He knew he had them. He knew that now. He knew it whenever he stood in his church. He looked around the pale yellow walls and inspected its saints and statues and he had some sense of Robert's restless presence. He knew he was there in every candle flicker, every expression and every word, but he couldn't find any definition to it all. So his son remained mysterious, and the things he might have done, the things he might have achieved, were a matter of suspense. He waited and wondered. It would be something to do with the church, with God, but he could never know, never even glimpse that point of view.

Of course, he had given up his God, in his own secret, determined way. He had never confessed that. He had never publicly suffered it, championed it, tested it, proclaimed it or claimed it. It just was. His life's story had demanded it. He always told himself that he did it for Robert, and for what Robert represented - a generation who wasn't yet ready to stand up for themselves. It had been his duty. He would never have acted in any other way. Murphy had to die. But another voice, a deeper, more troubling voice, told him that he had done it for himself. When he had stabbed Murphy it was for his own sake. He had to do it to live up to the name he wanted for himself. He had done it for John Devlin because John Devlin lived with the constant fear of being no one. He couldn't survive with that. He had a set of rules for being a man. He couldn't have written them down, he couldn't have even attempted to describe them in any way, but they existed all the same, moving his limbs, his eyes, his tongue. And one of those rules demanded he press a knife into Murphy. And one of those rules dictated that his son went off without a goodbye and died.

He lifted the young Robert onto his shoulder. His small chubby limbs seemed so fragile in his own clumsy hands. His fingers, pulling at his chin, soft, fleshy feelers, working out the outlines and confines of his world, were too defenceless, too vulnerable. It was awful the violence that could be done to them, the violence that was done to them. He saw it all of the time. Men beating their children, smacking them, punching them, making them bend. Was it right? He had never done much of that. But he had been fierce when necessary. Was that right? He didn't know of any other way. His own father had been quiet and strong. He had never lain a finger on him, but John would never have crossed him. He could see him now in his leather waistcoat, clogs and his rough cloth trousers tied at the knees. He didn't know what he thought about anything. He cut peat. He was the colour of peat. He smelled of peat. He would be buried in peat. He would still be the colour of peat. His skin would be grained, flaxen and wood dyed. He would be what he had been. That was something. But what had he seen? Questions like that didn't exist. So why now? Why did Robert, two Roberts, shake his composure and make him wonder what it was all for? Had he been so wrong, so bad, so misled?

Inevitably he was brought to Patrick. He was sitting quietly, holding himself in his usual, fixed, lazy pose. John could scarcely believe he was on the motorbus. It wasn't the sort of thing he usually did. John couldn't bring himself to believe that Patrick might be excited by something. He just never was. He was aloof, complaining and sickly, with a tendency to sound truculent whenever he was addressed. He was soft and incapable with a desire to appear tough. He didn't trust or turn to anyone, except a girl he had known at school. John had never been able to work that out. She used to come and sit with Patrick when he was ill in bed. God knows what they spoke about? Patrick never seemed inclined to talk, not quite cut out for it somehow. He simmered and stewed. It had obviously come to nothing. He wasn't sure whether he ever saw her now. It didn't seem likely. He just drifted, moving from job to job, farm work mainly, seasonal things. John was convinced it was just to get away. He spent his summers in barns and lofts, his winters here and there, sometimes at home, sometimes with Dora, sometimes with Peter. He never stayed in one place long. There was obviously some gypsy in him. John couldn't account for that. It didn't come from Julia, and he couldn't see how it could have come from Jones, the beautiful, blond miner. Jones at the very least seemed a settled, established character. So, there was no accounting for Patrick. He had sprung up, one on his own, a throw-back to some remote ancestry. John couldn't pretend he had done well there.

He pulled Robert closer to him. His attention, though, was on Patrick. Even now he was outside of the normal flow of things. His voice didn't join the others. Patrick never shouted, made jokes or cried out loud. His world was entirely interior, if it existed at all. He was much like Peter in that respect. He was another that John had not expected to see. They were men apart. They had broken their ties. But, at least with Peter, there was the ghost of a man that people remembered and mourned. Patrick had broken his bonds at birth. He had been a sickly baby with a recurrent brassy cough. He was still the same. He seemed tied up, disaffected and disorganised. His future looked bleak. It was obvious he needed to know who he was.

As he thought this a wave of temper flashed through John. He had always known that Patrick needed to know who he was. Patrick had always known that he wasn't one of them. That was more than certain. How that had been John couldn't guess. Maybe it was simply intuition, a gut feeling of difference. He refused to accept that it was maybe something to do with Kate and him. He was convinced that they had been proper parents. They had taken him in. They had brought him up. It needed no other proofs. The problem lay with Patrick. He chose to reject what had been given. Something innate in him had told him that he wasn't at home and it had dogged him all of his life. And, it was obvious to John, that it would dog him for the rest of his life until he was told. It wasn't doing him any favours living the lie. He had to be told. It might make all the difference. He might actually learn to trust the world, eventually even to love it and take part. John determined that he would tell Patrick the truth before the day was out. He knew Kate would put up a fight if she knew. He decided he wouldn't tell her. It would be easier like that.

Shortly after he had decided on his plan of action the motorbus ran up alongside Kate. She was walking with a basket on her arm from the railway station towards the beach. The motorbus slowed down and moved at her pace. Hugh went to the door and told her to jump on. She just kept on walking and waved the bus on with her free arm, not even deigning to turn and look at the machine. Jacques kept pace with her for a little longer, Kate constantly ushering the bus to move on, then finally he gave it up and accelerated towards the beach leaving her behind, still implacably refusing to acknowledge its presence. As well as the din of the accelerating engine there was a brief outbreak of laughter at Kate's expense. It disgruntled John, but he let it pass without comment. After all, he shared its sentiment.

Jacques pulled the bus up on a piece of rough ground overlooking the beach. He was the first off and stood by the door acknowledging everyone as they alighted, again instructing them on the time of departure. The children were the first off after Jacques, scrambling in a disordered push to get off and get to the beach. A grassy bank led down to a stone esplanade, then there was a drop to a band of shingle, then a vast stretch of tidal sand. The sea at St Bees went out some half a mile or more. The shingle bank was divided by a sequence of regular groynes that ran some distance into the sand. When they arrived the tide was out. From the rough ground it seemed far in the distance, a film of translucent blue that ran to a horizon of brilliant whiteness.

As the bus was pulling to a standstill John quickly handed Robert to Hugh and made sure he was just behind the children, so as to be in a position to catch up with Patrick who, having sat at the front, would be one of the first off. John came just behind him. He was amazed to be greeted by John Darcy, who was standing a few yards off by his trolley. Patrick and Marty were already with him.

"A fine day for it, Mr Devlin. God is on our side," John Darcy pronounced as John approached.

John nodded, but looked disdainful and suspicious. "How did you end up here?" he demanded.

"I set off on the road at the crack. The motorbus is a marvel to be sure, but still can't accommodate a trolley of these grand proportions."

"And why would you be needing your trolley, I'm asking myself John?"

"Beach essentials, Mr Devlin, beach essentials. It may be the holiday season for the majority, but I still have a crust to earn. I wouldn't deny myself an opportunity of the happy multitude, would I now?"

"You'll make your fortune one day Mr Darcy."

"Indeed I will Mr Devlin, and it's kind of you to acknowledge the fact."

"Not at all."

"Will you keep us company Mr Devlin?"

"No, I'll head down to the shingle and wait for Kate."

"Ah, of course, her natural inclination is to obstruct the modern world, and good luck to her, innovation only brings trouble in the end."

"Not obstruct, exactly, but it takes her a little longer than most."

John Darcy smiled. "God, man, but your loyalty's a treat. You have yourself the finest woman on the planet, you know that for a fact."

John didn't reply, but indicated that he would press on. He turned from John Darcy and looked directly at Patrick. He held him in his gaze for a moment. Patrick visibly recoiled from his attention. John attempted to make his suggestion seem spontaneous and natural. "Ah Patrick," he began as if he had just that minute realised he was there, "you can come with me. We'll go down to the shingle and wait for Kate, for your mother."

Patrick looked decidedly unsure and uncomfortable. He shook his head and took a step back. "I'm going with John Darcy and Uncle Marty," he stammered. "It's all arranged."

"But I want you to come with me," John said, an edge of temper clearly audible in his voice.

Patrick looked horrified. He shook his head again, forcibly. "No," he insisted, "I'm staying with them."

John glared at him, only just resisting the temptation to grab him and drag him physically to the shoreline.

Marty spoke up. "He'll be well looked after, you know that. No fears on that score. Leave the lad to us. We've planned a little game, and I wouldn't want the lad to miss out now."

John stood his ground for a moment longer, staring implacably at Patrick, then abruptly tore himself away without another word. He marched away down the grassy bank toward the shingle without once looking back.

The sun was high in the sky behind him. It made the sea in the distance glimmer, its colours bright and shifting, its sound coming in a gentle chorus. The shouts and screams of children outdid the surf. He could see Julie and Jane running. Hugh was with them, gambolling along sideways like a comic ape. The girls ran as fast as they could. They just couldn't stop. Their expressions showed their strange, spontaneous determination. Hugh thought it amazing. The seaside had set them off, the sand, the sea, the sound and smell of both, the sounds of other children playing. They were bursting with aimless energy. He loved every minute. He laughed as he went alongside them. But they didn't. They were in deadly earnest. And yet there was no purpose to it. They just kept running, keeping to as straight a line as they could. Hugh

273

would never forget that image of them, running for all they were worth, inspired.

As they moved away, parallel to the horizon, their figures becoming indiscernible, Peter came and stood over John. He too was looking in the direction of the girls and Hugh. Neither spoke for some time. They simply kept on gazing at the same image of the father and his racing girls. In truth, John somewhat dreaded this approach from Peter. He wasn't in the humour to listen to his old rigmarole, his annoyance and impatience with everything.

Eventually, it was Peter who spoke first. "Hugh's a great lad," he said. "He does things very well."

John turned to Peter. They were both squinting, Peter towards the far ground, John towards the near. There was something plaintive in Peter's tone that surprised John. Eventually, he nodded his agreement and said: "He loves his kids right enough, I don't think anyone would argue that. I often wish that he didn't have quite so many. It wouldn't do him any harm to leave my lass alone a bit more."

Peter smiled. "He's not the type to do that."

"Evidently," John said, smiling himself.

"Or Dora, for that matter."

"Be careful, now. That's my daughter you're calling."

"I'm sorry, I didn't mean anything."

"I know. I'm only pulling your leg," John said, unused entirely to contrition from Peter. "I know you didn't mean anything."

"It's good they have all these kids."

"Maybe, I don't know."

"I bully mine."

John looked more intently at Peter, surprised by the admission, but Peter said no more. Eventually, sensing that John was looking at him, Peter looked down and shrugged and smiled simply, but still didn't speak.

"Sit down, for God's sake, Peter, sit down."

Peter slumped onto the shingle, his knees up, his arms resting on top of them. He gazed blankly at the horizon. He began again. "I know I bully him. I tell myself I shouldn't do it. I make deals with myself, but I always break the contract. I don't know why I do it. I'm jealous of him sometimes. I know that. It sounds crazy, doesn't it. He's just a kid. I know that. But I am, all the same. Just sometimes. Usually though, I'm just angry, angry for no reason. Why the hell should I be angry for no reason? It doesn't make any sense, does it, but there it is."

John wasn't sure what to say. He had never heard Peter speak like this. He knew he should not disregard it, but he didn't know how to respond. He had learnt to be wary of Peter. It was difficult to break that reserve. After some thought he uttered: "You went through a lot. You all went through a lot. That can't be easy. It must leave a mark."

"What do you mean?"

"Well, the war and that, you, Hugh, and Robert of course. You went through a lot, saw a lot. That's what I mean."

"Christ, that was years ago. Everybody's forgotten about that. What the hell does that mean to anyone now?"

"I think about it all of the time."

"Well, more fool you then," Peter snapped suddenly.

John felt instantly wary of Peter, but went on nevertheless. "No, I don't think so. I didn't do very well by Robert, and I try to work things out in my head. Try to work out what he thought about it all. What sort of a man he became."

"There's nothing to work out. It was all one great big fucking sham. We got ourselves fucked up for nothing, nothing at all."

"You said it was all for poor little Belgium. Robert said. I remember him telling me as clearly as if it was just yesterday. It was a hot day like today, and he stood up to me, mouthing off about poor little Belgium. He was very impressed by everything you'd said. He would have gone off sooner if he could have, ready to stick up for poor little Belgium."

"Poor little Belgium. He should have told me to get lost, shouldn't he. Poor little Belgium. Just shows what a fucking fool I was, doesn't it. Poor little Belgium."

"I think you were right."

"What?"

"Right, I think you were right, and I was wrong."

"You're not serious."

"Of course I am. Why not?"

"Belgium?"

"Yes, Belgium."

Peter began to laugh, the sound quiet and reflective, but for once devoid of anger. "You're full of shocks, you know that," he said.

"I'm pleased."

At this point in the conversation they heard music start up behind them. It was a strange percussive music with a familiar fiddle. They both turned to investigate. It came from along the esplanade. There was a four piece band. Marty was at the front. They recognised him, despite the fact that he had dressed himself as if he were sporting Oriental wear, the veils and scarves concocted from the rags John Darcy collected. John Darcy was to one side banging a small drum, whilst Jacques was at the other side tapping a tune out of differing lengths of pipe. Behind the three of them came Patrick, his head bowed tapping pieces of coconut shell together. The music was dissonant, yet rhythmic. After a short prelude John Darcy and Jacques began to sing. It was a song about Arabia. It was unexpectedly effective.

Peter turned back to John and asked: "Why does Marty dress up?"

John gazed at the shenanigans for a moment longer, laughed quietly and replied: "Because he's the biggest kid on the whole beach."

"Do we approve?"

"Oh Jesus, I should hope so. Taking care of Marty is what makes us what we are."

Peter shrugged, but didn't look over impressed. He turned his attention back to the bright, glittering horizon.

John went on: "Do you think that's wrong then, a grown man dressing up like Marty? He's just a kid, an overgrown, excitable kid. The point about Marty is that he's harmless. He's so harmless he frightens the life out of me. I'd put up with a great deal for Marty's sake, though I'd never let on to Kate."

"That's what kids do is it, dress up?"

"That and other things. Did Bill never dress up?"

"All the time. I was always catching him decked out like Marty there, like the Queen of bloody Sheba. Always thought it was a bit weird myself. I've given him a few hidings for that over the years."

"You're way too hard on him."

"I know that. I said. I bully him. I admit it. All right. I can't say more."

"You could stop."

"Maybe I have. I think I'm more indifferent these days than anything else. Another year at school and he'll be off working somewhere. God knows where? I can't see him down a mine, somehow, but he'll be able to fend for himself."

"Good, not down a mine I mean. Good."

"Is it?"

John simply nodded. They didn't say anymore for a while. They gazed at the shimmering sea, John smiling, letting the sunshine warm through him, Peter sinking into his customary moroseness and disaffection with everything.

276

Eventually John turned back to Peter and looked him over, briefly, yet with feeling, for the first time in years encouraged to talk to him. "What happened to you Peter?" he asked warmly. "You were a champion boy. The tops. I really thought you were the best. Then you got sad. But it's gone on for a long time, too long, too long for all of us."

Peter turned his head somewhat towards John, not completely but obliquely. "Do you think I was saved for a reason?" he asked, his voice little more than a whisper, a hoarse, difficult whisper.

John shrugged. "I never thought about it, but I suppose so. Yes. Why not?"

"I think it was a mistake. It shouldn't have happened. I was there a long time. I got right through. Nobody got right through. It was a mistake." John tried to speak, knowing he had to contradict what Peter was asserting, but Peter spoke right over him, his voice strong again. "There was one time we had two kids join us, two new, soppy kids, can't have been much more than sixteen. They'd only been with us two weeks, when all of a sudden we had to do this attack. We were in reserve to a regiment in front of us, but the previous morning the Germans had come over under a barrage of smoke and captured the whole lot of them. The two battalions to either side couldn't get in touch with each other, so we had to get the ground back. Well, when those two kids found out we were going to do this attack they just started crying their eyes out. I mean it, literally, just sobbing away in front of everybody. It was just too soon, I suppose. Anyways, when we moved up we lost sight of them. They'd cleared off, right out of it. They were picked up by the redcaps three or four miles back from the action. Of course, they were brought back and charged, found guilty of desertion. As the youngsters had been in our platoon we drew lots to work out who was going to shoot them. The next morning they were tied to a post and had a white cloth pinned over their hearts and shot. Some of the guns had ball and others were blank so you weren't supposed to know if you'd shot them or not, but you could tell by the recoil of the rifle. Their parents were sent telegrams to say they'd been killed on active service. Their names were read out on three successive parades as a warning. Two weeks they lasted, that's all, two lousy, fucking weeks, a pair of stupid, soppy kids that shouldn't have been there at all." He stopped speaking and eyed John for a moment. A semi-formed, cold smile spread across his lips. He knew the question on John's mind. He uttered: "I said, you can always tell by the recoil. And I got through the whole lot. I don't think that makes a lot of sense somehow, do you? See, I shouldn't be here, sitting on this beach having this conversation. I shouldn't be here at all. Christ, it's not as if I can do anything great or wonderful, is it. I've got nothing to offer. Maybe that's it. Maybe I was just overlooked because I'm nobody. I'm nobody to God and he's nobody to me. But you wouldn't get that, would you? You don't know what the hell I'm talking about, do you? How the hell could you?"

John was about to protest, but Peter got to his feet hurriedly and, in some confusion, indicated that he had to go. The problem was he didn't know where. John lifted his arms and shrugged. "You could be kinder to a lot more people, Peter, including yourself. Think about Bobby, for God's sake. I loved..."

Before he had finished Peter marched off, his heavy footfalls displacing the shingle as he went. The songs from the Orient continued.

John stood up intending to walk somewhere, maybe down to the water where he could dip his hands into a sea dear to his heart. As he did Kate's voice began to harangue him from the esplanade behind him. He turned to her quickly. She complained that she had been looking all over for him. Why hadn't he waited for her? He had no idea where that was supposed to be, but he didn't defend himself. He shrugged in acquiescence. He knew in that moment that his plan for the day would not come to fruition. He would not tell Patrick the truth about himself. It wasn't just that Kate would obstruct him, and that she was maybe capable of that, it just didn't seem worthwhile anymore. In fact, it smacked of cruelty. Maybe they were all bullies, of one kind of another. It wasn't a very agreeable thought. He helped Kate down onto the shingle and told her he was glad to see her. She dismissed him, but was nevertheless delighted that he was willing to still say such things. They sat down together and watched their grandchildren play on the sands.

Peter made his way down the shingle and reached the sand. His boots made deep impressions in its damp surface. He walked along for a while parallel to the shingle, stopping every now and again to look out to sea. The water continued to glitter, its surface thin and dazzling. But everything on it, everything beyond the bathers jumping and diving in the breakers, seemed motionless. There was a stillness to everything. Each time he looked he felt his mood drop lower and lower. He couldn't quite account for it. Maybe it was simply the sound of the bathers, screaming in unison as the waves broke around their thighs. Each scream was a spectacular reminder that he was alone. He gave it up and walked on, only to stop and investigate it again.

Then as he walked some way further he heard his name called. He turned toward the shingle. Breda was sitting alone. He immediately marched up the bank of loose, yielding stones and stood over her.

Now that he was there in front of her she seemed unsure. He just stood there as if he was waiting to know what she wanted, not accepting that she had just called his name because he had appeared. In the end she simply shrugged and smiled.

He asked: "Why are you sitting alone?"

His question sounded like an accusation. She shrugged again, but didn't reply.

He gazed at her as if he couldn't work out why she was there at all. "Do you remember Mam and Dad?" he blurted out suddenly.

She looked at him warily and quietly said that she did. Of course she did. She reminded him that she was thirteen years old when they died. He continued to look confused, as if he were trying to work things out that wouldn't make any sense to him, at all.

"And how old was Alice?"

"Fourteen."

"Catherine?"

"Eighteen, I think."

"June?"

"Seventeen. If Catherine was eighteen she was seventeen."

"And me? How old was I?"

"I don't know, twenty, twenty-one. No, twenty. Twenty. You must remember."

"And Tom?"

"Why?"

"And Tom?"

"Fifteen, he was fifteen. Why?"

"And Stanley?"

"The baby, a kid. Why? Twelve. But just a kid."

"Did he remember them?"

"Yes," she said, unable to stem the tears that had been threatening since he had started questioning her. "Of course he remembered them."

"So what happened?"

"What do you mean?" she moaned, her words charged by their memory, and also by her growing apprehension of Peter.

He bowed down so that his face was directly in front of hers and demanded: "Where did it all go wrong? If everyone remembered them like you say they did, why did it all go wrong?"

She gazed back sheepishly at his fixed stare and then, suddenly finding the strength to challenge him from somewhere deep within her, snapped back at him: "Because we grew up mad and bad, mad, bad and sad."

"No!"

"Yes!"

He continued to gaze at her with his fixed unyielding stare, then suddenly broke away and marched back down the shingle towards the sand. She called after him, her voice growing more and more shrill. "You don't help Peter. You didn't help. You stood by as we fell apart. You let it happen. You let us go rotten. You did nothing. You let yourself get completely wrapped up in yourself. So don't blame us. We didn't know any better. Catherine said we were all hopeless but that you were the worst!"

When Peter reached the sand he rounded on her fiercely, glaring at her for a while, then he pointed at her and shouted: "Don't sit alone, there's no reason for it. Go and sit with someone. Run across the sand and find Dora Glyn. I don't want you sitting alone." He stopped speaking, looked at her for a moment longer then tore away and continued his march along the sands, still keeping the shingle parallel.

As he made his way from her Breda moaned, threw back her head, let out a shriek then put her face in her hands and began to moan. She was convinced that she too must be bad, mad and sad. Catherine was right. They all were. There was no way back for them. However, a few minutes later she got to her feet and made her way to the sands, and set off to discover Dora Glyn as Peter had instructed.

Later that morning Breda and Dora made sand-castles with all the Glyn children, except Mary, who had gone off, she said, to investigate rock pools with Bill. (They had actually sneaked off from Martin who had been determined to play with them all morning. Dora had had to console him with the possibility of an ice-cream later.) Hugh had left them to it. He said he wanted to listen to the Arabian band. In fact he went for a beer with Peter. The sun was virtually at its zenith. The tide was coming in quickly. Any castles they built would certainly not last long. But that was part of the pleasure, to build them quickly and watch them chance the waves.

They had been working furiously for a while, producing a mound of unshaped sand, rivulets of water already appearing around them where the sand-bed had been furrowed into permanent channels, when Hugh went to his mother and said he had seen Aunty June. He said he recognised her from photographs. He was sure it was her. Dora turned quickly to Breda, unsure whether she wanted her to hear. Hugh was far from being a fanciful boy, but she couldn't quite make sense of what he was saying. Breda had heard though and pounced on him immediately. Where was she? Where had he seen her? Hugh looked at his mother for permission. She simply nodded. He pointed vaguely towards the esplanade. Breda followed the direction of his pointing finger, but couldn't really make out anyone in any great detail. She went beside him and told him to tell her exactly. Her voice ran on after the question. It was just that she couldn't see. She didn't see where he meant. She couldn't work it out. Hugh looked at his mother again. Dora simply shrugged. She trusted that he thought he had seen her, but suspected he was mistaken. He had only been a baby when she last went away. It was more than likely he was wrong. She couldn't work out why he would have said such a thing. He uttered that she was no longer there. Breda turned to Dora in confusion. Was he playing games? Would he do that? He went on. He said that she had walked along the esplanade, stopped and looked at Uncle Marty then turned and quickly made off in the other direction, then made her way up the grassy bank at the far side towards the beach huts. Breda ran off straight away, Dora's voice trailing her, calling her name.

Dora didn't know what to do. She couldn't chase after Breda and leave her children. She was on her own. The tide was coming in. She simply shrugged, looked wistfully at Hugh and told him they should build more quickly. More castles, lots more castles, and more quickly.

When Breda returned Dora was standing on the lower reaches of the shingle, the children sitting higher up on the bank behind her. There was water around her shins. She was reluctant to step out. She could tell by the despondent look on Breda's face that she had been unsuccessful. She didn't want Hugh to take any blame. She began to describe the water overwhelming the castles. They had made so many, but it was all for nothing. The water was relentless, not rough or violent, but just overpowering. It had eaten at walls so that there were only ravaged keeps, collapsing citadels, macerated walls. She smiled forlornly and described it as really quite wonderful to witness. She ended with an open, incomplete sentence. If only every day were like this.

Breda looked at her earnestly. She spoke with obvious passion. She believed him. June had been there. She must be staying in one of the beach huts. Either that or she was hiding in one, taking refuge through some opportune door. She was going to go back and keep watch. She would find her.

Dora was torn by loyalty to Hugh and compassion for Breda. She asked Breda to reconsider. Why would June run away? Why would she not want to be found? She had nothing to hide. She had gone away because she was upset. She would come back when she was ready, when the hurt had changed. She wouldn't run away from her, just as she wouldn't have run away from Marty or Patrick. It didn't make sense. Maybe Hugh had made a mistake. He had only ever seen a photograph. She had to remember that.

Breda shook her head. She had a ready answer. June would have run away from Peter. She wouldn't be ready for that. Peter was too formidable. He frightened everyone. She wouldn't face him.

Was Peter there?

Breda didn't reply. She waited a moment longer then made her way back to the beach huts. She wandered around them for the rest of the day, listening to the remote barely discernible sounds of the private lives that were taking place inside them. She didn't discover June.

Dora stepped from the water, mournful of the fact that all her castles had been washed away.

As Breda ran off chasing after an appearance of June, and Dora and the children struggled to shore up their failing bastions and fortresses, Mary was convulsing on the Head. She had told Dora that she was going to play in the rock pools at the foot of the cliffs, but Bill had persuaded her to walk to the top.

The sandstone stacks between St Bees and Whitehaven rose out of a jumbled collection of rocky buttresses and outcrops, forming an arc at the north shore of the beach which jutted out into the sea. The cliffs that began there achieved height quickly, so that they were soon all of a level. A steep, though accessible, path started where the beach finished. To one side was the deepening ravine that dropped down to the rock pools then, after the arc, the sea itself, and to the other side rolling fields, lush with meadow grasses and flowers. The path was a dividing line between two distinct natures. As the path climbed up it followed the line of the arc that pushed out into the sea, then reached a promontory that looked right across the beach and far into the distance along the flat coastal plain. The path then climbed steeply again up a wide grassy embankment for some considerable distance until it reached the absolute height of the cliffs proper, then it continued level all the way to Whitehaven, sheer sandstone stacks seaward, fields behind.

They discovered that at a certain point in climbing the path all the laughter and all the other beach sounds suddenly stopped, and only the sound of gulls remained, crying regularly against the sound of the sea below, which was constant, but all of a level and like a type of silence itself, a fabric, tangible silence. It was Bill who pointed it out. He became excited and suddenly ran ahead, up the steep path towards the final summit, shouting aloud that the laughter had stopped. At first Mary didn't understand what he meant. He asked her to listen. What could she hear? The sea and the gulls. Exactly he roared. The beach is silent. They had left it behind. She didn't comprehend his excitement at having left it behind, but she recognised it. She was somewhat fearful of it. She knew she shouldn't have left the beach, and now that it was silent she was more aware than ever of her transgression. On the other hand she felt very grown-up that Bill had wanted her to go with him. He was so much older. He was almost a man. It had to be all right being with him. No one could accuse her of being reckless.

When they reached the summit the sandstone stacks stretched far into the distance, a sequence of bends, with a constant display of birds drifting on the up-draught. The guillemots and razorbills had gone, leaving the multitudinous shelves and fissures of the rock bare, but for the sheets of their grey encrusted droppings.

Bill found the highest point on the top of the bank and just gazed along the red brown shelves. He had an inkling to shout out with delight, yet also felt a temptation to cry. He didn't understand. It happened so often to him. He witnessed something he felt quite wonderful and it brought on those opposing tendencies, to applaud and to weep. It was crazy. He didn't know of anyone else who thought like that. Maybe that was why he had brought Mary. She was just a little girl, but he felt safe with her. He could say things and it didn't matter. She just listened. She was good at that. He knew it was odd. He should have been down on the sands with Hugh and Martin, maybe even trying to get to know Patrick, but he felt uncomfortable with them, not shy or reserved, simply curtailed. He wanted to declare his delight and his gloom, but he couldn't with them. It wasn't that they were unfriendly, they just didn't show any tendency to such thoughts. No one did. They did what they did, and that was it. He told himself he had too much imagination. He took it as a probable fault.

He was sure the gulls didn't have imagination. They made their sorties along the cliff stacks and over the sea with the single, thoughtless desire to make it through. They didn't have to think of where they were, or where they had come from. There was no dead mother, her touch gentle and desperate, joining with that flight. There was no father, his expression disappointed and aggrieved, overviewing that struggle. It only existed as it happened. It was the same on the beach. Martin was the king of the castle, but only whilst the castle stood, then he was something else, and he didn't regret no longer being the king, nor did he mourn the castle. But Bill did. As he ran up the grassy bank he was a soldier, an explorer, a cave man, and as he stood looking along the shelves of cliff he mourned their loss. He was always mourning the dead, the imaginary dead. He was always reliving their lives in his head. He rehearsed whole episodes that might have been, tender moments between mother and son, brother and brother, king and queen. And he also lived what might be. The testing moment of father and son. The declarative moment when inner worlds and outer worlds would explode against each other.

The world in his head wouldn't allow the world outside of him to be itself. He couldn't just shout out like Martin, because that's what boys did, and it was understood. He couldn't charge away along the cliff-top path, a brave warrior, plotting new ground, original man. He didn't let himself do such things. He was always jealous of his pleasures, distrustful, hurt by them. Nothing was safe, nothing secure, nothing shared. He loved where he was, and he hated it. It was delightful and he suffered it. His home was a joy and a dread. He loved the Glyns, the town, the streets, he loved his father, and longed to be loved in turn, but that couldn't be, because no one knew that he wanted to cry quite as much as he wanted to laugh. No one knew the burden of imagination he carried with him. No one knew how the shape of the cliff marked off against the blue, capillary veined sky, made him ache. He wanted to embrace it, love it, understand it, express it, but how? What did it mean being so overwhelmed by the world on your eyes? What did it mean to have a head spinning, and a stomach churning, because of the slow, lazy flight of a sea bird, its outlined shape passing through the elements of colour, space and time? What sort of a person was he? What sort of a man was he going to be? Why was it all so difficult? Why did it seem to him that the line of cliffs striding into the milky distance were reaching consciousness into memory into the future.

He turned to the sea. He reached out his arms like a priest. Maybe it was only through imagination that anything existed? One could either dispense with it, or give it reign. Well, why not the latter? He let his head spin.

He was a chosen child. He was special. He had dominion. It was a good game. He could conduct nature around him. The waves clashed in his head; the gulls through the empty spaces of his being. He contained them all. He was king of dreams. He was a man made by God. He was son of it all. He intended to shout aloud: Damn you father, son and wholly stupid, but his flight of fancy was brought crashing to earth by Mary.

She was gazing up at him, wondering what he was doing flexing his body and waving his arms, as if he were conducting the sounds around him. She didn't know what game it was, or what she was supposed to do. Then, for a moment, everything became singularly strange. Everything slipped out of joint. Time was going backwards. There was a voice calling from the deck below. It was her mother and a gull. She put her hand to her temple.

Bill saw her hand reach up, and caught a look on her face of sheer confusion and incredible panic. A second later she fell to the floor, issuing a strange scream of descent. She held herself tightly, her whole body rigid and fixed, her jaw clenched firmly closed. This lasted no more than twenty seconds or so, yet seemed to go on forever to Bill. He was just coming to the conclusion that she was dying when suddenly her face, body, arms and legs began to jerk violently, every inch of her pulsating as if it were being assaulted by thousands of needle pricks. There was foam and blood around her mouth.

He was rooted to the spot. He had never seen her fit before. He was terrified. The fact that a body could so suddenly lose control, that a face could be twisted out of all semblance of normality, was beyond comprehension. It was horrific. It momentarily annulled his natural tendency. He gazed at her as if she were a stranger, maybe even a freak. No matter that he told himself he should go to her and help, though what help he might give he couldn't even begin to conceive, he couldn't overcome his virtual repugnance. Then after a few minutes, the jerking slowed to nothing, and her body relaxed. For a moment she came round. She said something totally incomprehensible. It sounded like, put up in the starry pit, but he wasn't at all sure. She reached for a nearby flower and tried to pluck it but only managed to put her fingers together over the top of the petalled head. The world was upside down.

With an instant rush of affection Bill shouted out her name and rushed to her, knelt by her and cradled her head in his lap. She fell into a deep sleep. He pulled her up into his arms and caressed her. She had wet herself. Her pinafore was soaked. He put his face against hers and pressed them together tightly.

When she awoke she wanted her mother. She was scared, confused and in pain. She had bitten her tongue. Bill tried his best to comfort her. She quickly became hysterical. He still held her, but she fought to free herself, moaning all of the time that she wanted her mother. Bill was fearful of letting her go. He didn't want her running back to the beach in that state. What would his father say? What might he do? Besides, what would he make of the fact that he had gone off with Mary. It was hardly the thing for a boy of his age. Consequently he held her close, and continued to try to soothe her, whispering to her that everything was going to be all right. Eventually she gave a great moan of despair, let her face fall against him and began to sob. Her small torso gave such violent shudders that he feared she was beginning to have another convulsion. He lifted her face in his palms to look at her. She moaned that she was wet. Bill smiled. He whispered to her that the sun was shining. She would dry in no time. She put out her tongue. The flesh was torn. It was crimson and purple. He moaned in sympathy, and lay her face back against him. He stroked her and tried to console her, repeating there, there, over and over again. She became so still and quiet that he thought she might have fallen asleep again. He looked down at her face. She was staring blankly in front of her. He smiled. There was imagination in her expression. It was personal, remote and not yet mature, but it was there all right.

He whispered that she should get dry. She looked up at him and smiled. She would do as he directed. She trusted him. He would look after her. He helped her take off her pinafore and knickers. He lay them across a gorse bush. She lay down fully naked among the coarse grass, unashamed and relaxed. Bill sat beside her and neither looked at her nor didn't look at her. Her nakedness was nothing. They spoke very little. They thought their thoughts.

Later, when they returned to the beach, Mary told her mother that she had slipped climbing over a rock pool and bit her tongue. She made no reference to the fact that she had had a fit. Dora thought it strange that she should have the tell-tale sign of her convulsions, but had no reason to think she would lie. The notion that she might not be telling the truth made no sense at all.

Bill was satisfied by the experience. He didn't understand the feeling, but he was aware of it. For some reason it allowed him to feel less remote from everyone. He was even happy to play with Martin.

Together they constructed channels with their hands and lengths of sticks in the once again exposed sand. As they played he went up to Mary, brought her attention to the head-land away to their right, and whispered to her that together they knew something about that high ground. At a certain point the laughter abruptly stops, and when you come back down it starts again at exactly the same point. She didn't say anything, but smiled. It was their secret. That was such a grown-up thing.

They stayed on at St Bees for the whole day. Kate left first in order to catch her train. She was offered a lift in the charabanc, even if it was only as far as the station, but she wouldn't entertain it. John said he would walk her to the station, but she wouldn't hear of that either. She insisted she would make her own, safe way home. John let her go with a touch of frustration and regret. He didn't like her acting as if she were too old for things. She wasn't like that. It crossed his mind that he would have another opportunity to approach Patrick. He knew it was spiteful, but Kate had annoyed him with her irrational obstruction. He told himself that all of her obstruction was irrational and that had to include Patrick. Still, as she wandered off with her basket on her arm, it was a somewhat wistful look he gave her as he followed her progress out of sight.

As it turned out Patrick solved any dilemma John might have had about talking to him. He was quite drunk. He had been with Marty, John Darcy and Jacques all day, and they had been drinking for the greater part of it. They came to the motorbus singing and shouting. Patrick was actually the centre of attention. Marty and John Darcy were giving him frank advice on how to succeed with women. John was disgusted. He decided to simply ignore them. He didn't want the outing to end on a sour note. Besides there were too many children about. He determined to see Marty and Patrick another day. Their display was unforgivable.

There was some discussion about Jacques' fitness to drive the motorbus, but as there was no one else who knew how, along with Jacques' insistence that he had drunk very little himself and had only been keeping the band company, it was accepted that there was nothing else for it but to let him take charge of the vehicle.

The sun was a large orange ball, its outer rim just dipping behind the water, the sky crimson and turquoise, as they set off. The children continued to chatter loudly, still excited, whilst the grown-ups sat back against the hard back chairs worn out by the sea air. John closed his eyes and let the sounds of the engine and the children merge into one satisfying backdrop, and prepared to fall asleep. However, he was just nodding off when the bus gave a great lurch and he felt himself jolted. He woke instantly from his half-sleep. Jacques had driven the motorbus off the road into a ditch. The aisle side of the bus was wedged against a bank, whilst to the other side the windows looked out onto the deepening night sky. Thankfully no one was hurt, but they couldn't get off. The front of the motorbus was stuck fast in the ditch and the door was blocked. For a while there was absolute confusion as to what they should do. A consensus was developing that they would probably have to wait for the machine to be dragged out. John couldn't accept that. Kate would be terrified. She suspected the worst as it was. If they shouldn't return it would confirm her worst fears. He climbed over the bench and went to the door himself. It was impossible. He was tempted to punch Jacques, but he was too obviously shocked to understand what was happening. In the end it was Peter who took the starting-handle and went to the back of the bus and smashed the windows. He then carefully picked out the pieces of shattered fragments and produced an exit large enough for an adult to get through. Within minutes there was a band of walkers making a slow, weary trek back to Whitehaven, cursing Jacques and motor transport in general. Jacques, Marty and Patrick remained behind, fit only to sleep it off, though that proved less than comfortable. Patrick dreamed he was on a capsized boat and vomited.

McClean accepted Jacques offer to buy the motorbus from him. He wasn't really disappointed. His initial enthusiasm had waned over the last few weeks. As the summer developed he realised he missed his days around the docks. He was a sailor. It made sense that a mechanic should own the bus. Besides, Jacques was so embarrassed by the event that the offer he made McClean was very generous indeed. McClean bought himself a brand-new, enormous model boat and resumed his life by the shore-side. He even bought Marty a bottle of whisky out of the proceeds. Kate was never openly triumphant, but there was no masking her pleasure. It was assumed she felt vindicated; that she could say to herself that she had told them all so. To her own mind, though, it was another escape from the shocking inevitability of McClean's. The demise of the motorbus symbolically made emigration remoter than it had been. She prayed that that was how it would remain.

*

For the remainder of that summer of 1928 Breda haunted the beach huts at St Bees. They were a collection of wooden sheds and small stone built cottages. She worked for Wilson and Kitchin's, a wholesale and retail chemist, druggist and drysalters, sometimes in the Guinea Warehouse, sometimes in one of their numerous stores. She started at seven each morning, and worked though until six. As soon as she finished for the day she took the path over the head-land and searched for June. The Devlins scarcely saw her. She only really returned home to sleep. Kate tried to reason with her. She had learned from Dora the reason for Breda's obsession. She told her it didn't make any sense. There was no reason for June to hide. If she was coming home, then she would do it openly, and with a clear conscience. Breda justified herself by way of Hugh. She pointed out that he was a sensible, trustworthy lad, a mature lad, sentiments Kate couldn't dispute, and that she couldn't but believe him. June had been there that day in St Bees. The fact that she didn't want to be found could only mean that she was in trouble. For that reason it was urgent that Breda did find her. Kate didn't change her opinion. Breda's reasoning was unsound. Besides, she was looking increasingly tired and drawn. Kate didn't know what she was eating, and was pretty sure she wasn't sleeping much.

In late September Breda's visits became less frequent. She confined herself to her days off. And she no longer stole about the beach huts but sat on the esplanade and looked out to sea, simply gazing at the incoming and outgoing tides, the bar of horizon, and the outlines of the cliffs against ever deepening skies. The days were shortening quickly.

In mid-October she confided to Dora that she was pretty certain that June had killed herself. She concocted a detailed picture of the suicide. June had obviously returned home in some kind of trouble. She didn't elaborate on the nature of the trouble, but pronounced the word as if it were understood. Her only elaboration was to declare that the Kavanaghs attracted trouble. For some reason they were bad. Dora tried a number of times to argue that point, but Breda was adamant. They were bad through and through. Catherine had said it and she was right. They were all hopeless. She didn't know where it stemmed from, but they were too far gone to be redeemed. She listed numerous incidents as her proof, citing minor mishaps as well as their tragedies amongst her evidence. Nothing that Dora could say would dissuade her. They were bad and June was in trouble, and because of her trouble she was too ashamed to show herself. She had obviously seen them all on the beach that day and hadn't been able to face them. She had actually fled. Dora protested that there was only Hugh's word for that, but Breda was having none of it.

She shook her head sagely and pointed out that Dora knew he was an intelligent lad, that nothing really passed him.

She went on to describe in detail June's growing frustration and despondency. She had taken a beach shed for the summer, but her money was running out. She had decided not to approach anyone she knew for help. She had put a barrier up that she couldn't cross. In her heart, she obviously wanted to be home, but she couldn't make those last few steps. She had exiled herself. The loneliness of her hideaway, and the frustration of not knowing what her next step was, finally took its toll. She could see no way forward.

In a dreamy, wistful voice, Breda described in detail the final moments of June's life. She could see her clearly in her mind's eye. She had made a slow, terrible, desperate climb onto the head-land. The sun was just disappearing below the horizon. The temperature fell rapidly. The sky was covered with a thin patterning of grey cloud. The sea below echoed around the base of the cliffs. It seemed to produce thousands of voices, whispering in her head, encouraging her, calling to her, ultimately welcoming her. She took a step forward. An up-draught from the cliffs below made her whole body feel like ice. She was frozen to the spot. She thought of each one of them in turn. She began to cry, but it was too late. There was only Breda really left. Peter was still there, but he was a shadow, socially dead anyway. She was part of a dying family. She couldn't take it anymore. She couldn't face an uncertain, heavy future anymore. She couldn't face herself in the mirror anymore. She tried to pray, but couldn't. She just couldn't bring any words into her head. She gave herself to the elements, a diver, a beautiful bird giving herself to the waves. And the sea took her and hid her away as she had wished. It was all finally as she had wanted.

There was a long period of silence when Breda concluded her story. Eventually Dora shook her head and quietly insisted, carefully enunciating each word, that it wasn't true, Breda didn't know, it was all in her head. Breda smiled knowingly, and then very quietly whispered that she knew. She smiled again. She seemed quite satisfied by herself. Dora proceeded to try and argue, but Breda was through. She had described what she knew to be true and she was finished. She had nothing more to say. She had a family member to mourn.

Dora was at a complete loss. She didn't know what to make of Breda's story. She had never experienced anything so strange. She thought back to Robert. She tried to work out when she had first known for certain that he was dead. Had she known before they had received official notification? Was there a bond between brother and sister, sister and sister, that told one when the other was no more? Had she experienced that? The simple truth was that she hadn't. Quite the opposite. She couldn't really remember when she had finally accepted that the official word was accurate. Indeed, she wasn't entirely convinced that she believed it even now, eleven years later. That thought sent a shiver down her spine. She really didn't believe he was gone, not completely. She carried so many versions of him around with her it was inconceivable that she wouldn't meet one again. She threw up her hands in despair. What on earth did any of it mean, missing and mourning? She loved him now as much as ever. That was sufficient. That was real.

She told Kate that she was concerned about Breda. Kate treated that as an understatement. They were all worried about Breda. Pretty soon she would be skin and bone. Dora shook her head. It wasn't that. Besides, Breda was lovely. The thought seemed to tickle Dora. She repeated it as if it were something of a revelation. Breda was absolutely lovely. Kate raised an eyebrow as much as to say it wouldn't last the way she was going. Dora opted not to tell Kate about Breda's belief that June was dead. It was all too strange and fanciful. She confined herself to the suggestion that she thought Breda was having bad dreams. Kate queried the phrase. Bad dreams? Dora shrugged. Nightmares. She thought she was experiencing nightmares. Kate dismissed her with the mildly impatient assertion that as far as she could tell Breda hardly slept, so she didn't see how she could be bothered by nightmares. Dora insisted that, nevertheless, it was the case. Kate agreed to keep an eye on her. She was anyway.

What Dora could never have guessed was that the story Breda told her was Breda's own. It was herself she was talking about climbing the cliff, and herself she saw standing at the summit, listening to the beckoning waves. The only part that she hadn't foreseen was that the sea didn't take her, not completely. It washed her about against the rocks at the foot of the cliffs, and then finally deposited her, her body broken and bashed, on a worn mussel encrusted boulder.

The official verdict was that she must have had an accident. After all, the cliffs could be treacherous in poor weather. In the absence of any note there was no reason to assume that it was otherwise. The only things in her pockets were two photographs of June, one of her with a feather-duster and the other holding a jar of sweets, which had been on display in the Devlins parlour since Breda had moved in. Father Bond accepted the verdict as correct and buried her accordingly. Rumour persisted that

Breda's death had been no accident. Certain people even speculated about the possibility of foul-play. Surely she went out to meet someone? Why else would she venture out across the cliff path so frequently? Dora certainly was sure she knew the truth. Breda had committed suicide. She told Kate what she knew. Kate had never been in any doubt.

Dora went over and over her story. What had Breda been trying to tell her? Had she been in trouble? Was it the kind of trouble Dora could have helped her with? Nothing materialised. No one came along and agreed with Breda's assertion that she was bad, bad as all her family were. In the end, she punished herself with the thought that Breda was simply telling her that she was lonely, and she had failed to respond. She had failed her completely. Breda had asked for a lifeline, but Dora hadn't picked up the message. She knew she would feel guilty about that for as long as she lived. That thought was more agreeable than thinking it would have been better if Hugh had never said he had seen June. She never wanted him to feel that he was in anyway to blame. The blame was all hers.

Ironically, on the morning after Breda had taken her own life Kate received a letter from Aunty Dora. In it, among other things, she said she had bumped into Catherine in Lytham St Anne's. Aunty Dora didn't take too much account of it. She merely said it had been nice seeing her. She thought Catherine seemed to be doing all right. She was working in a hotel in Blackpool, and was down in Lytham on her day off. Aunty Dora had asked about June. She never implied that Catherine was anything less than forthcoming. The most recent news that Catherine had was that June had gone back to Manchester and was working in textiles again. She was under the impression that she was doing very well and had met someone quite special. She was planning on visiting her, now that the season was over. Aunty Dora had concluded her recounting of the meeting with the words: *So, we can all expect an announcement soon.*

Chapter Six

Monday, hot midsummer, 1932, Marty arrived in the cellar in the house on Mount Peasant with his coat tied round his waist like a skirt, his customary summer wear. Mondays were washdays. In fact, the boiler in the cellar in the house on Mount Pleasant was lit every day and the dolly tubs filled. Hugh, now eleven, claimed the job of lighting it and also helped Dora fill the tubs. He had become a tall, lean boy, with large hands and feet, who felt humiliated by his size, except when he was in the cellar where his strength was a source of pride. He was worshipped and rather feared by the other children who regularly sat on the cellar steps simply to watch him move the tubs on their rims. That was for the family wash. Mondays were different. Then washing came in from all over, turning the cellar into a laundry. Dora would remain all day, and when there was no school Hugh stayed with her. He would agitate clothes in the tubs throughout the day without complaint. Mondays were a constant pleasure to him.

Marty, who was a Monday regular, only ever stated a desire to have his socks washed; nevertheless, Dora always prized some other garment from him. This particular Monday she scolded him for smelling, pointing forcibly at the sweat marks that were apparent all over his shirt, and berated him for his wretchedly stained trousers, again gesticulating wildly at the offending garment. When she was through criticising his wayward hygiene she demanded all of his clothes, and instructed him to sit on the steps and keep his coat over his knees. He muttered under his breath, but acquiesced to her request. He gingerly slipped off his trousers, then his shirt and vests, (he wore at least two vests, even in the summer, more in the winter). He cursed her, accusing her of growing up vindictive, when the cold body of his fiddle fell against his exposed shoulder. She raised a mock threatening hand, but said no more. He slumped down onto the steps, draped his coat over his lap and pulled a baggy green felt hat over his face, then howled like a cat in the dark. This noise went on until John Darcy threw his washing down the steps and draped Marty in a toga of soiled cloth. Marty, who made no attempt to remove the laundry, stopped howling and merely hummed to himself.

John Darcy was another Monday regular. He remained a collector and bearer of gifts. His packman trolley was loaded with cups, mugs, blacklead, reddening stones, carbolic, sheets and bolsters. He could also be relied on for dolls, usually balding but fully clothed, and small metal soldiers. He often repainted the chipped soldiers himself from dyes he scrounged at the tannery in return for any expendable *poteen*, which he received via McClean. McClean had no scruples about handling illicit liquor, but he declined to sell it openly himself. (McClean would handle most things brought to him, but never sold on directly from his shop.) Martin was gradually amassing an army of pink coats, purple coats and black coats. His pitched battles all ended in confusion as no colours were entirely the same. John Darcy was the fundamental reason for Marty's Monday appearances as John Darcy could be relied on for a supply of non expendable *poteen*.

Although Uncle John Darcy, Dora insisted on the status, usually had something for the children, whenever he didn't he would grin widely, revealing the half-a-dozen teeth left in his head, and in the most grandiose voice insist he had procured some magical item. In this way a knotted bootlace became the dried corpse of a cobra de capello of a snake-charmer, and an old tea-cosy became a Sultan's head-piece. The children would look at the objects with some suspicion until Marty declared their wonder for all the world to see, and then they would fight for the right to be Oriental. The day regularly concluded with Uncle John Darcy wheeling Marty on his trolley around the docks, the two singing duets beside the coalboats and fishing smacks to the hobblers, returning with their earnings of sprats, coal-dust and meths.

"I see you're enjoying all the rewards of the sunshine Marty," John Darcy spoke up melodiously, stepping over his scattered wash in order to hand Hugh a small parcel. Hugh took it without comment. He was suspicious and resentful of Uncle John Darcy, and even great Uncle Marty, believing they made a sordid circus of the cellar. He was already planning on clearing them out when he was older. He was certain they were taking advantage of his mother's over generous nature and wondered why his father allowed it. He could only assume it was because his father was at work and so none the wiser. He put a bar of chocolate, a tin of cocoa and a bar of carbolic down in the corner, then sat on the lowest step and observed the two men disdainfully. They were vague and grey through the rising steam, already imbibing McClean's liquor. Hugh pressed his large fingers into his stomach and sighed.

Marty spoke bitterly. "Jesus man, but I've been stripped bare like a baby fresh born."

"God, but you're a pale specimen beneath your great-coat, Marty Boland, and the bits that show are a dead ringer for a turkey crop. You should go and sit on the steps and gain yourself a little colour. You'd have to watch for the butcher feller though."

"There's enough colour to me for the time being."

"Jesus, you're a man of prehistory who loves to dwell in caves."

"It would be a lot less exposing and irksome than this carry-on."

"I dare say you're right, Marty Boland," John Darcy agreed, then got to his feet, took the bottle from Marty's lips, and spoke up expansively. "But then, a clean *habillement* is not to be sniffed at, and young Dora does a magnificent job." He took a swallow from the bottle, then called down the steps: "I am afraid Mrs Glyn that I have not had the decency to collect all the washing, not even my own mother's I am ashamed to admit." He bowed, then resumed his seat.

Dora waved away his apology as unnecessary and called up to Mary and Martin sitting together on the top step: "Go and bring Mrs Darcy's and Mrs Ryles' washing. And wash Mrs Ryles' feet."

Feet washing was something that all the Glyn children had experienced at some time. It represented Dora's contribution to the congregation. They had washed so many feet they associated the need with old age. By this standard Kate and John were not old as they never needed to have their feet washed. On the other hand each child had experienced something of washing Grandfather Glyn's feet, which they did right up until the day he died. It was something they all hated, but couldn't avoid. At the slightest hint of dissent Dora scolded them into submission. "Was Our Lord not proud to wash the apostles' feet. Well you will be proud to wash your grandfather's." The trouble was they were all rather afraid of him. His face was too jaundiced, waxy and wizened to inspire devotion in a child. But they loved his birds. They had all stood at one time or another gazing in wonder at his aviary, watching the jewelled wings of his finches unfurl and spread, the old man beside them smiling with the certain satisfaction that he was instilling his own love into his grandchildren. His smile, though, which was toothless, moist and rather lopsided, in fact, something of an unintentional leer, terrified them, so that when he effused about the birds they responded with stunned, fearful silence.

At first neither of them moved. "Now!" Dora shouted, beginning her peroration on the feet of Our Lord and the apostles, as she stepped towards them. They instantly leapt up and ran from the cellar with John Darcy calling after them that his trolley was tied at the summit of the steps, and Dora's uncompromising words resounding in their ears, informing them that if they valued their skins they wouldn't forget Mrs Ryles' feet.

In fact, it was understood, if not declared, that Uncle John Darcy never did collect the washing during the school summer holiday. Throughout the winter he would brave any weather, dragging his loaded trolley through ice and snow, in order to bring the Monday washing, but summer was different. During the summer he migrated out of the house and slept with his trolley wherever his fancy took him. He had fads. Sometimes he would spend entire weeks by the dockside. During the day he would trade along the quays, bartering reddening stones for scraps, poteen for trinkets and valuables, with the regular hobblers, fishermen, migrant labourers and foreign sailors to be found there. At night he secreted himself and his trolley amongst the lobster-pots. He would lay awake listening to the sound of the boats on the water, the jingle of riggings, and the pull of the waves, content in the certain knowledge of his own freedom. At other times he would wheel his trolley out of town and ply his trade with the regular and seasonal farm labourers, exchanging knick-knacks and liquor for cheese and bread. Then he liked to sleep near a rookery and drift off to the plaintive caws of the roosting birds, once again satisfied by his own itinerant whims. His personal bundle of washing stayed with him and invariably brought him to the cellar each Monday.

Occasionally Patrick would sleep rough with Uncle John Darcy. He was the final member of the Monday laundry circus, though the least certain to appear. He had grown up into an isolated, apprehensive, sour man, drifting from one casual job to another. He had, in fact, more or less slept rough since he had left school and begun labouring on farms, spending weeks at a time in barns or under hedgerows. He had discovered that he could drift, yet still return. So far he had never lost the ability to return. There were variations though as to where he might find himself when he did. Sometimes he went to Kate, sometimes to Dora, sometimes with Uncle John Darcy, and sometimes he found himself in a bunk beside Uncle Marty. Latterly, however, he spent more and more time asleep in the graveyard.

It was Uncle John Darcy who first brought to light Patrick's apparent fascination with death. He told Kate that since the beginning of summer he had had a terrible time dissuading Patrick from wanting to set the trolley up in the graveyard. The news humiliated her, angered her, but didn't entirely shock her, coinciding as it did with the fact that she had finally told him that he was a Devlin by name and not by birth.

John had finally broken down her resistance. It had caused something of a rift between them for a while. John insisted that Patrick needed to know why he hated them so much. Kate flatly rejected any such notion. He did not hate them. He was naturally shy and hesitant, as any orphan would be. John pointed out that he didn't know that he was an orphan. Kate simply reiterated that it was only natural. John said he was retarded. He couldn't work out how Julia and Jones could have produced such a child. Kate flared up in a display of resentment and disappointment. Julia and Jones had not produced such a child. They had! Patrick was their child. She stopped short of blaming John outright, but he understood the meaning she was hinting at. He had not played the part of a proper father. He had let the situation drift. He decided not to pass on the matter. He defended himself by insisting that Patrick had never allowed himself to be loved, to be wanted, to be one of them. He had set himself against them from the start. Kate let the matter go. She couldn't maintain the row. It was too difficult for her. She was sure she had failed both Patrick and Julia, and she just couldn't work it out. Patrick was the child she had always wanted. Was it possible he did not want to be wanted? Was that ever the case before? She certainly didn't think falling out with John would help. She simply shrugged and left his comments unanswered. John changed tack. He suggested that if he found out from someone else then Patrick certainly would hate them. He pressed the point that Patrick had a right to know. He was a man. He had to know who he was. He offered to tell him, but she insisted that the task was hers. As she thought through the admission that she had to make she felt that she was disowning him, scoring a line through all the years he had been under her roof. It was such a heartless confession. She accepted that he had never been entirely happy, but in no way could he be blamed for that. The failure was hers, and she was willing to accept that it was hers alone. She would willingly bear it for the rest of her life.

He took the news with what seemed complete indifference. He listened to her tortured confession without comment. He simply shrugged. She thought she detected something of a smile crossing his lips, but dismissed the possibility. If it was possible, it was simply due to the strange emotions he must have been experiencing. She longed for him to talk to her, lay open his mind, tell her how he saw himself. Where had such a sickly, shy (the word retarded seared across her thoughts), struggling man come from? She would have given a great deal to work it out. In fact, if anything, he was more uncommunicative than ever after the admission. Indeed, he was more uncommunicative, sour in aspect and more liable to drift than before. Afterwards, he scarcely spoke to her or John, but seemed bound up in his own inner world. She felt he was lost to her. It was an agony she found difficult to bear.

Despite her frustration and revulsion at Patrick's behaviour she never gave up on him, but visited the graveyard each evening to see if he was there and, if necessary, bring him away. She was always relieved to hear whenever he managed to turn up at Dora's. It seemed to suggest at least some sense of lingering normality.

On this particular day he came onto the steps as Mary and Martin ran out. He peered into the cellar with his usual reluctance and foreboding until John Darcy held the bottle aloft, which he took without exchanging a word with anyone, then assumed his place on the stairs.

Mrs Darcy was a witch. Everybody was convinced of that. She was a wraithlike, emaciated woman, dressed in heavily starched black, with waist length wiry, matted, grey hair, who had an obvious abhorrence for the world. Anyone who had seen her did not doubt John Darcy's propensity for sleeping rough. Not that many did see her. Virtually no one entered Mrs Darcy's house on Ginns, and she only infrequently came to the door herself, though she was often glimpsed peeping around the threadbare curtain of her solitary window. In fact, it was not a house as such but rooms above a chandlers, the smell of wax and oil around Mrs Darcy's attributed to her manufacture of necromantic potions. Other than her son, Mrs Darcy only tolerated one regular visitor, Father Bond. The old priest, who had become very stout, his petechial neck hanging like folds of pig skin over his collar, and who walked with a limp and had a weakness in one hand, would knock lightly at Mrs Darcy's door, then whisper something at the chink before being admitted. This placed the old man in a very strange light with the children he confirmed. He was forever coupled in their minds with the witch of Ginns. All manner of strange supernatural rites and pacts with the devil were imagined. "For God sake," Dora told her own, "he's only calling off for a smoke. She's harmless enough." Her reassurance counted for nothing. Mrs Darcy remained an object of fear and vilification, and the priest was bound up with her. It was with some dread, then, that Mary and Martin

298

contemplated collecting Mrs Darcy's washing. Not that they had to see her. The washing was always left in a sack on the step. Nevertheless, they called for Bill Kavanagh en route.

Bill Kavanagh was now sixteen and worked in a tailor's. Peter had been surprisingly indifferent to Bill's choice of profession. When Bill told him he had a mind to be a tailor he merely said that Bill always had favoured his mother. He was often given Mondays off, a quiet day of business, if he had worked late nights for a couple of weeks. He was often asked to work late because he was good, skilful in design and pattern cutting. He hoped one day to complete a diploma in dress making, design and pattern cutting. He made skirts and shirts for all the family from waste material. He had made a beautiful tartan patterned dress for Mary from a heavy woollen cloth he claimed was to have been thrown out. The truth was that he had saved up and paid for the material himself. Over the years a closeness had developed between Bill and Mary despite their five years age difference.

He had of course, more or less, grown up with the Glyn children. Peter had often come looking for him to find that Hugh had accidentally put him to bed with the other children. He was always left until the morning. Sometimes he would stay for days on end. Ever since the day out in the charabanc Peter had tempered his abusive attitude to Bill, but had never overcome his disaffection for him. Bill had learnt from early childhood to seek approval elsewhere. Since the day Hugh had fed him black-pudding, bacon and cheese he felt a bond with Hugh. It was only natural he should have become a semi-adopted member of the Glyn family. From a young age it had always been Mary he favoured rather than Hugh or Martin. Indeed, at times he seemed to positively resent their presence. This had become particularly marked after they had taken their first communion together and had been confirmed by the experience they had shared on the head-land. Although well-built and muscular like his father, Bill was softly spoken and aesthetically sensitive, though he was in no way shy or retiring. Mary found that she had to be different for different people. For Bill she developed a sensitiveness to match his: with Martin she was simply wild.

"Come on out, Bill Kavanagh," Martin shouted at the open window of Bill's house, beating his hands against the frame of John Darcy's trolley which he had wheeled from the summit of Mount Pleasant across to Ginns. "Come on out, we've got a fight today!"

Mary ran up to him and caught his arms. "What the hell are you giving out about, Martin? Have you gone mad?"

299

"Come on, Bill Kavanagh, we've got to go to the witch," Martin continued regardless.

Bill Kavanagh came to the door and stood in the frame, frowning in the sunlight. His appearance threw Mary into confusion. She was unsure whether she should be angry or not. "We're collecting washing," she said, trying to speak calmly, whilst still struggling with Martin's arms.

"We've got no washing, you know that," Bill said casually. Mary felt sure he was being deliberately unhelpful.

"Who does your washing anyway?" Martin demanded.

"I do."

"You should bring it to ours. Loads do. You want nothing washing. It's girls' work."

"We don't have any girls in our house, Martin, or had you not noticed? Maybe you're not at the age to notice?"

"Isn't that just what I'm saying," Martin said, freeing himself from Mary's grasp. "Bring it to ours and it would be done for you."

"Aunty Dora does enough. Perhaps you should think of that."

"She doesn't collect the damn stuff. I hate pulling this trolley."

"Oh, let it go and I'll do it," Bill said, stepping from the door frame. "Is that what all the shouting was about. I don't mind. I was only doing a few repairs. They'll wait."

"It's not that I can't. I just don't like it. It makes me feel like a rag-and-bone-man."

"Well, that's certainly how you look," Mary said, and pushed him on his way. They jostled each other along the street.

"Who's fighting who anyway?" Bill asked, unsure in his own mind whether he was amused or bored. He was already wishing that Martin wasn't there. He knew Mary would act differently if he were gone. He would be more himself then, less stuffy somehow.

"He only said that," she said, giving Martin a heavy push along the street.

"No, I didn't," Martin countered, eyeing Mary ruefully. "I'm going to walk right into Mrs Darcy's and tell her to make us all a cup of tea."

"She'll boil your brains," Bill said, his tone matter of fact.

"Martin doesn't have the same concerns on that score as the rest of us."

"I'm not scared."

Bill said: "I would be."

Martin smiled gratefully. "You just watch me," he said triumphantly, then ran ahead calling out like an Indian brave.

Bill and Mary stood still and watched him as he charged ahead. Waves of heat rose from the cobbled street, forming a vaguely translucent veil. As he gazed ahead Bill's expression became concentrated and despondent. It seemed to Mary that he was struggling with some thought or idea that tormented him. She had seen the same look on a hundred previous occasions. He never explained it and she didn't know how to ask. Years later she would attempt to visualise it again, and as a woman understand it, but by then it was no more.

After a moment or two he snapped out of it. He gave himself a mild shake, turned to her and smiled instantly, affectionately, though somewhat forlornly, at her. "It's all so peculiar," he said, "this town and its goings-on. How the hell could you ever know if you were being yourself or not?" Mary made no response. He shrugged, conceding that it was difficult for her to respond. "Well, I suppose we'd better save him from himself," he said. He grinned broadly. "Save us all from ourselves." He pressed on with the trolley.

The sound of its slowly rotating wheels as it rolled forward across the cobbles struck Mary as in someway lonely and sad. A part of her wanted to run ahead and be with Martin, another part of her could not desert Bill. She walked on in silence.

They caught up with Martin outside the witch's house. The chandlers shop was empty. They stared at the closed door in the gable end. The washing was in a pillow-case, leaning against the step. Their three faces screwed up in the sunlight. Martin's was peach coloured and moist. He wiped the hair from his brow. It formed a little knotted crown. He turned to Bill and Mary: "To hell with it! I'm too hot to drink tea."

"Daddy says it's the most cooling drink there is," Mary teased. "Really. All the men drink it down the mine."

"But that's cold tea."

"The hotter the better, he says," she pressed mercilessly.

"I've heard that too," Bill agreed. "They drink it all the time in India and India is as hot as they come. Well, that's where it comes from, India and China, and they're both hot. You must know that, Martin."

"Well, I'm still too hot," Martin snapped sulkily.

Mary collected the pillow-case and dropped it heavily onto the trolley, grinning wickedly at Martin as she did. He scowled in response. She eyed him sternly for a moment, then stepped back, right up to Mrs Darcy's door. She held her hand up as if about to knock, then turned and faced him. She said: "I tell you what, I'll give her a knock and tell her you want her. How will that be?" She didn't wait for any response

301

from him, but immediately rapped her fist against the door. There was no answer. Mary smiled. She struck the door again with her fist. This time the door was eased open a few inches. The witch's head hung forward from her neck like a withered globe. Mary stepped back. The door opened some more. The melted face came to the threshold, but not beyond, her withered hands hanging onto the rim of the door frame. Her expression was apprehensive, appealing for some explanation. "What do you want from me," she asked, her voice timid and hushed.

Mary was running before she realised that she was. Martin was with her, shouting out loud and wildly, jubilantly. They didn't stop until they had cleared Ginns. It was some time before Bill caught up with them. He came along at a gentle pace, wheeling the trolley without any urgency. As soon as he came into view Martin began. "She's a witch all right, Bill Kavanagh," he called down the street excitedly. "Did you ever see the likes? Crikey, what a witch!"

Mary began to cry.

Bill didn't respond, but kept on his even pace towards them. As he joined them Mary bowed her head. She couldn't look into his face. She sobbed bitterly as she tried to speak. Her voice croaked. She spoke erratically, in short, punctuated phrases. "Did you see her hands, her face, the look on her face, her eyes, those eyes, and her voice, what a soft voice?" Bill let go of the trolley and stroked her shoulder.

"A witch, I'm telling you, a witch if ever there was one," Martin called out delightedly. He kept on dancing about her, chanting that she was a witch, definitely a witch.

"Oh, shut up, Martin, for God's sake!" Mary moaned, but to no avail. Martin kept on his excited shouts and exclamations. She looked up at Bill. Her expression was penitent. She was horrified at herself. She uttered: "I was cruel to her. I was really horrible. The way she asked what I wanted. I was terrible. I hurt her. I really hurt her. I shouldn't have done it. I can't believe what I've done." Tears coursed down her cheeks.

"She's used to it," Bill said quietly. "She's had worse than that. She gets that all of the time. You can stop crying. It won't do anybody any good. None of this is doing any good." As he spoke he swatted Martin across the ear. Martin froze. He eyed Bill ferociously, but nevertheless, didn't say another word. "Come on," Bill said, "at least we can get her washing done."

"We have to do Mrs Ryles' feet," Mary said. There was a note of horror and disbelief in her voice. Bill put his arm around her, and led her forward without a word. He smiled to himself. He felt strangely satisfied, elated in a way.

Mrs Ryles' feet were red and yellow with corns and calluses. The toes all overlapped and each curled under the other. The big toes bent sharply over all the others, and had large balls of bunions. Her Monday soak and scrub was the highlight of her week. She expressed her delight by munching her toothless jaws together as if sucking a sop of cake. Martin and Mary hated those two feet with their deformities and lumps, hated them more than anything else they could imagine. Martin had once urinated in the water in the bowl she used for soaking them and claimed, when finally she peered over her gross knees and viewed the yellow liquor, that he had seen a corn burst. *I never knew they were so acid*, she laughed and munched all the more powerfully.

Mary continued to whimper as Bill ushered her forward, and Martin was sulky, still smarting from the blow to his ear. Bill knew they were not up to the task. Mary would just cry, and Martin would do something stupid. He announced that he would see to Mrs Ryles' feet. He accepted the chore gladly for Mary's sake.

He helped the old woman pull her thick woollen socks from her thighs, over her club knees, easing them gently down her swollen, mottled skin. He held the stocking toe and pulled gently so it gradually slipped off, without being inside out. The revealed flesh was fatty, red and damp. He lifted her feet and carefully lowered them into the bowl. He let them rest for a moment, then he began to gently soap them, massaging his fingers into the bloated instep and ankle. Eventually, he ran his soap covered hands up and down her pitting legs. When she had soaked so long that the water had become tepid he lifted her feet onto a towel in his lap and roughly dried them, patting and rubbing them briskly. He then carefully pulled the towel between her toes, and finished by smoothing the towel around her sole and ankle. When he was through, the calluses had become white and porous, and the corns were like rubies. She shivered and giggled, delighted by the soak.

As Bill worked Mary watched him with developing interest. Pretty soon she put aside her own troubled feelings and stopped moaning. At first she watched with fascination, but as his hands moved along the fleshy leg, it was with increasing disgust. Eventually, the continued sight of him touching those mottled legs turned her stomach. Finally, she couldn't take it anymore and had to walk out. She stood in the street and simply faced the small house staring at it. Her mind was racing. Images of John Darcy's mother and Mrs Ryles flashed across her mind.

Images of emaciated flesh and bloated flesh. She sensed that her own cruelty and Bill's gentleness were somehow inextricably linked, but she couldn't work it out. She had been cruel and then incapable. Bill had been forgiving and then caring. He didn't despise her, but she was revolted by him, by what he had done, by the touch he placed on an old woman's diseased legs. He should despise her. He didn't despise her though. He forgave her. He took on her chores. She should thank him for that, but she had deserted him. What did it all mean? How could she make sense of the confusion she felt with Bill Kavanagh? He made her feel grown-up and childish at one and the same time. Which was she? Maybe she was a child. Did he know that? Why did he make her feel so good and yet lacking all at once? It was all so mixed up.

She had a long wait in the street, simply gazing at the house, and her thoughts just went on and on, but never came to any satisfactory resolution. All she knew was that she felt bad about herself, disappointed by her cruelty, disappointed for walking out on Bill, yet still disgusted by what he had done. When Bill and Martin finally emerged from the house she was no nearer making any sense of anything. They were eating cake. Bill had a piece for her. He offered it straight away, holding it out to her as he approached her. She refused it. He threw it down the street for the dogs and birds.

"How could you do that?" she asked.

"Well, you didn't want it, so why not?"

"No, wash her feet like that."

"Because you wouldn't do it."

"But you enjoyed it."

Bill's expression became instantly hardened. He eyed her severely for a moment, searching her features. He found her expression stubborn, recalcitrant, yet also perturbed and wounded. His annoyance faded as quickly as it had appeared. He smiled at her and shrugged. He spoke up softly and affectionately, yet with a perceivable passion. "Look, Mary," he said, "I'm determined never to run away from anything. Do you understand? If there are things to do or say, then I'll do it or say it. I want to be a witness, then anything bad doesn't matter, and the good is a bonus. If you slip through life from one prison to another, then so what? The important thing was to have been there. Do you know what I mean?"

Mary's lips parted. She wanted to speak, but couldn't. In that moment, his quietly sustained speech still resonating in her mind, she felt love and loathing for him, and also something that seemed like fear. She trembled inwardly. She trembled for him, but she couldn't account for it. Why did he make her feel so happy and yet so sad? Why was he poor Bill Kavanagh, and still magical Bill Kavanagh? She didn't understand it. She wanted guidance. The problem was that he was the only one able to give it, and she couldn't possibly ask him. How could she?

Looking at her strange quizzical expression, he burst out laughing, the sound of it rich and real. "Come on," he said, "we should get this washing to Aunty Dora, she'll be wondering what's happened to you two." Mary didn't move. She just looked at him, her mind elsewhere, adrift with her contradictory thoughts. Bill took hold of her shoulders and give her a slight shake. She looked right at him. He whispered: "Come on, get on the trolley, I'll take you home." She nodded and immediately sat, nestled in the witch, Mrs Darcy's washing. She understood that her friendship with Bill was intact, but recognised that it was entering new grounds.

By the time they reached the cellar the customary Monday argument had already begun between John Darcy, Marty and Patrick. It was unavoidable whenever Patrick was present. The routine was always the same. To begin with they got mildly drunk, and then they discussed love. Both John Darcy and Marty, despite their lack of experience, considered themselves experts on the subject, and insisted on telling Patrick all they knew.

Since his school-days Patrick had courted Gladys. She was probably the only person Patrick had ever made a bond with. She had taken him on. As a schoolgirl she had been small, wiry and robustly tender. She had badgered, bullied and coaxed him to be more outgoing, more fun, more normal. In fact, she had been something of a comical child herself, a bit of a char really, bustling about with her arms folded, ticking off all and sundry, in a grumpy middle-aged voice, play acting the part of gossip and know it all. She had been his quirky little friend. Strangely, though, she had grown up into a quietly plaintive, thoughtful woman, acting decidedly younger the older she became. In some ways, the only vestige of the funny little girl that remained was her loyalty to Patrick. As she matured and developed she had never abandoned him. She had shared his worst moments. When he had been sick she had sat with him. Her affection developed from testy but loyal urgency to calm patience. As she grew up she had increasingly suffered with him when he had been ill, suffered as he coughed fresh blood. It was possible that she did indeed love him, love him in her own peculiar, reflective way. But that certainly did not mean that she could ever contemplate marrying him. Over the years she had made that more and more clear. Whatever had drawn her to befriend Patrick survived, but it had not grown, had not grown as she had grown, and nor had Patrick. He was the same awkward, estranged being. She was his devoted friend. Marriage was not part of the situation.

Nevertheless, at every given opportunity, John Darcy and Marty formulated new plans to bring Gladys to the altar. Every plan, however, came down to the same basic principle, that he should simply go to her and demand her hand in marriage and not accept no for an answer. Patrick would express the hopelessness of the whole affair, lose his temper, then end up mournful and tearful. However, he quite often left the cellar on the pretext that he intended following their advice, though there wasn't even one occasion that anyone knew of when he had actually proposed, and no one believed there ever would be. Certainly, he sometimes sat outside the tannery where she worked mixing dyes, but he was always gone before her shift finished.

As Bill brought the washing to the head of the stairs, Patrick was getting to his feet. He lurched up the steps, groaning to himself. They met each other. Patrick put his arms limply around Bill's neck, and stared into his face. His expression was harsh and hopeless. "What would you do Bill, you're a solid, sensible lad?" he asked, his tone affected and sour, filled with that almost jeering quality his voice now always had.

"Tell him to be a man, for Christ sake," John Darcy called up the stairs.

"Be a man," Bill repeated with great simplicity.

Patrick grimaced, his whole expression appearing spiteful and sardonic. Bill could taste the warmth of his breath. "And how do you do that Bill?"

"I don't know, Patrick," he said coldly.

Bill pulled away, releasing himself from Patrick's feeble hold. Patrick fell against the wall. Before he could steady himself Bill pressed on, pushing between John Darcy and Marty. Hugh sat on the bottom step. Bill threw the sack over his head and playfully kicked his thigh. Hugh looked up very slowly. His face was grey and drenched. Bill touched him. He was soaking. The moisture beaded on his skin. "What is it, Hugh?" Bill demanded, scared of the frank fear apparent in Hugh's expression.

Hugh shook his head slightly. "I'll tell my dad when he gets in."

Bill would never forget the sound of his own voice screaming: "Aunty Dora!" It destroyed the cellar, leaving only the distilled image of a grey frightened saturated face. Hugh never did tell his father. He died of a ruptured appendix, believing he had developed some unusual man's trouble that he would understand better when he was older.

*

As no one could afford cars or carriages they put his coffin on Uncle John Darcy's trolley and wheeled it from the foot of Mount Pleasant through the market to the church of *Saint Joseph*. Father Bond waited beside the porcelain Christ before the porch, watching the procession thread its way between the vegetable stalls and fish counters. John, Peter, Patrick and Bill wheeled the trolley, wearing the same stiff black suits they all reserved for marriages, christenings and funerals. Hugh, Dora and Kate followed. Hugh's attention never wavered from the place where Kate had embroidered a silver cross onto a black sheet and lain it across the long slender box. Behind them came the slow black stream of the other mourners. The sunlight was severe. They sweltered in its intensity: a mirage in its brittle light. Father Bond limped forward to greet them. He raised a strong hand and a weak hand and said: "In baptism he died with Christ: may he also share his resurrection." The cortege then followed him into the heart of the church. The market again traded.

After the service Father Bond led the procession from the church back through the market, then up through the narrow streets of Ginns. On Ginns every window and door was closed. The procession moved along the terrace in almost complete silence, only the sound of the slowly hoisted trolley creaking over the cobbles announcing the passage of the dead. The cortege pressed on and left the streets behind. They were now surrounded by the sound of birds and insects. Flies swarmed the full flower-heads among the weld and yarrow, which burst out in long white veins clotting the hedgerow. Martin brushed his arm through the fibre stems, making a trail of soft down, yellow powder dusting and staining his black sleeve. The flies buzzed ever louder.

Eventually they reached the Catholic graveyard. It was a field set apart, the burial place of the *Irish streets*. Elder trees hung fragrant flowers between the bars of the black metal entrance gates. Around its margins the rush marsh had not yet been drained. Throughout the spring hordes of frogs congregated there and the croaking chorus of their orgy sounded over the silent graves. No one had any doubts that burial among frogs must be a lonely affair. All the petitions and injunctions in the world could not dispel that thought, though they strove to do so.

For Hugh the entire Catholic school waited in attendance. As the trolley passed through the gates there was an inclination, perhaps even the idea that there was an expectation, among the pupils to applaud, a nervous murmur passing along the standing rows. However, in the face of the severity of adult grief, they remained silent. As soon as she saw them Dora broke-down, choking on her own breaths. She wanted to fall to the ground and give vent to her need to shout out her complaints, her objections, her disbelief. Hugh should have been one of them. He should have been standing there, a part of that neat, awkward regimentation. Why was he not there? He had never done anything wrong. He had only ever been a good boy, a shy, awkward boy, like they were. Why was he not with them? It was appalling, terrible. She expected him to step out at any second and lift her under the arms and hold her up, smiling at her, his face bashful yet strong, as it was in the cellar, as it had been when he was dying. The thought pierced her. She wailed and shook. Her body was out of control. Nothing made sense. She was sinking.

Marty held on to her, and kept her on her feet, his long sinuous arms wrapped tightly around her. Hugh ushered the trolley on. Kate joined Marty in his desperate embrace. Together they urged Dora to go on, whispering consolations, yet crying with her at the same time. Without knowing why it should be, they thought she should go on, that she had to stay with Hugh, stay with the coffin until it was laid to rest. They somehow managed to support her to the graveside.

By the open grave, she knelt down onto the cinder path and let nine children hang onto her. Only Hugh actually watched the coffin as it was lowered into the ground, his attention still fixed on the embroidered silver crucifix. When the coffin was in place the sheet was pulled away revealing the unpolished box, made up of boards and panels. When the covering was removed Dora stood up and composed herself. It took some time, but eventually she managed it. She picked up a clump of soil, walked to the graveside and crumbled it through her fingers, like salt over the dull wood of the coffin. She choked on her own breaths again, but quickly controlled herself. She turned to her children and gestured that they all do as she had done and each take a handful of soil and throw it onto the coffin. One by one they acted out the ritual, then stood to the side frightened and yet too numb to show it, too empty to know what they felt. The adult world weighed on them. It was beyond comprehension. When they were all done Peter and Bill shovelled the earth back into place.

When Bill had finished he went to Mary. He did not want to go back for the funeral tea and wanted her to stay with him. It confused her. Her first thought was that she should go to her mother. She needed Dora's guidance. She couldn't manage things on her own. She had to be told what to do, told what was right. But when she turned towards her mother she saw that she had fallen to her knees again on the cinder path. Kate was pressed against her. They were rocking and gently moaning together. It was impossible to speak to her. She didn't know what to do. She wanted to do something right. Could she avoid going to the tea? Was it right staying with Bill? How could she know? She went to Marty and spoke to him. He smiled mysteriously and said: "No one is hungry." She took it as permission. Perhaps more, she took it as an indication. She stayed with Bill.

When the procession had gone the graveyard was spacious about them. Bill stood in front of Bobby and Polly's grave and studied the small uninscribed cross that fronted it. In his memory the events of that night when his brother and mother died were wild and terrible. It made him ashamed to think of it. And yet, it was a sense of shame he was not at all clear about. He felt it had something to do with an all too apparent exposure of feeling, but he didn't really understand what that meant. He was fearful of it, and resented it. He was living in a world of other people's feelings, a world of only vaguely comprehended crisis and skirmishes. He had suffered too much from it, from the excess of others. He felt denied it. He was merely its victim. When did his own reality come into focus, into question. When would he ever be able to say how it was for him. It was all so unequal.

He moved along the line of graves. There were very few. That fact hurt him. He was over represented. He read the names, ages and epitaphs. *Commended unto God, Into God's loving hands, God's eternal rest,* and then in his own father's immature hand, *In God's loveing care.* Is that how it was, he thought, each spirit risen into the pale blue skies of heaven, leaving the soulless corpse behind, the body sludge beneath the sod. There was something distasteful like shame in that. But, then, had Christ himself not suffered as a man, died as a man! But what did it mean, and what did it take, to suffer as a man? What the hell was a man? Was he a man? Was his destiny to be putrefying liquid and no more? Is that all the God dying as a man offered? He kicked out furiously. A small shower of cinders went over the bed of a grave. He repeated the gesture three times.

After that, he stood very still. What was happening to him? He felt ridiculous. He didn't do things like that. He wasn't suited to such displays. He took a step back as if to remove himself from his actions. As he did he remembered Mary and turned to her quickly. She was staring at him and looked frightened, maybe even horrified. His attention caught her unawares. Her confused emotions welled up inside her. She began to cry. Once she had begun she couldn't control herself. She shivered violently and began to retch. She tried to speak, but no words would come. She gestured to him, appealing for help, needing something to stem an emotional tide that threatened to sweep her away. He hesitated, though, unable to respond to her, momentarily paralysed by the sheer weight of need she expressed. He simply stared at her. He was sure she was about to take one of her fits. He didn't know what to do. His indecision lasted only seconds. Her obvious mental turmoil spurred him to action. He couldn't just leave her. She was Mary. She was special to him. He went to her and held her. He held her tightly. He held her tightly because he had nothing to say, nothing to offer. He knew it was all unjust, that there could be no sense, no consolation, no prize in Hugh dying, but there was no benefit in saying so. He regretted having asked her to stay with him. He hadn't thought it through. He had been thinking about himself, and now he had to contend with emotions he wasn't equipped to deal with, didn't want to deal with. He stroked her face. Her cheek was wet against his palm. She tried to speak but once again failed. He led her away, both arms wrapped around her, not through the gates and so back to the town, but across the marsh towards open country.

The rolling landscape spread before them like lain palm leaves, yellow, bronze and gold, toward a line of iron-green fells. The air was filled with skylark song. Swallows dipped and dived around their heads. The clover rich grasses snapped around their feet. As they walked along, slowly stumbling together, Bill felt the eruptions in her body calm, the shudders coming with less and less frequency. Still he led her on, away from the graveyard and the town. Eventually they reached the bank of a river. It was at a point where it had cut a looping meander through a reed-bed, almost sufficient to form an island. An alder tree had almost collapsed into the water. Its exposed roots held a shelf of red clay earth over the stream.

Bill released his hold on Mary. She smiled at him to reassure him of her composure. Still they didn't speak. He backed away from her and went and stood on the shelf and looked down into the water. It was slow and clear. Small fly skipped across the surface. He stood up. Mary followed him and came beside him. She touched his face, affectionately, grateful for the moment of peace she felt, however brief. Bill recoiled at her touch. "I'm sorry," he said quickly, surprised and ashamed at his action. "You surprised me, that's all."

"I'm the one who should be sorry," she responded. "I couldn't help myself. It was just..."

"You were upset."

"I dreamed that I'd killed him."

"Because you were upset. That's all. We dream because we're upset."

"No, it was more than that. It was my fault. I didn't want to get into trouble over Mrs Darcy, and I didn't. I didn't get into trouble. You see, it's more than a dream. I think it in the day and I dream it at night. I killed him, Bill."

"Stop it."

Mary felt the tide of emotion stir within her again. She tried to resist it, but knew it was impossible. She needed Bill to quell it. Her voice broke. "What should I do? I didn't mean for anything to happen. I was so horrible to poor Mrs Darcy, and then Hugh. I feel so bad. I feel so bad. I can't stand it."

"Stop it!" Bill snapped. "Stop it!"

"How?"

"I don't know," he wailed, "I just don't know." His words drifted hopelessly.

"Oh Bill..." Mary said and reached for him.

He tolerated her embrace but no more. For some reason that he couldn't fathom he found her touch a burden. He turned his head aside and gazed along the river banks, searching for the furthest point. Then a few moments later he pulled away from her. He knew he was hurting her, but couldn't help himself. He just couldn't continue to feel her weight against him. As he stepped back from her his mind was in turmoil. Why was he so antagonistic to her grief, so begrudging of her affection? All he knew was that it had something to do with the tiny crucifix fronting his grandmother's grave, but more than that he couldn't work out.

He collapsed to his knees and then rested on all fours at the edge of the alder shelf and looked down into the water. There was a bed of stones the colour of liver. Spouts of mud ruptured between the stones. The river was filled with mysteries. He turned his head and looked up at Mary. He had to say something. He had to explain. He had to hear something from himself, something that would make sense for him. As he spoke, his voice coming in surges, his attention alternated between Mary and the water below him.

"I don't know," he said, " I suppose I just feel it's important not to be disappointed. You know, feeling bad all of the time. I mean, I know that lots of things, maybe most things, who knows, are terrible, terrible and unfair and, well, unjust. God, dying is. Dying is certainly unjust. I know that for a fact. But, well, I suppose it shouldn't rule us, shouldn't take over everything. I'm not going to say that it isn't the case for some time, probably a long time. Of course it is. But it's not down to us to be disappointed all of the time, to have it block everything else out. Do you know what I mean? I don't think we've got that right, somehow. Does that make sense? I mean, we can't live our life through anyone else's life, can we? You can't go on dreaming you killed Hugh. It's wrong. You have to do your own things. I have to do my own things. My conscience is clear. I have nothing to be ashamed of. Why the hell should I?" He stopped speaking. His attention was firmly fixed on Mary. He wanted some response. He couldn't go on without it. She looked blankly at him, though. "I'm sorry," he said, and turned his head back towards the slowly moving stream. He spoke quietly. "I know I'm not making sense, but, well, I can't really explain what I mean." He smiled grimly. "I won't be disappointed though. I've made that clear. I won't be shamed into it."

"I'm sorry," Mary said, but her words were scarcely audible.

Bill turned to her once again. He gazed at her for a moment or two, then jumped to his feet, threw up his hands and immediately turned from her and walked off along the river-bank and into the bog. The marsh trickled with golden viscous streams. There was a smell of gas and metal, a smell of things turning rotten. Snipe sprang from the stinking quagmire and beat short tom-tom wings over the brown rush. At the water's edge two herons unfurled their wings in large slow beats and lifted themselves into the air. They rose higher and higher, over the shallow valley, like prehistoric creatures going ever further into the distance. The river emptied into a small bowl and the water wavered. Grey-green fish exploded into yellow mud. He could smell decaying animal in his nostrils. A single bone lay on the bowl bottom. There were primrose and the dog-ends of bluebells on the banks. There were skylarks and peewits overhead. The peewits were crazy against the blue still sky. He found the ragged remains of a dead sheep. It lay like a large rag in the rush. Blow fly had migrated into the dead head. He dragged the stinking bloodied remains and threw it into the bowl. Mary winced as the carcass hit the water. He held his hand across his mouth and nose and watched the water until the yellow mud settled back onto the river bed. He went back to Mary. He placed his two palms firmly on her shoulders. His expression was earnest and determined. He said: "I will not be a disappointed man, Mary. Life is so short. We should love well because life is so short."

"I think I want to die," she said.

He slapped her across the face. She was too shocked to respond. He slapped her again. She began to cry. He immediately held her as tightly as he could. "Never say that ever again," he said. "Never, never, never say anything like that. It's the most stupid idea of all. I couldn't stand it." She clung to him. She clung to him as if she were grateful.

That night Bill lay again with the Glyn boys, their heads at the feet of the Glyn girls. No one resented him that right. It had been his bed many times before. They knew he wasn't attempting to take Hugh's place. He hugged Martin and Robert. They were thankful for that. From the loft they could hear the whine of Marty's fiddle and Patrick sobbing as if he were moaning in his dreams.

*

Dora's numerous successful pregnancies went a long way to dissuade Kate from the belief that as a family they were cursed. Nevertheless, she insisted on being present at each confinement, as if by the sheer strength of her will she could protect them from the devil. It was, then, no surprise that Hugh seeing Dora waiting for him on the steps with that heavy, informative, look that announced the beginning of pain, should know that he would have to run for Kate before even a midwife. "Jesus!" he declared, recognising the certainty of progress in Dora's quietly troubled expression, "will I have time to change my trousers?" When Dora joined him he was pulling his Sunday best over his clogs and work trousers, without bothering to bend his knees. After a protracted struggle he finally tied a second belt at his waist and ran out. Dora eased herself down onto a chair and called after him: "Men should have this pain and give up being heroes." She knew he was beyond hearing.

It had been a great surprise to many people when Dora had *fell wrong* yet again. John shared their unease. The deaths of Julia, Polly and Anne haunted his memory as much as they haunted Kate's. In this instance he also thought it perverse that a birth should follow so quickly the death of the eldest son. "Will they never be through with it?" he demanded of Kate one night as he stood over the fire, allowing both his fierce disapproval and his fears to surface.

"It's not for us to question!" Kate responded calmly, aware of the concern at the heart of his question.

"Well, who should question it?"

"Maybe we shouldn't question God in this, at all, because it's God that sees to these things, therefore God you'd be questioning," she suggested, without certainty, wanting to sustain herself, sustain her own peace of mind.

"God?" John queried, his tone bitter and derisory. "Is everything they get up to the will of God then?"

"Yes!" Kate retorted. "Yes it is. They are all God's children. Whose else would they be?"

"Christ," John muttered, "the world is indecent enough. But I wouldn't blame it on a man's God, by God I wouldn't."

Kate eyed him with troubled sympathy, but he could no longer face her. Her resilience had undermined his anger. He turned away and stared into the fire.

"You know that a man and a woman love each other more when they are mourning than otherwise," she said gently. "They can't help it. Do you not remember, yourself?"

Yes, he thought, of course he remembered. And perhaps that was why it was so terrible. He did know the terrible agony that brought two people together. He wasn't of the opinion that conception should take place in the face of that, though he would have happily accepted it for himself if it had been the case. Once again he was faced with something that was beyond his control. Women in this family died giving birth. It was not his province. He was not allowed. It was terrible for him to feel so ineffectual. He feared for Dora. She had had too many pregnancies. The background to this one was all wrong. It didn't bode well. He couldn't vocalise the dread he felt. That wasn't allowed either. He reached down, adjusted the damper in the fire so that it made noise, a roar and splutter of flame. He didn't pursue the matter. Kate said no more.

He again stood over the fire and adjusted the damper the evening Hugh came for Kate. He gazed down into the contending flames, as Kate rushed about getting herself ready. Eventually his eyes smarted. He closed them. He again said nothing. Moments later the door closed behind him and the draught in the fire eased. Hugh and Kate were too preoccupied to have taken any notice of him and wonder at his silence.

314

When Hugh returned home Kate had already taken Dora to the bedroom. The children sat huddled together on the stairs. Their expressions were fearful and awkward. They disliked and resented this rupture of their routine. They looked at him expectantly, as if he could put it all to rights. He didn't want to have to face that. If he could have made them go away he would have. He wanted to be with Dora. Nevertheless, he knew his place and sat with them. Mary placed the four year old Patrick in his lap and put her own arms around his shoulders, her head resting on her own forearm.

He was still quite breathless. He had run all over Ginns looking for one of the two midwives who served the town. He had been forced to run from Ginns down into the market and along to the docks where a woman was confined on one of the fishing smacks. The sailors had been Danish and did not understand this man at all, running along the quay obviously wearing two pairs of trousers. When he finally discovered her she could only say that she would be along as soon as possible. He knew he should tell Kate, but felt that access to the bedroom was barred.

In order to pass the time he combed the children's hair for lice. This was a regular bed time feature, which he usually did after he had washed the boys. They waited in a quiet obedient line, then knelt before him, their heads hung over his lap. He put a newspaper across his knees, then pulled a fine toothed bone comb through their hair. Small golden brown lice and nits fell onto the black type. They would always remember the sight of the insects and empty egg cases dropping onto the paper as an act of love. He told the boys that they got nits from kissing girls and told the girls they got nits from kissing boys. The children went to school with the reproving sense that the other children were dirty. Not a single nit had the original name Glyn. Hugh had a lap of lice when he heard Kate call him. He thrust them, paper and all, into the fire and ran up the stairs.

The bedroom door was open for him. The room was lit by streetlight through open curtains. He could see Dora on the bed, her knees raised, draped by sheets and blankets. He couldn't see the colour of her skin in the semi-darkness, and her face was only partially luminous. He heard her moan, then breathe rapidly and deeply. He stepped into the room and began to pull the door behind him.

"No," Kate intervened irritably, "can't you see we've got no light in here. We're in the dark, Hugh. We're not seeing properly. We need the mantle changed."

Hugh backed out of the room. He felt excluded and embarrassed. He stood behind the door for a moment, his back against it, the handle still firmly in his palm, his head back, eyes closed. He listened for the sounds coming from the other side. His whole body bristled with tension as he heard the muffled sound of Dora's gasp. It didn't last long. He strained to hear it. He wanted to hear it. It was the only thing that could bring her close to him. It was the only way he could share her ordeal. He could hear her and remember it, then be aware for the future of what she had achieved. As he strained to hear, the voices of the children on the stairs interfered. Increasingly it was their voices he heard. Finally, he gave it up and bounced downstairs in temper. He shouted at them to clear the stair, but seeing their perplexed expressions regretted it, and with equal authority demanded that they remain. He threw up his hands and in a voice full of quiet repentance repeated the injunction that they stay put. Very gingerly they all sat back down. He sighed and went off to get the mantle.

He collected it from the pantry and went back into the confinement. The gas-torch was over the bed-head. He took the papery mantle from its box and leaned over Dora. He wanted to look at her, but was afraid Kate's eyes, even through the dimness, would pick him out. He didn't want her disapproval. He didn't want to have to work out what that disapproval would signify. He was a man and knew he should not be there. Birth was a mystery the workings of which were not for him to know. It was probably perversion in him that he did want to know. He didn't want Kate spying that perversion. However, he heard the onset of pain and had to look into Dora's face. He immediately recoiled at her discomfort and felt a surge of frustration and despair at his own insufficiencies, his face contorting with hers. He felt the mantle crumble in his fingers like dried insect wings.

"Clay to God man, are you useless and stupid?" Kate exploded, seeing the fractured mantle in his hands. "Get me another and I'll fix it myself."

"There isn't another," he said lamely.

"Then run to Ginns and ask John for our spare," Kate said, her voice chiding and commanding. The breaking of the mantle, along with the absence of the midwife, concerned her.

Hugh backed out of the room without further question.

He didn't knock but let himself into the house on Ginns. He found John as he had left him, still standing over the fire. He had a poker in his hand and was carelessly picking and prising at the melted crust of

316

coal. White flames spat out. He had not heard Hugh come in. He turned quickly on being addressed. The poker was a weapon in his hand. On seeing Hugh he was fearful. "Is anything wrong?" he asked quietly and weakly, his guts tightening.

"We have no gas-mantles," Hugh said. He looked shy and childish, standing there making the admission.

John burst out laughing. "So, your baby is being born in the dark, is it, Hugh lad," he said, "well, I presume it was conceived that way."

"What do you mean?" Hugh asked, piqued by John's suggestion, despite his continued awkwardness.

"Well, was it not conceived in the dark?"

"Do you mean carelessly?"

"No," John retorted, "I'm not saying anything of the sort. I would assume a thing like that could never be careless in marriage. Isn't that right? Nothing so important could be careless, could it? You wouldn't say so would you, Hugh lad? " He paused, eyed Hugh with mild amusement and added: "Mind you, it was careless not to have a spare mantle."

"I broke it."

"Ah, Holy Jesus, and I suppose Kate went altogether mad."

"She wasn't well pleased."

"But Dora's all right, that's the main thing, isn't it."

"She seems to be. She's lying in the dark. It's hard to say. I can't stand it when she cries out."

"Of course not," John said. "Of course you can't stand it. Who can? Who can in the their proper frame of mind?"

As he spoke he sat down heavily in an armchair by the fire. When he was finished speaking he pursed his lips together and eyed Hugh up and down. Hugh felt uncomfortable under his gaze. He detested the feeling he had of being a child. He didn't understand it. It seemed to have something to do with what was going on behind the closed door of his bedroom, but that didn't make any sense to him.

Once John had thoroughly looked Hugh over he took a packet of cigarettes from his pocket, put one in his mouth and offered one to Hugh. Hugh stepped forward, took the cigarette and lit them both. He continued to stand. They smoked silently for a while. John spoke first. "Does it not frighten you becoming a father again? The world would have thought you were through with that."

"No, I can't say that it frightens me. Are you saying that it should?"

"God but you're full of queries tonight, questioning everything that's said to you. Why's that I wonder? All I'm saying is that you're a miner and it's not gold you're digging up."

"Well, even if I was, it wouldn't be any of mine. I don't know. I suppose Kate is right, we bring them up on miracles."

"Did Kate say that?"

"Yes, Kate said that. Do you not remember? Something like that, anyway."

"Kate says so many things. I can just imagine it. A miracle, a prayer and the Holy Ghost, and a song just for good measure, that'll do for Kate."

"Do you not approve of what she says, Mr Devlin?"

"Oh, I approve. Why not? If that's what she wants to think. I don't believe in miracles myself."

"No, I didn't think you did."

"I believe in ghosts though."

"I'm surprised."

"You damn well know I don't."

"I only know what you tell me, Mr Devlin."

John laughed sceptically. He threw his butt into the fire, aiming at the strongest flame. "That's right," he said bleakly, but determinedly, as the butt flared up.

Hugh didn't reply but continued to smoke for a while longer, then tossed his butt at the front of the fire and watched it slowly burn up.

As Hugh's butt gradually ignited John said: "So, if we don't allow for miracles, what are we left with, Hugh?"

"Dreams, I suppose."

"Old men don't dream. There's only so many and you run out."

"Not so old."

"Old enough. Old enough not to want to dream, even if I did have any left. It might have been different if Connolly had lived, but he didn't, and that's that."

"Things move on."

"Of course they do. I know all about that. Everything moves on, and it seems like someone else's world, not your own anymore. I know all about that." He hesitated for a second. "I don't even feel angry anymore, just ashamed. Can you imagine that, Hugh lad, feeling only ashamed?"

"No, John, I can't," Hugh said. He had never before called John anything but Mr Devlin. The two men's eyes met in a brief, mutual smile.

318

"You know," John said warmly, "I wouldn't have been frightened either." For a moment Hugh was confused, then he remembered the question John had posed him about being afraid of being a father again. It brought him back to Dora. He had to get the mantle to her. The child conceived in the dark should at least be allowed to be born into the light. He had reneged on his duties. He stood up. John followed him with his eyes and continued speaking. "At one time I would have been father to as many children as God would have given. But he only gave two. Something happened to Kate after Robert. We were told that that might be it and it was. Still, you always manage to be grateful for something. We always end up thanking God for something, don't we. That's the way we are. Brought up to it I suppose, and don't know any better. Perhaps, when he burns us all we will be grateful for being warm. Well, I'm just grateful that Kate is alive. If I could meet my God I would worship Him for that."

"You'll meet your God, some day, Mr Devlin, as I reckon we all will. You're a good man, a decent man, fit for it."

"Maybe. We'll have to see. I don't believe he's so forgiving, though." He paused, then smiled broadly. "I remember when Dora and Robert were born. I remember it like it was two minutes ago. Marty was playing in the yard. My children were born with music in the air. Christ, I cried in his arms both times. I couldn't have cared less who saw me. I was overcome and I'm not ashamed to admit it, completely overcome. It seems we know things and then we choose to forget. I should have remembered crying in his arms. I should have remembered being that overcome that I didn't mind crying in Marty's arms. Marty cried with me. You can rely on him for things like that. Not much else, but things that might bother you later. He's good like that." He shrugged and turned pensively towards the fire. He stared deeply into the flames. "I'm pleased we couldn't replace Robert. As far as I'm concerned his ghost will haunt this world, my world, like Connolly's, until it is all brought to an end, whether that's burnt up or what, I don't know. But Robert'll be there at the reckoning. By Christ he will." His eyes were wide, glazed in the firelight.

"Is that what you think we are doing?" Hugh asked, his voice steady, but troubled. "Go on, tell me, Mr Devlin. Tell me you're not thinking that."

"The thought crossed my mind."

"Well, you're wrong," Hugh declared, angered by the suggestion, but unsure as how best to express it. "It doesn't work like that. God man, how could you see it like that? You're wrong. You couldn't be more wrong." Hugh fell silent. He was hoping for some response, some token comment that would put his mind to rest that John no longer believed what he had thought. John didn't turn from the fire, though. He just kept on staring into its depths, his eyes reddening in the glow. And Hugh kept his eyes on him all of the time, willing him to turn and apologise, repent of the monstrous accusation that he had made. But as Hugh looked at him, gazing stubbornly into the flames, a man exhausted of dreams, he felt a softening of his temper, and a wave of sympathy took over and replaced his anger, sympathy for this man whom he cared deeply about who seemed to have lost so much, so much more than Hugh could know. He spoke kindly. "I'm sorry, Mr Devlin, I'd give a lot to sit and talk with you a great deal more, but I'll have to get that mantle home or your woman will have the ghost of me."

"Help yourself," John said, pointing Hugh towards the pantry. Hugh went immediately and took the mantle box from the bottom shelf then went back to John to say he was off. He found that John was ready for him. "You know," he said, in a lively, matter of fact voice, "like all men who have never seen a child come into this world I have an image of it. Well, I think you have to. I see it like two hands waving in the dark, moving like a jellyfish across the bottom of the sea."

Hugh grinned: "I think you've been underground far too long, Mr Devlin."

John shrugged and smiled, as much as to say that Hugh was probably right.

When Hugh returned to the bedroom, which until then had been his and Dora's but was no longer his, the midwife had arrived. She was working by candlelight. He thought of mass. The candles formed a host of apparitions around the altar bed. Dora was shouting now. Hugh smiled restively at the passion. He was content with his analogy. It was the passion, this tormenting bringing forth of life. He thought of his own image. Two hands together, as if tied, fluttering with the fragility of a butterfly from the pupa.

As he stood there musing on the image before him, Kate took the box from him. However, instead of going to the gas-torch she immediately started shouting at him: "If God created man in His own image then he certainly forgot the brain. This is my memory-box from the bottom shelf. The new one is on the top shelf where everyone but a man would see."

The box Hugh had brought was empty. Kate placed an empty mantle box on her bottom shelf whenever her own mantle was finished, which she called her *memory-box*, to remind her to buy a new one so that she would never be without. She was obviously due a purchase. She marched out of the bedroom in order to get the mantle herself. As she left she commanded Hugh to watch the children. "Remember, there are nine of them. Try not to lose any. Pray that the unborn is a girl."

Kate returned before the baby was born. It came shortly after into the hissing strained light of gas, a light like dull dawn across a snow covered landscape, grey, blue and pink. Outside it was winter. Snow flurries touched the curtained windows. Kate's prayer had not been answered in so far as it was a boy she wrapped up against the cold. Dora had already chosen the name of Francis. The children crowded around the pink baby. Hugh looked at him. He thought of Hugh. A butterfly image came to mind. He went out of the house without speaking to Dora and stood on the Mount Pleasant steps. He could see the dusty snow swirling through the lights that ran straight and high from the docks. He felt it land on his shoulders, hair and face. He felt his ruby-red skin wither from his face. He lit a cigarette and smoked in the snow, trying not to shout out or cry.

Kate came every day of Dora's lying-in period and, despite the continued attention of the midwife, made her lie on her side so that she could inspect below her anus for any blood loss. Each morning the children waited at the foot of the stairs. "Clay to God childer," she exploded, "will you never stop tormenting your poor mother."

"When will she be back?" Martin asked sheepishly.

"Too soon!" she exclaimed.

Dora's absence was like a death in the house. For the period of lying-in the children mourned. Despite all of her own arguments to the counter Dora was forced to remain in bed for two weeks. Kate saw to that. And Hugh waited for Kate's permission to sleep in his own bed. Everyone waited and as they waited they heard Francis cry then become silent and as the silence fell on the house their minds filled with uncertain images.

Chapter Seven

By the beginning of 1934 Canning Pit, King Pit, Duke Pit and Ladysmith Pit had all closed on the grounds of being uneconomic. There was much speculation and rumour regarding further closures. The Miners Federation rapidly lost membership to the National Unemployed Workers' Movement. The Fed resisted the closures and found itself locked out. *Strangers* moved in, travelling nightly *ghost trains*. It was with this influx of *strangers* that an old friend appeared. On Saint Patrick's day 1934 Aunty Dora came home for good.

There was a party. A party for Saint Patrick and for Aunty Dora. She appeared old and more formidable than ever as she took her place, gazing straight ahead through grey, glazed eyes, serenely fierce. The lid of her *cockeye* now drooped, formed a salmon-pink lip, bright like an open wound. Martin and Mary approached her. Dora had instructed them. Her crenellated face, puffed up, rubicund, rounded and squeezed by her white bonnet, overviewed them mercilessly. A glint of humour puckered her lips and lent a brightness to her eyes. The children quivered but did not fail, in awe of her but at the same time pitying her. They were drawn to watch the slow birth like trickle of tears which laboured through her saturated eyelashes, wanting to know why she was so permanently sad. Mary was struck by a desire to stroke the offending lid, hypnotised by the flow of pearl like tears.

Aunty Dora picked up the direction of their attention. She grinned inwardly and proceeded to peel the raw flesh of her eye lid forward, stroked her lashes then let it go. "Do you like my cockeye?" she asked, her tone sinister and mocking. "Oh, I knew what you were staring at. My magic-eye tells me. I can see everything. I know just what you're thinking. It's a gift from God, you see, but as with all of God's gifts it has a draw-back. That's no criticism of God, dear me, no. Far from it. He knows best. Who am I to suggest that or otherwise. Tut, tut. We all have to have a burden. It keeps us straight. Mine is a cockeye. That's not much is it? A wee trail of tears." She paused and eyed them ruefully. "Well, what do you say? Do you think God is kind? Do you think it's a reasonable weight to bear?" They neither answered.

Martin was of the theory that the clear drops had more to do with gin than God. He had watched expectantly as the glass met her lips to be followed sure enough by a magical dew-drop.

"Has the cat got your tongues, then?" she pressed. "If God thinks it worthwhile to give an animal the power of speech, then he can presumably live with some backchat. And if he gives us the miracle of seeing he also gives us the problem of keyholes. Am I right? God, but would you listen to me, badgering the life out of you. Am I turned into a batty old, eccentric spinster, then? God help me."

She stopped speaking and eyed them closely for a few moments. A flash of fierce, tender humour spread across her face as she did. "Here," she eventually began again, and reached out and took a hand from each of them, "I'll read your futures in your palms." She held their hands fast in her own. "Do you think I can do that? Do you think I can peer into the what is to be? No answer, I suppose. Well, my eye says yes, so yes it is. You don't argue with an eye like this, do you?"

She pressed two hard knotted thumbs into their closed fists, pressed them deeply into their palms and slowly and firmly rotated them around. As she did she lay her head to one side and mused, as if deciphering the messages she was reading. A moment later she suddenly spoke up, her tone quick and light: "This hand will break rock and this one will hold babies. That's it."

She burst out laughing, the sound rich and textured, and released their hands, throwing them aside like a magician displaying her magic. And there was a certain magic in it as Mary and Martin felt a new silver tanner in each palm.

Aunty Dora didn't wait for any response but immediately stood up, removed her coat, a clear signal she was ready and wanted to dance, and approached John Devlin.

"Will you leave that corned beef and spud a minute," she declared forcibly, "there's a lady here wishes to dance. Come on, Marty, you scruffy, wastrel of a man, exercise that instrument and show us the only talent God gave you."

Marty was behind John Devlin, hunched over a bowl of broth. He looked up without raising his head. He frowned at her, slowly lowered his eyes back to the broth, then painstakingly blew across its hot surface. After his long, deliberate exhalation he brought the bowl to his lips and sucked loudly. He continued to tip the bowl until the greater part was gone. He put the bowl back on the table, slowly wiped his sleeves across his face, and only then acknowledged his sister. He nodded at her, gave a slight bow, drew up his fiddle and said: "Your man is now ready." He began *We only want the earth*, one of Connolly's *Songs of Freedom*.

Aunty Dora huffed but didn't respond. At that moment she loved Marty's eccentricity. It was reliable, and it was harmless. It was an element of homecoming that she could enjoy, one thing at least that didn't have to trouble her.

She turned her attention instead to John. She spoke up, her voice deliberately loud as if needing to announce her presence, test out its meaning. "Well, well, despite growing old and a mite sour, you remain the handsomest man in the world, Mr Devlin. But, for God's sake, before you say a word, don't think to compliment me, you'd only shame yourself."

"You never change in my eyes, Dora, that's for sure."

She shrugged and gave a brief, half-smile. She spoke more quietly. "No, I imagine not. I've just been explaining my cockeye to your grandchildren. Well, tormenting and terrorising them with it, if the truth be known."

"Does it have an explanation then?" he asked. "I don't ever remember being treated to an account of it." As he spoke he was already casting his mind back to the first tear-drops. He knew there was a mystery there. It rankled him at the time, and it still did all these years later. He knew he had been excluded from something, but didn't know what, something that Kate and Dora shared. He resented any such segregation, even amongst women.

She skewed her face. "Of course, it has an explanation. Why not? It's a warning, that's what it is, a warning to stop me believing any God forsaken old gibberish and rubbish some old man might tell me."

"There isn't a man would hazard his luck and not be straight with you, Dora. I feel pretty confident about that."

She skewed her face again, contorting it into a greater show of scepticism. "God Almighty, and would you just listen to that, and tell me the same." She gestured towards Marty who was still singing Connolly's song.

> *Tis passing strange, yet I declare*
> *Such statements give me mirth*
> *For our demands most moderate are*
> *We only want the earth.*

"We only want the earth," she repeated, deriding it. "I seem to remember straw in a cellar did for the likes of us. I don't particularly recall that we wanted the earth."

"Well, it doesn't do to look back sometimes. Maybe it's better to plan."

"And what do you do, plan for the worst so the best might not be so bad after all?"

He gazed at her steadily, and quietly said: "You'll have a bed beneath my roof, I can tell you that much."

"Oh God, why do men have to take everything so much to heart. You don't owe me. I'll fend for myself all right. I'll sleep in the yard, the shed, the grate. It's all the same to me."

"I said a bed."

"Please, don't be so serious, John Devlin. Don't you see, I'm fingering my way home. It's not easy, you know, not easy coming back." She ran her hands across her face as if she were deeply weary, eventually dragging her fingers down and across her leaking eye and good eye. "I feel out of sorts and, well, a bit lost already. I don't know where I might fit, or whether I'll ever fit. I don't know myself after all this time, always living by someone else's say so and permission. I don't know what I'm fit for and I don't want to impose. I'm a bloody orphan..."

John made to speak, but only managed to huff. He didn't know where to begin. He wanted to rubbish everything she said, yet at the same time he recognised her view of herself. It appalled him that she should feel so alien. It underlined so much about all of them. Were they not all liable to feel that they didn't quite know where they fit? He never for a moment lost sight of the fact that he was in someone else's country, but he fretted that he might have lost sight of the one he came from.

She instantly recognised his misgivings and wanted to mollify him. She said: "I would be honoured to accept your offer, John Devlin. It's more than I could have hoped for. You know that. You don't owe me. I'm grateful. I'm very grateful. I'll be able to pay my way mind. I never made a lot, but I never had out to spend it on. So, don't worry on that score. You set the terms, John Devlin, that's what I'm used to."

"Call it home, for God's sake," he replied.

She half-smiled. "So, you have your country now."

"That isn't what I meant."

She laughed. "Do you not think I know that. It's stamped all over you. You carry a dead man's wound every bit as much as I do, perhaps even a bit more. Actually I'd say a hell of a lot more."

326

He looked at her for explanation, but she just shook her head, refusing it. She wasn't about to elucidate. Despite everything they had their own world as well.

He thought immediately of Murphy, but surely she couldn't mean that. That history was buried and finished with and couldn't be unearthed. No, she didn't allude to Murphy. He'd have to live with that secret to the end. Only one other person now knew about that episode and he never uttered a word. The fact that they were the only two spoke so much of the lives they had led. And as to herself, he couldn't begin to guess. All sorts of images flashed across his mind, but they wouldn't quite fit with the stocky, unlovely woman standing before him. Her dead man was someone other than an admirer or lover. Her dead man maybe had more to do with mind than body. He just didn't know. They had their secrets then. That was the only sensible conclusion. That thought satisfied him. He smiled and briskly suggested: "I thought you had a mind to dance."

"To tell the truth my heart isn't in it tonight, not really. I'm a bit of a con when all's told. I'm not what they all think I am. It all takes time, I suppose, but I'll get there." She gave a hasty, embarrassed smile, and whispered: "Call it home."

She moved away. He let her go. He saw no reason to hold her. He agreed with her. It took time. Everything took time. He went in search of Kate. Having asked Dora, he found he actually had a mind to dance.

Aunty Dora resumed her seat. She felt emptied and restrained, rendered quite silent, without any voice, at all. She watched John and Kate as they danced. She recognised in their touch, its familiarity yet surprise, its display yet privacy, that they had found a home in each other, that they discovered each other shamelessly in mysterious adulthood. It was an experience that had bypassed her. She steeled herself. She refused to concede to emotions that threatened her. She told herself that she belonged nowhere, never had, neither in a place nor a person, but that it wasn't unique, or special, but ordinary, the ordinary experience of the very ordinary majority. She scoffed at herself, at desires that said *We only want the earth*, at desires that ground to nothing. She reached beside her and poured herself another gin. There was always that. She could sate her pleasures without recrimination. She smiled to herself and poured herself a large measure. When she sat up Dora was in front of her. She looked up, squinted, and said: "I'll be crying later."

"Well, you can do what you like now."

"That's right, whatever I like, whenever I like. What to make of that, eh?"

327

"Are you coming to live with me?"

"A mattress in the yard?"

"There's room."

"No, there isn't. There's no room at all." She smiled and cast her eyes across the dancers. She felt the weight of their proximity. Even now, in that brief moment, their sense of touch had deepened. They were an emblem of themselves. They were suggestive of contracts and commitments. She smiled again and turned back to Dora. She said: "I'll stay with Kate, that's the best place for me."

Dora felt the older woman's inertia, her awareness of lack. She saw that her smile was new and awkward. It was obvious she wasn't in a state of mind to enjoy her homecoming party. She clearly felt stifled and absent, in too many senses still removed. Dora didn't know what to do. She wanted the welcome to work, but not at the expense of what had been. She wanted it all to add up. She suggested: "I suppose you'll miss it, the house and all, for a while, miss it for a while? That would only be natural."

"No, I won't miss it. What would be natural about that? None of it was ever mine. I worked hard enough," Aunty Dora replied quickly but simply, emphasising nothing.

"But..." Dora began, imagining herself a world of borrowed comforts. "I would have thought, well... Oh, I don't know, the security, the people, the..."

"I miss the hotels," Aunty Dora cut in, regretting the implied abruptness of her previous remark. She knew it was unfair. Dora meant well. She shouldn't really be treated to anything but reassurance and comfort. She went on: "The hotels were good, really good. We had some great times in the hotels. We used to eat the leftovers with the commercial travellers who came down to the kitchens when the day was done. That was good. Some of those boys were the right lads. I could tell you so many stories of days and nights and the bits between. I've got the smells of rashers and linen and boot-black and all sorts. It was a whole world you know. It was all right in the hotels. I will say that."

"Come to me," Dora said, as if she hadn't really heard a word.

Aunty Dora shook her head. "No, I'll go to Kate. I'll go to Kate and hope it works out for the best."

Dora gave a half-smile, and gazed intently at her namesake, and with a strange insistence uttered: "You'll come to me eventually."

Aunty Dora was still working out how to reply to Dora's enigmatic statement when the dancing in the kitchen came to an uneasy halt and the music slowly wound down. She turned to see Peter Kavanagh, Gavin Duffy, Uncle John Darcy and Patrick Devlin fall fully into the room. All four were drunk. Patrick was crying and moaning quietly. His face was a thin wafer between his spread fingers. Uncle John Darcy was comforting him. It was a comic, meaningless comfort made up of broken, flabby sentiments that made no sense outside John Darcy's head.

Patrick had not been home since the previous autumn. His disappearance coincided with Gladys getting married. He didn't say anything to anyone, but just quietly slipped away. Such was the usual anonymity of his life that no one could have precisely recorded the day he went off. John Darcy heard word of him from time to time and kept Kate informed of his whereabouts as best he could. He had turned up at docks along the coast for a while, labouring in one warehouse after another, loading and packing. After that he had shown up on a whole series of farms where he had laboured on numerous occasions in the past. He didn't stay anywhere for very long. He didn't always leave of his own accord. The only comfort Kate had was that at least he wasn't frequenting the graveyard. Although he never said anything to Kate John was relieved that he was gone. He found his increasing drinking and reluctance to communicate more and more embarrassing. He told himself that he was not to blame, and certainly Kate was not to blame, but still he worried about other people's opinions. Nor could he ever quite escape the feeling of resentment that Patrick was alive, wasting himself, and Robert wasn't. It infuriated him, but he kept that entirely to himself.

When the music and dancing came to a complete halt there was a period of uneasy silence, broken only by the whimperings of Patrick and the senseless consolation of John Darcy. Eventually, Bill Kavanagh stood up and approached Patrick. He gazed at him for a moment from close quarters, his head to one side as if he were struck by both curiosity and pity. After that, he reached out and took both of his hands and led him, as if he were blind, to the table and sat him down. He then brought a bowl of soup and sat down beside him and began to administer it to him, holding the spoon at his lips, slowly pressing and working it in.

Relieved of his burden, Uncle John Darcy took out a bottle and began to drink. He then handed it on to Gavin Duffy who in turn passed it to Peter Kavanagh.

As soon as Gavin passed the bottle on he shouted out, demanding music. He repeated the injunction over and over. Music, music, music! No one answered. Indeed, no one had spoken in the room since the four had fallen in. As he shouted out he danced awkwardly and threateningly on Peter's arm, swinging his fists and feet, his face a grimace.

As Gavin stomped against him Peter watched Bill spoon soup against Patrick's lips, then wipe the dribbles that rolled across his emaciated face. The image of Bill's nursing disgusted him. It disgusted him that it was his son doing it. The scene was filthy. Suddenly, he picked up on Gavin's theme, and started marching him around the kitchen, sending him into uneasy reels, whilst stomping his own feet and shouting out, echoing Gavin's demand. Music, music, music!

Aunty Dora stood up. She had every intention of berating them their intrusion, but as soon as she got to her feet her anger failed her. She had an acute sensation of having crossed the mark. It wasn't her place to take these four to task. She didn't know the antecedents. She remained an outsider. After all, no one else had queried that terrible display of anger, and she was pretty sure that it wasn't fear alone that dictated that. John Devlin would not hold his tongue without good reason. So, with all those thoughts rushing round her head, she turned towards Marty. She smiled as much to say Saint Patrick belonged to them just as much as to an unholy virgin, then vociferously called out: "For God's sake, give them a tune." She sat back down, vaguely satisfied with herself, despite her feeling of uprootedness. Marty slowly brought the fiddle to his shoulder, hesitated for a moment, like a professional building the anticipation, then burst into his song, Connolly's *Rebel Song*, one to placate Duffy.

> *Come workers sing a rebel song,*
> *A song of love and hate,*
> *Of love unto the lowly*
> *And hatred to the great...*

Gavin stopped his awkward, marionette dance. He staggered towards Marty. He angrily shouted out: "No, no, no! Not that! To hell with that. Something else!"

Marty immediately stopped playing. There was a momentary silence in the room once again. Marty began to whisper.

> *With me whack fol the do fol.*
> *The diddle idle day.*

Gavin listened for a moment, his upper body swinging forward and backwards clumsily, his expression limp, then managed to hold himself erect and started clapping the tune, despite the absence of music.

John spoke over the sound of Gavin clapping, his voice quiet but strong: "What was wrong with the other?"

Gavin didn't turn to him but snapped out: "I don't care to listen to it tonight."

"Why not?"

"Because I don't care to listen to it any night."

"But I do," John said emphatically, his voice holding the final word.

Gavin turned on him, and spoke out quickly and savagely: "He died for nothing, a fucking martyr, nothing else, a martyr, not a socialist. He gave the country to the lawyers and they gave it up in loans. Oh, to hell with it. Why try to explain?" He fell forward, but kept his feet. He tried to smile, but failed. All the tightness in his expression faded away and he looked completely blank. His voice faded away to little more than a whisper. "A Capuchin friar gave him his death rites, a fucking Capuchin friar."

Hugh Glyn intervened. He spoke slowly and hesitatingly. Despite Gavin's drunken display he had a great deal of sympathy for him. He had fought long and hard for the Fed, more so than anyone else. Because of it he had been one of the first to be locked-out. Certainly he was relentless and somewhat possessed, but at least he had beliefs. It made his drunken outburst all the more disappointing. Of course, soon enough and they would all be locked-out. "Surely you can be as good to your Party as you are to your church, can't you? I would have thought that was all right. That's the case isn't it?"

Gavin turned two keen eyes on Hugh and quickly uttered: "But would your church let you? You can't take orders from everyone. So what would it be? Would you tell Saint Patrick that you've rioted and burnt? Would you tell Saint Patrick that you've taken up arms and broken the law? For Christ sake, you won't even tell yourselves that you might have to." He fell silent. He looked at those around him, slowly passing from face to face, his expression again blank. He shook his head and turned towards the door. He took a few steps, stumbled and fell against it. He pressed his palms fast against the wood to stop himself falling. Then he relaxed and let himself be supported by it. He turned his head to the side and called out: "Why are they removing all the Communists from office?" There was no reply. "Are you too far gone to answer?" Still there was no response. He grimaced, closed his eyes for a moment and let his head press against the door. A few seconds later he pushed himself up, flung back the door and stumbled out. Peter followed quickly behind him, pausing only long enough to cast a single, glaring glance at Bill. The door remained wide open.

As they made their exit Patrick tried to stand, presumably intending to follow them, but as he tried to take his first step forward he stumbled and went sprawling across the kitchen flags, bringing the soup bowl with him crashing over the pink stone. Kate and Aunty Dora picked him up. There was thick soup dripping down his front.

John Darcy made a move towards him, a single arm outstretched as if to draw him away. Aunty Dora rounded on him. She firmly stated: "He'll sleep in his mother's house tonight, and there'll be no argument" John Darcy raised his hands in submission. The two women each put an arm under his shoulder and lifted him towards the stair.

At the foot of the stairs Kate whispered across to her sister: "It's good to have you home, Dora. I can't tell you. Together we do things, make things happen. I've missed that, and I've needed it really. Welcome home." Aunty Dora didn't say anything. She simply turned to Kate and gave a brief, circumspect nod. Kate read it as mild embarrassment. A half-smile passed her lips. Dora responded in kind. They stepped forward together hauling Patrick behind them up the steep and narrow staircase.

In the kitchen Marty whispered once again.

With me whack fol the do fol.
The diddle idle day.

Francis began to cry. Hugh picked him up from a tent of blankets and rocked him. He held him tightly and felt him concealed. Only his cries gave him away.

With me whack fol the do fol.
The diddle idle day.

The Saint Patrick's day party was over.

*

1934. Cold spring. Strange things began to happen. *Ghost trains* appeared with ever greater regularity. Untime-tabled, occupied by *spooks* without a valid ticket of travel, the trains clanked through the night. More and more *strangers* slept in bunks in the grub houses and screen sheds of Canning pit and the disused buildings of Lady pit. Tents were erected in a single night on the slopes above Loft. In response to the influx of *spooks,* outside non-union labour, the Fish miners chose mass burial. The occupation had been preceded by a strike, the result of which was the appearance of even more *strangers*. During the strike a *Daily Worker* reporter, addressing the *Fed*, had made the statement: *The fight against Fascism has to be conducted underground.* He was taken at face value.

As long as the Fish men were underground no *spook* or scab could be. They went back to work and at the end of their shift refused to come to the surface.

On the fourth night of the occupation Peter Kavanagh and Gavin Duffy sat on a perch below the promontory of Loft. Across the bay was the coastal shelf where the trains wound beneath shallow cliffs. Below them was the sea, which was also the surface of Fish, Canning and Loft, the workings of all of them running in to each other and stretching out miles beneath the Solway. A not quite fully formed moon was reflected on it. They waited patiently, until finally, in the early hours, just as their sources had predicted, a train came into view, moving slowly along the shelf between two moons. In that light it was for all the world ghostlike. Its cargo was *spooks*.

Although it was clearly visible in the moonlight, from their viewpoint it seemed to move slowly and silently. It wound round large circuits of the coast, moving in and out of clear vision. It made steady progress and pretty soon they could hear it as well as see it. As it approached the final bend, before turning straight into the town, they fell flat on their faces amongst the stubble and cinders of the bank and inched forward to the edge of the promontory. Just as the train hit the apex of the corner it came to an abrupt stop. Peter and Gavin lay their heads flat against the ground, but kept their eyes on the coastal shelf.

They weren't surprised by the sudden arrest of the train's progress. It was what they had been waiting for. Earlier in the night, just short of midnight, they had assisted a group of unnameable miners in moving a coping-stone to a shelf on the shallow sandstone head-land. They had worked shafts for levers beneath it, which allowed a large enough group of men to drop it to the track below with relative ease. Gavin would have gladly moved the levers himself, but his mind was on a different prize.

They kept their heads down and continued to watch and wait. On the plateau above them the grub houses of Loft emptied out and were abandoned as the resident *strangers* went to assist the stricken train. As Gavin surveyed the developing confusion his face tightened into a satisfied grimace. He suppressed a desire to laugh out loud, but the sound stuck in his throat. He pressed his face sharply into the ground. He felt the tough grasses and cinders dig in. He had to control himself and keep his excitement in check. He had to be professional. He slammed his fist against the hard, rough surface. Peter whispered something to him. Gavin ceased beating the ground and turned to him. Peter was watching him calmly, patiently. Peter smiled. The gesture was cold and humourless. Gavin tapped him and they crawled up the cinder bank and looked over the plateau above.

The grub houses and screen sheds appeared deserted. Gavin lifted himself higher. There was no one. He looked back towards the coastal shelf. He could see the small, indistinct shapes of tiny figures rushing towards the derailed train. He was convinced that they had all run off to assist. Loft was theirs. He reached inside his jacket pocket and pulled out a fox pelt. It was scrawny and dog-eared. A rag of head, body fur and brush, precariously knitted together. He had bought it from John Darcy as a whim many years previously on the day of the funeral cortege for the Lady pit men and boys. He held it up, examined it for a few seconds, then draped it carefully over his head. His eyes peered through two triangular tears in its back, whilst its head, frozen to a snarl, dangled at the nape of his neck. He shook it and emitted a soft hideous moan. Peter looked on blankly, refusing to admit either approval or disapproval. He simply waited. It wasn't his place to have an opinion. That had been Gavin's promise. He didn't need to think anymore. He just had to act. That was the beauty of it all. He could never be wrong. Once Gavin was happy that the fox fur was firmly in place he tapped Peter on the shoulder and together they dashed, hunched over, across the plateau to Loft's sheds.

Explosives! These were Gavin's prize. A *gift* for Ireland. Being cold spring John Darcy had not taken to sleeping rough but was still with the witch. He had left his gift bearers trolley beside Loft's coal-hops for Gavin to transport his prize down to the quays and a certain little ship. Explosives! They were a symbol of Gavin's commitment to the I.R.A. It was certainly not a commitment approved by the Party. It was personal. It was a process of memory foretelling what experience had failed to achieve. His visions, *The One Big Union*, *The Socialist Republic*, had come to nothing but lock-outs, defeats, compromise, sell-outs, De Valera's bastard republic hemmed in by big ships, Cosgrave's blue shirt Fascists and Mosely's black shirt Fascists. But for a man of such austere, uncompromising principle, there was no way out. He had to continue the struggle. His experience, though he would have denied it vehemently, had drawn him to a state of thinking closer to Pearse and the notion of sacrifice, martyrdom, Christ crucified, and the conviction that *life springs from... blood letting*, than to the Party he adored. Gavin wanted a mass of blood letting. His anger demanded it. His memory demanded it. His fatigue demanded it. His vision demanded it. It didn't have to make too much sense anymore. It just had to happen. All his dreams and nightmares had to be for something.

He knocked firmly at the grub house door and then turned away. The watchman answered to the frozen snarl of a fox head. As Gavin heard the door open he made one last scan of the pit-head, then in one quick movement spun round and struck the watchman two clean blows to the head with a painted shillelagh, which he had kept as an ornament in his house for years. The watchman crumpled to the ground. Gavin's uncharacteristic display, though, proved to be a miscalculation. Even as the watchman fell his dog, a mastiff, incensed by the dangling head gear, was already mauling Gavin's arm. Within seconds it brought Gavin to his knees. He screamed with the pain as the animal tore into the muscles of his upper arm, and caught at the sinews of his neck. Try as he might he just couldn't shake it off.

The speed of the attack caught Peter off guard. For a few seconds he just stood transfixed, stupefied by the ferocity of the animal, before eventually discovering the presence of mind to pick up the club and strike at it. He smashed its skull with a number of repeated blows. The very first had brought it down. It was only as he raised the club to bring it down for the fifth time that he became aware of what he was doing. He suddenly stopped, still holding the weapon aloft. The silence shocked him. He realised that all he had been hearing was the repeated impact of the club. The dog's head was a macerated pulp. Its contents were seeping out. He felt ashamed and stupid. He knew he had been afraid, and fear had made him crazy. It had been so long since he had been afraid, so long since he had felt very much at all. He slowly lowered the club.

As he did Gavin howled at him. He turned immediately, reflexly towards the sound. Gavin was clawing at his wound, his spread fingers pulling at the torn flesh as if he could knit it back together. Peter had seen it so many times, men hugging their bodies as Gavin was, caressing their appalling wounds. Usually, they looked shocked and hurt, as if it were too incomprehensible to understand. Gavin was different though. He was glaring at Peter. His anger and resentment were obvious. He didn't need to say anything. There was no forgiveness in his expression. He despised Peter for his indecision. Peter knew he had somehow to make amends.

He dropped the shillelagh beside the dog and quickly, and roughly, frisked the watchman for his keys. Once he had acquired those he scrambled over to Gavin with every intention of helping him get to his feet. But Gavin didn't want him anywhere near him. As Peter came towards him he swung out at him with his good arm. Then, having hit out once, his anger overwhelmed him. He threw himself at Peter and tried desperately to strike at him with his one fist. Peter backed away rather than defend himself, but as he did he pushed up against the watchman and stumbled. Gavin tried to reach him before he could find his feet but, as he pulled himself forward, he was suddenly seized by a terrific spasm of pain. He stopped and held himself rigid, and again hugged and clawed at his wound. Peter seized the opportunity. He sprung beside Gavin and wrapped his arms around him, both supporting him and keeping his working arm secure. Gavin conceded to his hold. Pain and frustration had overcome his anger. He allowed Peter to help him to his feet.

Peter led him to the shed known as *Reserve Station*. The door read: *Reserve Station. Explosives. No unauthorised person to enter reserve station. No smoking, matches or naked flames within twenty yards of Reserve Station.* He unlocked it and went in. He took some rags that were cushioning the explosives and wrapped up Gavin's wounds, twining rags one over another up the length of his arm and around his shoulder. When the lacerated flesh was completely covered he set to the task of loading John Darcy's trolley. Gavin just stood and watched, looking on blankly as Peter heaved the boxes in place. Neither of them spoke.

In the early dawn, a liquid pale dawn, sun and moon in the sky together, the sky veined turquoise and crimson, they wheeled the trolley past the moored boats along the *Tongues*. They wheeled it casually, without urgency. They had managed to get well clear of Loft before the *spooks* had returned from the stricken train. The pain in Gavin's arm had reduced to a burning throb. It was the dawn of the fifth morning of the occupation. It was the morning the miners came up. They had been made promises of no victimisation, no scab labour, no lock-outs. They had passed the time chasing, catching and dissecting rats. Stories were already circulating the town that they had eaten rats.

Peter and Gavin spent the morning on the docks helping load boats for McClean. McClean was there himself, sitting on deck pulling his toy boat about the basin by a length of string, not supervising anything, simply enjoying himself. They received word that the men from Fish had come up, but they didn't hear any details. At the time the miners crossed the Prospect Road between Mount Pleasant and Ginns they were being questioned by the police. The police were, for the main part, *strangers* as well. The town's watch committee had drafted in reinforcements once the *ghost trains* had begun. They had been camped out in tents on the slopes along the cliffs from Loft pit. They appeared along the dockside in large numbers. Their accents placed them as far afield as Glasgow and Birmingham. Peter and Gavin were on deck packing crates when the police arrived. A group gathered along the boat.

"What's the load?" a voice from among the crowd of police demanded.

Gavin closed the lid of the crate, looked along the line, then asked: "Why? Who wants to know?"

A large figure stepped from the line and boarded the boat. He was a giant of a man with a large square head, ossified features and over large, bony hands. He walked straight up to Gavin and towered over him. He didn't look directly at him, but rather kept his head back gazing into the distance. He repeated the question. "What's the load?"

McClean answered. "Linen, just linen."

A half-smile passed the policeman's large, fleshy lips. He didn't turn to McClean, but continued to gaze ahead. "Why did he say, just linen? See, that gets me thinking. Why should I have thought that there would be anything else? You see the way my mind works."

"I don't know why he said it. He just did. It doesn't mean anything."

The policeman looked down at Gavin and eyed him closely. "It doesn't mean anything. You don't know. You don't know. Of course not. None of you bastards ever know anything, do you! Ignorant bastards you lot. Ignorant all the time. Is that right? Are you just an ignorant bastard?"

Gavin didn't reply. He just kept his eyes forward, not focused on anything in particular. He kept telling himself to be disciplined, to keep his anger in check, and not let the policeman provoke him. He was struggling with it though. He had checked himself a number of times already. His natural tendency was to strike out.

The policeman went on. He spoke with a quiet, amused insistence. "I want you to say it. I want you to repeat: I don't know anything because I'm an ignorant bastard. Have you got that? I don't know anything because I'm an ignorant bastard."

It was too much for Gavin. "Fuck you!" he snapped.

The policeman immediately grabbed his arm and twisted it. He brought him down steadily to the deck of the boat, continuously bending his already damaged limb as he did. Gavin howled in pain. A show of new blood soaked through his sleeve. The policeman felt it in his palm. He dropped Gavin to the floor and examined his hand. "How did you do that?" he demanded. Gavin didn't reply. He was holding himself tightly, hugging his arm as he had earlier, quietly moaning to himself. The policeman kicked him in the stomach. "How did you do it?" he repeated, shouting out the demand. He kicked him again. "Come on, tell me. How did you do it?"

"I caught it on a crate," Gavin gasped, taking quick short breaths as he struggled to speak.

The policeman turned to Peter. He demanded: "Name? Your name? Quickly. Come on."

"Kavanagh."

"Job?"

"Unemployed."

"Job?"

"Unemployed."

"What the fuck are you doing on the boat then? Answer! Quickly. Come on."

McClean spoke up. "I employ them for a bit of herring and chewing tobacco. That's all."

"His name?" the policeman demanded, indicating Gavin. Peter and McClean said nothing. "His name? Come on. Quickly. Name?"

Peter answered: "Duffy."

"Job?"

"Unemployed."

"You," the policeman said pointing at Peter, "open it. Come on. Quickly! Move! Now!" Peter moved gingerly towards the crate. Gavin lay beside it. The policeman barracked Peter as he approached the crate and then stood over it, pressing him to get a move on and stop wasting time. Peter broke the lid. He was instructed to empty it. He turned it onto its side. Rolls and scraps of linen spread across the boat floor. The policeman looked at the fabric for a moment, then pushed his foot through it, kicking it across the deck, then he walked over it. Having stepped over the fabric a number of times he strolled back to his starting point and stepped on Gavin's spread arm. He screwed his boot against it, then marched away, making his way off the boat. As he did he shouted further instructions to the other watching officers, who all seemed quite satisfied and amused by the entertainment.

Whilst the police occupied the quays the miners of Fish made their way home. There were no celebrations. They conducted themselves in mourning. It was an art they had learnt. An art that whole families practised. It was an attitude they assumed when passing unsympathetic shops, blackleg houses, or the police, enacting the death in the community

338

of all who were not with them, and therefore against them. When they reached Prospect, the road dividing towards Ginns or Mount Pleasant, the trouble began. A crowd of *strangers* and unsympathetic locals had collected on each of the roads. They had even spilled onto the grassy banks which rose above Prospect. There were no police present. All at once they converged on the miners and began to stone them. Grossly outnumbered the Fish men were forced to run through the barrage. They had to keep running until they were out of range well on the Ginns and Mount Pleasant roads.

John Devlin and Hugh Glyn were two of them. When John made it to his own kitchen he found Patrick there. Each was shocked at the other's appearance. John's blackened face was marked by a series of irregular stripes, his hair matted with blood. Patrick's face was the colour of rancid butter, marasmic. Patrick began to cry. He contracted into himself as if in pain, hiding his face in his hands as if the sight of John was too terrible to view. The streaks of blood that had dribbled down John's face seemed to send Patrick into a state of minor hysteria. He tried to look again, but failed. He rushed off to fetch Kate. John didn't understand. Patrick's nerves were evidently shattered.

A moment later Kate came in from the yard. Patrick trailed her. As he came into the room he began to whimper. Kate turned on him and ordered him to go to bed. He ran off instantly at her command, emitting strange wails as he went. On another day John might have laughed at the performance. Instead he just stared, his eyes fixed on the door where Patrick had bolted.

Kate gazed at him for a few moments, and then stepped up to him and began to undress him. She slipped off his waistcoat, unbuttoned his shirt and trousers and eventually stripped him naked. She brought a bucket of water and washed his entire body. As she knew he was ashamed she didn't look at his face. The blackened water ran onto the stone flags. When she had finished washing and drying him, she wrapped a towel across his head and covered him in a blanket. After that she went out. They had not broken their five day silence.

The majority of those of Ginns had come out. They didn't discuss anything but as a group began to march towards the colliery. The same had occurred on Mount Pleasant. The two crowds met at Prospect, where the miners had been stoned, and continued marching together. They were a combination of unemployed and retired men, women and children. Eventually they converged on Fish. They all shared the same single idea. They wanted to tear down its offices and structure brick by yellow brick.

As they drew towards the colliery a line of police officers filed into place in front of them, barring their path. The crowd halted. The two sides faced each other for a few minutes, without making any move. There was an eerie silence as they each weighed up the other. And then, at some signal that no one in the crowd registered, the police lines all drew truncheons. They charged the crowd. The protest was broken up. There were numerous beatings.

At 2 a.m. the following morning Gavin Duffy and Peter Kavanagh were arrested in their beds and charged with inciting riot. Throughout that day McClean was not allowed into the police station to give evidence that the men had been loading his boats when the riot took place. In fact, he too was threatened with arrest. And then, quite unexpectedly, in the early evening when Aunty Dora had for the fifth time tried to gain access to see Peter she was told she could take him home, he was free to go. The riot charges had been dismissed. Nevertheless, Gavin was still held. Copies of the *Soldier's Voice* had been found in his room, packed for shipment to the British held ports in Ireland, which called for all soldiers to join arms with the working-classes to overthrow Capitalism. He was charged under the *Incitement to Mutiny Act* of 1797. Gavin's response was to begin an immediate hunger strike.

*

"Cripes!" Martin said.

He was startled and fearful, yet slightly amused, by Dora's order that he had to go to the church of *Saint Joseph* where he was to act as a crutch for Father Bond in order to help the old priest make a journey across town. Before he could say any more she chased him out. He hesitated on the steps for some time considering his charge. Small children poked at the dust and moss in the step corners. Curlicues of black smoke rose into the cloudless blue sky. It was only when he thought the door was opening behind him that he shot down the steps of Mount Pleasant. However, he didn't go to the church, but ran down to the quays.

The *Sugar Tongue* was a wall of noise, composed of the labouring hiss and throb of numerous steamers. He stood there for a while immersed in the sound, daydreaming of foreign countries. He was aroused by the clatter of noise of a coal-hop tipping its load into a boat's hold. Aware, suddenly, of the time he had taken he called out, "Cripes!" once again, burst out laughing at his own failure, and set off at some pace across the market.

In the event, morning mass was not yet over by the time he reached the church. He waited in the porch. He could hear the whisper of voices through the door. He looked up into the bright spring sky. It was completely clear, at this point devoid of smoke, just blue and seagulls and the cool and whisper of the porch.

Shortly after he arrived Father Bond emerged. He immediately laid his hand on Martin's shoulder and told him to walk. His touch was light and not at all imposing, as if he needed guidance rather than support, yet somehow he effectively led the way. He directed Martin down Rope Street, along twisted lines of cottages and recessed courtyards, then through finger width alleys. On every other step his body seemed to give way, only to rise again on the next step, so that he rolled forward, yet his weight never bore down on Martin, only his touch. He made no conversation, but at various times grimaced, grinned and mumbled, as if conducting elaborate conversations in his own mind.

Eventually they came to a quarter of the town entirely unknown to Martin. They approached a number of large lemon and white buildings with steps and pleated columns, connected by a series of archways. They went through one of the archways into a cobbled courtyard. The courtyard was dingy and bare, quite unlike the facade. In a dull yellow brick building at the rear of the courtyard the police had their headquarters and their cells. The priest was expected.

They were led into a whitewashed cellar corridor lit by daylight through high metal latticed grills, and admitted into a cell. It was a dull little chamber. The walls were also whitewashed and rough, with light filtering through a ceiling and a high wall grill, insufficient to fully illuminate the space. The air was cool and moist. Gavin Duffy sat on a bench against the wall. His head was bowed into his hands. Only the crown of his dull sandy hair was visible. He was into the sixth day of his hunger strike. He made no acknowledgement that he was aware anyone had entered. Father Bond picked up a short three legged stool and placed it directly in front of Gavin. When he sat down he leaned his head into his own hands and began to murmur softly, a prayer. There was a hint of visible breath. Martin backed into a corner and forced himself tightly into it, his spine stretched straight, wanting to escape.

The priest concluded the prayer and signed the cross. There was a period of silence. Both men remained entirely still. Father Bond spoke first. His mouth was dry and his tongue stuck to his palate. His speech was slow and quiet: "You know that it is a sin to take your own life?" Gavin didn't respond. Father Bond repeated himself with rather more force. "You know that it is a sin to take your own life." Again Gavin didn't respond. Father Bond repeated himself impatiently and with noticeably increasing heat: "You know that it is a sin to take your own life."

Gavin looked up. He appeared drawn and washed-out, but uncowed. He quietly, but firmly announced: "I have no need of salvation, Father."

"How is it?"

A brief smile crossed Gavin's lips. "They've stripped me, beat me, humiliated me and kept me awake. If I fall asleep they bang on the doors, shout at me, prod me, laugh at me. They want me to go mad. That's how it is."

"Well, don't give them cause. Give it up!"

"Go to hell!" Gavin snapped, but at the same time smiled again. "I can suffer. I can suffer them. They can't take that."

"Don't be so presumptive," Father Bond retorted. He was patently angered and incensed by Gavin's suggestion. "Christ suffered the agony of crucifixion that you might be free from sin, don't dare take that accolade onto your own feeble shoulders. How dare you!"

Gavin eyed him coldly. "Leave me alone, Father. I don't need you here. I don't want you here."

Father Bond stood up quickly. For a moment he wavered as if he couldn't keep his balance. Martin rushed to his side. He felt certain that he would be blamed for the old priest's unsteadiness. For the first time he felt the weight of his touch bear down on him. As the priest steadied himself against Martin he declared: "I'll be back tomorrow."

"I have no power to stop you," Gavin replied, "but I want you to know that if I could I would. I don't want you here."

"You'll see me tomorrow!"

Back in the courtyard Father Bond stood for some time, breathing deeply. His breaths were laboured and noisy. His weight bore down heavily on Martin as he did. Martin quailed under his touch. He was quite unnerved, fearful of the priest's ferocity and fragility, terrified that he would not be able to support him and that he might drop him to the ground. He wanted to run away, but there was no escape. He could only wait and hope. Eventually Father Bond instructed him to make his way to the Sisters of Charity. His touch was again light, leading the way, no longer bearing down.

Being a Franciscan his allegiance was to his mendicant order rather than to a bishop, his motto theirs, *To help the sick,* therefore each morning following mass he went to the hospice of the *Sisters of Charity* known as the *Home of the Little Sisters* where those with infectious diseases, incurables, and the dying were brought. Martin shuddered at the request. He knew that Patrick had recently been taken there.

Martin breathed sharply in the bare dusky porch, strange aromas filling his nostrils, alcohol, gangrene, wound fungus, vomit and excrement. He felt sick. He held himself rigid and fought against it, terrified of committing such an indiscretion in that place. Father Bond led them into the hostel. The walls were whitewashed but, in the unnatural twilight that always existed in the room, looked grey. They were adorned with crucifix and Madonna. Along the walls were placed rows of closely placed beds. There were up to twenty in all. The nuns moved between the beds in long, stiffened, white robes, the sheer disks of their faces revealed beneath headgear which at first bandaged the head and then folded out into great exaggerated curves like swans wings. Their expressions were stark and severe. However, to Father Bond they showed obeisance, bowing to him as he stepped along the line of beds. By each one he signed the cross, prayed, then leaned on the mattress and said a few words to the ill or dying man. As they moved along the beds Martin caught glimpses of the nuns' work. By one bed they washed away vomit and excrement from a half revealed naked body. At another they wiped fungus from a wound. At another they bathed the red flesh above black stumps. He continued to struggle against the desire to be sick. In one bed a man hiccuped incessantly. The thought crossed Martin's mind that he was dying of it. For the first time in that place he smiled to himself. It eased the nausea in his guts.

By Patrick's bed, perhaps out of courtesy to Martin, perhaps in awareness of the proximity of death, Father Bond knelt and prayed. Martin immediately knelt beside him, but didn't pray. He stared at Patrick who lay unresponsive against his pillow. His flesh was pallid and moist, his expression fixed and distant. At first Martin thought Patrick hadn't recognised him but then, whilst Father Bond prayed, he leaned forward, stroked Martin's face and hair, then smiled grimly. He spoke with a guttural, strained voice. He said: "You're like a young angel, our Martin, leading the Father in here. Have you brought me a drink?" Martin shook his head. "Next time bring me a drink." Father Bond eyed Martin and shook his head. A nun joined them and knelt opposite, presumably assuming the end was near.

Such was the devotion demanded by the order that they were not supposed to leave the sick in order to eat, but only ever to pray. The sister had splashed broth onto her stiff white apron. "Sister," Father Bond said when he raised his head, "you have prayers down your front."

"Thank you, Father," she said with dignity, and immediately excused herself.

Patrick began to cough. Spots of blood splashed onto the white sheets.

For seven mornings Martin supported Father Bond on his round of cell and hospice. In the cell he leaned against the corner and tried to make himself as discreet as possible. The ferocity of the two men towards each other scared him. It was something new to him, and not something he could easily understood in men of their age.

Each day Father Bond began with a new question. On the second day he asked: "Who is your witness?" As on the first day Gavin cradled his face in his hands and made no response. It irritated the priest. He repeated it, demanding an answer. "I asked: Who is your witness?" Gavin looked up. He rubbed his face in his two palms and the colour rose in his sandy cheeks. Nevertheless, he looked more drawn and tired than he had the previous day. The priest tried again. "Who is your witness?"

"At the moment, Father, you."

"No, man, I am not your witness. The Lord your God is your witness.

"Then I will die for my God."

"You will die in his presence," Father Bond retorted, "but not for him."

"Then God is not my witness."

Undeterred the priest went on, his voice trembling, angered. "Well, who do you think is your witness?"

Gavin leaned forward. He considered for a moment and then spoke up, quietly yet harshly, with an obvious edge of disgust: "You ask me, in that voice, who is my witness? I'll tell you, his uncle for one!" Gavin pointed at Martin. Martin hugged the corner more tightly.

Father Bond turned briefly to Martin. "His uncle was a holy man."

"His uncle is dead!"

Father Bond closed his eyes and breathed deeply and deliberately. Gavin lay back against the wall.

Martin felt scared and confused. He had been brought, unwillingly, into this confrontation, but he didn't understand why. What did his uncle have to do with this? He knew about his uncle. His mother spoke about him often. But he was a soldier. Now he was a holy man. She had never said that. What did they mean? Why bring a dead man into it?

Father Bond whispered: "I will pray for you."

"Fuck you!" Gavin responded, without lowering his eyes.

Father Bond said his prayer, then signalled for Martin, and together they left for the *Little Sisters*.

"Did you bring me a drink?" Patrick demanded. Martin shook his head. "Not even a sip. Not a taste. Christ, have some mercy, will you." He sat up off the pillow and crawled across the sheet as if possessed. Eventually he leaned his palms on Martin's shoulders. His mouth opened. He tried to speak, but his words failed. His lips were cracked, his throat raw and his breath rotten. He tried to speak again. Specks of fluid splashed against Martin's chest. Eventually he said: "Please, Martin, a drink." A nun came and pressed him back to his pillow. Martin grinned. He looked the nun in the eye and wondered if she might think he had prayers down his front.

On the third day Father Bond sat for a while on his stool before speaking, weighing his half-dead hand in the palm of the other. Gavin sat in silence. He looked in need of sleep. Eventually the priest spoke. He too was in need of sleep. He spoke wearily, quizzically. "What do you trust in, Gavin?"

"Nothing."

"How can you not trust in something?"

"I am never disappointed, Father. Other things but not that. Angry, hateful, but never the other."

"Do you not think God will be disappointed in you, Gavin?"

Gavin laughed quietly. The sound had an empty ring. "Do you think I care?"

"I do."

"What damned right have you to come here and presume so much?" Gavin snapped out, summonsing the energy from somewhere within him. "What do you get out of coming here each day to punish me with your holy muck? I don't ask for it. I don't want it. I don't want you. Do you understand? Do you?" His voice trailed away.

Martin shuddered and pressed himself tightly against the corner, scared that he would again be drawn into this battle. And yet, at the same time he felt drawn towards Gavin, drawn towards his rage. He felt something thrill inside him as Gavin's voice broke out, and something subside as his voice faded.

"Are you not afraid, Gavin?" the priest asked, unperturbed by Gavin's outburst, and still inclined to coax something out of him.

Gavin didn't respond. He had been emptied by his outburst. He felt weak and uncertain. He stared ahead for some time. Eventually, he did manage to speak, but his voice was hushed and cowed: "I'm afraid every time that door opens and afraid every time it closes. I'm afraid of the night and I'm afraid of the day. And each day I'm more afraid than the day before. Each day I shake more. I cry for no reason. That is lack of food, I suppose." He paused. "I'm afraid of going mad." He paused again and seemed to be lost in thought, as if searching for ideas and words. When he continued his sentences were fractured. "I will carry on, though. I will. Take it wherever it's going. Fight on against Fascism, anyway, anyway at all. Can't succumb to Fascist justice." He stopped speaking. He looked directly at the priest, then smiled suddenly, as if out of recognition, even warmth. He seemed satisfied by himself.

"Are you drinking, Gavin?"

"Yes, I'm drinking."

"That is something at least."

Father Bond began to pray.

Gavin grimaced then grinned, then slowly shook his head.

Patrick perched on the edge of his mattress, his head bowed, running his fingers slowly along the canvas of his gown, carefully tracing the patterns of ingrained stains, a look of wonder and bewilderment on his face. Martin waited at the foot of the bed without speaking. He had never seen that look before; it made him think of Duffy in his cell. He was moved by a terrible pity for both of them, but most particularly Duffy because Duffy was alone. He spoke Patrick's name softly. Patrick looked up. The wonder immediately vanished and was replaced by a look of stupid greed. "A drink?" he asked, insisting on it. "A drink, Martin?" Martin shook his head. Patrick gave a sober vexed smile and looked away.

"Are you alone in this, Gavin?" Father Bond demanded on the fourth day.

"Christ, man," Gavin retorted, "do you mean, do I believe in God? Will you never give up?"

"I mean," Father Bond responded tartly, "is there a company of you? Is this your doing or have you been put up to it?"

"Put up to it, Father?"

"Yes, put up to it. Is your organisation behind it all?"

"My organisation?"

"Don't be so tardy, man. It's a simple enough question."

"All right, then, no, my organisation, as you call it, has not put me up to it."

"So, you are abandoning this world of your own free-will?"

"I'm not abandoning this world."

"Have you started to eat?"

"No."

"Then I repeat, you are abandoning this world of your own free-will."

"Look, I don't believe in any other world than this one." He paused and eyed the priest closely for a moment. As he did there was a noticeable relaxation of his expression. The suspicion and alertness reduced. He looked as if he had come to a decision that he was willing to concede something to this man who came to him every day, willing to own up to what was on his mind, willing to speak. His speech came in even measures. "All the labours a man could have, could hope to have, are here. I might be alone here, here in this cell, but I'm not alone altogether. I never did believe in that maxim. I thought it let us down. Ourselves alone. I'm never alone. I'm on the side of life. That's what I have been put up to. It will only be when everyone is set free, not just the Irish, but the Negroes, the Jews, the Indians, Chinese, everyone, that one person can be set free. That's the magnitude of the struggle. That's its greatness. When everyone comes together in one human bond then we'll all be set free. I don't mind being put up to that. Even to die here, alone, would be to be on the side of life. They can't take that away from me."

"It isn't the Catholic church which says you are alone," Father Bond responded with feeling, perhaps sensing some way to Duffy. "It's not the Catholic church which says a man must find his own route to God, discover his own salvation, interpret God to himself. The Catholic church has defined the way. The Catholic church isn't about the one, but the whole. Can you abandon that? Can you dare abandon that?"

"The *Quadragesimo Anno* states: *The political configuration of the people or the state is irrelevant as long as God is supreme...* The Fascists will have God, so Pope Pius will have the Fascists. So, Father, will the church stand up for me in court? Will it be with me when the police attack Communist Party members? Will it fight Fascist justice? Will it resist the beatings, imprisonment and murders of Communists and Trade Unionists? Will it fight, Father? Will the priests and pontiffs fight, Father? Do we have God on our side?"

"Yes, God is on your side."

Gavin smiled ruefully. "I pity you, Father."

"I will pray for you Gavin. What will you do for me?"

Gavin smiled again, but said nothing.

Patrick paced up and down the aisle between the beds flailing his arms from side to side. When he reached the corridor's limit he wheeled around and continued in the same manner. The Little Sisters informed Father Bond that he had gone on much like that for the greater part of the morning. Father Bond went to him. Both men held their place in the aisle. Patrick's arms swung at his side. The priest spoke up. He was commanding and insistent. "You must be obedient here, Patrick! Obedient. Do you understand?"

"Why?"

"Because you have need of obedience."

"The Sisters are obedient," Patrick replied, his voice flat and devoid of any obvious emotion.

"Of course the Sisters are obedient. Follow their example. Do as they do. Trust in them."

"Have you brought me a drink, Martin?"

"Of course he has not brought you a drink."

"Have you no sympathy for me?'

"Of course he has sympathy for you. That's why he will not be bringing you a drink."

"I'll die here without a drink."

Father Bond's voice failed him for a moment. He looked Patrick squarely in the face. His frustration was evident in his expression, his face puffed up and flushed. When he did finally rediscover his voice it burst out in strong, clear tones. "The water here is clean, refreshing and wholesome. Do you hear me, clean refreshing and wholesome. You will drink that."

Patrick smiled as if grateful. He said: "I want to be obedient, Father. I try to be obedient." He walked back to his own bed and lay down.

The next day Father Bond was impatient. He bustled into Gavin's cell and started speaking before he was seated. "Do you really mean to die, Duffy, or is this a game of sorts?"

"I'm willing to die," Gavin replied without hesitation. "I might even expect to die." As he responded he looked directly at the priest, obviously anticipating and prepared for the encounter.

"This is a perversity in you Gavin," the priest continued, still not sitting, "a terrible perversity."

"What would you have me do?"

348

"Give it up, for Christ sake, man. Give it up. This isn't the place for this."

"How would I fight them?"

"With the law, in the courts, through the legal system."

"Don't be such a fool."

"This is an old Irish game you're playing here Duffy. We both know that." His lame body swayed as he spoke. Martin feared he would fall at any moment. "You can't play it here. I know you want to fashion yourself another Thomas Ashe or Terence MacSwiney, and I know Connolly did it, but this isn't the right place or the right time. They're laughing at you, man. You're in their country. Can't you see that? You're making a fool of yourself with it. It means nothing to them. You're a laughing-stock. Do you hear me?"

"We'll just have to see! Like they say: Irish history exists as a witness in the Irish man's favour. Besides, didn't St Patrick himself hunger strike against God on the Holy Mount."

"Don't be ridiculous! Come on, Duffy, this isn't the country. Give it up. Tell them it was all a game. Tell them that you've chosen to end it."

"I'm not free to choose anything!"

"You're a sad old man, Duffy, just a sad old man. Do you really think you're going to achieve anything with this?"

"Get out!"

Father Bond shook his head. He held up his hands as if in frustration, but then let them remain and spoke his customary prayer then, when the prayer was concluded, he signed the cross. As he uttered his prayer Gavin lay down and closed his eyes. He made no response.

Patrick didn't demand a drink. He couldn't speak. He was vomiting blood. A froth of red bubbles spilled across his pillow and down his gown. He gazed at Martin. His expression was inviting and affectionate, and strangely adamant. One of the Little Sisters rushed Martin away. He resolved in his own mind to bring Patrick a drink.

On the sixth day Father Bond and Gavin seemed surprisingly relaxed together. The visit proved brief and easy. It was as if they both needed to redress something. The priest began with his customary question, but there was no force to it. "You know that this is a blasphemy, don't you?"

"Oh, the damage is done."

"No, the damage is never altogether done. There is always forgiveness, even after terrible wrong, there is always forgiveness. One may have to experience fire, self-loathing, the fall, but after that there is grace, the state of grace is there for you, as it is there for all of us."

"I didn't mean by me, Father," Gavin said, his tone vaguely apologetic. As he spoke he looked more tired than ever. His face was waxy and masklike. His eyes were lost in their sockets and brooded from their depth. As Martin looked at Gavin's worn and exhausted features he told himself that it surely couldn't be a crime to take a small shot of his father's bottle for Patrick. As was Gavin's need for rest, so was Patrick's need for a drink. His father would have understood that. His father would know it was the right thing. He fingered the small bottle in his pocket. He felt a definite sense of satisfaction as he did.

Whilst Martin fingered the bottle in his pocket Father Bond petitioned Gavin: "Don't blaspheme yourself, Gavin. It isn't worth it. The price is too great. The loss is too much."

"I will not blaspheme life by giving up the fight, Father. That price is good enough for me. I don't lose by that."

"We all need redemption, Gavin, all of us. I'll pray for yours."

Gavin smiled. It was a curtailed, half-hearted gesture, yet not without warmth. He said: "I believe that everything ends, Father, that it all comes to nothing. Forever and ever, nothing at all, absolutely nothing. And that makes me happy. Really, it does. It gives me hope. It makes me want to create things, and do things, to make things happen, to achieve things. It makes me a faithful man, Father. Do you understand that? I am a man of faith, a man of unshakeable, total faith. You can't touch that." He stopped speaking and continued to gaze at the old priest for a moment, as if he had more to say and was still formulating the words. But in the end he shook his head, lay down and turned away. Father Bond said his prayer. They said no more.

Martin slipped the small bottle of whisky under Patrick's pillow. Patrick accepted it without surprise or gratitude. He simply fished for it with his hand and immediately began to drink. He filled his mouth. A few drops trickled across his dry, cracked lips, across his stubbled chin then down onto his gown. He groaned appreciatively as the liquid passed down his throat. He lay back and stared fixedly towards the ceiling. His expression was peaceful. "Patrick," Martin said quietly, "you have prayers down your front." Patrick didn't smile. Martin left him to his reverie.

"Have you ever loved Christ, Gavin?" Father Bond asked on the seventh day.

"Though you speak with the tongues of men and angels your voice is a sounding brass," Gavin whispered ponderously. His voice was thick and dry making his words sticky.

"Gavin, you're not well. Your breath stinks, man. Your eyes look as if they're bleeding. Give it up."

"To hell with it. They can't keep me awake any more. I can sleep with my eyes wide open. I can sleep on my feet. I'm through the worst. Don't worry about me. I can fight them now. I'm all right."

"You're not, Gavin. You look terrible man. Can you not see yourself? Do you feel weak?"

"I don't feel anything. I don't need to feel anything. Not now. I'm ready now."

"It's not good. Give it up."

"It's too late."

"Have I lacked charity, Gavin?"

"I don't know what you're talking about."

"Towards you."

"Is this about you, then?"

"No, Gavin, don't accuse me. I don't ask for my sake. I want you to end. I implore you to give it up. In the name of Our Lord, Jesus Christ, give it up. There's no need for this. You've done enough. You've done more than enough. You don't have to see it through any further."

"I've done nothing, Father. I've just been kept awake so far. I don't count that too much."

"I do, Gavin. I want you to know that."

Gavin eyed the priest for a moment or two. He was moved to feel affection for him though he desired to loathe him. He wanted to hold on to his reason, and his reason told him to deny the other. He had to be astringent. The effort was too great, though. He was too tired. He couldn't help but respond to the affection of the old man. "Of course, I loved Christ once, Father. We are brought up to it, aren't we. We can't help ourselves. I loved the stupid story, loved it like an idiot." He paused for a moment. He attempted to smile, but it never quite formed. His lips were too dry. He went on. "Then I learnt to love his doubt all for myself. I can't deny that. I loved him for his doubt. Believe it or not, I suppose I still do."

"Our Lord had no doubts, son."

"Ah, but you are wrong there, Father, very wrong."

"It is time to pray."

Gavin lay down and stared at the ceiling, refusing to hear the words of the prayer. He felt calm and resigned. In his own mind he really believed he was through the worst, and there was nothing more they could do to him.

That morning they discovered that Patrick had gone missing from the hospice. Somehow he had escaped in the night. He was not expected to be missing for long as he had no clothes except for the gown the Little Sisters dressed him in. Martin was sent around the houses of Mount Pleasant and Ginns to see if he had found shelter in a loft or shed. He was nowhere to be seen. John and Hugh organised a number of search parties to look for him.

During the course of that day Gavin was quietly released. His health had suddenly deteriorated, declining faster than had been expected. He had begun to hallucinate. The authorities deemed it better he die elsewhere than in custody. He was delivered to Peter who, rather than return him to his own cellar, brought him to Kate. Kate spoon fed him. At first Peter thought to stop her, but in the end said nothing. The protest was over.

The hunt for Patrick went on all day without success. It was Bill who went to the graveyard after dark. It was a still, moonlit night. The little wooden crosses and slabs of stone were pearly. Patrick was clearly visible, lying on his mother's grave. When Bill came up to him he found that his expression was entirely carefree. He lay down beside him and hugged him, then kissed his stone-cold grey flesh.

Chapter Eight

During 1935 some magical and some unmagical events occurred. The last of the working mines closed. Any prospect of their reopening was not specified, not promised and, in reality, not believed in. Evictions were expected but when and from whom was not known. Ownership of the colliery houses had become a mystery. The barricades were prepared. John Devlin nailed his window sashes and cut boards that could be nailed to the inner frames.

In contrast, the opening of the Market Square cinema was an event of perpetual magic. Not that the *silver screen* was immediately available to the Glyn children. Kate said she clearly remembered seeing a film in a basement in the market before the war. Mathieson Lang played *The Wandering Jew*. She quoted from it: *It is ever in his hour of need that man calls upon the God he has denied.* Whether it was *The Wandering Jew* or Mathieson Lang himself which so affected her, no one could say, but Kate bore a stubborn prejudice against the movies. There had always been one or more cinemas on the other side of town, but it had been easy for her to object to them as being distant and expensive. The fact that the majority of people on Ginns and Mount Pleasant had been watching the movies since the days of the Mack Sennett bathing beauty brigade cut no ice with her. John had once tried to persuade her to see Rudolph Valentino in *The Four Horsemen of the Apocalypse* on the pretext that with such a title it had to be worthwhile, but to no avail. The magic of the movies had been disallowed.

With the opening of the Market Square cinema her complaints made no sense whatsoever. Nevertheless, she adamantly forbade any member of her family to attend. She was comic in her refusal to even discuss the subject, and the more comic she became the more determined she became. The cinema question was not resolved until John went from Ginns to Mount Pleasant and personally took the children to the Market Place. Still Kate marched down from Ginns, wearing an outsized bonnet, which she never did, and ordered them home. John stepped out of the queue, took her by the hand, and forced her inside. On pain of being humiliated she stayed. After that, as if to prove the corruptive force of the *pictures* she and John went every week.

Pictures were a spell that cast their strange powers over all who watched. They turned unsuspecting innocents into heroes. No one left the Market Place basement in the same frame of mind as the one they went in with. For the rest of his life Martin Glyn was a cowboy without ever really understanding why. By the time most films reached the Market Square they were already a couple of years old. It regularly showed old silent films, particularly on Sundays when part of the takings had to be forfeited to charities. Pretty soon Kate had caught up with the recent history of the motion picture. Names like Harry Lloyd, Douglas Fairbanks, Freddie Bartholomew, Jean Harlow, Charlie Chaplin and Leslie Howard became part of her life. The experience was dazzling, spiritual and amazing. For two, sometimes three, times a week she gazed with curiosity into unimaginable other worlds. "It is not really fair to Robert to come here and see all this," Kate whispered through the shifting grey light, and the purring of the projector during a screening of *Cleopatra*, "but he did call on God in the end." John didn't listen but sank in his seat, eyed the slave girls dancing around the burnished barge and dreamed of Araby.

The year was to bring an event of magic far greater than even the *pictures* had been. After twenty years or more absence *Lord Singer's Circus* returned. Like Noah himself, though, squat, wizened, and ancient, Lord Singer led the animals two by two into the valley. For Kate the appearance of the circus was a cause of pain. Unlike the cinema, where the connection with Robert was a personal matter, peculiar to Kate's way of thinking, the circus inevitably brought him to mind. She had strictly forbidden anyone attending the last time it came to town. It would only be sanctioned when Robert came home. Funnily enough, she made no complaints. Though she never told anyone, she felt that Robert was close to her, closer than he had been for a very long time. Perhaps the doubts and uncertainties which surrounded her made it inevitable that she should feel the need for him, and for the conversations they shared.

She went up to the plateau above the coastal cliffs where she once picked flowers with Anne. A web of small blue and yellow flowers carpeted the floor as far as the eye could see. There was perfume in the air. She could see the circus stalls in the valley below her. She whispered to Robert and Anne that the circus was back. She knelt down and prayed. She felt his presence pass through her. It was cold then warm. She felt it along her spine. He was with her. He was always with her. Her sense of foreboding at what lay ahead diminished.

The circus became a carnival. The town was invaded. Fairs came in. A bazaar of fortune-tellers, freaks and curiosities set up along the Strand. Madame O'Leary read the cards saying she could *peery into the future and the other world. Biddles Ghost Show* exhibited the other world, pale phantoms and mobile skeletons stalking the corridors and tunnels of its nightmare, the whole place ringing to the sound of screaming. Horses were bought and sold beneath the idle coal hurries where farmers came to trade and hire hands. The smell of toffee and nougat drifted over the dock basins replacing lime, coal-dust and fish. Braziers spat with black-pudding, white-pudding and sweetbreads. The smell of smoke and ash charged the air.

John Devlin walked onto the Strand in the company of Marty, nine children (Francis remained with Dora) and four elephants. The children ran close to the elephants feet, watching the slow drums pad softly on the cobbles. They were escorted by clowns and ridden by kings regaled in turbans and shimmering embroidered gowns. The elephants bore great ornamental caps on their crowns beneath which their vast ears hung limp between bells. Their trunks were painted with fantastic florid designs. John stopped and watched them move down the Strand. Ahead of him, by the first capstan, Gavin, Peter and McClean were talking. The subject would be evictions. John didn't want to face it. He didn't want to face them. He was in no mood for their astringent pronouncements. Besides, he didn't want to contemplate defeat. The town was too strange, too magical, too wonderfully exotic, a place for Gypsies, Jews and Turks, to consider its downside. He turned on his heels. The children had gone with the animals. Marty was with them. They were safe.

He walked along the bazaar taking it all in. As well as *Madame O'Leary,* and *Biddle's Ghost Show,* there was also a tent for *The Bearded Lady,* and another for *The Most Beautiful Woman In The World* and there was also a *Cinematograph.* The *cinematograph* offered the experience of flight, not the fictional world of the *pictures* but simulation. John wondered what Kate would have made of that and whether her strange prejudice would extend to such fantasy. He had half a mind to go in, but knew he could not justify paying the price. Instead he bought a bag of nougat and put it in his pocket for her.

He had no idea where she was. He assumed she didn't approve of the circus, though she had never said. He hadn't bothered to ask. He was convinced he knew the answer anyway. She hadn't been at home when he left, but he was pretty certain she wasn't on the Strand. She had probably taken herself off somewhere remote and quiet to avoid all the fuss. Her uncharacteristic objections to things troubled him. At first it was McClean's bus, then the cinema and now the circus. He half-feared she was losing her mind. It wouldn't be entirely surprising. They were assailed by uncertainties. They might be homeless at any moment. They had come all this way and were no better off than when they started. They were living hand to mouth. Everything was crazy. And it was all out of his control. They would be beaten and he was not in any position to act. He had been clipped and reduced to nothing. He didn't understand how it had happened to him. When had he become so obsolete? Is that what Kate really objected to, the fact that he was so ineffectual? It hadn't been like that before. Once when there had been trouble he would have acted. Murphy was the evidence of that, for Christ sake.

He suddenly stopped his own train of thought. He scolded himself for such thinking. He had to go on. They had to defend themselves. Murphy was the proof. He was the same man. He was still capable of such necessary acts. He knew he should have joined Gavin, Peter and McClean. He turned round. He could no longer see them. He was outside the booth of *The Most Beautiful Woman In The World*. He was curious and peered in. It was dusky beneath the tent canopy. There was only the slightest shimmer of pale light coming from deep inside. He made to go in, but as he did felt a hand press firmly against his thigh. He turned to find that he was being obstructed by a dwarf. He was broad and muscular, and returned John's gaze steadily, his expression amused and disdainful. He held out his open palm awaiting payment.

"I don't believe it," John said.

The dwarf burst out laughing: "Try the bearded lady, grandpa."

"I said, I don't believe it."

"Pay the admission fee and it will all be revealed to you, the most beautiful woman in the world."

"I can't afford it."

"Then you'll never know."

"I don't want to know."

"Then you've lost nothing, grandpa."

"No, I've lost nothing."

356

The dwarf turned away and began touting for trade: "Roll up, roll up. Come and witness the vision of a lifetime. The most beautiful woman in the world. Pay your money and be amazed. You've never seen anything like it. Don't miss the most beautiful woman in the world."

John repeated: "I don't believe it." The dwarf cocked an eye towards him and smirked, but simply carried on calling out his offer of a lifetime. John hesitantly took his leave, the calls of the dwarf ringing in his ears.

He made his way towards the capstan where he had seen Gavin, Peter and McClean talking. He told himself that he had to face them. It was unavoidable. If he didn't he would go mad. As he pushed his way through the crowd he saw that they were still there. He wondered how Gavin would be. He was supposedly cured of his short stay in prison, but there was no doubt the experience had left him scarred. At times his brooding predictions got the better of him and he tipped into raving. When the mood took him he ranted for hours about Fascist justice and threw down challenges to all and sundry to stand with him, whilst at the same time denouncing everyone as cowards and scabs.

It transpired that he was in a particularly morose mood. He scarcely acknowledged John as he joined them and took up his place alongside them. His attention was absorbed by the procession, which had become so congested that it had completely stalled. A dancing monkey was directly in front of them, decked in a small red suit and matching pillbox hat. It danced on a platform to the sound of a hurdy-gurdy. The music was virtually drowned out in the general clamour of the crowd.

McClean seemed bored, unimpressed by either the conversation or the circus. He was simply too listless to move on and leave it behind. He looked beyond the monkey to the open sea. Its antics had brought to mind the old emigrant parties. Over the years his business had changed. Sea items no longer sold. He more or less kept his stocks out of loyalty to the past. He didn't understand the change, but didn't worry about it. Tickets abroad were selling better than ever. The end of month Friday night parties, though, had become torch processions to the quay. Emigrants no longer found it permissible to dance.

John also looked out to sea. He saw fishing smacks, little ships, small and indistinct on the mauve horizon, sailing over the edge of the earth. He was drawn to them, but knew he had to dismiss them. For him the emigrant's journey had been made. Any further journeys were simply out of the question. Kate would never contemplate such a thing. He had already traded one country, another was too much. No, they had to stand still and close ranks. He turned to Peter. Having avoided the subject he found that he was the one needing to take the plunge. He asked. "How goes it?"

"What do you think?" Peter replied, his tone dispirited and sharp.

"It's a grand old show."

"Can you afford anything?"

"Not much." Peter skewed his face, but John refused to be browbeaten. He went on: "I've got a bag of nougat."

"Bully for you."

Gavin cut in: "Did you see the precious birds, Devlin?"

"No, I didn't see any birds."

"They were quite a sight, special altogether, the colour of the sea in winter."

"No, I missed them."

"And you didn't hear them, didn't hear their bugles? You never heard screeching like it."

"No, I missed it."

Gavin turned to him. His expression broke into a smile. It was sudden and brief. It passed as quickly as it came. "Never mind," he said in a blank monotone. "The Anson Estates have birds, birds of all kinds. Weird and wonderful, fiery birds, all the colours of the rainbows. Just the symbol for a man who owned a mine and closed it down. You might see them. If you're lucky, that is. Are you lucky? I can't remember." Having said that he laughed as he had smiled, abruptly and curtailed, then turned back to the procession.

The traffic had moved on, but was once again stalled. The monkey was now some way along the Strand. There was now a metal barred cage in view, in which a lone tiger was circling the confined space. It wasn't a large animal, possibly only half-grown, but was nevertheless striking. It was sleek and fit, its rib-cage protruding through its gleaming coat. Its circling was ponderous and obsessive, its behaviour apparently still wild. Gavin went up to it and peered in for a while, and then he began moving with it, taking steps along the bars and swinging his torso in time to the wheels of the animal. In response its movements became more erratic. It halted and pawed at the ground, then made sudden leaps and circles. It also began to make sounds, a low murmur seeming to emanate from its guts. Gavin answered it with shouts and jeers, seemingly taunting and tempting it.

The exhibition concerned John. He had heard reports that Gavin's behaviour at times was stranger than just his usual moods. Peter told him that he had been with him on a number of occasions when he saw things and heard things that weren't there. He also knew that he had been taken in a number of times by Father Bond when he had been found wandering and shouting in the streets. He had never actually witnessed such things himself. He thought this incident with the tiger might be one of those. Besides, he thought Gavin's behaviour smacked of pointless cruelty. He looked to Peter to intervene. He knew he was regularly with Gavin and assumed he would understand him. Peter simply refused to acknowledge John's unspoken promptings. John didn't press it. He could tell from the way Peter steadfastly gazed ahead that he felt powerless and incapable. He couldn't force that. He decided there was nothing for it but to take it on himself. He didn't like seeing Gavin so disturbed. Their involvement with each other went back a long way. Murphy joined them. However, just as he had determined to remove Gavin the drivers became involved.

Gavin's persistent shouts had finally alerted them to the fact that he was screaming at their animal. At first they contented themselves with shouting abuse at him. After all, it wasn't an unusual occurrence for people to torment the animals. Gavin seemed to relish their attack. They traded insults. Finally they threatened him. Gavin shrieked with laughter. Certainly one of the drivers was preparing to jump down when the procession again began to roll forward. Gavin shrieked again, but allowed the cage to move on without following. The driver let it pass.

As he returned to the capstan McClean whispered to John: "Duffy isn't mad, he just wishes he was." He walked off into the crowd before Gavin returned, the possibility of abuse from Gavin obviously too much to risk.

John waited. He kept his attention pinned on Gavin, looking for an explanation. Gavin looked ahead as if he were still interested in the slow progress of the procession. His expression kept altering, though, one moment appearing grieved, at another incensed, then appalled. His mind was obviously active and he seemed disapproving of his own actions. Eventually he smiled, but the gesture seemed hopeless and empty. At the same time he turned to Peter. He seemed to be appealing to him for some kind of support, but Peter had nothing to offer. Peter continued to gaze mindlessly at the passing exhibition. John could not question that. He didn't know what Peter endured on Gavin's behalf. Gavin turned to John and spoke up: "It seems I'm going a bit mad, Devlin."

"I think we all are, Gavin. It's not surprising is it."

"No, I suppose not. Good of you to see it like that."

"We see things as they are."

"I've had enough of these damned animals. Better off than us. Well fed, healthy and a decent prison in which to dream of the wild. That's a nice thought, isn't it."

John looked along the Strand. The parade stretched right along it making its sluggish, fitful progress. He had had enough of it too. He had had enough of dancing monkeys, restless tigers and piglike elephants. It was all misplaced. This wasn't the time for entertainment, frivolity, or indulgence. It was the time to take sides and signal acknowledgements. He turned to Gavin and placed his hand firmly on his shoulder. "We've all had enough, Gavin. Remember that. Don't exclude anyone. We're all involved. We always have been. Don't forget it. We go back together all the way. All right? Keep in touch."

The two men looked at each other for a few moments. Their expressions were firm, for a time almost serene, devoid completely of enmity. Gavin nodded his assent. "I don't ever forget Devlin. I'll never forget."

John's hand rested for a while longer on Gavin's shoulder then, without further comment, he marched away. As he abandoned the Strand and the bazaar a strange muffled cacophony of laughter and ululation gathered behind him. Its blended fragments tormented him. It defined a life denied him. It underlined what having no money meant. And in the animal roar, be it the bugle of elephant or the primeval screech of parakeet, there was the suggestion of the torment that having no home would mean. It was the worst of all states. It was a state worse than death. In his imagination John Devlin considered himself a beaten man, but in reality he didn't know how to express or represent that. He knew he would just keep on until there was no where left to turn. He didn't know anything different.

He had no clear purpose of what he intended to do when he returned to the house on Ginns. He had an overwhelming desire to see Kate. He wanted to say to her that for him she was the most beautiful woman in the world. He felt a niggling concern that he had in someway been disloyal to her by even considering peeping at the one who had claimed the title for herself. He felt the need to make amends. He wanted to explain that he knew what being beautiful really meant, that it described something of the pleasure and completeness his dancing partner had brought to his life. Perhaps he would say just how much he loved her.

Of course, he would have said nothing of the sort. He would have been awkward and evasive, then irritable when she failed to recognise his need to communicate. Everything would remain tacit, yet understood, as always, an act of trust. As with their faith, as with their futures, as with their very survival, it was all unstated, accepted, simply believed in, not a matter of words but actions, and most actions circumscribed. By the time he reached Ginns it was enough for him to concede that he desired to be with her. To express it would have been too much. It would have taken the heart out of him completely.

In the event Kate wasn't home. The boarded house with its musty air was mournful and oppressive without her. He was moved to tears and deeply shocked by that. He went out into the yard. He struggled with and derided himself. He wanted to be angry. He wanted to be angry and so eradicate the self-pity that was slowly consuming him. He wanted Kate. It was as these thoughts were turning over in his head that he became aware of the pig. He heard it nuzzling in the corner of its makeshift sty. He was immediately seized with the idea that he had to kill the pig.

Ever since John had brought that very first pig home in the presence of Julia, there had been a succession of pigs in the Devlin yard. They had all been given pet names, a Pinky, Curly, or Spotty, and they had all been Marty's bedfellows at some time. They were an essential part of the yearly routine. As once Dora named the animal now her children did. As she fed it so did they. They all shared in its care, and all shared in its profit. The animals were butchered at Advent and shared out among the whole family for Christmas. No one was ever openly sentimental. There was a tacit agreement that the pigs had a decent life but their function was practical. Of course, the killing took place with due regard for prayer and the praise for God that Advent demanded. It was unprecedented that John should want to kill the animal now. Indeed, he had never before killed the animal himself, but always paid a butcher, even if only with a portion of the kill.

He brought a carving knife and a steel from the kitchen and approached the sty. He was not exactly clear about the nature of the killing. He had some vague idea of pressing the steel across the pig's neck, then nicking its throat to make it bleed. There was some notion in the back of his mind that if the job were done properly then the pig had to bleed slowly. Try as he might he couldn't really work out what had been done over the years. As he came near, it continued to nuzzle about the sty, quite unconcerned by his interest. As he gazed at it nosing about it assumed in his mind the shape of a small deformed elephant, scrubbed naked and pink, its trunk sliced. He couldn't rid himself of that dreamlike transformation. Still, he determined to see it through. Deformed or not, he was going to butcher it.

He opened the sty gate and tiptoed towards the animal. It looked up and snorted. He didn't hesitate, but lunged at it. However, as he had the knife in one hand and the steel in the other he had no way of holding it. It skipped through his arms and bolted through the gate that he had inadvertently left open into the yard. He immediately chased after it and again lunged at it, but with the same result: it simply slipped through his arms. It ran along the fences of the chicken-run and the kitchen wall. He pursued it relentlessly, round and round the confined yet chaotic space, still with the knife and steel in his hands. It ran wilder as he ran. Its squeals began to torment him. He wanted it dead. He had determined on that course of action. It was infuriating that he couldn't see it through. He began slashing the knife through the air. At first he slashed in the direction of the pig as it ran madly around the yard. Then he slashed wildly all around him, no longer aware of where the pig actually was. He began to turn in a fit of fury, still slashing at the emptiness around him. And then, quite suddenly, he became still. He stood for a moment, then fell to his knees in the middle of the yard, quite breathless, beaten by both his effort and his failure. He slammed the steel and knife against the yard floor.

Dora found him. He was still kneeling, in the position of prayer, sobbing noiselessly, the knife blade and steel crossed before him like venerated objects, the pig nosing about him. She crouched down to him. She pressed her hands against his shoulders. She quietly asked: "What's wrong? What's happened? Tell me. Are you not well?" He couldn't answer. He kept on breathing deeply, his mouth and nostrils congested. She ran her hands along his back, feeling the depth of his breaths. She was fearful of his refusal to speak. He didn't seem ill, just out of breath. She tried again. "What have you been doing? What's been going on?" Still he didn't reply. She looked around and began to examine the scene. Slowly she pieced the details together bit by bit. As she did she began to laugh, the sound gentle and coaxing, yet reproving. She stroked his face with the palms of both hands. She said: "Surely you didn't try to kill the pig? Don't tell me that. For God's sake, it's still scrawny. There isn't a pick on it."

"Fat enough," he responded, through his laboured breaths.

"It is not and don't lie to yourself," she said with deliberate indignation, censuring him. "Besides, I take my pork at Christmas. I don't want you denying my children their Christmas treat. What the hell were you thinking about?"

He looked up at her, determined to face her, yet he felt bereft. He uttered: "We need the money. That's all there is to say."

"You don't kill an animal just like that.'

"It's only swine."

"But you've never killed it. You've never killed any of them, not a one of them. In all the years, not one. There's not a drop of blood on your hands of those poor little things. Christ, what on earth possessed you? Jesus, you've never killed a thing in your life."

He looked at her for a few seconds longer, then bowed his head. A moment later he pulled himself to his feet, walked to the kitchen door and threw the knife and steel indoors. He stood for a while leaning against the frame, needing the support it gave, his body drained by the strain of it all. After a while he turned back and faced her. He called to her. He spoke with great simplicity. "How am I going to keep this house?"

"Well, not by butchering a scrawny pig, that's for sure."

"It would help."

"How?"

"I'd sell it."

"Just once, then what?"

"I don't know."

"You don't know! God, leave the creature out of it. Its time will come soon enough." She stopped speaking and gazed at him intently. A vague, scarcely discernible smile passed her lips. She quietly said: "You don't need this house." She continued to gaze directly at him. He made no response. He didn't even acknowledge that she had suggested anything. She added: "Come to me. I want you to come to me."

There was a brief pause, then he burst out laughing. The sound was deliberate and harsh. "And what," he declared, "put your children on the street? Kick them out to let us in? Don't be so ridiculous."

"No, they'll stay."

He pulled himself from the wall and crossed the yard back to the sty. He looked inside. He felt foolish. He knew he had been rash, that he had let his torments get the better of him and he had achieved nothing. That was the worst. He had tried to take hold of matters but he had been found to be more than wanting. All he had left was his agitation. He turned back to Dora. He intended to make a speech about ownership. He wanted to say something about his yard, his work, his time, all the effort that went into making somewhere a home, but she was no longer looking at him. He turned to where she was looking. He discovered that Kate and Aunty Dora had returned. They were standing beyond the threshold of the kitchen door looking at him. They sensed that something had obviously happened, but they couldn't guess what.

He laughed out loud, the sound again forced and bitter, and called to them: "Dora reckons we don't need this house. What do you say, Kate, Dora? Do we not need this house?"

Dora spoke before he was through. "I want you to come to me. It will be simpler. That's all. It makes sense."

Kate didn't answer. She simply gazed steadily at John. She recognised the weight of his grief. It was terrible. Of course she knew its source. It was ancient for them. It was part of who they were. It explained why they were standing in that dismal yard. The phrase, I have no home anymore, haunted them. To give it up, to admit the need, was the worst circumstance imaginable. He was burning with it. She turned to Dora. "How will it be simpler?" she asked sharply.

"We would see it through, that's all, financially, I mean. I think we'd survive together, one rent, one set of bills, one kitty."

"Where?"

"Wherever you choose."

"The cellar?"

"There's no need for that."

Kate shrugged. She approached John and stood beside him. He was looking down into the empty sty. She said: "We would leave nothing behind. We would leave no one behind."

John didn't respond for some time. He continued to gaze down into the deserted enclosure, struggling with himself, struggling against the desire and need to cry and scream and protest. Eventually he called out: "We'll have to kill the pig anyway, you have no yard."

John Darcy's trolley brought John, Kate and Aunty Dora from Ginns to Mount Pleasant making successive trips from one to the other. John's indispensable yard treasures were saved. Kate guarded a diary that for explanation she called *The Psalms*. The pig was also saved, at least until Advent. John Darcy's witch mother agreed to keep it in her kitchen. People were afraid of pork that year.

The circus animals remained for two weeks. Their presence occupied the imagination of the whole town. The still of the night was textured by the primitive sounds of their shrieks and howls. When John lay down by the boiler in Dora's cellar he was certain he could hear the distant roar of wild animals and imagined all kinds of dangers assailing his subterranean dwelling. Consequently, his sleep in his new home was disturbed and fretful. Then, to cap it all, on the fourth night the tiger went missing. Its cage doors had been forced. Rumour had it that Gavin was responsible. He had, after all, been enthralled by it, and numerous people attested to the fact that they had seen him torment it. He was questioned by the police, but denied all knowledge. The town was gripped by panic. Over the next few days the animal was sighted everywhere. Terrible stories began to circulate about what it had done to innocent babies and frail old people. At night the streets were deserted. Even the soldiers who had been brought in to assist the police in the search for the animal refused to patrol after dark. However, it was in the middle of the night that Gavin Duffy, John Darcy, Peter Kavanagh and John Devlin, each wearing a balaclava, came to the cellar on Mount Pleasant having been to the Anson estates. They pulled John Darcy's trolley to the top of the steps and unloaded a cargo of sacks, each one stuffed with dead pheasants, and in one a single tail-less peacock, Gavin insisting they try the taste. The creatures hung in the half light to the sound of hurried, urgent whispers.

The next day the tiger was discovered on the south shore. It was a bay where the sea seemed to endlessly whisper and, due to a natural echo, answer itself, its voices numerous and overlaid. The arc was formed by shallow, but sheer, sandstone cliffs, and was crowned by slag from the mines, Loft, Fish and Canning, and formerly Lady. The shingle and sands of the south shore were studded with coal and coal-dust and because of it there was a constant concourse of beachcombers picking at the shoreline. That day John Devlin, Hugh Glyn, Mary and Martin had spent the morning on the south shore picking at the dust. In the mid-morning they were joined by Gavin Duffy, Peter Kavanagh and John Darcy. For a while they prospected together. Just before mid-day Mary had had enough. She shook her coal blackened raw hands and complained of fatigue. It was Gavin rather than Hugh who responded to her. He suggested that she go and wash them in the rock pools at the base of the cliffs and rest there awhile. It was there that she discovered the animal. She knew immediately it was dead. It lay between two slabs of sandstone, its face twisted towards the sky, its body sand blackened. She called to Martin. Together they touched it. At first they gingerly passed their fingers along its fur, then they firmly pressed their hands into its body, trying to shake it, move it, but with no success. After that they told the others. They all grappled together and eventually managed to drag it from the cliffs. They covered it with an old sheet John Darcy kept on his trolley for those occasions when he needed to display his wares (Gavin promised to replace it), then hauled it out along the harbour wall towards the lighthouse. When they reached the furthest point they weighted the sheet with a number of split sandstone rocks they brought on the trolley, tied the sheet into a tight bag and committed it to the sea. They were the only people to ever know that the phantom had been discovered. The rest had to learn to live with it. As the bag went under the water Martin began to holler and Mary began to cry.

*

One circus had scarcely left, leaving its litter of fantasy behind, than another took its place. The travelling circus of the *British Union of Fascists* rolled in. There was general agreement amongst trades unionists that they had been invited, most likely by an alliance of a small section of the county borough and a group of mine and factory owners (largely that section of the county borough men and the owners were one and the same). Their target was the local branch of the National Unemployed Workers' Movement, the leadership of which was almost exclusively made up of Communist Party members, including Peter Kavanagh and Gavin Duffy.

At a national level the Movement had been the driving force in organising the resistance against the attempts of Public Assistance Committees to means test benefit payments. (The Public Assistance Committees had taken over the function of the Boards of Guardians, when the Poor Law was reformed in 1930, a reform designed to put a stop to the practice of Labour run boards paying higher rates of relief than others, which had usually been the case locally.) Such was the climate against means testing that benefit payment was taken away from the Public Assistance Committees altogether, and an Unemployment Assistance Board was set up to introduce a national rate (a step which effectively marked the end of the Poor Law). However, when the national rate was announced, in the beginning of 1935, it was less than those which had generally been fixed locally. The Unemployed Workers' Movement organised renewed demonstrations.

In the Whitehaven area Peter Kavanagh led the protests, but the soul of resistance was Duffy. In Mount Pleasant and Ginns he was something of a local hero, a martyr even. His periodic bouts of madness only served to highlight his reputation, as to everyone's way of thinking his obvious afflictions resulted from the struggle. A section of the county borough members clearly remembered that when his roar went up: "No means testing! No fixing of relief rate! Barbarism or socialism!" it was enough

366

to invoke the crowd to protest and virtual riot, which was enough to break up numerous meetings of the Public Assistance Committee.

Throughout the spring and summer there were sporadic outbursts of protest, most resulting in minor scuffles which were easily broken up by the local police, some though ending up with attacks on council property and serious street disturbances. Then, in the late summer, as Lord Singer led his animals out of the valley, Gavin announced that he was preparing to organise a hunger march to highlight the plight of Whitehaven's most destitute. Although the organisation of hunger marches was a national policy within the Unemployed Workers' Movement, designed to expose the conditions endured in the most depressed areas of the country, such a march associated with Gavin took on a particular resonance. He had chosen hunger when he was imprisoned. It had been a deliberate choice. Hunger certainly went deep into the Irish psyche. It evoked the great famine and others since. It was the driving force of emigration. It was also symbolic of the political struggle. Gavin was well aware of all that. He knew he could invoke the militancy of the Irish streets. His announcement created consternation amongst sections of the county borough members. They feared severe civil disturbance and unrest resulting from such a march. The issues of unemployment assistance rates and possible evictions were out of their control. They wanted Duffy sorted out, in one way or another.

The first thing to happen was that Peter was arrested. The only permissible evidence was that of the arresting police officers who claimed he was responsible for inciting riot. Aunty Dora, who had been with Peter in the house in Ginns when he was arrested, found she herself was arrested, accused of a breach of the peace, when she turned up in the police station to plead his case. In the ensuing struggle she was lucky not to burst another tear gland.

After that a series of Fascist rallies were held. There was one in the Market Square, one on the cinder pitch of Fish Pit and one along the quays. With Peter under arrest Gavin led the opposition. He rallied the residents of Ginns and Mount Pleasant with the refrain: "The fight against Fascism is the fight for Trades Unionism! Down with Fascist justice! Barbarism or socialism!" The initial rallies broke up in a spate of minor skirmishes. On each occasion Gavin was targeted but protected by the Miners' Federation. During these disturbances the police presence was at first negligible, then negligent, then ultimately non-existent. With each successive rally the fighting became more sustained and intense.

In the late afternoon the Fascists gathered on the quays. They were now openly armed with clubs, bottles and knives. There was no policing of any kind. Once again Gavin prepared to lead the protest. It was at this moment the news broke that the long expected notice of evictions had been announced. To everyone's amazement there was only one. To further the surprise, it didn't come from owners but from the Public Health committee. The eviction was for Duffy from his single room cellar, on the grounds of sanitary abuse. This order was regarding a premises in which the only plumbing was a single cold tap. Duffy wanted to carry on with the protest but in the light of the Committee's pronouncement he was persuaded by the executives of the Miners' Federation and the Unemployed Workers' to return to Mount Pleasant and barricade himself in. The stand against convictions was too important to be allowed to fail. He was promised protection.

As evening fell, crowds gathered on the steps of Mount Pleasant. At first everything remained quiet. The Fascists remained on the quays and proceeded to go through their round of speech making. On Mount Pleasant only Gavin's voice broke the silence with occasional invective: "Barbarism or socialism!" Then, after dark, bailiffs began to appear at the foot of the steps. They made no move. There was a period of uneasy stand off between them and the crowd gathered on the steps above them. Minutes later and the bailiffs were joined by a crowd of Black Shirts who filed in lines around them. When they were all in place they started stoning the crowd, which was clustered closely together on the steps. Of course the Mount Pleasant and Ginns residents were prepared and responded in kind. They had been drilled by the Miners' Fed and Unemployed Workers' Movement. Grossly out numbered, the bailiffs and Black Shirts quickly beat a retreat. The crowds on the steps surged forwards. The Fascists were running. They gave chase and pursued them along the *Sugar Tongue* and *Tobacco Tongue*. Pockets of fights broke out all around the docks. Any number of Fascists were beaten up and thrown into the water. On this occasion victory seemed assured for the residents.

However, as the Miners' Federation, Unemployed Workers Movement and the people of Ginns and Mount Pleasant fought with the Fascists along the quays the police, together with a handful of soldiers, marched onto Mount Pleasant. A few shots were fired to disperse those who remained. Kate was one. When the shots rang out she lay down across the steps before her own door. As she lay there she heard Gavin's screams as they hauled him from his cellar then beat him with leather straps. She even heard the jokes they made as they did it. "Listen, Mick, this is the soldier's voice!" When news spread of what had occurred the town became strangely silent. The police and army easily restored order and quickly cleared the streets. The sense of defeat that gripped everyone was deep and embarrassing.

As soon as the police and soldiers left Kate went to Gavin who lay across the steps beside his stair-well. She asked him in. He refused. She brought water and bathed his wounds. He writhed on the steps. Again she asked him in. Again he refused. She offered him food and water. He refused. Finally, she sat on the step beside him, bent over him and began to massage his beaten body. He groaned under her attention. She wanted to soothe him and in some way let him know that she was keeping faith with him.

"How many more circuses will we have to see, Gavin?" she asked despondently. "I can't take many more." He did not answer, but moved and moaned. She removed her heavy fleshy fingers from his body and apologised. "I'm sorry. I want to help. I think I knew what was happening. I don't know why. I knew they were tricking everybody. They let us get carried away. We lost all our sense." She hesitated and stroked him again. He cried out. "I don't know how to help you, Gavin," she said hopelessly. She moved close to him and let his head rest in the well of her apron. She could see the bleeding points across his face, his arms and torso. She whispered monotonously towards his bloodied features: "Do you think it means anything that I knew but didn't know what to do? Just didn't know what to do. Is it always like that? Knowing but not knowing what to do. It's awful, Gavin. I couldn't cope with that. It's just too awful. Tell me, is that how it is?" His head remained like a stone ball in her lap. She sat forward to see his face which had turned into her apron. His eyes were open, staring fixedly forward, the look captured in them terrified and hateful. "Come in doors, Gavin, for God's sake, come in doors." He made no response.

"Oh Gavin, where is all this going? I don't understand. We didn't ask for all this, did we? We haven't done anything wrong, have we? I'm right aren't I? I just can't work it out. You look so bad Gavin. There's no need for it. You look like Jones when Dora and I saw to him. We left him in a state. I've never told anybody about that before. There was never any need. It's not that I ever felt bad about it. To be honest, I've never really thought about it that much, at all. Well, other things took over, more important things. But, well..." She fell silent thinking of Patrick. She threw back her head and stared at the space between the two walls.

It was narrow and oblong like a grave, its colours smoky, neither light nor dark, but a grey in-between state.

When she thought of Julia it seemed as if it were only yesterday. She could still see her, behind the door, weeping, the baby born in the worst year since the great famine. But when she thought of Patrick it was all so old. It made her feel old. Old and rather pointless. She had never really taken charge. She had taken Patrick but never held him. He had struggled and chosen his own anonymity, rather than concede to her. Was her identity so bad that a sickly child should malign it and refuse it and then die true to his rejection? There had been so many deaths. They were cursed. Was it because they were so bad? Is that why they were hated? She wailed aloud. The sound of her own voice shook her. She looked down at Gavin. The same fixed, aggravated stare remained in place.

"It was my fault, you know. It was all my fault. I was the first to emigrate. I don't know where I got the strength for that. It just seemed the right thing. God, when I think about it now. They none of them would have come if it hadn't been for me. None of this would have happened. None of it. There's so many died Gavin. I can't make sense of that. Is that all my fault? Have I killed them all? Have I killed Robert, Gavin? I think I'd kill myself if I was sure of that. He wouldn't be dead, would he? I mean that's the simple truth. If I'd never left he would be alive now, wouldn't he. I killed my own darling, Gavin. Mind you, we had the bogey men back home, didn't we? We did, didn't we? We were always terrified of the gombeen men. You'd remember all the songs, wouldn't you Gavin. It was never right there either. We were always hiding behind the window, scared the bogey man was coming to put us out. They've always hated us, wherever we've been. But what does that make us Gavin? Christ, what are we?" She fell silent again. She wanted to cry but couldn't. Even the thought of Robert wasn't enough to allow her to weep. She couldn't understand. She just felt debarred. Perhaps it was the presence of Gavin, his battered head resting in her lap. It wasn't enough to cry. The need for retaliation weighed against it.

"My father was one of the damned men you know. I kind of laugh at it now. I didn't have a clue what it meant then. Well, I was only a kid. When you're that age your father's just your father. He doesn't do anything wrong, or strange, or not normal, does he. You'd never manage to work a thing out like that. I think he killed a landlord's agent. It's like I'm confessing it for the first time. Why am I doing that Gavin? I can't believe it mind. Not the face I see. I wish I could see him laughing a bit more. There was only really Julia could bring him out of himself. I always get that shocked, uncertain look. I didn't know what the hell that was about. We're so stupid when we're kids. They call it innocence, I just call it daft. Shame to grow out of all the daftness though. I wouldn't have the world like this. I'm sure I wouldn't. I wouldn't have him looking like that, like to all the world he hasn't a clue. Christ, the poor sod. Sorry, I shouldn't say that. It makes it sound like I've given up on him. I haven't and never will. That isn't why I left. Well, I don't know why I left. It was the only thing, that's all, the only thing. There was only my grandfather at the end. He would only have fretted his way into the grave. I couldn't do that, couldn't be responsible. I just couldn't."

She stopped speaking and stroked Gavin's face, her lips pursed together in a semi-formed smile. "I've made John into a damned man, you know. Do you think he'll ever forgive me. I don't think he will. I told him we'd leave nothing behind and that we'd leave no one behind, no one that was ours. That can't be completely true though, can it? He knows that. He lies awake at night. I don't think he sleeps at all. He can't go on forever like that. He'll go mad. I'd never forgive myself for that. There's no man like John Devlin and I've took his home off him. He's in a cellar for God's sake, like some bloody caveman. So we got ourselves away from the bogey men for this. What's the point Gavin? I don't see it anymore."

She shook her head quietly. He was in this dreadful state for the sake of a cellar. He had been battered to unconsciousness for the small matter of a tiny underground chamber. If it wasn't so awful it would be absurd. "I don't know Gavin. Where is it all going to end? I hear terrible things. Well, we all do. I hear about the Jews and all the things that are happening to them. Well, there's so many refugees aren't there. You can't help but hear. It's in all the papers. I don't understand it, but I know about it. The stupid thing is I think it's something foreign, something over there and not really anything to do with me. Christ, I've got enough on my plate. But then here you are and they're still here rampaging around the town in their stupid uniforms like kids playing at soldiers. But they're not kids are they. They're deadly earnest. I mean, look at you Gavin. We're just Jews aren't we. We left one country and never properly arrived at another. We're just the same aren't we. So when they've hounded their own Jews will they come and hound us. Will there be Murphys everywhere I turn. I'm terrified Gavin. I'll admit it. I've never been so scared. Why do they want to do it Gavin? Is that a stupid question? I think it must be. Maybe if I had more book learning I'd know what it was all about and realise that was a stupid question. But from where I'm sitting it seems sensible enough to me. Why do some people hate other people Gavin, and some people love everybody? Anne loved everybody and she died. Julia loved everybody. Is that all there is when you love? There should be more. Is that what the ones who hate get out of it, more time to hate? If we're still here is it because we've learnt to hate? Well, maybe I have." She finally began to cry. She fought back the tears but to no avail. She spoke through them. "I don't hate, Gavin. I don't hate anyone. Come in Gavin, for God's sake. Let me give you a bit of cover. Please Gavin. It's all I have to offer."

He still made no answer. She was finished. She couldn't go on. She took off her apron and fashioned it into the shape of a pillow and placed it under his head. She went down into her cellar and waited for John to return, hoping he would know how to bring Gavin in.

In fact Gavin remained on the steps all of that night and throughout the next day and night. Petitions were made to him to come into someone's, anyone's, house. He refused them all. Kate sat with him often throughout his ordeal. She was relieved by John, Hugh or Father Bond, and on two occasions even by Martin. Martin never said anything to him other than to tell Gavin who it was sitting with him. After that, he simply gazed at him, counting over his wounds. Hugh wanted to bodily carry Gavin indoors, but Kate firmly opposed such an idea. She feared for his mind if faced with further coercion. Most of the time he simply slept curled like an animal on the landing of the steps. It seemed he was finally determined to die.

On the second day following Gavin's eviction Peter and Aunty Dora were released. They went straight to Mount Pleasant. They approached Gavin and found him in a cocoon of dried blood and excrement. News of their release had spread quickly and people crowded out onto their doorsteps on each of the landings. Peter looked up, past them all, to where the stairs ceased. Loft Pit towered over them. He crouched down to Gavin. "Gavin," he said, whispering his name, "Gavin, it's me, Peter Kavanagh. Gavin, it's time to come home." Gavin rolled onto his back. He opened his eyes and blinked at the sun. His eyes wouldn't completely open. The attempt was obviously painful. He turned away again. "Gavin," Peter repeated, petitioning him, "please Gavin, it's time to come home. It's all over. We're through here, Gavin. Please, Gavin. We can't do anymore."

Gavin rolled onto his back once more and again tried to open his eyes. The attempt proved as painful as the first time. Peter continued to encourage him, quietly repeating his name over and over. This time Gavin didn't turn away but instead lifted himself and tried to stand. Peter and Aunty Dora helped him to his feet. For a while they simply held him up, allowing him time to feel his residual strength, and then very slowly Peter led him up the Mount Pleasant steps.

Blank faces stared at them as they passed. Peter kept on. And then, one by one, everyone began to clap. No one remembered who applauded first but many believed it was Kate, her two flabby yellow palms raised defiantly in the air. The clapping grew in intensity until it became a tide of cheers and shouts. They had secured a victory after all. This was the sound they left behind them as they made their measured and laboured way to Ginns. So Gavin went to live in the house of a man who had once wanted to kill him.

*

Bill took charge of Duffy. He stripped his bloodied and dirtied clothes from him, then sat him in a bath before the fire. Gavin was stupefied and sat rigidly in the water, staring ahead. Bill soaped his body. Despite the fact that he was in his sixties his skin remained tough and elastic, and his muscles firm. Bill felt repulsed by his nakedness, and yet at the same time sympathetic towards it. It spoke of too many hardships, too many beatings, too much abuse. It seemed lifeless, despite its apparent strength. It was the colour and texture of lard. Nevertheless, Bill was gentle and thorough. After bathing him, he shaved him and cut his hair. His hair was thin and patchy, a series of colourless, fibrous strands. When he was through cleaning him up he rubbed ointment and grease into his mesh of cuts and bruises. When he was finished he put him to bed.

Gavin slept soundly for an hour or so then he began to call out and moan. This was the presage of a fever which was to last for a number of days. During that time it remained Bill who cared for him. He repeatedly wiped down his body with tepid sponges in an attempt to cool his burning skin. He consoled him and reassured him, doing his best to quieten him, whenever he clambered from his bed, evidently trying to escape his nightmares. For the whole duration of Gavin's illness Peter remained aloof, happy that Bill had taken it on, yet at the same time mocking him. "You do that very well," he said pointedly, one night, as he watched Bill sponge Gavin's face.

"Why should I not?"

"Why should you?"

Bill refused the challenge. He had long been of the opinion that there was no point contending with his father. He knew that they had no common ground. They tolerated each other without questioning why that was all. Bill merely said: "We could go on all night like this."

Peter seized on the comment. "Of course, unlike the rest of us, you have work in the morning. My son has the great fortune to be a tailor."

Bill let it go.

It was not easy living with Gavin. Even when the fever subsided he remained debilitated, something of a mental cripple. He lost all self-confidence and belief and rarely ventured out of doors anymore. Most strangely of all he never spoke about politics. If Peter mentioned anything he balked at it and left the room. Peter gave it up. His own commitment wavered without Gavin to guide him, without a clear programme to follow. The Unemployed Workers' Movement, the Miners' Fed, and the Communist Party had become stalled. Membership was declining both locally and nationally. The future was uncertain.

Gavin's personal habits became lazy and dirty. He spent much of the day in his bedroom, which had been Peter's, who now slept in the parlour, drinking and smoking (both the whisky and tobacco provided by Bill). He weltered in plumes of acrid smoke surrounded by the array of whisky stains and tobacco stains his negligence had made. At night he was regularly incontinent but rarely quit his bed, except when driven by his periodic nightmares. At times it seemed as if his fever had returned. He would call out and scream and start climbing the walls. At first Bill tried to comfort him and would attempt to lead him back to bed, but eventually he gave it up. There was no comforting Gavin. The mental storm just had to be lived through and endured.

One night when Gavin was shouting and clambering about his room Bill went to the kitchen hoping he might be able to get some sleep a bit further away from the noise. However, when he pushed the door open he found Peter already there, crouched before a blazing fire. Peter gave a start as the door opened and turned quickly, but seeing that it was only Bill turned back to the flames without comment. Up until then he had always denied that Gavin's night-time traumas bothered him, claiming that the sound didn't travel to the parlour. Bill pulled the door quietly behind him. Gavin's shouts and moans became muffled. Peter didn't move. He waited for Bill to break the silence. He spat into the fire. It sizzled and roared. An orange glow flickered across the walls. Bill sat down. They didn't speak for some time. Bill, though, was tired and needed to sleep before work. He had to break the silence. He said: "He's very troubled tonight. It's gone on a long time."

"He can't help it."

"I didn't say he could. He's kept me awake longer than usual, that's all. I'll be exhausted in the morning."

"I'm sorry about that. I'll have to tell him."

"I don't know what the neighbours think."

Peter lifted up, and sat back in a chair by the fire. "We don't get any complaints."

"Of course we don't. They're all frightened of you."

"What the hell do you mean?" Peter snapped. Bill merely shrugged, too worn-out to pursue it. Peter took his opportunity. "They admire him. They know what he's done for them. That's why they say nothing. He's one of them."

"Well, they might learn to despise him if he carries on like this."

"Put him out then! Go on, put him out!"

"You know I wouldn't do that."

"Why not?"

"It's not something I would do. It's not fair of you to suggest it."

"Fair, what the hell is fair about anything! He wouldn't be in that sorry state if there was anything fair! He's a fucking mess because nothing is fair."

"But what do we do about it?"

"Do? What do we do? We stand by him! We support him! We see him through! We fight his fights! Are you so removed from us?"

"I mean now, at this very minute, how do we help him?"

"Help him or help yourself?"

"How can you say that?"

"You seem very concerned by the neighbours all of a sudden."

"Of course. I'm concerned about everyone. I'm even concerned about you."

"Well, you needn't be."

"Of course I am, you're my father, so naturally I'm concerned about you."

Peter turned to him quickly. His expression looked severe, obviously angered. He snapped: "I don't need your concern."

Bill shrugged, but eyed Peter steadily, this time deciding not to pass. "Well, that's a shame. I think that's a shame, anyway. We all need someone to worry about us. It's only natural. I've always worried about you, well certainly since mother died."

Peter stood up as Bill spoke, challenging him to shut up. "I don't want to hear about it. Are you listening to me?"

"Why not?" Bill retorted, despite himself, for the first time in talking with his father unable to forego what might develop. "Maybe I need to discuss it. Does that not cross your mind?"

"There's nothing to say."

"There is for me! There's lots of things. Things I need to know. For instance, why do I feel so guilty about it? What did I do?"

"Stop it," Peter commanded.

"No, I want to know. Was it because I wouldn't go to bed? Is that it? Is that why I feel so guilty? Because I wouldn't go to bed?"

"Go to bed now Bill before you say anything else."

"No! Damn it! To hell with you ordering me about. Why can't you ever talk? Christ, look at you! Just look at you!" Peter grimaced under Bill's dismissive attention. His instinct was to strike Bill, strike at him and swipe away the problem. He felt his anger keenly, acutely aware of it spreading through his whole frame. Bill recognised his desire and derided it. He spoke up, taunting Peter. "The same old answer to everything? It must be all you've ever learned. It's pathetic. Well, come on then, try."

Bill waited for him. They were at the brink, twenty years in the making. However, at the point of crisis, they were deflected by Gavin. He came in quietly and stealthily like a thief. He was entirely naked. He peered all around, then having satisfied himself that he was unobserved began to paw at the walls like an animal climbing or digging. After a few minutes of this he stopped abruptly. He turned and looked directly at Peter and Bill in turn. A second later he screamed aloud, a piercing shriek, then fled in terror, leaving the door open behind him.

After he had gone Peter spoke first. His tone was unexpectedly calm, almost gentle, his temper seemingly having withered as quickly as it had grown. "Go to bed Bill, there's no need to be bedding down here. He'll sleep now. You know that."

Bill was confused. He was certainly unclear in his own mind whether he was through or not. He tried to summons the same passion he had felt only moments before, but the attempt was futile and in the end he had to recognise that it was gone. He hated admitting that it was down to Peter whether they acted out their antagonisms or not, but that was evidently the case. Peter remained in charge. He complied to what his father suggested without saying another word.

Bill didn't go to work that morning. He thought he might spend some time with Mary. Over the years their friendship had remained close, though not confiding. They simply found pleasure in each other's company. He knew she would be on the south shore scouring for coal. He went to the cinder plateau before the once again empty sheds of Lady Pit (now that all the mines were closed the strangers had decamped) where steps, cut into the sandstone, ran steeply down to the shingle and black sands, and stood there ready to catch her attention. Even in the early hours the beach was busy. He could see her, though, walking beside Hugh and John, her head bowed, working. He knew he should go down to them, but to do so would mean admitting, perhaps more for them than him, that he had no need to join them. He was in work. He wasn't a beachcomber. He had never been a beachcomber. Instead he just waited, certain she would eventually look up and see him and come to him.

In the early light the shore struck him as quite beautiful. A pale light spread across the sea, silk on silk, the sunlight milky and dispersed through mist and spray, the horizon fused. And the scourers moved against its sheen, slow, silhouetted, bonded to its fabric beauty. Mary walked to the water's edge, foam splashing about her ankles. He waved his arms at her but she didn't notice. Her attention, even as she paddled through the shallow incoming waves, was rooted to the black coal-dusted sands. He found himself in something of a quandary. He couldn't shout to her. From that distance his voice would be lost amongst the constantly whispering water, and the echoing, fissured rock face. And he couldn't go to her. He had no place on that shore. So, for a while he just stood and watched her, his two hands knitted together resting on the crown of his head.

She was agile, gracefully kicking through the foam, at first forcing her feet through the water so as to feel the force of the wave against her, then tiptoeing through it, stepping over each wave as it broke to nothing on the polluted sands. She was luxuriating in her break from her work. The experience struck him as personal and private. He smiled to think that there was something passing through her head as she played in the water, as she felt its weight, its feel, its touch, but he didn't attempt to consider just what those thoughts might be. He was sure he had strayed too much into her privacy already. It wasn't fair to spy on her like this. He took a step back. As he did he lifted his hands from his head and held them aloft as if making a symbol of atonement to her.

It was as he did this that she looked up and saw him. She gazed at him for a moment and then waved energetically. She took a few steps

377

towards him then, still in the midst of the shallow waves, stopped and splashed the water around her ankles. She did it as if she were doing it for his sake, looking up to him for approval, then laughing out loud at his continued attention. After that she came to him, running quickly across the black shingle. However, by the time she had climbed the steps to the plateau of Lady he had gone. As to why he had so suddenly dashed away he couldn't really have said. It was just that seeing her run towards him, roused from her personal reverie, had stirred in him a need to flee.

He spent much of the day wandering along the coast, following the cliff top paths between Whitehaven and St Bees. The breeding season was over. The guillemots, kittiwakes and fulmars had abandoned the sandstone ledges. Their barrage of sound was absent. Only their excreta remained, trailing messily across the split sandstone walls. Only herring gulls drifted above the cliff line, their raucous individual calls blending with the crashing tide below him. His thoughts centred on Gavin.

He pictured him screaming, his face contorted with incomprehension and fear, trying to lay bare the horrors which assailed him. He wondered if Gavin ever could be cured and if so what shape his cure could take. He remembered Gavin as a strict, brooding man, wedded implacably to his beliefs and opinions, yet, he had been destroyed, broken in pieces slowly and methodically. This town, these cliffs, its industry and its people, had defeated him, as it seemed capable of defeating anyone. There was a malevolence about it. His father suffered from it, acting out its belligerence, its desire to kick at something, anything, as long as it was a weaker party.

It seemed to him that the whole environment bickered all about him because, like the beady eyed herring gulls, the people he knew, were all fighting to survive. It made them hasty and quick to temper. And he felt victimised by them. He was unfairly judged and made separate. It was they who made him a tailor, a figure of fun and suspicion. It was they who tarnished it. There was no way out for him. He was being reduced year by year. He was just like Gavin. He was giving in to a life that gave nothing back, a life that took what he had, and claimed it wasn't authentic. He had had enough and needed release.

But where would he find it? He couldn't scream. He didn't have that temperament. He couldn't act out of character. He never had. He was always rational and stolid, despite the fact that he knew he was hemmed in by deception and lies. He had learned to live with those. He didn't share his secrets; though he would have been liberal with his love. That was what Mary seemed to recognise. He wasn't retarded. He needed to love. Perhaps that was all any of them needed, but none of them were either willing or brave enough to say so. It was too disarming, unmanly. But what did that mean, being a man?

He had almost been on the verge of stating something about love to his father the night before, at the outset of their argument. He had instinctively opted to say he was concerned about him. He would never have said he loved him. Not only because he had no way of knowing whether that was true or not, but also because his father would have derided it, even worse turned it into something perverse. These people, these men, didn't talk about love. So, if he had given in to his impulse, at best he might have said words to the effect that of course he was concerned about him, because they were supposed to love each other, father and son, and then quickly qualified that by pointing out it would be considered quite normal between them.

As he thought these things he picked up a stone and threw it towards the flocks of drifting, noisy gulls, then immediately turned away in disgust at his own violence. He rushed away. The desire to scream was large and real within him, but it wasn't voiced because he didn't know what to say, what to express, or how to say it. He didn't have the language, the intuition or the zeal. He simply could not admit that he had reached the crisis of his life.

As evening fell he went back into town. He went from pub to pub and ended up hopelessly drunk, which was entirely out of character for him. He ended up on the quays. It seemed unreal. His mind raced. Everything swirled around him at great speed. The lights on the water perplexed him. He couldn't differentiate between object and thought. He was reduced to tears but had no idea why. His mind filled with the images of people. He thought of Gavin, imagining him naked, climbing the walls, his expression horrified. He thought of Patrick, cold as stone, his face a chalk mask, lying on his mother's grave, and remembered kissing him, his lips pressing against that insufficiency, that absence of warmth. Then he thought of his own mother, her expression peaceful, her face a moon seen through rain, and beyond and behind her, somewhat vaguer but nevertheless there, his father, gazing obdurately back at him, his demeanour fearful and trembling. He closed his eyes and shook his head, but they remained. He opened his eyes and stared hard at the unfocused object world but they remained. They were his companions, his inner ghost world.

He stumbled on along the *Sugar Tongue*. He began to cry aloud. He knew he was but he couldn't stop. He was doing the unthinkable. He was being exterior. He didn't do that. But he couldn't call a halt. He had given himself to it. He would have to play himself out. Nevertheless, he wasn't saying the things he wanted to say. He was making animal noises, simply moaning aloud about his agony.

What he really wanted to say was that he loved them. He wanted to confront them with that aberrant word. And as much as he wanted to say it, he wanted to hear it. He wanted to be loved. After all, it wasn't so much, was it? It could be said. It didn't have to be stifled. It couldn't be gainsaid. He had loved what they had loved. Why was it so difficult to agree? Why was there a blanket refusal, an embarrassment, a shame invested in the word. It was a lovely word. Wasn't it a lovely word? He was sure it should be. But was he right or was he wrong? Was it, after all, just disgraceful, simply an idea that someone had the time and inclination to bandy about? Maybe so. Christ, why should anybody love? Maybe it was simply fraudulent. At the end of the day, they were all brought together by accident, by the chance of birth, death and misfortune. It brought up the shutters. He had passed from one prison to another, always dissatisfied, always yearning, always out of step, never at peace. He had no class to call his own. His life had been a sequence of punishment, making do and talking their talk, and living their life. He had never known a home, not in a place or a person. He was an immigrant in his own community. It was outrageous. He threw up his arms in despair. He spun round, his arms still extended, as if contending with heaven. This brought a new idea into his head. God. What did he feel about God?

He didn't answer himself. At that moment he fell amongst a pile of crates and lobster-pots. His body was hurt. He cried out in pain. He cried out with embarrassment. No one came to him. He shifted himself until he found a position where the pain was lessened and he was more or less comfortable. He fell asleep with the world rotating around him, blazing, eccentric, possible.

The morning was cool and pale, with pink light on the water. He felt stiff and ached. He found he couldn't easily move. His head was splitting. Nevertheless, he remembered the night before. He remembered his crying, his resolve, his love. He tried to move again. He felt his groin and trouser leg. They were cold and damp. He realised he had wet himself. He had learned to call out and be incontinent in one night. He groaned at the thought. Without thinking about it he began to masturbate. When he had finished he kicked the pots aside and pulled himself free. He felt dirty and ashamed.

He went to the south shore. It was as yet deserted. As always the sea whispered. He walked into it. The water was freezing against his skin, but he didn't hesitate. He waded right up to his thighs. When he had achieved that depth he turned round and round, then ducked beneath the waves three times, and then three times more, and yet again three times more. Nine times in all. One time for each month of gestation: one time for each month that created him, made him a man. After each immersion he came up gasping, taking great gulps of air, then dived his head beneath the water again. When he had completed that he stood up and faced the town. In the early dawn it seemed untroubled and at peace. He raised his arms and called out at the top of his voice, a single word, an affirmation. Yes. He had cleansed himself. He had baptised himself in water. His spirit soared free. He couldn't be chained anymore. His spirit was flying. He was a bird, an angel, a fish. He began to laugh, then bowed to the water, spread his arms before him and began to swim back towards the town. He knew what he had to do.

Less than three weeks later Mary ran along the station platform, calling to him as his train pulled away that he had to write often. He shouted back that he would, and also that he loved her. He proved to be true to his words. He wrote to her regularly. His letters were honest, open and frank. He told her that he had never really believed it possible for one man to kiss another man but if he had persisted in that thought he could only have died. Mary knew he was being hopelessly indiscreet. She knew she had to be secretive and extremely protective over him. She said his letters were full of jokes and that no one had ever really appreciated what a fabulous comic he was. She burnt them all.

*

In the late spring of 1937 Loft, Canning and Fish reopened after a closure of over two years. Government grants had been made available to revive four depressed areas, or special areas as they were renamed, West Cumberland being one. The apparent prosperity of the new company was indicated by the fact that it had acquired its own ambulance, a green, *Great War,* ambulance. It had been touched up and polished and was parked on the Loft cinders right on the promontory on display. The mine owners presented it as their commitment to their newly acquired asset. The miners were sceptical. Events over the years since the ambulance had first been used had taught them that it was better to refuse to be optimistic. They were pleased not to have given up trades union rights, but ashamed they could not resist exclusions.

John, Gavin and Peter were amongst those not taken on after queuing to be appraised for some five hours. John was informed that he was too old. Gavin was told that he wasn't up to the job. The decision against Peter was simply vindictive, a response to his previous union activities. He was given no reason, but was simply refused. Hugh's anger and representations on behalf of an ex-soldier achieved nothing. In fact, he came close to nearly losing his own job. He was curtly informed that the new company would hire and fire whoever they liked and that he could either accept that fact or walk away from it, but that he didn't have long to think about it. There was nothing for it but to walk out of the office without saying another word.

Peter told him he shouldn't have bothered. He claimed to be entirely indifferent on the subject. He said it was all unrealistic anyway. He pointed out his nursing duties as the evidence for that. It had been absurd to believe that they would take on Gavin. He was a shadow of his former self and Peter was in no position to leave him. If left to his own devices he would probably burn the house down. He added that despite being in London his son still paid the rent, so he better look after it. All in all, he was fairly sure that Gavin and he would survive.

As far as most people were aware Gavin could have been dead. He never ventured out, had few visitors, and Peter spoke little of him. Kate took them occasional meals and John or John Darcy would turn up with a bottle or two. Father Bond was his most regular visitor, but they spoke little. They simply sat together, smoked and sipped whisky.

From their cellar home, John, Kate and Aunty Dora, heard Hugh and Martin set off to Fish on that first morning. It was Martin's first job. He had a spent a year since leaving school passing most of his days beachcombing. He went into the pit, slightly made, but wiry, not lacking in strength, and sun-tanned. Kate was the first to rise. She shuffled about, still wrapped in her bed blanket, as the first spindles of grey light penetrated the gloom. The air was cool and damp. She went to Aunty Dora and found her also awake, gazing from her mattress into the half-light. "Did you hear them go?" Kate asked, giving no hint of what she felt.

John groaned as if still in sleep and turned over.

"Of course I did," Aunty Dora whispered harshly and gloomily, as she lifted herself up.

"It's good isn't it?"

"How should I know?"

"A bit of money, anyway."

"Well, they don't have to be grateful, do they."

"I suppose not. I didn't say they were."

"We'll see."

"It's better for them to be working. It's been too long. Poor Hugh. He'll be himself. And it's only right that Martin should have a break. It's only a shame, well..."

She heard John stir behind her and fell silent. She turned to him. He lifted himself heavily off the mattress and stood gazing at them for a moment, his expression cold and impatient. When they neither spoke he snapped: "I'll light the damned boiler."

Since coming to the cellar they had taken on the duties of the daily wash, taking it on themselves to light the boiler and start the first wash as soon as they woke, before even taking any breakfast. After the first wash Kate and Aunty Dora went to Mass and John to the south shore in order to scour for coal. He didn't envisage that routine changing now Hugh was in work.

Aunty Dora responded to him. She guessed what he was feeling, but wanted to register her disapproval of his taking it out on them. He didn't have that right. They weren't independent in that way. They were all pleased and disappointed. That's how it was. That's how it so often was. They all knew that. "For God's sake, just give me a matter of a second or two and I'll give you a hand. There's no need to kill yourself."

He snapped: "I can manage."

"I didn't say you couldn't."

"No," he said, already faltering, knowing he could either continue to sulk or simply concede. He chose the latter. When he spoke he was wearily conciliatory. "I know you didn't. I know you didn't mean that. Nobody means anything."

She sighed: "Christ, I'll be pleased when today is through, though."

John let it pass, but Kate couldn't. "What do you mean? Why? What does that mean? Why today?"

"It's been closed for two years, that's all."

"And? What of it? I don't follow."

"Two years is a long time, that's all. That's all I'm saying. It's nothing really. Just that. Two years is a long time. Oh, it's nothing. Don't set your face at me like that, Kate. I know all about your faces. I've grown up with them remember. Christ, what a woman. Tell her to keep her face to herself will you, John Devlin. Keep her in order, for God's sake. I could do with a smoke."

John held out a packet of cigarettes. Kate eyed the exchange with something like suspicion or derision in her expression. John wanted to tell her to quit making those faces, but he couldn't. He couldn't really speak. He was struggling with the stark awareness that the remainder of his life was likely to be mapped out in that chamber. It took some thinking through. He had to adjust to a new and troubling version of himself. He found himself underground, but he was no miner, and he certainly wasn't dead. What was he then? He didn't know. He pressed on with the wash. He was grateful that Kate didn't pursue the matter, but also busied herself with the wash.

In the early afternoon Mary came to the cellar. She had been sent by John from the south shore. She couldn't speak at first. She didn't know how to speak. Aunty Dora took hold of her and made her talk. In the end, she blurted out that she had seen the green ambulance leave its parking place and drive into town. She was sure it was probably nothing, nothing at all. It was just that she had seen it, that was all. She didn't know why her grandfather had sent her. It was a whim. Nothing else. He had whims. Everyone knew he had whims. She was humouring him. He needed that today. Didn't they think that too, that he needed humouring, that day of all days.

Aunty Dora released her, but didn't utter a word. She went to the corner and sat down. She gazed directly before her, unable to find any words to speak, condemning herself in her own mind, over and over again, for her foreboding. As she did Kate instructed Mary to go with her mother.

"Me?" she wailed, feeling both incredulous and fearful at the command.

"Go on, before I slap you. Go on, that's your place. You have to be with her now. Just in case, that's all. Just in case. Jesus."

Kate and Aunty Dora took the rest of the children into the cellar and played games, Grandmother's Footsteps, Pirates Treasure, games of stealth and secrecy, and Matthew, Mark, Luke and John, a game of verbal tag. They were determined to avoid the drab of simply waiting. Even before they had begun they had failed. The elder children, Julie, Jane and Catherine, felt they were too old for such things, but picking up the mood of the women decided to say nothing and play along.

For Mary being ordered by her grandmother to be with her mother represented the clear evidence of her coming of age. That fact would always be mixed in her memory with the harrowing details of their walk to the Infirmary. Of course she had felt grown-up before, and assumed she was. She had felt grown-up when she wore her mother's wedding dress and taken her first communion. She had felt grown-up whenever she had gone off secretly with Bill Kavanagh. She felt grown-up being the trusted guardian of his secret. She felt grown-up being a bakery girl, earning a little money. She worked for a few hours every morning in quite a busy bakery, Lavery's, one of the biggest in town. She hoped to learn the trade, eventually take a full time job if she was lucky and there was a vacancy. But this was different. This was the dawning realisation, the awful realisation, that life always intruded, that being grown-up was a burden as well as a relief. It was inescapable.

She remembered the Great War ambulance and the miners and other women already milling around it. She overheard them speaking as she and her mother approached. The talk was of *cuckoo shot, goaf* and *robbery.* They were meaningless words to her. Then, as they drew closer there was a developing silence, as one miner after another, one woman after another, became conscious of their presence and their voices became hushed. By the time they came up to the group not one of them was speaking anymore. They immediately parted and formed a clear passage for the two of them to walk through. Dora quailed and faltered. She did not want that right of entry. She wanted to be one of the women for whom it was all right. She would be able to express her sympathy as well as the next. She wanted to be one of them. It was Mary who held her and ushered her forward, leading her into the midst of the group, though she wasn't really conscious of what she was doing. She only had her grandmother's injunction to guide her. Mary recognised Martin amongst the crowd. He just stood there staring at them, his mouth slightly gaping, unable to speak or move. Mary gave him a slight nod. She didn't herself know what she meant by it, but it registered something with him. He closed his lips together and returned the gesture. She knew he had come of age too. In that brief exchange they realised that there had always been a compact between them but they had never before needed to affirm it.

As they walked through the crowd, each face still and passive, yet gazing steadily at them, one of the miners stepped forward. He seemed both irritated and anxious. His words came in an uncontrolled, but quiet rush. "When the roof came in he was there! I wouldn't have asked him. Honest! I wouldn't ask that of anyone. They hadn't sorted out the proper safety. It wasn't maintained properly. I wouldn't have wanted him to.

He just did. You have to believe that. Honest to God." Dora stopped and listened for a moment, but was quite stupefied and failed to register any meaning at all. Mary urged her on. They went into the hospital.

When Dora came beside Hugh she touched him all over. She ran her hands over his face, torso, arms, waist and legs, rapidly back and forth, shaping him, claiming him. She spoke at him. Her voice was shrill and frightened, and though devoid of weight, severe and penetrating. "Why did you do it, Hugh Glyn?" she demanded. "Why, damn you? Why didn't you let the roof fall? No one would have blamed you. You had no right. Damn you! No one else would have done it. It always has to be you. Always you trying to make it right. You shouldn't have done it."

Suddenly her voice trailed away. At the same time as her voice failed her massage became more robust. She ran her palms briskly all over him, covering his entire figure, until finally they came to a nervous rest on his exposed chest. She looked deeply into his face for a moment, a look of sheer panic in her eyes, then she began to shout at him, her voice demanding and desperate: "Don't let me hate you, Hugh Glyn, don't let me hate you. For God's sake don't let me hate you. Oh Christ, I love you. I love you."

Her voice trailed away again. She pawed at him, her muscles intermittently going rigid and relaxing in a fit of uncontrol. She reached for an arm to hold her. It was an arm that was no longer there. The realisation that there was nothing there took a moment to register, but when it did she began striking him, beating her fists against his chest. This lasted a matter of seconds, after which she collapsed over him and sobbed against his naked breast.

Mary stooped over her and caressed her, hiding her own face against her mother's back. She suffered. She suffered the hideous reality ceaselessly unfolding about her and she suffered the responsibility she felt placed on her. She wanted everything to stop, turn back, and then she would find that nothing had happened, that the world still made sense. But it wouldn't. It bore her senselessly on. She felt shock waves pulse through her. She was certain she was going to take one of her fits, and was not inclined to resist, even that was a hope for a way out. But it wouldn't happen. Nothing would go away.

As she lay pining against her mother's back Hugh opened his eyes. They were lined with dirt. Dora wiped them. She tried to control her weeping. She told herself that she had to do it for his sake. Somehow she had to keep it from him that his arm was gone. She kept on wiping at the dirt on his face, desperate for something to do. She knew it was ridiculous. It was all ridiculous. She just didn't know what else to do. Still, even as she laboriously worked at the dirt on his face she kept on repeating in a broken, pleading whisper: "Why did you do it? Why?"

When there was a momentary lull in her hushed tirade he answered her. His voice was hoarse and laboured. He said: "You don't think, just don't think. You know how it is. You'd expect me to do the same, I know that." He closed his eyes and breathed deeply, the effort to speak overwhelming him. A moment later he tried to speak again, but his voice failed him. He opened his eyes once more. He smiled. Dora moaned aloud. She recognised wonder, fear and love in his expression. Again she wanted to beat her fists against him, but she was beaten herself by this love between them. He struggled to speak, forcing his words. They came in stuttered fragments: "I loved Hugh, loved him, so much. Tell Francis, Francis, I love him. Tell..."

"Put your arms around me, Hugh Glyn, put your arms around me! Put your arms around me for God's sake."

Hugh smiled and closed his eyes.

Mary went out. She didn't really know what motivated her. She had some sense of the fact that she should leave them. She couldn't have put it into words or made proper sense of it, but it was something she felt to be instinctively right. She didn't say anything, but simply slipped away. Once away from her father's bedside she was overcome by a feeling of intense loneliness and fear. She had never felt anything so dreadful in her life. Indeed, she had never in her wildest imaginings conceived of a feeling that was so bad. She had assumed that she had felt as bad as it was possible to be when Hugh died, but that was nothing compared to this. She didn't know whether she was going to scream, faint or be sick. She told herself that she had to do something. She had to let them know at home. It gave her some vague purpose. She would go and tell them in the cellar. That was obviously part of her job. When she got outside the hospital she looked for Martin, but all the miners, together with the women, had gone. She guessed he would remain with them, for a while at least.

When she reached home she found she didn't need to explain. Kate refused the need. She simply crossed her hands before her, forbidding any words to be spoken, stepped away from her and slumped heavily onto a small stool and stared blankly into space. Aunty Dora gathered the children around her. She told them that they had to be brave, that they had to be wonderful and they had to pray. They just stood saying

387

nothing. Mary remained separate. Julie was the elder of that group now. She saw Francis gazing at her and suspected that he was going to come to her. She gestured him away. He frowned but nevertheless responded to her sign and turned away from her and pushed himself between Robert and John. They thought to complain, but really in the circumstances both recognised that that was really quite impossible.

Mary would never really know whether she had done well or not. For the rest of her life she would never be able to disentangle grief and love. She would always recognise that one was also the other, but that confusion made no sense to her at all.

Not long after Mary had come to the cellar Dora herself returned. She demanded her children. She didn't speak to them, though, or console them, but simply took Francis by the hand and immediately left again. It was many hours before she returned. Francis was asleep in her arms. The burden of carrying him showed in her whole demeanour.

When she had left she had gone straight back to the Infirmary, tugging Francis behind her, making him trot along. She had the utter conviction that Hugh must see him. She had never fostered the slightest suspicion that Hugh thought himself anything but the same father to them all. She knew he was devoted to Hugh. That was only natural. Not only had he been their first son, he was named after Hugh, and he was a striking shy boy. She had never considered that Francis coming after Hugh's death had been significant. She had to let him know that he had always been correct and equal. He was punishing himself needlessly. Wasn't it just like him, to be self-conscious and serious. He was more devoted to his children than anyone else she knew. Children were usually beaten, brought up to be mindful and know their place, but not hers. He had never lain a finger on her or them. He didn't even get drunk every week. She had always assumed that was something to do with the war. He always wanted to do things right. It was as if he had always known a day like this would come, a day when it was maybe too late to make amends. That was one thing he didn't need to do. He had to know that.

The urgency of her mission to get Francis to him briefly dispelled the weight of her suffering. It gave her a purpose that the senselessness of what was happening stole away. She only let her mind dwell on father and child. He couldn't go on, alive or dead, believing he had let Francis down in anyway. It simply wasn't true. She objected to it in her own mind. It was a deplorable idea. He had to know. He just had to know.

She felt her whole body go still as she stepped back into the Infirmary. Suddenly her confidence failed her. For a moment she couldn't approach his bed. She began screaming inside. It threatened to tear her apart completely. She began to panic. She felt a film of cold, wet sweat spread across her. She could feel her heart beating in her chest, its muscle pounding to the point of rupture. Then she felt Francis' palm in hers. It was warm and moist. She turned to him quickly. He was looking up at her. He didn't know what to do so he smiled. She knelt down and hugged him tightly. She owed it to him as well. He had to grow up without any doubts. He had to know the mountain of his father's love. She whispered comforting sounds to him, then led him into the large open ward.

She could see Hugh lying on his back, the wound of his severed limb heavily bandaged. Even from a distance she could see that it was blood soaked. The colour looked still red. It was obviously fresh. Her heart quailed. How many times had they already changed the bandage?

She drew Francis to the bedside, whispering to him not to be afraid. Much to her surprise he answered her. He said he wasn't afraid. He even asked why he should. He was going to see his father. As she came beside Hugh she immediately started whispering his name and telling him that she had brought Francis. He didn't speak, in fact he didn't even open his eyes, but she recognised a minor movement of recognition in his features, a relaxation of the taut stricken muscles. His face had been cleaned, but inexpertly with no attention to detail. Coal-dust still highlighted the myriad lines that formed his image. The dusted lines seemed to add to him, as if they revealed the characteristics that made him. He looked sensuous, fragile and instinctive, somehow both strong and defenceless.

She passed her hands gently across those defined, sketched lines, tracing the ever shifting image of him. She moaned with the sheer passion of her longing for him. She uttered beneath her breath: Put your arms around me Hugh Glyn, put your arms around me. Then she took Francis' hand and pressed it against Hugh's, palm to palm, entwining the fingers together so they formed a mesh, then she lay it on Hugh's chest. She was sure she saw Hugh's fingers tighten around the small hand clasped in his. She quickly looked to his face. He was trying to speak and he was trying to open his eyes. He managed neither. Then he gave up the effort. His whole face loosened. There was a sudden absence of pain. She recognised a smile, but then in the blink of an eye it was gone. She had seen it though. She would demand that truth as long as she lived. Then a striking brightness shone through his features and he gave a long gentle wail which seemed to reach forward then fall away like a long fading note. She knew he had gone. She waited for a moment, then released Francis' hand. She bent down and kissed Hugh on the lips, long and gently. Then she cupped her palm around his cheeks and whispered that he was just the job, he had always been just the job. After that she apologised to him and told him she needed to get Francis home, but that she would be back, she would never leave him. He had to understand she would never leave him, he only had to wait.

She didn't remember much about her journey home. She recalled thinking that the world collapsed, yet the world continued. How was that? Everything went on in the street as if nothing had happened. She couldn't understand that. She hated them for that. How could they carry on as if nothing had happened? Why didn't everything grind to a halt, albeit briefly, to acknowledge its loss? Surely that wasn't too much to ask.

Somehow she found herself down by the dockside. She didn't really know how she had managed to get herself there. She stood looking over the still, water filled basins. It was beside those basins that they had first made love. She remembered his face close to hers, vivid and bright, his breath visible as if his passion was forming language, but such words as only they could share. A gift to each other. She remembered drawing him to the shed on the promontory and the subsequent pain of his body, his body in her, the two of them joined. Of course it was painful, painful and ecstatic. How could joining be any different? They had fused, become one. How could she live without that, his body repeating that declaration, that desire. It wasn't fair. They weren't through. But then they would never be through. She would never be finished with that face, chilled and vivid, close to her, moving toward her, smiling, vivid and encouraging, absolving and exciting, the fluent marvel of him. And with that face of him, came so many others. They all rushed on her at once. He was so many Hughs, each one separate yet conjoined, himself and more, the one before and the one that came after, all Hugh, each one dependent, but vivid, flashing.

She thought she saw him as a child, and even then they loved each other. It was impossible. She had never known him before that day he had come home with Peter. Her father had brought him. He said she made a great healer of wounds. She said that she thought he was teasing her, but she knew he wasn't, not completely, anyway. And she was aware of him as a little boy then. Even though he was brisk and military, he was still a little boy. She knew what might make him laugh and what might make him cry. He always carried the capability. That was his perfection, to remember crying and laughing. He made bird songs to prove it. He sang like a finch. He was all nature. And he teased her in the yard, but at the same time he was loving her, drawing out its future shape. Then Marty climbed over the wall and the pig squealed, and somehow Hugh had manufactured it all because it was wonderful and he made the wonderful happen and it was effortless because he never showed-off, even though he could.

Even then, she knew that love was always tempered by the possibility of loss. Robert had taught her that. But if she had ever thought that it was impossible to be happy again, that it was impermissible, maybe, downright wrong, then he had brought his face to her, frank and vivid, pulsing with life, hesitant, equipped life, wanting to say it and perform it. And he never lost sight of it. Even when he sat by Mary's bed and the fever was burning her he never lost sight of the vivid and the wonderful. He had prayed and believed. He always believed. He had told her Peter was brave, fought like a hero and never chose to think of it as anything else. He broke up the cellar because he still believed in them all, and didn't want to give up on them, anyone. He would have died for Mary and considered himself fortunate, as long as she smiled. And he ran along the sands with Julie and Jane and the wonder in his face was greater than theirs. He could scarcely believe he had effected such wonder. He had survived a war for that and never lost faith. How was it he never lost faith? What gave him such appetite? And he thought he had let Francis down, pulling on his two pair of trousers and running off down the street. He couldn't have let anyone down. Then breaking the mantle in his nervous fingers. Such a look. A child capable of laughing and crying.

She howled with luxurious, blissful, exquisite, indescribable pain.

He had loved her. She had loved him. They had made love on that dockside. No one could take that away.

She looked down at Francis. He too looked capable of laughing and crying. She smiled at him. He didn't know what was happening. She bent down and scooped him up. She whispered that they were going home. He lay his head on her shoulder and within minutes was fast asleep.

When she went in Mary was the first to go to her. Dora smiled at her, placed her index-finger to her lips and hushed her before she could speak, then whispered: "I can't believe I don't have him to love anymore. I can't accept that. He has to be here, Mary. He has to be."

"I know."

Dora smiled again. "I must have some suppers to make."

Mary shook her head: "Not tonight."

"Is your grandfather home?"

"He came but went again."

"Go and get him. He might have his eyes closed, but he won't be asleep. Tell him I need him. He needs to know that. Make sure he knows. I need him."

So Mary went to the south shore below the plateau of dead Lady, where the sea whispered without saying anything, knowing already that this was the worst day of her life and that it would always remain so.

*

Whenever she was able, which was dependent on her hours at the bakery, Mary became John's regular companion on the south shore. His pain and loneliness had been so great the day her father died that over the subsequent weeks and months she couldn't countenance leaving him alone. Now that the mines were reopening less and less people frequented the shore. In fact, it was quite often the case that for hours at a stretch they were the only two. She was sure he stuck to the south shore because the mine that topped it was dead. It didn't so obviously underline the fact that he was through with being underground, reliant on public assistance handouts and grants. In the clasp of that whispering cove they became intimate without ever expressing their secrets or innermost thoughts. They were simply content to share each other's company.

Mary took all of Bill's letters to the south shore where she could read them in secret then burn them, letting the ash blow across the shingle, secure in the knowledge that their secrets were safe. They were extremely anecdotal and cryptic. She imagined a strange, wonderful city with remote but amazing characters.

As she read her letters John would fish the beach, no longer prospecting just for coal but anything that took his fancy, blanched wood, razor-shells, veined stones. Then they would come together and look out at the horizon, keeping their own thoughts.

Mary wrote to Bill. She told him about the terrible event of her father's death and how she now spent any spare time she had available with her grandfather on the south shore. She told him that it was there that she read his letters. He replied that he had seen Saint Peter and the Lord himself on that beach. They had called his name. He couldn't do anything but answer. She should always remember that he had seen St Peter and the Lord. It meant that heaven was more than a possibility. He was bitterly sorry about Hugh. He was such a true man and that was special. She found his response strange because he had never exhibited any tendency towards holiness. True, they had shared their first communion together, but she remembered him as shy and awkward, far from pious. Indeed, over the weeks, it was an increasingly different, unfamiliar Bill who wrote to her.

He wrote: *To the east of Haverstock Hill is the Tailors' Asylum for old, crippled and deranged tailors. It's not surprising that a city with so many mannequins should be so caring of its tailors. In his rooms in Chalk Farm Art has a mannequin. He laughs about it and says that's what attracted me to him. He might be right. He was certainly surprised at how well I dressed it up. It's a constant source of laughter and tears between us. This city is so cut out for tailors I wish I was something else. Oh, how dearly I wish I was something else. How much I'm finding out. There are things here worth witnessing, things we never realised were happening. We really should be witnesses, a good witness. It would be wrong to grow old not witnessing something, to never act on impulse or dictate, be irresponsible, not thinking things through. The world is such a vast mechanical, made up, monolith. It's a real plunge into nothing, into such a flagrant world.*

Mary drew a mannequin in the sand, but was uncertain whether it should have features. She tried to remember all that Bill had written. *Imagine a mile of mannequins,* came to mind. What did he mean? She left it with a moonface. Slowly the sea claimed it, running along the channels of its traced figure. She went to John. He was crouched among the boulders and rock pools, tapping at a starfish ingrained onto the algae rich rock. He pulled at one of the stars. It snapped into his fingers. Mary gave a start. John stood up, still holding the point of star, and laughed out loud. "Don't set on so," he said, "it'll grow again. It can afford one of its rays. It would certainly prefer to give up this than its entire self." He tossed it into the incoming waves. Water splashed about the pools. John remained. He spoke against the sound. "It's like rock when it's out of water. It would take a hammer and jump to move it. But when it feels the water on its back it just eases loose and is free. Can you imagine that?" His face looked bright and greedy. She reached out and took his hand. He took hers freely. They clambered away from the tide and stood together thinking about what they had offered the waters.

Bill had his wish and no longer worked as a tailor. He wrote: *I have been saved, saved a thousand thousand times over.* Art worked as a nurse for the insane and managed to secure Bill a job as a helper. He was certainly cut out for the task, after all, he had nursed Gavin through various crisis. *To think I will not be assigned to the Tailors' Asylum. You cannot imagine the relief that brings me. No one should have to face such a dreary future. Not that I don't respect tailors. Don't get me wrong. It has never been that. No, never. The Kavanaghs have always worked warp and weave. My mother and aunts all made their way in rag. The Kavanaghs have such dark souls though. Where have the Kavanaghs come from? We haven't been like ordinary families. Why was that? No, I've got nothing against tailors. I just have to make clean breaks. Clean, clean, clean breaks. Oh dear!*

His letters took on an even stranger turn than previously. He began to populate them with the strange characters he now met, the patients he nursed. He became obsessive over certain ones and would write at length about their antics, telling of their movements, their speech, their fantasies, their wildness. There was a burgeoning excitement in all he wrote. He had found a place, *a home* he called it, where he could be at one with those around him. *Nothing has ever made quite so much sense as these people's decision to quit. My little immigrant soul is at peace. Though they'll never understand it, maybe never even know it, but how I admire them. They don't realise their own bravery. They don't recognise their own genius. We should all be such spirits. They dazzle and dance. They reckon with salvation. Kiss Saint Peter from me. He has proved a tramp king.*

Mary didn't understand half of what he told her. His aphorisms were beyond her understanding, and he made little or no attempt to explain. As she read his letters she couldn't work out whether he expected her to understand or not. Surely he wouldn't say things for the sake of it. There had to be a belief in her ability to comprehend. She, therefore, increasingly suffered from her lack of understanding. She so much wanted to able to reach out to him, wanted to make contact on his terms. She knew that when she wrote there was no artistry though. She presented him with the basic facts of home. She surmised that it wasn't enough, but really could'nt conceive what would be enough. His letters entranced, intrigued, entertained and unnerved her.

He wrote: *Can we ever extract the little Catholic boy from his cherished domain, this sentimental lover of God's things, Stabat Mater Dolorosa? Can I ever know what I'm really capable of, what history might demand of me? I don't know that I ever could have known, but I might find out, might be called upon. Why did we never realise such things, the size of the globe, the people in it, trundling, always trundling, round and round, lost, completely lost, or debarred, kicked out. The world doesn't like its strangers, and yet we're all strangers at heart. I remember after Gavin Duffy was evicted your grandmother said something about the Irish just being like Jews. You weren't there. It was one of the times she came to see him, bringing him some broth and bread. She was right, but only half right, I think. We are all dispossessed. That is the texture, the pattern, the weave. All crazy and remote, looking through peepholes, savage little eye slits, just mirror men. You see the mannequin can never know itself except in admiration, and we are too disgraced and put out for that. God, it's so crazy. True exiles dream of home, I dream of the high seas.*

His letters increasingly troubled her. It was something more than the fact that she didn't understand much of what he was trying to say, but the tone of them seemed strange, even disturbing. She really couldn't say why. When she read them over she reassured herself that it was only her lack of comprehension that bothered her and left it at that, but she wasn't entirely convinced. Of course, the truth of the matter was that there was nothing else she could do, but leave it at that. To share them with someone else and see if they shared her concerns was simply out of the question. As such his letters became another instance of the maturity life pressed on her. She was responsible for something given in obvious faith. She was both perplexed and flattered by it. It was part of the same injunction that had made Kate order her to go with Dora, and it was the same force that brought her to John.

She was pretty sure in her own mind that her company saved him from premature senility. Without her he seemed so remote and alone, given to such random exploration and random thought. By the same token he brought her down to earth, a very real earth, a black coal-dusted earth. He drew her back from her flights of fancy with Bill's letters to tangible sands. So, in many respects they managed to guide each other, and so save each other from the inexplicable. They probably needed it as much as each other. Perhaps, as Bill's letters became increasingly remote, she needed it rather more than John.

Bill wrote: *Can I really call Christ to mind, my Christ, the butchered man, man of flesh, skin, muscle, bone, blood and salt tears, give meaning to his flesh, reasons to the sheds, vans and ruins that cover the globe? They make a brute of beauty, pervert the eyes, make pack hounds. Man love is disgusting and a crime, so strike him down, brother soldier, brother child. It's a grave affair. Stay indoors Mary, only sneak out to hear Saint Peter, from time to time, but beware he whispers dangerous things, delectable things.*

She stood by her grandfather one day and watched him handle a bone-white shaft of wood he had picked up. He was so obviously possessed of vision as he rotated it in his hands, extracting the visual possibilities from it, that she was filled with wonder at his imagination. It struck her that a lifetime underground had stifled him. He had spent his time in the dark, in confined spaces, when his spirit sought wide spaces, the shore and the horizon beyond. He was not so terribly different to Bill in that, except Bill had heard his voices and made his escape, his discreet and personal escape. He could not have survived where they were. She knew that. But how well did any of them survive? She felt a surge of pity for John. He turned to her and displayed his find as if he had deciphered its hidden form, and smiled. She felt like crying.

He put his arm around her. "You're becoming a sad and serious girl, you know. You mustn't forget to smile. Your father would not want that, in any way. He only ever wanted you to be happy."

She broke down. "I miss Daddy so much. I miss him and miss him. Will I always feel like this? Will I always feel this bad?"

"Yes, you'll always feel it, but you'll learn to live with it and even love it."

"Love it?"

"Yes, love it, because it's your love. There can't be any pain where there was no love. Do you really not want any pain? I shouldn't think so. Between grief and nothing, choose grief."

"Oh, grandfather," she moaned, but could say no more.

He whispered a single: "Amen."

Some of these people are possessed of death. It permeates everything about them. It fills their faces. It should be present as dread, but seems only to create wonder. Their possession infuriates me. I don't know why. I despise sick beauty. I despise what is so obviously perverse. Isn't that strange. How can I say that? That's really rich coming from me. I should boast! God, but I'm in with a crowd and half though, aren't I! And it's all I've ever wanted, you know. I see that now. I've got what I want, what I deserve I suppose, because I reckon everyone deserves the best love their imaginations can aspire to. And we are in love, Mary. So in love. That's why I get so worked up I guess. You know, someone actually said to me: Life is totally death, death in nature, death in art, death in sex. I couldn't take that. These deathmongers seem so selfish to me. It's obviously my mother who makes me feel like this. God help me! Don't say that this isn't the job for me, after all. I'm sure it is. Of course, it is. I just have to avoid certain thoughts. Art is so funny. He laughs at everything. He is certainly not possessed of death. He is totally outrageous. He scares me at times. It's a risky business. I never was brave. I never wanted to make a stand and here I am, an outcast on my own island. God but life is confusing at times. Does the Lord still whisper? I heard his voice: Lord, who shall abide in thy tabernacle? who shall dwell in thy holy hill? He that walketh uprightly, and worketh righteousness, and speaketh the truth in his heart. Is it possible? I wonder. God, listen to me, a preacher man. You should have a good laugh at that.

Mary burnt the letter. It formed a brief marigold in her hand. Then she watched the black scraps scatter along the shoreline and disappear from view. She wondered if she should say something to someone. Was it right to keep Bill's communications all to herself? But who should she speak to? He mentioned no one, asked after no one, certainly not directly, not by name.

He wrote: *I could never really belong, say I am bold, tenacious and courageous, a paid-up member, one of the crowd, the family crowd, one of the prospective ghosts, a story man. I don't really want to belong, but I've loved what they loved, I know that, wanted what they've wanted, cried when they were hurt. Christ, I've even nursed their wounds. At the end of the day I'm a Kavanagh, God help me, to put along all my other sins. Hear me, I've wanted to be in the world too. We all want to be in the world. But would you ask them all a question from me? What is the world in? The old priest will say in the lap of God and that will be a beautiful answer. Which God though. A great big brown God. We are all exiles, at the end of the day, at the finish. Your grandmother is a wise woman. Of course we are all Jews, all part of the same stubborn, dogged tribe, God help us.*

He never really needed to ask about people by name. She always told him as much as she could when she wrote. He didn't acknowledge what she said, though. She considered that he had obviously drawn a line between his two lives. Did she have any right to transgress that? Obviously not. His life had to be safe with her. She could say nothing. When the last charred leaves of that letter had been swept away she went to her grandfather. She asked: "Why does grandmother pray so much these days?"

John laughed out loud. "Does she? I hadn't noticed. I suppose it's something she remembers well. At our age you have to do things that you remember well. That's how it is. I mine for fabulous objects."

"Is there a tendency to become more holy as you get older."

"No, not at all." He studied her for a moment, half-smiled then asked: "Why? Do you feel holy?"

"No more than usual. No more than I should. I think."

"That's enough. Just as much as you think."

I am no longer with Art. It couldn't go on. Not really. He was rather wild and wilful. It's not the time. The bigots have the floor. They'll be running the show and what then? Oh yes, what then? What lies will we all cook up? Dead nature, dead art, dead sex. What transgressions we contemplate. What options we assume. What mannequins we are. Back to that, I'm afraid. Dead dummies dressed up for balls! Well, dear, all dressed up with no where to go. What a sham, charade, and waste of energy. What a life really. It's all so phoney. I think he liked the sound of his own sweet, shrill voice. I never met so many people in love with tragedy. If only they knew our people, Mary. Our sturdy, irrepressible, tragic breed. I begin to love them more and more. Yes, over and over. Is that righteous enough? God help me! I feel a bit lost here after all.

"What is a bigot, grandfather?" she asked.

His arms were full of seaweed. She had no idea what he intended to do with that. He considered for a while before eventually saying: "We are all bigots of one kind or another."

"But meaning what?"

"Meaning we are blind and obstinate. Meaning no one gives anyone else a chance. Meaning we cherish the other man's failure. Meaning we see the rank in everyone. Meaning we despise the person that isn't us. And the whole thing in reverse."

"Is that how you see things?"

"I don't see anything anymore. I'm blind to most of what goes on. It's how I feel. I just wonder what on earth has happened to me that I find myself here."

"What about other things, charity, love, and things."

"Those as well."

"What?"

"Bigoted and soiled."

"Please, grandfather."

"I might be wrong. I've been wrong before. I've done wrong before. Luckily I didn't learn to love it."

"I don't believe you."

"You think I do love it."

"You've never done wrong. You're more holy than you make out."

John burst out laughing. The sound blended imperceptibly with the swirling waves.

I think a lot about that corpus Christi when we took mass together. Old Father Bond's a saint of sorts. He fought to bring me home, save me, secure me from exile. I haven't repaid him well. I'd like to say to him thank you for my past, my faces, my lips, my story, my home, but I don't think he'd want to listen to the likes of me. Who in the whole wide world would listen to the likes of me? We're secret men, bogey men, break the traditional mould, who keep our stories to ourselves, close to our saggy chests, our bravery under wraps, our courage in a pot. Sure, I'd like to be a big strong soldier like daddy, maybe a big strong Christian soldier, go fight a war, a proper war, a war for all the people, but all war is disgusting, so I'll have to let the people down. That's too bad of course. It would be something grand to look back on. But then, I hate nostalgia really. It makes me imagine things that weren't real, at all. I don't believe any of it. I wish I could. I wish we were the people I say we were. At the end of the day we're just a bunch of poor old dummies, kitted out in rags, our heads stuffed with notions and schemes. Don't pray for me, just whistle. Once, you know, I wouldn't go to bed and Mammy died. I think of that. What would have happened if I'd gone to bed? I'll never know. I don't even know my own story. But if I could see her face again, even for a minute, a second, say her name, I might be able to profess my faith. Christ I miss her! Who the hell am I to say this to you? Forgive me. God bless. I don't think grace is just around the corner.

Mary went to church. She wanted to talk to Father Bond but when she saw him bustle around the altar, plucking dead flower-heads, she couldn't speak. She wanted to explain to him how much she missed her father and then hopefully find out something about the extent of pain. But when she saw him, for some reason that was inexplicable to herself, he didn't seem the right person after all. When she had thought it through beforehand she had intended to pray, then ask his blessing, but when it came to put her plan into practice it slipped her mind. Instead, she simply went up to the altar step and told him Bill sent all his best. The priest pulled himself around, cradling a weak hand, smiled at her and said he was pleased about that. Bill was a good boy. He always deserved to be a good Catholic boy. Yes, he was grateful.

I don't know who else to write to. Bill always spoke of you so fondly and generously. He really loved you. At least I know you're real. It wasn't always easy to tell with Bill. He used to talk about you a lot, but he said so much, and changed his mind so often that I wasn't sure. When I went through his things I found the letters you wrote to him wrapped up in a red ribbon. I haven't read them I just took your address. I suppose in a clumsy, pining way I'm asking your permission. I know I should have returned them to you. I so much want a piece of him though. He used to tell me the most ridiculous lies. I don't know why. I should have known I suppose. I deal with people who see and hear things, imagine all sorts of things that haven't really happened, but they're not lies. Mind you, I'm not sure I know the difference anymore. Is a lie different to a dream? And which is the worst. He told me in the beginning that he was an orphan brought up by a reclusive maiden aunt who never spoke to him. Later, he told me his father ran a small textiles factory, manufacturing evening wear for women, and that his mother was an artist. I don't know if he forgot the first story or simply changed his mind. He was always doing that. He always mentioned you, though, always in the same generous, loving way. To be honest, it got to the stage where I thought he was making you up. You were always his friend, though. You might be surprised to know the different places you're supposed to have come from. I don't honestly remember him mentioning Cumberland but he might have done. Perhaps you understood him much better than I have. I of all people should have understood something of what was happening, but sometimes you can be too close to someone to know. Love is like that, I suppose, and we were in love. I hope you don't mind my saying that. From what Bill said I'm sure you won't. I loved him from the very first. He was such a comedy. I'll never forget that first night. We were in a pub in Fitrovia. He was pretending he didn't know what was going on, but he did. He was a country boy and not. He was always like that, a country boy and not. I used to show him off all the time. He was confident, funny, a bit too serious, a bit too crazy and the complete opposite. I guess I don't know what it was like for him. I was too busy enjoying him to try and understand him. I know I shall never forgive myself for introducing him to people who had tried to take their own life. He couldn't cope really with other people's pain. He took it all on himself. He was a real sucker for it. I didn't see that at the time. He couldn't be happy unless everyone was. Well, that's not possible. We tend to be a little volatile in our group and a bit wrapped up in ourselves. He didn't ever approve. A bit false in his eyes. He was quite a puritan at times. Oh, poor Bill. The last few months were very strange. He changed from being a bit insular to suddenly being very public. He became concerned by everything. He accused me of cowardice and repinement. He became rather reckless and did some odd things. I didn't know what he was up to at all. I'm afraid that sometimes with people like me, and people like Bill, we start off hugging the shadows and shunning the limelight, basically because we're not sure of ourselves and certainly not sure of the world, and then we go mad, really outrageous. I guess we just have to see how far we can go, how much we can get away with things. It usually ends up by being beaten up in the street some night. But then, Bill was a big boy and could handle himself. No, I don't know. He was certainly pushing against something. I mean, the things he did. He marched to Whitehall with the Spanish Volunteers claiming that he had been to Spain. Honestly, if we got talking to someone in a pub in the evening he'd launch into these stories about what he and his comrades did in Catalonia. He would make out that he went with volunteers from his local town. He'd have a list of ready names as well. Later on, he would be quite angry about it all, going on and on at me about why people listened to such rubbish. You never knew what story was coming next. The strangest thing he did was to attend Fascist meetings in Bermondsey. I don't know what he was trying to prove. He hated Fascists. I know that. I can't work out what all that was about. He probably just wanted to get at our group. Well, his group as well. I realise that. We have to keep ourselves very much to ourselves. You can appreciate that. I think he was deep down more afraid than any of us. He couldn't live with it. He had to put it to the test. He was funny at times, though, marching out singing his favourite psalm: He that goeth forth and weepeth, bearing precious seed, shall doubtless come again with rejoicing, bringing his sheaves with him. He was happy for a time, I'm sure of that, but for some reason he woke up one morning and I think he felt very lonely. He was at home in London and then he wasn't. Deep down I think he wanted to go home, but I don't think he thought that was possible. He should have gone home. At least he'd still be with us. It's so tragic. He really did want to go home, but as with everything with him he always made everything so hard for himself. He was so crammed with longing, shame and rage. It's a hell of a mixture. A real bomb. I suppose it's inevitable that he had to explode. I don't understand that he didn't realise how much I loved him. I know that he wanted to go home, but please write and tell me that there is no objection to my burying him here. It would mean a great deal to me if I could. If there is an objection I shall understand. God bless. Arthur.

There was no objection to Bill being buried in London. Peter said that he had made it his home and so be it. No one went to his funeral, though there was a collection for flowers. The fact that he had taken his own life sufficed to excuse people from attending. Arthur wrote once more to Mary to say that all had gone well, considering. She knew what he meant and felt deeply ashamed. On that same day she told John he was right, everyone was a bigot. He made no response. His mind was on the distant thread of horizon. Mary's days of being on attendance with him were numbered.

*

It was Martin who persuaded Mary to go to the dance on the other side of town, though when she later told the story she always claimed it was her idea. It was a Guy Fawkes dance, organised by the town shopkeepers' association. She would never have been allowed to attend, even with Martin to look after her, if she had asked for permission. No matter that she now worked full-time in Lavery's bakery, from six in the morning to three in the afternoon, and in little over a month she would be eighteen years old. Kate said all the shop owners were Freemasons, not to mention the fact that on bonfire night they burnt effigies of the Pope. It was out of the question. Girls from the Irish streets didn't go to dances on the other side of town. She probably would never have gone, never dreamed of going, had it not been for Tommy McKee.

Tommy McKee was a local man, quite involved with the church, organising the collection, seeing to minor repairs, that sort of thing. He had read the lesson on All Saints day. He didn't have a good voice, in fact, he more or less stuttered his way through it, but he saw it to the end. He had been sitting in the kitchen in Mount Pleasant, in a chair by the kitchen fire, drinking tea and eating fruit-cake, when Mary came home at the end of her shift. He was brief but polite, a sombre, unassuming man. Nevertheless, it was a surprise to find him there. She assumed it was a church matter. He stayed for about thirty more minutes more following her arrival then excused himself. It was then that Dora confided that he had proposed marriage. He was two years Dora's junior. Hugh had been dead for eighteen months. Mary didn't know what to say.

Dora pressed her for a response. Mary eyed her carefully. Her mother didn't show any signs of excitement or passion. In fact, she was extremely matter of fact. There were no indications of anything remotely akin to a girlish infatuation, which wasn't particularly surprising. Tommy McKee wasn't the figure of a man to evoke such a feeling. It was ridiculous. Tommy McKee was a drudge of a man. Mary felt a sense of revolt develop within her, but she couldn't put it into words. It was all too nonsensical. Eventually she asked her mother very simply if she loved him.

Dora remained calm and profoundly matter of fact. He was a decent, hard-working man, an iron-ore miner, who never missed a shift. The iron-ore mines were busier than they'd been for years. He had told her that. The country was arming. There was a demand for iron-ore. The issue of love was immaterial. He was thirty-eight years old, had sober habits, drank and smoked in moderation, and had put a bit of savings aside. He had proposed marriage in the full knowledge of Dora's children. Was she really in a position to decline? Once again Mary didn't know what to say.

There was a period of silence. Neither mother nor daughter knew how to continue. Mary's mind flooded with images, brief pictures of people, her father, her grandparents, the other children, singly, then in groups, impressions and outlines, rather than clear figures, but these images didn't become ideas or words. She had nothing to say. She didn't know how to express the fact that her head was bursting with all these people, and together they formulated her shock and, perhaps, even revulsion at such a proposition. The terrible thing was that the most vivid image of all was that of Tommy McKee himself comfortable by the fire, drinking his tea and eating his fruit-cake, a cake Mary herself had baked. All of that chaos of thought was distilled down into a vacant gaze at her mother.

Dora made numerous aborted efforts to speak. Each one resulting in nothing more than facial expressions and hand movements, those at least indicating her willingness to try. The silence lasted a few minutes. Finally Dora took a grip of herself and began. She ended up making something of an impromptu speech. To begin with her voice was flat and slow. Her mouth was dry and her tongue clicked against her palate. But gradually it came stronger and stronger.

"Look, Mary," she said, "I know it's not easy, not easy on you. You get the worst of it, because you're the one I talk to. Well, you're a woman, well... you know what I mean. Who else? Martin? He's still a little boy in so many ways. He didn't get that thoughtful streak that some in the family have. The others are still children really. I have to talk to you Mary. It's how we've become. Well, you know how it's been these last eighteen months. It hasn't been easy. I've hardly had the chance to miss him, hardly had the right, really. And I do miss him. By God, I miss him. Don't ever think anything else of me. I'm burning right through me even as I say it. But I've got ten children. I've got a cellar with three more. What am I supposed to do? I've got myself a job and I work hard. God, I go out to work every morning before most of my children are even awake and quite frankly I come back sometimes too tired to care. I don't want it to be like that. Your dad's children were everything to him, the roots of him he said. He was soft like that, and hard, don't forget that, everything. He was rich and difficult. Did you recognise that? Were you aware of the complex pattern of him? You never saw him that night in the cellar. Well, how could you? What am I saying? Oh God, Mary, I can't bring his children up like this. I have the welfare here every other week, and I make sure they're all dressed in their worst so I might get another handout. What was I supposed to say when Francis asks right out, right in front of them, can I go and put my proper clothes back on now? I can't go on like this forever." She hesitated for a moment and drew a breath. She pursed her lips, exhaled long and hard, then began again. "I'm lonely, Mary. I'm lonely and I think I'm getting lonelier."

"You're beautiful," Mary protested weakly, unable to articulate more than that.

"I have ten children. It should be eleven. I wish it was eleven. I wish we were more than that." Mary moved to say something more, but Dora spoke up over her, strongly. "But it isn't going to be. Not like I want. I can't bring him back. Do you know what I'm saying. I can't do the impossible. I can't dream him here. Look, he doesn't want to take Hugh's place. He knows that. He knows he can't. He doesn't want that. Do you hear? That isn't what he expects. He says I'll always be Hugh's wife, really..."

"You can't even say his name."

"What?"

"You're not saying his name."

"Tommy. He's called Tommy. You know that. You know him. And he'll always be just Tommy. He said that. He doesn't expect to be called anything else. Tommy, just Tommy."

"Just Tommy."

"It won't be a cold, disgraceful arrangement. Don't get me wrong. I'll be his wife. I know that. I've weighed all that up. He's a decent man, Mary. I could do a whole lot worse."

"You'll die of boredom," Mary snapped petulantly.

Dora smiled at her, then slowly shook her head. "I've had Hugh Glyn."

They left it at that. Mary neither condoned nor condemned her mothers proposal. Dora didn't press her. She assumed she needed time to work it out. She didn't disguise to herself the enormity of what she was asking of her children. She reminded herself that she was not expecting them to love Tommy McKee, just accept him, in the same way she didn't expect Tommy McKee to love them. She didn't bring herself into that equation. She was immaterial. She had spent her love. She insisted to herself that life could be navigated without it. She had loved so much, a brother, a son, and most powerfully, a husband: most powerfully because its demonstrations were so powerful. She longed to have his hands and lips touching her skin again, his body inside hers, panting out that terrible affirmation, yes, yes, yes. But, no, it was never going to be. It seemed that life was a confrontation, a contest, between love and loss. And love didn't stand a chance. She determined in her own mind that she was going to accept Tommy McKee's proposal.

Mary left Dora standing in the kitchen and went outside. She sat down on the steps and looked across the town. The daylight was already failing. A thick grey and yellow haze sank down over the skyline, draping everything. The quays, tanners and railyards were indistinct, known landmarks lost in a blur of smoke and fog. Still, there was the distant rumble and hiss of machinery, the day still active.

She felt her mood sink lower and lower. She began to cry. It wasn't a great show of emotion. Just a few tears trickled across her cheeks. She felt an enormous weight in her chest. If she had needed to speak she would have choked on it. There was no pleasure or savour in anything. What was the point? She hung her head, resting her face in her palms. She didn't close her eyes, but gazed abstractly at the step beneath her. She was empty of all feeling, except for a sense of deep and profound disappointment. She remembered Bill saying that it was so important never to be disappointed, but Bill was dead, so what sense was there in that? What sense was there in anything? Nothing added up, nothing amounted to anything. There was nothing to dream of, and the things worth remembering only made matters worse. There was no escape.

It was as she was musing in this fashion that Martin came down the steps, having finished his shift down Fish. He stepped behind her and put his dirty fingers across her eyes and asked her to guess who. She felt an instant leap in her mood as he spoke to her. She pulled his hands away and quickly turned to him. She sighed his name aloud, the whole weight of her emotional turmoil exposed in pronouncing his name. His expression changed instantly from fooling to something more serious. He said her name twice, as if he were trying to rouse her from sleep. She smiled faintly. He whispered to her that she was crying black tears.

The coal-dust from his hands had smeared across her eyes and cheeks. She said that she was feeling a little bit sad, that was all. It was passing already. He shook his head. He didn't believe it was passing. He said her name again in the same quietly urgent fashion as before, and she smiled in response in the same restive manner as she previously had. He put his hands beneath her shoulders and lifted her up. Then he announced that he was taking her to a dance. He wasn't prepared to accept no for an answer. He knew lots that were going. They weren't going to say anything to anyone, they were just going to go. She didn't argue, she merely wiped her hand across his coal blackened face and said that he did have that thoughtful streak, maybe more than any of them. He simply shrugged his incomprehension at what she meant.

The dance took place in a hall on the other side of the valley. If they looked back they could see the dark outlines of Mount Pleasant and Ginns carved into the hillside opposite them, the workings of Loft, Fish, Canning and the dead Lady surmounting them. There were no lights to see on that side of the valley. However, away to their left there were little pockets of fires dotted here and there along the valley side. Occasional fireworks burst over the dock basins. The waters lit up in sudden flashes of colour. Then the darkness came down quickly again. Dogs howled all around the valley. Outside the hall there was a large unlit bonfire. They went inside.

At one end of the hall there was a small stage. The band were already in place and playing. It was strange listening to music that wasn't provided by Uncle Marty. Mary felt it was disloyal. At the other end of the room there was a bar. There was a small group of men gathered around it drinking. As Martin and Mary came in this group looked them over. Their attention troubled Mary. She was conscious that they might not be wanted. Martin told her that the miners would be along soon enough and everything would be all right, they would have a good time. He then went to the bar and bought them each an orange-cordial. One of the men followed him with his eyes right back to the place Mary had chosen for them to sit. When he realised that Mary had been aware of his interest he smiled. She gave a circumspect nod in return.

They sat for a further forty minutes or so, scarcely talking. On a number of occasions Mary threatened to go home. She felt out of sorts, and besides so little was happening. Martin persuaded her to wait a little longer. Then the band ceased playing and someone came on stage and announced the lighting of the bonfire. The small group of people gathered in the hall went outside.

The bonfire was just as it had been, leafless branches and unidentifiable rubbish, silhouetted against the near dark. There were now many more rockets bursting over the town. The screams of their ascent filled the night air, followed by explosions of colour. Faces were illuminated briefly, gazing skyward. A few minutes later there was a low rumble of singing. Very quickly it grew in intensity. It became a raucous, haphazard chorus. It had started low in the valley, but was obviously getting closer. It was coming along the road Mary and Martin had taken to reach the hall. Very soon they could see lights appearing on the side of the hill, torchlights. The fireworks continued to break across the docks. Dogs howled ever more loudly as the fireworks exploded. Someone went with a taper around the base of the bonfire. It started to crackle and snap. Single flames reached up through the spines of branches, spurted and leapt to other branches. The inner core of the bonfire began to assume a shape, revealed by the lines of flame. Soon the whole structure had taken light. It roared upwards. A halo of flame appeared above the pile, sending a shower of sparks and smoke into the night sky. The side of the hill came into focus.

At the same time as the bonfire became a conflagration a crowd appeared on the crest of the hill. They were singing, chanting and laughing. They carried numerous effigies, held shoulder height, a whole row of floppy, awkward stuffed Guys. They marched right up to the bonfire and one after another launched their dummies into the flame. Pretty soon the bonfire was loaded with a number of lopsided, disfigured forms, their outlines dissolving in the roar of the fire.

Mary shuddered as the flames licked up over the collapsing outlines. The flames themselves screamed as the dummies caught. It was horrific. She couldn't help but think the Kavanaghs had lost family through fire. She didn't know the details, but she had heard it spoken about. She turned away. Martin was no longer beside her. She looked around for him. He had gone off to join the group. It was obvious he knew them. He was helping them throw yet another Guy onto the fire. She shouted to him angrily, annoyed that he had deserted her and disgusted that he was taking part in such a performance, calling his name over and over. Eventually, he turned to her but simply gestured for her to join them. She shook her head. He burst out laughing and turned back to the task in hand. As she looked on he started to shout out wildly, rejoicing in the fact that the dummy had landed right on top of the fire. Mary looked up at it. It seemed to stand above the flames for a moment, its stuffed arms spread out to the side, its head and torso riding the storm below.

Fireworks broke above its head. Although they were off in the distance the angle was such that it looked as if they were just above its clownishly drawn face. A moment later it suddenly collapsed right down into the heart of the fire as if it had fallen through a chute. There was a roar of approval. Mary flinched and turned away again.

As she did, a hand touched her shoulder. She looked up. It was the man at the bar who had smiled at her. She realised she had seen him before. He was a butcher who worked in a shop a few doors down from Lavery's. He delivered the meat for their pies sometimes, when the boys weren't available. He wasn't a butcher boy. He was fully qualified. He was at least ten years older than she was, maybe more. He had a pint in his hand. She could detect the faint sweet smell of dead-meat from him, as well as the aroma of beer and cigarettes. He smiled at her. He asked her what she thought of the fire. She didn't seem to be enjoying it too much. Was she scared? There was nothing to be scared of. When it died down a bit they could throw some potatoes in the ashes and let them cook, and later when it died down a bit more they could pick them out. She replied that she wasn't scared at all. She added that she was only pleased that she hadn't recognised anything that looked remotely like the Pope tossed onto it. He considered her remark for a moment, then burst out laughing and went off.

Shortly after, Martin came back and led her into the hall. The room was now more or less packed. There was dancing and singing. Martin was in the heart of it with a group of lads just about the same age as him. Mary was on the edge of the group. She watched the others dancing and listened to the band play. She found the boys a little tiresome. They were like kids. Maybe her mother was right. Martin was still a little boy at heart. Eventually, their conversation got round to war. Of course, it had been the topic of conversation for months. They universally denounced Chamberlain's agreement with Hitler as treachery. They virtually outdid each other in their willingness to fight. And then all burst out into a round of laughter when somebody demanded to know where the hell Czechoslovakia was, anyway? Another said that what he really wanted to know was, just what exactly was a Jew?

Mary wandered off. As she stepped away Martin called to her. She turned and smiled, and gestured that he continue with his friends. She wandered around the edge of the hall, watching the dancing couples. Once again the butcher approached her. He asked her if she would care to dance herself. She declined, but he insisted. He turned out to be a fair dancer himself. They danced to a few tunes, then he said he had to have another drink before he could manage another step. He offered her but she refused. He smiled and went off. He returned with a small glass of something for her. She held it at arms length. He burst out laughing and pressed her to at least try it. She put it to her lips. It was sweet and abrasive at the same time, but not at all unpalatable. She drank it down. They danced a few more, then had another drink. She found that after the second she was slightly tipsy, and it wasn't such an awful feeling. For the first time that day since she had sat on the steps she didn't feel too bad, at all. And the more she danced so the more the feeling grew in her. What did anything matter? There was no point fighting everything, you would only lose in the end. She threw herself more into the dancing.

She had no idea how long this had gone on when the music came to a halt. Someone came onto the stage and announced that it was the time to choose the Bonfire Queen. The crowd in the room broke out into excited applause. The man held up an envelope and a box, which were evidently prizes for the winner. He waved these in the air, building up the excitement, and then with a great flourish in his voice, declared that the queen was the lovely beauty with black hair dancing with Josh Tinnion, the butcher. The crowd parted, following the direction he was indicating. Mary looked back horrified. She couldn't be the Bonfire Queen. She wasn't supposed to be there. To make matters worse, as she looked towards the stage, a photographer appeared. The man on stage announced him as a photographer from the Whitehaven News. That was too much. Mary turned and fled. As she exited through the door she heard Martin's voice behind her calling her name, over and over.

She had every intention of running all the way back to Mount Pleasant, but as she came out into the cold air she felt suddenly quite dizzy. She stopped and tried to steady herself. She didn't feel quite right, at all. She looked around. Everything had a strange, unreal quality to it, as if lines didn't quire connect as they should. She gazed at the bonfire. It was reduced to a pile of glowing cinders. There were a couple a people beside it, raking sticks through it, causing small sparks to ignite in the air. For some reason they made her want to cry, they were so lovely. She took a step towards it, but stumbled. She might have fallen, but she felt her arm taken. She assumed it was Martin. She turned towards him. It was the butcher, Josh Tinnion. He smiled and whispered that she was silly running off without her prize. His face was ruddy in the glow of the embers. He had a long, lean, yet rather square face, with skin that had a thick, leathery texture. His forehead wrinkled with clearly defined lines.

His hair was piled high on his forehead, cut severely up the sides, but then long on top, with a wavy quiff oiled into place.

He supported her and they strolled forward. They went past the bonfire and began to descend down the valley side, not down the road by which the crowd had come to the hall but down a hillside path. He spoke to her all the time, but she didn't really hear a word. His voice was just a texture amongst the other night time sounds, not a particularly pleasing or soothing texture, but not disagreeable either. They stopped on a promontory. He bent over her. He was quite a bit taller than her. He brought his face close to hers. Again she was aware of the aroma of dead-meat, cigarettes and beer. He kissed her. She didn't resist. As his face came across hers she felt she was sinking. He helped her down onto the ground. He put his hand up her skirt and parted her knickers. He lay on top of her and penetrated her. She wasn't aware that she made any sound at all. In no time at all he was standing over her, helping her to her feet. They continued down into the town.

She didn't remember getting home. The last thing she could bring to mind was climbing into bed beside Julie and Jane and feeling intensely cold, then later Martin coming to the door and whispering her name, but she let on she was asleep.

Martin came to her door and called her name for the next three days, both before he went to work and as soon as he returned. She didn't answer at any time but pretended she was asleep. She told her mother she felt unwell, but didn't need a doctor. It was just a touch of flu. She simply lay there for three days, without eating and without really thinking. The only consideration that did cross her mind was that it would have been different if her father had been there, he would have knelt by the bed and stayed with her all the time, but she quickly dismissed that idea. After three days she got up. She simply said she was feeling a little better.

That afternoon, much to her shock and mild horror, Josh Tinnion knocked on the door of Mount Pleasant. It was Aunty Dora who came to fetch her. She said there was a man wished to talk to her. He didn't actually say much at all. He invited her to go for a walk. She wasn't sure, but didn't know what else to do. She went with him. He led her back across town, and back up the hill where the bonfire had been. As it was a cold, fresh day if she looked back across town she could clearly see Mount Pleasant and Ginns in the distance. He stopped at a row of houses almost directly opposite Mount Pleasant. He asked her to go inside. She was uncertain, a bit confused. Did he want to introduce her to someone? Nevertheless, she went in. She found the house completely empty. She looked around more confused than ever. He said he had bought it for her. If she wanted it then it was hers. She could be Mrs Tinnion. She only had to say.

They were married the following March, the same month the Germans invaded Prague and finally completed their take-over of Czechoslovakia. The papers were full of invasion. The talk was more than ever focused on war. Before the marriage Josh Tinnion had promised to become a Catholic. He went to Father Bond for lessons. He joked about them. The lesson consisted of his doing the priest's garden for him. The lessons were supposed to amount to a certain number so that they could be completed by corpus Christi when he would be able to take his first communion. He persuaded the priest to allow the marriage to take place earlier as it would have a direct effect on his tax payments. Father Bond agreed, accepting Josh's solemn vow to complete his conversion. After the wedding he never went into a Catholic church ever again. When their first child was born, despite all of his assurances, he insisted that it was to be baptised a Protestant.

On his wedding night he got hopelessly drunk. The marriage wasn't consummated until the following afternoon, in the house facing Mount Pleasant, by which time he felt less hungover. It was as quick and dispassionate as the first time on the hillside path. Once again Mary could detect the sickly sweet smell of dead-meat, as well as cigarettes and beer. At nine o'clock that night he washed and dressed and said he was going out. When she questioned it, he told her he went out every night at that time for a few pints. When he had gone she walked out onto the bank and looked out across the town. She could see the outlines of where her whole life up until that point had taken place, Mount Pleasant, Ginns, the south shore. So much of it remained, so much of it was lost. She fell to her knees, but didn't pray. She didn't expect to be happy any more. What was there to pray for?

Five months later, just a matter of a few weeks before Britain declared war on Germany, Dora married Tommy McKee. She wore a simple dress, something she would have worn any Sunday to church. Francis, dressed in a little suit with short pants, held a horseshoe throughout the ceremony. At the end of the service he was ushered forward to hand it to his mother and step-father. He held it out. Tommy McKee moved to pat him on the head, but immediately checked himself. Dora took the horseshoe, then she quickly picked up Francis and nestled his face up against hers, pressing him so tightly he couldn't look either right or left.

*

At the end of May 1940 while the *little ships* were crossing to France John stood ankle deep in water, his boots tied around his neck, his breeches tied above his knees, watching little ships leave the harbour. The fishing smacks pulled their drag-nets slowly across the bar of the horizon and the coal steamers entered the still waters. Plumes of black smoke fanned into the empty, sun bleached sky, and gulls floated high in the vault. He could scarcely hear them cry. He could only hear the endless susurrus of the surf. The sunlight was petalled on the surface, appearing in mobile flashes in the element of mirrors.

He moved along the beach, kicking his feet lazily through the shallow waves. It was his beach now that Mary no longer came, now she was on the other side of the valley. Indeed, hardly anyone ever came for very long anymore, usually only taking the time it took to exercise a dog. The beachcombing when whole families would pass the entire day there was suspended, maybe even finished. It was his own land. He knew it and often smiled to himself about it. He imagined they called him old John and the south shore old John's beach. Without understanding how, he had become a little bit eccentric, like McClean with his boats and John Darcy with his trolley. He was therefore surprised, and somewhat troubled, to find Martin approaching him. Martin never frequented his beach.

He paddled right into the water beside his grandfather and started speaking to him immediately. His voice was shrill and excited. "Grandfather, will you talk to my mother?"

"It depends. What about?"

"About me."

"Surely you're old enough to talk for yourself, Martin."

"Not what I have to tell her."

"Are you in trouble?"

"I don't think so. I don't know though. No, of course not. Not like you mean."

"Well, if you're not in trouble you can talk to your mother. You know that. You don't need me."

"It's about joining up. I just don't know what to say to her. I don't want her upset and feeling bad about me. I don't want her feeling I'm letting her down."

412

John turned his attention keenly to Martin and looked him over for a moment. His perplexity made him look out of sorts and comic. "Listen, Martin," John began benignly, "I've been giving this a bit of thought and to be honest I reckon it's all quite simple. We are neutral in all this and bound to stay so, so if it comes to it we'll get you a place on one of the coalboats going home. We'll get you to hell out of all this. Your mother will understand that. God, Martin, I don't think there's anyone would understand better. She's not going to feel let down. Why ever would you think that?"

"Neutral!" Martin exclaimed incredulously. "I'm not neutral in this. This is my country."

"Martin, Martin," John reasoned, realising the extent to which he had misunderstood. "This isn't your fight. This isn't our fight. This is what we've been waiting for. Let them slog it out and tear each other to bits. Let them destroy each other for all we care. God, you never know, but maybe even history will stop. Can you imagine that Martin?" He stopped speaking for a moment and smiled. The gesture was sour and harsh. He quietly added. "And then we'll die for God and God alone. God and no one else."

"You don't believe that," Martin declared bitterly. "Even my grandmother doesn't believe that and she prays like some kind of bloody saint. What the hell is all that about? Oh no, don't let God interfere. This is my country. Do you understand? This is my country and this is my fight and it's a damn good fight, the fight Mr Duffy was always talking about, the fight against Fascism, and I'm not skulking in some damned coalboat for anybody. Don't forget my father was a soldier."

John didn't respond. He began to walk away, dragging his feet through the shallows, keeping the shoreline parallel. His mind was racing. The idea of Hugh being a soldier was too difficult to argue. Of course Hugh had been a soldier, as Robert had been a soldier. Robert had tried to talk to him the way Martin was talking to him now. They were both so convinced by themselves, so convinced by the fact that they wanted to do what was right. They declared it with the certainty that they were involved with such a larger world than him. He suddenly felt the insularity his beach existence had become. He felt its weight bearing down on him as he ploughed forward. He wanted to counteract that feeling. He could only think of one way. He had to speak out, brag even, and tell of his own exploits, detail the enthusiasms and skirmishes that made up his own history and by the same token the history of those like him. He wasn't some damned eccentric skulking out his days on

413

a barren shore. He had stood his ground. He had kept faith. He had damned himself for a dead son.

He turned back intending to berate Martin with his dealings. He found that Martin was just a few feet from him. He had followed right behind him. John groaned inwardly at the figure Martin cut. He looked so impetuous, impatient and untried. When John did eventually speak his voice was wretched and cowed. "Oh Martin, if it doesn't all come to an end for us, if history never halts, fighting their battles and not our own, we'll never get beyond these beaches, we'll just be defeated by it. Our degraded faith, whichever one, Martin, whichever one, poor old Duffy, just washed up, washed up and pointless. It has to mean something, the dying has to be for something."

"You don't believe any of it. I know you don't. You know what this war's about. You know what we're up against."

"Of my country I am ashamed," John said, his voice weakening even more, in fact, virtually failing.

"I don't know what you're saying. I don't understand. I really don't."

John suddenly spoke up strongly and fiercely. "I'm talking about nation destroying nation, this nation destroying mine, some people making life unliveable for other people, some people making life hell, and the possibility of peace."

"And what do you do when someone destroys your peace?" Martin demanded, agitated and aggravated by the progress of the conversation.

"Kill him!" John said simply, but emphatically. "I kill him!"

"You mean you fight!"

John eyed him sharply. "I know what I mean, and I mean I kill him. I mean I play my part and I damn myself, damn myself a million times, a million times over and over, damn myself with everyone else, until we're all washed up, us and the cats and the dogs and the goats and the monkeys, and all the rest, the whole damned lot of us, all on the shore of a single nation, a single nation. Do you hear me?" He fell silent abruptly. He felt exposed and awkward. He looked fixedly at Martin, appealing to him, and very quietly added: "We're all immigrants without God. Thank God." He shook his head and turned away. "Oh, to hell with it. I was born a long time ago."

Picking up the altered note in John's voice Martin asked: "Will you talk to her?"

"No, damn it, you talk to her."

"I know I'm not the breadwinner anymore, well, you know. But, I'm in a reserve profession," Martin moaned. "I'm a miner. How will she understand?"

John turned to him again. "You talk to her, and when you talk to her count yourself lucky you don't have a father, not a real father, anyway. Now, leave me alone." He again turned away, and began to make slow tentative steps forward, inching into deeper waters.

Martin hesitated for some time, but gaining no more attention from John began to walk away. After a few steps he stopped. He looked at the old man slowly moving away from him, the water around his knees, then called to him: "I'll leave you now but I'll talk to you before I go. Promise me that you'll speak to me. I won't go without you speaking to me."

John stopped wading, but he didn't immediately respond. He didn't really know how. He wasn't sure what was being asked of him. Martin called to him again. His voice was demanding and compelling. John couldn't deny it. Not this time. He called out as if he were shouting to the sea in front of him: "Of course I'll speak to you. Of course, I will. I'll speak to you." He heard Martin kick through the shallows then march away across the shingle. When he was gone there was a terrible silence.

John stood still for a while gazing ahead at the vast surface of water that stretched in all directions from him. It shone in broken fragments, a mosaic of shimmers. Its surface moved slowly up and down his leg, a few inches above the knee. He felt it like a caress. It was hypnotic and dreamlike. The light seemed to distil before him into a single intensity, a whiteness, singular and sharp.

He inched forward some more, sliding his feet across the sandy sea-bed, his soles breaking the surface. After a few more steps his foot hit against something solid and sharp. He bent down and fished about with his hand, the water up to his shoulder. He pulled out a long, slender piece of metal. It was heavily corroded, its entire surface encrusted with rust, but it was clearly a knife. He turned it round and round in his fingers, the oxidase staining his fingertips a dirty brown, then lay it across his two open palms and gazed at it. The skin of his hands beneath the metal was thick and leathery, marked by numerous small scars, the fingers marked by a patterning of heavy tobacco stains. They were soiled hands. They had been stained long before by the same type of tool, perhaps even the self-same tool. He held it aloft in the sunlight. Its texture disappeared and only an outline remained. He turned it again in the severe light, attempting to extract its precise shape from its corrosion.

As he turned it he heard a slow murmur come to him. At first it was like the whisperings of the surf, reaching and receding up the shingle, but then it became defined into a single lowly uttered voice, then gradually a number of voices, all reciting the fifteen decades of the Holy Rosary. He wrapped his two palms firmly around the knife, virtually concealing it, and lowered it to his chest, and listened. The voices seemed to be coming from somewhere in the sea before him. He peered hard into the sunlight that remained distilled, harshly white, bright and brittle. He was sure he could see vague shapes. They were scarcely even outlines, just shadows, an intimation of something, whether near or far he couldn't say. He simply had an inkling of their presence.

The recitation went on, no stronger, no weaker. He wanted a clearer sense of the shadows. He stepped further into the water. It inched up to his thighs. The light seemed to grow correspondingly brighter. The outlines of the figures became no clearer, but their features flashed briefly into focus, only to disappear as quickly, as if they had been illuminated by a sudden brief torch. The revelation was enough for him to recognise members of his own family, family he had not seen for half a century and in some cases more. He could see his father and mother, his grandparents, a number of his brothers and sisters, even those who had died in childhood. Of course, they were all dead. With that realisation there was a moment of greater revelation. The light burned fiercely on their expressions. And still they simply carried on reciting the Holy Rosary. But as they did there was an indication of a smile on their expressions, a smile indicative of calm satisfaction. He knew it was for him. They were smiling for him. And with those smiles they were summonsing him, chanting the termination of his exile. He was being called back across a sea dear to his heart, back home, to his own country. He responded, inching his way gingerly into ever deeper water.

As the water washed about his waist he heard fiddle music. It drifted across the waves, subdued, but gay and lively. He turned round. He could see Marty on the shore. He was dressed in a long white coat that came down below his knees, which he wore completely unbuttoned, and his hair was long, flowing over his shoulders and down his back. And as he played he danced to his own tune, his coat flaring around him and his hair swaying. He jigged along the shingle, skipping, spinning, and bowing like a dancing figure in a child's kaleidoscope. And all the time he fiddled and danced he kept his eyes on John and laughed all the while.

John followed his dancing antics as he played back and forth along the water's edge, and then as the tune continued, its tempo changing fluently from time to time, it was accompanied by clapping. He turned to the source. He saw Gavin Duffy dressed only in a pair of ragged breeches, his face, torso, arms and legs below the knees smeared with coal-dirt, like war paint applied by the fingers, forming irregular abstract patterns. As John's attention lit on him he tossed his head in acknowledgement, but kept on clapping, smiling as he did, then called out: *The tragedy is letting them have the last laugh Devlin, don't forget that, man. We had the first laugh and by God it was a good one.* But Gavin, are you not mad? John called back. Gavin burst out into the most uproarious laughter.

There was further clapping. Peter Kavanagh was on the other side of Marty facing Gavin, keeping time, dressed in full uniform which was immaculately clean. He saluted John, missing only one beat, the movement fluid and in time. *I got it wrong, didn't I, Uncle John. I shouldn't have made out I was going to be happy when he had to go away.* John was about to reply, uttering words to the effect that Anne loved him, when he saw Anne herself, slowly dancing down the shingle, her skirt flaring as she turned. She looked as lovely as she had on that first night he had seen her, the night Bobby went away. She smiled, blew him a kiss and called out: *I never knew so many people ready to be happy. I think that was a piece of magic, don't you.* He nodded his head weakly.

A moment later and the beach was crowded. It was like the night of Bobby's going away all over again. John Darcy was there with his mother. They were singing together, the sound catlike and comic. McClean was there, dancing a sailor's reel, his pyknic body moving like a puppet on strings. Hugh and Dora and all the children were there, including young Hugh. (There was no Tommy McKee.) Dora held out her hands for him to come and dance, but he shook his head. She nodded sceptically, implying that he would later. The Boland sisters were there. Julia burst out laughing and asked him: *What on earth happened to that ridiculous little runt?* He was about to say they had kept more, many more, when she burst out laughing again and said: *I heard you tried to kill it with your own bare hands. You wouldn't sacrifice a runt, John Devlin, surely not, not even a sickly stray. I know you better than that.* Dora Boland just eyed him calmly, flicking a torrent of tears from her

417

weeping eye in his direction. They splashed on the water in a spray of colour, violet and indigo.

All the Kavanaghs were there. He caught sight of Tom and immediately called out to him, asking him what he'd been up to. Tom shrugged proudly. *I was arrested in the Dublin port for handling explosives and sent down for a couple of years. I became a soldier though, and fought with Frank Ryan's crowd in Spain. It was really to get at those old bastards the Irish Brigade. I can look him in the eye for sure and not give a damn.* John had more to ask but he was gone, lost amongst the turmoil of the dancing crowd. Catherine and June danced as if they were a mirror image of each other, one on either side of Marty, replicating each other's moves, producing a wild and vigorous display. When they were through they burst out laughing, put their index finger to their lips and shook their heads. They refused to speak. Instead he heard Bobby's voice saying: *What about Polly, what about Polly?* John felt his spirits run wild at the prospect of seeing Bobby, and there he was his handkerchief pressed against his mouth, looking more as if he were stifling laughter than a fit of coughing. You never told me about the black miners, Bobby, John called. But Bobby waved his hand as if he were incapable of talking, his congestive state too much to contend with. John's spirits shrank back in disappointment. He heard himself wistfully uttering Bobby's name over and over.

At the same time as he spoke Bobby's name he heard the Holy Rosary grow in volume behind him. He turned quickly. The horizon was clustered with vague, shadowy apparitions. The Holy Rosary and fiddle music contended. He turned back quickly towards the beach. He cried out: Where's Robert? Where is he? You can't hide a whole heaven, can you? Where is he?

As soon as he had spoken the fiddle music began to wind down, slowly and discordantly, fracturing. And as the music wound down the beach began to depopulate, each figure disappearing without his noticing the moment of departure. Pretty soon there was only Marty left. The music ground to a complete halt. Marty lowered the fiddle and made a bow, a large ostentatious bow. At the same time as Marty ceased playing the Holy Rosary became deeper and more intense, as if the voices were coalescing into one. He turned back to the horizon. He took another step forward. The light grew brighter and brighter, a sheer brilliant white. He could no longer see any figure clearly, the light was too intense, but he was still aware of them, as if they were moving behind a partially transparent screen. He took another step. As he did he heard his name called behind him

He turned yet again to the beach. He could see Kate at the top of the shingle bank. Marty was still there, his figure statuesque by the water's edge. Kate extended her arms. *Will you dance, John Devlin,* she said, *God but I have a mind for it, tonight, you and I, what do you say?* Where's Robert, he asked? She shook her head. They gazed at each other for a moment or two, then very quietly she joined in the recitation of the Holy Rosary. Then as she moved through her decades the voices now behind him began to fade.

He closed his eyes. He kept on listening. He could hear the gentle surge of the swelling tide and he heard Kate's voice in it humming her rosary, and then far off and remote the echo of it, coming somewhere from the sea. He spun round suddenly and flung the knife as far out into the water as he was able. He saw it hit the surface and vanish, the broken water recovering as quickly as it was disturbed. The horizon beyond was still and blue. There were little ships dotted along its margins. There was silence. The Holy Rosary was either concluded or suspended. He called out: "*Lord, give ear to my prayer that goeth not out of feigned lips...*" He waited a moment as if he expected an echo to return to him then, when one was obviously not forthcoming, he smiled, shook his head, wheeled around and slowly made his way back to the shore. He knew there was a dancer waiting for him. It wasn't the time to think of another country.

Chapter Nine

A three-quarter moon hung above the Orne. The river in the valley was red, and the moon was red shining through haze, dust and smoke. Martin lay down in dust on a hill on the west bank. He listened as bombers came from the north and dropped their target indicators, then their loads. He could hear Welsh spoken all around him. He pressed into the dry ground, screwed up his face and closed his eyes. The incomprehensible chatter grew louder and louder. He wanted it to stop. He wanted it all to stop. He opened his eyes. The valley thundered. Vivid lights streaked the purple sky. The thud of landing bombs could be felt as well as heard. He peered into the red bowl.

Duffy whispered. Martin heard him across the concrete, his voice hard, precise, yet tinged with a note of lassitude. *Fire the capitalists! They are your enemy!* Not Duffy, Donald, a mortar sergeant. *Oh, Martin!* "Mary!" he called aloud. *Oh, Martin.*

"Women soon, maybe," Donald said, moving to lie closer to Martin.

Martin shuddered, taken aback by his sudden awareness of the sergeant beside him. Flares pumped across the sky. The horizon erupted into a series of orange beacons. Again, again and again. *Martin, Martin, Martin.* "Shush!" Martin said wearily. "Shush, for Christ sake!"

"Don't take on," Donald said impatiently but sympathetically. "I know what you mean, though. I wouldn't like to be amongst that lot tonight. Let's keep to hell out of it." He burst out laughing. The gesture was bluff but well intentioned. "I'd much rather be swimming!" He paddled his arms along the dust.

"I see they're speaking Welsh again," Martin said sullenly.

"It's not deliberate. They're excited, a bit afraid, unsure. It's not against you."

"It is deliberate," Martin snapped. "And it doesn't help me."

"How the hell did you end up in the Welsh Fusiliers anyway?" Donald demanded, amused and at the same time marginally annoyed by Martin.

"Because they wouldn't let me join the navy."

"A swimming man!"

"Fuck you, I said. If I can't join the navy then put me any damn place you like. So, here I am stuck with you lot."

"And what a bloody treat, young man," Donald laughed, "to be here amongst such men watching Caen kicked to bits. What a magical bloody show, eh? Right bloody show." As the sergeant spoke Martin eyed him strangely, as if he didn't recognise him, his laughter seeming grotesque and vulgar. Martin thought of Duffy again. Recently he came to mind more and more often. The sound of harsh, self-censuring laughter continued in Martin's head long after Donald had ceased. Martin reached out but his hand grasped nothing but dust. Donald spoke again, his voice once again familiar and cheerful. "What the hell would induce anyone to join the navy. All that fucking water to die in, for Christ sake."

"My grandfather had his own beach."

Donald roared his scepticism. "I never took you to be landed."

"His own personal island too."

"Away with you, you little liar!"

"Calls it home!"

"Can you believe it, but before I joined this man's army I couldn't swim. Not a stroke. But look at the cut of me now. Four years in Minehead just jumping off the sea-wall into the big blue yonder. Best four years I ever spent really. Bloody marvellous."

"Shush!" Martin said fiercely. He looked into the valley. Bombs still plunged towards the city. Caen shimmered beneath the three-quarter moon. Martin groaned and let his head fall heavily against the ground. "Shush!" he repeated defiantly. "Someone might hear."

"You're crazy Martin, you know that, absolutely crazy."

"You would be crazy if you weren't a Welshman. And, anyway, you're still crazy. You're all fucking crazy." He quickly looked back and shouted aloud: "Speak English, you bastards!"

There was momentary silence, but that was quickly breached by a roar of laughter.

Caen lit up with a further wave of bombs. Martin beat the ground, then uttered into it: "Stop! Stop, for Christ sake!"

"It won't stop tonight, Martin, boy," Donald said. "They'll bomb away until dawn."

"No," Martin said wearily, "I don't want that to stop."

"What then? Not the Welsh? That won't stop either. Be fair."

"No," Martin said, with the same note of fatigue, "they can go to hell. I shouldn't have said it."

"They love you really, you know."

Martin balked at the suggestion. He looked again at the city in flames beneath the moon, its skyline a strange shifting contention between shadow and light; its tall chimneys reaching into the heavily streaked sky then vanishing into hazy darkness. *Fire the capitalists! They are your enemy!* What should I do, Mr Duffy, Gavin? Oh Christ! *Martin, Martin, Martin!* "Mary! I'm sorry!" The ground quivered beneath him. He gripped his hands before his chest.

"Praying, boy?" Donald laughed, but then as soon as he had said it he quickly apologised. "Look, I'm sorry, I didn't mean anything. I just, well, you know..."

Martin grinned, lay on his side and uttered: "I've got dust all down my front!" He could see the clusters of Lancasters and Halifaxes as they crossed the moon. Within moments they were gone and the moon's face returned large and turquoise. Artillery took up the bombardment. The air swelled with thunder. "Of course I wasn't praying," Martin said petulantly. Donald shrugged as much as to say he didn't care. Martin closed his eyes and despite everything fell asleep.

He awoke to a soft, liquid dawn. Donald was asleep by his legs. The artillery were still pumping their loads towards the city. He stood up. The city looked beautiful in the valley. Gentle pink sunlight trickled through the haze, dust and smoke like liquid on a muslin frame. Pale mauve shapes formed mysterious presences in the mist along the valley floor where the Orne presented a currentless silver thread winding beyond sight. In the yellow cornfields that spread across the entire valley floor hundreds of tanks had collected. He went towards them. He began to whistle as he climbed down.

When he reached the valley floor he was greeted by an irate cocoa coloured faced man glaring at him, holding up his hands to bar him. He was dusted and dishevelled. He carried knives, a tommy-gun, a bandoleer, hand-grenades, rope, pick handle, spade and a copy of the Daily Mirror. He barked at Martin. His voice was severe, yet not unfriendly: "Hey pal, the bridges are down over there. Do you understand? All down. Okay, pal."

"I'm not crossing the river," Martin answered.

"Shit you ain't, pal!"

"Are you crossing the river?"

"Every damned last soldier."

"Good luck, then."

"Fuck that! Don't court luck pal, make sure you can swim or catch yourself a piggyback. Okay pal."

Martin grinned his agreement, then turned back up the hill leaving the cocoa coloured soldier to his preparations.

That morning they followed the tanks into the city. It loomed, in its own still netting, out of the yellow plain. Moving down the hills they could see the single surviving chimney of the *Colombelles* steel factory, and the distant suburbs still held by the Germans. But as they descended into the valley the tanks came before them level with the city and the corn and mustard fields spread long yellow waves around them, so the city was no longer decipherable. As they marched a white horse came towards them through the corn, an old farmer leading it through the mass of advancing troops. As he did he periodically lifted his cap to announce: "Vive la France! Vive l'Angleterre!" His voice was dry and sticky. The horse was old and lean, a decrepit looking cart-horse. Behind it a pall of smoke and dust hung over the valley and the city waited. It seemed to Martin strangely peaceful.

However, there was no entry into the city. At the first cross-roads bulldozers were shovelling masonry and rubble into bomb craters which had made it impossible for the tanks to continue. For the rest of the morning the Welshmen simply had to wait and watch the bulldozers make insignificant indentations on the walls of rubble that obstructed them.

Then, in the early afternoon, they were ordered to enter ahead of the tanks. They clambered over bank after bank of dry rubble. There were trees, poles, petrol pumps, wires, cars, trucks and railings chewed and churned in the heaps. To begin with progress was slow, but then became impossible when heavy firing forced them back from the next cross-roads.

Martin ran from the gun fire. He fell into a mound of dust and pressed himself hard into it. Fragments of shattered masonry pressed painfully against his body. He could hear sobbing overhead. The *sobbing sisters, the wailing Winnies*, they called them, the German mortars. He began to count, much as Kate and Aunty Dora counted, fingering the beads of their rosary. Christ, he had dust down his front. He stood up and brushed himself down repeatedly. *Martin, Martin, Martin!* "Mary! Oh God, Mary, I'm sorry." He looked around and caught sight of Donald across the street, sheltering under a still standing arched doorway, calling to him. He ran to join him.

Donald led a group of them through the partial structure of a still remaining house. The front and the roof were gone. Sunlight shone on exposed rafters and lintels. The rear remained intact. As they made their way through the ruin it became suddenly dark and airless. Martin looked back. He was choking on the dust heavy air. Through fractured frames he could see dust spiral through the sunlight, pouring in a steady beautiful trickle. He stood still for some time simply watching it. *Martin, Martin, Martin!* "Mary!" he called out hopelessly. As he did he felt her hand slip into his, small and cold. He wanted to cry with relief. He looked down. He saw the face of a child, a young girl, the look on her face patient and unafraid. He was immediately roused from his reverie. All around him were children, grubby, dishevelled children. They were all silent, expressionless, simply watching.

"Christ!" Martin uttered, then howled through the gloom towards Donald: "Are they all alone here, do you think?"

"Seems like."

"Damn!"

Donald considered for a moment, obviously unsure what to do next. His gaze quickly scanned the children, without resting on anyone in particular, then with a sudden display of resolve he called out, ordering his men: "Come on, we're going." He ran at the rear door and kicked at it until it snapped from its hinge. Masonry fell into the empty frame, light rushed in and dust poured through the beam. Beyond the threshold lupines and gladioli were visible. "Come on!" he screamed at the soldiers who were still waiting. All at once they responded to his command and ran out, one after the other, bursting through the lupines and gladioli. They made unhindered progress following a path of gardens. Caen was in bloom, the scent of flowers blending into the dust laden air. The sound of fighting drifted, vanished and returned in sequence, left them, then circled them.

When the line of gardens ceased they regained the road at another cross-roads. There was a strong presence of troops already gathered there. A few hundred yards ahead there was a courtyard from where there was heavy firing. Dense mortar fire was returned. They moved slowly forwards. The firing moved away. They entered the courtyard sheepishly. No one mentioned the silent children.

The buildings in the square had been badly damaged, whole facades torn away revealing exposed floors like open dolls'-houses, with doll's-

425

house furniture and doll's-house wallpaper. A cloud rested within the square, the weight sunk from it, leaving a trailing discoloration and insubstantial mist. The sunlight splintered and was hot. A small steeple pointed into it. Martin traced its still extant contours with his eyes. His eyes watered. He pressed his eyelids. He heard voices deep within him. *I will pray for you! What will you do for me?*

Donald arrested him from his musing by calling attention as a group of nuns descended from the steps of the church. It was a sign of respect, a symbol of military order. All at once the square began to fill with people. The church doors opened wide. Old men, old women and children came down to the soldiers bearing armfuls of flowers. They came from cellars and side-streets, converging silently together. Men wearing the ridged helmet of the French army and carrying arms, the long rifle of the French army, German rifles and even British sten-guns, stood ready for inspection. Some wore the uniform of the French army, in the main shabby and creased, but most wore tattered civilian clothes. Everyone wore the Cross of Lorraine.

"Father, I pity you," Martin whispered to himself.

In the courtyard they raised the Tricolour. Straight after, it appeared on all the balconies. They sang the *Marseillaise*. The courtyard filled with the sound. They exchanged flowers. And then shots rang out. The crowd cheered and began the *Madelon*. More shots were fired. It was only then, as people fell, that they realised they were under fire. Again they ran for the cellars and lay back down amongst the shattered walls and casements.

Martin lay with Donald amongst a heap of parlour furniture. The walls of the house were absent. The courtyard had fallen silent. Only the Tricolours moved in the light breeze. The fighting sounded ever more distant. *You know that this is blasphemy!* Martin whispered to himself. *Martin, Martin, Martin!* "Mary, oh Mary, what should I have done?" he whispered beneath his breath. He shook his head. His mind was racing. The face of the unresponsive child was consuming him.

"Christ! Look at the Sister!" Donald exclaimed.

Martin roused himself. He saw one of the nuns tiptoeing her way across the courtyard. He stood up. Donald dragged him down, shouting into the courtyard as he did: "Sister, for Christ's sake, will you get down! Get down!" Still she came on. No shot was fired. Eventually she reached their parlour. Donald glared at her and shouted: "What the hell are you playing at?"

She was defiant, yet sympathetic. "I refuse to be afraid forever, sergeant. I have sacrificed enough." Donald turned away from her. He couldn't look at her. He felt outraged and humbled. She stepped forward, ducking under fallen beams. She smiled benignly towards Donald, then turned to Martin. His eyes remained steadily fixed on her. She smiled at him, then reached out and took hold of his hands. She weighed them in her own for a moment then spoke up, clearly and intently: "We want you to know that as the guns are in the church we do not mind if you explode it."

Donald turned back, eyed the old nun clasping Martin's hands for a second, then burst into scant, abject laughter. Unperturbed, she turned to him, gave a slight bow, then smiled with great simplicity. Donald fell silent. He shuffled awkwardly, confused as to how he should respond to her obvious sacrifice. He certainly recognised it as such, despite the charm and sincerity of her offer. He spoke quietly, almost solemnly. "I don't think we need blow it up, but I wouldn't mind knocking the top off, if that is agreeable."

"Just as you like," the old Sister said, releasing Martin's hands from her own. She then straightened herself and dusted the front of her habit, evidently satisfied by the transaction.

"Sister," Martin said, his voice quiet, appealing, yet tinged with humour. "Sister." She turned to him. He didn't say anymore. She waited patiently for a moment or two, then gestured him to continue, to express what was on his mind. He grinned in response, then dreamily declared: "Sister, I hope you find happiness in heaven."

She looked immediately formal, and with some severity said: "We will all find forgiveness, and that will be our happiness, our joy."

"Even after terrible wrong?"

"Martin," Donald interceded impatiently, smiling awkwardly at the sister as he spoke, "the sister doesn't really have the time. Now, take a piat upstairs and blow the steeple down. And don't miss."

Martin gazed blankly in front of him for a moment, but just before Donald was about to repeat his order he suddenly jumped up and made his way from them without another word.

He climbed a rickety stair to the second-floor. He peeped out over the ledge of a fractured window. The sun had sunk behind the steeple. The courtyard was in shadow. He continued to stare at the slender roof for some time, outlining its blackened shape with his eyes, as if he were trying to make some sense of it. His mind was blank though. It made nothing of the job. He gave himself a shake, aimed and fired very quickly. Seconds later the sunlight returned, orange-red, just above the point where the roof collapsed inwards.

Members of the resistance, each one wearing the Cross of Lorraine armband, stormed the church. Minutes later they brought out dead bodies and left them on the church steps. Martin descended. He went to examine the corpses. There were twelve in all. They had been stabbed numerous times. A ring of small boys, no older than five or six, smoking, carrying knives, gathered around them. The old nun returned to the church, tiptoeing up the steps between the corpses. She stopped at the porch. She turned to Martin and smiled. From her expression it appeared that she was grateful.

"Sister," Martin asked, "how many were in the steeple?"

"All of them, I believe," she said gently. "Come, join us in prayer."

Martin went up a few steps, then stopped. He suddenly rounded on the boys and demanded that they remove their cigarettes before the Sister. They took no notice. They began to slap the corpses with the flats of their blades. Martin went on to the doorway. He could smell beeswax. He stopped. "Sister," he called, "I have work to do. I pray all of the time."

She smiled, bowed to him and said: "We forgive you. God will understand. His presence is everywhere. Let Him give you the strength you require. Remember, the liberation of these people is correct and lawful. We have waited a long time. We have endured terrible privation."

Martin intended to say thank you, but found he couldn't speak. He backed away a few steps then turned and marched away.

When they moved out of the square the sun had sunk. The wind had grown stronger. The flags flapped noisily. In the distance artillery poured concentrations into the Colombelles factory. All around bulldozers were pushing right through Caen. "Shush," Martin whispered, "Shush." There was no one and nothing to hear him.

*

A serried row of poplars stretched into the distance marking the line of the road. The rising sun was blood-red. The sky was streaked mauve and purple, sketched in veins, some straight, some swirling. It didn't seem to have any depth. It was a pall covering them.

428

The road was straight. The fields around were flat. They were dull yellow, crimson and purple. The darkness was just rising. Outlines were indistinct. The trees were grey and purple shapes. The landscape had no suggestion of movement. It wasn't mobile but still. But there was movement overlaid.

Soldiers pushed forward. Martin and the Welshmen pressed ahead. They had left their trucks with most of the mortar equipment and were making their way on foot. The outline of the next town was in view at the end of the straight road. They had orders to check that the town was secure, then pick up the trucks again. Rank upon rank of troops went before them and came behind them. They were like the poplars. But the poplars were still. It wasn't the same soldier. They moved on and were replaced. Their postures gave their individuality away, but not their difference. They brought up dust. It was a cloud across the straight road.

There was also a steady stream pushing against the soldiers. Even in the early dawn they were already on the move. They were a dishevelled, sombre retinue, stretching as far as the poplars, as far as the soldiers, moving against them, leading overladen carts or pushing wheelbarrows and prams. Men, women, children and dogs. At one time Martin had found these processions bizarre, maybe even quizzical. He had never considered them funny. They were too tedious and repetitive for that. They had seemed like so many John Darcys, Uncle John Darcy, wheeling their pathetic possessions. But they weren't John Darcy. They never smiled. They never made the funny, pointless bows that John Darcy made. They never made his ridiculous speeches. Were they really free? Were they really liberated? Could their expressions really be the expressions of liberation? Donald said they were liberated. Martin wasn't convinced. It was all too meagre and messy to be absolutely true. All too filthy and meagre.

It was the same everywhere. People were on the move. Maybe the whole of Europe was on the move. It seemed like it to Martin. Everywhere he went, wheelbarrows and prams. He remembered his grandfather, grandmother and great Aunty Dora coming to squat in the cellar. They had put everything onto a trolley, John Darcy's trolley. It had taken a number of journeys. They managed it though. They transported everything they had ever owned on that trolley. They had even transported a pig to John Darcy's ancient mother who was reputed to be a witch. Mary had knocked on her door and Hugh had died. Was it because she was a witch? Were you still a witch when you were as old as she was? Maybe, once a witch always a witch. Were there witches making their plodding way down the straight road? Who could tell? They were all one. They were like the soldiers, individual but not different. His grandmother hadn't looked like that. She had worn a smile of sorts. It wasn't a proper smile. He knew that now. He hadn't realised it then. It was a make do smile. Great Aunty Dora had smiled right enough. She had even laughed as he remembered. Why was that? Why had she laughed taking up residence in a cellar? He should have understood that. His grandfather hadn't smiled at all. His grandfather never really smiled. He moved his lips. But what that meant was impossible to say. He went to his beach and kept his thoughts to himself. Was that fair? If he died Martin would never know what his thoughts were. They might be brilliant, wonderful thoughts. He could do with them now. He could think them as he made his way down the straight road. He could have thought them as they struggled out of Caen.

The fighting had been terrible breaking out of Caen. It went on and on. They had scrambled for days amongst rubble. They were filthy and exhausted and stunk of sour sweat. It wasn't funny anymore having dirt down your front. It was tedium. He never felt clean anymore. He never felt comfortable. He never felt complete. He always had aches and felt fatigued. His ears buzzed. Sounds had become muffled. He walked around for days like a deaf man, a dazed man, not knowing what he was doing. Everyone else seemed so sure. The Welshmen seemed to be in their element. They rushed and scrambled about, shouting, ordering each other here and there. But it made no sense to him. He couldn't work out the style, the pattern. How did they know? Dig that hole! Lie in that slit-trench! Run like hell! Crouch and fire! Shoot! All the time shooting and diving, but no longer swimming. That was done. The best years were finished.

Even when they broke out into open country there was no let up. In fact, it was worse. The Germans were visible, standing their ground, only backing away inch by inch. It went on for weeks, that slow slog, that shooting, pushing down long straight roads. The serried rows of poplars marching away. Fixed sentinels, overviewing those great upheavals of people. Wheelbarrows and prams, overladen, collapsing. What would Duffy have said? He would have had a slogan. What would that have been? He tried to keep Duffy's slogans in his head. What had he said before he was evicted? He remembered he had said something. It had been repeated numerous times. Most people smiled about it. After all, Duffy was finished. They had won regards Duffy. Hadn't they? That was the case. Duffy was a lunatic. Everyone knew that. But he had told the old priest that he didn't want him, that he didn't need him. He wasn't eating then. And he said his uncle was a holy man. He was a soldier and a holy man. Had he seen the same things? Why didn't he know? Why had he always been a cowboy? It wasn't doing him any good now. He wanted to know about the soldier and holy man. His mother loved him so much. He cried when he thought of his mother. Grandfather said you could always talk to her. He was right. It was terrible crying. No one saw. There was too much happening. Besides they all had dust in their eyes. Their eyes streamed with it. Maybe they were crying. He didn't think so. Where the hell was the Rhonda? They were all so sure of it. One of them, a man called Albert, the loud one, was always bragging about the men of the valley. He seemed to think he was taunting Martin with it somehow. The men of the Rhonda. As if they were the only ones worth anything. To hell with them. To hell with everything. He could scarcely hear anything anymore.

A few miles from Caen they passed through a gorge. It opened into a triangular stretch of land rising up to a bank of trees, all in a line across the horizon. There were escarpments running in a series of steps to each side of the spreading incline. Every few steps they trampled on pieces of body. The steps were choked up with equipment. It was all burnt out or wrecked. There was every conceivable kind of vehicle, tanks, trucks, armoured-cars, staff cars, amphibious-cars, wooden carts loaded with ammunition, stores and food, all completely smashed up. Motor engines had been wrenched from their bearings by the force of explosions and hurled some twenty or thirty yards. Panther tanks had their turrets shorn off, the hull of the tank on one side of the road and the turret on the other. There was a smell that was at times sweet then overwhelmingly rancid. Blow-fly infested the pieces of body. He saw one crawl around an empty eye socket, performing a stuttered dance. Lots of men vomited. Martin didn't. The vomit made him retch though. It was fresh. The smell was vegetable and sour. The other was already done with, impersonal. The distributed corpses, the disarranged body parts, the exposed guts, had become strange grotesque pictures, but pictures nevertheless. It was too much to think about. It only existed in small physical incidents. He remembered Donald accidentally standing on a corpse and the body moving like swamp beneath his boot. The guts ruptured. The stench was disgusting. He was close to being sick then. Donald had reacted violently. He screamed orders and swore repeatedly. There was black and green fluid all over his boots.

What would Duffy have said? What would a soldier, a holy man, have made of it? How did he die? No one said. He had died though. He had died in a war. Maybe all soldiers died in a war. But, of course, that wasn't true. Peter Kavanagh hadn't died. He was no fun, though. He had never been any fun. His father had always been fun. They hadn't killed him. He never said though. No one ever spoke. Why did they never speak? What were they ashamed of? He had never thought about that. Maybe it was just the same. Was it periodic then? Eventually everyone fought in a war. Everyone struck down the enemy, even when they had given it up.

He didn't blame anyone. It was how it was. They overtook Germans pushing wheelbarrows and prams. They all abandoned them with the same simple gesture. One push and the things simply rolled away. Sometimes they came to a halt and stood there unattended. Sometimes they collapsed into the side of the roads. Whatever, they always looked pathetic. It was as if the Germans knew they would be overtaken, captured. Many were shot. It was just a matter of luck. A small group of soldiers on their own never took prisoners. It was only when you weren't sure. You were always sure though. Would he never talk about it? Was that why they never said? How would he ask? He was such a simpleton really. There was so much he couldn't work out. He should have worked harder. But maybe that was more stupid than taking prisoners.

There were some Germans that could never be taken prisoner even if there had been a will for it. Albert said they were fanatics. He added a whole barrage of swear words to go with that. They were the s.s. troops. They tied themselves to the trunks of trees with belts or stretches of rope so that if they were wounded or killed they wouldn't fall. Martin had seen their grotesque posturing, hanging away from the tree, heavy, clumsy and ugly. A dead-weight dangling sideways, the head thrown onto the shoulder. Some of them were kids younger than himself. It wasn't always easy to tell. Most of the corpses were defiled.

He saw one of the Welshman take his rifle and swing the butt against the suspended head of one of them. The skull cracked open but nothing came out. The Welshman was disappointed. He expected that it would launch into the air like a football. They had all seen soldiers kick heads like footballs. Somehow, it didn't register. They just booted them down the long straight roads. It would last for a minute or two and then be finished with. It was the same as kicking a piece of sod. Bits flew off and it became reduced, eventually unusable. It was never a real thing.

Nothing was. The dead were just monotonous. Martin was learning to hate them.

At least hating them was something. Most of the time he didn't think or feel anything. He couldn't resist that. He was a deaf man. The world mumbled. It was terrible. He wanted to hear what was being said, but he couldn't. Everything was too quick and chaotic. When he could hear it was just a parody. Besides, most of the time it was all in Welsh. French, German and Welsh! How could he be expected to make any sense of that? The ridiculous thing was the Welsh laughed about his dialect. He didn't understand that. He didn't talk like his grandfather. They would never have understood him. He wouldn't have cared. He would have kept himself to himself. Of course he wouldn't have been there. But he talked before Martin left. Martin had insisted on that. There hadn't been much need. His grandfather searched him out. He made a point of it. It was a bit too serious for Martin's liking. He was pleased now, though. His grandfather knew things. He didn't speak Irish though. Did anyone speak Irish? Why didn't he know? He was such an ignoramus really. He didn't know anything. He should have known that. He had never said he was Irish, though. He'd never claimed that before. He hadn't realised it then. He should have known he was Irish. He should have worked that out. He had decided he was Irish now. He wasn't sure why exactly. It was probably being with the Welshmen. They were so sure that not being English was a good thing, something worth bragging about.

The funny thing was he had seen Albert lose his head because a German wouldn't speak English. He didn't understand that. Albert spoke Welsh. He was always speaking Welsh. Even when he spoke English it sounded Welsh. Why had he suddenly lost his head? Albert was loud and big, but all right. He didn't push anybody around like some of them. He didn't usually do terrible things for the sake of it. Not like some of them. Some of them seemed to enjoy what they did. Martin wasn't sure. How was one supposed to behave? No one said. A soldier was a soldier. Over and over again he came back to the same questions. What would Duffy say? What would his grandfather say? What would his own father say? It never crossed his mind to wonder what Father Bond might say. He was in another world.

The incident with Albert happened shortly after they had made their way from the gorge. They traipsed over the horizon, the trees running parallel to them, and before them there was a series of downs. As they came to the crest of the hill they overtook a group of Germans. They were obviously stragglers left behind by the main group. Somehow they had survived the carnage in the gorge. A corporal stepped out of the group and offered their surrender. He walked towards Martin and the Welshmen, his hands in the air, his fingers spread, at shoulder height. He kept repeating: La guerre - nicht bon. La guerre - nicht bon. He was obviously worn out and terrified. He was tall and lean with a thin, cavernous face. His eyes flicked nervously from soldier to soldier. La guerre - nicht bon. Albert stepped up to him and frisked him roughly. He had a leaflet in his pocket. It was in English. It was titled: *Welcome to the continent*. It ran on: *Who on earth put it into your head the idea that America and Britain are threatened from the continent. Have we ever attempted to invade your coasts?* As Albert read aloud the corporal nodded continuously, inanely, and made half-hearted attempts to smile.

Albert suddenly screwed up the leaflet, snarled and tried to push the leaflet down the German's throat. As he did he shouted at him to speak in English. He kept on, calling him filthy names, and demanding that he speak in English. The German made no real attempt to defend himself, but kept his hands in the air, shoulder height. He choked on the leaflet that Albert continued to try to stuff into his mouth. His hands wavered like fronds wafted by a current. Eventually Albert forced him to the ground. He started to strangle the corporal. No one moved to intervene. The German started to kick one of his legs. It was a quick, jerking reflex. Martin had seen pigs do it when they were being butchered. Then the jerking stopped and the German lay completely still. Albert stood up and backed away. He put his hands to his face, his fingers spread around his jaw, then turned and looked from one person to the next. No one met his gaze. A moment later Donald ordered them to get a move on. Before they continued they shot the other Germans. They left them by the roadside.

The red sky was diluting to rose pink. The veins were widening and lightening. Martin's platoon had left the main road and were coming close to the town. Donald repeated that all they had to do was mop up any stray Germans, whatever that meant, and make sure the town was secure. There had been reports about sporadic fire. It wasn't much, but had to be checked. German snipers managed to cause havoc at times. The columns still moved along the main road, spreading far into the distance to their right. Soldiers and civilians. They were visible across the wide flat fields, grey outlined figures, moving beneath the skyline, surprisingly silent in the roseate dawn. The town ahead was a cluster of irregular pale lemon and olive walls, and red tiled roofs. Its colours were dilute and fused, as if rubbed to a dull yet luminous sheen in the rich early light. Soldiers fanned out across the approaches, moving stealthily across the wide flat fields. Martin and the Welshmen kept to the road, following the line of poplars.

As they came to the fringes of the town they couldn't hear any firing. The town seemed deadly silent. There were a number of farmsteads that seemed completely deserted, apart from two animals, a cockerel that stood on a shed roof and a pig nosing around a small enclosure. The cockerel made no sound, but opened its wings stiffly, only to furl them back against its side a moment later. It repeated that display over and over. More than likely they would come back and claim the animals. Foul and pork. It would be a welcome change. If all went well. At each building sections were detached to check for snipers.

The farmsteads gave way to a winding central street with narrow streets leading off to either side. The houses were shuttered. Soldiers kicked in the doors and made a check of each house. They found that they were all deserted. They continued along the empty street. The central avenue curved round to the right. It formed a blind bend. Donald fanned them out to either side. They pressed against the walls and carefully inched forward, keeping their backs to the wall. They came around the curve ready to fire.

There was a stretch of straight narrow street. Sunlight began to break across the roof tops. The street remained in darkness, though, a series of shadowed, decrepit walls, and a dusty throughway. A few yards in front of them there was a woman on her knees. Her hands were clasped together, and her head was bowed. She was silent. Above her there was a body, the body of a man, hanging from the balcony of the house. Further along the street there were other hanging bodies. They hung from the houses and from street lamps.

Martin was one of the first to move ahead. Donald and a group of the other Welshmen were with him. They had abandoned any display of vigilance. They lowered their rifles and walked forward. They stopped a few feet away from the woman. She remained silent. She may have been praying, she may not. She remained hunched, propped in an attitude of prayer, but silent. She had a shawl over her head, but her face was free of any cover. Her expression was completely blank. She wasn't silently mouthing anything. She didn't really seem aware of anything. She certainly paid no heed to the soldiers standing a few feet from her. She was obviously aware of the figure of the man dangling above her. She didn't look at it, but she was facing it, poised below it.

435

Martin looked up at the strangled corpse. It hung from the rails of a small window balcony. The balcony was a frame of thin black metal. The rope had been knotted to the inside of the frame at the base and stretched up and over the balcony rail. It hadn't been long enough to clear the entire frame. The body didn't hang loosely. The shoulders were pressed against the metal bar. The head hung forward. The hands had been tied together at the wrist but he had obviously struggled to hold onto something behind him and had succeeded in getting the knot caught on the under-frame. His elbows stuck out to the side like angular stumpy wings and his shoulders were rolled forward, twisted out of their sockets. The corpse was awkward, twisted and fractured.

One of the soldiers went up to the woman. He stood for a while just looking at her, assuming that she would respond to his presence but then, when it was obvious that she was entirely impervious to him, he put his hands beneath her arms and eased her to her feet. Martin didn't understand that need to get her to stand. It served no purpose. She looked around as if she were only now in any way aware that the soldiers were there. She looked mildly embarrassed. She looked from soldier to soldier, confused, apologetic. And then awareness of the body suspended over her hit her once again and all expression vanished from her face. She looked quickly up at the corpse, as if she had been guilty of negligence in her observance, and for a moment looked as if she might make some response, a word, a gesture, a sound, but the moment passed quickly and she fell again into her trancelike devotion. There was obviously nothing to say. It was beyond understanding. The passion she felt could not be described.

The same soldier who had helped her to her feet now ushered her away. She complied mechanically. The soldier directed her towards the house, passing her from his hands in that direction, but once free of him she kept on along the street where the other bodies were suspended. Martin felt an urge to intervene. He wanted her to kneel again. It was obvious she wasn't through. He made to call to her, but found he didn't know what to say. It was a matter of language, a matter of words. How could he call her back? He couldn't name what he was calling her back to.

He had seen her as he had seen his grandmother so many times, in that devotional position, separate and distinct, alone with their murmurings, counting out the decades of the rosary, and wanted her to continue. He had seen them all, his mother, his great Aunty Dora, his sisters, but it was his grandmother who seemed remote and otherworldly when she prayed. He had always assumed it was because she was the most holy. The most holy and maybe the most old fashioned. His mother said she wasn't nearly as holy as she made out, not at all. She never explained that, but she always said it with a mischievous, knowing smile. She obviously knew something. Why didn't he know? Maybe he was too young. But he was here. How could that be? He was too young to know why his grandmother prayed all the time, but old enough to see a broken corpse. It didn't make sense. It must have been his fault. He should have listened more. If he had he might know what to shout out. As it was he didn't say a word. The desire stalled on his lips. The woman walked ahead in her slow mechanical manner. The soldiers followed.

Martin stood back for a while and gazed at the clumsy corpse strung up at the balcony. His eyes slowly passed over the dead figure, taking in details. The dirty soiled clothes, the pendant feet, the squashed face, pulled by the rope. He had a desire to touch it, to feel whether there was warmth or malleability. In fact, he wanted to embrace it. He didn't know why. It was just a thought. If he could have done it he would. He knew it would have had to be a secret thing. Soldiers did not embrace the corpses they came across. They would never make any progress that way. But it would have been acceptable to do it just once. He thought of the people he had seen touching the body of the crucified Christ. He had never really understood that. He could clearly see it in his mind's eye, though. Furtive fingers reaching out and stroking the ankle, the shin, the thigh. Fingers pulled across the porcelain flesh, moving in a disarray of disbelief, which of course was belief. Disbelief at the scale of the crime, the execution of God, the beautiful pale, porcelain God, his face fixed in that perpetual peace of pain, but with the belief of notice, the gift of grace. Was that true? If he called out would the lovely Christ corpse respond?

Duffy didn't think so. He said he could suffer all on his own. Father Bond said he was presumptuous to take that accolade onto his own feeble shoulders. But Duffy was a good man. He wasn't showing-off. He said he loved Christ as well. Martin didn't understand. Duffy said he didn't want the priest, didn't need him, but he said he loved Christ, loved him for his doubt. How could he love him? It was too much. Martin agonised with his memories. The face of Patrick, drawn and withered, obviously close to death, kept interrupting his recollections and he couldn't understand why. He hadn't thought about Patrick since he had died. Why did he think about him now?

Martin wailed inwardly, but was still incapable of speaking aloud. He couldn't bring his mind to a single, definite thought. He wanted to feel rage and disgust, and as a corollary a desire for revenge, but it felt like weariness and boredom. If there was disgust it was for the corpse as well as the murderer, and it was also for himself. Disgust that he didn't pull down the body and bury it. No, it had to be left, proclaiming itself, telling the world of its disgusting struggle to keep alive, survive. He wouldn't offer to remove it, and no one would suggest it. But he knew it should be concluded. It should be allowed to be finished with itself.

He squeezed his face tightly in a fit of frustration. He didn't know what he was thinking. But he wanted to cry. He wanted to weep below the pendant feet of this dirty corpse, but couldn't. He wanted to weep as he had seen women weep at the feet of Christ. But he was evidently incapable. It was a terrible admission. He didn't know what to do with the dead. They no longer had any meaning. They were everywhere. On this street alone there had to be more than a dozen. There couldn't be enough praise in the world to do justice to the numbers that demanded it. He threw back his head defiantly. He was a soldier. He didn't count the dead. He had to let them go.

He followed the others along the street. Their progress was slow and methodical. They didn't stop at the other corpses but noted them. There were fourteen in all. Despite his boast he had counted them anyway. Soldiers obviously did count the dead. Fourteen gibbets. The number of the stations of the cross. War was like that. It was never shy of its symbols. And Martin didn't shy from the figures but passed his eyes over each one, studying the details, trying to ascertain something of the torture that had taken place, the moments of struggle, the hands and eyes and words used. He wanted to bring the story alive, piece it together, body by body, resurrecting each one in a brief moment of imaginative recreation.

When he reached the end of the street he knew that he would never be the same again. He couldn't have described the alteration in easy terms. It wasn't that he had come into the street a child and left it a man. That was too glib. He had left it a wraith, a monster, a shade, a disbeliever. He had counted the dead.

As he turned away from the final hanging corpse he felt a moment of intense grief. It was like a necklace draped across his sternum, a fullness in his throat, momentarily capable of overwhelming him, bringing him to his knees. It was a desire to weep freely and without thought. But he suppressed the feeling. He just had to work.

The soldiers continued following the line of the street. The woman remained ahead of them, still walking like an automaton. The straight street was intersected by another broader avenue, which ran to both right and left and obviously formed another point of entry and exit to the town. The woman walked off to the left. Donald divided the platoon, sending half one way and half the other, ordering them to stay vigil and check every building. Martin continued to follow the woman. After another hundred yards or so they found themselves in a broad square. The soldiers filtered around the outer perimeter. There was a crowd of women gathered in the centre. They turned and faced the soldiers, but didn't respond. Martin had never experienced anything like this. They were always welcome. Women cheered when the soldiers appeared, but not this time.

Eventually one of the women stepped from the crowd and approached Donald. She began to speak immediately. She spoke in French. Donald couldn't get her to stop. One of the Welshman went to her and began to respond to her. Martin was bemused. He hadn't realised that one of the Welshman could speak French. It seemed odd. He hadn't really expected that a soldier could speak French. It meant he was something else. Of course he was something else. They were all something else, but that was gone. Maybe it would never be again. But here was a Welshman speaking French. He obviously spoke three languages. Maybe he spoke more. It struck Martin as quite unbelievable.

The woman explained that the s.s. had executed the men. There were more than the bodies in the street. They had killed hundreds. It was a random reprisal because Resistance fighters had carried out acts of sabotage against the same s.s. division. They weren't even from the same town. They had led hundreds of people away, herded them into barns and set them alight. The bodies in the street were just reminders, trophies. She shrugged and threw up her arms. There was nothing more to say. She turned away, but immediately checked herself. She threw her hands above her head and then started banging her temples with the fingers of each hand. The s.s. were still in the town. It wasn't over. They were still executing civilians.

Donald shrugged at the news. It didn't seem likely. German troops had abandoned this sector some time before. There were just pockets of resistance left. Still they had to be vigilant. There could easily be stray snipers. Donald asked for more information. Where were the s.s. troops? She pointed straight ahead. The end of town. They had everyone else from the town with them. How many troops? Plenty. She returned to the huddled group of women.

The woman who had headed the soldiers was lost. She must have made her way into the crowd when the other woman was talking. Martin attempted to search her out amongst the other women but with no luck. She had moved on. He would probably never see her again. Her image would remain with him though. He knew that. Her kneeling shape had become a part of him. Whether it was a good part or a bad part he didn't know. If he had taken the thought a step further he would have decided that there was no such division. He didn't have time to think though. Donald ordered them forward. It was possible that there were s.s. troops still in the town.

The woman was right. They soon discovered that there were indeed still s.s. troops there. Martin's platoon caught up with them on the far side of the town from where they had entered. They were unaware of the soldiers converging on them, ducking from doorway to doorway. They were engaged in setting light to a pile of bodies. It was impossible to estimate how many. They were stacked in layers, one pile across another, perhaps five or six high. There were women and children among the dead. The s.s. troops stood to attention as the pyres went up in flame. While the fire raged one of the victims, a woman, rose to her feet. She had either somehow survived or shammed death all along. She stepped from the pyre and approached her executioners, begging for pity, her burning hands clasped together, flames licking around the entwined fingers. The troops she approached responded to her with a burst of gunfire. She stopped, rooted to the spot. She turned her head to the side, her face contorted with the pain, each muscle held rigid. A second later and the flesh on her face melted and the bones became visible. At that moment she gave a violent shudder, began shaking her head from side to side, then collapsed backwards.

As she hit the ground the Welsh platoon opened fire. The s.s. troops were caught off guard. It was too late for them to find cover. Some crouched behind the pyre, but they couldn't keep close enough to avoid being a target. The exchange was over quickly. The Welshman hauled a few bodies onto the pyre, but quickly gave it up as too much effort. It wasn't up to them. It was the civil authorities that had to clean-up. They had done their job.

Donald ordered them to push on and rejoin the main highway. They didn't speak as they left the town behind. The sun was bright across the wide flat fields. The landscape was laid out in regular lines, its colours primary and vivid. The road was long and straight. There was a constant flow of traffic. It went in both directions. The soldiers were individual but not different. The civilians were the same.

*

They had been sitting in the back of the truck on bags of potatoes and turnips driving with mortar equipment for two hours. They had gone no distance farther forward and no distance back. They had only been somewhere different, directed down one-way traffic lanes by military police. Having been held up at the last cross-roads, whilst the one-way priority altered its twenty-four hour rota, they could now no longer see the dust of the advance trucks. The road stretched before them yellow and straight. Martin lay down on the truck boards and rested his head on a sack of turnips. He watched the sun sink low in the sky. It was bright orange coming to earth, its liquid effulgence shadowing the poplars, plane and growing clusters of lime, turning the countryside from yellow to lime green. The trees turned blue in the distance and across the horizon the corn red. Among the shadows of the poplars the roadways were littered with abandoned equipment, jeeps and trucks stripped to the chassis labelled with signs which stated: *Free Parts*.

The truck slowed to a halt. Martin lifted himself from the floor. To either side of the road lime trees in wide open spaces stretched back towards dense woodland. Amongst the trees there were gliders. They were twisted and broken. They made grotesque patterns in the maroon evening light. How long they had been there no one could have accurately said, but they had probably been part of the earliest assaults. They were certainly deserted now. An old woman hailed them from the verge. She was a large, rounded woman, in peasant dress, with a shawl resting over her head. Her voice was guttural, but not unmusical. She beckoned them to follow. She had an insistent, but not urgent, smile.

"Go and see what she wants, will you, Martin," Donald said impatiently, irritated by this further obstacle to their catching up with the forward trucks. Martin pulled himself lazily to his feet and jumped down. The old woman immediately moved away, still beckoning, and now pointing. A little way in the distance, through the line of trees, Martin could see a small farmhouse. "Go on," Donald pressed irritably, "it might be eggs or something. Just hurry up, for Christ sake!"

Martin trailed the old woman. Every few steps she turned to ensure herself that he still followed, each time beckoning him, coaxing and

441

reassuring him at the same time. As they approached the farmhouse they were met by a young woman. She carried a basket of flowers on her arm. She greeted the old woman with a kiss. She then turned to Martin and offered him the flowers, holding them out to him at arms length. They were a massed tangle of small white flowers like stock. Martin took one of the small cruciform blooms. She offered them again. He took another. She smiled quizzically. For a moment she looked anxious and disappointed, but then shrugged as if it were of no matter. She smiled again and beckoned him to come quickly.

She went on ahead and opened up the farmhouse. Martin followed her in. The old woman came behind. They began to chatter to him. He didn't understand a word. Eventually he worked out that they wanted him to go upstairs. He hesitated, but they were so eager and excited that he felt unable to refuse. He made his way behind them. They climbed a rickety, wooden staircase to an uneven landing. He followed them into one of the bedrooms.

He saw a bed framed with flowers and lace. Lying in the midst of the luxury was a dead glider-pilot. His cocoa coloured face had been scrubbed clean. It was translucent grey amongst the cruciform petals. The young woman placed her new flowers across the old. When the offering had been lain down the two women knelt and prayed. Martin knelt with them. When they were through they looked towards him. Their expressions were both triumphant, appealing. They had done their best and now wanted their charge taken away. They had created an angel, but were through with it. Martin indicated that he would leave but return. He dropped his own two flowers onto the makeshift catafalque as a token, then made to leave.

The old woman stopped him. She spoke hurriedly, still excited, and started beckoning him again. There was nothing for it but to follow. She led him back outside to a pigsty with a sow and piglets. She picked out one of the piglets and placed it in his arms. The young woman brought two bottles of Calvados. He left them indicating he would be back.

Albert had been a butcher before joining up. He leaned out of the truck to accept the pig, his face glowing with affection. "Ah, come to me, Charlie," he said tenderly, taking the animal in his arms and kissing its snout. "God, Charlie, I'll kill you so sweetly and so tenderly you'll carve like a dream, by God you will. You're a grand wee boy Martin. Did I tell you I was a butcher? I don't mean now, before like. A proper butcher, master-butcher I was, before all this fucking useless butchery. God but I'll take proper care of this wee feller."

442

Martin hadn't known that Albert was a butcher. The image of his sister Mary flashed across his mind. She had married a butcher and she wasn't happy. And it was all Martin's fault. She was unhappy on his account. And the butcher was still at home with her, making her life hell with his drinking. Someone secured him a job at the pit, but he hardly ever had to go. He'd never gone underground. It was all a con. He sold black-market meat. He had become a bit notorious. Martin resolved he would do something about it when he went home. After all, he wasn't a kid anymore. He couldn't stand by and let Mary be unhappy. He would do something.

He shouted up to Albert: "I'm keeping the wee feller for a pet, Albert, I think you should know that before you start taking its guts out."

"Tell me just once that the boy is cracked and I'll shoot him myself, go on just give me the word."

"I'm telling you, I have a definite mind for it."

"Don't be disgusting, boy. You couldn't be giving yourself to lie in pig shit. Don't be altogether daft man. Pig shit is the most liquid imaginable, the most liquid shit of all shit, well..." He hesitated and let his voice trail away coyly: " Well, after... need I say it..."

"Go on, you're obviously dying to."

"Well, after English shit, Martin, it must be said. English shit is just like English beer, all froth and water."

"I wouldn't know Albert. My shit is all Irish, did I not tell you, the greenest shit in all Europe."

"Well, as long as it isn't yellow we won't lose any sleep over it will we."

"*Oh, that I had wings like a dove: for then would I fly away and be at rest,*" Martin pronounced loudly. Albert skewed his face disdainfully, unimpressed by Martin's outburst. Martin smiled bitterly and said: "Keep the fucking pig. I was only having you on. What the hell would I want with it? We gave up on pigs years ago when they stole the house on Ginns."

Albert held the piglet aloft making it squeal. He said: "I won't let anybody down."

Martin didn't answer. He lay down in the truck once again. As it pulled away he allowed himself one backward glance. The trees shadowed the farmhouse and hid it from view. He settled down, content in his own mind that the airman was at rest, everything for him complete and finished. *Lo then would I fly away and be at rest.*

As he lay there in the gathering gloom Albert spoke to him. His tone was measured, and had a note of contrition: "I knew a lot of men from the last war, men from the Rhonda like, who deserted the British army to go and fight in Ireland. I don't mean those bastards the Black and Tans after the war. No right in the middle of it. Went to fight alongside the Irish." He paused as if he expected a response, but Martin didn't speak. Albert went on, his voice lowering as he spoke: "Same idea that drove the Volunteers to Spain later on, I suppose. There was a lot Welsh went to Spain. The Welsh have a good record, you know Martin. They've fought Fascism long and hard. We're a solid people, Martin, stand shoulder to shoulder. It's the only way to win. I didn't mean out earlier. It was just a bit of chat. I didn't know you were Irish. You're a good lad, Martin."

As Albert whispered to him Martin thought of Gavin. He could clearly see his face in his mind's eye, his weary restive expression as he sat in his cell, keeping his faith. He supposed that Gavin would have volunteered for Spain if he had been young enough, maybe still would have if his health had held up. He didn't know anyone who had gone to Spain. Why was that? There had been enough talk. He had an inkling that Peter Kavanagh had a fancy to volunteer but someone had said it wasn't his fight. He didn't really know who had said that. He supposed it was his grandfather, but how could that be, he was always on the south shore. Maybe it was the priest, but he was barely able to talk at the best of times. He'd had God knows how many strokes over the past few years. All he really wanted was to retire to his cell and pray. He professed the desire quite openly. That was so ironic. He had gone every day to complain to Gavin about his attitude in his cell and now that was all he wanted for himself. Well, whoever had said it, Peter Kavanagh had stayed put. Martin felt it was disappointing, maybe even shameful that he didn't know anyone who had been to Spain. He whispered to Albert: "Were you in Spain then?"

Albert's response was tentative and defensive: "No, I couldn't. Not really. No, I was never in Spain."

"I was only wondering. It's not important, not really. I don't know anybody, that's all. Can't quite work that out really. Still, same fight now, isn't it. We're here now." He fell silent for a moment. Gavin remained on his mind. He couldn't rid himself of his expression as the old priest badgered him. Then, if he tried to imagine Father Bond, it was the same expression. What did it mean? What lay behind that exhausted, yet determined look? Where did it come from, that aggravated assurance, that unwillingness to ever concede? It was marginal but amazing. He shuffled and repositioned himself so that he could see Albert. He quietly asked: "Who is your witness, Albert?" Albert shrugged. Martin didn't know whether he was shrugging because he couldn't say or because he didn't comprehend the question. He went on: "Not God, then? God isn't your witness?"

"I don't object if he's yours."

"My uncle was a holy man. He died in the last war."

"I'm sorry."

"I don't know. I was never holy," Martin uttered. "I was reared on it though. My grandmother prays like mad. Is that holy or is she scared? You never know with people." He turned away and viewed the darkness of the woods. How many dead soldiers lay secretly at peace amongst ceremonial flowers in there? Witness was a terrible burden. There was such a pressure to disclose and have it said. There was so much he felt that he should want to say, but somehow he couldn't conceive of any words to shape it. He smiled to himself. Maybe he should have listened more in school. He had never been very conscientious when it came to that. He closed his eyes. He felt the motion of the truck. It was soothing and restful. He gave himself to it. He felt at peace and sleepy. He nodded off. His mind had gone blank.

He didn't know how long he slept for but it can't have been long because when he woke up it still wasn't completely dark. He peered into the gloom without moving. He felt out of sorts. Consciousness was painful. He couldn't work it out. Something nagged at him. He cast his mind back. It must have been the dead pilot. He wasn't sure. He just knew something didn't feel right. He opened and closed his eyes a number of times, trying to rouse himself fully, trying to shake off the cloud that weighed on him.

As he was coming to he heard Donald call out over the sound of the truck's engine: "Apparently the bridge ahead isn't down. It's good news."

Martin sat up and asked: "Are we crossing the river?"

Albert shouted out furiously: "Like shit! Not tonight! No, chance."

"Well, we're not sitting in these woods."

"But they'll know exactly where we are if we take the bridge, that's just stupid, suicidal."

"I know that, I know. We'll stop short of the bridge. But we're not staying in these woods. We'll just go a little further."

445

Albert sighed: "The only killing tonight will be wee Charlie, and I'll make sure he doesn't mind."

They drove for a further twenty minutes or so and then the woodland began to fall away to either side and they entered a broad plain. A few plane trees and apple trees afforded a little cover, otherwise the plain stretched ahead of them opalescent in the moonlight, the truck headlights casting only weak beams into the opening void. Their route was unclear, difficult to ascertain in the dark. At this point Donald ordered them to stop for the night.

As soon as he gave the order Albert began to cajole the animal, petting it and asking its forgiveness, promising it a first-class death. He brought it in his arms to Martin and told him to hold it, then went on to explain that he intended to break its neck with his rifle. The animal became restive as he passed it on. Albert exhorted him to hold it still. The piglet squealed and squirmed. Albert brought the lever to its neck, hesitated briefly to ask its forgiveness once again, then brought it to bear. The animal gave an enormous jolt and broke free of Martin's grip. Albert grabbed it and thrust his knife into its neck. The animal coughed and choked. Blood bubbled in its throat. The air rushed from its lungs. Albert began to sob, his voice blending with the dying note of the piglet. "Jesus, Charlie," he moaned, "I didn't kill you I murdered you. Jesus, I wouldn't have murdered you!" He turned fiercely to Martin: "You bastard! What the hell were you playing at?" Then he turned back to the dead animal and wailed again: "I wouldn't have murdered you."

"It was you that made a mess of it, not me. Don't start on me. Anyway it's only a fucking pig, what's the big deal?" Martin railed in his defence.

Albert rounded on him: "The Irish always were cruel to animals."

"Well, it could be worse, couldn't it!"

"Could it?" Albert challenged. "Could it really? Tell me?"

"Oh, cook the fucking thing will you, and get off my back."

Albert squared up to Martin. Martin met the challenge. They eyed each other for a while, but neither made a move. It was Albert who let it pass. He shook his head and turned away. He picked up the dead-meat in one hand and held it up. Blood dripped onto the truck boards, splashing towards Martin's feet. Martin smiled.

When the meat was cooked Albert again complained about the killing. As he took his share he started muttering again that he had murdered the thing rather than killed it. He had never intended to murder it. That was someone else's doing. Martin had had enough. He intended

446

to have it out. They might have come to blows, but as he prepared to face Albert he heard the distant drone of planes. He stopped dead still. A barrage began.

The plain ahead erupted in discrete splashes of colour. The pale horizon broke into sheaves of orange and yellow. Then the barrage moved nearer. Target markers dropped before them, then shortly after came the loads. Everything around them became lit up by eerie daylight. They began to run. They made for the plane and apple trees. Once in the orchards they fell flat on their faces and lay among apple pulp. The sickly sweet aroma of bruised fermenting fruit filled their nostrils. They lay quite still, unable to move. The sound and light moved away. Still they waited. They couldn't bring themselves to move. Eventually they slept. The last thing Martin heard was Albert moaning quite close by to him. He assumed he was asleep and was moaning in his dreams. He didn't check.

The dawn damage inspection found the truck to be in working order. A pale sun settled over the plain before them. Its map of villages, lanes, tributaries and portioned fields was clearly visible, laid out in a vast yet neat arrangement of limes and yellows. At first pods of dust marked their progress until light showers followed a sequence of clouding, clearing and reclouding. The sky coloured into rich pink and mauve sheaves. The rain drummed gently but insistently onto the dry earth.

When they reached the bridge they discovered evidence of a German retreat. There were guns overturned by the side of the road, a half-track armoured-car still burning, ploughs and horse rakes left to block the road pushed aside and signs posted stating: *Keep to the centre of the road.* They were obviously trailing the British army as much as the German. That incensed Donald. His orders to the driver to get a move on were suddenly impersonal and bombastic. The mood in the truck was awkward, contrite, dissenting and relieved.

They crossed the bridge and made for the village just beyond. The farmers, already back in the fields, scarcely bothered to look at the truck as it trundled past. They found the village badly damaged. Entire squares and streets were reduced to masonry. The villagers, though, were determined to carry on. As they made their way through the demolished central square, inching through the rubble, a postman, well turned out in his blue and red uniform, waved at them, then cheered and grinned, as he delivered a letter to an old woman, who did likewise, at the gates of a villa where only the gates remained. They were both seemingly impervious to the fact that the address on the letter had ceased to exist. The soldiers

447

made no response. A young girl came alongside the truck, her arms full of flowers. Her expression was embarrassed and fearful. Martin leaned towards her and took one. She smiled, relieved and obviously grateful that someone had responded. She impulsively handed Martin the entire bunch and rushed away. Martin stood up and called out: "*Oh that I had wings like a dove: for then would I fly away...*"

Donald intervened and ordered him to sit down and shut up. He then instructed the driver to get the hell out of it, and make sure they were back with the army before they were all charged with desertion.

*

The route from the Seine to the Somme ignoring Paris is relatively straight passing through rolling farmlands where in late summer the days are still hot and the evenings remain light and warm. On this route, much to Donald's relief, the truck caught up with the bulk of the army, and became subject to orders. Progress between the two rivers, though never uncontested mile for mile, was steady and decisive. Against the thrust of army still came the steady reflux of people, men, women and children pushing wheelbarrows and prams, containing all that remained of all they had owned, lining the roads from one shattered village to another shattered village, picking their way between the discarded equipment which littered the roadsides.

As Martin viewed this steady march of dispossessed humanity his thoughts were constantly of Gavin. He saw him in his mind's eye, beaten, bloodied, but still capable of the challenge: *Socialism or barbarism!* He tried to imagine what he would say about this flow of bedraggled people. How would he would sum it up? What would be his analysis? What would be his answer? What bombast would he explode in the priest's face when questioned about his witness? Martin could see him in his cell, suffering and deteriorating daily, tasting the grit of loneliness and the outrage of torture, but never relinquishing the thoughts and ideas that had motivated him for a lifetime. *Socialism or barbarism!* Here only barbarism prevailed.

At the same time another voice whispered within him. *Lo that I could fly away... Martin, Martin, Martin!* It was all he could do to stop himself from crying aloud. But what would he say? Which words applied in this broken, ruined landscape of uprooted people? He knew the ones he wanted. He uttered Mary's name beneath his breath. Thinking of her always brought him back to his senses. His love for his sister was deep and profound. That love was the only sanity he could hang on to, but she was unhappy and it was his fault. He should have done something. He had let her run out the door.

These conflicting voices he heard grew in him with each passing mile. They preoccupied his thinking, awake or asleep. The clear lines between reality and thought were no longer easy to calculate. As they approached the Somme he felt he was encroaching on someone else's war, the sense of which was buried somewhere deep within him.

They reached the downs of Picardy in the night. There was moonlight. They could see the Somme as it flowed between patchy woods and within soft rolls of landscape then on into Amiens. The town was their target. They were part of the detachment ordered to take it. It was shelled and mortared throughout the night, then before dawn they were ordered to progress on foot. The bridges were not down. The reasons for the night-time attack had been met. In the early hours, before the pale liquid light of dawn illuminated the downs into recognisable farmland, they crossed the river. The moonlight moved within its straight black channels. They pressed on quickly and again came onto the pale ghostly tumuli of Picardy. Dew and mist draped its risen bellies of earth and its sunken gullies.

They came to the small village of Hamlin, a hamlet of a few houses and scattered farm buildings. As they moved through the farm's paddocks curtain fire exploded above them and hung low across the sky, forcing them to dive for cover. The ground was moist and cool beneath them. The paddocks glowed white under the fire. Martin scrambled forward across the saturated grasses and rolled under a hedgerow for cover.

He pressed himself hard against the knot of trunks. His whole body felt rigid. His breathing was rapid and shallow. He covered his face with his palms. It was like breathing into a mask. He listened to his breathing rather than the firing. His breathing came more quickly. He could feel his heart beating inside his chest. He could hear blood vessels thump behind his ears. He was going to burst. His body was going mad. He had to scream. He had to get this madness out. He opened his palms. His mouth gaped. Air rushed in. He forced it out. It came again. He took control. He still breathed quickly, but now deeply. He began to register the mingled perfumes of sodden earth and plants. It was a musk smell. It was better than the firing. He concentrated on the aroma. His breathing came more slowly and deeper still.

He inched closer to the trunks. He pressed himself against them. He felt the solid shapes buttress him. He was slowing down. He pulled at the foliage and draped it over him, across his shoulders and down his back. He felt sealed. The firing was somehow removed. He curled himself against the ground. It was scrub beneath the hedging, granular but moist. He inhaled it as if it were flesh. It tingled in his nostrils. He luxuriated in it. He was in a haven, a cocoon, a private bed. He began to explore his space.

He passed his hands through the leaves clustered around him. They were soft to the touch. He lifted his head and pressed his face through the foliage. He peered through to the other side. He could see a graveyard. Its rows of headstones shone out clearly in the light. They were Great War gravestones. At first he just gazed at them, dumbfounded, and then he began to count them out slowly. He had scarcely started when he stopped himself. It was absurd.

He turned away and lay back down. His cheek nestled against the damp earth. He reached out a hand and slowly clawed it through the soil. He crumbled the dirt through his fingers. He looked back across the paddock he had crawled across. There was a break in the curtain fire. The light faded. The grey light of dawn seeped across the downs. He didn't want to face it. He closed his eyes. As soon as he did he could hear his name called. *Martin, Martin, Martin!* He squeezed his face tightly. He didn't want to hear it. He didn't want to be called. He didn't want to move.

His body shuddered with a sudden chill. It triggered something. He felt his heartbeat begin to increase. He turned over in frustration. He didn't want it all to start again, the fear, the agony, the cowardice. As soon as he turned over he was aware of the gravestones just a few yards away. He found himself uttering the name he had wanted to avoid. "Robert! Robert! Robert!"

He was aware of his own voice. It came rapidly and monotonously. He didn't know whether he was speaking aloud, in his head or dreaming it. "Robert, were you scared? Were you scared all of the time? Why is it like this? I can't stand it! A little girl gave me flowers and was blown up! I saw people screaming and clambering right over each other in the middle of a bonfire, like lots of Guy Fawkes. Not a bridge was down. That's not true. Did you know that, though? I'm so scared I make things up all of the time. Did you make things up? La guerre - nicht bon! A German soldier said that. What the hell did he think I was? I slapped him down! Liar, liar, liar. I beat the bastard till he was black and blue. Who the hell did he think he was talking to? La guerre - nicht bon! I'm a cowboy. I was playing with guns. No I'm a soldier, a miner. I said goodbye to Grandfather. I left him on the beach. He's not a holy man. Why does Grandmother pray all of the time? Did you pray, even here? I don't..."

He became silent. He could hear trucks rolling into the village. A moment later and he heard his name called again. *Martin, Martin, Martin!* He looked across the gravestones. Pale light filled the sky. The moon was vanishing. He began to cry. He uttered under his breath: "Stay with me? Please, stay with me."

He began to laugh amongst his tears. He spoke aloud. His tone was harsh, sardonic and bitter: "Do you think I could fly?" He stood up. He dusted himself down. He had dirt down his front. He shook himself. He had to dismiss such thoughts. He had to clear his mind. He was going slightly crazy. He knew he had to fight himself. It was a crazy thought in itself. He shrugged. He felt at once incredulous and fearful.

He walked towards the arriving trucks. He felt as if he had been dreaming and just woken up. Vestiges of it remained though. He knew he wasn't through with it. The boundary was down, breached, and he couldn't erect it again, not easily. He would just have to see it through. In that he was like everyone else. He was one of the whole just seeing it through. It was all out of his hands.

He met Donald. Picardy burnt. "Don't worry about anything," Martin said warmly, "we are cowboys really." They jumped on the truck. They went on to Arras, Douai, and then on into Brussels.

*

Martin was drinking in a bar in *Les Boucher,* and though it was as yet still only early evening he was quite drunk. He went to the door and gazed through a portal window. Soldiers were fighting in the street. A steady curtain of rain slanted down onto the cobbled alley. He saw one of the soldiers, a Canadian, fall to the ground, blood seeping from his face, mingling with rain water. A group of kids fell on his prostrate body and rifled his pockets. The other soldiers continued to tussle and skirmish. Martin opened the bar door. He could hear the rain, the groans of the soldiers and the rummaging of the kids. He balked at the noise. "Keep it down!" he snapped. "There is a holy man here." The uproar continued. "Well, fuck you!" he shouted, letting the door swing to. At that moment the Welshmen began to sing. He moaned out loud, returned to the bar and slammed his glass down. "They're off, then," he said irascibly, gazing at his own dogged features in the mirror along the rear bar, addressing himself to Donald who was alongside him.

"They're singing about home, man, leave them be," Donald said kindly.

"I'm pleased for them. I hope they live to see it."

"Martin!"

"Maybe I should sing myself," Martin declared, and he turned, faced the Welshmen sitting round a table a few feet off, and with every intention of singing *The Wild Colonial Boy* raised his hand for quiet. The Welshmen continued unabashed.

> *Good-bye Piccadilly, farewell Leicester Square*
> *It's a long long way to Tipperary*
> *But the greenest shit lies there...*

"Bastards!"

"It's only a joke," Albert called above the continuing refrain. "Come on sing yourself, if you have a mind to it, man."

"I wouldn't sing for a butcher," Martin said bitterly, uncompromising. Albert glared at him and appeared suddenly tearful, whether angry or hurt Martin couldn't say. He didn't know how to respond. He was too drunk to mitigate his insult. He decided simply to leave. He turned away from Albert and fled. The song broke up in howls of derisory laughter behind him.

Outside the bar the soldiers and grubby kids had gone. The fallen Canadian was also gone, though the cobbles where he had lain were still marked with blood. The drizzle still fell, heavy but warm. He could see its rapid sheets crossways in cafe lights. Flags and buntings, red, yellow and black, hung straight and heavy from shuttered balconies. He took a few steps forward, then staggered and fell against the wall. He closed his eyes. He was certain he was going to be sick. He breathed in and out deeply, struggling against the desire to be sick and the desire to sleep, the desire to absent himself. He kept on breathing. Eventually he heard a voice, a woman's voice, a calm and composed voice, asking: "You are all right, Monsieur?" Martin nodded but kept his eyes closed. "Where you want to be, Monsieur?" Martin couldn't answer. In his stupor he was trying to work it out. Had she said his name? Where was he? Had he miraculously been taken home? Yes, he thought, he had heard her. *Martin, Martin, Martin!* "Mary," he uttered, quite softly but clearly. He opened his eyes and peered around gingerly.

He saw a small, neat featured girl. She was heavily made up. She had piercing blue eyes, and an inquisitive, coquettish expression. She was dressed, in common with so many Belgian women, in a red skirt, yellow blouse and black scarf. The drizzle had drenched her so that her clothes hung to her skin, revealing the spareness of her figure. It had also made her makeup run. It gave her a dishevelled, tragic air. She met Martin's gaze for a moment, then pushed her hand into her knot of dark curling hair and burst into a peal of crisp laughter. "No, Monsieur," she declared, "no, no, no, she, well..." She waved her hands carelessly through the air in no particular direction. "Gone, long time, maybe. I think. Must be. I am Yvonne. My name, Yvonne. I see you earlier, in *Les Boucher*. You look sad, angry, perhaps. I don't know. I see you, you know."

Martin withered under the attention of her gaze. He shook his head, uncertain of her interest and confused by it. "I'm just a soldier."

She laughed again, the sound mildly defiant, gently rebuking him: "We are all soldiers, huh, I think. All of us. There is a war, you know."

"I'm sorry."

Yvonne came closer to him. "Where are you go, Monsieur? Brussels not so safe. I do not think so. Perhaps not so good idea, walk too far."

"I don't know. I seem to have lost my way." He looked up and down the alley. The drizzle continued to slant across the lights. The alley was a series of shadowy corners and yellow lights. There was no one else to be seen. He turned back to her and shook his head. He couldn't think straight. He had drunk too much. He fell back against the wall and shrugged, conceding to his disordered thinking. He closed his eyes, sighed deeply and uttered: "I seem to have lost my guide somehow."

"You look only one, perhaps, I don't know. I see you, just you. In Les Boucher, I mean. Just you."

"Perhaps I was."

"I don't know. Perhaps I am, well, not right. I say I see. No more. Perhaps, if you want, I guide. I know Brussels. Of course. Well, if you like?"

Martin inhaled deeply, then nodded his head without opening his eyes. "Yes," he said, "that would be good. Yes. Thank you."

"Brussels is not so safe, I do not think. Not so safe for soldiers. Not soldiers, just one. The Gestapo. You know. I don't think Gestapo all go. Not yet, perhaps. No, Brussels not so safe. Bang, bang!" She held her fingers at his chest and fired an imaginary gun. He opened his eyes in response to the pressure of her index-finger. She smiled. "What then?"

"I shall be dead. And when I am dead I shall be an angel like you."

She frowned. "No, do not say such things. I do not think that is so good. No, I do not like."

"I'm sorry. I say things aloud that come into my head. I know I shouldn't. I'm sorry. I never used to. I'm not quite myself. I was never like this."

She shrugged. "Perhaps, no more, yes. No more. I do not like. I do not want you say. I am sorry." She stopped speaking and studied him for a moment. She hung her head from side to side as if weighing him up. She frowned, looked quizzical then smiled. She shook her head and laughed faintly. "I do not think you walk Brussels alone. Brussels is not safe. Many bad things in the city and perhaps bad in city now. Not bad as then but, not so safe. I do not think Brussels so safe."

"I'm not alone."

"You all right with me?"

"Of course. I trust you."

"Trust?" she repeated, either sceptical of the word or unsure of its meaning. Martin couldn't tell. She shook her head sympathetically. "You all right with me. Perhaps you better say no. But... You say no all time and..." She shrugged and pouted her lips, clearly uncertain of the right word. For a moment or two she seemed quite frustrated, but eventually settled on something she considered satisfactory. "Nothing. You say no and nothing. Nothing no good. No." She burst into light, cheerful laughter, and threw up her hands inviting some response. Martin merely shrugged. She mirrored his gesture, as if she understood his apparent weariness, then reached to him and took his hand. He willingly allowed it to be taken. He wanted to be led. He had not heard such laughter for as long as he could remember. It came from a different time altogether. He couldn't quite accept that it was real, but he was content to allow the illusion. He pulled himself from the wall and prepared to be guided.

He found he had sobered enough to walk. They made their way down the alley away from the bar. It ran straight for a while then twisted away from the oblique cafe lights and seemed to plunge into semi-darkness. Cats and dogs scuffled in the gloom, gnawing at scraps and pieces of rubbish. Figures were hunched in doorways. There were Belgian girls dressed in the Tricolour with Allied soldiers. Their vague animal groans echoed along the alley. Martin and Yvonne went on, ignoring everything they passed. After a time they began to climb. The gradient wasn't laborious but nevertheless rose steadily. A short time later, without warning, the lights of the city were revealed far below them like a star filled sky. Martin was astounded. He gripped Yvonne's hand tightly. "I can see *The Bear*," he whispered.

Yvonne made no reply. He turned to her. She was looking at him. Only the bold contours of her face were visible, though. She smiled. She pressed her fingers lightly in his palm and immediately began to descend towards the firmament, bringing Martin with her. He was aware that with each step he was coming to, no longer staggering, but much stronger, his mind clearer. And as his mind cleared he realised that he desperately wanted to do something he had never done before. He wanted to make love to her, make love to a woman. He couldn't go on being just a boy. It was ridiculous. He stopped her and looked her in the face. It was still a relief of light and shade. He couldn't speak. He couldn't say what was on his mind. She had the face of a child, the child he had seen in the house in Caen, looking up at him, trusting him, wanting to be trusted by him. He felt disgusted by himself. He whispered: "Thank you."

"Thank you? Why? For what?"

"Guiding me."

She shrugged. "It is nothing. Really. You know. Here, this place, is *Les Marolles*. From here, out of these desperate little streets, the best of the city really, do not you think, I think, look... from here the Nazis gathered their slave-labour. Many peoples. And more, perhaps, of course, much more, those bastards. They turn everyone into a whore." She spat on the floor, then shrugged, her expression unchanged, still childlike. She continued thoughtfully. "The Nazis take everyone, men, women, childrens, but most of all Jews. No Jews now. No Jews at all. I do not think they will come back, not anymore. They hate Jews. Why Jews? They are crazy, maybe, crazy with hating. Who knows, who knows ever?"

"My grandmother said we were Jews, Irish Jews, all the Irish, Jews. She prays all the time, I don't know why."

He smiled weakly. Yvonne shrugged in response, then with renewed resolution said: "Come, we go on, come meet my best friend, my best friend in all the world."

Through the drizzle the streets appeared dingy and inchoate, inhabited by an array of cripples, witches and decrepit scrounging kids. Old unkempt women with disfigured faces lifted their heads from the gutter and eyed them malevolently as they passed. Martin's mind's eye filled with the image of Mrs Darcy, her witch's face peering fearfully through a partially opened door. She would not have been out of place there. Would any of them?

They picked their way through the huddled figures until Yvonne stopped at the entrance to a small cafe. It was in keeping with its surroundings, dirty and forlorn. Inside a group of old gnarl faced men sat together at a small table without talking, and a couple of soldiers lay slouched across the bar. Behind the counter there was a flame haired girl with sharp, birdlike features. Yvonne introduced her as Ivi, her very best friend in the whole world. The two kissed and embraced across the counter. When that was concluded Ivi looked Martin up and down a number of times. The action was deliberate and challenging. At first her expression was grim and distrustful, but that quickly evolved into amusement, so that by the time she was through she was laughing out loud. Still laughing, she poured a glass of brandy and indicated that Martin take it. He picked it up but didn't drink. He wasn't sure. He was wary of being as drunk as he had been, but at the same time was nervous of being sober.

"Go on, drink it down liberator," Ivi insisted, her voice languid and hoarse, suffused with boredom. "It's all right. It won't kill you." Martin put the glass to his lips and downed it in one. Ivi smiled and poured him another. This time she placed the bottle beside the glass. "Easy liberator," she whispered. "Easy."

He held the glass to his lips, but only inhaled at its contents. He had to do as he was told. He had to follow orders. He had been taught that. It made sense. An order was something that made sense. He put the glass to his lips and sipped. It trickled over his tongue. It was raw and burnt. He had been so unwise earlier. It had been painful taking a whole glass. She had not intended that. He turned to Ivi. She had half an eye on him. She was watching him. Did she suspect him of something? Well, she was wrong, he was a good boy. As she watched him she smoked lazily, taking long draws on her cigarette, and spoke with Yvonne. He didn't understand a word, but it didn't matter. Their voices, hushed but intermingled, two distinct pitches, one deep, one fluid, making a texture, an easy, pleasing texture, reduced the other voices going round and round in his head. There were too many voices. He scarcely understood a word.

He didn't know how long they stayed at the bar. He had no sense of time passing. He guessed he must have fallen asleep. He must have been dreaming. He had certainly relived details of his journey there, once again fighting every inch of ground from Caen to Brussels, the hand of a little girl in his, the woman's face disappearing in fire. But he had somehow also finished the bottle. Had he done that before he drifted off?

He didn't remember that. But then he didn't remember anything clearly, just voices, words he didn't understand, La guerre - nicht bon, and faces, dishevelled, staring faces. It was all just fleeting, chaotic impressions, making a montage of memory. He must have been dreaming.

Ivi, picking up the empty bottle, roused him. She dangled it over his glass, shaking two drops more from it, then went off. He followed her with his eyes. The room was spinning. He felt quite sick. Everything he looked at was vivid and intense. Ivi went along the bar to the two soldiers, who were still there slouched across the counter. She inhaled deeply on her cigarette, lifted their heads by the hair and kissed them hard on their mouths, then pushed them away, drawling: "Go on, back to where you have to be, liberator, it's all over now." The soldiers protested incoherently, but nevertheless fell from their stools and stumbled to the door. The old men followed immediately after them.

"What will we do with no war?" Ivi queried, frowning quizzically, even dejectedly.

Yvonne smiled. "Be just us, normal, perhaps."

Ivi shrugged, then began wiping down surfaces, turning off lights as she went.

"I have to go," Martin said uncertain, startled by the dark.

"Go? Go where?" Yvonne asked.

He had no idea. His mind was swimming. He stood up. He saw himself in the bar mirror. He scarcely recognised himself. He was dishevelled and dirty. He looked like an old man. The lines on his face were wrong. They were too marked. He didn't stand to attention like that. He wasn't nearly so sullen. His gaze wasn't so ponderous. He had become a stranger. How was that? "Look," he said, his voice hollow and dejected, "I have prayers down my front."

Yvonne laughed and brushed his jacket. "Cognac, it is Cognac. You make a mess like a baby, a big baby boy, that is all."

Martin stared at his reflection for a moment, then spoke up in tones so low they were scarcely audible. He spoke directly to his reflection as if speaking to himself. "I should have buried a pilot but I didn't. How could I have been so lazy? How will he ever fly away and be at rest." He turned to Yvonne. He could say no more. He was enraged and confused, choked suddenly by the emotion he felt. For a moment neither knew how to proceed. Ivi broke the deadlock. She suggested: "Catholic, yes? A Catholic soldier, yes?"

"Of course."

"So, take him to Ferdinand." She extinguished the final light as she spoke. She led them to the door in near-darkness. She opened the door onto the street. A slant of light broke across them. Ivi shrugged, eyed Martin quizzically, then stepped up to him and kissed him gently on the lips. She exhaled an overwhelming perfume of tobacco. It reminded him of home, his grandfather in the cellar. It was an ever present aroma. She then turned to Yvonne, smiled and kissed her. Martin had an urge to say he wasn't worthy, he had been swimming for years, but the door closed on him. He turned to Yvonne. She gestured for him to follow her. He couldn't refuse.

She took him to the Church of the Immaculate Conception. On the threshold she dabbed her fingers in a font of holy water and signed the cross. She turned to him and whispered: "They save many lives, the Capuchin Fathers. The Fathers here. They were very good, they make a safe place, a good place when the Nazis hunt slaves. We are very grateful. They make lots of lives."

The church was small and silent. It was lit only by candlelight. There were small pools of gold. The guttering flames picked out the averted faces of Christ and the Madonna. Martin quailed under their presence. He had failed to bury the airman. He felt guilty. He had no right to be here. He was unequal to the confession. No wonder they would not look at him. No wonder they held their expressions in that dreadful way. He had let them down. He had failed so miserably. He had trampled across dead bodies and scarcely flinched. He had watched homeless people trudge by him without a word. He had seen people burn like stuffed dummies. He had seen a man with broken shoulders pinned to a wall. He had passed by without a prayer. Not a Hail Mary, Our Father, or Glory be. He had not knelt. He had not uttered the prayer before the crucifix. *O Good Jesus. They have pierced my hands and my feet; they have numbered all my bones.*

Now as he stood at the threshold of the church his mind raced with prayers and psalms. They all ran together into one wailing, withering howl. He heard brief, recognisable fragments. His grandmother's voice, Father Bond, Mary, his mother, his grandfather, even Albert, whom he had never heard pray in reality. But as soon as he heard a distinct voice it was drowned out by another. They came into his head, layer upon layer. He tried to hear particular and precious voices but they were lost. Important words were simply washed away in the general roar. He couldn't really make sense of anything. The roar swallowed it all. It was a roar that was as visual as much as it was vocal. It was made up of candle flame, face and body. They danced before his eyes, picture within picture, merging and breaking apart, to an accompaniment of sighs and screeches. His journey to that moment in time was encapsulated in an instantaneous, concurrent repetition of word and image. His head was bursting with them. They caused physical pain. He felt the weight of them all, and the loneliness they imposed. They ushered him to that point but abandoned him. He was on his own.

He reached for Yvonne's hand. She took it and led him down the aisle. She knocked three times at the vestry door. A moment later a figure appeared in the doorway, a hooded figure, his face almost completely obscured. Yvonne spoke. "Father Ferdinand? I have a soldier, a Catholic, a Catholic soldier. I think, perhaps, he has troubles, much troubles. I think perhaps, very good, you talk, Father? I think good help."

There was a period of silence. Martin was certain he could sense the interest of the priest's eyes on him. It made him feel awkward, shy and out of sorts, as if he were a child being chastised. He was unable to meet the other's attention, yet at a loss as where else to look. He simply gazed into space. Father Ferdinand eventually broke the silence. His voice was that of a young man, pleasant and melodious: "I am Ferdinand, Father Ferdinand. You can speak to me. You can speak in this place. You need have no fear. This is a haven for you as it is a haven for all of us. Where sin has separated us from God, His love will reunite us. God does not want to see you burdened. If you are troubled I can hear your confession. Remember the words of St John: *That which we have heard, which we have seen with our eyes, which we have looked upon, and our hands have handled, of the Word of life, declare we unto you.* Go ahead. Remember, there is fellowship here if you require it."

Martin turned towards the hooded figure. He felt compelled to answer. He had not learnt any disobedience. He wasn't Duffy capable of saying he didn't want the priest, didn't need the priest. Maybe he did. Maybe he couldn't do without what the priest had to give. When he spoke, though, his voice almost failed him. His mouth was dry and his tongue stuck to his palate. He uttered: "Father, there is a dead man here."

"Tell me about him?"

Martin licked his lips a number of times. When he again spoke his voice grew more fluent so that he was able to say more, but it remained essentially hushed and broken. "I saw him. I thought he had cocoa on his face but it was probably mud. He told me the bridges were down. I had the chance to bury him but wouldn't. I let him down. How will he ever fly away and be at rest?"

"Did he die with you? In your presence, I mean."

"No, no, not with me, a long time ago. Yes, he died a long time ago. I don't know when. He is among the flowers. He can't fly. He will be there for ever and ever."

"You knew him well, though?"

"He was a holy man, Father. Everybody said that. He sings psalms for me. I have nothing in return, absolutely nothing. I wasn't the brightest at school. I didn't work very hard. I know that. I couldn't even bring myself to bury his body. That was bad. I know I'm bad. I'm selfish and lazy. I should have buried the body."

"It is the soul which is the concern of God. You need have no trouble on that count. Have confidence and trust in God." Father Ferdinand lifted his arms and promulgated his next sentence. "Give thanks to the Lord, for he is good."

The priest stopped speaking and there was another period of silence. Martin realised that he should have responded. He had been invited to confess. He didn't know what to say. He felt fearful. The priest would punish him. He had to behave properly. He was like Patrick. He had to be obedient. Eventually he stammered a reply. He didn't know where it came from, but he recognised that it was right. "His mercy endures forever."

Father Ferdinand continued: "You may go in peace. You are a good man. I can see that. Go in peace and say your prayers. The Lord has freed you from your sins."

Martin took a step back. He didn't know what was going on. This was too strange. Why was the priest hooded? He heard Duffy's voice. He didn't want the priest's prayers. He could do very well without them. Then he saw Patrick. He felt more like Patrick. His voice was sticky like Patrick's. Maybe he had prayers down his front? He grinned at the thought. He immediately bowed his head. What would happen if the priest had seen his response? What would he say? He quickly uttered: "I have no rosary, Father."

"There is no impediment to prayer," Father Ferdinand replied firmly.

"No, of course not. I'm sorry." He backed away, then turned to leave. He was stopped short by the fact that he came up against the altar platform. The altar itself was just a few feet from him. It was decorated with gladioli and grapes and draped with the Belgian flag. The tabernacle was right behind it. He signed the cross, then slowly turned to the vestry door. Father Ferdinand was still there. Martin hesitated then quietly uttered: "Thank you, Father. I am grateful. I am really. I know you mean well. I have been told of all of the good things you have done. I know it is a terrible thing to be in a cell all alone. I know that."

"We have to remember what it is to be a true disciple of the Lord. Do not forget. *If any man would come after me, let him deny himself and take up his cross and follow me.*"

Martin didn't immediately reply. One image had fixed itself on his mind, that of the dangling figure and his somewhat stunted crucifixion, his arms pinioned, his shoulders torn from their sockets. He shook his head slowly, but decisively. "I don't think I can suffer anymore, Father. I'm tired now. Mr Duffy said he could suffer and that they couldn't take it away from him, but he was a strong man. He knew about all sorts of things. I'm sorry Father, but if that's what God wants I'd rather give up. I've had enough. I'm not strong. I don't want to be left alone though. I don't understand that. I'm terrified of being left alone. I always imagined I was a cowboy."

Father Ferdinand didn't reply. Martin grew fearful. He was sure he had unwittingly offended the priest. His nerve failed him. He turned away and fled down the aisle away from the dressed altar.

Yvonne called to him from the porch door. He was already someway down the street. "Where are you going?"

Martin turned and called back: "Was I bad? I think I was bad. I didn't mean to be bad."

She came up to him. "No, you were not bad. I do not see how. You were all right."

"I don't mean to be bad. I don't mean to be rude. Not even to John Darcy's mother who everyone knows is a witch." He looked into Yvonne's face. He was moved by an intense desire for her. He whispered: "I am so lonely, when I said... well, I don't know..."

She placed her fingertips against his lips. She shook her head gently. "I have somewhere. Everything is all right."

They walked through the dead city to the dead suburb of *Etterbeek*. She told him she lived with friends, good friends. Ivi might be there. They had done things during the war. She didn't say what. She took him into a large shuttered house. As the door opened he could see a staircase along a corridor. There was a door off to the right. When the door closed behind them the stairwell was in darkness. There were voices coming from the room. He couldn't make out how many. There were men and

461

women. It sounded as if they were arguing. It wasn't a heated argument, just a mild dispute. Yvonne took his hand. She led him towards the stair. They went up to the first-floor. The sound of the continuing row faded below them. When they closed the bedroom door behind them they completely banished it.

The room was dark. They could only just see each other's shape in the gloom. They held each other for some time without speaking. Eventually Yvonne helped him undress. Her fingers ran across him, shaping him in the dark as she stripped him. She lay him down between cool sheets. He waited for her. He could hear her undress. She came beside him. They caressed each other for warmth. They began to laugh quietly. She put her arms around his body and drew him to her. "Oui," she said. "Viens à moi. Oui." Martin embraced her as if she were an element he could finally and convincingly surrender to.

When he awoke the pale colourless light of dawn seeped into the room. It formed bars across the walls where it reflected the window shutters. He felt cool air on his body and stretched into the sheets for warmth. Yvonne moved along the length of the bed. Her body was milky-white in the weak light. He listened to her furtive movements with his eyes wide open. She reached to the floor at the foot of the bed. He sat up quickly and reached along the bed to pull her back to him. She fell back startled. He stopped and stared at her. She held his trousers in her hands. He shook his head and crawled towards her. He began to cry. "Not for money," he moaned, still coming towards her. His voice broke out in a series of defiant howls: "Not for money, for Christ's sake, not for money! I trusted you! You were my guide! You took me to confession! He said there was fellowship! Christ, it was all rubbish, wasn't it. A pack of lies! Just to get the better of me. Lies! Lies, lies, and more damned lies."

She backed away from him, uttering his name over and over, imploring him: "Martin, Martin, Martin!"

He called out: "Mary! No, liar! Liar! You're not her! No one is her!" He swung his fist against her face. She fell below the shutters. He heard the heavy thud of her falling. The shutters remained still. Yvonne also lay still. He knelt down beside her. He began to sob. He held her head. It was limp in his grasp. His hands were covered with blood. He shook her. There was no response. He took her hands. He felt a string of beads pressed between her palms. He heard voices below him. They were coming up the stairs. He stood up. "*Why seek the living among the dead?*" he whispered under his breath.

462

He opened the shutters. He walked naked onto the balcony. All around him the grey-white houses were sunk in white mist. The sky contained a pale fire which streaked its surface. He felt the cold air cover him. He heard bird wings. He flew. He screamed as a sword between air and earth tore him in two. Flags fluttered freely in the morning air. A taxi passed the street end.